ALSO BY YAEL HEDAYA

Housebroken

Accidents

EDEN

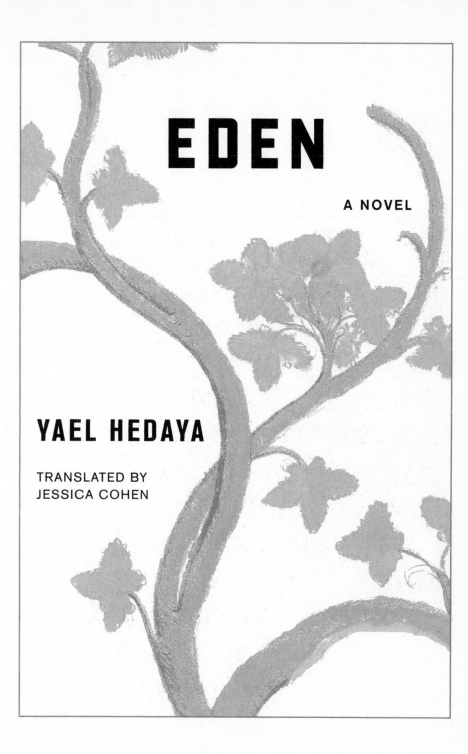

EDEN

A NOVEL

YAEL HEDAYA

TRANSLATED BY
JESSICA COHEN

METROPOLITAN BOOKS   HENRY HOLT AND COMPANY   NEW YORK

Metropolitan Books
Henry Holt and Company, LLC
Publishers since 1866
175 Fifth Avenue
New York, New York 10010

Metropolitan Books® and ⊞® are registered trademarks of
Henry Holt and Company, LLC.

Originally published in Israel in 2005 by Am Oved, Tel Aviv.

The quotes from *Past Perfect* are from Dalya Bilu's translation
(Yaakov Shabtai, *Past Perfect*. New York: Viking, 1987).

Library of Congress Cataloging-in-Publication Data

Hedaya, Yael.
  [Eden. English]
  Eden : a novel / Yael Hedaya ; translated [from the Hebrew] by Jessica Cohen.—1st U.S. ed.
    p. cm.
  ISBN 978-0-8050-9265-3
  I. Cohen, Jessica.   II. Title.
  PJ5055.23.E33E4313 2010
  892.4'36—dc22   2010007149

Henry Holt books are available for special promotions and
premiums. For details contact: Director, Special Markets.

First U.S. Edition 2010

Designed by Kelly S. Too

Printed in the United States of America

1 3 5 7 9 10 8 6 4 2

For Noa and Itamar

PART ONE

DAFNA

So what is the moment? What does it look like? What shape does it take and when does it occur, that instant which is not a moment and yet is everything? And why does it slip away from her time after time after time?

Because to talk about the moment of conception sounds trite, too small for the occasion and utterly imprecise. And to speak of the encounter between sperm and egg sounds silly, like the press releases she formulates every day (a historic meeting, a once-in-a-lifetime summit) and also untrue. The lab technicians have seen Eli's millions of sperm swimming obediently, though perhaps unenthusiastically, toward her eggs as they sit in little petri dishes like parked cars, waiting for someone to break into them, start their engines, and drive them away. The simple fact is that nothing has happened.

Even the disappointment no longer mattered very much, and not because she had grown used to it. "It's disappointing all over again, every time," the nurse said when she gave Dafna the results over the phone and heard her slow, restrained *okay*, more of an exhalation than an utterance, because her heart never said it was okay, not once, but her lungs mechanically filled with air to push down the sobs. The nurse had it wrong. You didn't feel disappointed all over again, every time. The disappointment settled like another story on a vast construction project with an unknown completion date, a building with scaffolding made out of hopes, now removed, and from month to month it looked more like a tower block, a concrete monster with closed-in balconies. Sometimes the nurse said, "It'll be okay, Dafna; it will work for you in the end, too," and the *for you* stung more than the disappointment, more than the word *end*; and besides, *what* would work? What was it that would work in the end? She no longer knew whether this thing, which was not working, would fix everything that was broken and start her life again. But she didn't care. She just wanted it to work.

She was standing in the kitchen waiting for the kettle to boil so she could mix the sunrise potion concocted for her by the Chinese doctor, in whom she no longer believed but did not yet doubt enough to strike him off her list of alternative practitioners whom she'd visited in recent years: the ones who said her womb was too cold and the ones who compared it to a burning-hot oven, the ones who named her spleen as the source of the trouble and the ones who blamed her kidneys, the ones who said everything was fine, just fine, and likened her ovaries to nuts or tubers and her fallopian tubes to lilies. Perhaps she felt a little sorry for the Chinese medicine guy, because there was something pathetic and dated about his office, because he had not asked her to listen or visualize or believe, instructing her only to stick out her tongue, and she had felt that she was sticking her tongue out at everyone, at the healers and the Chinese doctors and the alternative practitioners, all of them, and at Eli waiting downstairs in a café, sipping a double espresso that had no ill effect on his excellent sperm count, much like the five cigarettes he smoked every day, no doubt poring over some legal file or reprimanding an intern over his cell phone, waiting for her to finish her appointment with the guru du jour—and yet for six months she'd been drinking the potion every morning, and still: nothing.

Now she thought that she would like to implant a tiny video camera in her body, to roam the expanses, spy into corners, slide down curves, and attach itself to the sticky walls of her womb—which quite possibly were not sticky enough, and maybe that was the problem: embryos tumbled off them like mountain climbers plunging to their deaths from a slippery rock wall. A camera would catch everything, projecting the images onto a screen and she would watch: a video clip of her body. She would fast-forward and rewind it, freeze it, examine every frame, every angle, especially that one instant when it all came to a head, the moment that could not be defined, the moment that had been driving Dafna out of her mind for seven years.

Because the idea of a single moment when a pregnancy takes hold is false. There might have been dozens of pregnancies that had taken hold, maybe even hundreds. When she was young she hadn't been careful (her friends called her irresponsible, and the guys she slept with said she was playing with fire, but they still came inside her, and she had only started using contraceptives when she got married, a fact she now found ridiculously insulting), and she realized that what had seemed at the time like tempting fate was in fact prophetic intuition, and perhaps, she thought, as she poured water into the Duralex glass—chosen as her lucky glass, refusing to replace it even after it had disappointed during the last in vitro fertilization—perhaps hundreds of pregnancies had taken hold, but something (what could it be?) had made them change their minds, spurred them to press their ejection buttons and flee. These treacherous cells preferred to grow parachutes over placentas; they quarreled when they divided or disliked the lodgings they found: it was too cold or too hot; she knew all the permutations. She was all too familiar with the mechanics and the details of the hormonal environment, and she knew the statistics for women her age. Still, that moment remained mysterious and elusive and critical—a celestial instant; that was how she thought of it at first, though lately it seemed all too earthly, subterranean and dark—a moment from another world and, in some clear and wounding way, not of her world.

The mixture of ground leaves and roots and whatever else was in the glass swirled around, painting the water a nauseating yet promising greenish earth-toned hue. She looked through the window at the backyard, still obscured in darkness, and she could picture its borders lined with jasmine, hibiscus, and honeysuckle bushes—and oleander. "If we have a child we'll have to pull it up, it's poisonous," Eli had said, not long ago, and his *if*, which used to be *when*, scared her more than the thought that their child would swallow a leaf or a flower. She gazed at the lemon cypresses, black and hulking like dozing beasts, and at the lawn, which glistened with moisture in the halogen white that filtered out through the kitchen window. Daylight would soon break and turn the square of darkness into their garden: a phosphorescent green lake of lawn touching a patio tiled with flagstone, adorned with a complete set of oak garden furniture, 9,530 shekels—odd that she remembered this price, of all the fortunes they had spent on the house—and the fancy grill, and of course the rockery, Eli's pride and joy, built from pebbles, centered around a small pool lit with bluish underwater spotlights. The water made a trickle that sounded like a recording, and goldfish swam indifferently in the pool, playing their parts as ornamental fish. When the mid-October sun rose she would see the neatly pruned bushes, and when the last patches of darkness unraveled she would think what she thought every morning when she looked out: in all the world there was no uglier beauty.

Hunched over with her arms resting on the marble countertop—wearing a nightshirt that once, before a hundred washes, dozens of injections in her rear end and her stomach, several intrauterine inseminations, four IVFs, and God knows how many glasses of Chinese silt and needles, used to have a bunny print—she thought she looked old, like her mother, on whose land the house she and Eli lived in had been built (the old house was about to collapse anyway, Eli had said, when she suggested they renovate it instead of tearing it down). The plain, modest house had been destroyed with chilling simplicity, and even the contractor, who was no stranger to tearing down homes, had complimented the structure for seeming to surrender willingly, as though the bulldozer's touch was merely a tickle that sent it crumpling to the ground and rolling around with laughter, churning up clouds of dust. The contractor, a Gulliver with a frizzy red mane of hair, with whom they later fought and were embroiled in a court case, reminded Dafna of her father, a large man who had bequeathed her his physique. "The burning bush," Eli had affectionately nicknamed the contractor before he started referring to him as "that shit." The contractor had a habit of nervously chewing his lower lip, just like she remembered her father doing when he was tense or thoughtful—her father who had wanted to live in the countryside.

A few weeks after her parents left their home in Petach Tikva and moved to the moshav with their three children—eight-year-old Irit, five-year-old Dafna, and Gadi, a two-month-old baby—her father had suffered cardiac arrest and died in his sleep.

Dafna remembered waking up that Saturday morning to the sound of her mother sobbing. She was dashing around the house wearing a slip, which she had never done before and which amused Dafna and her sister, whom their mother quickly sent next door to the neighbor, the widow Sonia Baruch, along with baby Gadi and a bottle of milk. Only after breakfast, when their mother came in, her eyes red and puffy, and whispered with Sonia in the hallway, and they heard the two women sniveling, and Sonia came back into the kitchen and told them they would have to stay until evening, and outside in the yard people started to gather—only then did they realize something terrible had happened.

Eli, like her father, had also wanted to move to the country. He would pace their penthouse apartment in north Tel Aviv and complain that he couldn't breathe, he was suffocating, he was spending too many hours at the office, in offices in general, in court, and he had to get out and work the land, at least on weekends. "Yes," he said, "you can laugh all you want, but I have an urge to work on the land." The person who ended up actually taking care of their half acre was Bobo from Thailand.

Dafna's father was forty-one when he announced to her mother that he had a unique opportunity to buy a two-bedroom house in Eden for a steal, and they wouldn't even have to sell the apartment in Petach Tikva. "You'll see, Leah, it will be paradise for the children." After his death, the house remained exactly as it had been when he bought it and the garden just a thought: a square of lawn that Dafna and Irit and, later, Gadi watered obediently twice a week. Every winter the lawn fell into decay, seemed finally on the verge of death, and then came to life again in the spring. That lawn, she thought, was a yellowing, angry longing for her father, who had left them with the promise of a different life and with so much work.

When her mother died, five years ago, Irit and Gadi agreed to split the profits from the sale of the apartment in Petach Tikva and give Dafna the house on the moshav, which no one imagined would become one of the most expensive areas in Israel. "We made a good deal," Eli said, although he had initially objected and claimed Dafna's siblings were cheating her. "I was wrong, big-time," he conceded, whenever she reminded him of how he had tormented her for stupidly giving up her share in the apartment for a crumbling house that, granted, was sitting on half an acre of land, but who needed half an acre in a place like that?

In the late nineties, Eden, originally a farming collective founded by Polish and Hungarian immigrants in the early nineteen fifties, emerged as one of the most desirable communities in central Israel. Young families, mostly from Tel Aviv and Petach Tikva, purchased entire farms for ridiculous prices and built houses that looked as if they had all been designed by the same architect: one- or two-story stucco buildings in pastel shades—lemon yellow, pale pink, baby blue, or pistachio green—with large Dutch-style windows in smoky colors. Their flat roofs seemed to mock the mossy red slate that capped the original old houses, which were gradually disappearing along with their owners as they died or moved to live near children in the cities and suburbs. There were a few who stayed, a handful of elderly couples, one widower, and several widows, who began to resemble their houses: the opposite of pastel, the opposite of designer. There was an odd contrast between the owners of these crumbling buildings and their land, which by the first decade of the millennium was worth millions.

When prices soared and the elderly homeowners and, more markedly, their children lost their financial innocence, the wealthy began to arrive. In the past two years a few giant estates had sprouted up alongside the old houses and their newer pastel-hued neighbors. Hidden behind high walls with electric gates that opened onto double and triple parking bays, these mansions, precisely because they were hidden, looked enviously ostentatious, quietly terrifying, and masterful, like yawning lions sprawled among herds of zebra. Now Eden comprised three distinct classes: upper, lower, and elderly. The last had its own subgroups: those who held on to their land, sometimes to the chagrin of their children; those who wanted to move and left the negotiations for their children, who sometimes demanded such high prices for the condemned house and land that their parents had to keep living in Eden, unable to attract a buyer; and the third most vulnerable group, the elderly who had no offspring to shield them from those who coveted their property. Shortly after moving to Eden, Eli told Dafna his idea for a new business venture: Why shouldn't he represent these people, in return for a modest percentage of the sales, and make sure no one screwed them over? She said she hoped he was joking, and he said, "Not really, but I gather you don't like the idea."

"It stinks," she said, "taking advantage of these people."

Insulted, Eli asked why she called it *taking advantage* when all he would be doing was mediating, even offering protection. After all, if he weren't taking care of them, the buyers would just trample all over them. "You could say I'll be the son they never had. A child gets something from his parents, doesn't he? Didn't you inherit this house?" He reminded her that he himself had inherited nothing: his father's apartment in Jerusalem's Nachlaot neighborhood had been rent-controlled, and when he died it reverted to the owner. Everything he had ever owned had been bought with hard work and sweat. She asked how much exactly he was thinking of taking, assuming anyone would be foolish enough to use his services, and he said, "One or two percent, just like an agent. And don't play innocent, Dafna, real estate lawyers take hefty sums just for sitting in their offices drawing up contracts." Besides, he said, he was getting sick of being a criminal lawyer. Not that it wasn't profitable, but sometimes he envied his colleagues who made a fortune without ever leaving their desks, while he worked his ass off. "So what do you care if I sniff around a bit to see if there's any demand for this kind of service? What do you say?"

She said no. She thought about people like Sonia Baruch, who, if she had still been alive, living alone, would have been one of Eli's victims. Her home had stood abandoned for several years after she died childless, and on Saturdays families would drive by, stop their cars, and peer through the fence at the house, which hid defensively behind tall weeds and thistles. The site became a destination for all sorts of potential buyers who had heard about the abandoned property that stood on well over an acre of land. It was a good thing she and Eli hadn't lived in Eden at the time, so she hadn't seen the silent fight over the house with her own eyes, the cars circling like sharks dizzied by the scent of injured, isolated real estate. The house was eventually turned over to the Public Trustee, which office quickly sold it to a couple from Ra'anana named Shuki and Iris. They later boasted of having made the deal of a lifetime by buying the land in 1998 for less than a million shekels. Today, it was worth that several times over.

It disgusted her. To think that the place where she grew up, whose secret beauty, she believed, was in the rich, rebellious wildness of the flora that grew undisturbed between the houses, separating but also connecting them with a greenish glue, this place where she had spent an admittedly lousy childhood but which was still hers, had turned into a real estate amusement park. As though along with the land and the houses, what had also been traded in was a childhood spent hiding among bushes and tall, wild weeds, roaming orchards and fruit groves—those faraway days of small loneliness and big plans.

Every place that had once stood for something had been ruined, which only made it all the more symbolic and nostalgic. When she moved back with Eli in the summer of 2000, almost nothing of the old Eden was recognizable except the grocery store, although only the old-timers still shopped there. It stood on a paved square in the middle of the moshav, with heaps of cardboard boxes and plastic crates full of bottles near the entrance, and a pay phone that looked like a museum exhibit, because who ever used it other than the Thai workers?

No, she had not wanted to come back here, but Eli had insisted. And not just because of him, he explained, not just because of how stifled he felt in Tel Aviv—and he was amazed she didn't feel the same way; how could she not?—but because it was much healthier to bring up kids in the country. "Think about the future," he said, and she felt he did have a point; even though they were already having difficulties and were about to leave her ob-gyn and switch to an infertility expert, it had never occurred to her either that five years would go by and they still would not have a child or that Eden would not be the same Eden, not really.

That was what pained her. She tried to explain it to Eli, though she knew she was wasting her words. She couldn't help seeing a parallel between what had happened to Eden and what had happened to the country. She also sometimes saw an analogy between Eden's evolution and her own: uncontrolled weight gain as a result of the hormones and the occasional attack of binge eating but inside—nothing. Nothing was growing.

No, she didn't want Eli sniffing around, but knowing him he'd probably already done it behind her back. "Since when do I go around behind your back?" he protested. "Your back's too big for me to do anything behind it anyway."

It was a compliment, because that was what he loved about her so much, he said. That was why he had fallen in love with her, because of her strength and her idealism and the fact that she still cared about what happened in this country. Unlike who? she had asked him. "Unlike me," he replied, "I admit it." It wasn't that he didn't care, he added, so much as that he believed it was all a lost cause anyway, that caring wouldn't do anyone any good anymore. What ultimately stayed with her, and grew bothersome and gnawing, was not his cynicism or his civic laziness, as she privately called it, but the thing with her back. She had never been petite, always a broad woman, especially around the shoulders. "Like an Olympic swimmer," Eli used to say affectionately. But now, after moving back to Eden, she had gained eighteen pounds, all of which seemed to have settled on her back.

When the estate was first divided up between Dafna and her siblings, she and Eli rented the house in Eden to a young couple with a baby who had just come back from a long trip to India and were looking for somewhere quiet. They lived there for two years and were easy tenants. They never asked for anything to be repaired and never called them when something broke. When they left, the neighbors who had bought Sonia Baruch's house told Dafna and Eli that their tenants had been a serious nuisance, with raves and drugs and stray dogs they fed who kept hanging around the street even after their benefactors had left.

"A real pain," said Shuki from behind the wheel of his Mitsubishi SUV one afternoon when they came to see the now-vacant house. Shuki owned a security company and was trying to be friendly. They stood chatting with him, apologizing for the distress they had unwittingly caused.

"Why didn't you call? We would have done something, talked to them, made them leave, you know?" Eli said. "I'm a lawyer. I would have kicked them the hell out."

"We wanted to, but you know, every time it quieted down a bit we decided to lay off, and anyway we were doing renovations, so part of the time we weren't living here. We just moved in a year ago."

"You did a great job on the house," Eli said, even though it was ugly. He asked where they were from.

"Ra'anana. We had a piece of land there too, but not like this. Come inside, have a look."

"Some other time," Dafna said.

"So are you going to live here now?" Shuki asked.

Eli said probably and looked at Dafna.

"You really should. You can't match the quality of life. By the way, I'm Shuki." He held out his hand.

"Eli. And this is Dafna."

"Nice to meet you," Dafna said.

A woman came out to the driveway wearing sweats and running shoes. "This is my wife," said Shuki. "Iris, these are the owners of the shack."

"Finally!" Iris exclaimed. "So, are you going to build?"

"We might renovate," said Dafna.

Iris grimaced. "Are you crazy? Pull it down and build. We had an amazing contractor, if you want the name, and we have a young architect couple, they've just graduated, so they're pretty cheap, and they're talent to die for. You should get in on them before it goes to their head. Would you like to see our house?"

Eli looked at Dafna. She said she'd love to, some other time. They had to get back to Tel Aviv.

"Do you have kids?" Iris asked.

They both said, "No, not yet, and you?"

"A son, he's three. He's at tae kwon do now."

"After-school activities? They have that here?" asked Dafna. "Since when?"

"What are you talking about?" Iris started jogging in place. "There's stuff here to die for; really, you should pop in next time you're here; we'll bring you up to speed. They built a pool here last year, but I'm sure you know that."

"No, no. A pool?"

"Wait, didn't the board ask you to pay?" Shuki asked.

Eli shook his head.

"You'll get the bill, you can be sure of that. So you really have to stop by; we'll tell you everything."

"We will," said Eli.

"Cool." Shuki took a pen out of the bag on the seat next to him and wrote his home number on a business card, pumping the gas pedal as he did so.

"So, your offices are in Holon?" Eli asked, when he looked at the card. "Traffic must be a bitch in the morning, huh?"

"If you leave before six-thirty it's okay. One minute later, disaster."

"Well, maybe we really will stop by one Saturday."

"Saturday sounds great. You'll come over; we'll do brunch. Iris found a shop nearby that makes real bagels, just like in America." He shook both their hands and left.

They traipsed through the empty house, assessing damages and potential. Some of the tiles they stepped on were blackened, some were cracked, and others wobbled and made a crunchy sound.

"Tear it down, Dafna. We have to," Eli said, and she nodded. "Look at this place," he said, when they stood behind the house in their vast private field, surrounded by waist-high thistles. "I'm telling you, you made the deal of a lifetime." He looked out to the horizon, past the orchards that spread beyond their land and the odd little grove they abutted. He glanced at Shuki and Iris's house to their left and his eyes lit up. "We could put a pool in the yard, you know? If we have any money left over."

"But we won't," Dafna said.

"I know, I know, we don't have to do it now, but it's cool, isn't it? Just the idea! Do you get what we have here? Do you get it?"

The thought of a pool filled her with sorrow: a thorny memory of endless summers with her widowed mother, squashed between her adolescent sister and her asthmatic little brother. Almost every morning during summer vacation, the four of them used to march to the bus stop, unless someone drove by and volunteered to take them to Petach Tikva, where they spent the day baking under an umbrella at the public pool.

The three females loathed the pool, but Gadi needed physical activity, according to the family physician, Dr. Moshe, whose clinic they went to once every month or two. "As much sport as possible," ordered the doctor, whom Irit and Dafna hated because he kept winking at them and held his stethoscope to their budding breasts for too long when he examined them. Their mother always said, "Once we're here, won't you check the girls as well?" and he always agreed. Once, when she was eleven, he told everyone to leave because he wanted to ask Dafna a few questions about *womanly things*. "But why don't you want to ask Irit?" she asked, and the doctor—who was a little afraid of the older girl because she talked back and had once told him he had bad breath—said Irit was grown up and there was no need, but that Dafna was at a sensitive age. Dafna's mother said all right, they'd wait outside, although Dafna thought she detected a flash of discomfort or apprehension.

The doctor dragged his chair out from behind his desk and sat opposite her, with his knees touching hers, and asked how school was and how she was doing. She mumbled that she was fine and her gaze roamed the walls, lingering on colorful photographs of smiling babies and one poster she especially liked, of three ruddy cocker spaniel puppies crowded together in a wicker basket. "I'm glad to hear that," he said, and asked if she knew how babies came into the world. She said she knew. She thought that would be it and she'd be able to leave. "I'm glad to hear that," the doctor. "Why don't you tell me how, then? So we can be sure you really understand." She made a face and said she knew and that was that. She looked away from the wall and stared at the floor. "You're a lovely girl, do you know that? You're a special, sensitive girl, not like your sister." She looked up at him and noticed for the first time that his eyes were green and that he had a transparent protrusion on one of his eyelids, which looked like one of those tiny snails you find stuck to blades of grass. "You look like your father, may he rest in peace," he said, and added that it was such a pity, poor man, a wonderful person dying like that, so suddenly. He'd only met him twice, he said, when he first came with her mother and the baby, but it was obvious that he was a man of great stature. When he saw Dafna's tears—which were brought on not by the memory of her father's passing but by having been abandoned by her mother, whom she could hear scolding her little brother as he ran around the waiting room—when he noticed her tears the doctor hugged Dafna, pressed her to his chest, and whispered, "You can cry, honey, it's okay." She stood up, shoved him away, and ran to the door, wiping her eyes on her sleeve.

When she emerged, her mother asked if she wanted to stop at the toy store near the bus stop. She could buy that big talking doll she had wanted last time they were there. Dafna said that was a year ago and she didn't want the doll anymore. "Then something else," her mother offered, thinking she had to compensate her middle child yet not knowing exactly what for.

Shortly before she died, Dafna's mother told her about having had three abortions. The first one had been two months after Irit was born, and the second and third—"Two in six months," she boasted—were about a year before Dafna was born. When she heard her mother on her deathbed bragging about these secret abortions, it occurred to Dafna that she might have come into the world simply because her mother was afraid to have another one, whereas where Gadi was concerned—and this was no secret, as her mother had spoken of it all these years with unknowing pride, although it now occurred to Dafna that perhaps it was very much knowing and that her mother even enjoyed offending her daughters—"We had Gadi because we wanted a son."

She remembered one of their last conversations, on the balcony of the house (which at the time did not yet have a garden in front or a backyard, or hedges and fences, or a patio), with her mother slumped to one side in the old armchair that had once belonged to the cats Dafna and her siblings had raised. The bowel cancer had finished gnawing away at her insides and the only thing left to do was to wait. Her mother knew without being told about Dafna's attempts to get pregnant, and Dafna looked back nostalgically on those days, even though they were the days of her mother's dying and even though she had been forced to take care of her because Irit was on bed rest with her second son and Gadi was busy with his crumbling marriage—still, she remembered those terrible days with nostalgia, because she and Eli were at the beginning of the road then; it hadn't yet occurred to them that something was very wrong, and they had not yet set foot on the long path of disappointments that lay ahead.

It had been a September evening, cooler than usual for an Israeli autumn, and the weather reminded her mother of the only time she'd been overseas, ten years earlier, on a package tour. She'd been to see the foliage in New England (she struggled to pronounce the name without an Israeli accent) and it was cold, just like now, she said, and asked Dafna to go inside and bring her the off-white cable-knit sweater she'd bought in New England at a seaside village tourist shop. She hadn't worn it since because she said it was too warm and heavy for Israel, but mostly because she thought it was ridiculous on her and made her look like some kind of Norwegian fisherman. But now she asked for it because she was really cold, "like in New England," and Dafna thought that more than being cold she simply enjoyed enunciating those words over and over again. When she came back with the sweater and helped her mother, who could barely lift her arms anymore, to put it on, her mother cuddled up and ran her fingers along the thick cables, her eyes focused on a distant point in the sickly lawn, and said, "Not everyone was meant to have children." When Dafna looked at her huddled on the armchair, swallowed up in the sweater, nothing but skin and bones, with a distended stomach that suggested not cancer but another unwanted pregnancy, her mother looked back at her and said, "It's not a tragedy, Dafna. It's really not."

But she was wrong. Not in what she said, but in the fact that those were more or less her final words, and words uttered on one's deathbed have a grating sting that penetrates deep under the skin and trickles into the blood with a poison whose effect is delayed and continuous. It was not what she said, although that was insulting and infuriating, but the fact that she tried to console Dafna and was no more successful than she had been all the other thousands of times. When she died, Dafna's anger gave way to a sense of failure, which was followed, of course, by sadness and longing and then guilt. No matter what she'd said, Dafna thought, when she reconstructed that conversation over and over again, her mother would have imprinted her with this tattoo of sadness. She realized that those who die destroy the living with their final words, and she promised herself that she would save her children from that; when she was dying she would stick to small talk—weather, food, shopping, maybe politics—protecting them from some accidental but haunting truth.

She heard Eli fart in the bedroom and the motorized blinds hum their way up, and wondered if he remembered that they were invited to Irit and Mani's that evening for a birthday dinner for their eldest son, Lior. Irit had Lior and Assaf, and Gadi, who had divorced two years ago, had Gila and Gaya, and his second wife, Anat, was already expecting, and she was two years older than Dafna. She had tried to like Anat at first, because Gadi's first wife, the mother of his two daughters, had caused him pain. She used to tell herself that she shouldn't think of her just as Gadi's second wife, and eventually she was able to view the petite, slender economist as just Anat. She even grew to like her, until she became pregnant, which Dafna calculated had happened before they got married and was perhaps the reason for the marriage. She was already pregnant when they celebrated her thirty-ninth birthday. Dafna remembered how Anat had refused the champagne they'd bought especially, gently and discreetly pushing away the flute. And ever since they made the official announcement shortly afterward, hand in hand—"We're pregnant!"—Anat had reverted to being just Gadi's second wife.

Yesterday Dafna had called her to ask if they had the amniocentesis results—Irit had told her they'd had one; Gadi and Anat did not share these things with her so as not to cause her pain. Even Anat's voice sounded pregnant when she replied, "Yes, we got the results on Sunday, and everything's fine, thank God." It was a girl. The doctor hadn't been sure at the last scan, and had even scared them a bit by saying, "Maybe it's a boy with a little penis," but it wasn't, it was a girl, and everything was fine, "thank God."

"So now you can finally start enjoying this pregnancy," Dafna said.

"You think so?"

Dafna said she was sure, and sent big hugs to her and Gadi and the fetus. She detected a tone of surprise in Anat's voice, and a certain relief, when she said, "Wow, you too, Dafna, I mean hugs and everything, and thanks. You know I think about you all the time, like, I don't know if it's okay to say this now, but I know you're trying; Gadi told me."

"Yes, I know, but never mind that now; I'm just happy that everything's all right with the amnio."

Anat sighed. "You have no idea the anxiety we went through; you have no idea. I thought I would miscarry just from that."

"Why on earth would you miscarry?" Dafna exclaimed, and even said *thank God* herself a few times before she hung up and kept sitting on the lawn chair, staring at the orchards and the spindly grove beyond them, until the cordless phone in her lap rang and Eli announced that he'd be late and asked if she was okay, because she sounded a little strange. She said she was fine and sat there until it grew dark.

This evening, she thought, Anat will come to Lior's birthday dinner with a deep glass bowl full of chocolate mousse, which she'd promised, and with her stomach, which Irit had reported was compact and looked like a small basketball; other than that she hadn't gained an ounce. She'd be with Gadi, whose freckles, which had faded with age, seemed to have regained their color since he'd met her, and they'd sit on Irit and

Mani's couch, and perhaps Anat would wonder about the new white sofa they'd recently bought at IKEA—how long would it take the baby to destroy it? And her heart would sink, as Anat would put one hand on her belly and the other in Gadi's hand, and he would look so happy, with his freckles and his couch-destroying baby girl. And having dispatched the evil eye that had silenced them till now, they'd debate out loud whether to call the baby Or or Alma, or perhaps Aya, and Eli would say, "Alma, go for Alma, that's a hot chick's name," and Dafna would hate him because Alma was the name they were keeping for *their* child, and Yonatan if it was a boy, and what did it say that he so easily conceded the name they had worked to agree on all these years.

Now she heard Eli brushing his teeth with the electric toothbrush, which he claimed was the reason he brushed twice a day, two minutes each time, and enjoyed it. He had bought her one too but she preferred the old kind. She found the buzzing in her mouth unpleasant, as if she had swallowed a wasp, and now she felt the dim vibration of the brush in her limbs and something in her shuddered, as though the hum was passing from Eli's mouth to her knees. She missed him, she missed the man she had known before the accessories, the man before this house, before the inexplicable infertility, when he himself had been a little more inexplicable: a cynical Jerusalemite lawyer, "cracked and Syrian, just like the olives," as he sometimes said of himself. When was the last time they'd had sex?

Ten days ago. Not something worth straining to remember, but still the act of remembering involved a certain effort, because she tried to forget the few couplings with Eli as soon as they were over, despite the fact that she was the one who insisted on them, demanded them, out of an urge, she thought, because she would suddenly look at him and want him, but mainly because she was afraid to turn into a person who had no sex. When he saw her looking at him that way, with the hungry gaze he had once loved, which used to turn him on just like her red hair had—*Gingy*, he used to call her when they first met, and she thought it was horribly clichéd and common, and it was one of the things that bothered her about Eli, but those words, including the Gingy he had long ago stopped saying, had turned over the years into one mass, a clump of pasta forgotten in the sieve, until she could no longer separate what bothered her from what didn't—now when he saw that look he would come up to her and ask tenderly, and sometimes, she suspected, pityingly, "Do you feel like it?" She would nod as if he'd offered to share a snack, and then came the usual moves. They were so set in their patterns that they could have left written instructions for another couple to clone their intercourse, the one and only remaining routine out of what used to be a rich repertoire, the one that was easiest, most comfortable. Unlike the stereotype, they did not favor the missionary position— they'd been saved from at least one cliché—but did it from the rear, with Dafna on her stomach, a holdover from the days when they thought they'd be able to have a child naturally, and the first doctor, the one from the HMO—she missed his innocence, his ordinariness—had recommended that position. Perhaps it would really be better if they saved themselves the effort and just sat comfortably and watched from a distance as the other couple humiliated themselves, and pointed at them with a stick as if they were a diagram, to highlight their mistakes. When it was over—quickly, thank God—they could look each other in the eye and say, *See? Is it worth it?* Then Dafna could shake her head and say, *I don't look like I'm enjoying it. Am I enjoying it? But you came*, he'd say, presenting his winning argument. *I came, but that doesn't mean I enjoyed it.* He'd shake his head sadly and they'd agree it was unnecessary, it was terrible, and they weren't going to do it anymore, okay?

But no. Every few weeks, mostly when they were taking a break between one IVF and the next, she couldn't help herself. Eli blamed the hormones, but she knew it had nothing to do with that. Quite the opposite: most of the time she felt swollen and sore, and there were the eighteen pounds that had made her, officially, a large woman, a tall, full-figured, broad redhead. It was not the hormones that made her horny but the fear that this is how it would always be: she and Eli alone in this house, with the garden furniture that cost 9,530 shekels. She didn't want to adopt, she told everyone who suggested it. She knew there were new options—Ukraine, Latvia, Georgia—but then again Georgia was closed off now; the Georgians didn't want to give babies to a terrorist state. No, she couldn't think about that, because it would be one thing if they had a diagnosis, if someone just said to them, "Take a deep breath, it's not going to happen." But the unexplained was something you could not abandon, something that was both mysterious and predictable and so much like them: the unexplained was their adopted child.

Besides, seven years was not so much time, said the people who had tried for ten or more and had eventually succeeded, the people who looked like they had come home from a long trek on a lost and dangerous continent, the kind that thousands travel to but from which only a handful return. She hung on every word uttered by these infertility warhorses. She knew two such couples, and one of them now had two children, born a year apart. "A screwup," said the mother with a weary smile. "Turns out you're most fertile right after giving birth, so watch out." As if Dafna herself was in the midst of this dangerous twilight of fertility. As if she were the one breast-feeding a two-week-old girl while her one-year-old tried to pull the baby away from the breast. Dafna found it strange to see this woman instantly converting her infertility into excessive fertility, forgetting who she had been and playing her new part, plump and exhausted. She envied her and sometimes hated her, but this woman gave her hope, and after every visit or phone call she thought, *Seven years really isn't that long.* "Who are you kidding?" Eli said, when she tried to cheer herself up, diffusing the house with this new perspective like air freshener. "Seven years? That's a long time. Very long! But it'll be all right, Dafna, it'll work out in the end." In those moments, more than ever, she felt truly betrayed.

She thought of how Anat's impudent pregnancy had played tricks on her love for her little brother. Because at first she had hoped something would go wrong. When Irit called one evening, a few days after the announcement, to tell her that Gadi and Anat had spent the night in the ER because of bleeding, Dafna had asked anxiously, "And?"

"And nothing. It stopped, and there's a pulse, and everything's fine. The doctor said it happens. You remember it happened to me with Lior?"

"Yes, and with Assaf too, no?"

"No, with Assaf it was cervical insufficiency. They had to stitch me up, don't you remember? Come on, I was on bed rest for six months, when Mom died."

Dafna said she remembered, of course she did.

"Anyway," Irit said, and Dafna could hear her boys fighting in the background, "Gadi says they were scared, but thank God everything's okay."

"Thank God."

Irit said she had to go before the kids murdered each other—not that she cared. "Cut it out! Enough!" she screamed, right into the phone, but Dafna wasn't really listening. She hated herself so much for having even been capable of wishing tragedy on her own brother. "So we'll talk later," Irit said, and of course they didn't.

The silt sank to the bottom of the glass and a dense, milky light began to trickle over the backyard. Dafna emptied the glass in three gulps and heard the alarm system beep when Eli punched in the code to neutralize it. He came into the kitchen and touched her shoulder, both to say good morning and to move her aside, and took the coffee out of the freezer and walked over to the espresso machine and asked what the smell was. She pointed to the empty glass and he said, "You've started already? When did you get your period?" She said yesterday, and he yawned and said, "Oh, right." She asked if he remembered they were going to Irit and Mani's that night, and he said he did. He turned on the machine and went over to the French doors and opened them wide. He always opened those doors, as if something noxious had built up in the house overnight. He asked if she wanted coffee, and she said not yet, she wanted to wait a little, to give the substance time to work. She searched his face for the contempt, but this morning he looked truly indifferent. "So what time do we have to be there?" he asked.

"Seven-thirty. I still have to buy a gift for Lior."

He said he could go past Toys"R"Us if she wanted, his hearing had been canceled and he had some spare time in the afternoon.

"I'd love that," she said, and told him she had a busy day preparing for the next evening's demonstration. "Are you coming?"

"We'll see; I'm not sure what kind of day I have yet. Is it okay if I let you know tomorrow morning?"

She nodded. It was obvious that he wouldn't come to the demonstration, just like he hadn't gone to the other ones. In fact, she thought, she would prefer it if he didn't come, so he wouldn't see her running around, worried, fussing with signs, instructing volunteers, counting heads, chasing down the few journalists who turned up, remembering at the last minute that she'd forgotten to revise Gabi's speech. After all, she knew this demonstration, like the previous ones, would look slightly ridiculous and sparsely attended. It was supposed to have taken place a month ago, but it was postponed because of the terrorist attack at Maxim's restaurant, which had happened three days earlier, and now the evenings were chilly and people wouldn't show up. But she knew, hot or cold, either way it wouldn't be more than a few dozen, and she would rather Eli not be there, so he wouldn't be able to dump on her what he dumped on her the whole time anyway, so as not to provide him with more evidence, solid this time, for his claim that this new social movement she represented wasn't worth shit.

"What will you get him?" she asked, and he said he'd see, maybe a remote-controlled jeep. "He has one," she said, as the coffee aroma swallowed up the sharply exotic traces of her concoction.

"So what should I get?" he asked. He poured milk into the little pitcher and started to froth it. "Something else with a remote?" When he saw her looking at the machine he asked, "Should I make you some after all?"

"No, not yet. Actually, yes. I'll ask Irit what he doesn't have."

"Okay, you can let me know later. I'll go in the afternoon sometime, not before. I have meetings at the office."

They took their coffee and sat facing each other at the table, and he asked if she was starting with the shots today. She nodded, and he asked if he should stop at the drugstore. She said no, she'd already bought all the ampoules yesterday. "But remember to clear the seventeenth or the eighteenth in your diary, the nineteenth at the latest."

"Okay, but I really hope it isn't on the eighteenth, 'cause I have a court appearance first thing in the morning. But don't worry. When was your retrieval last time?"

"On the thirteenth day."

"Oh, yeah. Right."

She remembered how ceremonious Professor Ferber had sounded when he told her they'd retrieved nine eggs. "Nine!" he'd announced, because they'd only seen six on the ultrasound. He was counting on those extra three, "the stowaways," as he called them. "Those'll be your triplets." He laughed, but when he met them three days later, for the transfer, only three embryos had been fertilized, and his expression was cool. "Still, that's also something. Two of excellent quality and one so-so." But none of them had taken.

"I don't think it's likely you'll have the retrieval on the eighteenth, is it? That's a little early, no? What does that come out to, let's count it."

"It comes out the thirteenth day. Clear that day."

"Sure, I'll clear it, don't worry."

She was seized by a spasm of longing for that distant era of five minutes ago, with the light just before sunrise and the kitchen a moment before Eli had invaded it, flooding it with their life, with her failure.

REUVEN

"That woman's pipe was whistling all night, kind of a high-pitched hum." Reuven tried to mimic the sound so Rina would understand exactly what he was talking about, but she'd heard the pipe too, although it hadn't stopped her from getting a good night's sleep. "It's a hum of wastefulness, of her generation's irresponsibility toward the state, toward the moshav, toward God!" he yelled from the bathroom, and flushed the toilet on the low-flow setting. But then he felt like taking a crap, which was odd because he never took a crap in the morning, always in the afternoon, when he came home from the office, roughly between three and four. He ignored the dull pressure in his stomach and was about to head to the kitchen for his instant coffee, but when he washed his hands under the weak stream produced by the new water-saving faucet, the pressure became an urge, and he pulled his pajama bottoms down and sat on the toilet, angry with himself, because now this unexpected crap would cost him one-and-a-half tanks of water.

"*Sheeeeeee.*" He whistled the syllable of wastefulness again. "*Sheeeeeee,* all night long! It's enough to drive you crazy! I mean, doesn't she hear it? Doesn't she know she has a leak?"

"She hears and she knows," Rina answered from the kitchen, "but she doesn't care."

"I'll show her *doesn't care,*" he said, as he passed a stream of loose stool into the toilet. "I'll have a talk with her husband."

"What would you do that for? He doesn't live there anymore. Talk with *her*, she's nice."

"I *will* talk with her. I will." *Nice*, he scoffed to himself and tried to remember what he'd eaten the day before that had brought on this upset stomach. He reviewed yesterday's menu and found nothing out of the ordinary. "Do you have a stomachache, too?" he asked his wife, who quickly appeared in the hallway.

"You have a stomachache?"

"Diarrhea." He sighed, and although he thought he'd emptied his bowels, he kept sitting on the toilet, just to be on the safe side.

"What did you eat?" As she stood in the bathroom doorway, her face, which always took slightly longer to wake up than the rest of her, was suddenly glowing, eager to contend with this new domestic health crisis. "Did you eat something at the office?"

"Nothing." But then he remembered the sesame bread with *zaatar* that Ali had brought from his village. "Maybe some of that sesame bread the Arab brought."

"Sesame bread can't cause anything."

"What do I know?" He looked at her as she leaned on the doorway and nibbled on a slice of toast with cream cheese. "Maybe he touched it with dirty hands, the louse." He sighed and tore off some squares of toilet paper, ready to wipe as soon as he was convinced his bowels were done playing games with him.

"So is it serious?"

He shook his head.

"You're sweating terribly." She came closer. "Maybe you have a fever?"

"I don't. I only ate a little, not much, and I didn't touch the *zaatar* at all."

"Thank God. That's where all the germs are, in those little twists of newspaper."

"Yes." And it was an Arabic newspaper! He decided to risk it and wipe. When he finished, even before pulling up his pajamas, he pushed down on the larger flush handle, and stood watching the water swirl down. Just as he'd feared, one tank wasn't enough, and a frothy cloud of stool floated on the water. He sighed and waited for the tank to fill up, debating whether half a tank would be enough this time. So as not to risk being wasteful again, and not to give Rina the evidence she sought to prove her annoying claim that it was the water-saving devices that ended up wasting water, he flushed the large handle again.

He agreed to have tea with lemon instead of coffee and sat down at the table under the neon lamp that meted out its miserly light. Then he got up to open the window, look out onto the street, and listen to his neighbor's whistling pipe across the street. Like his own, it was one of the older houses on the moshav, but Alona Segal and her half-American husband, who was no longer exactly her husband now because they were separated, or whatever it was called these days, had renovated it five years ago, when they bought it from Berkovich's widow, after her sons moved her to an assisted living facility, where she'd died within a month—"From a broken heart," he'd told Rina, but she'd said it was no broken heart, she'd been sick for years. She could never see the big picture, the complex maneuvers that led to these simple, miserable results, and although he looked down on her for that, he always reminded himself that this was the reason, among others, that he'd married her. He had wanted a practical woman who wouldn't bother him with nonsense.

He was forty-two when he met her, still a bachelor, and in some ways also a virgin. He had been with a few women, three to be precise, but they hadn't been right for him. His elderly parents, Ze'ev and Gita Brochstein, had been among the founders of Eden, and even in their old age, he thought sadly now, they had tended to the peach and nectarine groves that he himself had leased after their deaths to a farmer from a nearby moshav. The chicken coops he'd done away with. He missed his parents, although he did not by any means feel that he'd betrayed them, even when he watched the Thai workers in the groves and the farmer who leased the lands drive up in a Toyota truck to give them orders. No, he had not betrayed his parents because they themselves had claimed—especially his mother, whom he missed with a prolonged physical pain, a sort of ulcer that had accompanied him ever since her death sixteen years ago, five years after his father had died—they had both claimed that he was not made of the stuff of farmers. Even today's farmers were not made of that stuff, his mother used to say with bitter resignation.

"No, Rubi, you were not meant to work the land," she said, giving him the exemption he had longed for since childhood, stressing the word *you* as if there were others who could be considered, other sons who might be better suited for the job. But Reuven was an only child, and his mother had no great expectations. That had made things easier for him in the past, but now, when he thought about it, he found it slightly insulting. She had only asked for one thing, both his parents had, although his father never said much, giving only the slow nod that always accompanied his mother's words. "One thing I ask of you, and even beg you to promise me," she used to say—and his father would nod as though the plea were addressed to him, too—"that you find yourself a good wife. Someone good for you." Again that emphasis, as though she were discussing not her only child, a bachelor, but a fragile and extraordinary creature that the world could not accommodate. "Find yourself someone right, and don't let any *tzitzkes* and *pulkes* and *tucheses* muddle you up"—here there was a cynical roll of the eyes—"you need a woman to take care of you and the house and the children and everything else." And because the plea was made when he was as young as fifteen, the breasts, thighs, and especially the rear ends of women became fixed in his mind as a continuous threat, a gang of seasoned swindlers whose winks and calls should make a decent person cross to the other side of the street. And the fact was that the three women he had been with before he met Rina had been blessed with bodies as straight as rulers, as had Rina, who came to replace a secretary on maternity leave at the local council, where he was working at the time as a clerk in the business licensing department, the department he managed today with unbending severity.

She was a widow who had lost her husband in the Yom Kippur War, and when they met she was thirty-five. But other than her age, which made his mother suspicious of her reproductive abilities, it was love at first sight. He was sorry that his father was not alive to nod his background harmony on the day he announced his engagement. His mother responded by declaring that now she could depart in peace, but she stayed alive for another five years and was even rewarded with one grandson. Dudi was an ideal baby, smiley and chubby; from the day they came home from the hospital he slept through the night and had no special demands or any kind of fussing and nonsense like other people's babies.

Reuven looked out at the one-story house across the street, which was hidden by a living fence of jasmine and honeysuckle. Most of the renovated houses on the moshav were new, but the woman and her soon-to-be-ex-husband had left the old structure intact, knocked down the inside walls, and turned it into one big space containing the living room and kitchen. They built extensions on either side of the house, one a huge bedroom facing the backyard, the other with three smaller rooms. They painted over the original plaster with a pale shade of yellow, replaced the standard floor tiles with faded yellow tiles that looked as if millions of feet had already walked over them, laid a parquet floor in the bedroom, and generally amazed and horrified Reuven by managing to make an old house look even older.

"Interesting. . . . Her car isn't there," he said, when he noticed the woman's silver Mazda wasn't in its usual place near the gate.

"Maybe they went somewhere."

"Where would they go? Don't the kids need to go to kindergarten? There—listen!" He pricked up one finger as though trying to isolate a single note in a symphony.

"Yes," Rina said, and squeezed lemon into his tea. "I hear it. So go talk to her, go on; she's a nice woman."

"I will talk to her. Don't think I won't. Nice woman. . . ." He sat down at the table again, debating whether to eat something or let his stomach rest. Rina suggested toast, and in his mind's eye he suddenly saw the sesame roll he'd devoured, the one Ali had placed on the table before leaving to do a job. "This is for you, Mr. Reuven," he'd said, as though presenting a bottle of poison—that Arab, who only even had a job thanks to Reuven. The council didn't list him as an employee, there was no formal position, and even if there was, why on earth would they give it to an Arab, even one who was a citizen? It was Reuven who had convinced the residents of Eden to pay Ali a modest monthly salary out of their own pockets in return for odd jobs that no one could precisely define but were clearly essential. In between jobs, Ali would hang around Reuven's office as if he were his deputy, and now he was trying to kill him.

Rina asked if he wanted some cottage cheese on his toast, it wouldn't do any harm. He said no, just toast, because he suddenly felt his bowels rumbling again. He blew on the tea she served him and waited for the slice to pop out of the toaster and land in the sink before Rina, who had been distracted lately, could catch it. He had repeatedly suggested that she move the toaster, but she said it was convenient where it was, and anyway there was no room left on the counter, what with all the appliances. If she moved the toaster, where would she put the mixer and the blender? "The toast!" he warned, a second before it popped, and she lurched to the corner like a basketball player, caught the flying slice, and carefully handed it over with both hands, as though she had captured a bird for him.

Toast in hand, he went to the window again, and said it was intolerable. He thought they might need to talk to someone. But who? Maybe Friedman, the council chair, because this wasn't the first time it had happened; he'd mentioned it politely a few times, and Alona had always apologized and promised to get someone to fix it, and she had; he'd seen the plumbers, kneeling on the asphalt and fixing the broken valve. And her peculiar husband, the half-American—"He's not American," Rina would correct him, "he has an English name but he grew up here"—he'd talked with that Mark guy a few times, too, going all the way to the Italian restaurant he'd opened without a license at the edge of the moshav, right in the woods, on land the council had agreed to lease to him practically for free. After a few hearings, they'd reached a compromise to allow him to continue operating the restaurant, but Reuven had personally seen to it that the council required Mark Segal to pave an access road at his own expense, so the restaurant traffic wouldn't pass through the moshav. He was convinced the cost would be beyond the guy's ability, but he had dug a dirt road—Reuven wondered where he got the money; everyone was a thief in this country nowadays, everyone—and privately he had to admit that Alona, his separated wife, was a very good-looking woman, even beautiful in a certain way, though somewhat wild and unkempt. More than once he had imagined her naked. Not that he lacked for opportunities to really see her almost naked at the pool, with her *tzitzkes* hanging out and her big *tuches* wiggling right under his nose like an accusing finger.

Once, when she was in the water with the kids, the son—what was his name? He remembered the girl's name, Maya, because he liked that name, but what was the boy called?—the boy, who was in her arms, afraid of the water, had pulled down her bathing suit strap and her

breast had been exposed for all to see. Since she was busy calming the
boy she hadn't noticed, or had but didn't care—that was just like her
generation—and he saw a dreamy breast, white and dazzling against her
tan skin, as though someone had whitewashed it, with a pink-brown
nipple that gathered bluish veins toward it like a spiderweb, a trap. He
wondered later who else had seen it. Everyone had looked so busy that
he thought he was the only one who had witnessed this wonderful
sight, which lasted for an eternity, until her hand suddenly reached out
and pulled up the strap and shoved the breast inside like a pillow into a
pillowcase, matter-of-factly, without panic. Although he was disappointed
he was also happy, because he did not want her to expose everything to
him—not that way, not at once but slowly, when they were together,
after she put her vandalizing kids to bed and he happened to be there,
helping her fix something around the house, opening a clogged drain or
replacing a light socket. He was good at fixing things and, as the entire
moshav knew, because he helped them all happily, he had good hands,
and he wanted to put those hands on her, on that Alona, damn her.

Except that recently she hadn't needed his services. Two years ago,
when she broke up with the guy, Reuven had turned up every time a
repair was needed. She didn't ask but he offered, insisted even. Whenever he ran into her at the grocery store, or when he walked by the front
yard and the gate was open and he saw her there, with the kids or
alone, he would ask if everything was okay in the house and if she needed
help with anything. Usually she thanked him and said everything was
fine, but sometimes she mentioned that something was broken or needed
to be checked, and he would offer to come and have a look; maybe he
could fix it and save her the money. She would protest, at first sincerely,
then just to be polite, so he had become a regular fixture in her household
that winter, after her husband left. He would turn up in the early evening with his toolbox, which always impressed her—or perhaps, he
thought now, she was just pretending—but either way he was flattered
by the effect he had on her and the kids, who liked to scatter his tools
around the house. "No problem, let them play," he always said, even
though he was annoyed by their behavior and the way their mother
couldn't control them, and a few of his tools got lost. He would start to
repair whatever was broken and refuse to eat or drink anything. "Maybe
later," he'd say and wave a dismissive hand at her apologies for being

busy with the kids, making their dinner, bathing them, putting them to bed. (What sort of a notion is that, he thought, *putting them to bed*? When Dudi was little no one called it that. You didn't put children to bed—the kid just went to sleep whether he wanted to or not, and that was that.) "I hope I'm not in the way," he would say, and Alona would reply, of course not, she was grateful to him for coming. While he fixed whatever needed fixing—she had a lot of problems with the electricity, he remembered, and all the window frames had leaks that no amount of silicone could seal—he would devour the messy house with his eyes and inhale the smells wafting from the wood-burning stove.

Once he remarked in a friendly tone that it was much cleaner, safer, and more economical to install a central heating system. She looked at him and said that central heating was less fun and less romantic, wasn't it? He wondered if she was coming on to him. His heart told him it was impossible, but other organs suspected it might be true. She said the stove was nice, you could roast potatoes and marshmallows, and once a year the wood was delivered and there was a storeroom in the base-ment, and no, it wasn't hard for her to go down and bring up the wood, it was the only exercise she got, and he thought about her going up and down the stairs, her wonderful breasts swinging like pendulums. Yes, that's how he would like her, on top of him, even thought he didn't like being on the bottom, and Rina used to sometimes complain, back when they still had sex, that he was square and conservative. But with Alona, he thought, he would be willing to try things, like being on his back, for example; why not? Anything, whatever she suggested, whatever she wanted, whatever didn't hurt or get in the way. Anything. He was sixty-two, he still had something to offer, something to try out.

He had looked at her from the top of the ladder where he was perched, dislodging a broken light socket with a pair of pliers. He had to be careful not to lose his balance when the boy ran out of the bath-room naked and she hurried after him with a big towel. She bumped into the ladder and apologized, grabbed the boy and picked him up, wrapped him in the towel, and took him into the children's bedroom. The girl, who was as beautiful as her mother, appeared in the living room wearing her pajamas, with her hair combed back, and curled up in the armchair and asked to see a video. "Just a minute," her mother answered from the bedroom. "Let me finish up here, and then I'll come."

The girl started to whimper—*Come now!*—and Alona shouted, "I'm coming!"

Reuven offered to put the tape on: "Just tell me which one." The girl eyed him suspiciously, and her mother said there was no need; she had to learn how to wait. The girl shrieked, "I don't want to wait! I always wait!"

Reuven said, "It's fine, Alona, I'll be happy to put the tape on, just tell me which one. I'm getting down now." But the girl had screamed *I want my mommy to put it on!*

Alona had emerged, holding the half-naked boy waving a diaper in his hand. How old was he then? About eighteen months. And the girl was three. That's how you leave a wife, with two babies at home? Reuven mused. But Mark hadn't gone far, he'd stayed in the moshav, renting from the Blochs, who had bought their house as an investment and renovated it but never lived there.

Because he was on his way down the ladder, standing two rungs up, the abandoned woman's face was very close to his groin, but she didn't notice because she was lecturing the girl, who buried her face in the arm-chair and scissored her legs up and down. Embarrassed, he was unsure whether to go up or down. "Listen to me carefully, Maya," she told the girl, who had kicked the cordless phone and a copper bowl filled with dried flowers off the coffee table. "We've talked about this a million times. I can't do two things at once. You have to be a little bit patient, do you understand?" From the depths of the armchair came a muffled wail: *I don't want to.* "Well you'll just have to, and if you're bored then go get a game or a book, or watch Reuven." Maya's head peeked out from under a pillow: *Then I want Reuven to put it on!* "No!" said Alona. "He's busy, too." Reuven was about to get off the ladder, but the woman turned to him, and perhaps she suddenly noticed the bulge in his pants— although he found that hard to believe, since it wasn't a real erection but just the beginning of something—and she took a few steps back and said, "Absolutely not. She'll wait."

He was sorry, because he wanted to hurry up this pointless putting-to-bed process so that he could finally say, You know what? I will have a coffee now, if it's not too much trouble. And she would say, Gladly, and he'd sit at the huge table in the kitchen, which was really part of the living room, and this was another thing he didn't understand: What for? But that's the way it was with all the young people. More than half the moshav looked like that now, and those windows, the huge frames with lots of little squares, which cost too much money and caused a lot of trouble. He would watch her movements as she made him the coffee. She would look tired but he would ignore it; after all, he was doing her a service, saving her a lot of money she'd have had to pay some crooked electrician who didn't know how to do his job, and he deserved at least a drink.

He strained to ignore the lower body of the toddler in her arms, with his tiny penis, and although he had seen naked children before, he had trouble determining whether it was normal or abnormal in its smallness and could not help wondering whether it meant anything about the size of his father's penis, although what bothered Reuven about that thought was not so much the size as the fact that who knew how many times and in how many ways it had penetrated this tired and beautiful woman? "I'm sorry," she said, and sighed. "Three is such a difficult age."

"Well, kids—I know how it is," he replied, and climbed back up the ladder.

"Come on," she said to the boy, "we'll change your diaper on the couch."

The boy waddled over to his sister, who sat fuming in the armchair. "Get away from me, creep!" she screeched, and for a moment Reuven thought she was talking to him. "Maya, I'm warning you," Alona said, putting a tape into the VCR and turning the TV on. The weather forecaster's face switched to an animated lion cub standing on a cliff. "That's not the beginning!" the girl yelled. "I want it from the beginning!"

Reuven disconnected the light socket and placed it on the upper rung of the ladder, pulled a new one out of his pocket—he had refused to let her pay for it because he had several spares at home, and this annoyed him later—and the boy got up and started running around the house again, pulled his clean diaper off, and then stood under the ladder and put his foot on the first rung. His mother scooped him up. "Let him watch," Reuven said. "If he's really interested, maybe he'll learn something." She propped the baby on her shoulder, and again Reuven could not avoid looking at the little penis that shrank like a turtle's head and disappeared between his chubby thighs. "I think he's making pee-pee on you," he said, and Alona quickly disengaged the boy from her shoulder.

Patience, Reuven told himself as he installed the new socket, careful not to touch the wrong wire. "There's no need to turn off the power," he'd boasted when Alona suggested it, "I know what I'm doing and you need light now, don't you? With putting the kids to bed and all." Half an hour from now they'd be alone in the kitchen, sitting at the heavy wooden table, which looked old and could do with a coat of varnish. He had once offered to come by sometime and give it a polish, but Alona had smiled and told him it was like that on purpose; they wanted it to look old. He couldn't understand it, just couldn't, but he no longer wanted to understand, he just wanted to sit with her in the quiet house, sip the coffee she'd make him when this exhausting day was finally over—the kids still looked completely alert—and maybe, who knew, she would gaze at him with those beautiful eyes, which, although he wanted each and every limb of her full body, were definitely what excited him more than anything else, and she'd invite him to the bedroom with the parquet floor, which he'd never been in because somehow it was the one room where nothing ever needed fixing, but he'd seen it many times when he'd walked past the open door, and there—they would try to be quiet because of the children, and he wasn't one of those noisy men anyway—he would make love to her even though he did not love her, but he desired her as he felt he had never before desired anyone, not Rina and not the three before her, not even the ones who came later, in his imagination.

He had never been unfaithful to Rina, and it seemed to him that now, at the age of sixty-two, he was not only permitted but obliged, at least once, because soon it would be too late, and in any case he didn't think Rina would mind if she knew, although she never would; Alona seemed discreet. Rina had lost interest a long time ago, not that she was ever a great catch in the bedroom, and it was obvious to him that all the accusations she used to hurl at him about not being daring or original and refusing to try out new things were in fact covering up for her own frigidity. Once or twice a month she'd consent, and then she was full of criticism and suggestions for improvements, as she called them, and once, more than a decade ago, she had even given him a book he'd refused to read, but he sometimes looked at the diagrams and the pictures, shocked and curious, and then hid it under a pile of wood in the shed so it wouldn't end up in Dudi's hands.

Dudi wasn't interested in girls anyway, what with his job in the army. He came home tired and irritable every evening and shut himself up in his room for hours, sitting at the computer with that Internet of his. Reuven rued the day he had agreed to hook up to it—he'd already threatened to stop paying the massive phone bills, but Dudi, without even turning to face him, said very simply that if he did that he would kill himself. Rina tried to reassure Reuven when he came out of the boy's room in a state and reported what he'd said. She'd told him that was how young people talked these days, everyone threatening suicide. Yet something in him—some part of him that knew Dudi deep inside—understood that in his case the threat could come true. The boy was quiet, always had been, but it was worse in the last couple of years, since he'd grown taller than Reuven and his voice had plunged a whole octave lower.

He was now certain that another trip to the toilet was unavoidable, yet he kept standing by the window, listening to the whistling pipe as if it were a signal from a radio station that had stopped broadcasting. He hadn't been inside the house across the street for two years. Every time he offered, she said there was no need, really; everything was fine, "You must have done such a good job last time that nothing has broken since." Her compliments made him proud, even though they sounded like the way you would praise a child, but he was still disappointed.

He sometimes ran into her in the supermarket at the giant shopping center near the Rimonim Intersection, a ten-minute drive from Eden. He would nod in her direction, or stop to chat if she looked as though she was not in a hurry. Once he asked, "So how come I don't remember you from when you were growing up here, when you were little?"

"There's not much to remember," she said, and told him she'd spent most of her childhood at home with her father. She wasn't in a youth movement or anything and didn't hang out in the square by the grocery store with the other kids in the evenings. She had left Eden before her army service, at seventeen, and gone to live in Tel Aviv with her cousin, a student, because she had a year between high school and the army.

"Really?" Reuven was surprised.

"Yes, I didn't get along with my mom, so she didn't object. She was all for it, actually. My dad was pretty broken up, but he couldn't do anything."

Reuven was shocked: How could a seventeen-year-old girl go and live alone in the city with some student cousin? But that probably explained why he didn't remember her.

When he met her in the supermarket or at the gas station, he usually settled for a polite hello, but once, at the beginning of summer, on a blistering hot day, he saw her standing outside the supermarket with her kids, who were clutching ice-cream bars that dripped on their chins and clothes, which didn't seem to bother their mother much. She was holding the handle of an overflowing shopping cart with one hand and pressing a cell phone to her ear with the other, conducting a noisy conversation with a lit cigarette hanging from the corner of her mouth—like some kind of skank, he thought. He hated women who smoked, but for her he would make an exception. She was wearing her pool clothes: an oversized men's undershirt with her black bra showing through the huge arm openings, thigh-length cut-off jeans, and flip-flops. He waited for her to finish her phone call, grinning the whole time at the children, who glared back at him, and when she hung up and put the phone in her bag, she gave him one of her weary smiles and asked how he was. She raised a hand to wipe the sweat off her forehead and revealed an armpit covered with black stubble like moss. He said he was fine and offered to push the cart to her car.

When they reached the Mazda he stood behind her and waited for her to open the trunk, but the boy dropped his ice cream on the asphalt, started to scream, and refused to be strapped into his seat until the lost ice cream was returned. "It's gone," the woman told him. "You didn't have much left anyway, just one bite, it's no big deal." But the boy looked at his sister, who clung to her mother's bare thigh and slowly licked her almost-whole ice cream, and cried even louder. Reuven watched her struggle with the toddler, her upper body in the car and her ass hanging out, bent over like she was asking for it, really asking for it, and the way she fought with the boy, trying to force him into the seat, made her rear end jab at the air right in front of Reuven's eyes, begging him to come at her from behind, he thought. As much as he tried to lower his gaze, focus on the huge boxes of cereal in the cart, and smile at the girl, whose ice cream was drawing a sticky white stripe along her mother's right thigh, he could not: his eyes were fixed on the wriggling ass in front of him, and suddenly he had a real erection, a full and painful flourishing of the hint that had started that day on the ladder, that winter after the American had left.

"I'm really sorry," she said, when she finally pulled herself out of the car, her face flushed and sweaty, while the boy—Ido! He finally remembered the kid's name—stared at them both with an accusatory look as two rivers of tears made their way down the white mud on his face. "I'm sorry to keep you in this heat. That's it, I can manage now," she said, and tried to take the cart. But he insisted on helping put the stuff in the trunk because he was afraid to let go; the cart was hiding his midsection. She said it was fine, she'd manage, and told the girl firmly to get into the car. The girl did as she was told. "Give me the cart, I can manage," Alona said again, after walking around to the other side of the car and buckling the girl into her seat. She looked surprised when he refused to release his grip from the handle and practically yelled for her to open the trunk, but when she did it was almost completely filled with books, papers, toys, and swim rings that no one had bothered to deflate.

"There's no room," he mumbled, and she said—angrily, he thought—that there was, but he still refused to let go of the cart. "I don't think we'll be able to get anything in there," he said, hoping she would bend over again to make room but also now praying for the opportunity to leave so he could turn his back on her and hurry to his Subaru, parked on the other side of the lot.

She leaned into the trunk, pulled out a large cardboard box full of books and bent down to put it on the pavement, her rear end sticking way up and touching his hand on the handle for an instant. "Oops," she said, "sorry, I'll put this in the front," and he said okay and was about to explode; he fixed his eyes, which were glazing over with the terrible pleasure about to flood his body at any moment, on the duck heads of the swim rings peering out at him from the depths of the trunk. All he could see at that moment was a moist, yellow mass, and he no longer heard the voice of the woman, who must have been talking to him as they hoisted the bags into the trunk.

"I'll take the cart back," he said, and before she could protest, before he could remember the five-shekel coin trapped in the handle as a deposit, he turned his back and hurried away with the empty cart and the erection, it too suddenly emptied, not with an ejection of sticky wetness but as if its air had been let out.

He put the five shekels into an envelope and wrote on it, *This is yours, from the supermarket, Rubi Brochstein*, and put it in her mailbox the next day.

Sheeeeeee! He felt his brain shatter from the impact of the prolonged whistle of the pipe. *Sheeeeeee!* He chewed his toast impassively and suddenly could no longer hold it in. He put the toast on the counter and ran to the bathroom, pulling his pants down on the way, and barely had time to sit on the toilet before his bowels emptied out again, furiously this time. He heard Rina's flip-flops slapping down the hallway, and her voice asking, "What happened? What happened?" A spasm of pain seized his stomach; no way could one sesame roll be responsible for this. His wife pointed out again that he was sweating terribly, and said he looked frightening.

"Then be frightened," he whispered, and wasn't sure if she had heard him, but he knew his words were not really directed at her but at Alona, about whom he had not stopped fantasizing since that incident at the supermarket.

One day near the end of summer she had come to the council to settle a debt, and he'd met her in the hallway and invited her into his office. "I have the best AC," he boasted, "and you can leave the check with me; I'll take care of it."

"I forgot to thank you for the five shekels," she said, "you really didn't need to do that."

When she got up to go he insisted on shaking her hand. "You have nice perfume," he observed, when he walked her to the door, and she said, "Perfume?" and sniffed at her wrist. "No, that's from the kids' wipes."

After she left he stood by the window and watched her getting into her Mazda, then locked himself in his own small bathroom, determined

to reconstruct—and this time, to finish—what had started on the ladder
and continued in the parking lot. He used the hand that smelled of the
wipes to jerk off, excited and scared and mostly annoyed because it
took him so long to get hard. All he used to need was a thought or the
trace of a memory, but now, at sixty-two, he apparently needed the
presence of the ass itself, the ass that was probably settling at this minute into the driver's seat of the Mazda, and the legs, which today had
arrived in a skirt, slightly spread, the right foot on the gas—there, he
thought, he hadn't completely lost it after all, because his organ started
to harden a little, and he quickly summoned up the rest of the memory
from that one time, the only time, when Alona had given him a ride to
the garage where his car was being fixed. "I'm on my way to go shopping," she had said, when she saw him standing at the bus stop just outside the moshav.

"Okay then, thank you very much," he replied, and when they got
on the main road he noted to himself that she drove like a man. Since it
was winter and she was wearing a long coat, he could only imagine her
thighs rubbing against each other by the movement of her foot on the
gas and brake pedals. He felt that this woman who was driving was in
charge, and as she talked on her cell phone he listened to the deep, slightly
gravelly voice of a man who sounded like he had just woken up, coming
from the speakerphone.

"A young writer," she explained, when the call was over. "I'm editing
his first book."

"Talented?" he asked, as if this too were an area of his expertise,
although he hadn't read a book since high school.

"Super talented," she said.

In the bathroom, he turned that winter drive into a summer journey
to a shared orgasm and dressed the driver in her swimsuit. Once he
stopped feeling the edge of the little sink pressing into the small of his
back and surrendered to the almost imperceptible thrusting of his hips
forward, over the toilet, he knew that he was back on track, that this
erection would not let him down, because he was feeling what he remembered feeling years ago, when he was about to empty out—but suddenly from the other side of the door he heard the heavy footsteps of
work shoes and froze. Then came Ali's deep, moist cough, and a clearing
of the throat and spitting.

If he's spitting into my trash can I'll kill him, Reuven thought, touching his shrinking organ. But Ali wouldn't dare, he reassured himself. He must have spat out the window, into the planter. Generations of geraniums had flowered on that Arab's phlegm, he told himself, as he pulled up his underwear and pants and debated whether or not to flush the toilet so the Arab would know he was here and wouldn't do anything in the office.

The phone rang and Ali said, "*Ahalan*, yes, *baruch hashem*, God willing," and promised someone in Eden he'd be there by lunchtime to remove a dead cat.

Another wave of pain gripped Reuven's stomach. Rina wet a towel, pressed it to his forehead, and stood over him while he emptied his bowels again and again, like a truck unloading dirt, never ending, and he found himself giving in to the cool touch of the towel and his wife's comforting words, "Let it all out, Rubi, let it out." The *sheeeeeee* in his ears and the burning in his anus and the poisoned bread all swirled around his head like lassos. This is a terrorist attack, he thought. That man had worked on the moshav for twenty-five years, and Reuven had personally helped him once, back in the first intifada, when they put his eldest son in administrative detention. "He's a good boy," the Arab had sobbed shamelessly, in tears. "He helps his mother, he's a good boy, he didn't do anything, I swear to you in God's name."

Reuven hadn't even thought twice—or maybe he had, but he'd decided to rise above himself and call someone who had grown up on the moshav, a former Mossad guy whose parents owed Reuven's parents a favor. Since the two sets of parents were no longer alive, he called in the favor himself from the Mossad guy, reminding him pleasantly of that incident—*When was it? Must have been at least thirty years.* "Thirty?" the guy had said, "longer!" That time when Ze'ev and Gita had loaned the Mossad guy's father a tractor, after his was stolen, and in the middle of picking season, no less. "I remember, sure, it was a Ferguson," said the man. Reuven said no, it was a John Deere. "Oh, that's right," said the man nostalgically, "the John Deere, sure." Then, as though it were another amusing detail from the tractor story, Reuven casually mentioned Ali's eldest son, Khaled, who was a good boy and a university student. Reuven said that he could personally vouch for him. The man said, "Okay, okay, I get it, I'll see what I can do. I'll make a few calls, but I'm not promising anything."

The boy was let out that same day, and the next day Ali appeared in the office and shamelessly got down at Reuven's feet and thanked him. Then he hurried out to his beat-up Peugeot station wagon and came back with crates of food: fruit and vegetables that looked as small and apologetic as the man who had grown them, and thin, crumbling pitas that his wife had baked, and a green, dirty-looking jerry can full of olive oil, made by Ali's brother in his own press, that people came from around the country to buy. Reuven, embarrassed, thanked Ali and then lied almost every single day when Ali asked, "So? How was the pita? And the vegetables? That's organic, that is. In Tel Aviv they pay a fortune for something like that."

In his heart Reuven thought, organic, my ass! They use sewage to water their vegetables. "Excellent," he said. "Really something special." But he threw it all out, including the filthy jerry can.

A painful spasm cut through his stomach again, and he sighed and hunched over. This is a terrorist attack by any definition, he told himself. How could that man sleep at night? He had no God. And now he, Reuven, would die like a dog on this toilet.

MARK

But why the sadness? He always seemed accompanied by fear. He couldn't help smiling when he thought about the word *fear* and the momentous significance it had acquired a few days ago, when Ido came home from preschool and announced, "Daddy, today we saw fear!"

At bedtime that night, he asked Mark to show him the fear in a book he'd brought home. They were in the kids' room, which, try as he might—and at first, right after the separation, he had built two beds with his own hands and painted them in soft hues, and on a trip to Italy he'd bought linens with much prettier characters than the Disney ones they already had, but they preferred Disney—try as he might the room still looked like a copy, a ghost of their real room, the one at Alona's.

"Fear?" he asked, and stroked the boy's hair. "What do you mean?"

Ido repeated his demand that his daddy show him the fear, until Maya, who was sitting on the rug arranging shells they'd collected on the beach on Saturday, said, "He means the picture with the clothes."

His five-year-old daughter sounded grown up, but he also detected her mother's impatience in her voice. He flipped through the book until he found the picture his son wanted: a pile of clothes that scared a girl named Hannah Banana, because at night it looked like an elephant.

Ido was pleased. "Yes, that one," he said, and turned the page. "Now show this fear!" He pointed excitedly to a picture of a plant that Hannah Banana, on that same dark night, thought was a monster.

A foggy, grainy notion of fear had been with Mark for the past few weeks, something dull and throbbing, but more than frightening he found it bothersome, saddening, as though he were waiting for something but did not know what. Or did not know how to go on living as if he were not waiting.

He felt the sadness while he sat in the kitchen drinking cappuccino, debating whether to defrost one of the croissants he had baked with the kids or eat something later at the Trattoria. After getting out of bed, he had walked around the house in his dinosaur-print boxers, then gone out to the garden and let his bare feet delight in the damp lawn that needed mowing, and all that time he felt, like he did every morning recently, as though his body were wrapped in a heavy, damp sheet of fearful sorrow. He couldn't shake it when he sat down to phone his supplier and learn what had happened to his durum flour, which he needed to make pasta for the weekend. He also asked about the organic eggs that had arrived mostly broken the day before.

"That's how I got them from the farm," the driver claimed. "It's not my responsibility."

But Mark had already spoken to the chicken farmer, a childhood friend from a moshav near Jerusalem who also supplied him with home-made ricotta and mascarpone, and he knew the hundred and twenty eggs were whole when they left the farm. He told the driver in a quiet but firm voice—the voice he used when he wanted his kids to know that he was angry or disappointed, a voice that held no anger or disappointment but rather an artificial calmness that impressed them—that he knew accidents could happen, but he also knew that the truck was overloaded and the egg crates had been placed next to large containers of organic olives, which the driver was hauling from the same farm to a restaurant in Tel Aviv.

"How do I know? Trust me, I know." He demanded that the driver go back to the farm that same morning and pick up fresh crates, "At your own expense, of course," and that he make sure they were transported properly this time; otherwise not only would he file suit, he would make sure his restaurateur friends, including the one who had ordered the olives—"Yes, Raul, he's a good friend of mine"—stopped working with him.

For a moment he felt he had stunned not only the enemy but himself as well. In his imagination, he had conducted hundreds of these conversations, with suppliers, importers, drivers, Ministry of Health officials, and VAT clerks, and especially with the people at the local council who hounded him. But whenever he opened his mouth, the flow of quiet demands and stylized threats always turned into a trickle of flattery. This morning, though, something, perhaps the increasing weight of his small sadness, had launched a precise and lethal rocket of decisiveness.

He listened to the silence on the other end of the line, sipped his cappuccino, distractedly stroked Popeye's head—he was the oldest of Mark's three dogs and had rubbed up against his bare leg on his way to the food dish—and then the driver said, "Okay, fine, okay, I get it," and promised he'd do his best to be there that afternoon with the eggs.

"Don't do your best," Mark said, "just do it. Thank you very much." He hung up, satisfied. Distracted by his victory, he filled Popeye's dish with dry food, even though he usually only fed the dogs in the evening, and looked at the mixed black Lab slowly gnawing away. He noted that the dog was getting senile; it was a good thing the other two had already gone off on their morning rounds and wouldn't get to enjoy Mark's error. He hunched down on his heels, holding his coffee mug, stroked the dog's faded fur, and said, "Hey, Popolo, what's up?" He wanted to boast of his accomplishment with the driver, and Popeye lay down on his side and put his head on the pillow, his snout touching a yellow Lion King sock. It was Maya's lost sock, which they had given up on, and Mark was about to go over to the pillow and retrieve it— Maya would be happy when he called that evening to tell her he'd found it; or maybe he'd drop by later; or maybe he wouldn't tell her at all, because he thought he'd already thrown out the other sock— and suddenly he felt the sadness touch him again, like the small, sticky hand of a child. He hurried to the phone to call his wine supplier and then Alona, to ask how Maya was, since she'd had a virus with diarrhea yesterday.

Since the separation, his wife had become his best friend. They talked on the phone every day, sometimes more than once, sometimes not about the children, and the truth was that he could not start his day without chatting with Alona. It was strange, he thought, but now, two years after the temporary separation, which had apparently become permanent, he loved her more than he had before they married. Now

he even thought he was in love with her. And not because he had redis-
covered her, not something mature that attaches itself like a contemplative epilogue to a turbulent marriage that has ended—and he wondered
now if his marriage to Alona really had been turbulent and if it really
was over—but the opposite: he was in love with his wife like a boy, a
love that was as hesitant as it was certain, a love that held equal por-
tions of euphoria and panic, a love that he intended to do nothing about
other than simply keep it like a pet, a boisterous puppy whom you could
pet and then gently push away when it crossed the line. A love you
could train.

They had no intention of living together again, but they did not have
any urgent need to divorce either. He had told Alona how he felt about
her now, and she'd admitted that she too had new feelings for him.
"Feelings with round edges," she called them, unlike the serrated emotions of the past. But she didn't want to get back together, she liked it
this way, and there was no point in confusing the kids again, especially
Roni, his daughter from his first wife, Jane.

Mark said, "You're right, you're absolutely right, but still, I'm completely in love with you."

"Great, me too, sometimes."

"Alona, I'm serious," he said.

"Yeah, me too, so what?"

"So nothing," he said, and to some extent he was relieved that she
had exempted him from taking responsibility for this love, from proposing that they do something about it. He could continue to be in love,
rejected and desired at the same time, an emotional nuisance but now
also a crutch.

"Yes, believe it or not, I'm finally starting to rely on you," she said,
"but don't delude yourself, Mark. It's not you who's matured, it's me."

Unlike Alona, he had never been alone for more than a few months.
He was incapable of it and saw no point in learning solitude, as both
Alona and Jane had suggested when they broke up with him. They
thought he needed to teach himself how to live alone. With himself. Just
for a while. Instead of rushing straight into a new relationship. But what
was the point of struggling to learn how to live alone? he wondered—
even though he felt sure there was a certain charm to it, a strength, as
they both claimed, as if they were egging him on to taste an exotic dish,

promising nothing bad would happen and he might even like it, when it was clear that being alone would always be a temporary stage for him, a symbolic and redundant step on the way to a new togetherness.

From the day he lost his virginity at sixteen with Sharon Lipsky, his girl for two years, he had always had girlfriends. Even as a little boy, he used to ask girls to be his girlfriend, sometimes two or three of them at once, just to be on the safe side.

He met Jane a few days after he broke up with Laura, whom he had dated when he was studying film at NYU. Emotional and confused, but also more self-confident than he had ever been, he abandoned Manhattan and film school and went to Chicago to study at a prestigious culinary school. He rented a car and towed a U-Haul full of clothes, books, tapes, a couch, a full-size mattress, and piles of expensive copper pots and kitchenware that he had accumulated during his two years in New York. When he crossed the border into Illinois he knew he had done the right thing by leaving behind a fictional career as a director, a studio apartment in the Village that he was a little sorry to give up, and Laura, a medical student, his ticket to New York. She had found him the cheap apartment, which belonged to a relative, and had insisted they keep living separately even when they'd been going out together. She told him, after the fact, about the abortion she'd had shortly after they met. She said she hadn't wanted him to stress and beg her not to abort, she'd wanted to save both of them from that, and although he felt betrayed, he knew she was right. He would have made her life miserable until she had agreed to have the child, not because he wanted it, but because a baby would have fit perfectly into the screenplay of his life. A filmmaker and a doctor raising a baby girl together—clearly it would have been a girl—in a loft in SoHo or Chelsea, poor but happy, having friends over every evening for elaborate dinners that he would cook while she breast-fed. She was right not to tell him, but he was angry anyway. Laura was also his ticket *out* of the city. They came back one night after a screening of student films that had included his own, depicting a view of Manhattan from a dog's perspective. Throughout the three-minute film, the camera focused on the sad face of Roy, a pointer that belonged to one of Mark's classmates, with a sound track composed of the rattling of a subway train's wheels and the dog's panting. Laura said she wanted to break up because he was holding her back, imprisoning her in a fantasy that wasn't hers and wasn't really his either, if he wanted to be honest with himself; his film, to put it gently, was not exactly a breakthrough, and she was sick of being the partner of an artist who wasn't really an artist and knew it. "You want to cook, go learn how to cook. You're a wonderful cook, Mark," she said. She wanted to focus on her studies; she didn't want a partner at all; there would be time for that later, wouldn't there? As they lay in bed in the dark, she looked into his astonished eyes and something in him breathed a sigh of relief, that same something that didn't want to make movies but to cook, the domestic something that New York and Laura, and he himself, had disdained up until that moment.

Chicago was no less exciting than New York, and he liked cold winters, and Laura had set him up in a big loft two blocks from culinary school, with a great roommate, a friend of a friend called Jane Lerner. She was an artist herself, a real one, "Some sort of sculptor, I can't remember exactly, but I think you'll get along," and of course he fell in love with her.

Everything that had been complicated with Laura was simple with Jane. At first he attributed the ease with which they became a couple to the fact that she was five years older and, at thirty, knew a few things about life that he did not yet know. He gobbled up this knowledge like a chick whose food has been masticated for him. Something about Jane projected not only deep, mysterious knowledge but also the slow tranquillity of a spiritual guide. Jane knew what she wanted. Jane knew what Mark needed. Jane, he noted with satisfaction when he moved his stuff from the improvised room she had set up for him in the loft to the open area where she slept and worked, was what he wanted to need.

There was no answer at Alona's, which seemed strange. At eight-thirty in the morning she should have been at home after taking the kids to school. She should have been sitting in her office, making last-minute revisions to the manuscript of a young writer she couldn't stop talking about, a twenty-seven-year-old boy who had written a first novel that read like a third novel. "It's so polished it makes you want to throw up," she joked.

When she suggested that Mark read a few pages to see what she meant, he refused, saying he wasn't in the mood to be impressed by young talent right now. She asked if she smelled a whiff of jealousy, and he said, "Not at all, quite the opposite. The last thing I'd want to be now is a promising young man. I'd rather be an old man who's disappointed." He knew this would sound absurd to her; she couldn't imagine someone not wanting to be more than they were, or at least to be someone different.

Perhaps that was why she told him once that his real problem was that he was emotionally lazy, he wanted someone to feel the big things for him and leave him the lower octaves of emotions. "You were never looking for a partner but for a filter," she had said. But now he felt things changing. Maybe it was the fact that he had three kids, or the fact that next Saturday he would turn forty-four, not a milestone age or a round one, but still significant to him. Forty-four created reasonable distance from his thirties without bringing him much closer to the daunting twilight zone of forty-eight or forty-nine, one minute before he officially became a grown-up, the thing he had feared becoming his whole life: a man.

"We have to celebrate forty-four big-time," he told Alona, when she asked if he wanted the kids to organize anything for him.

"Big-time?" she asked. "I was thinking a cake and balloons, same as usual." But he said he was thinking hors d'oeuvres and osso buco, and of course a cake and balloons for the kids, and an adult dessert for them. "Okay, whatever you want," she said.

"Yes, I feel celebratory this year," he declared. They settled on Sunday evening, and he made a list of ingredients, but then he wondered if he really felt celebratory this year or just lonely, a pre-man squeezing out another evening with his family, using an admittedly excellent excuse, but still an excuse. Alona was wrong about the emotions, he thought. Lately he thought his range was broadening, which gave him both pain and a certain pride; the fact was that his ex no longer had a monopoly on sophistication and depth and anxiety, which used to be her exclusive domain. True, in the past she had read him as if he were one of her manuscripts, albeit less polished and ingenious; he had never been able to hide his emotions from her, simple and domestic as they might be, nor had he tried. But now there was one thing he could not share with her, and perhaps he didn't want to: this new sadness—fearsadness, as he called it privately—which was completely his own.

He got dressed and decided to walk to the restaurant. At this hour of the morning the moshav streets would be silent. Most of the residents worked in Tel Aviv and had left long ago, leaving Eden to the handful of elderly residents, and the few farmers who still worked their lands, and to people like Alona, who worked from home. But where could she be now?

Yesterday he'd tried to sleep with her again, and her refusal now suffused his body like the scent of sex that hadn't happened—saddening and arousing. He had brought the kids home from an afternoon excursion to the mall and helped her with bath time and bedtime, even though he knew she preferred doing it alone. "It just goes faster when you're not here, Mark," she always said, and then there'd be the speech about his lack of boundaries, how the children took advantage of it, how when he was there they stayed up till eleven or twelve, and then you couldn't wake them up in the morning. But yesterday he had really tried, badgering them to get into bed, reading them only one story and announcing that Alona would come in to read the second one, knowing the second one was the one that tended to stretch out endlessly, the one the kids begged to hear over and over again so as to postpone the moment when they would be exiled from the grown-ups' lives.

When Alona came into the room wearing one of the Indian tank-top dresses she bought at the Bezalel Market, he asked if he should make something to eat. She nodded. "But something light." He went into the pantry, whose contents he knew by heart, took out a can of whole tomatoes and a jar of anchovies, found the Kalamata olives he'd brought from Italy, and started to cook the puttanesca sauce she liked. "Something light!" she repeated when she came into the kitchen and saw garlic and chili frying in the pan. Maya had studded her hair with pins when they'd played hairdresser before bath time. Alona stood next to Mark and pulled out the pins, placing them in the dish of pacifiers on the counter. There were hairpins with flowers and butterflies, and a few cheap-looking ones in glowing colors that Maya especially loved. He put his hand on the back of her neck and asked if she needed a massage, and she said, "Yes, I really do, but just a massage."

"Stir this, then," he commanded, and handed her the wooden spoon. He rubbed her neck and shoulders while she stood with her back to him and hummed with pleasure, her head bowed. "You're forgetting to stir," he whispered, knowing his whisper was too seductive. She put the wooden spoon down on the counter, and he rubbed her shoulders hard and whispered in her ear, "The garlic will burn."

"Let it burn," she said, and wondered out loud, in a pampered voice, why she could never do just one thing. He asked what she meant, trying not to kiss her ear. "Like get a massage without stirring sauce, for example," she explained. "Or talk on the phone without washing dishes. Drive without giving pep talks to depressed young writers—"

"And good-looking young writers," Mark added.

"And good-looking ones, although he's not my type; I'm sick of being a crutch for the egos of guys like him. Or, for instance, read a book without always thinking about something else."

"Like what?" This time he could not resist, and his tongue fluttered over her earlobe.

"Like Maya having diarrhea, and if she still has it tomorrow she won't be able to go to kindergarten, and that will mess things up for me 'cause I have a ton of work, and I have to be in Tel Aviv at lunchtime."

"I can take her to the restaurant with me," he offered, wrapping his arms around her stomach.

"Thanks, but I'm sure she'll be fine, it wasn't serious." She took the spoon and stirred the garlic and chili. "Shouldn't we add the tomatoes?"

"Soon." He pressed his lips to the back of her neck. "You missed one." He pulled a beetle-shaped pin from her mess of hair.

Alona turned to him and said, "Stop, Mark, we said we wouldn't."

It occurred to him that he loved not only her but her refusal.

It was full of energy, and it reminded him of the way Alona was when he first met her. The refusal re-created the old tension between them, except now it was a pleasant tension of anticipation rather than failure, and it was clear to him that she would give in eventually. She hadn't slept with anyone for two years. She always told him about her various "almosts," and he listened like a friend. There was a photographer who worked on a book jacket with her, and a guy who gave her shiatsu treatments about a year ago, when she had those terrible headaches, but nothing came of it. She didn't think the photographer was attracted to her because, even though he flirted like crazy, he went out with all kinds of models, so what would he see in her? And the shiatsu one, they kissed and made out for a while one day, but they realized it wasn't right.

"I'm horny as hell," she would complain, and he'd say he couldn't understand how she could survive for two years without sex. It seemed inhuman to him, and she said, "I *am* inhuman, as we know. That's why we broke up, isn't it?"

Mark also let her in on the details of his relationships since they separated, especially the one with Michal, an architect from Tel Aviv whom he dated for almost a year and only recently broke up with. He liked the way Alona couldn't stand her. She would say things like, "She's the perfect woman, Mark, what can I say? And she sounds very maternal, too. Bottom line, she's made for you." He agreed, but he unraveled the stitches anyway, because he felt it wasn't fair to bring Michal into his family chaos. Still, he knew that more than trying to protect Michal, he was protective of his chaos, of his family, and of Alona, who repeatedly rejected his advances except for that one time, a month after the separation, when they were both very confused and pre-missing each other.

"But why, Alona?" he wondered. He really did want to know. And she said that if they hooked up one more time they'd be back together again, and from her point of view it would be fine just sleeping together, but he wouldn't be able to take it. No, he'd dig a tunnel home using teaspoons of sex, and she wasn't up for that; she'd rather suffer and just fantasize about men.

"About me, too?" he asked.

"Sometimes, when I'm really desperate."

Mark pretended to be hurt. "Well, unlike your stinginess, I fantasize about you all the time."

"Because of the kids. Because you're afraid you'll lose them if you don't fuck their mother every so often."

"What are you talking about? What's that got to do with anything?"

She demanded that he tell her exactly what he saw in his fantasies, and he confessed that it was nothing, really; he just saw *her*, at home, in the car, in the study, just daily things.

"Then it's not fantasies, Mark, it's homesickness."

How well she read him. And how he loved being a text. He loved her rejection, even as he wished to erase it.

His Trattoria stood in the heart of a small eucalyptus grove that used to be larger and far more impressive, according to the old-timers, before it was almost completely destroyed by a fire twenty years ago. What remained was a U-shape of growth, in the center of which he built his restaurant out of stones from a ruined building that a friend in Jerusalem found for him. He borrowed money from the bank and from his brother Danny, who lived with his wife and three children in LA and had made a fortune from a start-up that Mark found boring to hear about and could never completely understand. Danny generously offered to lend him the whole amount: "What do you need to get mixed up with the bank for? With me you'll get much better terms." But Mark preferred to split the amount between his brother and the bank, and to this day he wasn't sure exactly why. Perhaps he was slightly insulted by how eager Danny was to help him, because it was Mark, the little brother, who always needed helping out. It was part of the Segals' genetic code, and what had once been his parents' role had passed on after their deaths to his big brother, who not only expressed no surprise that Mark had decided to open a restaurant now, of all times, but even encouraged him and said he viewed it as the epitome of Zionism, real Zionism, in-your-face Zionism, the new kind. "Maybe it's culinary Zionism?" Mark joked, but his brother didn't get it and just kept up his excitable speech, saying he thought it was an awesome time to open a restaurant.

"Way to go, bro!" he enthused, and did not say a word even when the Trattoria lost money for two years and Mark asked to borrow another twenty thousand dollars to pay his taxes and debts. "It'll work out," Danny said, after the elections. "Sharon will go in there and show those fuckers which end is up. I mean, it has to end soon, right? They're dying of hunger over there, those shitheads."

Mark hated himself as he mumbled into the phone, "Yeah, you're right," and thought how nice it must be to be right-wing. He remembered how, as a boy, he used to trail after his brother to activities in the leftist Shomer Hatzair youth movement and then to Peace Now demonstrations. And now this brother was not only richer and more successful than he was but also much more handsome. He was "Danny the hunk," who during the first intifada had spent thirty days in military prison for refusing to do reserve duty in the West Bank.

Mark thought of the new right-wing views his brother was cultivating out in California like a middle-aged potbelly. His brother gave him the money without a second thought and said he shouldn't hesitate to take more. "That's what I'm here for," he said.

"For my Zionist endeavor," Mark added, and Danny said Yeah, exactly.

The Trattoria consisted of one single space with high ceilings, antique stone tiles, large windows with stained-glass panes painted by a neighbor from Mark's days in Jerusalem, an open kitchen where patrons could watch him cook while they sat at old wooden tables from the flea market, and his pride and joy: a big wood-burning stove that, in winter, emitted a soft warmth that felt like overseas. There was an expansive wood deck off the front, shaded by a canopy of vines. Alona had told Mark he was making a terrible mistake: he'd never make back his investment, and they didn't have any money as it was, so why get into debt? One of his best friends, Raul, had offered to employ him as a chef in his Tel Aviv restaurant, with a good salary and a share in the profits, but Mark didn't want to be an employee, he wanted his own place. Alona claimed that what he really wanted was an Arab-style house, which was why he had painstakingly reconstructed the dump he used to live in, the house where his first daughter Roni was born, in Jerusalem.

He walked by Alona's house, which was legally his also. After all, they'd bought it mainly with his money, after he'd sold the little house in Jerusalem, the apple of his eye, the house he'd bought with Jane when they came to Israel, the house that stood on the edge of a terrace, its arched windows offering a view of the wadi. Hippies, he thought longingly. We were hippies, Jane and I, and Roni was our little hippie baby. But the nostalgia soon succumbed to the usual wave of terror that always threatened to explode inside him and always retreated at the last minute: Roni's birth, which had started one February night in that house and had almost ended in tragedy.

Now almost a month had gone by since he'd talked to Jane. She lived in upstate New York on a farm she'd bought for pennies and fixed up a little, but at the moment she was in an artists' colony in New Mexico, living on a grant. The last time they spoke, she told him how awful Roni's summer visit had been, how much tension there was between them, and how they hadn't stopped fighting. "About nonsense, Mark. It's like she just wants to fight, like that's the one thing she really wants to do."

He tried to reassure her. "Yes, she wants to fight, that's true. So what, Jane?"

"So it does me in. It just does me in."

He had the feeling it wasn't the fights with Roni that were troubling her, but a delayed reaction—five years too late—to the fact that she had let Roni go.

When he walked past Alona's house and saw the Mazda wasn't outside, he thought that what bothered him most about the separation was that his natural right to know where Alona was at any moment had been revoked. Not that she hid her actions from him. On the contrary: Alona loved to update him on what she'd done and what she was going to do, where she'd been and where she hadn't had time to go, what had happened and what they'd had to eat. But the fact that he had to be informed about these things, instead of knowing them because he was automatically included, saddened him. He realized that this was what he liked about serial couplehood, which Alona and Jane both mocked him for. He liked to include and be included without the matter being subject to change or discussions or negotiations. Not to take a kid to preschool because it was his turn, not to cook dinner as gesture of goodwill to a tired ex.

He continued down the street until he reached the restaurant, where the two young dogs broke into a run and Popeye faltered behind him, lost in canine thoughts. Far away, on the main road that led to the moshav, he saw the council bus taking the high school kids to school and wondered if Roni was on it or if she hadn't woken up and was still deep in adolescent sleep in her room next to his little kids' room.

She lived in both houses, his and Alona's, although in fact she did not live anywhere: she roamed from one house to the other, moved by her moods, usually preferring Alona's home and choosing his mostly when he traveled abroad two or three times a year. He knew she'd gone to a party in Tel Aviv the night before. Alona had told him she'd gone with Adi and Shiri and had promised to come home with them in Adi's parents' car. Roni was one of the only kids in her class who didn't have her license yet. He paid for driving lessons, and for six months now a teacher had been picking her up regularly, but she couldn't take the test yet because she'd only turn seventeen in February. "She's a great driver," the teacher promised. "She's careful and alert and she has excellent coordination, and I promise you she'll pass the first time." But Roni seemed to approach the whole issue of driving with boredom, as if it were just another grown-up chore.

He hated driving too, afraid to switch lanes, hesitant to pass. Initially, Alona thought it was sexy. "You're like Woody Allen," she said, every time they went anywhere—she always drove. He agreed, slightly flattered, and reminded her that he had once wanted to be a filmmaker. "I wonder what would've become of you if you'd stuck with that?"

"Nothing. Same as what became of me anyway."

"Oh, yes. I like that about you, too. Your self-pity."

But later she found it annoying. "It's not annoying," she said when they were having one of their endless, circuitous conversations about their relationship, "so much as it's just demanding. You steal energy from people. You treat people—and I've noticed, Mark, that you do it with the kids, too—like sympathy ATMs: you punch in the secret code, and voilà! A wad of attention."

"The kids?"

"Yes, the kids." Then she shocked him by replaying a family outing. "Did you notice how Maya doesn't take her eyes off you even for a minute?"

"So what? She's at the age when she's supposed to fall in love with me, isn't she?"

"No, Mark, she's worried about you. She picks up your moods with her sensors. And Ido? Don't you see how he's always trying to please you?"

"But that's natural, Alona, every child wants to please his parents."

"Yes, but he's literally terrified, Mark."

"Terrified?"

"Oh, come on, Mark. That whole thing yesterday, when he brought you his toolbox so you could see how neatly he arranged everything. Why do you think it was so important to him?" When he said he had no idea, she reminded him that a week earlier Ido had lost the expensive toy drill Mark got him for his birthday.

"So? I didn't make a big deal out of it, did I? I told him it was all right, that I lost things too sometimes—"

"Yes, but five minutes later you started sulking."

"But not because of that!"

In his mind's eye he saw that afternoon: the kids were sitting on the rug in the living room watching television, and Ido came over to him while he was making spaghetti Bolognese in the kitchen. "Dad, I lost the new drill you got me for my birthday," he said, and burst into tears. Mark hugged him, picked him up, and set him on the counter to comfort him, but he suddenly grew distracted, lost in an unexplained but very familiar funk. It wasn't the drill; he didn't really know what brought it on. The boy watched his every move, waiting for forgiveness but refusing to accept it, shrugging his shoulders when Mark suggested he help chop the tomatoes with a real knife. Alona came home from a meeting in Tel Aviv and Mark told her that Ido had lost the drill but it was okay. "We'll find it, right, Ido?" The boy nodded, with tears in his eyes. One week later, after dinner, he had appeared at Mark's side while he was washing the dishes, placed his open toolbox on the floor, and said, "Look, I tidied everything." Mark bent down to examine the plastic tools, screws, and nails arranged in little compartments, and he stroked his son's head and praised him. The boy kept standing in the kitchen for several moments, looking back and forth from the tools to his father.

"It must be fun for you to be blind," Alona had said.

Now he turned left, walked a few hundred yards through the thorny brush already flattened by his many walks to the restaurant, and reached the dirt path that led from the main road to the Trattoria. Brutus and Olive ran ahead, kicking up clouds of white dust, and Mark stopped to tie the shoelaces on his heavy Timberland boots, which he wore year-round because he liked the way they hugged his ankles and the workmanlike image they gave him. He waited a moment longer, hunched down, for Popeye to reach him, then stroked the dog's head, stood up, and kept walking, wondering if the driver would really turn up with the eggs.

The weekend had been busier than usual, an excellent couple of days. The small parking area hadn't been big enough for the fifteen or sixteen cars, and some had parked on the side of the dirt road. It had been so surprisingly crowded that he'd had to wake Roni and ask her to come and wait tables. "Get some clothes on and get over here, I'm going crazy." At first she protested sleepily, and then Mark heard Alona urging her to go and help her father, and she yawned into the receiver.

"Okay, Dad, I'll come, but you owe me big-time."

She arrived wearing low-cut shorts that exposed the waistband of a pair of boxers—his? Perhaps. They looked a lot like his, anyway, with a familiar floral print. Her midriff shirt revealed her pierced navel; he had grown used to that, but not to the way she walked around without a bra. He would never get used to that, but what father could?

Roni scattered her sassy teenaged womanhood all over the house: her clothes, her underwear, her pink Gillette Sensor that was always covered with stubble from her armpits and legs—she shaved right in front of him, carrying on her small talk—her gray canvas backpack that she parked everywhere like an occupation flag, and her books. "You have to give her credit for one thing," Alona said. "The girl is a book-worm." Lately she'd been reading a lot of Kafka and Thomas Mann and Dostoevsky, in old translations. Her books upholstered every avail-able piece of furniture, lying spine up on tables and chairs and the kitchen counter. Then there were her tank tops, earrings, and hairpins, even though her hair was cropped short, and the occasional tiny, transparent pair of underwear, which it pained him to look at, and pens and note-book pages. Didn't she have any secrets? he wondered. Alona said, "Of course she does, don't worry; there's no such thing as a sixteen-year-old girl without secrets."

And now there was the smoking. What had started a year or two ago by stealing the occasional cigarette from Alona had officially turned into a habit. *There's* a secret, he thought. She'd asked him not to tell her mother. "It'll break her heart, Dad," Roni explained, "she hates cigarettes so much." Why upset Jane, the health freak, the vegetarian, who only smoked joints? So he promised he wouldn't tell.

He thought back to a conversation one Saturday morning at the res-taurant, earlier that summer, when she was helping him set the tables for lunch. "And you, Roni? Do you ever smoke anything?"

"What?" She looked at him with her blue Jane-eyes and ran a hand through her black hair like she did when she was embarrassed, when she was going to lie.

"You know, weed. Do you ever smoke it?"

She folded a napkin and placed it on the table, moved a wineglass with her fingertip, and said carnations in vases were tacky. "Dad, carna-tions are for wedding halls; you have to upgrade your taste in flowers.

They sell gorgeous irises down the road, and tulips—yeah, tulips would be perfect."

"Roni, answer me, please." He wondered if she'd noticed the geriatric hoarseness that had crept into his voice. "Do you smoke anything?"

"Everyone does."

"Okay, but swear to me that you never touch anything else."

"I swear." She held her hand to her heart, smiling.

He believed her, or wanted to, but that whole day, which was also a very busy Saturday—in general, he noted, the summer had gone well; the Trattoria wasn't making a profit yet, but it had stopped losing money, and his brother said, "You see? The country's recovering, didn't I tell you? Bibi was right; we're out of the recession" to which Mark had replied, "You call this a recovery? This is the swan song"—that whole day he was restless and kept watching his daughter as she dashed among the diners, taking orders, chatting easily, serving food.

You could say what you wanted about Roni, but she was a fantastic waitress, and some customers complimented him after the meal not only for the food and the setting but for the girl: "Keep your eye on that one," a man around his age once told him in a tone that gave him goose bumps; he looked like a businessman, eating dinner with a group of well-dressed forty-something men.

That Saturday, after the last of the customers had left, Mark drove Roni to Shiri's house, where she wanted to sleep over, and then hurried to Alona's. He was so upset he could barely explain himself: "It's too much for me, to be a parent. I'm only just realizing that."

"Only now?" Alona asked, and he told her he didn't believe Roni; he was convinced she was dropping acid at these parties. Alona said she wasn't, but he couldn't calm down. Something inside him had cracked, stunned from that morning's conversation.

"And what about Shiri? Why does she always have to sleep over there, doesn't she have a home?" He said he couldn't believe he was sounding like such an old man.

"Don't worry about it," Alona had said, and offered to make him some tea. "Every parent automatically turns into an old person." It was one o'clock in the morning, and he asked if he could look in on the kids for a minute. "Okay, but quietly, Mark. Ido's been waking up from the slightest thing lately."

"I know, I know," he said, and tiptoed into the room. He stood there for a few moments looking at Ido, who slept with his rear end sticking up and his knees and elbows folded under his body, like a rabbit, and at Maya, sprawled on her back with her limbs askew. He stood frozen, listening, searching in the dark for their breaths. As though sensing his presence, they both suddenly moved: Ido curled in as though he were about to sit up, and Maya turned to her side, opened her eyes for a moment, seeing yet not seeing him, then closed them and let out a small sigh, as if to say: Poor Daddy.

He left the room and joined Alona, who was smoking a cigarette in the yard, sitting on one of the old garden chairs that had also been purchased at the flea market. He hugged her from behind, wondering if she knew how much he needed to get laid, not because he was horny, not because he loved her, but because he was afraid—there, he thought now, standing on the deck at the Trattoria, maybe that was the moment when the fearsadness had started, that Saturday night at the beginning of summer—and Alona, reading him as usual, said, "Mark, it's not a good idea." He wondered if his best friend was taking revenge on him for all the times he'd refused her when they'd lived together. Too many times, he thought, when he left her place, got into the Hyundai, and drove less than a minute to his rented house, the house in which all of his children had rooms but where no one really lived.

But what could he do? His body knew only two options: passion or withdrawal. When he felt bad, or when something was bothering him, any physical contact struck him as an imposition, indifferent to his condition, and he would dive inward, angry and lonely. Sometimes great excitement or happiness provoked the same response. "I can't concentrate on two things at once," he explained, "either I'm sad or I'm screwing." But he was inconsistent: sometimes depression or an especially upbeat mood demanded immediate sex to unload the excess of electricity charging his body. Alona, and Jane before her, found this maddening. For them, as for other women he'd been with, sex was part of the sentence, not the period or question mark at the end.

He took the keys out of his pocket and unlocked the Trattoria door, waiting for Popeye to clamber up the wooden stairs of the deck and stand next to him, panting. He walked inside, filled a bowl with water, and placed it outside. The dog walked over to it indifferently, as if he knew out of habit that he was thirsty but did not really feel it. He drank a little water, then slouched under a table.

Popeye was Roni's dog. She had chosen him, at the age of two, from among the five puppies born to their neighbor's dog in Jerusalem. She'd approached the big straw basket of puppies decisively, ignoring their mother's token grunt, bent over, and picked up the only black one. "This one," she said. Mark looked at old Popeye and remembered how he'd hoped Roni would choose a different puppy, a cheerful, mischievous-looking white one that had charmed him. But Roni wanted the black one, who looked undistinguished, chubby, and sleepy. When he said, "Are you sure? There are some really cute puppies here"—in those days she used to say *this one* about almost everything—Jane shushed him and said, "It's her dog, Mark, let her choose." Popeye was his dog now. And Popeye, the vet said, was suffering terribly.

But Roni wouldn't hear of it. "Absolutely not," she said, even before he finished telling her about the latest checkup. "He's not suffering." She caressed the dog, who, when she wasn't trying to save his life, she ignored. "He's just old. Would you like to be put to sleep just because you're old?" She sounded so schoolmarmy and so sweet when she asked that question.

"Honestly, yes. If I was suffering, then yes."

"But I wouldn't. I would just like to die happily of old age."

"But if you were suffering, it wouldn't be happily."

"But how do you know? Does he look like he's suffering to you?" They both looked at Popeye as if he had the answer. Roni went up to the dog. "Look, he's wagging his tail. He's happy, he still has joy in him."

And those words, which his daughter repeated again and again, always broke his heart and gave Popeye the extension he did not really need because no one was seriously considering putting him down.

Mark made a cappuccino and thought that if the durum flour hadn't arrived by tomorrow, he'd compromise and use regular flour. It wouldn't be the end of the world; he'd made pasta with regular flour before. He debated whether to make gnocchi—it wasn't really winter yet and it was still warm; gnocchi sounded heavy—maybe the spinach and ricotta ravioli he'd done last week, which had been a big hit, unlike the porcini ravioli, which Roni said was salty and too weird. He decided to wait until afternoon for the eggs and flour and wondered if he should call the driver again and find out if he was on the way. He sat down outside and phoned Mickey, the farmer near Jerusalem, to ask if the driver had already been to his place, but Mickey was unavailable and he was afraid to call the driver. He suddenly hated himself for being dependent on so many people and afraid of so many people, when the whole point was to be independent. It'll be okay, he told himself and dialed Alona's number again, the first number in the cell phone's memory, but there was still no answer.

Olive and Brutus ran up and emptied out the water bowl, and he went to fill it again and thought about what to make himself for breakfast. He peered through the glass doors of the large refrigerator. He was almost out of prosciutto; he wasn't sure if there would be enough for the prosciutto and fig appetizer, which was one of the most popular summer dishes. The chalkboard menu changed according to what was in stock and his mood. The Trattoria was open three nights a week, Thursday through Saturday. In light of the recovery he wondered if he should open for dinner the rest of the week too, but he decided to postpone the decision until spring. It was almost winter, and in winter, his restaurateur friends told him, people go out less. "Don't take any chances," said Raul, who owned a successful bistro in Tel Aviv. "Just be happy you're full on the weekends, and see how it goes after winter. Look, *my* place is practically empty all week. Who's gonna drive all the way out to your godforsaken spot at night, even if you do make the best osso buco in Israel?"

Mark remembered his birthday dinner, which was set for Sunday, and for a moment he managed to extricate himself from his helplessness. He debated which appetizers to make for the birthday. Maya wasn't eating anything lately, and Ido ate everything. Mark wondered if the toddler was pretending to be a gourmand just to please him. Maya had gone through a similar phase two years ago, when he and Alona separated; she used to want to taste everything and claimed everything was yummy. He'd been so proud of her, and of his cooking skills, and so pleased with the fact that while other kids lived on hot dogs and French fries, his children enjoyed roast leg of lamb and seafood risotto. It hadn't occurred to him to suspect that their culinary sophistication and maturity were covering up for simple childish misery. He felt suddenly angry at Alona and dialed her number again, almost without thinking, but there was still no answer. He was angry at her for always ruining things for him, for acting like a camera, documenting his behavior, like a reality show, except that later, in the editing, the gray, normal bits were cut, leaving only the horrifying, sensational scenes. It's a good thing we broke up, he thought. It was a smart move. Now all he had to do was learn how to really separate. He went over to the fridge again, ravenous, but he was too distracted to decide what he wanted, so he sat down on the deck again and rubbed his foot on Popeye's back as he lay dozing under a table. Here come the jealous ones, he thought, smiling to himself when Brutus and Olive, the mixed German shepherd and the little pinscher, got up together, as if on cue, and came over to be petted. You'd think she was the perfect parent, he told himself as he downed the rest of his cappuccino. The kid likes food and that's all.

The phone rang and he picked up immediately: Mickey from the farm. "Your dopey driver was here; he just left." Mark breathed a sigh of relief. Mickey said the guy had spent almost an hour arranging the egg crates in the truck. "You should've seen it!"

Mark suddenly felt sorry for the driver—perhaps he'd gone a little too far; it was so easy to scare people lately. The driver was a chubby man around his own age, with a round baby face. Once, when they'd sat on the Trattoria deck and Mark had served him coffee and tiramisu, he'd told Mark he lived in Ashdod, he had two daughters and a son, and his wife was on dialysis, waiting for a kidney transplant. Mark thought about him arranging the egg cartons like he was building Legos, and his heart fell.

"What else is new?" asked Mickey.

"Everything's good," Mark said, and hung up. He decided to play it safe and make a stock of spinach-ricotta ravioli for the weekend, and some fettuccine and a few simple sauces. For the entrées he'd use what veal he had left, and he'd phone his butcher soon and ask him to set aside a cut of sirloin for carpaccio, which he had to have. The menu planning was starting to work its relaxing magic.

He went inside again and opened the refrigerator doors, and as if the decision had been made without him he knew what he wanted: an omelet with salami, something simple and comforting. He took out three eggs and sliced a few rounds off one of the spicy salamis he'd brought from Italy, and his cell phone rang again and he hurried outside to answer it. The driver said he'd be there in half an hour, and Mark thanked him and said he was waiting for him with coffee. Only then did he notice that the morning chill had lifted and turned into the definite buds of a heat wave, and suddenly he did not feel old but too young, a child with three children of his own and a restaurant. He looked out at the fields he'd walked across, felt his feet baking in the heavy shoes, went inside, took some paper and a pen from the drawer under the cash register, went back outside, and sat down to make a list of things he had to do that day: *Moish—sirloin, Raffi—herbs, lettuce, arugula, tomatoes, zucchini, red peppers, eggplant, figs.* He crossed out the figs because he remembered the prosciutto was almost finished; besides, there weren't any good figs on the market; the season was over. He wrote down *Book Roni for Fri–Sat*, added three exclamation marks, either out of urgency or boredom, and suddenly the sadness returned. He caught sight of it out of the corner of his eye, a snake emerging from among the thistles, vapors of heat dancing in the air, illogical, ill-defined, but completely present, like the fear in that book Ido had brought home from preschool.

ALONA

Even before she woke up, she knew what she would write on the note she stuck on her computer monitor every morning. The note always had one word, which she replaced every day, to serve as a flashing bulb of inspiration or warning. Yesterday she'd written RELAX and had added, as usual, a huge exclamation mark to remind herself of the urgency. She always felt ridiculous when she scribbled the very same punctuation marks which she methodically, sometimes contemptuously, crossed out in the manuscripts she edited, especially those written by the youngest or oldest of her authors, whose writing always had a sense of urgency. *If you create an atmosphere of exclamation, you won't need the exclamation mark itself*, she liked to suggest. To justify her own usage, she told herself that in literature it was forbidden, but in life—and how childish this maxim sounded—it was allowed. The addition shouted out geometrically: *Urgent, urgent, urgent!*

Everything was so urgent.

She'd spent the night in a state of tension, her ears alert to the sounds coming from the children's room, breaths and murmurs, the first signs of discomfort: a child tossing and turning, the soft squeak of Ido's bed legs, Maya's sad sighs, like an old lady's, or the plastic click of a dropped pacifier. An orchestra tuning its instruments, followed by the first note, drawn out and hesitant, or sometimes determined—*Mommy!*—propelling her to their room like a bat flying out of its cave.

With half-closed eyes and a sleeping heart she would approach whichever child had woken up, usually Ido, and instead of reassuring him she
would scold. Even when she caressed a cheek or picked up a pacifier and
stuck it back between a pair of lips parted like a fishlike mouth on a
damp circle on the pillow, or pulled up a crumpled blanket, or peeled
back another, she felt as though her presence was diffusing not tranquillity but caution: *If you wake up again I won't come,* or *I'll come but I'll
be angry.* Later, back in bed, she would listen to the crickets chirping, and
the loud *tsk-tsk* emitted by the geckos, who hung like miniature dino-
saurs from the walls of the house, and her own heartbeat and the rustle
of the leaves: the tapestry of nocturnal sounds in which a single thread,
the one that led to the children's room, was always wrapped around
her finger. In the morning she hated herself for not lingering in their
room to miraculously glue back together the shreds of their sleep but,
instead, fleeing back to her bed to save what little remained of her own
time to rest.

Mark was much better at these things. She claimed it was part of his
disorganization: "Because you don't have a daily routine, you're not
too concerned about your nights." But she knew it was more complicated than that; in parenting, as in everything else, they were opposites.
Mark lived for the moment, while she feared to give them so much as
an inch. Mark seemed not to know the difference between an inch
and a mile. That was why she had fallen in love with him. She kept
reminding herself of this as she watched him refuse to live a separate
life within their shared life. More than anything else, he symbolized, for
her, the chance to be someone else, to blend and wallow with him until
she became a new hybrid creature, something that would still be her
but would defeat the person she really was. But the blending and the
wallowing had left them both even more impenetrable, as though the
marriage had created another protective layer that prevented any chance
of fusion.

She knew that when the kids were at his place they slept in his bed.
There was no one to carry them out and whisper a sleepy speech about
how everyone had their own bed and had to sleep in it. On the contrary: Mark looked forward to his son climbing into bed with him.
Maya had stopped doing it, and at first Alona was glad, thinking her
education had succeeded. But lately she thought, What have I killed in

her? With Ido, there would be a little shove at the mattress, like a knock
on the door, and the boy would crawl on all fours to the vacant pillow,
dragging along his gear—blanket, pacifier, water bottle, toy—as if he
were going camping.

"Why don't you like sleeping with them?" Mark used to ask, when
they still lived together and waged three-way battles every night, between
her and them, between her and him, while the kids sat between them on
the bed awaiting a decision. She would reply that, first, she didn't understand how he could manage to sleep; Maya was like a kicking mule and
Ido was a cobra who wrapped himself around you. And second, if the
pair got used to it they'd never leave. She reminded him of friends whose
son still slept with them at the age of nine—nine!

"Mark, do you want Maya and Ido sleeping in our bed when they're
nine?" Mark would retort that, first, he didn't care and, second, he didn't
believe it would be forever, because at some point they'd give it up of
their own accord, wouldn't they?

"Yes," she said, "maybe," but forever became irrelevant, because she
and Mark had been sleeping in separate beds for two years now, in
separate houses, and twice a week and every other weekend the kids
snuggled up with their father in his bed, two blocks away, with his permission, upon his invitation, and the rest of the nights they waged
remote-controlled battles with her.

The crumbs of sleep she'd squeezed out of the night aroused an angry
appetite for more. "If you just let them sleep with you, you'd sleep like
a baby," Mark liked to say. She was angry, as usual, at herself more than
at the kids. Ido had been crying in his sleep lately, but there was no way
of knowing what was troubling him. When he awoke to the touch of
her hand on his face—a dark screen projecting an invisible horror
movie—he looked surprised and annoyed, as though she were the one
who had disturbed his sleep, rather than the other way around.

Maya had been complaining of a stomachache for days. The day
before yesterday she'd woken up twice, at midnight and at one-thirty,
and asked to use the bathroom. Two false alarms. The third time, while
Alona sat waiting on the edge of the bathtub, toilet paper torn and
ready in her hand, and watched Maya stooped on the toilet, elbows on
knees, humming a Sukkoth song she'd learned in kindergarten, she
briefly considered how pretty the girl was, and her heart soared and

then sank with compassion when Maya strained her stomach muscles. She wanted to tell her it was all right, there was time, not to force it, but the girl's legs, tanned and covered with a down of fair hair, swung back and forth and her heels hit the toilet bowl rhythmically, disclosing the stupid truth of this 3 A.M. episode: Maya was faking. She couldn't be suffering so badly if she was playing around on the toilet. That's not how you behaved when you were suffering. "Get up! Enough with these games," Alona snapped.

Maya straightened up and said, "But I have to go poo-poo."

"No, you don't! Come on, enough already." She took the girl's arm and stood her up and pulled up her short pajama bottoms and marched her back to her bed. Maya shrugged Alona's hand off her shoulder. Alona covered her with a sheet, said, "Good night, and don't call me again," and went back to bed. Before she fell asleep she scolded herself for not picking up on it sooner, at midnight, when Maya had sat on the toilet and told her a story about something that had happened in kindergarten, she couldn't remember what. Maya had recounted the story in detail and then started asking questions about the cosmetics scattered around the sink. "What's that one? What's this one?" She wanted to know if she could put on a certain cream and eye shadow tomorrow when she went to kindergarten. If Alona hadn't collaborated, patiently explaining about the function of each product and promising to put some of the silvery eye shadow on her in the morning, maybe her daughter would not have had the will for more nighttime woman talk. But how rare were the moments when they were alone, just the two of them, and in fact why not enjoy them, even if they occurred at impossible hours? If only she were more relaxed. If only she were cool and flowing, as Mark described certain women they knew, pointing to their maternity as if it were a dress he wanted to see her wear even though it was wrong for her figure. But it was hard to blame him. Mark was a child, and children hated boundaries. If she'd been stricter at midnight, she might have spared herself and Maya the wake-ups at one-thirty and three.

At five, when napping gave way to a deep, indulgent, post-struggle slumber, Alona heard soft sobbing and sniffling in the room and smelled something bad. She opened her eyes to find Maya standing over her, rubbing her tearful eyes with one fist and holding her soiled pajama bottoms with the other. "I have diarrhea," she whispered. "It came out in bed, and my tummy really hurts."

"Then why didn't you call me?" Alona mumbled, her head refusing to lift off the pillow.

"I called you quietly," the girl whimpered. "I called you, but you didn't hear."

RELAX! she'd written down yesterday morning, when the house had officially woken up, two hours after she'd changed the sheets in her daughter's bed, put her into the shower, and washed her, caressing her back and whispering reassuring words. When she asked if her tummy still hurt, Maya nodded her bowed head and said it was nice in the shower. On a tender moment's whim, Alona said, "Then let's wash your hair."

The girl cheered up. "Even though we already washed it?"

"Yes, even though we already washed it," Alona said, and shampooed Maya's hair, although she had no idea why she was doing it. She watched as Maya hesitantly picked up Ido's water pistol from the bathtub floor, unsure whether the strange nighttime treatment encompassed a prohibition on playing, and told her, "Maya, we're not playing now." But she took the pistol herself and filled it in the sink, and as she did so she glanced at her face in the mirror and did not know whether what she saw was the reflection of lack of sleep or of a wonderful intimacy. Maya aimed the pistol at the ceramic tiles. She looked at her daughter playing in the bath, a crest of foam on her head, and her eyes settled on the childish nudity, in which she could detect the shadows of a long-gone infancy and the suggestion of the girl Maya would soon be. There was something shocking about it, and something touching. When she's fifteen I'll be fifty, Alona thought. She glanced at her wristwatch, which lay next to the sink, and was hit by time again, like a spasm: it was 5:30 A.M. "Let's go, Maya, enough; get out and we'll try to sleep some more, okay?" Alona knew that the woman who had lost her sense of time with her child was only a fata morgana of a different parent, a better one. Maya gazed down at the flow of water swirling the foam around her feet and said, "It's like the sea." It occurred to Alona that the words *no, enough, come on,* and *okay?* were the four cornerstones of the language she was constructing with her children.

"It was fun with Dad at the beach," Maya said contemplatively, as she dried herself with a large towel and then silently put on fresh pajamas.

"Do you need to go again?"

Maya shook her head.

"Are you sure?"

The girl walked to her bed and lay down on her back.

"You'll tell me if it hurts you again?"

Maya nodded, and Ido sat up in bed and stared.

"Back to sleep!" Alona ordered, and he lay down.

"Good night, Mommy," Maya said.

"Good night, my sweet." She kissed Maya's forehead, which felt a little warm, but no, not now, she thought and went back to bed. Before falling asleep she heard a rustle in the yard, maybe footsteps. She perked up to listen, but could not tell if it was an animal or a person or if it was footsteps at all. She hit the mattress again, surrendering to the familiar grip of terror that had started after a woman and her two kids were murdered on a kibbutz. There was also a family or two in some settlement, she couldn't remember which one and how many were murdered, and whether there were also children. "It's not because they were settlers," she explained to Mark, when he teased her for having a selective memory, a political memory, for not being moved by the deaths of settlers. "I remember the kibbutz incident because it was a single mother with two children about Maya and Ido's age, kids with pacifiers."

And it never left her. Their house was probably the only one in Eden, except for her mother's, that didn't have an alarm system. Mark had a principled objection: "Is that what we moved to the countryside for? To live like this?"

"Oh, come on, Mark! Is this what they founded the State of Israel for? To live like this?"

"Okay, maybe you're right, but you don't have to get hysterical about it. And if it makes you feel better, I don't even turn my alarm on."

She said it didn't make her feel better at all, in fact it infuriated her, and she hoped—no, demanded!—that at least when the kids were sleeping he would overcome his childish principles and use the alarm. "And get that security guy over here to give us an estimate. How long have you been putting that off, Mark, two years?"

But why did she need him to do it? She sat up in bed again because the rustles, which may have been footsteps, sounded louder outside her window. Tomorrow she'd open the Yellow Pages and call the first company she found, because she was a single mother now, too. The rustle suddenly turned into a cat's screech. Grateful for the deferment she'd been given, she promised herself that she'd take care of an alarm first thing in the morning. She'd put two notes on the computer: RELAX! and ALARM! She fell asleep, but not before her brain automatically scanned all the escape routes from the house, only to find, once again, that there weren't any; they were done for either way, and what good would an alarm system do when you could easily murder a woman and two children in minutes?

An instant after she fell asleep the sunlight was dancing on her eyelids and the sound of galloping feet rolled down the hallway like tam-tam drums. Ido stood over her and declared, "I slept well, Mommy!" She said, Great, and he jumped onto the bed, lay behind her, and pressed his feet into the small of her back. She turned over and they looked into each other's eyes. She put her hand on his shoulder, and he put his on hers. A miniature Mark, she thought, as she did every morning when the boy stole her for this one minute before his sister woke up. "I slept well, Mommy," he repeated. She'd had children for almost five years, but was still amazed every time she discovered the existence of this compasslike mechanism that always aimed at happiness. How many times had he woken up crying in the night? And yet he wanted to be happy, and he wanted her to be happy. He was a baby, but he knew that sleep was important for her, that sleep was apparently a synonym for happiness.

"Yes," she said and kissed his nose, "you slept very well." Ido said he wanted to watch a video, and she said "Soon," and went into the kids' room, where Maya was sitting on the rug playing with her brother's tools. She announced that she didn't want cornflakes because they were gross. She wanted Squares. "But we don't have any, all we have is cornflakes," Alona said.

"But I want Squares! That's what I want!" Maya wailed, and the exclamation marks conducted their morning march into the house.

Ido ran into the room carrying a stack of video tapes and started screaming, "That's mine! My saw! She's touching my tools, Mommy!!"

Alona pulled some clothes out of the closet as the kids both tugged on the saw.

"I don't want that dress," Maya announced, "I want this one!" She ran with the saw to the laundry hamper and took out yesterday's dress, which Mark had bought her for Rosh Hashanah.

Ido lay down on the rug and kicked and screamed, "She took my tools! That's mine!"

Alona said quietly, "Come on, give him the saw already, Maya," and asked her to pick another dress. "What about the orange one with the fish?"

"No! I want this one!"

"But it's dirty, Maya, pick something else."

Maya held the saw and the dress to her chest and ran into the kitchen. She dragged a chair over from the table and stood on it to open the cabinet above the oven. "We *do* have Squares, Mom! See? I told you we did." Ido, whose sister had now turned from thief into hero, hugged Maya's legs, and she screamed that he was knocking her off the chair: "Mom!" She dropped the cereal box that Alona had hidden when she was on a health-food kick, and the cereal scattered all over the floor. Ido crawled around, shoving pieces quickly into his mouth, and Maya screamed, "Look what he's doing! He's eating off the floor!"

The phone rang: Mark wanted to coordinate plans for the afternoon. She could hear his espresso machine hissing in the background. She went over to the storage closet to get the broom. "Who's screaming there?" he asked affectionately, "Maya?"

Alona said yes, and he asked why. Alona said she couldn't talk, "Later, okay?" She leaned over to sweep the floor, pushing Ido away with her foot.

"I want to sweep! Me!" he begged.

"Not now, I'm in a hurry, we're late."

"What?" Mark asked. The boy tried to grab the broom, his face smeared with chocolate filling from the cereal, and Maya took the milk out of the fridge, and Alona looked at her and realized she was wearing the dirty dress. Mark asked if he should make sandwiches for the afternoon, because he might take them on a picnic. He had to go to the mall today and there was a new branch of Erez Bread there.

"What?" she said, and her husband's loneliness shot like a spray into her ear. Ido was pulling on the broom handle, and Mark said something about roast beef; he knew Ido loved it but Maya preferred regular pastrami, didn't she? Alona looked at her daughter sitting at the table eating the salvaged cereal, and a sharp set of teeth suddenly pierced her thigh. "Ido!" she shouted. Mark asked what happened, and she said she couldn't talk now and hung up. She dragged Ido to his room, trailing the clutched broom behind him, pushed him into the room, and asked if he wanted to calm down with the door open or shut. He lunged at her and punched her stomach. "I see you've decided," she said and shut the door, pulling back on the handle. "It's too bad that's how you chose," she added.

He tried to open the door and yelled, "Let me out!"

Maya appeared, holding her bowl of cereal in both hands. "What did he do, Mommy?" she asked.

Alona told her firmly to go back to the table. "We don't eat food here, it'll spill, and this is not a show, Maya, we don't need an audience."

"But what did he do? Just tell me."

"He bit me, okay?"

Maya smirked and Ido tried to shove the door open, and Maya suddenly put her bowl down on the floor, splattering milk on the tiles, and said her tummy ached, "It really hurts!"

Alona knew she would continue to be haunted by last night, and that although Maya might not remember the night itself, something from it, the mistrust, her mother calculating the minutes as though time were money, would scar her. If only she had been a different mother, she might have brought happier, calmer children into the world. But now was not the time to worry about that, now was about survival, and that was something she was good at. She took a deep breath and said in an almost imperceptible voice, "Go to the bathroom, sweetie, I'll be right there." She let go of the door handle and Ido shot out like an arrow, tears and snot paving their way through the muddy chocolate caked on his cheeks, and she knelt down and surrounded his body with her arms. "Enough, enough, chickie." He started to whimper, and she kissed his forehead and told him to go and sweep a little. "There are still some crumbs left. But then we have to get dressed and hurry to school, okay?"

The boy wiped his tears and nodded and rode the broom to the kitchen like a happy witch, or maybe not, but she didn't have time for that now; that would haunt her later.

She went into the bathroom and asked Maya if her tummy still hurt. Maya, sitting on the toilet, nodded. "But I can't make poo-poo again," she apologized. Alona asked if she wanted to wear the new skirt they'd bought last week. "With the shirt Daddy got me?" she asked, looking up hopefully.

Alona thought about the shirt Mark had chosen. He'd said he thought it looked cute, and Alona had told him five-year-old girls shouldn't walk around with bare midriffs. But he'd already shown Maya the shirt and promised she could wear it the next day. "Absolutely not," Alona had said and hidden it on the top shelf—the same mistake she made with the cereal, she thought now; she should have thrown it out or given it to someone. "Yes," she told Maya, "with the shirt Daddy got you."

"Relax," she said to herself in the car half an hour later. She'd dropped the kids off and was now reconstructing the series of mistakes she'd made that morning. Not mistakes, she thought, when she walked back into the postwar silence at home. Her good friend Ma'ayan, who had four kids, was right.

"Stop tormenting yourself," she always told Alona. "You don't make mistakes, you're a mom." Ma'ayan was the one who had suggested that she write down one word every day; "Word of the day," she called it. "I did it once, when the kids were little, and it worked. It really worked." Alona, who always disparaged this sort of undertaking, asked mockingly, "So is it like putting a fat picture of yourself on the fridge when you're dieting?"

"No, it's like putting up a thin picture of yourself, the kind that hasn't even been taken yet."

"Okay, it's a good idea. I'll think about it." But it never occurred to her to do it until a week ago, after a tumultuous separation from Ido, who had clung to her thigh for several minutes like a baby koala and refused to let her go until the teacher disconnected him and motioned to Alona to leave, hinting that her presence was what caused the boy to

suffer. She'd gone home, sat down in her study, and found herself pulling out a white piece of paper from the printer and writing down random words.

She looked at the column of words she'd written, a laundry list of
meanings:

SYMPATHY

UNDERSTANDING

IDENTIFICATION

Then she moved on to imperatives:

SYMPATHIZE

UNDERSTAND

IDENTIFY

And suddenly an unexpected word landed on the paper like a moth:

SLOW

It reproduced itself on the next line, and over and over again, all the
way to the bottom of the page: SLOW, SLOW, SLOW. She decorated the
last one with a fat, optimistic exclamation mark because she suddenly
realized what the problem was: there was a contradiction between what
she knew about life and how the children lived it. Her time with the children was like the Chaplinesque sound track of a record playing at the
wrong speed, and she had to lower the speed so she could delineate the
noise into patterns of notes. No more screams and threats and crying
and exclamation marks, but music. If only she could learn how to time
herself on *their* watch, the one that did not really exist but still managed her life. Because the kids were teaching her a new language, a
foreign language, one she was struggling with. It was the language of
time as they knew it, a language she might have known once but could
no longer remember. "We're in a hurry, we're late, come on, enough,
okay?" These were all synonyms for time, and since the kids did not
speak that language, they responded wildly, just as she probably would
if someone insisted on speaking to her in Sanskrit or Chinese, some
language in which she could not decipher even a single note.

Last week she had written her debut word—SLOW!—on a yellow
note and quickly pinned hopes on it, as though the word were a teacher

in an intensive language program. She stuck the note to the side of her monitor and looked at it, and for one childish moment she thought she could feel life without time, but then the phone rang and the washing machine repairman announced that he was on his way, and later, still breathing with artificial slowness, she called her publisher's production manager to find out the timeline for the cover of one of the books she'd finished editing, and he told her they were postponing the publication for Book Week.

"*What?* It was supposed to come out on Rosh Hashanah, and it didn't because the jacket wasn't ready!"

"Well, that's exactly it, Alona, we missed the holidays, so there's no reason to rush."

"Yes, there is! We promised the author! She was going to switch to a different publisher."

"But she didn't."

"This is not right!" In her mind's eye she saw the expression on the young writer's face. Three publishers had fought over her debut novel, and she'd decided to go with Subtext *just because of you, Alona, because I want you to edit it.* The doorbell rang and Alona told the production manager she had to run. "But I want you to know that I won't let this go without a fight." She opened the door for the repairman, who complained about how hard it was to find the place, and she offered him coffee, instant or drip.

"Drip, but not too strong."

She led him to the washing machine that had flooded the house over the weekend, made him his coffee, put it on the kitchen table, and said, "If you need me, call." She went into the study and thought about calling Subtext's publisher to complain, but she decided the repairman might need her. She sat down at her desk and picked up Uri Bruetner's manuscript, the first novel that read like the work of a seasoned author rather than a twenty-seven-year-old kid. She looked for the page she'd been working on the day before but she couldn't find it.

"Excuse me, Ms. Segal," came the repairman's hesitant voice from the hallway, and she jumped up and went out to him. "Where's the main?" he asked. "I have to shut the water off." She went outside with him and pointed, then went back to the study and sat down in her chair and stared at the note she'd stuck—when? How long ago had it been?—to the monitor: SLOW! She knew that as soon as she'd written it, the word had fallen prey to the daily particles that gradually cohered around it, like a heat wave, a conspiracy, as though the day were a biological entity, excreting enzymes that took control of the word and digested it, leaving behind their waste of letters in the evening.

Still, she did not give up, and the next day SLOW! gave way to LISTEN!, which a day later surrendered to UNDERSTAND!, which had no chance to begin with, and then she decided to give TENDERNESS! a chance, but she thought the commands might be more efficient, so the next day she wrote, FORGIVE!—both the children in advance and herself retroactively—and yesterday that ridiculous RELAX! had come along, which she could easily have replaced with MARK and done away with the punctuation.

Had she met Mark two years before she did, or even one year or one month, she would have labeled him a loser and moved on to the next blind date. She was thirty-three, tired of men who hesitated or caused her to hesitate, endless hesitations that were so eventful they seemed to substitute for the relationship itself. Deep in the centrifuge of blind dates, she had begun to see life alone as a friendly place, a small apartment with great potential.

She met him at the publisher's launch party for an anthology of American short stories. It was a barbecue on Herzliya Beach, on a cool evening in early spring of '98. A few months earlier she'd been appointed senior editor, after the publisher had stolen her, as he liked to say, from a competitor. Mark did the catering for the party. He was working with his friend, Raul, who today owned a bistro in Tel Aviv, and whom she knew from various other events and parties; she had tried to seduce him two years earlier. But Raul had a girlfriend, who later became his wife. "I'm dying to fuck you," he'd told Alona one night, when he walked her to her car after a party and she draped herself over him drunkenly, her nose and lips nestling in his neck, her hand gently pushed away from his pants zipper, "but I don't cheat on Inbal." Then he said he didn't think she should drive and he would get her a cab. "You can come and pick up your car tomorrow." She remembered that she'd argued and insisted she was fine and then vomited on his shoes.

Raul hugged her warmly when she arrived at the beach party. They had run into each other a few times in the intervening years, and each time they did, she thought she reeked of alcohol and vomit, and that she was ugly, not at all like Inbal, whom she had never met but who was obviously her complete opposite in every way: tall and slender, someone who had never tried to seduce a man in love with someone else in a parking lot after too many shots of tequila.

Raul was always happy to see her. "I love you," he'd say. "If I wasn't taken, I'd marry you, I swear." He whispered in her ear that Inbal was pregnant and they were getting married in August. "You're coming to the wedding!" he scolded her even before she could say anything, before she could protest that they barely knew each other, that apart from small talk shouted into ears in noisy bars and clubs, and dozens of hugs and cheek pecks and one failed seduction attempt, they knew nothing about each other and it was doubtful they would find anything in common in the light of day. "I'm sending you an invitation," he said; "write down your address." He pulled a notepad and pen out of his apron pocket and shoved them at her, and she wrote down her address and phone number. Raul took the pad back and dropped it in his pocket without even looking, and then a short, thin man walked up to him—he had spiky salt-and-pepper hair and wore a matching apron—and asked if he knew where the Tabasco bottles were because he couldn't find them anywhere.

"They're in the back of the van; I'll go and get them. This is a good friend of mine, Ilana."

"Alona," she said. Had he looked at the notepad, he would have known.

"Alona, yes, of course. I'm sorry, honey, I'm a little stressed out today. This place is a madhouse. Alona, this is Mark, my partner. Have you put the ribs on the grill yet?"

"Yeah," Mark said, and added that there was a mad rush for the chorizo and he didn't think there was enough.

"So they'll eat kebabs," Raul said, and took the keys for the van out of his pocket. "Okay, bye, sugar." He kissed Alona on her cheek and left her standing with Mark, whose face she now noticed was dripping with sweat and whose orange apron, which was too long and reached down to his shins, was covered with grease stains.

"Hard work, manning the grill," she said, with a smile. He nodded and wiped his forehead with the edge of the filthy apron. She said she had a tissue and started to dig through her bag, and he said he had to get back. "Then keep me a chorizo?" she asked, even though she didn't like them. He said he would, and hurried away. Two hours later, when she was about to leave and had started to make her way to the parking lot, she heard someone calling her name. She turned and saw Mark standing behind the grill, waving a chorizo speared on a fork.

"I totally forgot about it," she said, when she went over to him. He said he'd guarded that sausage all evening. When she apologized and said she'd already had dessert and was stuffed, Mark whistled, and out of nowhere a black Labrador appeared. Mark tossed him the chorizo and said, "Your gain, Popolo."

"Popolo?"

"Popeye. Popolo is his nom de plume."

"So he writes? 'Cause we're always looking for new material."

"No, but my daughter does."

Her heart sank with disappointment. He was married. And although she wasn't interested in him, it saddened her, statistically speaking, to know he wasn't available. "How old is she?"

He looked at the Lab, polishing off the chorizo, and said, "Almost ten. She lives in the States with her mother, and I miss her so much. She writes me letters. Short stories, really. Half Hebrew, half English."

"When did you separate?"

"Five years ago. She couldn't live here anymore—Jane, I mean. My ex-wife."

"Is she American?"

"Yes. We met in the States when I was studying there."

She asked what he was studying and he said it was a long and not particularly interesting story. She asked if he saw his daughter.

"Sure, she comes here in the summers, for two months." He looked at the dog. "And I go there once a year. But it's not enough."

"No, of course not."

"It's really not enough," he repeated, and looked from the dog back to her, and she thought he was about to cry. "I'm just dying, I miss her so much."

The infiltration of a ten-year-old girl into this evening turned the atmosphere serious. Alona could practically feel the small talk evaporate like sweat or perfume.

"Do you have a picture?" she asked.

He looked at her in surprise—later he said that was the moment he fell in love with her—and said he didn't have his wallet on him. "That's her dog," he said, and pointed at Popeye, who was sprawled at their feet.

"He's handsome. He looks like a good dog, too."

"Yeah, he's an excellent dog."

She later confessed that that was the moment she decided to sleep with him. "The way you talked about Popeye, so seriously. Who calls a dog *excellent*?"

"So what do you say, maybe we can get together some time? I'll show you a picture of Roni."

"Sure." She asked if he had a pen and paper, and he started searching, and then she remembered she had an electricity bill in her bag. She took out the envelope and tore off a piece and wrote down her number, feeling his eyes track the motion of the pen, swallowing up the numbers, and then he took the paper and looked at what she'd written and asked, "Is that a five or an eight?"

"Five. I guess my five and my eight are kind of similar."

The next day he called and asked if she was up for coming to Jerusalem. He was cooking dinner.

"For who?"

"For us. I mean, if you come."

She said she'd be happy to, and he said he lived in Ein Kerem, and as she drove her Renault Clio down the windy hills, she started to feel what she already knew: this man would conquer her with his tenderness and then drown her in it. She would marry this man and fight with him her whole life. She might even have children with him. This short, thin man had been sent to her as a goodwill gesture but also a warning: Had she learned nothing from all these years?

RELAX! she'd written yesterday, after taking the kids to kindergarten, forgetting the reminder about the alarm system. She put down her pen and went to make some coffee, and when the water boiled she changed her mind and steeped some herbal tea, because caffeine would contradict the calmness. Before going back to the study she started to pick up clothes and toys off the floor, and on the low worktable that Mark had built—and that was also why she had fallen in love with

him, because he built things—among shreds of paper and newspapers
cut up with plastic scissors, and lengths of colorful Play-Doh snaking
over them, she found the missing page from Uri Breutner's manuscript,
with her comments in the margins. The page was cut in two, and she
was filled with angry longings for the children who had created this
mess, because after she sat down with her herbal tea and taped the
torn page together and put it back in the manuscript and looked for
the point where she'd left off the day before, she envisioned them on the
way to kindergarten, sitting quietly in their car seats in the back, Maya
in that awful midriff shirt, Ido staring out the window, his tranquil face
giving no hint of the terrible scene that was about to occur a few minutes later.

Once again, he didn't want to her to leave. He wanted to stay home
with her and sweep the floor all day. She knelt down and held his hands
and explained it was impossible. He asked why, and she said she had to
work and he had to go to preschool.

"But why?" he repeated, and it was a genuine question, a desperate
desire to know.

"Because that's how it is, chickie." She pressed him to her chest and
felt the dampness of his tears on her neck. "Grownups have to work and
children have to go to school; that's your job."

He pulled away and looked at her curiously. "Really?"

"Yes, you work here; this is your job."

"And Maya, too?" He wiped his eyes with his hand.

"Maya, too. Maya works at kindergarten."

"But my job is harder, right?"

"Of course," she said, and the teacher stood by the door and winked
at her.

"Because she's a girl and I'm a boy," he went on.

The teacher said, "That's right, Ido."

Alona wanted to correct him, but he was three; let him think whatever he wanted. She was in a hurry and there was no time now for feminist correction. The problem seemed resolved, and she could give him
one last hug and deposit him with the teacher, who was starting to show
signs of impatience.

Suddenly the boy's face turned grave again, and he asked, "But what
is my job?"

"Wow, the boy has a difficult question. Well, Mommy, tell him—what is his job?"

"Your job is to be a boy in preschool."

Alona glanced at the teacher, who looked satisfied, but Ido clung to her neck again and whimpered, "But I want to sweep with you!"

"Later, Ido. Later you'll sweep with Mommy, right, Mommy? Because you have a lot of dirt at home, right?"

Alona nodded eagerly.

"But I want to do it now! Now, I want to!" He beat her with his fists.

"I have an idea! We'll give you a broom and you can sweep the yard, okay?" said the teacher.

"That's a great idea," Alona said.

"No! I want to sweep with Mommy!"

"Come on, Ido, I really have to go." She stood up and he wrapped his arms around her thigh, but the teacher motioned for her to leave. With a sense of relief, she fled, got into the car, shut the door, and turned the engine on. She switched on the radio—it was the end of the eight o'clock news, and they were forecasting a heat wave—and cranked the air-conditioning up to the highest setting, which drowned out her son's sobs still drifting out of the preschool window.

She looked at RELAX! again. The word was undoubtedly mocking her now. It was a compromise between the person she wanted to be and the person she never would be, because "cool and flowing" were not going to happen. They just weren't. And not because she didn't want to be like that, but because at thirty-nine (she'd be forty in the spring) she finally knew—and it was a pity she hadn't known this ten years earlier, but how could she?—that the struggle to be someone else was not only exhausting and futile but dangerous. Yes, dangerous, because it distracted her mind and robbed her powers, and now that she had children she could no longer allow herself the luxury of self-hatred. Not at all.

She felt a tinge of pity that threatened to ruin her workday and hover like a leitmotif over Uri Breutner's wonderful text; this kind of talent hardly ever came along. Although perhaps it wasn't that Breutner's manuscript was so wonderful, more that it blinded her vision, because at certain moments it all seemed fake, the suffering seemed false, too elegant, too stylized. Not long ago she'd gone to his birthday party in a Tel Aviv bar. He was twenty-seven and took every opportunity to embroil her in childish heart-to-heart discussions about life. He was interested in life, he said, "life itself." He talked about things like death and truth and bored her to death, although she was obviously attracted to him.

But so what? How could she not be? He had that puppyish distress and sloppiness, just like Mark when she'd fallen in love with him, just like Mark still had, and she'd happily sleep with him, too, she'd sleep with anyone now—not happily, perhaps, but with relief. It had been two years since the last time, the unnecessary time, a month after they'd separated. *The crybaby night*, she called it privately, to make herself not miss him or want more, even though she did—but no! No way. "But I don't want to leave home," he'd cried into her sticky embrace, under the big comforter. "I know it's what we have to do, but I don't want to." She felt like she had slept with a little boy. "I don't want to, I don't want to," he whimpered into her neck.

She reassured him, caressing and murmuring into his ear. "Stop, Mark, we have to, for the kids. We're not happy together."

He said he knew that. "But I don't want to."

She said it was just a trial separation: "Let's see how it goes. Worse comes to worst, we'll get back together, okay?" He sniveled. "Okay? Okay, Mark?" Just a minute ago she'd had an orgasm, and now she was consoling him.

How typical, she thought angrily, when she took a shower after he fell asleep. She didn't usually shower after sex, but she felt she had to wipe away his tears. How typical, she told herself as she soaped her body, hoping he wouldn't wake up and see her in the shower and be insulted. But so what? What's wrong with *typical*? Maybe he was right and she didn't know how to accept *typical*. She treated *typical* like an enemy, a cliché in a text. What's wrong with a twenty-seven-year-old man who wants to talk about life? And what's wrong with a forty-two-year-old man sobbing a moment after he climaxes?

"Did you put your diaphragm in?" he'd asked when they got into bed. When she said she had, he asked when she'd had time; he hadn't seen her go to the bathroom. She said she'd done it before he came over, even before he brought the kids home from the play, because she knew she would sleep with him that night. "Really? You knew?" he asked, and looked disappointed and slightly betrayed.

Perhaps that was why he had cried afterward, she thought now, staring at the word RELAX! She turned away from the note as if it were a failed charm, and thought about calling the preschool but decided not to, because the sounds of the children in the background, the commotion in which she would not be able to isolate her son's voice even though her ears and heart would try, those sounds, an amorphous childhood sound track to which she had no access, would make her feel even guiltier for abandoning him there, crying and kicking, for not being able to summon up the compassion required to tell the teacher to leave them alone, and then to sit down on the floor near the door, hold Ido in her lap, and tell him stories instead of lies. She would tell him that although she remembered almost nothing of her early childhood, she vividly recalled the terror of being left alone at preschool. "And my mother," she would have told him, had she thought about it, "I mean Grandma, Grandma liked to make her life easy, so she used to promise me that when she came to pick me up she'd buy me candy. But you, chickie, you're a lucky boy, you have candy strewn throughout your day, so you can't be bribed with it. Anyway, Grandma would leave me there with that promise and walk out even before I had time to consider if it was a good deal. She walked out because not everyone had cars back then, and she would run up the street as if a monster were chasing her—no, not a real monster—until she disappeared around the bend that led to our street, and I'd still be standing there, holding on to the railing." She wondered if her mother had also tormented herself every morning as she hurried to catch the bus to the institute she ran, or whether this guilt was something unique to Alona's generation.

Maybe she would call the preschool after all, she thought, and went out to the yard to smoke and reconsider. If she heard that everything was all right, she could finally relax. But what would she do if they told her Ido was still crying? Or, worse, if she heard him crying in the background? She put out her cigarette and stood up, trying to shake off the worry that was biting at her workday before it could swallow the whole thing. "I fell in love with you because you're the suffering type," Mark always said, and at first it turned her on: here was a man, finally, who was attracted to what had chased away all the others. "It's hard for you to be in the moment," he said, and she thought, How could you not fall in love with someone who can pull out such accurate diagnoses? She had a problem with the moment, she knew. She was always outside of it, a minute or two behind, never fully in it, as though the moment were a whirlwind she feared getting swept up in. Mark had picked up on it the minute they'd met.

"Why are you so tense?" he asked, when they had sat down for dinner on his vine-shaded balcony suspended over the wadi. "Are you in a hurry?"

She said she wasn't. "Why do you ask?" She told him the house was amazing, the balcony was amazing, the vine canopy was amazing. "Do you think I look tense?"

He said he wasn't sure, he didn't know her, "But it looks like you're not all here."

"I'm here! I'm completely here." But she knew he was right, and that an octopuslike force in her soul was constantly reaching out its tentacles, looking for something to grasp. One arm had already turned the lock and opened the door to her apartment in Tel Aviv, her single apartment on Shlomo Hamelech where she suddenly wanted to be.

He started to tell her that, until five years ago, Jane and Roni had lived here, and to this day he hadn't really reorganized his life. "As a divorced man, I mean." He pointed at a window. "See? There's her room."

"Oh, really? Can I look?"

He walked her inside and they went into the living room, where a Japanese screen concealed a double futon. A low wall tiled with Armenian ceramics and colorful pieces of glass separated the kitchen from the living room; farther down, near the front door, she noticed another door. It opened on to a large, beautiful room, almost as big as the living room, with a high ceiling and two arched windows with deep sills, which also looked out onto the wadi. "This is Roni's room," Mark said, and flipped a switch. A pale orange light filtered through a lampshade of parchment paper illustrated with deer and rabbits. "It's from some reservation in Arizona," he said when he saw her looking at the lamp-shade. "We bought it there last summer on a trip." She said it created a nice, soft light, and her eyes scanned the smooth old floor tiles, the red wool rug, and the wooden bed painted in a faded pale blue. "I built that," he said.

"Really? You know how to build things? Are you a carpenter?"

"Amateur, an amateur carpenter."

She said it was very impressive and tried to picture the girl. "You promised to show me a picture."

He pointed to an old dresser in the corner of the room. The doors were covered with pictures, and she walked over to look. "This is her," he said, pointing to a large black-and-white photograph. "It's a little out of date, I took it a year ago."

"She's lovely," Alona said as she studied the girl's features. She had a round face, like his, but her large eyes were different. "Are they blue?"

"Yes, she looks like Jane."

"But she has your mouth. And chin. And she has nice hair, like yours, doesn't she?"

"Yes, real black." He stared at the photo. "Except mine's already full of white."

As they were about to leave the room she noticed a shelf above the bed lined with books in English.

"Do you know this one?" he asked, pulling out a book. "*Goodnight Moon.*"

"No, I don't."

"They have it in Hebrew. It's one of her favorite books, and mine, too. She's a little old for it now, but I still like it so much I sometimes read it to myself."

Alona paged through the book, smiling.

"It's about a bunny who goes to sleep and says good night to all the objects in his room. Look how much detail there is."

"And who's this?" she asked, pointing to an elderly rabbit sitting on a rocking chair, sewing.

"I guess that's the grandma," he answered, standing close to her. "Or maybe the nanny, it's not clear. That's part of what's so great about it."

She felt his shoulder touch hers, and his neck gave off a whiff of cheap soap.

He turned the page. "Now she's not there anymore. She disappears, and Roni always asks where she went. It's kind of a game, we guess where she went."

"So where did she go?" Alona asked, when they left the room.

Mark put a hesitant hand on her arm and immediately pulled it back. "Where?" he said, when they went back onto the balcony. "I don't know. I guess she's in the other room, watching a bunny talk show on TV. Or maybe she went to play bridge." He placed a dish of osso buco on the table. "I hope you're not vegetarian."

"I'm the opposite of vegetarian," she said, and knew she would sleep with him that night, and that in the morning she would not feel like she wanted to flee, or like he wanted her to flee. She did not know that three years later this man would bring home, to the house they renovated together in Eden, a copy of *Goodnight Moon* for their little girl.

"What's going on, where are you?" he asked, as he watched her taste the osso buco and the orange-tinged mashed potatoes.

"Nothing, nowhere, I'm just focusing on the food." But she felt another tentacle slithering toward some place where there was no room for men like Mark.

"You don't have to eat it if you don't like it," she heard him say, "I won't be insulted."

"You have no idea how delicious it is." But she couldn't enjoy the meat, or the mashed potatoes, or the asparagus, or the salad. And she couldn't enjoy the panna cotta he served afterward with coffee. It was glossy and quivering, with a puddle of caramel in its center that teared down the sides. She couldn't enjoy it because she couldn't enjoy it. To her, this did not seem complicated but horribly simple. This poor man, she thought, as the tentacle twisted. Look at him: an open book. Another tentacle waved an accusatory finger: this man is amazing. Yeah, because he's pathetic, the first tentacle shot back. But what difference does that make? Alona thought, and lit a cigarette.

"I don't smoke," Mark said, when he brought her a copper ashtray. "Only weed, sometimes. An old habit from Jane."

"I can't." She looked into the dark wadi. "It gives me panic attacks."

"Really? You should smoke with me one day. You need to smoke with someone you feel comfortable with, someone who will watch out for you. Well, not with me actually, 'cause you don't feel comfortable with me." He grinned.

"Why do you say that?"

"Because it's obvious. Look at you, you're tense as hell; you look like you're having a panic attack right now."

Later, when they lay naked next to each other on the futon behind the screen, he told her that was what he liked, among other things: that anxiety of hers. He'd liked it from the first moment he saw it yesterday, on the beach.

"What did you see?" she asked, combing her fingers through his soft hair, which was damp with sweat—he's the type that gets sweaty, she had noted earlier, when she helped him clear the dishes; it seemed strange, because he was skinny and looked light, almost bodiless. "What did you see?" she repeated, seeking a diagnosis, because men had told her this before, usually as a reason for their incompatibility.

"I don't know." He looked up at the high ceiling, whose iron supports were exposed where the plaster had crumbled. "It's like you're always busy with something. I don't really know you, but it looks like you're troubled, like you're not having fun. I don't mean fun in the sense of fun."

"Then in what sense?" She stroked his chest. She'd only just noticed that he had almost no hair on his chest.

"In the sense of, I don't know. . . . Come on, don't get me tangled up." He turned onto his side and hugged her.

"Well? You started something, so finish it; don't leave me hanging."

"Your mind is always working."

"Everybody's mind is always working, isn't it?"

"No. There are people who know how to rest."

"Really? Name one."

"Me, for example."

"You rest?" She giggled, or tried to, when he put his cheek on her stomach.

"I'm resting now." He rubbed his lips over her belly button.

"Me, too. Don't I look like I'm resting now?"

"You really don't," he whispered into her stomach. "You look like you're asking yourself how you're going to get out of this, how you got into bed so quickly with a sensitive, vulnerable, kindhearted guy who cooked you a dinner you didn't really enjoy, and who isn't really your type, aren't you?"

"No way!"

"Then stop worrying. I know how to take care of myself."

"But it's not true that you're not my type. I don't even have a type. Maybe I used to, but not anymore. And I really enjoyed the food. It's the best meal I've had in ages."

"So what if you didn't enjoy it? It won't kill me."

"But I did! I swear!"

He got up to bring them a drink, and as she lay in bed she suddenly realized that she hadn't enjoyed the sex either, because of its status: it was famine-ending sex, which was supposed to be something different, celebratory and electric, ecstatic almost, and not so nice and easy and comforting.

Yesterday, before he'd brought the kids home from the mall—he'd ended up dropping the picnic idea—she'd almost been tempted to look for her diaphragm—she no longer remembered where she'd buried it— because why not? What was the worst that could happen? The thought that she'd spent half of her thirties, which were about to be over in the fall, without sex was horrifying, irrational. She'd been able to justify her avoidance of Mark for the past two years, but now there was no longer any point. It was obvious they would never get back together, so why not? And after two years it might even be exciting, like sleeping with someone new.

She remembered that she hadn't asked Mark if he was planning to give the kids dinner, and she called to check. Yes, they'd already eaten and were on their way. "We'll be home in fifteen minutes, tops." How easily he called his former home *home*, she thought. Two years ago it would have annoyed her, but not anymore. She went into the bathroom and started rummaging through the cabinet under the sink, but she stopped herself. No, she thought. Really, no. Why would she even think of it? She heard the car outside, the doors slamming and the gate opening, and the kids burst into the house in a frenzy and collapsed on the couch and asked to watch a video.

"No, it's time for showers now."

"Just one!" Ido begged.

"You promised!" Maya said.

"What did I promise?"

"That we'd watch a video when we got home from school," Maya said.

Mark walked in, carrying their bags full of dirty clothes and artwork. She was about to say goodbye to him but he asked if she wanted him to give them a bath, since she looked a little tired. "Did you work today?"

"Yes, a little, but I couldn't really get into it."

"Then let me do it—I mean, if it's okay." He also offered to make the two of them some pasta or something for dinner, and she thought she didn't need to worry about the diaphragm because she was supposed to get her period at the end of the week anyway, but no, she told herself again, absolutely not.

As always happened when Mark spent the afternoon with the kids, the night was relatively quiet. Ido woke up only once, and Maya slept through. When Alona opened her eyes and surrendered to the temporary caress of a morning breeze, listening to the bamboo blinds tapping against the window, she thought she had found the formula: she would write several words today, which together might be able to create the miracle that was too much for one word. And really, she thought, just like with the children, and with Mark and herself, it turned out she had excessive demands from words, too.

She got up and went to the study and tore off a yellow note and wrote SURRENDER TO THE MOMENT! She stuck the note on the monitor but changed her mind, pulled it off, and threw it in the trash can. There was no joy in surrendering, and no benefit either. DEDICATE YOURSELF TO THE MOMENT, she wrote, without an exclamation mark. A little New Agey, but so what? She left the room, wondering that the kids hadn't woken up yet, and went into the kitchen to put the water on to boil. She started to scribble the day's chores on the magnetic board attached to the fridge but stopped; that list negated what she had just written down a moment ago. Perhaps she should start practicing her new skills. She would drink her coffee alone, in the yard, and smoke one cigarette, even though she had forbidden herself to smoke before breakfast, but the new rule superseded all the old ones.

She put the box of remaining Squares on the table, took out the kids' plastic bowls from the dishwasher, and when the kettle boiled it occurred to her that she had unintentionally formulated an ingenious rule, the kind that canceled all other ones, and she suddenly felt a little shiver: maybe today she would sleep with Mark. She leaned on the counter and gazed out to the street. Something looked different this morning, almost foreign. She opened the window and twisted her face. The water valve was whistling again, and she'd just had the plumber over two weeks ago.

"Mommy!" came Maya's sleepy voice. "Mommy, come here! I told you to come already!" her daughter commanded.

She heard bare feet pounding down the hallway. "I slept well!" Ido announced and wrapped his arms around her thigh. She leaned down to hug him. "Yes, you really did sleep well." The boy smiled proudly, and she thought this morning she would stay at preschool with him for as long as he wanted, and maybe it would be a kind of shock therapy, and her willingness to stay would take the sting out of the separation. But then she scolded herself for falling back into her old ways: Why think about what's going to happen in an hour when I can simply—she hated the word but told herself to give it a chance—flow with it?

She straightened up, and before heading to the children's room she took a long breath and tried to convert the uprising in her heart into a new smile. Maya was starting the day off with power games—so what? She glanced out the window again and saw what had only been hinted at a moment before: the exclamation point she had banished from her note was now stationed defiantly outside, in the space usually occupied by the Mazda. When she hurried to the front door she found the door was locked and the keys she had left there were gone.

ELI

Anything is amazing if a sixteen-year-old girl does it to you. Anything. Even if she doesn't know how to give head, the fact that she's sixteen is what does it. And also the way that she tries so hard, which at first he found pathetic, but only for a moment. (If he'd allowed that moment to last, if he'd given it more credit than he had decided it deserved, he obviously wouldn't have slept with her at all, no way.) That sweet earnestness—it takes years to learn how to give a blow job without effort, without choking, years of trial and error, and maybe a couple of good girlfriends to teach her, as Dafna once told him in a moment of candor, when they'd only just met, after he complimented her on a blow job. She'd done it wrong for years, she said, until one day a friend demonstrated on a Coke bottle, as a joke.

"What was it?" Eli asked that day, lying on his back, and stroking her neck. "What were you doing wrong?"

She giggled shyly. "I didn't know you had to hold it."

"Hold what?" he asked, smiling up at the ceiling.

"The weenie," she whispered, and he thought that was when he fell in love with her: she could go down on him like a pro but she couldn't say *dick*. That was the kind of woman he wanted: a woman of contrasts, someone who would put a little zigzag into his straight life.

"But why do you have to hold it? To help the erection?"

"No, the opposite—to control it, so I won't choke."

"Oh, that makes sense. But didn't you figure that out on your own?"
She shook her head into his thigh.

"How come?" he asked, and she said that sex, like anything, turned
out to be a pattern, and that what you did the first few times was what
got fixed in your mind as a method, a style, perhaps even a destiny. "Not
with me," he said, and privately complimented himself for the long
road he'd traveled since the first time he got a blow job, when he was a
soldier.

"I don't know, I guess I just thought that's how you did it." He asked
about her first time. "I was nineteen," she said.

"Me too. I got my first blow job in the army, and it was so awful,
with this dumb-ass girl from the base. She bit me! What about you?
Who was it with?"

"I'm embarrassed to say. I think I bit him, too."

"Come on, tell me, don't be embarrassed."

"It was with a lifeguard on the beach," she said, and buried her
face in his leg. "A group of us girls used to go to the beach every
Saturday—"

"Which beach?"

"In Tel Aviv."

"But which one?" he insisted, as though he were planning to track
down that lifeguard and put him on trial.

"I don't remember. I think it was the Sheraton beach."

"How did it happen? Was he old?"

"No, young actually. Maybe twenty-one. And he was hot."

"One of those macho types?"

"Kind of. He hit on all three of us, but I was the only one who didn't
have a boyfriend. I didn't know what I was doing—"

"And I didn't know what was being done to me," he interrupted,
remembering. "I just came right into her mouth, poor girl. I don't think
I enjoyed it at all."

"I definitely didn't. It was pretty disgusting. I was horrified by myself,
and by the taste of it. I didn't know it was salty." She crawled up the
mattress until her face was close to his and snuggled up next to him,
resting her hand on his chest as though seeking belated consolation for
that ancient blow job.

He hoisted himself up on his elbows and said, "I just had a revelation. You'll laugh, but I realize now what the basic difference between men and women is. For you, the first time was insulting. For me, it created ambition."

"Maybe, I don't know. It was obviously a lot more complicated than that." He said of course it was, but he asked in what way. She said she couldn't remember and didn't think she even knew at this point—or, rather, could no longer feel what had gone through her mind when she was nineteen because her mind was different now, and maybe what now seemed like humiliation was only humiliating in retrospect, viewed from a mature perspective. He nodded, trying to understand. "Because nineteen seems like a little girl to me now, even though at the time I thought I was pretty grown up. Now that I *am* grown up, it seems terrible, like I was cheated."

"I felt a bit cheated, too." He ran his hand through her red hair, which was thick and fragrant and heavy. "Have I already told you that I love your hair?" he whispered.

She nodded.

"And have I already told you that you give incredible blow jobs?" He tried to imagine their future together, and although they'd only known each other for a few weeks, he knew this was the woman he would marry. Because unlike the others, there was something about Dafna that he'd only encountered before as a passing shadow in his secret longings, a combination of pink, redheaded babyness and deep, brown maternity. He knew it was a cliché, but so what? She had it and that was that, and he wasn't about to give it up.

Now he looked at the sediment in the bottom of the glass, the glass she believed would bring her good luck, although he had no idea why. He'd realized long ago that he would never be able to really know what she was going through, and he thought about himself, about what he would go through in roughly ten days, and he very much hoped it wouldn't be on the eighteenth, just not on the eighteenth, because on the eighteenth he had a court appearance in the contractor's case. He thought about what he would go through when they drove to the hospital together and sat silently in the car through the regular traffic jam. She'd say it was a pity they hadn't left half an hour earlier, and he'd say it wouldn't have made any difference; if you don't leave before six-thirty you get stuck no matter what. They'd sit there, she with her ovaries bursting with hormones, Chinese mud, and desperation, and he silently fuming over jerking off into a cup—it was cruel, he knew, to think about it that way, but that's how he saw it now, because after their fourth IVF, six months ago, he'd realized it was never going to happen. They were never going to have a baby this way.

Something in him saw it very lucidly. It was one of those moments in life when you know something, when a simple fact strips off in front of you and faces you naked and says, Here I am. Fuck you. Whaddaya gonna do about it? It had happened to him a few times before, and he was always right. Eight years ago, for example, on the morning his father died, he knew it. He clearly saw his father lying on his side on the balcony of his apartment in Nachlaot. And he had another flash, a moment of sheer lucidity, a moment you could practically hear crackling, that morning in May when Dafna was about to go to the hospital for a blood test and he knew it would be negative.

He got out of bed that morning, went into the kitchen, and looked at her sitting by the table eating cornflakes with banana, reading *Ha'aretz*. She was already dressed, her hair washed and damp, still glistening from hair mousse, and when he said good morning she said she was leaving soon. He wanted to say, Don't go, honey, there's no point. They'd been trying to get pregnant for almost seven years, and at that moment he felt as if their roller coaster was stuck and he was sitting up high looking down on everything. When the fear dissipated, he saw something he'd never seen before, which stood before him like a person or an object in his field of vision for a fraction of a second and then disappeared: complete failure.

But he said nothing, and she left, and at lunchtime he called her office to find out if the results were in, and she said, "Not yet, in an hour."

He said, "Let me know, then," and she said, Of course, and he felt as if he were cheating her, as if he had joined the ranks of frauds. "How are you doing? Are you okay?" he asked, and she said she was swamped with work, which helped a little; she'd been fine in the morning but now, with only an hour left, it was getting really difficult. "It'll be okay, Dafna," he said, and hated himself because he knew it wouldn't, not this time and not the next time. It would never be okay.

"Eli?" she said.

"What, honey?"

"I have a good feeling," she whispered into the phone. "I mean, I think it's positive this time."

He asked why she thought so. "Because of the sore breasts? You had that last time, too, didn't you?" He tried gently to divert her from the path of hope.

"Not because of that, I don't have the pain anymore—"

"Really?" He wanted to say scoldingly, *Then there you go, that's the answer.* "Why, then?"

"I don't know, just intuition." She said she had to go, she needed to call a journalist.

"Then call me as soon as you find out, honey."

Before she hung up she suddenly asked, "So what do you think? Do you think it's not it?"

It was if one of his negative thoughts had managed to filter through the mixed messages after all, and he said, "I don't know, Dafna, I really don't know anymore. But if you have a good feeling about it, then maybe."

"You think it's negative, don't you?"

He said he didn't know, he really didn't know. "Let's wait until two and then see."

That hour, the longest hour in his wife's life, flew by for him, and he felt like only a minute had passed when DAFNA OFFICE flashed on his cell-phone screen. When he answered, he couldn't resist saying, even before he heard her voice, "It's negative, right?" He heard her muffled yes, and then the tears of a woman sitting in an office behind a closed door. Then came his "It'll be okay," and his offer to meet her for lunch.

"I have no appetite and I'm busy; I have a crazy day."

"Then I'll see you at home?"

"Yes, I'll see you at home." She sniveled, and lingered a while longer in the silence, as though she did not want to end the call because to hang up would be to shut off this failed cycle of treatments definitively.

"Won't you change your mind? I can come by your office. Let me take you out for coffee at least." But she said no, and he said, "If you change your mind, I have time this afternoon."

"Okay, we'll see."

He reminded himself to go past the florist later to buy her a bouquet, or maybe not, maybe something else, because he'd brought her flowers the last two times. Maybe he'd get perfume this time, or jewelry. It never occurred to him that he needed comfort too, because it was obvious that he was the appeaser, the compensator, even though it wasn't his fault: he was proud of his amazing sperm counts. "Let me tell you," Professor Ferber had said, when they first saw him a month ago, after leaving the previous expert, "it's rare to see someone your age, and a smoker at that, with the sperm of a kid."

"A kid?" Eli had asked, insulted.

"Well, an eighteen-year-old boy, a soldier in Golani."

"Oh," he'd said, reassured. So no, he was not at fault here, but still, he was the one who felt guilty, and he wasn't good with sorrow.

Not good at all. And he didn't think this whole business of their unexplained infertility, Dafna's, to be precise, was in any way connected—not even in a loose or symbolic way—with what had started up last winter with the girl. The love of his life, he wanted to call her secretly, but he knew he didn't love her so much as lust after her. And in fact it wasn't really lust for her sixteen-year-old body so much as a yearning to keep watching this version of himself that fucked her. Wildly. Irresponsibly. Sometimes a little violently, but only because she asked for it. She said that was how she liked it: rough, with hands tied, with biting and harmless lashings with his tie or her stockings. The first time she suggested he tie her up and then she tie him up, he asked if that's what the boys in her class did, too, if that's what was popular these days. She said she didn't know what the boys in her class did because she didn't sleep with them.

"Only with grown men?" he asked, after their second or third time, when they were lying naked on a couch covered with dog hair at her father's house, under a quilt her mother had sent her for a birthday.

"Yes, only with grown men."

"Really?" he asked, stroking her genitalia. He suspected she applied some sort of lotion there, something sweet. "Do you put honey down there?" he asked once, and she swore she didn't. "Don't you want to be with someone your own age?"

"No, and you?" she said, and they rolled onto the rug, laughing, she with a childish unrestrained giggle, and he with the artificial chuckle of a wicked old man.

No. He was not in love with her, but that was irrelevant. That was not the point. It was something else, something more exciting and dangerous, not even sexual, because that would make it all so cheap, so much more criminal than it already was. Rather, it was something elemental and even innocent: it was about life. He wanted life, he did not want projects. When the thing had started, he'd already known about the great failure awaiting Dafna. He had started to digest it, and he only hoped she would come to her senses at some point and agree to adopt. When he thought about it, he realized he'd spent his whole life busy with some project or other, like getting into the University High School after his two older brothers had barely completed their high school equivalencies. And then his mother's sudden death from a stroke, when he was in the army. What a project it was to reorganize his father's life in the little apartment in Nachlaot. His brothers had just opened their liquor import business in Eilat and saddled him with the whole thing, as usual. And then law school, and the exhausting clerkship, and the new law firm, and then Dafna. And now he wanted something simple, something sweet like the taste of the girl's cunt—he had never come across such sweetness. Or maybe he just didn't remember.

He had never cheated on Dafna before, either, and even now it didn't seem like cheating but more like an experiment or—as he sometimes told himself when he was on his way to meet her, once every week or two, at her father's house, or in his SUV, and a few times on the beach—a costume: he was dressing up as a forty-one-year-old man fucking a sixteen-year-old girl, like in the movies. He was the scoundrel who had sex with minors. He was that pathetic, loathsome man. Once, at the beginning of his career, he'd happened to defend someone like that. He was a nice, solid guy, could even have been his buddy, a friendly computer programmer, married with two kids, who was accused of statutory rape of a fifteen-year-old girl.

Eli had presented the judge with an innovative line of defense, claiming the law was antiquated and should be reinterpreted because today's minors were not the minors of the past. Had His Honor had the opportunity to meet any fifteen-year-old girls? Was His Honor aware that boys and girls had sexual intercourse at age twelve these days? Had His Honor ever watched *Rebelde Way* or *Chiquititas* or some of the other telenovelas so popular in Israel? Could one really argue today that a girl of fifteen was innocent? Was this really exploitation?

"Whether it was or was not is not for me to determine," said the judge. "The law is still the law, and this was a violation of that law." His client took a plea bargain that gave him six months of community service.

When Eli left the courtroom, he ran into the girl's parents in the hallway. They were young, in their thirties, and had sat silently in the front of the courtroom during the hearing. A mixed Sephardic-Ashkenazic couple, the man was very fair, a redhead like Dafna, and the woman was of Iraqi descent. "Her parents are a little primitive," the client had told him. "Her dad's a bus driver and her mom's a secretary at an accounting firm."

At first Eli felt angry. The woman reminded him a little of his mother, although his parents were both Syrian, not Iraqi. Something in her unhandsome, angry face and the black hair pulled back and pinned to her head with plain clips looked like his mother; she had also been a secretary, for a notary in Jerusalem, until she gave birth to her first son, Shabtai, and since then she had stayed at home. How could you call them primitive? "And the girl? What's she like?" he had asked the client at their first meeting.

The man had sighed. "Out of this world, such a lovely kid. She's gifted, did you know that?" He spoke of her as if she were his daughter and not the girl he fucked in his Skoda.

When Eli met her parents in the hallway, the mother came up to him and put her hand to her neck as though there were a necklace there; he looked back and saw his client sitting down on a bench next to his wife and hugging her. The mother said softly, gently, that she just wanted to ask him one question, if she could. "Go ahead," he said awkwardly, "but I'm in a bit of a hurry."

She asked if he had children. When he said not yet, she said, "Only someone who doesn't have children could say things like that, like you said to the judge." Then she turned and left.

And now it was happening to him, too, the same thing, the same out-of-this-world thing, and every so often he thought of that mother and did not know if he was angry at her or missed her, her scolding, the primitivism that was like his mother's, who had not been fortunate enough, as his father lamented, to see him go to law school and graduate with honors. "Poor woman," his father would say and nod sadly—his

father, whose widowhood and retirement from his job as a land sur-
veyor had nailed him to that balcony over Nissim Bachar Street.

After the fourth failure, in May, Dafna had surprised Eli by suggesting
they go to therapy. "Something bad is happening to us," she had said, in
that same weary tone with which she now asked him to set aside the seventeenth, eighteenth, and nineteenth. When he'd asked what? she'd said,
"Something bad, Eli. Something very bad."

They were sitting in the garden waiting for guests they'd invited for
a barbecue, to celebrate his win in the Arbel case. It was a spontaneous
celebration—they had a freezer full of sirloin steaks and lamb chops
from the barbecue three weeks earlier, for Dafna's birthday, which had
worked out exactly the same day they'd implanted three embryos in her
womb and she'd thought it was symbolic; something good had to come
of it that time, it simply had to, and Eli had said, "Maybe."

"Full acquittal," he had told her, "and the judges reprimanded the
prosecutor. You should have seen it, Dafna." He spoke without looking
at her, leaning back in the wooden chair, sipping a bottle of Heineken
and smoking his fourth cigarette of the day—he would smoke the last
one with Zvika, his partner, standing together by the fish pond. Zvika
loved the fish, and they'd rehash the acquittal of the businessman who'd
been accused of conspiring to murder his partner. Eli liked Zvika a lot.
Their partnership was a perfect match, a gamble that had paid off, because
he'd hardly known anything about Attorney Zvika Streusin when he
was a district attorney who impressed Eli with his virtuoso court appearances. When Eli left the firm and was planning to open up his own, he
approached Zvika one day in the cafeteria at the Tel Aviv District Courthouse and asked if there was any way he could persuade him to leave
the D.A.'s office, Zvika put down the *boureka* he was eating, leaned
back, wiped his mouth with a greasy paper napkin, and said, "Talk. I'm
listening."

Dafna liked him too, maybe because he was single, and spending
time with him was like sitting in a deck chair on the beach of your prior
life, this time as a bemused spectator. She would roll around laughing
when he told them about his Internet dating and one-night stands, and
every so often there was something that lasted for a few months and
seemed promising. And she would scold him good-naturedly for what
she called his irresponsible behavior with women. The three of them

would meet once or twice a month at restaurants or for dinner at their place. "Let's invite Zvika," Dafna would suggest every so often.

The Arbel acquittal came in May, after Independence Day, and Dafna agreed to invite a few people over. Eli said, "You're great, I appreciate it, and anyway we have to do something with all that meat in the freezer." They sat outside waiting for the guests: Zvika, who said he might bring a date but eventually came alone, and the next-door neighbors, Iris and Shuki, who were desperately trying to befriend them and had invited them to countless brunches. "So here's our chance to invite them once and be done with it, no?" Eli had said.

"Whatever, invite whoever you want," Dafna had responded, reminding him that it was his event, not hers, and his victory, less than a week after her failure, the one that had completely surprised her and was, she said, the hardest one of them all, because she'd been counting on at least one of the three embryos taking, just one, because it had been her birthday. But instead he'd bought her a stationary bike because she always claimed she wanted to work out and didn't have time. As they sat in the garden waiting, she said, "So tell me what happened in court," but he knew she wasn't listening. Even without looking at her he felt her staring at a distant point beyond the garden.

He went inside and came back with the verdict and started to read her a few choice passages. "Now listen to this, are you listening?" he said. He recited the paragraph in which the judge reprimanded the prosecution for choosing to ignore the well-known fact that there had been a long-standing dispute between the partners, Arbel and Ben-David, and that Ben-David had been heard in public saying one day he'd find a way *to screw him* and *put him in jail for the rest of his life.* He started telling Dafna what he'd already told her many times during the trial, about his brilliant idea of bringing in Mahmoud, who had once interned with Ben-David and who told the judge it wasn't the first time Ben-David had complained to the police that someone was trying to murder him: he had personally accompanied him ten years ago to file one such complaint, against a neighbor who'd objected to Ben-David adding a floor onto his apartment.

Dafna suddenly turned to him and said she suspected Ferber was a charlatan and that she regretted leaving Brand. "I mean, Brand is proven:

Brand helped Ellah and Micha; Brand saved Daniela and Hagai. Eli, we just rushed into it."

He said they hadn't, they'd made the right decision, her intuition had been right. "You'll see, a change of scenery will be good. And anyway, did you forget about Orit and Avi? They left Brand and it worked on their first time with Ferber. Did you forget, Dafna? That's why we left."

She nodded and said she didn't understand why Ferber couldn't see them until September. Who did he think he was? They were paying to see him privately!

"So we'll take a rest, Dafna. Nothing's going to happen if we wait another month or two. What's the big deal? It's not like you're forty or anything."

"No, I'm not forty or anything, and I wasn't forty when we started trying, seven years ago, and what good did that do me?" She stood up and started pacing back and forth. She plucked a few leaves off the pink oleander, tossed them onto the lawn, and wiped her hands on her pants.

"What's up, Dafna?"

She sat down next to him and said, "We're growing apart, Eli, we're really growing apart."

When she said that, he had the hint of a feeling he hadn't had for a long time: sorrow. Basic, simple sorrow.

Now, as he watched her sip the weak latte he'd made her—and how many times did she need persuading before she deigned to have a cup of coffee?—he thought that he was not sad so much as exhausted. He admired Dafna but also hated her a little, and he didn't mind being the bad guy. First, because someone had to take that role, and second, because he wasn't, not really. He was just pretending, playing the jerk, and that filled him with energy and rejuvenated him. Besides, the only person who knew he was a jerk was him. During the last few weeks he'd almost been tempted to tell Zvika, not because he wanted to share it with him: on the contrary, he was afraid that the minute he told some- one, the minute he put it into words, the story would lose its charm and become an anecdote, an incident, almost a case. No, he didn't want to share, he wanted to confess. That's what he wanted. He wanted absolution, and Zvika would absolve him, he was sure of that, but he'd also tell him he had to end it, because of the girl. *Think about what you're doing to her, did you ever think of that?* Zvika would say. And Eli would reply, "Of course! D'you think I don't think about that? I know very well what I'm doing to the girl, I'm doing her good, and it's a good thing she fell into my hands instead of some asshole who would take advantage of her. And let's just for a minute talk about what the girl is doing to me." But this was a land mine, because Zvika would demand that he tell him exactly what the big deal was. *And if you need it so badly, why don't you screw a twenty-two-year-old on the side? Something a little more stable, a little more legal—what's wrong with a woman of twenty-two? Twenty, if you insist.* And Eli would say he didn't see it as screwing on the side at all, that was just it: with a twenty-two-year-old it really would be just getting some on the side, an affair any way you looked at it. But with her it was different. Zvika would say he wasn't buying any of that crap; there were less dangerous ways of coping with a midlife crisis. *And no matter what you say, she fell into your hands, Eli. You're the asshole who's taking advantage of her. And another thing—did you ever think about what would happen if you got her pregnant?* And he'd say, "That won't happen. She's on the pill." And maybe he'd tell Zvika how wonderful it was to be afraid of exactly that.

At first he hadn't believed her when she said she'd been on the pill since age fifteen. "But what about AIDS? Aren't you scared of AIDS?" he asked her.

"Of course I am, but not with married guys."

"Guys? You mean there are others?"

She told him about the driving teacher.

"Him?" Eli was horrified. He'd seen the guy on the moshav a few times, when he came to pick up students in his white Corolla. "What's his name?"

"Yossi," she said.

Yossi was a lot more suited to the role of statutory rapist than he was, with that bald head and potbelly and those shorts and sandals. "Is he married?"

"Yes."

"Have you been to his house?" He interrogated her as if she were a witness in court.

"Why would I do that?"

"Then where do you do it?"

"In the car."

"But where, in broad daylight? Here, on the moshav?"

"Yes, on the moshav, and no, not in daylight. In the evening. We have our places, don't worry."

And she took him to those places, narrow dirt paths that were practically impassable—he had no idea how the Corolla got through them—hidden in the fields around the moshav, in the peach and nectarine groves, in the orchards. He couldn't help thinking about Yossi and about the girl's father, who had no idea what he was paying for. He found it all so infuriating that he lost his erection and excused himself by saying that he was a little nervous doing it here—anyone could come along.

"Are you afraid of jackals?" she asked, and in the dark he wasn't sure if she was serious or joking. That happened to him with her sometimes.

"No, I'm afraid of people," he said, and tried as hard as he could to banish the driving teacher from his mind as he lunged over the lovely creature sprawled on the backseat with her knees up in the air, like a baby having its diaper changed. And as if she too, at that moment, felt the dissipation of her status as goddess, she got up and started to suck on him, hard, with her teeth, and he remembered his first blow job, from that girl on the army base, and it was very similar, except this time it wasn't awful but wonderful.

Well, I hope for your sake and for Dafna's that you know what you're doing, Zvika would tell him, if he made the stupid mistake of confessing. Even though Eli knew he would never tell Zvika, he enjoyed playing the conversation in his mind. He would say, "I know what I'm doing," and explain that there was no reason to worry about Dafna: she wouldn't get hurt because she wouldn't find out. Zvika would say he hoped at least he wasn't coming inside her, *because she might be snowing you about the pill, you never know.* And Eli would say, "I come in all kinds of places, you have no idea the places I come. A few days ago I came in her armpit." Zvika would burst out laughing, nervously, and Eli would say, "Yeah, have you ever tried that?" Zvika would say he'd tried it all, but not that; he didn't even know it was an option. Eli would tell him it was her idea, that she'd said, "Come on, let's try it, what do you care? Let's see what it's like," and he'd pulled out of her and said, "Are you sure?" and she'd said yes, she was sure, it sounded cool, and he did it, he came in her armpit, and she said it was like taking a temperature, and when he was done he pulled a tissue out of the box but she said, "No, don't wipe it, I want it to dribble, it feels nice. You know, my little brother calls it the 'arm-bit!' " How would he tell Zvika all this, when he himself didn't understand why it was so wonderful when she ordered him to do all kinds of things? "Let's try it with our eyes open. Now let's try it without talking at all." How would he explain to Zvika that he was the one who felt like a toy, and not the other way around? *You're totally nuts*, Zvika would say, and put out his cigarette in disgust. Before he'd changed the subject he'd say, *It's your life, do what you want, but be careful, that's all I'm saying. Just be really, really careful.* Eli knew very well why he'd resisted the temptation to tell Zvika all those months, even though he wanted to so badly: Zvika was more Dafna's friend than his.

He wondered if, under different circumstances, if he wasn't in the picture, there could have been something between them. An affair. A fling. Zvika had often told him that Dafna was amazing, stunning, that she reminded him of that Botticelli picture, except that, unlike Venus, there was something dark and nervous about her, which for some men was a turn-on. "You know what I mean? It's like there's something frenetic inside her, under her skin." Eli would say of course he knew; after all, he was the one who'd married her, because of that, among other things. He tried to remember exactly what it was, that thing that had attracted him so much.

When he first met her, at a housewarming party thrown by a couple of friends in Tel Aviv, she reminded him of a gecko. A combination of gecko and cheetah. She had almost translucent skin and a springy body that was not sculpted, he thought, but animal. Later, when he sat next to her on the couch and she told him about her job as a morning-TV-show producer, someone else sat down beside him and squeezed him closer to Dafna so that her leg touched his and their thighs conducted a conversation. He somehow knew that physically, at least, she was stronger than he was. He even thought she was taller, and for some reason that excited him.

All the women he'd dated before her were alike, which only dawned on him when he saw Dafna naked for the first time, a few nights later. All his other women had been short and very thin, almost brittle, and they were crushed under his weight in bed and in conversation. When he met Dafna, suddenly he had the urge to be the one who was crushed.

He was thirty-two at the time, a salaried lawyer in a big law firm, and lived in a one-bedroom rental on Zeitlin Street. His apartment was sparsely but carefully furnished. The living room had two white leather couches, a glass and metal coffee table, a TV and a stereo system that had cost almost twenty thousand shekels, and a white wool rug. In the bedroom was a cherrywood bed, two matching bureaus, and a wardrobe with sliding doors. The kitchen had a built-in oven he never used, a microwave, an espresso machine, a food processor, and an electric citrus press. "A decked-out bachelor's pad," Dafna said, the first time she visited. She was the only woman he went out with who didn't love the apartment. Later, when they were a couple, she admitted that she was a little stunned by the fact that they were together; she hadn't thought it would work because she was a former moshav girl and he was a pseudo-yuppie.

"Pseudo-yuppie? What's that?"

She said it was someone who revealed yuppie tendencies but could still be saved.

He asked what was wrong with being a yuppie. "It's not like you're really different," he added.

"Me? I'm a simple country girl making her way in the big city."

"Define *simple*. Define *country*. What's the country? Do we even have a countryside in Israel? Or maybe you're talking about some prefab house behind a shopping mall?"

That irritated her. "When I was little there was a countryside. Eden absolutely was the country. I grew up in the country in every sense of the word."

"And what are you now, a cheesemaker? No, honey, you're a TV producer. If I'm a pseudo-yuppie, you're a super-yuppie."

She screwed up her face, whose milky tone reminded him, back then, of a porcelain doll, except for the freckles, which turned him on. She said his outlook was pretty limited, and that not everyone who worked in media was necessarily a yuppie.

"But lawyers are?" he said, trying to fight back.

She said it wasn't the profession, it was the personality. "That's what I'm trying to say—"

"Then don't say anything," he interrupted, knowing he was losing, and he fell on her and put his hand over her mouth. "Just like all the girls who work in TV, you talk too much." Those were the wonderful days when arguments were foreplay for sex, not the other way around.

And behind all the witty retorts and the opinions and the amazing sex (was that what had won him over? could it be?) and the leftist views that bothered him a little at first, he identified in her, right from the start, a restlessness that was very much like his and yet different, as though beneath the gecko skin, behind the brown cheetah eyes dotted with green sparks, another wild creature was darting around, small and furry and ravenous. What surprised him was that he liked it. When she ripped into him in front of her friends, it did not hurt his feelings but filled him with confidence. The bemused contempt with which she viewed his lifestyle—she agreed to date him despite the fact that he was a lawyer, and not, like all the others, because of it—and the fact that he made ten times what she and her friends from TV ever would, that contempt paradoxically flattered him. He felt that Dafna was the final stage in his personal evolution, in the process of making his life different from his parents' and brothers' lives. His brothers were also successful and his father was proud of them, but not like he was proud of Eli. And now, unlike Shabtai and Yoram, Eli had not found himself a good woman but a different one, a woman who was slightly complicated, "an intellectual," as his father said derisively, spitting out the consonants like nutshells. It wasn't because she was Ashkenazi, his sister-in-law Avivit was also Ashkenazi, Romanian on both sides. It was something else. "She's not for you, Eliko, listen to me. For once in your life, listen to someone more experienced than you," his father said, and in his mind's eye Eli saw his father sitting on a light-blue Formica chair with a dish towel spread over his lap, peeling apples with a hypnotizing circular motion, the peel curling down like a snake around the knife. In his memory he saw his father sigh and say, "You don't marry a woman who's taller than you. The girl looks like a giraffe, and you look like a poor little spider next to her."

He turned up with a sour face at the wedding, which was held in a restaurant in Jaffa. He looked gaunt and angry and wore his favorite suit, his only suit, which Eli and his brothers teased him about. They always asked if someone had sewn it for him in Gaza. "I'll buy you a new one for my wedding," Eli had tried to convince him. "Why not? We'll go to a tailor if you want." But his father had refused. Shabtai and Yoram, who suddenly looked like their father, walked in with him, each holding one of his arms, and Dafna, who stood beside Eli wearing a dress that in no way resembled a bridal gown—another crack in his father's heart—said he looked like he'd come to a funeral. When they stood under the chuppa, Eli's father looked at him with great sadness, as if he already knew something.

Dafna was not the final stage in his evolution. No, because there was the whole business with the children. "I want four," she declared, when they talked about getting married. "I want at least four, and I hope that's okay with you. There were three of us, and I want four."

Eli said four was too many. "There were three of us, too, but four is a litter."

They compromised on three. "But the first one's a girl," she said.

He agreed. "That's fine. I want to have girls."

When they stopped using protection, about a year after the wedding, they amused themselves every month thinking up names while they waited for her period—and unlike today, back then the waiting was shared and celebratory. What was the name she'd picked? He could hardly remember now, because they never spoke about it anymore. Amit, he thought. Yes, Amit; he'd vetoed that one. "Where did you come up with Amit? It's a boy's name!" He objected to the whole fashion of giving boys' names to girls. "Why not the other way around? Would you call your son Naomi or Rachel?" Eventually they compromised on Alma for a girl and Yonatan for a boy. Almost a decade had passed since they met, since he fell in love with her, since he fast-forwarded the movie of his life with dizzying speed. "Kiss of the spider woman?" she used to tease him, and he regretted having told her, back in the days when they could still talk about things, how his father had disliked her. "Oh, my poor little spider," she would say sometimes in bed, running her fingers through the thick hair on his chest. "What will become of my poor spider?"

. . .

He wished he hadn't promised to stop by Toys"R"Us. He had a busy morning and wasn't sure he'd have time in the afternoon. It was clear that his ten o'clock meeting would run late. And he was alone this morning. Zvika was away on reserve duty again, the second assignment in six months, and this time they'd sent him to guard some settlement near Nablus. "If I were you, I'd refuse," Eli had said when the call-up arrived, even though this wasn't true, and in any case he'd been doing his reserve duty in the military AG for the past ten years.

He sat in his SUV in the Ganot traffic jam and decided to call Dafna to ask if she could pick up something herself, he didn't think he'd have time, he was already late for his first meeting and had forgotten that the second one would probably be long. He was about to hit the first number in his speed dial and call home, but he was afraid. These little gestures he made—and he made sure to organize a few of them every week: shopping, tune-ups for her car, dropping in at the Income Tax or the HMO or the pharmacy—he needed these time-consuming errands. It wasn't to cleanse his conscience; he'd taken on the role of fixer and organizer a long time ago, when they'd only just started the fertility treatments, because he felt he had to do something, something that might not balance out her suffering against his, he knew that was impossible, but something that would clarify to her that, unlike what she thought, he was involved in her life, and that her life was not, as she claimed, a boat slowly sailing away from him.

"A boat?" he'd said mockingly when she threw the image at him two weeks ago, after their twice-quarterly sex.

"Yes, that's how I see it. A boat, a skiff, carried away on little ripples, almost imperceptible even to me, by the way, and you can't bring it back."

"Oh, no? Why not?"

"Because there's no way. The boat isn't tied to anything; there's no rope."

Eli sat up in bed and looked at her lying on her side, on the new sheets she'd bought with her holiday gift vouchers, sand-colored organic cotton or something like that. She looked like a beached baby whale, and her heavy, oily nakedness suddenly frightened him, or rather worried him—she'd already told him she'd gained eighteen pounds in the past two years, but there was something odd about those pounds, something watery, edematous. "So what you're saying is that the situation is basically hopeless? That if there's no rope, then I'm out of luck?"

"No. The rope is the child we might have one day." She said this into the sheets, with her eyes closed, but not in her former contemplative way, when she would close her eyes and whisper some statement about them. This time it sounded pained, as if a terrible ache was coursing through her ocean-mammal body. And it wasn't the sperm he had just wasted into her because maybe, you never knew, they did know people who had tried for years and then it had happened precisely when they weren't trying.

He would stop at Toys"R"Us and get it over with. He liked the store, and Dafna couldn't stand it. Toy stores reminded her of what she didn't have, but he felt like a kid in them, impressed by what today's children had but also a little alarmed. It wasn't that his childhood seemed so wonderful, and he didn't miss it, but still, he remembered endless afternoons spent in empty fields which in the seventies had become construction sites. He remembered planks and big rusty nails, countless games and dangers, and an elderly Arab guard at the construction site near his house, who they said was a pervert and grabbed little girls and rubbed up against them in his hut. That Arab was practically a hero to them, not a criminal.

He would drive over to Ga'ash at lunchtime and run into Toys"R"Us; it would calm him down. For his kid—and he knew he wouldn't have one, but so what; he was allowed to keep up an imaginary education of the child he'd never have—he'd never buy a computer. Maybe not never, that seemed excessive, but definitely not before he was twelve, or at least ten.

"Yeah, right, I'll believe that when I see it," Dafna said, when he told her that his boy—or girl, she said—or girl, he said, wouldn't sit at the computer all day like a zombie. "No, our boy will play outside, like I did, and like you did, right?" She nodded. "That's why we moved to the moshav, right?" And she said, "No, we moved to the moshav for you. I was perfectly happy in Tel Aviv." Lately they argued about almost everything.

Now, sitting in the SUV crawling along the North Ayalon Highway, he thought about the eighteenth, and it was obvious to him that Dafna's eggs would not wait until the nineteenth. No. Chances were the retrieval would fall on the eighteenth, and if that happened—and it would, he knew it would—he was totally screwed. For the first time in his solo career, he'd gotten hold of a juicy civil case. About a year ago, he'd managed to win the full acquittal of a contractor accused of negligent manslaughter. A wing in an office complex he'd built in southern Israel had collapsed and buried two homeless people from the Ukraine who were sleeping in the basement. Now the contractor had decided to sue the state for five million shekels, compensation for emotional distress and damage to his reputation. Even though Eli warned him that he didn't specialize in civil charges and would have to do a lot of research and he might be better off with another lawyer, the contractor insisted that Eli had to represent him: "You're a shark, and I trust you blindly."

There was no chance he'd get a postponement now, and Zvika was on reserve duty. Not that he knew the case, but he could have improvised. They didn't even have an intern anymore. The old one had finished a month ago, and the new one hadn't started yet. Not that an intern could help on the eighteenth, but still. And suddenly Eli felt like everyone had abandoned him—Zvika, the interns, and mostly Dafna. He wanted to call her up and ask her to drop it this month, not even start with the injections. Maybe they should just try it naturally this time, why not? That's what happened to Tzippi and Micha in the end, remember? And in his fantasy Dafna replied, *Why not? Good idea, let's give it a rest. Why get stressed out? You're right.* But he didn't dare call her.

He knew she'd left home ages ago, and might be stuck in the same traffic jam he'd just gotten out of. She had the big demonstration tomorrow, and her boss, that Gabi Drixler guy, had been on her case for weeks now because he didn't like the slogans she'd proposed. Eli couldn't understand why Dafna had left her TV job. She hadn't made great money there, but it wasn't bad, and she'd been about to get a promotion. They'd offered her a great contract, which Eli had personally reviewed and annotated, and they'd added managers' insurance and a continuing education fund and almost double the standard vacation time. But about a year after the intifada started, this Gabi Drixler had come along. Drixler was a businessman and a permanent fixture on the morning talk shows. He said he was starting a new movement and offered her the job of spokeswoman. Eli still wasn't convinced that Dafna didn't have a bit of a crush on him.

Eli remembered the first time the three of them had met, at a Japanese restaurant. Eli had checked out this Gabi guy and been relieved to discover that he didn't look all that hot; he was a bad dresser, a chain-smoker, and had a funny boyish haircut, parted on the side. What kind of leader does he think he's going to be with that side part? he'd wondered. He listened to Gabi explain his agenda. Dafna was already convinced, and the meeting was really so that Eli would give the green light.

"I'm purposely defining it as a social peace movement, not a political one, because everyone's sick of politics. Politics is a bad word," Gabi said.

"And society?" Eli asked, sensing Dafna's intent look. "That's not a bad word?"

"First of all, I want to make a conceptual change," the babyish leader went on. "Meaning the ideas, in the big-picture sense, are the same ideas of Meretz and Peace Now, but from the get-go I'm not defining it as a political movement, so we can attract the people who hate Meretz and Peace Now. So I'm defining it, right from the get-go, as a social peace movement—"

"Define *social*," Eli interrupted, pushing his salmon roll across the plate. There was no getting around it: he just didn't like sushi.

"Define *social*?" Dafna's guru sounded confused. "*Social* is me and you. *Social* is everyone who's sitting here. *Social* is us." The little man shoved a slice of smoked eel into his mouth and swallowed it whole.

"*Social is us*," Eli mimicked later in the car, on the way home.

Dafna said it was because of cynicism like his that we were in the shape we were in now. "Because we don't believe anything can change, we've stopped trying—"

"*We* in the social sense? Or *we* as in *me and you*?" he asked mockingly.

He didn't give her the green light she hoped for because he knew she didn't need it. She knew what she wanted and thought it would be nice if he wanted the same things, but ultimately she did not need his permission. On the contrary: he was usually the one who had to insist on bringing things he liked into the house, objects or furniture that Dafna derisively called *brands*. If it had been up to her, they wouldn't have built this house at all but just renovated her mother's old dump. She hated brand names, hated SUVs, and now it felt like she hated him, too—hated him as a concept. A few days after the sushi meal, she told him she was quitting her job. She spent weeks trying to come up with a name for the movement, assembling and dismantling acronyms. "How about SOP, for Social Peace?" Eli suggested. "Or maybe PIS—Peace In Society?" But his teasing only inspired her and eventually led to CUSP— Creating Unity for Social Peace. And one day Eli came home with the SUV, a gold Toyota Prado.

She didn't say a word, not even about the color, and he had actually wanted to consult her on that. He spent weeks deliberating between gold and silver, until Zvika, who had a blue Pajero, said if it were him he would pick gold. He asked if Dafna knew and Eli said, "No, don't tell her, it's a surprise."

"Surprise, my ass," Zvika said. "I know you, and you are headed for a world of trouble." Then he added that if he were Dafna, he'd seek a divorce.

Eli parked underground at the office building on Pinkas Street and waited for the elevator to take him to the tenth floor. He had to find a solution for the eighteenth. It scared him. He could send the sperm with Dafna, the way they used to do at first, but they had had an accident, which cost them a whole month, and he was pretty sure she still hadn't forgiven him. She claimed *that* month could have been *the* month, and he said she only said that because they'd lost it, and he wasn't willing to collaborate with this guilt trip.

He complained that it was hard for him to masturbate in the hospital and he preferred to do it at home, with or without her help. He said he couldn't set another foot in that horrible Room 4. "You don't know what I go through there," he told her, and when the doctor said they could bring the sperm from home as long as it stayed at body temperature, he said, "You'll see, now it'll work for us. I'm telling you, I know my sperm. It's a little shy."

For six months, they took the sperm from home. Dafna, with the utmost gravity, would jerk him off. He remembered the determined expression on her face, biting her lower lip in concentration. He told her he couldn't do it like that—she looked like a drill sergeant. Then one rainy day, when they were driving to the hospital together, Dafna sitting next to him holding the plastic cup under her jacket, against her stomach, a driver behind them slammed on the brakes and rear-ended them. It was at the light just before the turnoff for the hospital, and fortunately they weren't hurt, but the lid wasn't fastened properly and the cup rolled on the floor and spilled out on the mat.

The doctor was amused by the story and said they could try again the next day. "But why not this afternoon? It might be too late tomorrow!" Dafna protested.

"Let your poor husband rest a little," the doctor said with a wink. Then he burst out laughing again and said, "Come back tomorrow, but maybe you should take the bus this time. Although, perhaps that's not the best idea—just imagine if a terrorist blew himself up next to you! What would the body-retrieval volunteers say about the little plastic cup they'd find next to your body?"

When they left, Dafna begged Eli to overcome his stupid inhibitions and kindly masturbate in the hospital from now on. He said, "Fine," but the ultrasound next day showed that Dafna had already ovulated.

He walked into the office and said good morning to his secretary, Liat, who told him the clients had just called to say they'd be late. "Coffee?" she asked.

He said he'd have some at the meeting and shut himself in his office. The windows looked out onto the Ayalon Freeway and the tall buildings along its eastern side. The eighteenth flashed in his mind like a warning light; maybe she would agree just this one time, just this month—and who knew? Maybe this would be their month, too?—to take his sperm with her and he'd get there later, to be with her when she woke up and take her home. No big deal, right? After the meeting he'd call and ask if she wanted him to come to the demonstration the next day, even though he knew she'd say no, she didn't need him there getting in her way. And he'd ask, So what's happening with the slogans? Did you come up with anything? And maybe he'd offer to help; they could brainstorm together. After all, she'd once told him he was a pretty good copywriter. Maybe he'd even try to come up with a couple of slogans himself, and when they drove to her sister's tonight he'd surprise her by pulling out a few brilliant ideas. Then later, as if coincidentally, he'd bring up this matter of the eighteenth.

But he knew he wouldn't have the courage, and he knew he wouldn't be able to think of any good slogans; he was no longer sure he even objected to the security fence. And anyway, what did the fence have to do with social issues or poverty? He didn't understand that, and when he asked her, she'd launched into a totally baseless speech about how the fence was suffocating the Palestinians and would cause them even greater distress than they were already in. It would starve them, and now there were people going hungry on the Israeli side of the fence, too, so the fence was a kind of symbol; it separated the hungry from the hungry, when really they should be united if anything was ever to change here. He said, "Oh, very convincing," and she delivered her regular line about how it was because of people like him, etc. And he said, "Yeah, right, and people like you will bring peace."

But maybe the business with the eighteenth was simpler than he'd thought. Maybe he could request a postponement from the court; just tell them the truth. Medical reasons were grounds for postponement, and this was a purely medical reason. But what would he say, and how would he phrase the request? He needed to ask someone, someone who knew the judge and would know if he had any chance. He knew a few clerks at the district court who might help. He could also wait for Dafna's ultrasound next week, which would give some indication, but by then it might be too late.

He sat at his huge desk and tried to quiet himself, to ease the tension in his rigid neck and shoulders. His cell phone rang and his brother Shabtai asked if he'd had time to go over the documents. He was supposed to advise Shabtai about a lawsuit a hotel in Eilat had filed against him for being late with supplies. Eli said, "No, sorry, not yet." Shabtai said okay, whenever he had time, and Eli promised he'd do it that day, if possible, and asked how things were going. His brother said everything was fine, thank God, and they were probably going to take Yuval's cast off tomorrow. "Great news," Eli said, and promised to call later, after he reviewed the papers.

When he hung up, he leaned back in his leather upholstered chair, massaged his neck, and thought about Rosh Hashanah, six weeks ago, when the Eilat tribe had descended upon their home.

His brother Yoram had wanted them all to sleep in a hotel, but he and Dafna protested: "A hotel? Are you crazy? There's room for everyone here." Over and over again Eli asked Dafna if she was okay with it, really okay, and she said of course, what's the problem?

Dafna liked his family, especially Mali, Shabtai's wife, who considered herself an expert on fertility matters and was proud of having overcome her difficulties getting pregnant with the first son, Amir. Throughout the holiday she tried to convince Dafna to go and see some kabbalist in Eilat; "Women come from all over the country to see him. He has a hundred percent success, you should come. Have a little vacation, stay with us, get some rest." But Dafna politely refused—she had a lot of work, demonstrations and all that—to which Mali responded, "Oh."

Eli's family made a supreme effort to avoid talking politics, and the holiday passed pleasantly, with the house alive and noisy. But on the last evening, just when Eli and Dafna were about to drive everyone to the airport in two separate cars, Yuval, Shabtai's twelve-year-old boy, climbed up the rock garden, after betting his big brother he could catch a fish with his bare hands, and slid and broke his leg. Instead of driving to the airport, Eli took the boy and his parents to the emergency room.

Something strange and slightly scary happened to him at the ER. Up until this moment he hadn't had time to stop and think about it, to try and figure out exactly what it was. He was sitting with his brother and Mali and the boy, waiting for the doctor. The ER was crowded.

"It's always like this on the evening after a holiday," said Mali, "everyone suddenly gets sick."

Shabtai kept apologizing for holding him up. "Next time maybe we'll bring the car, so we can be independent. Or maybe you could come down to Eilat some time? You never come. Maybe you can come for Passover?"

"It's no big deal, really," Eli said. He looked around at the people besieging the front desk. A nurse was trying to push away an Ethiopian woman with an infant in her arms.

"Those are the ones I really can't stand," Mali hissed. "They act like they don't understand Hebrew, but pushing in line they know very well."

"Maybe you should go home," Shabtai said. "Dafna's waiting; she probably wants to go to sleep. We'll take a cab back."

Eli said it was out of the question, and Yuval wanted something from the vending machine. His mother replied, "You're not getting a thing after all the trouble you made today." Yuval started to whimper and said his leg hurt and he was thirsty, he wanted a Coke. "I don't care if you want Coke. I'll get you some water from the fountain," said Mali.

"Oh, come on, what's the big deal?" Eli said, and took a ten-shekel coin out of his pocket. "I'll get him a soda." Despite his brother and sister-in-law's protestations, he got up, mainly because he wanted to flee the waiting room for a while.

He walked down the main corridor, where the soda machines were. He passed them by and went out through the automatic doors, and, since he hadn't brought any cigarettes, he did something he never did: he bummed one from a fellow smoker outside. As he stood there smoking the cigarette, which was too strong, he suddenly panicked. Although he was eleven years younger than his brother, thinner, and dressed— compared to Shabtai, at least—as if he'd walked off the page of a fashion magazine, they had exactly the same face: his mother's face, with the hooked, vulture nose, brown-black eyes very close to each other, joined eyebrows, and long, crowded eyelashes. He saw himself at fifty-two, like Shabtai, lying in the king-size bed with a ruddy whale beached beside him as he drowned in organic cotton sheets.

He pulled out his cell phone and dialed her number. He hadn't dared put it in the phone's memory, but he knew it by heart. When she answered, he heard a commotion in the background, plates and forks clanging and the hiss of an espresso machine. He asked if she was at the restaurant waiting tables, and she said no, it was closed on the holidays; she was in Tel Aviv with some girlfriends. What was he up to? He said he just wanted to know how the holiday had gone for her, because she'd said she hadn't been into the family dinner. She said fine, it was really fine.

"I bet the food was amazing," he said.

She said yes, and he asked if she needed a ride to school the next day, but she told him there wasn't any school the next day. Then he remembered that he'd have to go to the airport anyway, and he wished so badly he could see her right then, right at that moment, to just leave his brother and his family with money for a cab and go to Tel Aviv.

"So what are you doing tomorrow? You'll probably sleep all morning."

She said maybe, she wasn't sure; she'd arranged to meet a friend to study for a literature exam. He asked since when did she study for exams, and she said, "Here and there, you know."

"So, d'you think you'll study all day, or what? Because I'm pretty free tomorrow. I could pick you up in the afternoon, we can go to the beach if you feel like it."

"Maybe, we'll see, I don't know. I don't feel like going to the beach now."

"Okay, give me a call if you feel like it then."

She said she would, and he thought about his nephew, Yuval, waiting on the bench for his Coke. He was less than five years younger than this girl. "So you'll call?" he said.

He was trembling, but not with passion, and his voice might have broken a little, because she asked if everything was okay. "You sound a little sad."

"I'm not sad, it's just a pain to wait here so long."

"Take care of yourself then, okay? I'm sending you a kiss, you know where." He said he did, and she added, "And a bite, too." He giggled, a giggle he'd invented especially for her, and she said, "And you know what else?"

"What?"

"I really wish you were inside me now."

"Why are you doing this to me, huh?" The *huh* was new, too, designed for her.

"Bye, then," she said into the phone, and he wondered if the girlfriends, or whoever she was with, had heard the whole conversation. "Bye, sweet pea." Her lips sucked a kiss into his ear.

"Bye, sweetie," he said, and went inside to the vending machine.

The last time they'd met she told him she really wanted to be an old lady, so she could feel what it was like to sit on a bench all day and feed the birds. He asked if she thought that's what old people did, sit on benches feeding birds all day. "Are you five years old or something?"

"If I was five, I'd probably turn you on even more."

"Watch it. You can't say things like that, even as a joke."

She sighed and nibbled on his shoulder and said it was a drag to be young when there were so many things she still had to go through, so many good things that would still happen to her, but probably bad things, too. She said that what seemed fun to her about being old was that everything would be behind you.

Liat came into the office and said the clients would be there in five minutes. He thanked her, and when she left he called Dafna to find out if she'd asked her sister what to buy her nephew, but she wasn't around. Maybe she was already at the office, in a meeting. He stood up and went over to the windows and thought, as he sometimes did when he had a few minutes to kill, that if he had chosen an office with a southern exposure he might have been able to see the building where Dafna worked, on Ahad Ha'am Street. He could at least have been able to make out the street and imagine that he could home in on her big office window in the old building. Dafna thought it was a beautiful building, but he didn't like that kind of architecture. It was a landmarked two-story structure, with high ceilings and ornate floor tiles, but it had been designated as unsafe.

When they built their house, Dafna had taken him to a factory in Jaffa where they made those kinds of tiles. He'd vetoed them but had given in on the Dutch-style windows, even though he couldn't stand them and claimed aluminum windows were far more practical and affordable. "You have no idea what they can do with aluminum these days; it's not what you think." But she refused even to look at samples. How they'd fought on the design of the house! he thought now, as he watched the traffic crawl across the Ayalon. It was as if they were designing not their house but their fate. As if every piece of furniture, every object, every accessory, was one that would determine what would happen there for years to come.

"I don't want my child growing up to be nouveau riche!" she yelled at him once in a moment of anger, when they were fighting; he couldn't remember about what, maybe the marble in the kitchen.

"And I don't want him growing up to be stuck up," he spat back at her.

He thought that, instead of luring him away from his family, Dafna was rolling him back into their court. And what was strange was that when he looked at her through their eyes, he began to see his mistake. Although, in fact, he couldn't say for sure whether it had been a mistake, because it was obvious that if they'd had children he would be thinking different thoughts at this window, or maybe he wouldn't be standing there at all.

He thought again about the eighteenth, about what he would go through when the receptionist handed him a plastic cup and he walked to Room 4 and sat down on the couch and debated whether to leaf through one of the porno magazines that were never changed. Once he'd complained about it to Dafna, and she said she knew what he was talking about because they didn't update the women's magazines in the ultrasound waiting room either. She'd been flipping through the same ones for—how long had they been doing IVF, four years?—four years! And suddenly that fact had registered with them both.

Maybe he'd skip the magazines and just fantasize. But last time he'd had some trouble with that, because he'd agreed with himself that he would not bring his main fantasy subject, his only one, into Room 4. Not out of guilt or respect for Dafna but out of a strange fear that if he brought her in there, then something of her, something in the scent of her sixteen-year-old body, would remain in the room and feed all the other guys' fantasies. The way she faked orgasms, for example—and it was obvious that she was faking: she came like a girl who'd watched too many porno movies, some of them with him. Or the way she agreed to have anal sex, convinced it was part of the package of growing up. Last month her father had been away in Italy buying black squid-ink pasta and Gorgonzola, and they'd done it on the living room couch, with those dogs sprawled nearby, and the TV with the nightly news on in the background.

"Are you okay?" he kept asking, trying not to hurt her, and she nodded seriously, biting her lip. "Does it hurt?"

"No. Ow, oh!"

"Then why are you saying ow?"

"Because it's so good," she whispered.

Before, she'd suggested getting some butter from the fridge, and he'd laughed, "What for?"

"You know, for . . . Don't we need it?"

"We don't need it; I won't hurt you," he'd said, and she'd looked disappointed.

Wow, he thought now as he sat down in the swivel chair.

Liat knocked on the door; the clients were there. Should she show them in?

"Give me another minute," he said. When she left, he closed his eyes. They had reached new heights that night. *He* had, he had to remind himself. Because, after all, she was faking. But maybe faking it, at her age, was also a kind of height for her. He'd been so loud he thought the neighbors had heard something; he'd heard a window slam in the house next door, just as he'd shouted while ejaculating into her ass ten times the amount he would struggle to squeeze out on the eighteenth of the month in Room 4: "Roni, Roni, my Roni!"

PART TWO

RONI

How long since I last saw you, a week? A month?

Now I am a mass of love more transparent and profound than any other love. Today I sat in the school cafeteria, and the fresh mint tea completely drugged me. This girl in my class read her poems about love and coalescence. She has a boyfriend who illustrates her poems, and there were pictures of sex. Of harmony. Of a body inside another body that is one body that is purple glue, but anyone who hasn't seen us together doesn't know what that purple is.

Sometimes you are a man-thing for me, and I love to watch you and touch you. I think I know your body better than my own. And when you touch me there is so much humidity in the air, it's a whole other climate.

Now I see your shoulders when you breathe. It's all one breath. The boyish stomach, the most wonderful, the strongest penis in the world. When you walk out of the shower your whole body emerges from the water all at once. Sometimes I want to be your mother. When we meet up I'll wash your hair, and when we sleep together I'll go wild. I'll go crazy.

Since she had no intention of sending what she had written, she didn't sign it. She had dozens of these notes, which she wasn't sure could even be called letters. Not that it mattered. Although sometimes she thought it did—to identify these notes, which poured out of her without any control, without her wanting to have control, like sex with him—words that burst out of her at home, on the bus to school, in class, at parties, in the Trattoria, where sometimes she had to drop everything and run to the storehouse to sit and write. What should she call them? How to define this relationship? Because it suddenly seemed important. It was suddenly crucial; if she found the definition, perhaps she would also find the way back to him.

She was late for the school bus. When she woke up in the big bed in Shiri's room, she found a note on the pillow in Shiri's sweet handwriting, nothing like her own unruly script, which she believed represented her more than anything else, represented who she truly was: illegible, almost like her. It disgusted her to look at Shiri's chubby letters, and again she had the fleeting thought she'd been trying to suppress for months: why were they still friends?

I tried to wake you up a hundred times, you nutcase, and you told me to leave you alone, so I did. It sucks. I have a rehearsal today, so I had to leave. My parents know you're here, and we left you a key on the kitchen table to lock the door. The alarm is off, so you can leave. The party was *amazing*, right? I have to tell you about G. Call my cell when you wake up.

Bye, love as always, forever and ever, yours eternally, kisses,
S

She always signed *S* instead of Shiri. She thought it was sexy. But Shiri was clueless about sex, *real* sex. All the melodrama, mainly over boys she fell in love with, and all the diva mannerisms and the secrets—a million secrets, but not a single one was real—they did nothing to change the fact that Shiri Silver was a good girl with a cardiologist father and a VP mother at an IT company, parents who tried to be so understanding and considerate, *young in spirit*, they called it, they could make you puke.

And so could Shiri, recently. She was no longer really a soul mate but sticky residue from another era that had ended about a year ago. Shiri had adopted Roni when she came back to Israel at the age of twelve and didn't know anyone on the moshav. It was right for then, for who she was, an angry, confused girl who dreamed of falling in love with someone who would be her Zorba the Greek—her favorite book at the time, although now she didn't think much of it and found the writing weak—someone passionate and wild and smart and sexy, not a baby, someone who would show her what life really was. Because it was just not possible that life with her pathetic mother in America, and now with her father, who had turned out to be not much better an option and in some ways even worse—although she didn't regret coming back to Israel, because otherwise she wouldn't have met the love of her life—it was just not possible that this was real life. Because if it was, suicide was better. Still, she'd never considered that seriously. That was one thing her parents didn't need to worry about. On the contrary: she wanted to live, but live differently. She wanted a life with magic and passion and true love, not girlish love like her friends had. She wanted the kind of love that produced amazing sex, like in *Last Tango in Paris*.

When she saw the movie last summer, she realized that she and Shiri had nothing in common anymore. They watched it together on cable. She thought it was genius: the depression and the alienation she found so sexy. Shiri said it was gross—what was she even doing with him? But Roni didn't answer, because what could you say to such an idiotic question? It wasn't something you could explain; you can't explain art, or the razor-sharp loneliness of two strangers, and how sexy and real and right it is.

During the scene with the anal sex and the butter, Shiri got the giggles, which seemed to Roni like blasphemy. "Yeah, I liked that film, too," Alona said, when Roni told her the next day that she thought Bertolucci was a genius. They were folding laundry together. "Though I wouldn't say *genius*," Alona added, "and he's made better movies than *Last Tango*."

"But don't you find it terribly powerful?" Roni asked, a little disappointed.

Alona thought about it. "Yes, but it's a little age-dependent. Don't be hurt, but I saw that movie three times, at different ages. The first time I was eighteen, and the last was about eight years ago, when I was thirty-two. They were showing it at the Cinematheque and a friend who had never seen it really wanted to go, so we did, and I came to the conclusion that it's a load of bullshit. The whole designer depression, in that pretentious Parisian apartment? I mean, really! With Marlon Brando looking like he has rabies, and Maria Schneider with that come-on accent in English. *Yecch!* And the sex? Honestly, who fucks like that? Do you know how much strength a man needs to lift someone up and fuck her against the wall? Do you know how many men have broken their backs because of Bertolucci the genius?"

But what did any of them know about genius, even Alona, who understood literature and whose tastes Roni valued, often asking her for book recommendations? And what did they know about sex? Her mother was growing cobwebs down there, for sure, and her father—she couldn't imagine him doing it; that was too disgusting. And Alona? *Her* she could imagine having tired of sex on her back, the sex of mothers who can't be bothered anymore, but that wasn't it at all. No, the thing was that sex—and this is what they were trying to show in *Last Tango in Paris*, which no one understood—was redemption, and Roni had an urgent need for redemption. Redemption with boys her own age was impossible, because they just hadn't suffered enough to know anything about it yet, and so since the age of fourteen or so she'd been looking for someone to fuck her like Marlon Brando did Maria Schneider: angrily, passionately, pouring all his loneliness into her, because she could contain it, she could; it would be her real matriculation. And it would be someone she could return the favor to by also saving him from something, it didn't matter what, maybe from himself. Because it wasn't Marlon Brando who fucked Maria Schneider but Maria Schneider who fucked Brando. That's why he was the one who died in the end.

She got out of bed and went into the kitchen. On the table she found another note, this one from Dalia, Shiri's mother:

Roni, good morning. We heard you had a nice time last night at the party and that you had a little trouble waking up this morning. Your dad called. He asked you to call when you got up. There's hot coffee in the machine—just remember to turn it off when you leave—and there's cheesecake in the fridge. Take some. Have a good day. Maybe you'll still be able to make it to school? Dalia. P.S. If possible, please smoke only in the yard. Okay?

Dalia Silver. If you put Roni's mother and Alona and Dalia Silver into a blender, they wouldn't mix. There would be three separate layers:

oil, water, and something else, maybe foam. Her mother, Jane, would be the foam, with her flakiness, and Alona would definitely be the oil; Roni always thought of Alona as a heavy, deep, soupy person, and that's why she liked her, even though she could be annoying. On the other hand it seemed insulting to compare her mother to foam: foam evaporated, so it was like giving her the evil eye. It was like at this very moment, standing in the Silvers' kitchen, something terrible was happening to her mother in the States. So she changed the formula: Dalia was the foam and her mother was the water. Water wasn't an insult or a compliment: water was transparent, which suited her. But at the last moment, before the image cemented in her mind and could no longer be changed, she decided it was better to be true to her mother than to fear for her, so she restored her foamy status.

She had been very preoccupied with truth lately. Before she met Uri, she hadn't thought about it much, but with him, because of their amazing conversations, she realized that part of their rare compatibility had something to do with the fact that they both constantly dealt with truth as a concept. With *the frustrating beauty of truth*, as he called it: "It's like looking at a goddess. You don't know if she really exists, but you want to believe in her, and either way you can't touch her."

"But what if you can?" Roni had asked, contributing her own wisdom, which Uri said he loved so much. "What if you *could* touch it? Then she wouldn't be a goddess anymore. She'd stop being an object of worship, wouldn't she? You'd get sick of her once you could possess her."

Uri said she was amazing. "Your mind is so great, it's amazing to talk with someone like you. Maybe it's because you're a baby"—at first she was insulted when he called her that, but later it became her nickname— "that you think that way. Fresh, new, kind of natural."

She tried to squeeze out more compliments. "You mean, you can't have these kinds of talks with women your age? I would think that would be even more interesting, no? They have more experience."

"Yes, but experience ruins the imagination. And anyway, they don't really care about philosophy and all that, they just pretend, as part of the seduction. But with you, we didn't have that whole seduction game. You didn't do anything, you were just you; you just appeared one day and that was it. You appeared in front of me like truth, like a goddess."

And she felt lucky: the whole world was full of shitheads, but she had appeared before *him*.

She met him in the last place she would have expected to meet the love of her life: at home. Alona had been editing his debut manuscript for months, and Roni had often heard her talking about him. Usually she praised him, but every so often she threw out some sarcastic comment, because Alona just had to ruin things for everyone, mostly for herself. The truth is that Roni felt a bit sorry for her because she didn't have anything truly special and rare in her life, apart from the children—obviously they meant a lot to Alona, and she knew she would want two or three kids herself one day, maybe even four, and obviously she loved her little brother and sister, it was scary how much she loved them—but still, Alona seemed a little extinguished, a little ordinary, living her life for those two wild little creatures as if there were nothing else in the world.

Once Roni asked if Alona didn't miss her old single life in Tel Aviv. It sounded so cool. Even before she finished the question, Alona said, "No. Not at all. Not for a minute." And she remembered wondering—when was that conversation, a year ago? How could that be?—wondering if Alona had ever had a crazy love like she did. She had asked her about it not long ago, but indirectly, so she wouldn't give anything away. Alona replied, "Of course. I loved your dad madly." That was a disappointing answer, a wimp-out even, especially from someone like Alona, who you could tell must have had a pretty crazy life once. Besides, no one could love her dad madly, he wasn't the type. You could love him quietly, you could love him forever, *that* you could do, but not madly. Not like she loved Uri Breutner.

His book did not yet have a title, and even though they'd stopped seeing each other, she kept trying to come up with one, because she knew from Alona that they were still looking. Maybe if she found something cool, she'd have the courage to call him, which he had asked her not to do. She would call him just to be magnanimous and give him a title that would blow him away, just blow him away, and remind him of who she really was, and maybe he'd understand what he hadn't understood the whole time they'd been together, all those amazing months: she wasn't just his baby but a sharp, sophisticated woman, with depth and fuckups and depressions, like the women he once said he loved. When she told him she thought she was that way too, deep and fucked up and depressed, and it was so difficult being her, he said, "Yes, but you're not a woman yet. You're the lovely, silky chrysalis of a woman."

She had jumped out of bed in a fury that was half real and half not and stood naked in the middle of the room and said, "Then make me a woman." She loved those words, which she might have heard in a movie, but she hated herself.

He laughed and said he couldn't; it wasn't something he or anyone else could do; only time could make her a woman. "Although I don't think you need to be in any hurry. What's so bad about being a baby? The day will come when you'll miss it terribly."

And then she was angry, really angry: who was *he* to sit there at the height of his twenty-seven years, eleven-plus miserable years older, and patronize her like that? What did he even know about her life and about how bad it really was to be a baby? That was the first and last time she had the sneaking suspicion that perhaps she was wrong, that perhaps even Uri could not contain her, contain who she really was, that he was just as pathetic and clichéd as the rest of them. But after she finished reading his book she realized that he could. Someone with that kind of talent could. Perhaps she just needed to give it time, and perhaps, as he said, he was just scared to death by the thought that he had something going on with a sixteen-year-old girl—and she *would* be sixteen in February.

She'd never read anything like it before, and she read a lot. Every time she was at his apartment he gave her a few pages. When he took them out of the printer she went into the kitchen with them or locked herself in the bathroom. She wouldn't let him be next to her while she read. She wanted to concentrate. Every word was important, vital. After a few weeks, when she'd read all three hundred and twenty pages, she felt she knew the text far more profoundly than Alona did; she saw hidden things and found her own image in it. She knew he'd written the book before they met, but still, something of her was there, she felt it, and although he said the couple in the book was based on him and his ex, Zohar, of whom she was not at all jealous—Zohar was six years older than Uri and they'd broken up because she wanted to have a baby—she still found the two of them in there.

Every time she heard Alona say something about the book, especially to her father—they talked on the phone once or twice a day, which
seemed sick, because what did they break up for if they were joined at
the hip even more than when they'd lived together? How could there be
so much to say about the children? Every time Alona said something
disparaging, Roni got annoyed, both because of the criticism itself, which
sounded petty and completely wrong coming from someone who was
jealous because she herself didn't have his talent—"That's why you
became an editor, isn't it?" Roni had blurted out a couple of years ago
in a moment of anger about something else, she couldn't remember
what—but mainly because of the fact that outside of his Tel Aviv apartment on Nachmani Street where she'd spent ten sweet mornings, eight
afternoons and evenings, and six enchanted nights, she had no special
existence as his reader, as someone who loved that book like no one else
in the world could.

Uri was impressed that she read so much. "I didn't know girls your
age read at all," he said, when he came to their house one day to work
on the manuscript with Alona, because Ido had an ear infection and
Alona couldn't get to Tel Aviv. "I thought there were studies about how
today's youth are virtually illiterate."

Alona said, "Roni ruins the statistics for everybody. She just finished
Death in Venice, and I told her I'd get her *Magic Mountain* in English,
because she prefers reading in English."

Roni quickly protested that she didn't prefer reading in English; that
wasn't true at all. She was afraid he'd think her Hebrew wasn't good
enough, that she was an immigrant or something.

"I think I have a copy in English at home. Remind me next time we
meet," Uri told Alona, and they both looked at Roni.

She had just come in from school and the whole conversation had begun
because of her huge backpack, which had aroused his curiosity. "This is
Uri Breutner," Alona had said. "Our new acquisition."

Roni said, "Nice to meet you," and Uri asked if she was carrying
rocks in her bag.

"It's books, believe it or not," Alona answered, and Roni fumed, like
she used to when she was eight and took piano lessons, and every time

she memorized a new composition her mother would make her play it for guests. It was completely unlike Jane, who was generally a space cadet and not at all the overbearing mother, but it was important to her that her daughter be an artist, like she was, so she encouraged her to write, and every week she gave her money for a book, and every time she talked with Roni's father she reminded him to send books in Hebrew so Roni could keep up her bilingualism. Her dad used to send all kinds of young adult books, adventures and sci-fi, and a few about the Holocaust, which bored her to death and made her feel a little guilty.

That was how her love of adult books had begun. But also, something in her had an urgent need to grow up, which she was able to do through reading, especially Kafka, Dostoevsky, and Thomas Mann in Hebrew. The words she didn't understand but made her feel dizzy, and she used to engrave them in her vocabulary and use them on all sorts of occasions: in poems she wrote, in letters to her father, everywhere.

When she returned to Israel and went to junior high, her composition teacher told her she was a talented writer and that her essays were at least two levels ahead of everyone else's. She even said her Hebrew was very impressive, considering she hadn't grown up in Israel. But she asked Roni why she wrote about such unusual topics, like death and sex, and whether she didn't think she should talk to someone about it. Roni said, "What's so unusual about that? You think death and sex are unusual? Did you think about the fact that while we're talking, right at this moment, someone is having sex somewhere in the world, and someone is dying?"

Undaunted, the teacher replied, "Yes, obviously. But someone is being born, too. Right?"

Roni thought, Okay, you win. But who cares about birth? Later she told Alona about the conversation. She was pretty naïve in those days, when she'd only just come back, and she used to share almost everything with Alona, secretly praising her father for his choice, because after all he could have set her up with a real bitch for a stepmother. She told Alona that what the narrow-minded teacher didn't understand was that art, real art, did not engage with joy but with sorrow, not with happiness but with suffering, not with birth but with death. Right?

Alona had said, "Not at all. The opposite." And just like two years later, when they talked about *Last Tango*, she added, "Don't be hurt, but I think it's age-dependent, this question." Then she said she certainly understood Roni. "When I was your age—and I can't believe that sentence just came out of my mouth, *when I was your age*; I guess I've *really* grown old—I thought the world was a terrible place, somewhere I couldn't fit in. And I admit it, I wrote poems. Oh, the poems I wrote! My mom has bagfuls of them in the basement, which I forbid her to look at, but I can't even read them myself because they give me hives. Poems about death and passion and sex, you wouldn't believe it. Never mind that I didn't even have sex until I was eighteen, that didn't stop me from being a high priestess of erotica at fourteen. Do you know what I wrote once? This'll crack you up. It was a poem, but I only remember one line from it: *The universe is raping me now, turning me in my grave.* Eeew!"

Roni thought it was actually a lovely line, but she didn't say anything. And then, as usual, Alona got carried away with one of her monologues about writing, her favorite topic, and how, when you're very young, words are a kind of sexual energy you don't really know how to channel, and that this, to her, was the difference between an unripe writer and a mature one.

"It's like learning how to make love. To linger on the foreplay and not rush to orgasm. So what did you tell the composition teacher? Did you tell her to go fly a kite?"

But Alona didn't understand. Even Alona—and Roni found it slightly horrifying to think about it now but she had worshipped Alona, simply worshipped her when she came back to Israel, maybe because she had to worship someone and her father was out of the question; he was the most annoying creature on earth, second only to her mother.

Now, as she took a mug out of the cabinet and poured herself some coffee from the machine, switching it off immediately so she wouldn't forget later and burn down the Silvers' house, which Shiri had once said was worth more than a million dollars, she realized that her father, in fact, was in a whole different league of annoying. Like the way he'd acted all weekend, after someone broke into Alona's house and stole her car. He kept going on about the Palestinians as if they were all to blame for the burglary. "Maybe they should have their own state, but I'm not so sure it should be here. Let them go to Jordan or Lebanon," he said, when they were setting the tables for brunch on Saturday in the Trattoria.

Roni said she couldn't believe he was saying such disgusting things. "What's the big deal? Just a couple of poor car thieves looking to make a living. Because of *us*, by the way, because we're starving them."

"You don't know what you're talking about, Roni. They almost killed Maya and Ido and Alona! Do you know what could have happened if someone had woken up?"

"What? What could have happened? Tell me. Would they have raped her? Murdered your two sweet children?"

He said he didn't want to talk about it. She followed him into the kitchen, where he stood staring at the pots as if he had no idea what to do with them.

"You're not really a right-winger, you're just a baby," she said.

"How do you know? Maybe I've turned right-wing! What's so bad about that? It's very reassuring." He took a deep breath, like he always did when he was about to deliver a sermon, and said, "You know what, Roni? This conversation is pointless. There's something you won't be able to understand until you grow up a little, which is what it means to be afraid for your life and, worse, for your children's lives."

"Okay, I get it. As usual, I have to grow up before I can understand. As usual, you're really mature and understand everything, and as usual I'm not."

"Yes, as usual," he said, and phoned Alona to ask if she wanted to come for lunch with the kids. The restaurant would be full, but still, it would be nice if they came.

Roni guessed Alona was saying no, because her father started nagging, as if he were afraid that now, at this moment, terrorists would go and murder them. When he hung up and the first couple of customers came in and sat down at the nicest table, the one by the window, she approached them with a smile. After she took their order, she went into the kitchen and found her father standing at the oven mumbling to himself. "What is it now?" she asked.

He said he'd forgotten to put rosemary on the focaccias, and it was too late and they'd be awful.

"So what's the big deal? They taste fine without rosemary. Did you put salt on?"

"Yes, but they'll still be awful."

He punched his funny little fist on the marble counter, and she touched his shoulder—that always annoyed him—and said, "Who needs to grow up now, Dad?"

"I just don't understand why she's so stubborn. The kids love coming here, and it would have taken care of lunch for her; they could have had something healthy for a change, instead of all the junk she feeds them."

She took her hand off his shoulder. "Dad, statistically there's more chance of a terrorist attack here, in your restaurant."

He sighed and said, "Yes," in a quiet, distant voice, and she thought his eyes looked a little damp, but that was really not something she could deal with. It was better to die than to see your parents cry. She had been relieved when a large group of people, two families, walked in and she could go over to them.

She looked at the big clock on the Silvers' kitchen wall and debated whether to call him now and get it over with. It was eight-thirty and he was probably in the restaurant, sitting there worrying about her, as usual. She took the milk out of the fridge and wanted to take a slice of cheesecake, but she decided to put that off because she felt the urgent need to smoke a cigarette and read her notebook. She wanted to look at what she'd written the night before in the bathroom of that club after drinking a pint of Tuborg. Shiri always made fun of the way Roni got drunk from one pint of beer. Not that Shiri was a drinker; she was watching her calories. If she talked to her father now, or stuffed herself with cake, that painfully pleasant tension that was coursing through her body would melt away, the tension of missing Uri, whom she hadn't seen since last fall, except for one time when instead of getting the bus to school she'd hitched a ride to Tel Aviv with a neighbor and spent the whole morning in the café on Yehuda Halevy, where she could watch his building.

She'd staked it out for three hours, imagining him sleeping on the mattress on the floor, in the front room, with the old wooden blinds that were always lowered because of the street noise. He'd be sleeping on his side with his mouth gaping, the blanket bunched up between his legs. She drank cocoa after cocoa for three hours, because she hated coffee, and in her imagination she made love with him. Her eyes were fixed on the third-floor window, and it was the most amazing and intense and dangerous thing she'd ever done; she wanted so badly to tell him about it. She looked at the building and thought about the precious mornings they'd spent together, sleeping in late and then going down to the café, where they sat silently reading *Ha'aretz*, each taking a section, like a couple.

At lunchtime, when the light clouds covering the sky began to drizzle with something that looked more like restrained tears than rain, the waitress had asked if she wanted to move inside. She said no and asked for the check, and as she was about to leave she saw him walk quickly out of the building and turn east, toward Petach Tikva Road, where it was easier to get a cab when he needed to run errands. When she saw him move farther away down Nachmani and stop to take a pack of Winstons out of the pocket of his denim jacket—the one she'd worn a few times on the mornings they went down to the café—she dug through her backpack and took out her own pack, lit a cigarette, and turned west onto Rothschild to catch the number 5 bus to the Central Bus Station. For the first time since meeting him—for the first time in her life, in fact—she felt she really was a baby. That she contained a million desires and possibilities, and a hunger, and that she was helpless.

She'd only slept over at his place six times, during a wonderful week in January when her dad went to Milan for a food convention and she could lie to Alona and tell her she was staying at her dad's house. Other than those few magical nights, she always had to catch the last bus home. For that, she never forgave them, her father and Alona and her mother, all of them, even though she knew it was not their fault; they couldn't be blamed for something they didn't even know about. But that didn't make any difference. They were still to blame for the fact that in the middle of everything, she had to get up, quickly get dressed, and run to Rothschild to grab a taxi and catch the last bus. Then she'd get off at the intersection and wait, sometimes for an hour or more, for a ride into the moshav. She wasn't afraid of hitchhiking as much as she feared the bothersome questions: "So, big night out on the town, hey?" asked the drivers who knew her; "What's a nice girl like you doing out at this time of night?" asked the ones who didn't. And there were a few older women who lectured her about how dangerous it was to do what she was doing: "These days, especially. Do you want to get yourself kidnapped and murdered?"

Sometimes there were kids from school, coming back from a night out in their parents' cars. They were the ones who gave her the funniest looks. It was as if they knew, as if they grasped that she was betraying her entire age group, not just by being out on her own at night, talking about all kinds of parties in Tel Aviv that never existed, which they knew full well, but also by her appearance. She went for the grungy look, as if it hadn't gone out of style. She didn't shave under her arms, because Uri said, "I love you that way. Nature girl. No makeup, no bra." And that's what she loved about him, the way he wasn't hung up on how she looked, like the boys in her class were. With Uri, everything was real. He always wore the same jeans, something from the seventies that he didn't even know was from the seventies, and faded, ripped T-shirts, and he was unshaven, but not because he'd planned it or put any effort into it, just because he couldn't be bothered. "It's not like I have anywhere to be," he said.

Those rides were a disaster, and she couldn't wait to take her driving test in February, praying she'd pass the first time. Her dad had promised she could have the car whenever she wanted. She just wished it could have happened *last* February, and this one stupid year hadn't separated her from the license, because maybe if she'd been independent, if she'd had a car, they would have become a real couple, and she would have come and gone whenever she'd wanted, and maybe she'd even have had a key to his apartment. She had thought that after high school she might get an exemption from the army on psychological grounds and get a waitressing job in the city—she had experience and she liked waiting tables—and she'd find an apartment, preferably in his area. Uri had never lived with anyone and he said he didn't think he could, so she thought it would be healthier to live nearby but not get in his way, and then he could spend the night at her place sometimes, too—an exciting thought. She might have had to live with roommates, but that wouldn't have gotten in the way. It hadn't occurred to her that this love story would be over before winter ended, because a love like that should never be over. Not a love like theirs.

She got her backpack from Shiri's room, returned to the kitchen, and took an ashtray out of the dishwasher. It was the same one she'd used yesterday, before they went to the party, and Dalia Silver had already washed it, of course. She went out into the backyard and felt old, really old, like Nechama, her step-grandma, the only grandparent she had. Her father's parents had both died of cancer within six months of each other when Roni was three, and her maternal grandmother had committed suicide more than thirty years ago, when her mother was seventeen. Her grandfather had married another woman almost immediately, but Jane hadn't had anything to do with him for years. Roni had always respected her mother's right to be angry at her father forever, even if that meant she didn't have a grandfather.

The truth is that when she compared Jane to other mothers, she knew she had nothing to complain about. They had a reasonable life together after her parents split up and Jane took her back to the States. More than reasonable, even. It was a bit like in the movies: they roamed from place to place, following the teaching jobs her mother got. First she taught at a college in Philadelphia, and later, when Roni was seven, they moved to Idaho, but her mother hated the place and the art school, so they moved in the middle of the year to Connecticut, which was where, Roni thought, her mother really wigged out and got the nomadic bug, because since then they'd never stayed in one place for more than a year. By the time Roni was nine she was seeing a psychologist regularly, even though her mother couldn't afford it, and neither of them needed the therapist to tell them that what was lacking in Roni's life was stability.

And then her mother made what she called—jokingly, though Roni knew it was more a message than a joke—the *ultimate maternal sacrifice* and settled for three years straight in a suburb of Minneapolis, where she taught sculpture at a high school and made heroic efforts, as she said, to give them both stability. But it didn't do any good, because you can't give someone stability retroactively, as her father said every time he talked with Jane and tried to convince her to let Roni come

back to Israel and live with him—not despite but *because* he was getting married again and you could not ask for a more stable life than the
one Alona would give them. The idea of returning was actually Roni's.
At first she used to hurl it at her mother every time they fought, on the
wooden deck outside their little house and in diners. She would tell her
mother she wanted to go back to Israel and live with her dad, and if
Jane didn't let her she didn't know what would happen. Not that she
was threatening suicide, "But you've already screwed up my life enough,
don't you think? Maybe you should give someone else a chance?"

"My life won't be the same without you," Jane had said once, and
that sentence stuck in Roni's mind. She recalled exactly what she'd
answered, frightened to the depths of her soul. "Oh, Mom, really, don't
make such a big deal out of it. It's not like you won't see me again or
anything." Her mother had shaken her head and held the white coffee
mug to her mouth, not to take a sip but to hide her trembling lips. She'd
smiled and said no, thanks, when the waitress came over with the coffee-
pot, and she'd told the waitress she was fine, and those two words, more
than all the others, had lodged in Roni's mind: *I'm fine.*

She had no idea why she'd thought of that now. Perhaps because
whenever she was at the Silvers she thought about her mother, not just
in a comparative way but as a sort of show of loyalty. She was no longer
angry at her mother, although she knew that if she ever had a daughter
everything would be different. There was only one thing for which she
could not forgive Jane: for the pity she had aroused, for the misery that
she herself was unaware of.

She sipped her coffee, dug through her backpack for her cigarettes
and lighter, lit a cigarette, and sat down on the damp lawn. She hugged
her knees and felt the bottom of her boxer shorts soaking up the dampness. She ran her fingers over the grass, gathering droplets, and drew a
wet heart on her thigh, even though hearts weren't really her style.
Since meeting Uri, she'd felt as though someone had turned her volume
button all the way up; she experienced everything with shuddering
intensity, as if there were a bass line vibrating inside her body. Take
nature, for instance, which she'd never found particularly exciting, and
in fact had little patience for; she always avoided school trips, with her
hysterical father's blessing. But now she felt in tune with the earth, connected, capable of bringing rain if she danced. Nature was sexy. Every-

thing was sexy. And she felt a sudden urge, almost like when you had to run to the bathroom, to write something.

She took her notebook out of the backpack, propped it on her knees, and looked for what she'd written the night before, at that horrible party in a new club at the Tel Aviv port. She couldn't even remember what it was called, but Shiri had said it was the bomb and they were lucky to get in. She flipped through and stopped at an older piece, which gave her a shiver of longing, but not just longing; it was also the chill of literary accomplishment. This was one of her best pieces, the only one she had ever been bold enough to show Uri, convinced it was good enough to impress him:

I see her, wonderfully, groaningly alive, wrapped in a blue sweatshirt, sleeves rolled up, an ingenious thought flits by in front of her, and she lies in wait and thinks, and suddenly she grabs it and devours it, the thought, and she becomes a clever animal—and it is you. Walking to the fridge, which is essential and present in your home—there is no right thinking or writing without nourishment and without eating, and then whatever comes. I cannot write all the goodness that is with you, that is you, that is us. What happens inside when you sleep with me are things that do not happen to anyone else, or maybe they do—you explode me. I explode you. I love you.

Uri had read that passage and said, "No shit, you have talent. It's raw, but it's talent." She asked if he really thought so, and he said he did, but she hadn't shown him the piece to get his literary opinion. No. That was her role. She had shown it to him because she'd thought he would pounce on her and undress her and make love to her. That her words would seduce him the way his seduced her. But he sat there quietly, and then he asked if she'd told anyone. She said no, of course not, and he said, "Good. I hope it stays that way." After a pause he asked, "Isn't it difficult for you? Don't you feel like you just have to tell someone? Doesn't it make you feel kind of lonely?" He said he sometimes felt terribly lonely, because no one, no one in the world apart from his shrink—and she didn't count—knew about this thing. Not his friends, and certainly not his family. No one. Not even Zohar, whom he talked with once or twice a week, and sometimes they met for coffee. And sometimes, he said, he felt like walking into a bar and getting trashed and just confessing to whomever, to the first victim who sat down next to him. "I'd just say, 'You know what? I have a thing going on with a sixteen-year-old girl. I'm sleeping with a sixteen-year-old girl, would you believe it?' Roni, isn't our thing driving you crazy with loneliness?"

It was, but she liked the loneliness. She worshipped it a little, even, that loneliness they shared, the loneliness of a secret life. She found it beautiful, pure, and never for a moment felt the need to tell someone, because it was impossible to tell; that would be like telling a hand or a foot or a lung. Uri was a limb—how do you tell a limb? And besides, she felt the loneliness brought them closer; it was their true covenant, like in *Last Tango in Paris*. It amazed her that everything, in fact, had come true, even though Uri was relatively young, not a middle-aged man, but there was something about him that reminded her of the Brando character. Like the fact that she didn't know much about him. He wouldn't even tell her his therapist's name. She only knew he'd grown up in Ramat Hasharon and he was a wonderful writer and he was amazing in bed and Zohar had hurt him, even though it wasn't her fault, because obviously a woman in her thirties would want a child. And obviously she, Roni, would heal his sadness; she did not want a child, she wanted him.

She read the passage again and thought she might have been wrong to show it to him. Perhaps that last line, *I love you*—she'd wanted to erase it as soon as she'd written it—had scared him. He'd told her a million times, "I'm crazy about you" and "You're amazing." He'd even said *I love you* a few times, and so had she, but always as an answer: "Me too," that kind of thing.

But then she'd suddenly saddled him with this independent *I love you*, and the fact was that not only had he not pounced on her and undressed her and made love to her after he'd read it, but in fact that evening he'd been a little withdrawn. He said he was preoccupied with the book, and Alona was getting on his nerves with her demands and cuts. He said he had to do some work on the computer, and she could read or watch TV and he'd join her soon. After about two hours, during which she looked through practically every book in his collection but found nothing she could concentrate on, she went into his room,

sat on his lap, and asked what he was doing. He said, "Nothing, annoying rewrites, I'm almost done." She said she had to leave soon, and he
took his hand off the mouse and pulled her to the bed, but he still
looked unfocused and irritable, even while they had sex, and for the
first time it wasn't that great, it was a little ordinary, and on the bus on
the way back to Eden she reassured herself that it was okay; even in
love, even in a love like theirs, there had to be room for something a
little ordinary sometimes.

She read the piece again and decided to forgive herself. That was not
the reason they'd broken up. It couldn't be. She flipped back a few
pages, to November 14, one of the only two dates she'd written in the
notebook—the fourteenth and the twentieth of November, 2004—because
afterward she'd stopped writing dates—after all, she was really only
fifteen still, and if anyone ever found out about Uri and put him on trial,
the dates would become evidence. But mainly it was because dates, in
her view, would have made it documentary and banal. She looked for
November 14, which was about midway through the notebook, but she
stopped at a different piece, a much longer one than the texts she wrote
for Uri. It was a silly, soppy passage that she was a little ashamed of;
she'd planned to pull the page out and burn it a million times but she
hadn't had the guts. She had written it for Eli, not because she was in
love with him, not at all, but because, a month after it ended with Uri, she
had felt the need somehow to denote the beginning of a new relationship.
But it wasn't over with Uri, she knew that. It was just on hold. He'd said
he didn't want to see her again and had asked her not to call him
because he felt he was starting to fall in love with her, really fall in love
with her. "And that's an irreversible stage, Roni; you know we can't
really be a couple, so let's put an end to it before it gets too painful for
both of us."

What got to her now was that she hadn't even tried to fight. She'd
agreed with him. She'd been terrified that if she protested, if she begged
him not to leave her, begged him to give them a chance—after all, once
she was seventeen that would change things; she'd have a driver's
license—she'd been afraid that if she took that route she would disclose
some childishness and prove to him that he was right and she really
was, as he said, a baby.

So she didn't protest. She said she understood and thought it would be hard for her, but she understood. "But can we meet every so often? You know, just for coffee or something?"

And Uri had said, "No, Roni. Because I won't be able to keep my hands off you, you know that." She was flattered: he could meet with Zohar sometimes, but not with her. He wanted her more. But it hadn't occurred to her that not being with him would be so intolerable, so impossible, and deep in her heart she knew that after his book came out, soon—she knew from Alona that it was in the final stages and was scheduled for publication before Passover—he would calm down a little, his mood would change, and maybe then, if he happened to run into her, everything would start up again, and this time it would not end.

She hadn't been planning to find someone else. On the contrary, she'd decided to swear off men, so her body would not forget Uri, so the imprints he'd left on her in invisible ink would not be erased. But then two of them came along, as if God, in whom she did not believe and neither did Uri, had sent her a gift as compensation, two for one: Yossi, her driving teacher, and Eli, her neighbor. And it had started up with both of them around the same time.

The truth is that Yossi disgusted her. He was short and had a hard, round potbelly that reminded her, the first time she slept with him—*on* him, really, because he said he liked it when she was on top—of the exercise balls from gym class, on which you had to lie and roll back and forth, on a floor covered with mattresses. The first time she slept with him—she didn't write the date down because it wasn't date-worthy, but it hadn't been raining and it was quite warm—he gave little screams when he came, and she remembered a movie she'd seen on cable, *Deliverance*, the scene where a gang of hillbilly perverts rapes one of the men, the chubbiest and weakest of them, and forces him to squeal like a pig.

Yossi was in awe of her. He said he'd never had such good sex, and asked if it was good for her, too. She said it was amazing. He asked if she was on the pill, and she said of course she was, and he pulled a wet-wipe from the box he always kept in the car and wiped himself off and asked if she wanted one too, and she said she didn't. Without planning on its becoming something regular, she found herself agreeing every time he asked, after her driving lesson, "Any chance of doing the nasty?" And then he would add, "So, how's my slang?" and she'd say it was coolio, and he'd switch seats with her. He'd tell her she was a great driver, and promise she'd pass her first test: "Trust me." And then they'd drive onto the dirt path on the other side of the moshav, not the restaurant side, because her father sometimes walked there and the dogs would definitely find her. Every time she slept with him she was pretty passive and couldn't figure out why he was so excited, and she remembered to tell him she was coming, even though she wasn't. And every time they did it, she thought about Uri, about their first time, on November 20, 2004, when she went clothes-shopping with Shiri in Dizengoff Center in Tel Aviv.

Shiri had a new boyfriend, a guy from twelfth grade who had the lead in a play she was in, and she desperately needed something to wear to a party in Jerusalem they were both going to that evening. When they left the mall and walked around Bograshov for a while, Shiri suggested they get some coffee—"Or cocoa for you," she added condescendingly—at Arcaffé on Rothschild. Roni protested—it was a long walk and it was starting to drizzle—and Shiri said, "Don't be such a bore. I thought you liked rain. Why are you in such a rush to leave?" Tom was picking them up two hours later in his brother's car to take them home, and anyway she wanted to walk down Sheinkin Street later; she'd promised to buy her dad a jazz CD at the Third Ear.

Even before they got to the café, she saw him. He was standing at the number 5 bus stop on the corner of Nachmani, leaning on a fence outside a building, reading a book. She hadn't thought about him since they'd met a few days earlier, but when she saw him standing there, unshaven, unkempt, his fair hair not tied back in a ponytail like it was before but loose, touching his shoulders, and he was entirely focused on the book he held open with one hand, a cigarette in the other, she felt as if she'd been thinking about him but just hadn't known it, as if she'd missed something terribly and now she knew what.

She told Shiri she was going to say hi to someone, "That guy standing there? He's that writer, Uri Breutner, whose book Alona is editing." Shiri said fine and crossed the street with her, and they walked over to Uri, who looked up from his book and gazed at them both and said, "Roni?" and she said, "Yes."

He asked how she was and what she was doing in Tel Aviv, and she told him they'd come to buy clothes for Shiri, emphasizing that it was just for Shiri, so he wouldn't suspect that clothes were important to her. He asked if they'd found anything, and before Shiri could answer in detail and embarrass them both, Roni thought of *Magic Mountain*. "Did you remember?" she asked.

"No," he said. "I'm glad you reminded me. I really do have to meet Alona next week, so I'll give it to her." But suddenly a week seemed like a very long time, and she asked if he'd mind if she picked it up now, because she had nothing to read. He said he was on his way somewhere, and Shiri started to get restless. "But I'll be home in an hour, or an hour and a half, if you want to drop by."

"Okay, we'll see," she said, and he said, "See you later, then, maybe," and she said, "Cool." A bus pulled up and Uri tossed his cigarette on the sidewalk and stepped on it before boarding.

When they crossed Rothschild back to the other side, Shiri said, "But you can't get the book from him. Tom's picking us up in two hours; we're meeting him on the corner of Rothschild and Sheinkin."

"I don't know if I'll go back with you," Roni said. Shiri asked why the book was so urgent, and she said it was a book she'd wanted to read for ages. "We'll see. I may drop by his place. You don't have to wait for me; I'll take the bus home."

Shiri said, "Whatever. But is it really worth schlepping home on the bus? It's only a book."

Two hours later, Roni climbed up the steps of the old building on Nachmani, which smelled of dampness and frying foods and something else—freedom, she thought now, as she tried to remember the smell. The smell of rapid heartbeats, the smell of Tel Aviv. It reminded her of that time when she made her first visit to the States after coming back to Israel. Her mother was supposed to meet her at the airport and drive her to a house she'd rented by a lake upstate, but she got the dates mixed up and thought Roni was arriving the next day. It was only JFK, where Roni had been a million times, but those twelve hours she spent roaming the huge airport alone, waiting for her mother, who was completely hysterical when Roni called collect from a pay phone—she managed to get on a flight that night and would meet Roni early in the morning—those twelve hours, during which she wandered in and out of fast-food chains, buying something small each time, so that the few dollars her father had given her wouldn't run out, the hours during which she meandered from gate to gate, sitting down to rest or to stare, next to people waiting for flights, and the stores she went in and out of without even noticing what they sold—all those hours she had oscillated between the terror of abandonment and a sense of wild, wonderful freedom. When she finally saw her mother standing on the sidewalk by the taxi ramp, afraid, guilty, looking for Roni, she walked into her embrace—no, it wasn't an embrace, she remembered now, but an almost animalistic lunge—she went slowly, almost unwillingly, a different person from the one she had been when she'd boarded the flight.

When Uri opened the door he looked surprised, as if he'd forgotten he'd told her to come by. He asked her in and apologized for the mess. She asked if he lived alone or with roommates, and he said, "Alone. I've never lived with roommates. I don't get along with people very well."

"Me neither," Roni said, and he said she didn't look like the type; she seemed social, and that friend of hers, what was her name?

"Shiri," Roni answered, suddenly ashamed of her.

"Shiri. She looks sweet."

Roni said she really was sweet, a little *too* sweet.

He smiled and asked if she wanted a hot drink.

"Tea," she replied, because she didn't have the courage to ask for cocoa.

He made tea for her and instant coffee for himself, and she looked around, inspecting the place as if she were examining the possibility of a different life. She said the apartment was awesome, she wouldn't mind living in a place like this, and she loved the floor tiles and the high ceilings; Alona and her dad had tried to imitate this kind of house, but it really wasn't the same.

"But the quality of life you have on the moshav you can't get anywhere else. Everyone's getting out of Tel Aviv now, and rightly so."

She asked why he wasn't getting out, and he said he was lazy, and he didn't have a car, and anyway he couldn't really see himself living in the country; how could you live without corner stores and cafés and people? She said he was right.

"And you? You're really stuck, I bet, 'cause you're too young to have your driver's license yet."

She said she was taking lessons.

"You started early. Isn't it a waste of money?"

She said it really was kind of dumb, but since everyone in her family was such a bad driver, her father had recommended that she start early, take her time, and be extra prepared when she took the test. But she suddenly wished she could take back her words, especially *my father*, because she was afraid that bringing him in here, into this apartment, would spoil something.

"Your father runs a restaurant, right? That sounds pretty cool. I bet you eat well." He took a pair of mugs out and put them on the living room floor because there was no table. Other than an old-people's prickly couch and one armchair, shelves full of books, a stereo system, and an old TV, there was nothing there.

Since he placed the mugs side by side and sat down on the couch, she sat down next to him and they were quiet for a few minutes, until Uri got up and said, "Don't let me forget."

He went over to the books, pulled out *Magic Mountain* in English, and said it was supposed to be a good translation. She asked how the book was, and he handed it to her and said he didn't know, he'd never read it. She instantly lost her own desire to read it and said she'd really liked *Death in Venice*, which wasn't a gay book at all but something else. He asked what, and she said, "Haven't you read it?"

"No, the truth is I've never read any Thomas Mann. I can't be bothered with those Germans."

"Not even Kafka?"

"I read Kafka in high school. I think it was *The Metamorphosis*."

She said *Metamorphosis* was amazing, and he should really read more Kafka.

"I know, I know, but when I'm writing I don't have the patience for anyone else. Here and there an Israeli book, to find out what the competition is doing." He grinned, and she told him she only read translated literature; she'd never read anything Israeli. "Really? You're missing out." She asked if he could recommend something, and he said, "Loads." He got up again and went to the bookshelves, ran his finger over the books, and said he was debating whether to start her off with Grossman or Shabtai. "They're both difficult; they're both crazy."

"Give me the craziest thing you have," she said, and he turned to her with a smile and looked at her, and she thought, That was when it started. That was when he realized the girl sitting on his couch had a fascinating depressive potential.

He said Shabtai wasn't the craziest but he was the most obsessive. "If you're into obsessive."

She said she loved obsessive, and she got up and stood next to him and looked at the book he was holding, *Past Perfect*. "This?" she asked.

"If you're up for it. It's not easy."

She said she liked difficult. "So what should I take? This or *Magic Mountain*?"

He told her she could take both, as long as she was careful; he was pretty possessive about his books. She said she would just take *Past Perfect*, and when she finished she'd take *Magic Mountain*.

They sat down on the couch again and he lit a cigarette, and she took hers out of her backpack. He asked how long she'd been smoking.

"I don't know, ever since I can remember myself."

He leaned back and blew smoke rings. "It's kind of funny to hear a girl your age say 'ever since I can remember myself.' How much self do you have to remember?"

She leaned back too, took a deep drag, and said, "It's not the quantity but the quality."

He said she was wicked sharp, and she said not always, and he asked when she wasn't, and she said most of the time; most of the time she didn't have anything to say, and she found everyone pretty disgusting and depressing and preoccupied with crap. He said he felt the same way. Outside the drizzle turned into rain, and she said, "Wow, it's pouring, and I don't have an umbrella."

He looked at her again and said, "Then wait it out here." He asked how she was getting home, and she said buses and then hitching a ride, and he asked if she wasn't afraid to take buses these days. He himself hadn't been on one in two and a half years, he only took jitneys and cabs; even though with his luck some terrorist with modest aspirations would probably decide to get on the number 5 jitney. She said she didn't exactly have a choice, and he said she really should get her driver's license. She said she knew, but it wasn't her fault; you had to be seventeen; it was such a lame law. He said most laws were lame, and she said that was so true, and the rain grew harder and Uri got up to shut the blinds and the window, "Not that it does any good, 'cause the window isn't sealed and it leaks."

He went into the kitchen and came back with a rag and put it down on the floor beneath the window, and the room grew dark, and he turned on the floor lamp next to the books, and a warm orange light illuminated the space. He asked if she was hungry; he had some Bolognese in the fridge that his friends had brought yesterday for a birthday dinner for someone at his place. He could heat some up for her; it was really good. She wanted to tell him that her father made amazing Bolognese sauce, but she said no, she wasn't hungry. She wanted to say that she'd split a sandwich with Shiri earlier and had ended up eating Shiri's half because Shiri hadn't liked it, but she didn't want to bring Shiri in here either, definitely not Shiri, and Uri, as if reading her thoughts, said, "So tell me what it's like to be sixteen."

She decided to tell him in the only way that seemed close to the truth, and even though her whole body was trembling with fear, she turned to him, took his hand, and placed it on her chest. When he did not resist, when she saw him staring at her with a stunned but slightly amused look, she peeled off her thin black sweater with a swift movement that she'd practiced during many hours of daydreaming, put his hand on one breast and then on the other. "You don't wear a bra?" he said, and his voice sounded faraway, disconnected from the hand that softly stroked her breasts. She said she didn't like them, and he said that was a turn-on. "But Roni, I don't really understand what we're doing now. Would you please tell me what we're doing?"

She said, "Shhh, don't speak," and pressed her lips to his and they kissed. She had only slept with one boy before, a kid from her class called Eilon, six months earlier, and it was hard to even call it sex, but she was a great kisser; not long ago she'd kissed a first-year architecture student at a party, and he'd told her she kissed like a pro and asked for her number; they talked a few times, but nothing came of it, mainly because he was afraid.

Uri suddenly stood up and said, "Listen, let's stop this now, okay? It's not cool." She asked if he was attracted to her, and he paced back and forth, and said obviously he was, even though he didn't have any special attraction to young girls. "But what difference does it make, Roni? There's zero chance that anything could ever happen between us beyond what just happened, and even *that* I have to let sink in. Zero chance. I'm twenty-seven, almost twenty-eight."

"So what?"

"So what? You're asking me so what? And your stepmother is editing my book?"

"She's not my stepmother."

"Okay, so she's not your stepmother. Whatever, that doesn't have anything to do with it."

"But you're not the first. I've already slept with someone before."

He said he didn't care, for all he cared she might have been at it since she was ten, but that didn't change the fact that it was wrong, it was criminal, and he didn't need that now, not at all, and by the way she didn't either.

She told him not to tell her what she did and did not need, okay? "Don't patronize me." She said she knew very well what she needed. She got up and pulled her sweater on and picked the book up off the floor and shoved it back onto the shelf and said she was leaving. He said it was pouring, she should wait a bit, she couldn't go out like that, and she said she could. "And don't worry, I won't tell Alona anything."

She hurried to the door, and he said, "Roni, sit down a minute. Enough with the sulking, okay? Wait for the rain to stop and I'll walk you to the bus."

She said she liked walking in the rain and she wasn't sulking and she didn't need him to walk her. She sat down on the couch and hugged her backpack and suddenly felt confused and tired, wishing she hadn't given up the ride back to Eden, wishing she didn't have to go back there at all, because how could she, emotionally, go back to her room in her dad's house, which was right next to Maya and Ido's, and their toys and clothes always invaded it like viruses, and how could she go back there when she'd been so close to getting out? And her lips started to tremble and tears flooded her eyes, and Uri, who looked startled, went up to her and held her hands.

"I'm really sorry. I feel bad. It was lovely and sweet. But that's it; let's forget it, okay?" She said she couldn't forget it and she didn't want to.

He offered to make her some more tea, and she agreed. She lit a cigarette and leaned her head on her arms and looked at the room and at Uri from the side, and when he came back with tea and a dish of cookies he asked if she felt like reading a few pages from his book, to change up the mood a little and pass the time until it stopped raining.

She said, "Yes, wow, I'd love to," and he said he'd print out some pages in the other room. When he left, she walked over to the window and looked at the rag, which was sopping wet. "Uri, the rag's full, should I wring it out?"

He said, "Yes, thanks, you can do it in the bathtub," and suddenly everything was fine between them, everything was so domestic, and she carefully rolled up the wet rag and took it into the bathroom, and when she sat on the edge of the tub and wrung it out, she examined the small room. The ceiling was full of peeling paint and the iron beams were exposed. A clump of fair hair sat in the strainer covering the bathtub drain, which was dotted with crumbs of plaster, and on a little plastic shelf stood a bottle of Hawaii shampoo and a cracked bar of soap, in which a large pubic hair, a little darker than the hair in the strainer, was embalmed like a fossil.

She got up to pee and looked in the toilet bowl, which had streaks of excrement on it, and the water at the bottom looked dark and rusty. But there was a scent of rain and perfume in the air. It was Fahrenheit: she spotted the open bottle on the shelf above the sink, next to a glass with a frayed toothbrush. She debated whether to close the bottle so it wouldn't evaporate, but she was afraid, she shouldn't be touching his stuff, so she went back to the living room and put the rag back on the floor, and Uri appeared and placed a stack of paper in her hands.

"Do you really feel like doing this?"

She said she couldn't wait to read it. "Alona talks about you so much I'm dying of curiosity to find out who this phenomenon is."

"Really? She talks about me a lot?"

"Yes, all the time."

"What does she say?"

"Good things, only good things."

When she sat down to read he sat next to her, but she asked him to sit somewhere else because she couldn't concentrate. He got up and sat on the armchair opposite her, and as she read she felt his gaze burning little holes in her skin, like the holes made by a ray of sun trapped in a magnifying glass on paper.

"Stop it."

"Stop what?"

"Stop looking at me like that."

He said he'd go into the other room and she should call him when she was done. She read, focused on her new role, folding the corners of pages where she found typos or extra spaces, and she could hear Uri on the other side of the wall the whole time, moving a chair, coughing, until thirty minutes later she had formed an opinion about the text and she got up and went into the other room and said, "You're a genius."

"Really?" He got up quickly from his chair at the computer. "Are you serious? Because I really value your opinion; you read a lot, more than me. I never read Thomas Mann."

"Really." She put the pages on the bed, and he went up to her and gave her a friendly hug.

"Wow, you are so cute, it's too bad you're so young. So, the rain's let up a bit, huh?"

She said yes, she thought it had.

"Take the book, then. You can give it to Alona when you're done."

"Okay."

He went into the living room and came back with *Past Perfect* and put it in her hands. He asked if she had a jacket, and she said no. "It's a little cold, isn't it?" he said, and she shook her head.

She felt overcome with sadness again. Two hours from now she'd be at home, in the midst of the bath time and bedtime hysterics. How could she go back to that world after she'd visited this one? How could she leave the deep, damp smell of rain and Fahrenheit and liberty, and the draft and the stupid rag and the bad tea and the traffic noise that invaded the room through the blinds? To leave all that, and Uri, seemed like leaving the last chance in her life to be someone else or, in fact, to become her, the real her.

Her lips trembled and she started to cry again, and Uri hugged her and said, "Don't. I'm really sorry if I hurt you."

"No, I started it."

"It wasn't all you. To tell you the truth, as soon as you walked in here there was this kind of atmosphere of—I don't know—danger."

She said she liked danger, and thought about the atmosphere when

Maria Schneider and Marlon Brando met for the first time in that apartment, two strangers.

He said he didn't, he was a coward and probably lost out on things because of it. He knew it, he was losing out on something amazing.

She said, "But I want you so much."

He giggled and said he'd never heard that sentence in real life, only in the movies. "I want you so much, too. Wow, it's fun to say that. You are sexy in a way I can't even describe, and I don't want to. Roni, I don't want to." He sighed and sat down on the bed. "This is tough, so tough." He ran his hand through his fair hair, which she later learned was a regular gesture of his, something between thinking and resting. "Why did you even come here?" he whispered, as if to himself, and since she assumed he was thinking about it and there might still be a chance, she might not be exiled back to the kingdom of omelets-for-dinner and cartoons, she sat down next to him.

"Just one more cigarette, okay?" she said.

And he said, "I'll have one too, then." He took one of hers, and they sat next to each other on the bed, smoking, rocking back and forth a little, flicking the ashes into the ashtray on the floor, which she now noticed contained a few roaches, and she asked if he had anything to smoke.

"No, I'm all out. Do you smoke?"

"Sometimes. I have some at home, actually."

He asked if she lived with Alona or with her dad. She said wherever she felt like. Sometimes she spent weeks in one place and weeks in the other, sometimes a night here and a night there, wherever there was less chaos. He asked what her brother and sister were like, and she said, "Amazing. It's fascinating to watch little kids."

"Yes, but I would go crazy if I had to live in the same house with them."

"Yeah, sometimes I go crazy, too. But sometimes it's fun. They have a crazy way of thinking."

"Like you," he said, and suddenly looked very focused, as if he were deciding something. "Listen, what are you like when it comes to dependency? I mean, do you get clingy? I guess what I'm asking is, how much experience do you have?"

"I have enough. I had a boyfriend for six months, and I'm the one who got rid of him. And loads of guys hit on me and I just brush them off."

"Because I really want you, Roni, and I'm struggling with myself because I'm scared, and I don't want you to leave here feeling like I don't want you or something. It doesn't seem fair for you to leave that way."

"You don't want me."

"I do, but I don't want a whole thing. I'm with myself now, and the book, and I don't have space for another person in my life. I broke up with someone not long ago, a bad breakup, and bottom line, Roni. . . . You know what? Forget what I just said. Just go home. Get out."

But she did not get up. She kept hugging *Past Perfect* to her body and staring at the speckled floor tiles, some of which were cracked and sunken. Then she lay on her back, and so did Uri, whose every movement she could suddenly predict, as if she had directed the movie but had not yet watched it. He lay on his back next to her and she sighed, and so did he, and she turned onto her side, and so did he, and she said, "Let's lie here for a while, quietly, and then I'll leave, I promise."

"Okay. Have you always had short hair?"

She told him she had, except when she was a little girl, when she went through a pigtail-and-braids phase.

He said Roni was a nice name, and she said yes, so was Uri.

"Why is your dad called Mark? Is he American?"

She said he was named after his grandfather, Marcus, who had died just before Mark was born. She asked what his parents were called.

"Mine? You want to know about my parents?"

"I was just wondering what they're called."

"Moshe and Rachel. I think the rain's completely stopped now, hasn't it? Do you hear anything?"

She said she didn't and kicked her shoes off onto the floor. Uri took his off too, and she undid the buttons of her jeans, and then his, and said, "We'll just touch a little, you me and me you, and that's it, no sex."

"Okay."

She carefully put her hand through his fly and gently hovered over the erection that stretched out his underwear, and he put his fingers down her pants. "Boxers?" he said, and she nodded and pulled her pants off and used the opportunity to take her sweater off again, and she lay on her side wearing underwear with a pattern of blue hearts, and Uri took his pants off too and stayed with his underwear and sweatshirt.

"Sweatshirt too," she said, and he took it off, and she said, "See? We haven't done anything."

"Not yet," he said, and turned her on her back and crawled down to the bottom of the mattress, and without taking her underwear off he started licking her there. "You're totally wet."

"I know," she said, even though she'd never once been wet before. "It's 'cause I'm so turned on."

"Has anyone ever licked you?"

"Sure." But that wasn't true. She and Eilon had made out a lot and they'd had intercourse, but that was it.

Uri pulled down her underwear and looked at her. "You have such a lovely pussy."

She propped her head up a little and said, "Really?"

When he licked her he said she tasted great. "You're so tasty. Tell me when you come, okay?"

She started to squirm and sigh, feeling like it was a particularly important scene in the movie. It felt good but she didn't know whether or not she was about to come, because she never had, with Eilon or with herself, even though she almost had, a few times. Since she didn't want him to get tired or sick of it, or to think he wasn't good at it or that it was her first time, she started to whisper that she was coming, and when she fake-came he lay on top of her and kissed her.

"Here, taste how good you are."

She licked his lips and said, "Come to me, be inside me."

"Are you sure? Are you on the pill?" and she said yes, even though it was only two weeks later, after they'd met two more times, that she went to the gynecologist and got a prescription. "I have rubbers," he said, but she said no, she wanted to really feel him, and he said he also wanted to really feel her, and she suddenly knew that whatever she said, he would repeat, and whatever she asked, he would do, and that he would believe every word, every sigh, every fake sound.

When he entered her she realized Eilon hadn't made love to her, Eilon had just gone in and out a few times, and he always came outside. She realized Eilon's penis was a just a weenie, something babyish and pale and shy, and he'd never even let her look at it or touch it afterward; he always pulled his pants up and went to get them a drink from the kitchen; and this, exactly this, was how it was supposed to be: filling and a little painful and totally crazy. She suddenly grew fearful: what if she got pregnant? It wasn't the pregnancy that scared her, because obviously she'd get an abortion—she had some money saved up—but that he would find out she'd lied.

He started moving quickly inside her, and she could see the minute he closed his eyes that he was about to come, and she whispered in his ear, "I want to taste you, too."

"I almost came," he said, and pulled out quickly and lay on his back, and she sucked him, amazed at how different it felt when he was inside her, and now in her mouth, and how difficult it was for her to breathe, and she heard him say "Wow" a few times, repeating the word over and over again, and she looked at him out of the corner of her eye, at his face that looked so tormented, so beautiful, at his long hair spread out on the mattress. "Wow, you're amazing." He sighed, and she saw it as a sign to pick up the speed. "I'm going to come," she heard him whisper, "Wow, I'm going to come!" He sat up and held her head in his hands and tried to pull himself out, but she motioned no, and he said, "But I'm going to come," and again, "Wow," and she motioned yes, and to show him how much she loved him, how serious she was—how all this was nothing to her even though she was about to gag—she swallowed it all.

"You're the tastiest thing I've ever eaten in my life," he said, after they lay quietly for a few minutes. She said, "You too," even though that, too, like her orgasm, was a kind of lie, because she hadn't expected it to be so salty and overbearing. She'd always thought it would be like those chocolates with the filling, which you sink your teeth into and your mouth gets flooded with sweet cream. It wasn't like that, but still, like the streaks of crap in his toilet bowl and the hair with bits of plaster in the tub, it didn't disgust her but the opposite: it only made her fall in love with him, out of a conscious decision, like falling in love with life itself, she thought, even though life was pretty disgusting, too.

She got up from the lawn, suddenly hungry, though still a little nauseated from drinking the night before. Now, after Uri, she didn't know why she let herself get dragged to those parties, where she was over-come with extreme and uncontrollable longings for him. Not that she could control how much she missed him normally—and missed herself, the person she had been for three months: someone with a secret, some-one with an alternative. But the parties were like being thrown back into the prison cell of childhood.

She took the cheesecake out of the fridge and placed it on the table next to Dalia's note. It was missing only three slices, and she guessed that each member of the household had eaten exactly one symmetrical slice. She found that funny: a cake like that wouldn't survive more than five minutes at Alona's or her dad's, those two gluttons. Lately, since breaking up with Uri, it disgusted her to see the way people gorged themselves, the way they lived like animals, with no asceticism whatso-ever, like Uri and she had had when they were together. They had suf-ficed with each other's bodies, because that was all you really needed. When they were together they didn't eat anything except the occasional pretzels or *bamba*, and once he ordered a pizza, but that was it. They had tea, and Uri sometimes drank arrack, and they smoked a lot of cigarettes, as well as the weed she brought, and they had sex and talked and had sex and talked.

Since the breakup, she had also become a glutton. She didn't have a weight problem, so she wasn't much bothered by the four or five pounds she'd put on. What did bother her was that she was no longer capable of enjoying anything. Nothing. Not cakes, not food, not even cigarettes or alcohol. Even weed didn't do it for her. Nothing. Absolutely nothing.

She happened to pick up the phone one day when her parents were talking—about her, of course, because what else did they have in com-mon; it was wacky to wonder what had even led those two to marry each other—and she heard her father telling her mother that she'd been eating a lot recently and had put on a few pounds. He wasn't worried about the weight but about what it meant. "Do you think she might be going through something? Has she told you anything?" he asked. Jane brushed off his anxiety as usual. "She's a growing girl." When Roni had once told Alona that her mother treated her like a little girl, Alona said, "The day will come when that's exactly what you'll want. A mother, period. But it'll be too late, because by then you'll be forty."

Roni did not hate her mother, as Jane liked to claim at every opportunity, but she pitied her, although she'd never had the courage to say it,
knowing how much it would hurt her, until she'd blurted it out last
summer during the totally unnecessary visit.

She had trailed along with Jane to some gallery, to attend the opening of a show by yet another of her intolerable aging artist friends with
their ethnic jewelry, silver rings, and chunky necklaces. She sat in the
corner on a stone bench, sipping some herbal tea that her mother handed
her in a paper cup, dying, simply dying for a cigarette but not daring to
smoke because her mother would have dropped dead. Although maybe
it wasn't such a bad idea to kill her now instead of listening to her telling her girlfriends, "Look at Roni, isn't she a beauty? That's me, thirty
years ago, exactly!" Jane was fifty and suffered from various meno-
pausal symptoms, but instead of keeping quiet about it like other mothers, she let Roni in on every ache, every late or abbreviated period, every
secretion. "Thank God I don't have hot flashes yet. And you know what's
sad? Because my mother committed suicide at such a young age, I don't
even know what to expect and how she got through it. But see, at least
you'll know what's ahead for you. I'm passing on important information."

Roni listened with a sour face, hoping her lack of collaboration
would convey to her mother that she was not up for these confidences.
Jane should talk to her best friend, Barbara, who looked like she hadn't
menstruated for twenty years. Thank God Roni had got her first period
in Israel, because otherwise who knows what kind of celebrations and
tribal rituals her mother would have organized.

Her dad had told her that Jane cried on the phone when he called to
let her know, and then he'd asked her awkwardly, "Roni, are you managing with it, by the way?"

She'd said, "Yes, Dad, I'm managing," and that was it; they never
spoke of it again.

She sat in the gallery watching her mother chatter with her friends,
laughing at their jokes like a retard, flinging her head back as if she
were being filmed for some Hollywood movie. She looked at her straight,
light-brown hair, always shoulder height, threaded with silver and white
strands; she wouldn't dye it on principle. She had small, droopy shoulders and large breasts, like Roni's own. "It definitely runs in the family.

My mother also had absolutely perfect breasts, *that* I remember, although mine are a bit larger. And yours, Roni, are rounder, and perkier of course, but that's only natural."

Okay, Roni thought, but why do we have to talk about it? Her mother was short, not even five-two, and even though she herself was already five-three, she knew she wouldn't pass her by much because her father was a dwarf at five-six, and even though it had nothing to do with her own height, Alona was also a dwarf, and Roni suddenly felt trapped in a kingdom of chattering, gobbling midgets. Even her siblings, whom she loved so much, seemed insufferable as she sat in that gallery, and all she wanted was to not be connected to anyone, to break free, to be homeless and without family.

Her mother came over and sat down next to her and asked if she was all right. She took out her organic lipstick and a small mirror and painted her lips a disgusting eggplant shade. She commented on how cool the crowd at the gallery was.

Roni knew she was sad but she hadn't realized she was also furious. "Cool?" she said. "What planet are you living on? Don't you know that only old people stick that word into every sentence?"

"I see you're in one of your moods, Roni, so I'll let you be. Just don't ruin this for me, because I'm actually enjoying myself."

"What could you possibly have to enjoy, Mom? You left your husband, you spent ten years flitting from one place to another, you don't really have a career, and—let's face it—you haven't had much of a breakthrough as an artist, and I'm pretty sure you haven't been laid in about ten years. You have a horrible, evil, adolescent daughter, and five minutes from now you won't ever have your period again. So what exactly are you enjoying, would you mind telling me that?"

It wasn't the first time she'd seen her mother cry. Jane cried easily and often, claiming it was purifying and refreshing and healthful. But it was the first time she had made her cry.

Jane hurried outside and got into the car and sat there for about twenty minutes with the windows rolled up and the air-conditioning on. When Roni went over and tapped on the window, Jane waved her away, and when Barbara came out to find out what had happened, Roni told her Jane wanted to be alone for a while.

The summer was ruined, she knew that already, but something else

was destroyed in that gallery—destroyed for good, like a rickety building that spends fifteen years swaying until a bulldozer bashes it in. What
had been shattered was the idea that someone could contain her, or even
just tolerate her. Because her mother had now proved that even she, like
all the others, like her dad and like Alona, despite everything, was weak.
That the less understood Roni became, the more dangerous she grew.
And in that last summer in the States, she understood that what she
needed more than anything else was someone who would get turned on
by danger and not fear it. Someone dangerous, just like her.

Eli looked a little dangerous, which was why she slept with him. It
didn't make her forget Uri, not for a minute; that wasn't the purpose
anyway. But there was something about him, unlike piggish Yossi, something dark and wild and desperate and hungry. It wasn't a hunger like
her dad's and Alona's but something different, a sexy hunger, which she
liked. And the sex was so different from sex with Uri that she didn't
even feel she was betraying him. In fact, every moment with Eli, who
was always neat and shaven and wore button-down shirts in soft fab-
rics and tailored pants and expensive leather shoes, and sometimes,
when he'd had a court appearance earlier in the day, a suit—every minute with him brought her closer to Uri in some back-asswards way.

She did not write the date in her notebook, but she remembered their
first time. It was February 15, two days after her sixteenth birthday,
exactly a month after the breakup with Uri and a week after she slept
with Yossi. It occurred to her now that perhaps Eli wasn't so much
because of Uri as because of the driving teacher, the way you eat something bad and then quickly swallow something else to get rid of the taste.

They knew each other to say hello, and once he'd given her a ride to
Tel Aviv when she was with Uri. She hadn't really given him much
thought and didn't think he'd noticed her—just a neighbor giving her a
ride—until one night when she came back from a party in Tel Aviv. She
had left early because she suddenly felt depressed, and the idea of waiting another hour or two to go back with Shiri and a few boys from the
moshav, one of whom had a car, seemed horrifying. She caught the last
bus and stood at the intersection outside Eden, waiting for a ride. A
Toyota SUV stopped, and the man who rolled down the window looked
familiar.

"Eli Nachmias, remember? Your name's Roni, right?" She was

reassured to discover that he knew her. When she got into the car he said he didn't usually come home so late, but he'd been working on a case in his office in Tel Aviv. "It's too bad I didn't know you were coming from there; I would have picked you up."

She told him she was at a party, and he said that sounded awesome, and she said not at all, it was horrible. He smiled and said, "I see," and turned up the radio. She couldn't remember what was playing, but she did remember the strange wave that suddenly flooded her in the closed-up SUV with the music blaring. It sounded like he had about eighty speakers in the car, like she was still at the party, but everything felt okay now, and she even felt like partying. As if he'd read her mind, he asked if she liked to dance. She said, "Kind of. Depends on my mood." He asked what kind of mood she was in now, because she looked a little down. She said her mood was improving, and she really felt like a beer; it was too bad there wasn't a pub or anything nearby. He said, "There is. Not a pub, but they sell beer at the gas station."

"Really?"

"Really. Should I turn around and get you a beer?"

Later, after they'd slept together a few times, he claimed she had seduced him, that her move was totally transparent, and what could he have done? She said that was ridiculous, and she really didn't think that was what she was doing at the time. They drove back to the main road and turned left, toward the gas station at the intersection. He stopped and left her in the car with the music turned on loud, and suddenly it was all fun, really fun; she didn't know why, but she hadn't felt that way for a long time. She was excited, happy, flowing, even though she wasn't really a flowing sort of person but an anxious one, with lots of bothersome thoughts, and a sad one, but suddenly a switch flipped in her mind and turned off all the heaviness, and she felt light and sexy, but not in a familiar way, because with Uri she hadn't felt sexy but something different, much larger, more principled.

When Eli came back with the beer and sat down and gave her his beer to hold, she suggested they go somewhere in Eden, to the orchards, even though she'd been there only a week ago with Yossi, or perhaps because of that. She tried to guess if Eli thought anything was going to happen between them, and she considered whether she wanted something to happen. She didn't exactly have an answer, but she was having a good time, a really good time, and now she understood Shiri, who loved parties so much, who loved to let loose and always made fun of Roni for being so uptight and heavy, so self-conscious. "How do you ever enjoy things?" she would ask. And Roni always answered, "I don't." She wasn't about enjoying but about observing. That's what she liked to do; that's what she knew how to do.

In the SUV, after two or three sips of beer, with the music blaring, she felt as if something in her was learning to stop observing and start enjoying, except she didn't know—and now she thought she understood the trap—that the part that was learning to enjoy was just as desperate and miserable as the part that only knew how to observe. It was all an illusion, and that's how she felt the minute Eli swiftly pulled out of her, not like Uri, who used to stay inside for a while. Eli unsheathed and quickly pulled up his pants and asked if she was cold; she was completely naked, although he hadn't undressed. She said she wasn't and thought it was a stupid question.

"You came, right? I felt you come," he said.

She nodded. "You bet I did."

"Yeah, I felt you coming really hard. You were all trembling."

Later, when he took her back to Alona's house, after they sat quietly in the SUV for a few minutes, he said he was kind of in shock by what he'd done. "How old are you?" She told him she'd just had her sixteenth birthday, and he said, "Shit." When she asked why, he got a little annoyed. "Why shit? Do you have any idea how long I could go to prison for this?"

"But why would you go to prison?"

"I know, but still. Shit, shit, shit! I mean, I knew you were young, but I thought you were seventeen or eighteen." Then he went on talking to himself. "Actually, no. It's obvious you're not."

She told him not to worry, she'd already had an older boyfriend and they'd only recently broken up. He asked how old he was and she told him twenty-eight. He laughed bitterly and said, "A kid." She was about to get out of the car when he said, "So, Roni, d'you think we should meet again?"

"Sure, why not?"

He took her cell phone number. "I'll call."

"Okay." She got out of the car.

. . .

He called the next morning. She was at school and he caught her as she was going in to her Bible class, and he told her he couldn't stop thinking about her; she was something else, she was really something, and he hadn't even showered yet; he didn't ever want to shower. He asked what she was doing that night, and if she felt like getting another beer.

She said she had to study for a test, and he sounded disappointed. She didn't tell him that she had showered for a whole hour until the hot water had run out. When Alona heard her getting out of the shower at 2 A.M. and asked if everything was okay, Roni had told her she was fine, she'd just gotten really sweaty at the party and the cigarette smoke had clung to her skin.

"How late are you studying?" Eli asked insistently.

"I don't know. Late. But we can meet tomorrow if you want." She didn't know why she said that.

"Definitely."

She'd lied to him. She didn't have any plans to study that evening, but she wanted to rest, to think about it a little, about whether she even felt like meeting him again and starting something up. So she added, "Actually I'm not really sure about tomorrow, but call me in the afternoon, okay? I'll be home after three."

"Okay, I'll call."

But instead of thinking about it, she walked around sorrowfully all day, and when he called, at exactly three, she wanted to banish the new sadness so she agreed to meet him.

And that's how it had started. It had been going on for more than six months, twice a week, or sometimes once, and sometimes only once every two or three weeks, except when her father was away and they met every single night. But in February, she knew, everything was going to change. She would pass her driving test, drop out of school—her dad couldn't do anything about that—and move to Tel Aviv.

She put the cheesecake back in the stuffed refrigerator and thought about her dad, who put so much work into the food he cooked at home, as if he'd forgotten it was just the two of them or perhaps because of that. It angered her to think that he went to so much trouble just for her. It made her feel sorry for him, and when she felt sorry for him the same thing happened as when she felt sorry for her mother: a terrible, rocking sadness came over her, which only reignited the anger.

She remembered what Alona had told her once, four years ago, when she came back to Israel and fought with her dad over practically everything, almost intentionally. Maya was a baby and Ido hadn't been born yet, and her father, who was afraid of her—he seemed to have been a little afraid of her since the day she was born—used to send Alona to appease her. Alona would come into her room with yellowish stains on her shirt from milk and spit-up and sit down next to her on the bed. Sometimes she was with Maya, sometimes not, and sometimes she breast-fed as she talked, and it was disgusting and hypnotizing to watch the huge breast with blue veins and a brown nipple like an animal's, and her little sister sucking madly, one hand clutching the breast, kneading and pushing it, the other tugging on her own ear over and over again.

She remembered once telling Alona that the baby looked depressed. Alona had looked at her in surprise, but not really, and said, "Why do you think so?" Roni said she didn't know, that's just how she looked with those rhythmic movements and that weird thing she did with her ear. Alona said she wasn't depressed, she was hungry. "She's too young to be depressed. But you, Roni. What about you?"

Roni said she wasn't depressed but angry, she was angry all the time. And not just that: she was sad, too, and sometimes she didn't know which was stronger, the sadness or the anger. Alona said, "Both, probably." And then she said the words that had somehow stayed with Roni all this time.

"I don't know if it's a good thing or a bad thing, but as you get older, the anger melts and only the sadness remains." And Roni remembered thinking, Of course it's a good thing. A majorly good thing.

ALONA

They found the Mazda and the cell phone after two days, but the camera was gone. It drove Alona crazy to think that at this very moment someone in Gaza or in some refugee camp was getting a close-up look at her life and at the kids, because of course they would have developed the roll of film.

Mark said she was crazy. "Why would a thief spend the money and take the time to develop that film? You think anyone cares about it? He probably just tossed it out and sold the camera for a few shekels. Don't worry about it, I'll get you a new one. Let it go."

But letting go was not an option.

"That's what happens when they lift the closure," said one of the police officers, the older of the two who arrived. "That's what happens when you give those shits any breathing room. See?" he added, as if having identified her as a leftie the moment he walked through the door—or even before, when he saw the house from the outside. Now he seemed to hope the burglary would teach her a political lesson. His young partner sipped the Turkish coffee she'd made and said there really had been a significant drop in car thefts since the beginning of the intifada, except when they lifted the closure on the Territories. "They're having a field day now."

Based on the footprints in the backyard, the policed surmised there were two or three guys, probably from Gaza. There was a known gang of Gaza car thieves that worked the area; two days ago four cars had been stolen on Ganei Zur and two in Pardesim. They had come in through the laundry room window, taken the keys out of the front door, and fled with the car. They hadn't even touched her handbag, which was on the bureau right next to the front door. But, after the car was located in a field with the cell phone still in the hands-free holster, and returned to her without a scratch—only the preset radio stations had been changed, and when she turned the engine on the car was flooded with Arabic music. She wanted to take some pictures of the kids, because there were only a few pictures left on the roll of film, but she couldn't find the camera. The police said if it wasn't in the car, they'd probably never find it, but it was no big deal; she'd gotten off easy.

She tried to remember what was on that roll of film, because she'd developed the last one sometime in the spring, and there were only five or six pictures left on the new one. But what was on the remaining thirty? It was suddenly critical that she remember what she had photographed. She wasn't in the pictures, she knew that, because she had taken them all. It was only the children, which made them somehow more vulnerable; she was not there in the pictures to protect them from strangers' looks. There were a few of Mark and the kids that she'd taken in the backyard, and some of her mother from Rosh Hashanah. Her mother had protested and said she didn't want to have her picture taken because she looked as pale as a ghost. An entire summer—one whole summer of one leftie Israeli family, yuppie occupiers in Oshkosh swimsuits, faces smeared with ice cream—was now on display in some refugee camp.

But she knew that wasn't it. The theft of the camera bothered her, and the notion that a family was sitting in Shaati right now—she tried to remember the names of other refugee camps but could not, and for a moment that bothered her, too; what did it say about her?—the thought that a family was sitting there scribbling mustaches on Maya's and Ido's faces, spitting on their images, on their popsicles, and the idea of a Palestinian mother looking at those pictures, just looking curiously—it sent shivers up her spine. But what really troubled her, so much that she couldn't even talk about it with Mark, because she would blame him for everything—if they'd had an alarm system, this wouldn't have happened—was the simple fact that at some point last week, on the night between Wednesday and Thursday, perhaps around 3 A.M.—the older policeman had said that was the most popular time for burglaries because that's when residents sleep most deeply—two or three Palestinian men had been here in this house.

It was clear to her that she and the children had survived a terrible disaster, and it didn't help that the younger officer said car thieves came with only one purpose, to steal the car, and that's why they hadn't taken her handbag.

"And the camera?" she asked.

"That *is* weird," he admitted, "but maybe it was just sitting there, like you said, on the bureau, and they couldn't resist the temptation."

"Yes," she replied, "but imagine what would have happened if I'd got up and bumped into them. What if, God forbid, one of the kids had woken up crying? They could have slaughtered the three of us, just out of fear!" And when she said that, she realized she had never uttered the word *slaughter* out loud before. To her it was a word for right-wingers, but it had just come out of her mouth, and it had a rather comforting sound.

"But that didn't happen," the young man said, and the older one added, "You were lucky."

And then Mark, the idiot, who said he'd tried to get hold of her all morning and she hadn't answered her cell or the home phone—it turned out the phone was off the hook; the children must have been playing with it the night before—Mark rushed over as soon as she called him, right after the police left. He was sweating and seemed terrified and said an alarm wouldn't have done any good anyway, they could neutralize an alarm blindfolded; loads of people around here with alarms had been broken into. "Are the kids at school?" he asked suddenly. "How did you take them? Why didn't you call me? I don't understand!" he shouted, and ran into the kids' room, as if he did not believe that they really weren't there, that they hadn't been murdered.

"They're at kindergarten!" she yelled, trembling slightly, allowing herself to light another cigarette at home, because after all she and the older officer had chain-smoked in the living room while he'd filled out the report, so one more wouldn't make any difference; the house had already been defiled, and now it was full of cigarette smoke. She said she had no idea why she hadn't called him. She'd been confused, and the first thing she could think of was that she had to take the kids to school, so she found her spare keys and left the kids watching TV and opened the door and ran to the neighbors, the Brochsteins, and Reuven was very nice, and he drove them to school and brought her back and waited with her until the police came.

"That pain in the ass?" Mark asked.

"Yes, that pain in the ass. He was a real angel." When she was about to call the police but realized her cell phone was missing and the phone was off the hook, she thought maybe the burglars had cut it off, like in the movies, but then she remembered that she'd seen the kids playing by the phone outlet the night before.

Mark sat down opposite her on the armchair and said she was irresponsible; it wasn't the first time the kids had left the phone off the hook. "Why don't you make sure it's on before you go to sleep? What if someone needs you urgently, like your mother? What if I have to tell you something? What if Roni needs you?" She told him to go to hell, if that's what he was worried about now.

Silence prevailed in the living room, where only a few hours ago two or three Palestinians had passed without leaving a trace, and where a few moments ago two policemen had sat, as evidenced by a full ashtray, coffee cups, and a dish with crumbs from some lemon wafers they'd polished off in a second, even though they weren't fresh, which bothered her a little now—how could she have served the policemen stale cookies?

Mark sat facing her, worrying and misunderstood, as usual, her *go to hell* echoing through the burglarized house like a gong. He asked what she was thinking about and said she looked like she was somewhere else. She took a final drag on the cigarette and put it out in the ashtray, next to her three Winston butts and the policeman's three Time ones, and remembered how she used to love it when he asked that question; he said the way she disconnected sometimes was sexy.

"Obviously I'm somewhere else. I'm always somewhere else. Wherever you aren't," she said.

He sighed and was about to get up, and then he said, "Okay, Alona, I really don't think this is the time or the place to start up again with settling old scores. I thought we were done with that."

She said it was precisely the time and the place. "And no, we're not done with that. The children and I could have died; you could have found us here slaughtered, like that woman and her kids on the kibbutz, and all you care about is that the phone was off the hook?" But she knew what was bothering him. She knew what he could not forgive her for.

And indeed, after they sat quietly for a few minutes and she lit another cigarette, he turned away from her and looked at the wall and said, "I just think it's a little weird, Alona, that you didn't call me first."

And that, among other things, was why they had separated. He claimed she was incapable of truly being part of a couple. Women of her type, he said, expertly diagnosing her problem, bachelorettes who had lived alone for too long, "are far more dangerous than all those men you hate so much, the aging bachelors with commitment issues. Because yes, on the surface you certainly want a relationship, you're mature and all that, you believe that all your years of being alone, not to mention your biological clock, have prepared you, more than anyone else, to be the ideal partner. But it's a lie." Whenever they fought, he told her over and over again, "It's not a commitment issue." They had fought since the moment they moved in together, two months after meeting, when he left his house in Ein Kerem and moved to Tel Aviv. "Because you don't have any problem with commitment. It's something else, something much deeper, much more pathological; you have no idea what it means to think in two. To feel in two. To suffer in two and be happy with someone else. Maybe you thought it was a hardware issue, that if they took you and put you in a couple, you'd figure it out. But no, Alona, it's a software issue. It's like a bug, and there's nothing to do about it. There just isn't."

At first she argued. Because, after all, everything he said about her could equally be said about him. He had lied too, she said. Maybe not intentionally—although she wasn't convinced—but still, he'd lied. "You, who had long-term relationships with women, who in fact had *only* long-term relationships. You, who were married and had a child; you gave the impression of stability. An island of sanity in a sea of dangerous bachelors. And you fell in love with me. And that was the biggest lie of all."

When he asked if she thought he'd deceived her, that he wasn't really in love with her, she said, "You were in love, Mark, you absolutely were, but not with me. You were in love with the concept of a single woman finally redeemed from her bachelorhood and coming home. To you. Like Lassie. I was your project, Mark, except you didn't take into account that projects sometimes fail."

He said he definitely had taken that into account—had she forgotten that he'd been married once before? He already had one failed project, and after Jane he had had two serious partners, and he hadn't treated either of them like a project but like a beloved.

When he said *beloved* it scared her, she wasn't sure why. Maybe because now *she* was his beloved, and that was a huge responsibility. She was far more beloved than Jane, who he claimed might have been mere puppy love. And more beloved than the next two: Gali, whom he dated for two years and still wasn't convinced she wasn't bisexual, and Rachel, whom he almost moved in with, but she decided to end it because she said he was suffocating her. And not only more beloved but a better match, which he realized from the moment he met her. But she had nothing to compare him with, and the truth is that what bothered her more than anything else was the fact that Mark insisted on holding the only card that was really worth anything, the winning card: the fact that whichever way you looked at it, when it came to couplehood he knew a lot more about it than she did.

In the first few weeks after they met, she had felt that being with him was like being with the complete opposite of what she'd known before. There was something both exciting and reassuring in that. Today she thought Mark was right: when she fell in love—and it happened on that first dinner—she fell in love with the total opposite of something, not with Mark. And today too, when she thought about the term *falling in love*, she remembered that first morning in Ein Kerem, when she woke up in his bed and panicked for a minute but quickly calmed down— perhaps because of the house, she thought, when she analyzed that morning over and over again in her mind, and because of Jerusalem, and the smell of the wood-burning stove he'd lit even though it was spring, because he was addicted to the scent of burning wood. Mark wasn't in bed, so she got dressed and went into the living room. The old wooden doors to the balcony were open and she saw him sitting there with his back to her, facing the wadi. On the table were two plates, two mugs, a pot of coffee, and a basket full of bread and baked goods. "My freezer was full of stuff I baked for an event last week," he said, when she kissed the back of his neck, amazed at how easy it was to kiss the back of this man's neck, "so I defrosted them."

Falling in love with Mark, she thought later, after they broke up, was willful: a decision, similar in its impossibility to other big decisions she'd made in her life, like not sleeping with a man on the first date, or that double oath she'd taken when she was fourteen, that she would never marry someone like her father, who was weak and fearful and very maternal, and that she, unlike her mother, would marry young.

As a girl, her father had reminded her of a rabbit. Something in him trembled on the inside, and he had a mane of furry gray hair—he was always proud of his hair—that contradicted his gaunt, fading appearance, his narrow shoulders, his slightly sunken chest, and his short legs, which carried him around swiftly, almost in a panic.

Shimshon Pressler was the most beloved X-ray technician at the state health fund branch in Petach Tikva. He was the one they called whenever a child needed an X-ray, because he had a special approach and no one was afraid of him; maybe they also thought of a friendly furry animal when they saw him. He was a modest man and very domestic, unlike her mother, who lorded it over a home for retarded children in Netanya, developing a career apparently not out of ambition, or even a sense of educational mission, but simply out of a fearful desire to flee her home. She left most of the work of raising her only daughter to her husband.

When Alona started to mature, at twelve or thirteen, the rabbit became a monster. The tenderness and domestic pleasantness, the meals he cooked, which were always waiting when she came home from school, were no longer a comfort but a threat to the proper order of things. How she envied her friends whose mothers stayed at home! She promised herself that, first, she would be that kind of mother and, second, when the time came she would fall in love with a strong, aggressive, charming man, who would control her. Just like it should be.

Now she sat with Mark and waited for the alarm technicians. He had insisted on being there, not only having dropped his objection to the alarm but showing real expertise, which, to her surprise, did not annoy her but the opposite: in the last few days, since the break-in, she had felt so exhausted and startled that she was afraid that when she had to give instructions about the type of alarm and the location of the sensors, she would not know what to say or would no longer care.

They were supposed to arrive at ten but had called to say they would be at least an hour late, and she said that in the meantime she would do some work in her study. She had to finish Uri Breutner's manuscript that week, there were only a few touches left.

"Sure, try to work a bit," Mark said. "I'll wash the dishes and then read the paper." He asked if she'd had breakfast, and she said she'd had a cracker and some cottage cheese with the kids. He asked if she was dieting again, and she said no; well, maybe a little; she'd eaten like a pig all weekend, eaten and smoked, and he said, "You're allowed, you're traumatized." She said yes, but she had to pull herself together.

She went into the study, sat down at the desk, and looked out at the backyard. That was where, the police believed, the burglars had come through. There, on a lawn dotted with accusatory yellow patches from underwatering, two or three Palestinians had stepped only a few days ago. She wondered what shoes they'd worn, what clothes, and it occurred to her how odd it was that the Palestinians had disappeared from the landscape, like details in a huge faded mural, thoroughly retreated into a dark background, and how the more they disappeared the more their presence became something general, theoretical perhaps, if not for the terrorist attacks. And here three Palestinians had been walking around her house, emerging momentarily from the mural and then receding into the background.

She settled in her chair and glanced at the stack of paper. The novel didn't even have a name yet, and it would have to be copyedited next week if they were going to publish it before Passover. She suddenly heard glass breaking and rushed to the kitchen. Mark was hunched over a shattered plate. "Sorry, it slipped out of my hand." She told him to sweep thoroughly because the kids walked around barefoot, and he said, "Obviously." Since she was already in the kitchen, she went to the fridge, took out a peach yogurt, and asked if he wanted one. "No, you know I can't stand all those diet foods." She said there was regular yogurt, too. "Maybe later," he said.

She looked at him hobbling around on his heels, examining the floor tiles for shards, and what had completely abandoned her over the last few days now bashfully stole back. The technicians had said they'd be there in an hour, but an hour meant at least two, so there was time, they could do it now, and she didn't even need a diaphragm because her period was due any minute.

Mark said, "Go on, do some work, take advantage of the time."

But she said she couldn't concentrate, and the yogurt had just made her hungrier. She took another one out of the fridge, and he asked if that would fill her up, and she said, "Not a chance, but there's nothing else in the house apart from junk food." She sat down at the table. "I smoked so much, Mark. And in the house! I'm ashamed."

He said she should be, but it wasn't the end of the world. He went over to hug her and she turned to face him, remembering the precise angle at which her lips would meet his, but Mark straightened up and said, "Did you hear about that boy?" She asked what boy, and he told her about the son of a couple on the moshav, "We don't know them, some couple called Shuki and Iris, they have a six- or seven-year-old son, something like that, who was apparently sexually molested. It's not clear exactly what happened, 'cause the kid isn't really talking, but at school they noticed he was behaving strangely. At first they didn't pay much attention because the kid just started the first grade, and anyway, long story short, after meeting with a psychologist it turned out the boy had been through something, some kind of assault, right here on the moshav, and they suspect it might be Ali, that Arab who works here."

"How could it be Ali? Isn't he a bit too old for that? Why do they always blame the Arabs?"

Mark said that just because everyone always blamed them didn't mean they weren't sometimes guilty.

"Okay, but Ali? Do you really think so?"

He said they also suspected the Thai gardener, the one who lived with that farmer and worked for half the moshav. She said she knew who he was, but why would he be a suspect? Mark said the Thai worked for this couple, Shuki and Iris, and for their neighbors, that lawyer Nachmias and his wife.

"The one from CUSP?" Alona asked.

"Yes, the redhead. The tall one." That's how he knew about the story, from Eli Nachmias. He'd met him at the gas station the day before. They were both getting their cars washed, and while they waited they sat talking for a while. "He's a nice guy, you know? At first I thought he

was a yuppie windbag, but he's not, he's a really good guy. Did you
know he's a Jerusalemite too?"

"No, but go on with the story."

"Eli says it probably happened when they left the boy with the babysitter one afternoon, a couple of months ago. They went off to a big sale
at IKEA and left the boy with a thirteen-year-old girl from the moshav.
A girl in the eighth grade, do you get it? The boy was playing in the
yard and she was watching TV, and she must have forgotten about him.
Eli says you can't get anything out of her either, 'cause she's really scared,
asleep at the wheel and all that, but she says that after about thirty minutes or an hour, tops, she went out to see what he was up to and found
him swinging on the swing and crying. She thought he might have
fallen or something, but he said he hadn't and he wanted to go inside
and watch TV, and ever since then he's apparently been acting a little
weird, but because he just started the first grade everyone thought it
was only problems with school. Then he started having nightmares and
they took him to a psychologist and things started to come out, and he
said there was a monster in the yard."

"That's what he said?" Her heart winced. The story was very distant
until Mark said *monster in the yard*, and then she saw Maya and Ido
and their own private monsters.

"Yes, that's what Eli said Iris told him. A monster in the yard, that's
what the boy kept saying, and till this day, by the way, he won't go out
there, not even with his parents. At first they thought maybe a dog had
bitten him. Their neighbors have that crazy Rambo, do you know him?"
She asked if that was the dog who was always tied up at the entrance to
the pool, and he said yes, and she said he did look a bit dangerous. "But
it wasn't the dog, because d'you know what the poor kid said? He said
the monster in the yard had a different kind of pee-pee, not red like
Rambo's. And then the penny dropped. But they can't get anything more
out of the child because every time they ask him who it was, he gets
hysterical and won't talk."

"But why Ali? And why the gardener?"

Mark said the gardener had been working there that day. "He'd just
finished at Iris and Shuki's and started on the Nachmias yard, so he was
there, but of course they're not sure, because the boy's seen him a few
times since, and he hasn't responded unusually. But again, he could be

in some crazy state of repression. And Ali? I guess they just suspect him because he was in the area, too. There was a broken pipe on their street, and he was coming and going all day, waiting for the council people to show up. Anyway, it's horrifying, isn't it?"

She said it was. It was horrifying. She asked if the police were investigating, and he said, "Yes, they've already taken Bobo and Ali in for questioning, but nothing came of it. They both deny it, of course, and unless the boy cooperates and says who it was, or at least who it wasn't, they're pretty much at a dead end. A thirteen-year-old babysitter! I mean really, who leaves a child with a thirteen-year-old girl? She needs a babysitter herself."

Alona reminded him that they'd often left baby Maya with Roni when she was thirteen, and he said Roni was different.

"Roni is responsible, Roni wouldn't plunk down in front of a tele-novela while her little siblings were being raped outside."

"Don't say that, Mark! Don't say that!" The phone rang and the technicians said they were at the entrance to the moshav and asked for directions to the house. "You see, they did get here early. They asked if we had a dog in the yard," she added, laughing. "I guess they also have traumas with dogs. Where are the dogs, anyway?"

Mark said they were at home; he'd come over in the car. "I don't know what's going to happen with Popeye, Alona. He can barely walk, and the last two weeks he's lost his appetite. The vet says it's probably old age, which makes it even worse, because it could easily go on for another year or two. Maybe more."

She thought about Popeye, Roni's dog, who lived in two homes like his owner. He used to follow her everywhere she went, until she realized that even the short distance from Mark's house to hers was difficult for him, so she just left him there. When Mark went outside to meet the technicians she thought of how his house had become a sort of old-age home for Popeye, the final station. Maybe that was why he had insisted on accompanying Roni at first: not out of canine loyalty but out of that survival instinct of the elderly, who pretend nothing has changed and keep on doing little tasks like cooking, shopping, repairs, and babysitting, even when they're no longer able, even when they cause more harm than good.

She suddenly felt relieved that her mother wasn't eager to take care of the kids. Nechama even liked to say she was happy that after so many years of taking care of other people's kids, and such difficult cases, she was exempt now and finally free to live her own life. It wasn't clear exactly what life she was talking about, but Alona was relieved that she would not have to one day tell her mother that she wasn't fit for babysitting, the kids were wild and undisciplined and you had to chase after them, and she couldn't do that anymore. Her mother's legs, like Popeye's, had betrayed her.

Alona often saw her mother in the mornings on her way to the grocery store. She would stop every few feet to hold on to a utility pole or lean on a fence. She looked like she was collapsing and recovering at the same time. Alona sometimes stopped to offer her a ride, but her mother—who whenever she saw Alona behind the wheel acted as if she were chasing her, as if her daughter were the problem and not her own legs—would say, "Go on. Go on, Alona!" It wasn't clear if she was banishing her because she insisted on maintaining some level of physical activity, as the doctors had ordered, or if she was ashamed to be caught that way, laboring up a silly little hill while her daughter watched sadly from an air-conditioned car. Alona's mother, who used to be as solid as a rock, had become something else, a substance that was crumbling softly, quietly, like chalk. Like Popeye, but without the canine advantage of ignorance.

Mark said he would cope with the technicians. "You've already told me where you want the sensors, so go and work." She nodded, smiled at the three young men in the doorway, and went into her study. How pleasant it was to be led. Nothing in her protested. On the contrary, something in her sought more, the same something that had previously enjoyed blaming Mark, of all people, for being a chauvinist. Mark, who would explain in that muffled anger of his that the point was not men and women, but couples.

The first time it happened was when the trouble with her mother started. A few months after Maya was born, her mother fell on the street and never really got up again. She broke her right arm and left wrist, and her face was bruised, but mainly she was deeply insulted, as if that little pothole in the sidewalk just outside the grocery store, the pothole that had always been there, had been waiting all these years, only for her, with patience and cunning. She could not use her hands for two and a half months. She refused to hire a nurse or a caregiver to live with her for a few weeks, and she wouldn't move in with them, either, although Mark offered. He said it would be easier for them to help her if she stayed with them, now that they had Maya and were less mobile. In the end Alona had to insist on helping, and she would go to her mother's house twice a day to do housework, cook and feed her, take her to the bathroom, and wash her in the shower, with two-month-old Maya strapped on her in a carrier the whole time.

That was where Maya gave her first heartbreaking smile, in the shower while her mother bathed her grandmother as she sat on a plastic stool Mark had bought. They were both silent—after all, you could not speak in that position, Alona thought, and she knew her mother felt the same way. She carefully soaped her back and breasts and asked her to get up for a moment so she could run the washcloth between her legs. Her mother's head was bent forward and the water ran over her thinning, doll-like hair and onto her heavy body, dotted with bruises and blue marks. "Like old people's wallpaper," she said embarrassedly when she saw Alona looking at her, and Alona thought, No, not old people's wallpaper, but old-age wallpaper.

And then her mother looked up and said, "Look! She's smiling!" They both looked at Maya, whose face was peeking out of the carrier with a large smile, not the grimace of a stomachache. Alona thought how sweet and lovely it was, and later she told Mark, who got excited and spent the whole evening trying unsuccessfully to get the baby to smile again.

But at night, when they lay in bed, she felt a huge, unexpected wave—she had been so busy all day that she hadn't felt it approaching. A terrifying breaker of sadness flooded her, and she told Mark she was going outside to smoke.

"Now? Try to sleep a little."

She said, "Now," and went out into the yard and lit a cigarette and burst into tears. She hoped Mark wouldn't follow her out, so he wouldn't see her that way, so she wouldn't have to explain, to tell him that this first smile they had celebrated today would be engraved in her heart as a chilling moment.

"Let me help," he kept insisting after her mother fell, "let me do something." She agreed to give him small jobs here and there, cleaning, buying stools, installing a handrail in the bath. Mark did the errands and she cried almost every night in the yard.

Those nightly escapes into the yard did not stop when her mother got better, and one night, when she came back to bed, Mark scolded her because it seemed like she was going back to being a heavy smoker. She'd been able to stop while she was pregnant, and now she was breastfeeding. "So why go back to it, Alona? You said you'd try."

She told him angrily that these nighttime cigarettes were her salvation; she wasn't going outside to smoke so much as to cry. "To cry?" Mark lifted up on his elbows. "But why?"

And she said, "Why? You really don't know?" He asked how he could know if she didn't tell him, and she said, "That's just it." And then they argued over who was entitled to feel more hurt, she for his not guessing or he for being expected to know.

The same issue continued to come up at almost every opportunity, and she would say it had nothing to do with couplehood, that's just the way she was, loneliness was part of her DNA, not a fault but a trait, and how could you teach a lone wolf to lick her wounds in company when instinct told her to retreat to a lair? She said the same thing to a counselor they saw when she was pregnant with Ido, when life with Mark seemed to revolve solely around proving her capacity to share, or at least some desire to learn how to share. It was a terrible period, that pregnancy. Maya was a year old and just starting to walk, and toward the end of the pregnancy she began her tantrums. The counselor did not reject the wolf claim outright but suggested that, as an exercise, she try to force herself to let Mark in on things that bothered her, even if she did not feel the need to do so.

"Initiate, Alona," she said encouragingly, "initiate, even little things." She tried a few times and felt silly, but she did not view the therapy as a total waste because it allowed her to understand that there was not one particular thing that bothered her. It was not events but a leitmotif, an atmosphere that threatened her emotional autonomy.

She shut herself up in the study and tried to work on Uri Breutner's text while planning the minute details of sex with Mark. After the technicians finished working in the hallway outside the study and moved on to the living room, she even thought of taking a shower—she never used to shower before sex with Mark, but because this would be a sort of first, she felt she had to prepare herself. At least going to the pool with the kids had forced her to shave her legs and armpits regularly. But then she decided to abandon the idea. After all, there were three strange men in the house, and someone could walk in on her in the bathroom.

There was one thing she hadn't spoken about with Mark or with the police, something that the use of the word *slaughter* had automatically canceled out: rape. She could easily have been a rape victim that night. She could have been raped right in front of her children, she thought with a tremble, and maybe slaughtered, too, together with them. She wondered if Mark might be just a little bit right when he accused her of childishly insisting on not hating *them* but ourselves, when in fact there *was* no more ourselves. Because who was left, apart from them and a few of their friends who all went to the same demonstrations and signed the same petitions? "And between us, Alona, when was the last time you were at a demonstration?"

"Allow yourself a little hatred," he told her once. "What do you care? It won't make you any less enlightened or conscientious. Try it, it's addictive." She knew he was only half joking. It wasn't that she hadn't tried, but the only thing that came out was fear. When she told Mark not long ago that yes, she was afraid, all the time, and that she'd taken the kids to see some friends near Rehovot one Saturday, and when she drove down Highway 6 she remembered that there'd been a terrorist attack there, a car had been shot at, and the whole way she kept thinking she could see snipers, dozens of invisible snipers, like toy soldiers, standing on the stone walls alongside the road. "I was doing eighty miles an hour," she confessed, and he snickered; what was there to be afraid of on Highway 6, that road, of all roads? "There's something frightening there: the topography? I don't know."

"Are you crazy?" he said. "Do me a favor and don't drive eighty again."

She waited impatiently for the technicians to finish and leave. Then she would listen to Mark's explanations about the system. He would probably insist on giving her the details of every little thing they'd done, and he'd teach her the secret codes, and they'd have about two hours left until she had to pick the kids up from school. It occurred to her that it would be a little weird to say goodbye after this and each go their separate ways, and Mark would probably take advantage of the opportunity to suggest that he pick the kids up, even though it wasn't his day, and he'd insist that they spend the afternoon together. He would trespass. But what difference did it really make? Maybe she'd even suggest that he take them himself—that would make him happy—and maybe she'd be generous after they had slept together and say he could take them to the park for a while if he felt like it, and she'd stay and do some work because she hadn't done much this morning. And he'd suggest taking them grocery shopping, and maybe to the mall.

"No, not to the mall," she'd say. It had been three years since she'd dared to set foot in the mall.

He'd make fun of her, as usual, and say the mall was the safest place to be: "Have you seen what kind of security they have there?" And he'd talk about the chances of being killed in an accident or dying of cancer, but he'd say, "Okay, not to the mall then, just the supermarket," even though he thought there was actually a bigger chance of a terrorist attack at the supermarket, with that elderly security guard who sat there on a bar stool and gave everyone a general nod of approval without checking their bags. It was strange, she thought, how different they were: he wasn't afraid but he was hateful, and she had only fear, for now.

And Mark would offer to cook them dinner, because all they had at home was junk, and she'd say okay, and she'd wonder if he was scheming to stretch out the proximity rights derived from their afternoon into the night, and if he might even sleep over. "What do you care?" he'd say, "just so you don't get stressed out about the alarm. After all, it's your first night with it." And she'd say it wasn't a good idea, it would confuse the children to find him there in the morning, and what would Roni think, and he'd say the children were much smarter than she thought, they didn't have to find him there in the morning to know he was there—he *was* there, wasn't he? In all sorts of ways. And Roni would just have to deal with it. And she would imagine their first night together in two years, and the sex she'd have soon would probably not be enough, it would only make her want more; she hadn't forgotten how hard it was to satisfy her hunger back then, after the great fast of her early thirties. Mark had been stunned by her appetite back then, and very flattered. So why not, in fact? Why not?

At one-thirty Mark came into the study and said it was done. "They've left. You're protected from every direction. Come on, I'll show you how to operate it." When he saw the worried look on her face, he said, "It's not complicated, don't worry. The code is your year of birth, so it'll be easy for you to remember." Only a few days ago he'd voiced a principled objection to alarms, and now he was so gleeful about the new toy.

"Okay, I'm coming," she said, and the phone rang. Uri Breutner was having another panic attack, and she motioned for Mark to wait. He said okay and left the room.

For the last few weeks she'd turned into Uri's shrink. He was in a crisis. He was so anxious about the book coming out that he even once threatened to cancel the contract. He said he couldn't do it; the book had to be shelved. He was certain of it now. Shelved, if not burned. "Because it's bad, Alona, it's bad."

She would reassure him, saying not only was the book not bad, it was amazing. "Uri, you're talented and you know it, so snap out of it, please." And he would say he couldn't. He would calm down for a day or two, but then make the mistake of reading the text and realizing something he hadn't seen before.

"It's trash, Alona, absolute trash." He hadn't been sleeping well for the past few weeks. He took Xanax and it made him blurry: "See? I'm all dopey now, can you hear?"

And she said, "Then don't take it. What do you need that for? Smoke something instead. You smoke dope, don't you?" They'd even smoked together once, a few weeks ago.

They were supposed to meet at their regular café to work on the opening passage, but Uri called when she was on her way and said he wasn't feeling well, so she went to his apartment. It reminded her of many apartments she'd lived in and made her feel old and motherly. She brought him a latte from the café, and a croissant, which he gobbled down as if he hadn't had eaten for days.

"When was the last time you had some food?" she asked, looking at him sprawled on the scratchy couch in that pseudo–living room that reminded her of all her own pseudo–living rooms. He said he couldn't remember; yesterday, maybe? He ate her croissant, too, which she offered him, saying she was on a diet. He said he couldn't understand her dieting thing—why would she be on a diet when she looked so hot? She said, "Hot?" and he said yes, and she said, "Warm, maybe. Extra-warm on a good day."

He said, "No, really, Alona, you look fantastic," and she wondered if he was attracted to her, and if she was attracted to him, and if someone like her, who hadn't had sex for two years, was even qualified to decide whom she was attracted to and whom she wasn't.

He kept coughing and blowing his nose loudly. There were crumpled tissues all over the floor and an unpleasant smell in the room, a sour masculine smell of sweat and dust and self-pity. When she asked why the windows were closed and said it was a little warm, he said the noise from Yehuda Halevi was intolerable. He was thinking of leaving Tel Aviv.

"Where to?" she asked.

"I don't know. Maybe Ramat Gan, or Ramat Chen, or Ramat Ha'Hayal. Maybe Ramat Efal, just as long as it's a Ramat." He said he was sick of this city, he'd had it up to here with Tel Aviv. He told her Zohar had recently moved into a cute little house in Ramat Ha'Hayal.

She sat on the armchair facing him and asked what was up with Zohar and if he'd been in touch with her recently. He said they met every so often. Actually, not every so often. More than that.

"And?" she said, hating the badgering, auntly tone.

"And nothing. Actually, I don't know. I miss her something awful. She read the book, did I tell you?"

"No! Tell me."

He said that at first she was angry at the way she was depicted. "I don't know, Alona, maybe I just need to go for it. She's thirty-four, so it's legitimate, you know, for her to want a kid, isn't it? And I want to have a kid, too. Not right now, but in principle." Then he said he'd been thinking about how his separation from Zohar this past year had done something to him. It had been a crazy, intensive year; things had happened to him. Then he suddenly fell quiet.

"What? What happened?"

"Nothing." He looked away and said he really should open a window, it was a little stuffy. "The book and all that. I'm just exhausted, and I feel like I need to rest, to go home, and Zohar is home for me, and I'm thinking, What's so bad about a kid, really? What's so bad about home?"

"Nothing. A kid and home are wonderful things."

He said he'd see, he still needed to think about it; he'd decided not to decide until the book came out because it was blinding him and damaging his judgment skills. Maybe he didn't miss Zohar so much as he was anxious about the book coming out. "Which reminds me, do you feel like smoking something?"

At first she panicked; weed always made her nervous, and having to enjoy herself made her nervous, but she said, "Do you have any?"

"Yeah, a little. Not great stuff, but it's all right."

She wanted to tell him to go ahead and smoke, it wouldn't bother her, but that she personally would prefer not to. But in the end she said, "Okay, let's go for it," because she was afraid to seem old.

He rolled a joint and let her light it, and she took a small drag and passed it back to him, and he sucked on it quickly and gave it back, but she faked the next few drags. It suddenly seemed important to her not to get high, and when she saw Uri relaxing, leaning back on the couch and closing his eyes, she scolded herself for being so heavy, as Roni sometimes called her, and a control freak. When Uri gave her the butt and said, "Take it, the last one's for you," she held it up to her lips and pretended to inhale, and told herself that if there was one advantage to being forty, it was that she no longer needed to apologize to herself for who she was: heavy, a control freak, a babysitter, an aunt. Why try so hard to be someone she wasn't, when she no longer hated who she truly was?

She watched Uri run his fingers over his neck and chest, half scratching, half caressing himself, and told herself he was obviously bad in bed, you could see it on him. He was so self-centered and tortured, almost deliberately so. She asked if everything was okay, and without opening his eyes he said, "Everything's fine. And you?" She asked if he had the strength to do a little work, and he said, "Soon," and she said okay and watched him stroke his beard stubble and thought that in fact she'd already slept with him, with all sorts of versions of him, twenty at least. She wondered if she missed those men, in this kind of apartment but with different kinds of pretending, and she realized she really didn't. Mark had saved her from that, although not Mark so much as the kids.

She knew Mark was probably right in some way. She hadn't really been looking for a lifelong partner but just trying to hitch a ride into a different life.

Uri got up to get the manuscript and asked, "Should we work?" Then her cell phone rang and Ido's teacher said Ido had a fever.

"How high?" she asked.

"One-oh-one point six," the teacher said.

Alona said she was in Tel Aviv and it would take her about an hour to get back. "Is he all right in the meantime?"

"For now, yes. I gave him a teaspoon of Acamol. Try to get here quickly, okay? Because we're about to have lunch, and then we'll put them down to nap. Do you want us to keep him awake?"

Alona said, "Yes, I'm leaving right now."

When she hung up, she apologized for having to leave, and Uri said there must be something going around; he thought his own fever had gone up a bit. "Touch me and see if I feel hot."

She leaned over and put her hand to his forehead, which was cool and damp. "You don't have a fever. Okay, I have to run, and I'll think about the book's opening on the way. Maybe I'll come up with something. But you think about it too, and we'll talk this evening." He walked her to the door.

All she could think about on the way home was Ido. She'd suspected he had a fever that morning, but she purposely hadn't taken his temperature so she wouldn't have to decide whether or not to send him to school. Now she felt guilty, even though he hadn't been all that hot. She pictured him sitting on a kindergarten mattress, refusing to eat lunch, sucking his pacifier, and waiting for her. "Your life as the woman you once were isn't over when you become a mother," Ma'ayan had once told her. But her good friend was wrong. It *was* over, and thank God for that. She would never have the courage to tell Ma'ayan—who at twenty-three had married her boyfriend from the army service and had never had time to become the woman she once was—that there was something wonderful about being erased.

She finished her phone call with Uri, promised to call again in the evening to see how he was, and reminded him that they had to pick a title

this week. When she left the study she found Mark reading *Ha'aretz* on
the couch in the living room. He'd already swept up the mess the technicians had left, when they drilled in the wall, and washed the dishes.
When she said, "Okay, I'm all ears now," he asked if this Uri Breutner
wasn't getting a little carried away with his anxiety attacks. She said
she couldn't wait for the book to come out already, so he'd get slammed
by the critics and be done with it.

"You think he's going to get panned?"

"Yes, and I know who's going to do it, too. But he has to go through
it once."

Mark asked if she wasn't being a bit cruel, and she said maybe she
was but she was sick of his whining and of everyone wanting something from her.

"Am I cruel?" she said, when they stood together by the alarm control panel and Mark explained the functions of the various buttons.

She always remembered—and this might have been the biggest insult
in their relationship, an insult she dragged into her world with the
children—she always remembered his accusation that maybe her problem in life was that she lacked tenderness, basic tenderness. When she did
feel it, it was planned and therefore valueless. But now he said, "No,
you've changed. You have changed a little since I met you. It comes to
you more naturally these days." She asked if he really thought so or if he
was just saying it, and he said, "Since when do I just say things?" Then he
asked her to concentrate. "Pay attention. You don't want the whole thing
to get messed up if you press the wrong button."

"Okay, enough, I get it." Her shoulder rubbed against his when she
took a step back.

He put his hand on her shoulder and said, "Congratulations, you
now have an alarm. If anybody murders you, at least there'll be a lot of
noise in the background."

She asked if he felt like staying and making something to eat, but he
said he had to get to the restaurant; someone was coming to fix the air-
conditioning at three. "But it's almost winter," she said, and he said yes,
but last weekend they'd been sweltering in there, and a few customers
had complained. "Yes," she said, "Roni told me it was hot."

"I'm going, then. Do you want to come and have something to eat?
I have some pumpkin ravioli in the fridge." She said no, and for a

moment it occurred to her that they could go to the restaurant. No one ever went there at this time of day. But no, she thought, that was crazy, she was long past the age of doing it on the floor or up against the counter. "Then what will you eat?" he asked as he took his keys, wallet, and phone from the kitchen counter, where he always left them.

"I don't know, I'll find something."

"We'll talk later, then."

She said yes and closed the door and suddenly regretted it. The idea of doing it in the restaurant kitchen or storehouse seemed exciting, but before she could even walk back into the study, Roni turned up, earlier than expected. She said she wasn't feeling well and had hitched a ride back with a teacher who lived in the area. She was going to take a nap. Alona watched as Roni tossed her backpack on the floor, walked into the kitchen and poured herself some water from the bottle in the fridge, then dragged the backpack into her room and shut the door behind her.

She looked moodier than usual, and Alona knocked on her door. Roni opened it, holding that notebook she always took everywhere, and asked, "What's up?"

"Nothing. You said you weren't feeling well. Are you okay?"

"I'm fine, I had a headache, but I took a pill and it's gone now. I'm a little stressed out, I have a history paper to hand in tomorrow, and at four I have a driving lesson."

"Okay. If you need anything, I'll be in the study."

"Everything's fine, everything's good." She smiled and closed the door.

When Alona sat down at her desk and scanned the list of titles under consideration for Uri's book, it occurred to her that Roni might have walked in and found her and Mark in bed. It was a good thing he'd left, ignoring her signals, unable to detect them, as usual.

ELI

And what if this Yossi character gets cloned? What if he turns into a long row of identical lovers, all middle-aged men like himself? Although he didn't think he would be jealous, he realized now that what scared him was the knowledge that he had an accomplice, a kinsman. Because more than he wanted exclusive rights to that body—which seemed to have given his life what it had always lacked: a bit of healthy craziness—he wanted to believe that Roni was a gift he'd been given and had long deserved, not something he'd stolen for himself. But if he had an accomplice, that meant there was a crime, and that was not something he could tolerate.

When he teased her about it—what was she even doing with that fat sweaty guy?—she said it really was embarrassing. "The piglet," she called him. But she felt bad calling it off now. She would take her driving test in February, and then she promised exclusivity. "So meanwhile, just try not to think about him, okay? It's not like it is with you, not at all." And just as it was easy to frighten him, it was easy to console him, so he calmed down and gave a little grunt of protest into her body.

This evening, they'd finally met. They hadn't seen each other in over a month, and he didn't know if she was avoiding him, if she really was busy or just a little moody, as she said, or God knows what. He didn't really care. He was addicted, badly, and so the truth did not matter. But she acted a little weird when she got into the car. She threw her backpack onto the floor and gathered her feet under her to sit cross-legged, as usual, but something looked different: ponderous and distant somehow. She sat silently for a few minutes, focused on a broken nail she was trying to bite off her thumb, and eventually she spat it out on the floor and said, "Can we not stay here today? Let's go somewhere."

"Fine, but where?" he said, and reminded himself to shake out the floor mat later.

"I don't know, it doesn't matter, just drive. I feel like getting out of here, I'm sick of this place. I'm sick of everyone."

He said, "Okay, whatever you say. I can see you're in a combative mood."

She said, "I'm not," and he drove onto the main road of the moshav and took a right at the intersection, toward Geha Highway. "So what's up?" she asked, and he wondered what to say. What *was* up? He quickly replayed the past month and realized that not much was happening: the holidays were over; yesterday he'd lost a case he'd known he would lose; Zvika was still on reserve duty.

He stole a look at her. It had been just over a month, a record he never wanted to break, and now he wanted to make sure all her limbs were in the right place, that this was the same girl who had curled up in his arms in the backseat on the evening after Yom Kippur. That had been hard to explain to Dafna. He'd told her he'd left a file at the office that he simply had to go and get. Now he looked at Roni as if to confirm that it was the same girl, because maybe she'd grown up in the meantime; with girls her age you could never know, and he suddenly felt embarrassed when he remembered Yom Kippur.

The sex had been nothing special. Their first so-so time, which had scared him a little. They embraced afterward, much more than usual, and on the way back from the beach in Herzliya she fell asleep. He looked at her differently on that drive home. Compassionately, he thought, with a paternal feeling that sent a shiver down his spine, because how could he sleep with her again? But when he looked at her sleeping, curled into a ball by his side with her head leaning on the door, her bare feet touching each other, toes against the gearbox, he realized he was probably exaggerating. His erection hadn't been steady right from the start, maybe because of the look on Dafna's face, which had stuck in his mind when he left the house, and because of her *Why can't you just go*

to the office tomorrow? Who works on Yom Kippur? and his aggressive
Everyone—I can give you a list! Maybe that's why he couldn't concentrate. The sagging hardness, the limpness of his penis, that bowing sensation, sent his mind urgent and confusing messages, and instead of
giving up, instead of taking a rest, he had panicked: she was sixteen—
and a half, as she liked to emphasize—and obviously this kind of thing
had never happened to her before, certainly not with that Yossi, who
sounded like a guy with a constant hard-on. That was the problem with
girls, he realized, while he moved quickly inside her, praying she couldn't
feel his dick shrivel for an instant, and then, as if finding a new strength,
or an ultimatum, filling up again inside her. Girls her age fantasized
about men his age, just like men his age fantasized about young girls,
and anyone could shatter those fantasies at any minute. He couldn't be
the one to do that because then she'd realize who he was and what he
was and what he was doing to her, and so he fucked her wildly that
night, except not with the wildness she liked, the kind she found sexy,
but with the desperation of a drowning man clinging to a slippery wall.
Maybe that's why she fell asleep right afterward, because he'd exhausted
her, or maybe scared her—or, worse, bored her. Maybe that's why she
looked weird when she got into the car this evening. Maybe that's why
he wanted to see her again so urgently, so he could make amends.

He kept looking at her now, turning his head from the road to her
and back, and when she saw him looking at her like that she smiled,
hoisted up her black long-sleeved T-shirt, turned her breasts to him, and
said, "They really missed you."

He said, "I missed them, too," and reached out and gently pinched
her cherry nipples.

"So what's going on with you?" she asked again, leaning back and
looking at the road. He said not much, same as usual, and as if she
could read his mind, as if she wanted to annoy him, she said, "And
how's Dafna?"

She knew about the fertility treatments. One of the first times they
met, she asked why they didn't have kids, with a naturalness not unlike
his nudity under the coat he spread over her in the backseat of the SUV.
It was a particularly cold night, and the heater wasn't doing much good,
and he remembered urging her to get dressed, and she said, "I don't feel
like it. So tell me why you don't have kids. It's, like, a little weird, isn't

it?" He said it wasn't weird, and then he told her, at first somewhat apologetically, as if Dafna's infertility would repel her. But in fact it fascinated her, and she listened with her mouth agape, eyes fixed intently on the steamed-up window. As he talked about the fertility treatments, he stroked her foot on his lap, massaging her toes through her thick wool sock. She wanted to know every detail, what exactly these treatments were, and what was the difference between insemination and fertilization. When he asked why she was so interested, she said, "What do you mean? Everything interests me. And anyway, it's about you, isn't it? I'm interested in hearing about you, as my lover"—lover, she said, as if she were a forty-year-old cheating on her husband—"and besides, it's sad that you don't have kids, isn't it?" At that moment he felt a sharp sliver of ice melting inside him. Of course it was sad, he knew it was sad, no one had to tell him it was sad, but when this girl he'd only known for a few weeks said the words, it was a different kind of sadness, an intolerable kind. And since that day he tried not to talk about it much.

He reported drily about the big failure last spring on Independence Day, but he didn't tell her how the failure had destroyed Dafna, so much so that she said she wanted them to see a counselor. In the summer, when Roni asked what was happening, he had told her they were taking a break because of various technical and bureaucratic things. Now she asked if they were still on a break, and he said no, they were probably having a fertilization later that month. Dafna had an ultrasound the next day, and the following week they would do the extraction.

Roni said, "Oh. Wow, I'm keeping my fingers crossed for you." If she were older, he thought, she wouldn't keep any fingers crossed. On the contrary, she would hope it wouldn't work, so she could bask in the tragedy of the barren wife. Then she said, "Listen to this dream I had," and she told him that a few nights ago she'd dreamed Dafna was pregnant. Eli said no kidding? but he was startled; what was she doing dreaming about Dafna? "Sometimes my dreams are prophetic," she said. "Did you hear about the kid on the moshav, the one who was sexually assaulted?"

He said, "Sure, he's our neighbors' son."

She told him that a few months ago, right before it happened, she'd dreamed she was walking around the fields near Eden, but she was little, five or six, and alone. "And I'm walking around, and it's dusk, winter, and everything's wet and cool and really beautiful and full of mud, and suddenly I see Popeye, my dog. I call out to him but he doesn't respond, and I call out again and he doesn't respond, and I try to get closer to him—he's standing in tall grass and all I can see is his head and tail—and when I get there I see it's not Popeye at all, it's some dog that looks like him. I pet him, and he suddenly turns into a different dog, a weird one, and he starts grunting and chasing me, and he has this red penis, like dogs have, and I slip in the mud and fall, and he tries to climb on top of me and rape me."

"And does he manage to do it?" Eli asked, as if this were the important part of the dream.

"No, but I'm scared and I call for help, and he keeps making that humping motion that dogs do, and I can't get up, and I shout, 'Mom!'"

"You called out for your mom? Not your dad?"

"Yes, obviously. When I was little I lived with my mom."

And he thought, What is she now, if not little?

"And then I woke up."

"It's a pity I wasn't there. I would have saved you." But he shivered, because he suddenly realized that the dog in the dream might be him. "So what did you dream about Dafna?" he asked, driving south on Geha, still not knowing where to.

She said she dreamed Dafna was pregnant, not from fertility treatments or anything, the dream wasn't detailed about that, but she was very pregnant, sitting on a wicker rocking chair on a porch outside an old house, surrounded by loads of cats.

"Cats? With you it's either cats or dogs," he said, trying to cover up the embarrassment this dream caused him, or the hopefulness. "And then? What's the outcome of this dreamed-up pregnancy of my wife?"

"A redheaded baby. I mean, I didn't see it, but that's what she had in her belly."

"Dafna's a redhead."

"I know."

"And what about me? Was I there?"

"No, just her. And she sat there in the rocking chair, with her huge belly, and it was a lovely quiet dream, not a lot of action, no sound track even."

"And where were you?"

"I wasn't there. I played the part of the dreamer."

"Cute dream. Redheaded baby," he pondered out loud. Maybe Dafna was giving birth to herself.

He slowed down and stopped on the side of the road leading to the Hiriya landfill. The aimless driving and the talk about Dafna were getting on his nerves.

"What's wrong? Why did we stop?"

He said they had to decide where they were going. "We can't just drive around like this all evening. We're almost at the end of the highway." He said he thought they could park somewhere around there.

"At Hiriya?"

"No, nearby." He remembered that there was a dirt path leading to nowhere, and there'd never be anyone there at this time of night. "What do you say?"

But she kept sitting upright in her Buddha position, without answering, and said she was dying for a cigarette. "But you won't let me smoke in the car, right?"

He said he would prefer her not to, and reminded himself again to shake out the mat and get rid of the incriminating fingernail. He unfastened his seat belt and moved closer to her, pulling her shoulder to him, and felt her fossilize. He remembered Yom Kippur again. "What's going on, Roni? You look a little sad."

"Nothing. Nothing's going on. I'm always a little sad."

"Really? I hadn't noticed."

"So you mean I look like a cheerful person to you?" she asked, as if he'd insulted her.

"No, of course not. Not cheerful, God forbid, but not sad."

"Because you wouldn't be this attracted to me if I was a happy-go-lucky type."

He thought about it for a minute and said he would be, but maybe a bit less.

"You're a depressive guy, too," she asserted.

"Depressive? I wouldn't say that. Irritable, maybe."

"Yes, you are."

"Maybe, if that's what you want me to be."

"Yes, that's what I want you to be." After a pause she asked if he felt like taking a trip to Jerusalem.

"What?" he asked, surprised.

"So you can show me where you grew up and all that."

He asked why she suddenly felt like going to Jerusalem, and she said she really loved Nachlaot. She'd walked around the neighborhood a while ago, after she went to a show at Pargod with Shiri. He said, "Oh, Pargod. That's a couple of feet away from where I grew up."

"So let's go. Why not? Let's go!"

He took his hand off her shoulder and said, "Okay, if that's what you feel like." He fastened his seat belt and merged into traffic.

"You have to exit here," she instructed.

He said he knew that, and he felt angry. Jerusalem? Now? He'd been waiting for this for more than a month, and now he was getting drawn into a nostalgia tour. He wondered if there was anywhere there, a field or a construction site, where they could fuck later, but he couldn't think of anywhere. He was amazed at how little he knew the city now. It had been fifteen years since he'd left, at twenty-six, practically a boy. His father had wished him luck when Eli told him he'd been accepted to do his articles in a big law firm in Tel Aviv, which was an opportunity not to be missed. "Of course, of course," his father said, but at that moment something in him hunched over like a stalk whipped by a gust of wind; it bent over and then straightened back up, but not all the way.

When he was at law school at the Hebrew University, having left the home on Nissim Bachar Street that his two older brothers had left long before, he still visited his father at least three or four times a week. He sat with him on the veranda and told him about his studies and about his aspirations, good-naturedly pushing back his father's questions about appropriate women and when he would find himself one. "It'll work out, Dad," he would say and pat his shoulder affectionately, "there's time," and his father would say *I trust you*. They passed endless afternoons in half-silences and words of worry and encouragement on that veranda, which barely had enough room for two chairs and seemed to have been built for one person only.

After he moved to Tel Aviv, he hosted his father for a weekend in his rented apartment on Zeitlin Street. It was the one and only time, and it clarified for them both that they had parted ways, that in fact they had never been on the same path. Something about his father's presence, his clothes, which looked tattered and even a little dirty against the cold white background of the leather couches and the practically empty book-shelf, and the wool rug, and the double bed he had made up for his father with a new set of pale-colored sheets—something in the appearance of the old man walking bemusedly between the two rooms, making a squeaky noise on the tiles with his eternal black shoes—which suddenly seemed to Eli like an immigrant's shoes, even though his father had been born in Israel—and the way he examined the marble counter in the clean kitchen, which, in a demonstration of defiant modernity, was equipped with a microwave, espresso machine, and electric citrus press, shaking his head from side to side in that familiar, quiet, impressed look of his— something about all that defiled the apartment, threatened the pseudo-yuppieness, as Dafna called it a few years later, as if all at once his home had been invaded by an elderly, gnarled spirit of Jerusalem. He was ashamed of thinking that way, but when he saw his father sitting on the couch in his light-blue cotton pajamas, which looked like hospital paja-mas, watching the huge flat-screen television—Eli had placed the remote control in his father's hand as if the gesture were a huge compliment, a ceding of control, but his father was unable to operate it—when he looked at him as he watched a talk show on the national channel, his eye-lids growing heavy and the remote control drooping on his lap, and then as he suddenly shook himself awake and his head snapped up, his hand grasping the remote again as he mumbled a few words of awe and dozed off again—that whole time Eli felt an acidity bubbling up inside him, try-ing to dismantle and melt away what this man, his father, had brought into his home. But what was it, in fact? Not just that Jerusalemite feeling, not just the aromas of the Mahane Yehuda Market that had infiltrated the glistening supermarket that was his new residence. No, it was not only that but something else, something general. It was the loneliness between parents and children and the moment at which the child—he, Eli—who had enough struggles without this, realized that the responsibility for this loneliness was on his shoulders from now on; the only person who loved him unconditionally did not belong in his world and, moreover, was there as an invader.

The next day they toured Tel Aviv in Eli's silver VW Golf. He drove past the sea, the promenade, Old Jaffa, and Malchei Yisrael Square, while his father the tourist sank back in his seat like a small child. When they got back to the apartment it seemed slightly hostile, just like he felt, and he couldn't wait for his father to wake up from his afternoon nap so he could drive him home to Jerusalem, which on that wintry Saturday evening looked as if it had been waiting impatiently to suck the old man back into its gut, ingest his insult, and spit out the son.

His father's Jerusalem died shortly after he did. Maybe it was just his imagination, but somehow, after his father was buried, he felt as if the city turned its back on him. Once its elderly citizen Avraham Nachmias had passed on, Jerusalem owed nothing toward the rebellious son, the snob, the pseudo-yuppie who had long ago abandoned it, and it seemed now to vent a hostility that had been on a low flame during the ten years after Eli left. Now that the father was gone, it was as if the city finally allowed itself to settle the score, to strike back at him with the same contempt he had felt toward it since leaving, since becoming a Tel Avivian—although he never really did that, just like Dafna said. He was a pseudo-yuppie hybrid who would never ripen into a real yuppie; he was a Jerusalemite who hungrily lunges at the city and swallows it whole but chokes on it.

"That's the problem," Dafna always claimed, and perhaps she was right. "That's your source of restlessness. That's why you want to move to the countryside," she said, when they still lived in the rooftop apartment on Budenheimer. "Not because you really love the country and want to work the land; that's a joke. But because you hate Tel Aviv, you hate it but you can't admit it, because what would that say about you? But you can't go back to Jerusalem anymore either."

Apart from court appearances, he intentionally avoided Jerusalem, and not only because of the situation. Something else, something more profound, prevented him from going, and when he thought about Jerusalem, especially in autumn, when he tried to reconstruct his days there, a screen dropped down in his mind, as if Jerusalem were a peepshow and his allotted time was up; he had to drop another coin in the slot to buy a few more minutes, over and over again, forever.

They passed Ben Gurion Airport and he asked Roni if she was sure she wanted to go to Jerusalem, if she didn't have to be home at a particular time. She said, "No. Actually, yes," and took out her cell phone and called her dad and told him she was in Tel Aviv with friends. "Not Shiri, other friends, you don't know them. . . . No, no, not from school. Look, you don't know them." She said she'd probably just spend the night at Alona's; her backpack was there and everything. Then she called Alona and said she'd be home very late, definitely not before one, and when she hung up she said at least Alona didn't get on her case.

"She's convinced I have a mysterious boyfriend, but she doesn't know the half of it." Eli said he'd never thought of himself as mysterious, but thanks, and suddenly she said, "Oh, no, I forgot the code again," and she told him they'd just had an alarm system installed because someone had broken into the house and stolen Alona's car, and she kept forgetting the stupid code. She phoned again and asked what the code was: "No, don't worry, I'm not writing it down. I'll remember, I'm telling you." She huffed and he could see her memorizing a number in the dark.

"Isn't there an alarm at your dad's?" he asked.

She said there was but it was easy because the code was her year of birth, 1989. Then she said, "Oops! Now you can break into our house!"

"I think I already did."

She smiled, finally looking relaxed, put her hand between his legs, and said, "I really feel like going down on you," which was the cue for him to pull off to the side of the road, but now he'd gotten himself into this Jerusalem tour, and who knew if they'd have time afterward. As it was, he'd have trouble explaining to Dafna why he was getting home so late.

"I have an idea," he said, removing her hand from between his thighs and holding it to his lips. "Listen, d'you feel like going to a hotel? We've never been in a hotel, you know with a Jacuzzi and all the little luxuries."

"Wow, what a weird idea. That sounds cool, but it's complicated, isn't it? It's a major production. We can't go in together; I'd have to sneak in."

"I know."

"Okay, I'm cool with it."

He knew the desk clerks would be on to him straightaway and kick him out—but maybe not. Hotels were desperate for tourists, and he was a kind of tourist, too. He had to find somewhere cheap, clean, and decent—the word *decent* sounded dirty to him now—and in his mind he scanned the various neighborhoods and was already regretting the crazy idea. Why Jerusalem? Roni asked where they were going and he said, "We'll find something."

"Something nice?"

"Of course."

As if connecting with the fear and regret that had started to seep through him, she said, "Actually, it doesn't have to be nice, does it? What do we care if it's nice or not."

"Of course it has to be nice."

Roni turned the radio on and asked where that CD they liked was, the Moby album that had been the background to so many of their meetings. He told her to look in the glove compartment. When they drove past Sha'ar Hagay and started up the mountains to Jerusalem, he remembered what Dafna had told him soon after they met, in the days when they still fed each other stories from their pasts, each inspecting the other's emotional digestive system. He remembered one story of hers that always scared him a little, about her winter tryst in a hotel in Ramallah, just before the first intifada.

She was studying theater and comparative literature and living with two roommates in Rehavia, on Alfasi Street. She was having an affair with a lecturer. "Not from my department," she stressed, as if it mattered, as if it were an extenuating circumstance. It was someone from the social sciences, Oded, or maybe Eran, he couldn't remember now. He was nineteen years older than Dafna and married.

Eli remembered how that had shocked him. Not the age difference—Dafna was twenty-one and the lecturer was forty, which was no big deal—but the fact that Dafna had had an affair with a married man. He'd never had a relationship with a married woman. Something in him rejected the idea from the outset. It seemed impractical and immoral, he told her. She said he was conservative.

"Affairs aren't supposed to be practical, and certainly not moral. Isn't that the whole point?"

As he watched Roni dig through the glove compartment for the Moby CD, he thought he understood for the first time that his thing with her was a terrible sin—toward himself, toward his values, which he was actually fond of, and toward a few other things. Like love, for example, which he believed in: he had never for a minute stopped loving Dafna, even now, when anger and pity competed every time he looked at her, every time he touched her. He was slightly disgusted but he still loved her completely.

And he believed in couplehood. He couldn't understand all those single women who had babies on their own. Couldn't understand it and couldn't stand it, he told Dafna, who was outraged, of course. And his left-wing positions were also pretty flexible, circumstantial, and maybe a show for Dafna. He badgered his law partner for not refusing to do his reserve duty in the Territories, when his own reserve duty was the occasional short and relatively pleasant stint at the Military Attorney General and he hadn't carried a weapon since the age of twenty-four. He had a problem with the foreign workers, too: he employed the Thai gardener, Bobo, who was the legal employee of one of the farmers on the moshav and lived in a trailer in his yard, but he supported the government's expulsion policy—for the Palestinians, he told Dafna, so they'd have somewhere to return to when all this was over, so their jobs would still be there.

"When all what is over?" she asked mockingly.

"You know, the intifada. Don't be difficult. When there's peace and all that," he said boldly, knowing he was infuriating her and slightly enjoying it.

"Peace? When there's peace they won't have to be our slaves anymore."

"Of course they will. It'll take them at least thirty years to build their own economy."

"No, there won't be real peace until they have a real state, with real jobs."

"Come on, Dafna, don't be ridiculous. You're naïve."

But he was the naïve one, he thought now, as he looked at Roni bopping her head around to Moby's beat, which he really couldn't stand. She hugged her knees in and looked out at the winding road. He was the naïve one if he thought he could keep on being who he'd been his whole life, a conservative liberal who believed in couplehood, who insisted on love, who knew that one day there would be a child in all this, too,

Ukrainian or Georgian or Romanian, but theirs. Naïve if he thought he could go home in the early hours of the morning the same person he was when he left, a person he actually liked, a good, decent person.

Dafna couldn't take the lecturer to her apartment because one of her roommates had a class with him, and they obviously couldn't meet at his place, so their relationship, if it could be called a relationship, was conducted in Dafna's car. She said he was hysterical about leaving evidence in his own car, in case his wife literally smelled something. It was Dafna's first car, a Ford Fiesta she'd inherited from her sister when she married, and one day, after almost a year of backseat sex—"Good sex?" Eli remembered asking, and she'd said, "In retrospect, not at all"—she suggested that they get a hotel room. Or, rather, insisted.

She insisted, she said, because something in her suddenly rebelled, demanded an upgrade, or at least that they do it once like human beings, in a bed. So she told Oded or Eran—two years ago she told Eli she'd run into him by chance at a conference on the Middle East; he was wearing a suit jacket with faded jeans, had gained about twenty pounds, and his hair was thinning, limp and colorless, not gray but worse than gray; she said she had goose bumps and slight nausea—she told him she wanted to go to a hotel for once, and he said, "Acceptable." ("Acceptable? You slept with someone who says *acceptable*?" Eli teased, and she said, "Yes, it's hard to believe, but yes. And by the way, I've heard you say an *acceptable* or two here and there.")

The lecturer told her to drive to East Jerusalem. When she asked why, he said, "I'm sure you don't think it's a good idea for us to go to a hotel in the western part of the city, do you? Someone might see us." She said he was right, and regretted the whole thing, and wanted to say they should forget about it and just go to their usual place in the Jerusalem Forest, but she didn't because it seemed like a point of principle.

"A principle?" Eli had exclaimed at the time, and he remembered now where they were sitting when she told him the story, and that was weird, because unlike Dafna he didn't usually remember those kinds of details, only the content or, as she called it, the point, the bottom line. But now he could picture the bar in the trendy Florentin neighborhood, although he couldn't remember its name and wasn't sure it even had one, it was just like Dafna to take him to a secret little place. They sat next to each other on bar stools and Dafna told the story to his profile, which turned to her occasionally, and he remembered that it seemed strange, that there was a contradiction between this exciting Dafna who wore a tight black turtleneck that nicely enveloped her small breasts, this Dafna who wore jeans—which had long ago stopped fitting her— and the one who a few years earlier had let some horny married guy take advantage of her. And it was strange that this woman, who made fun of his apartment and his wardrobe, and even had a problem with his VW Golf—"Only yuppies drive that car"—it was strange that back then this woman had thought it was such a principled issue to have sex in a hotel.

"I was young," she said, sipping beer on tap. She drank Guinness, which also surprised him. It seemed unfeminine but it turned him on. She drank Guinness and he sipped a gin and tonic and felt—what did he feel? Almost feminine, he remembered now. Feminine and clean and scared next to this redheaded live wire sitting next to him, whom he didn't really know yet. "I was young and stupid," she said, and recounted how they drove to East Jerusalem, passed Damascus Gate, and kept going east, and she asked if there was a specific place he had in mind or if they were just driving. Oded or Eran said he thought maybe it was better to go to Ramallah, he'd done his reserve duty there once and knew there were some places on the main road, kind of guesthouses; he even thought he'd seen a hotel sign on some of the buildings.

"I don't know, I guess my disgust threshold was pretty high, and my insult gauge was screwed up," she said, which reminded him of what she'd said about her first blow job, with the lifeguard, "and maybe I wasn't mature enough even to be insulted. Which means that maybe, theoretically, what happened wasn't really degrading, you know?"

He said he did, even though he wasn't convinced. He was fascinated by her, taken aback as though she were not a strange and attractive twenty-eight-year-old but a retired prostitute recounting her life story in a dingy bar. Dafna ordered another beer, and he was impressed by her drinking capacity, which she had lost in recent years. She said it was because of the hormones: "It's like I'm constantly pregnant, even though I never am." These days a few sips of beer or wine were enough to make her dizzy and nauseated, and to threaten her with the loss of control she so feared. That was why she hated throwing up, she said, unlike him, who wasn't bothered by it and in fact sometimes enjoyed it.

But loss of control was the name of the game back then, apparently, and they drove on and arrived at a building that seemed residential, and the look on the desk clerk's face was more political than any she'd ever seen before in a Palestinian. It was a victorious look, she said, like he was saying, You may be screwing us, but you have no choice but to screw at our place. "Welcome, *tfadalu*," he said, and they climbed up to the third floor and went into a room that didn't even have a number, one of four rooms on the floor. The whole building seemed abandoned, as if no one was there other than them and the Palestinian ghost clerk.

The room, she said, was freezing. The windows were open and there was a smell of cleaning materials and the starch used to wash the old linens—a white sheet, two pillows in white pillowcases—and two folded woolen blankets. "It smelled like a hospital and orphanage and soup kitchen and I don't know what else. Everything but a hotel. It was pretty clean but it was like a meat locker in there, and the heat wasn't working. Why would they turn on the heat for two Israelis just there for a quickie?" Oded or Eran sat down on the bed, took his shoes off, covered his feet with the folded blanket, and said, "*Brrrr.*" He suddenly looked grandfatherly, and he asked if she was satisfied, if the place was okay. She said, "It'll do," and lay down on the bed with all her clothes on, including her coat.

"What kind of coat did you have?" Eli had asked, and when she fell in love with him she said it was those kinds of questions that were one of the reasons.

She said she couldn't remember, probably a leather jacket, knowing her, or a corduroy one. She covered herself with a blanket and was totally passive, for the first time. She usually tried to impress him. "I did tricks like you wouldn't believe," she told Eli. But that night she didn't move, hardly breathed, and insisted on keeping her sweater and coat on the whole time, as well as her socks. "And the sex," she said—and Eli wanted to console her, to put a hand on her shoulder, to kiss her or something, but she was obviously in some kind of private trance that had nothing to do with him and never would—"it was so bad, so meaningless, so humiliating in a way that all the others in the backseat of the car hadn't been, and not only did I not come but I didn't even fake it. Like I'd died, you know?" He said he did. "But I still took in more details than when I was alive. Everything was magnified: his grunts, the robotic movements, the fact that he didn't really invest any effort in me, barely touched me, just exhaled an *umpf-umpf-umpf* in my ear, like a marathon runner who'd run all the way to Ramallah." Then she burst out laughing.

She might have been drunk already, and Eli laughed too, finally daring to put his hand on her fingers, which were constantly fiddling with a box of matches on the bar. Even though he had already slept with her, he had yet to attempt this kind of comforting touch. He laughed, but he was very sad and shocked. After that, she told him, she didn't want to see the guy anymore. Something in her was no longer capable of it, and she told him it was over; they'd exhausted it. The guy didn't really protest. "Moved on to the next co-ed?" Eli asked, and she had said she thought so.

They were stopped at the Sakharov Gardens light, right outside Jerusalem, listening to Moby. The image of that room in Ramallah, which he had never seen, haunted him. Not only because of Dafna—she wasn't why he felt this way—but because of a larger, more general miserableness that had quietly climbed up the Castel Hills with them. It was something almost philosophical, he thought, although he wasn't one of those people who busied themselves with abstract questions. No, he wasn't the type. He stole another look at Roni, and the car filled with sounds he did not like. He may have liked them when he was with her, inside her, but now they depressed him and made him, to his surprise, miss home, and Dafna, and especially that moment in the bar in Florentin, when her candor had borne something else: trust, not only in him but in her story's ability to build something. It was a sort of faith that he had, too, the faith that you can break your past up into little pieces, into chiseled stones, and use them with a little cement of compassion to build your future.

"What's up?" Roni asked. She hadn't said a word since Sha'ar Hagay. "What's up?" she asked again.

This time he answered impatiently. "Nothing, Roni, nothing's up. Are you okay?"

"A hundred percent," she said.

She looked scolded, and he felt a little sorry. "We'll be there soon, and I have an idea for where to go," he said, even though he had no clue what they would do when they reached the city.

"Yeah? Where?" she asked, encouraged.

"It's a surprise. I'm going to pamper you, it'll be awesome." Maybe he'd take her to the American Colony Hotel. That was a beautiful place, and it was in East Jerusalem, so what could go wrong? But that hotel in Ramallah stuck in his mind again, the Palestinian fleabag. If he went to the American Colony now it would be ironic, as if he were settling a score with that lecturer of Dafna's, upgrading her cheap affair. And maybe it would really be a double betrayal, to take the girl he was sleeping with right under his wife's nose—after all, their backyard faced the fields that his four-wheel-drive plowed through like a comb in a tangle of hair—to take Roni to the American Colony would be a betrayal not only of their shared present but also of Dafna's private past. He did not want to do that, because from one minute to the next—and by now he had entered Jerusalem and turned onto Herzl Boulevard—his memory of that night in the bar in Florentin was becoming magical and painful.

He remembered that he had paid for their drinks. Dafna always protested that she wanted to pay for herself, but he never let her. *A conservative Jerusalemite*, she had called him, and he said, "What do you care? It's your gain." They'd walked out to the street, and since they had only known each other for a few weeks and had slept together only twice, it was not yet obvious that they would spend the night together. Dafna said she would get a cab home. She lived in Kerem Hateimanim back then, in an apartment that reeked of poultry and meat from the butchers in the market, and he said, "No way, I'll take you."

He drove her in his silver Golf and asked if he could come up for coffee, and she said she was exhausted; the story about Ramallah and the three beers seemed to have tired her out. He said he was tired too, and she said, "Okay, but just a quick one."

She made him a cup of tea unenthusiastically, and it was obvious that she wanted him to leave, but he stayed. They sat on her old couch, the one she'd bought at the flea market, and she laid her head on his lap and said his car would probably get keyed; there were all kinds of thugs who walked around at night keying people's cars.

"So they'll key it," he said. "I don't care. I want to get a new car soon anyway."

"What kind will you get?" she asked, without lifting her head up, "A black BMW?"

"All right, that's enough. I'm not that bad."

"I know, I'm just kidding. I'm being mean. I'm exhausted, and I'm falling asleep on your lap."

"That's okay," he said, and was surprised that she really did fall asleep. She didn't seem like the type who could fall asleep on someone's lap, and he liked that she was, and he found himself sitting on the couch until dawn, afraid to wake her, napping with his back against the wall, his hand stroking her red hair, afraid to move, to undermine what he felt was building up between them. It was something new, something he'd never had before with a woman: friendship. When the morning light flooded the room through the slits of his eyes, he thought it might even be a true friendship, and a love he had never known before.

Roni pointed at the block of hotels to their left and asked if that was where they were going. He didn't even know their names. "No, those are horrible."

"Where, then?"

"Honestly? I have no idea."

"So there's no surprise?"

"No."

She looked disappointed, but she said, "That's okay, we can drive around for a while. Let's go to Nachlaot."

"Actually, there *is* a surprise," he said, and made a U-turn at the next light.

"There is? So we *are* going to a hotel?"

"Not just any hotel, the most beautiful hotel in the Middle East!" He plotted out the shortest route to East Jerusalem and turned onto Bezalel Street and then down toward the old Cinematheque. He wanted to tell Roni that as a boy he'd watched countless foreign movies there, which he hadn't liked and hadn't understood; he really went there to meet girls from other schools, like from the Music Academy. Those girls favored the hippie look, and they always attracted him. They used to sit in the cafeteria drinking mint tea and smoking Nelsons, and he was in love with them all. He drove past the old Cinematheque without saying a word and went on toward Damascus Gate and turned left, unsure if it was the right way.

Roni looked out of the window curiously. It was almost eleven and the streets were empty. "Wait, is this East Jerusalem?"

"Yes."

"Wow. I don't think I've ever been here."

"Really? How could that be?"

"I just haven't."

"But you were born in Jerusalem, weren't you? I thought you grew up here until you left with your mother."

"Yes, but I think the intifada had already started and you couldn't walk around the East anymore."

It suddenly hit him: 1989, the secret code. He knew, of course, how old she was, but he'd never thought about her year of birth. When Dafna was screwing her lecturer in Ramallah, Roni hadn't been born yet. Obviously she'd never been to East Jerusalem; obviously it was just a name for her. 1989. And suddenly her being sixteen was not exciting at all but impossible. He almost missed the American Colony but remembered the turnoff at the last minute. He parked outside the beautiful building and turned off the engine, as if not wanting to declare his presence.

Roni turned to him. "Here?"

"Yes, this is the American Colony." He wasn't sure what he expected her to do.

"It's an American place?"

He laughed. "No, it's an Arab place. Come on." He got out of the car, but then it occurred to him that it might be better for her to wait inside. As it was, he wasn't sure how to handle the occasion. He'd never gotten a hotel room like this, without a travel agent, in the middle of the night. But Roni jumped out and hoisted her backpack over her shoulder.

A cool silence welcomed them when they walked to the front desk, and he heard Roni whisper, "Wow, it's lovely here, look how beautiful!"

He hissed at her impatiently. "Shhh. . . . I know. We can look at it later."

He stood at the counter and grinned widely, madly, at the young woman behind the counter, who asked him in English, with an expressionless face, how she could help him. He told her matter-of-factly that he needed a room for one night. No, he didn't have a reservation; he was in town for business and had heard good things about the hotel, which really was very lovely. He looked around.

The young Arab woman said, "Thank you, but we're fully booked."

"Fully booked?" He hadn't taken that into account. It was early November, tourist season was over, and there weren't any tourists anyway, even in high season. "Fully booked?" he asked again, and the clerk, who looked straight into his eyes the whole time, stole a glance at Roni and said, "I'm sorry, sir."

He wanted to ask who exactly they were booked up with; who even came here, anyway? Foreign press, he knew that, but surely journalists weren't taking up every last room. Then he heard Roni say, "Oh, please, pretty please!" in perfect American English. The clerk smiled and said she was sorry but they were full. Roni told her in quick, casual English that she was very disappointed because she lived in the States with her mother and she was here to visit her father in Haifa, and today she'd come with him on a tour of *lovely* Jerusalem, and he'd promised to take her to the most beautiful hotel in the Middle East. "So please, just for a few hours? So I can at least tell my friends at school that I was here?"

But the Arab woman repeated, "I'm sorry."

"Bummer," Roni said, when they sat back down in the car. She fastened her seat belt and folded her legs underneath her and said she really needed a cigarette. "Let's stop somewhere and I'll get out to smoke."

"Not here, this isn't a place to stop; are you crazy? We're in the Wild East," he hissed. He drove onto the main road and turned toward Musrara.

"So what should we do?" she said. She did not sound as desperate as he felt, although in fact he wasn't desperate so much as he was tired and wanted to go home. He wondered if Dafna was asleep yet. She had an ultrasound the next day and had to get up at six and he still didn't have a solution for the eighteenth. She'd told him yesterday that the extraction would almost definitely be on the eighteenth. But he wasn't angry at her anymore. No, he needed her now. He made a right onto Jaffa Street and passed Mahane Yehuda Market—"Is this the *shuk*?" Roni asked, and he said yes distractedly—and he suddenly fantasized about getting into bed, hugging Dafna from behind, and telling her about his adventures, about getting kicked out of the American Colony. He would whisper, "They hate us, Dafna!" And he wouldn't even care if she said, We deserve to be hated. Anything she said would comfort him now.

"That desk clerk really bummed me out, but it's okay," Roni said, and thrust her left hand between his thighs, massaging his groin, as if she knew he needed comfort. But not that kind, he thought, not now.

Still, he was so hard it was painful, and he said, "Let's take a different route home." She said Yeah? and he nodded. When he turned onto Herzl Boulevard again and Roni asked if they hadn't been there already, he said, "Yes, but wait." He took a right on the road leading to the Jerusalem Forest. As he drove, looking for a place where they could stop, the girl leaned over and started to rub him.

Roni murmured, "I want you to lick me."

The magic sentence always turned him on, and he said, "Then let's stop," and drove off the narrow road onto a very narrow path that was probably meant for hikers, not cars. The Toyota pushed its way through the forest, butting past branches and thorny shrubs. With one click he closed all the windows—all he needed was a car full of twigs and thistles. The windows were getting scratched now, and the car was full of screeching sounds.

Roni sat up and said, "It's a pity to ruin all these bushes, isn't it? You're really thrashing them."

He said, "It's okay, they'll grow back," but he stopped, turned the engine off, and pulled the hand brake up.

"Look, we can't even get out; we're in a cage of thorns," she said.

He turned to her. "But we don't need to get out." He gestured at the backseat with his head. She quickly slipped between the two seats, giggling excitedly, and lay flat on her back. She took off her shoes and pants and lay there in her boxer shorts, which he recognized from one of their previous times. They had a green dinosaur print.

"Screw her," he said.

"Who?"

"The front desk clerk."

She giggled. "You're still thinking about that?"

"Yes, a little. Man, I have a hard-on like a rocket! How do you do it?"

She smiled and said, "I'm a magician."

"You're a witch."

"Good or wicked?"

"Very wicked." He turned her over on her stomach.

"But wait," he heard her protest into the upholstery.

"What?"

She turned her head and said, "Didn't we say that—you know—that you'd lick me?"

"Let's do it like in *Last Tango*, okay? Don't you want to? I really want to."

She paused for a moment and whispered, "Okay," and slowly, but not slowly enough, he made his way into her rear end and for the first time he knew he was really hurting her. And for the first time, he didn't care.

NECHAMA

A man leaves his home in the morning, takes his wallet, ID, checkbook, keys, and some medical documents in a plastic bag, and sits down in the car next to his daughter, who drives him to the hospital for a checkup scheduled long ago, a checkup that is not urgent, and yet he is afraid of it because it is unpleasant. The car leaves the moshav, stops at the intersection, and merges into traffic, and the man looks at the familiar sights and perhaps exchanges a few words with his daughter, who probably tries to reassure him because that's what she's been doing her whole life. He's been fasting for twelve hours, and perhaps, despite the fear, he is hungry, and he's thinking about the lunch he'll have at the cafeteria after it's all over, because he knows the hospital, he's had tests done there before, and he knows the menu and knows what to order. On that particular day he might be considering the meat quiche, which he is especially fond of, and he has no idea that this is the last time he will drive in this car and see these sights, that this is his last conversation with his daughter, that he will not eat lunch at the cafeteria, and that he will never go home again.

Even now, ten years after Shimshon's death, Nechama could not banish the notion that her husband had been cheated. It was supposed to be a simple colonoscopy. Shimshon had complained of stomach pain for months, and he'd lost weight, and obviously they had considered the worst, and even though now, at seventy-eight, she knew there was some mercy in the death he had suffered, she still felt shivers every time she remembered him leaving the house. He was wearing his gray pants and the maroon sweater Alona had bought for his seventieth birthday, and although there was no need for a coat that day, he'd insisted on taking his parka because they'd said it would start raining in the afternoon, and he always believed the forecasters. He believed everyone—and indeed it did start to rain that evening, but Shimshon was no longer conscious and the coat had become a nuisance.

A nuisance, and immediately following that, a memory, which still hung on the hook in the entryway, faded from the sunlight that bathed it every morning through the window. Nechama had carried that parka on her arm all evening, as she darted in and out of the ICU where Shimshon lay with what the doctors said was an infection—not from the test, that was impossible—a necrotizing fasciitis caused by streptococcus bacteria.

The test had revealed nothing unusual, and when the sedative wore off, Shimshon began to complain of weakness and chest pain. At first no one thought it was serious, and the doctors told him to lie down in the recovery room for a while longer. He fell asleep, and Alona went downstairs to get some coffee. When she returned, she found the doctors surrounding her father's bed. There had been a sudden drop in his blood pressure and he'd lost consciousness. When Nechama arrived, at seven—Fleischman, who drove her there, said it was probably nothing, maybe a reaction to the sedative, and there was something reassuring in his words, even though she did not believe him; Fleischman was a simple and foolish man, but a nice one, and he even offered to come and pick her up afterward, but there was no afterward—she took the elevator up to the ICU and ran into Alona, who told her that Dad's systems were failing. You could see she'd been crying all afternoon, and she said she needed some fresh air and a cigarette. When she left she gave Nechama the parka, which remained on her arm until a quarter to midnight, when the doctors pronounced Shimshon's death.

She always knew he would die before she did. Not because he was five years older, and not because nature ensures that the world fills up with widows, but because Shimshon was weak. He walked through life as if on a tightrope; a mere breeze was enough to unbalance him. The first cracks in his daily routine had emerged when Alona left home,

even before her army service, although he still worked part-time at the
health fund back then. But the real blow was retirement, which left him
confused and lost. It was not just retirement, he claimed, but something
general and continuous: this life, as he called it, in Eden, in this dump,
when his heart still beat with the hope of returning to Tel Aviv, which
they had left forty years ago because of her job. She was a special ed
teacher in the regional school, and later, after Alona was born, became
director of the school in Netanya. They could have gone back to Tel
Aviv then, it was the same distance from Netanya, but the idea became
buried under what was their life at the time: his work at the health fund
and their little daughter. He said he wanted Alona to grow up as a city
girl, with everything the city had to offer, but he still enjoyed watching
her run around the yard, barefoot, cheeks flushed, just like in the movies. He even built her a little petting zoo, with some chickens, guinea
fowl, rabbits, guinea pigs, and white doves. Alona was such a beautiful
girl, with an eager face and bright golden curls, an agile little body, and
an almost manic laugh. And so he agreed, without anything ever being
discussed, to postpone their return to the city for a while so that another
child could enjoy the countryside and the petting zoo. He announced
that he did not want a son but another daughter, another Alona, whom
he found so wonderful. But the second daughter never came, nor did a
son, although they tried. She had Alona at thirty-eight, and had gotten
pregnant easily, but they couldn't do it again. Back then they didn't have
the treatments they have now, and today Nechama believed that, ultimately, that was what had truly crushed him.

But it was not how he should have died, deceitfully, as if he'd been
kidnapped.

"Maybe you feel a bit guilty, Mom," Alona said. "You were the one
who pressured him to have the test. He didn't want to, he was afraid."
She replied maybe, but she knew that wasn't it. If it had been an illness,
like cancer, a heart attack, or a stroke, or even an accident or a terrorist
attack, she would not have felt the way she had for the past decade. She
would not have been left with the sight of his back retreating down the
path, his small body bending over to sit down in the car, his mottled hand
waving goodbye through the window: not a dramatic farewell flourish,
just an ordinary wave. And then the car reversing out of the driveway,
driving a hundred yards or so and disappearing around the bend, and

that was that. Every so often, when she remembered the waving hand, she thought perhaps the motion had been weaker than usual, docile, as if he knew. And if he did know—and this, too, gave her no peace—why didn't he fight? Why didn't he get out of the car and say, "Let's put the test off, Nechama, it's not urgent."

"Like a lamb to the slaughter," she told Alona during the shiva, "that's how he went." Alona got angry. "Really, Mom, stop it; don't torment yourself. Anyway, everyone goes to their death like a lamb to the slaughter, and it doesn't matter how they die." But even though she knew her daughter was right, she could not shake off the vision of that defeated, knowing hand.

In three weeks, on November twenty-fifth, he would have celebrated his eighty-third birthday. Every year around this time, in the autumn, she remembered the day of the colonoscopy, February 21, and reconstructed it in great detail, as if she could go back to that day and, if not mend something, at least understand. Every year, from November to February, it all became magnified in her mind, the fury and the wondering and the speculation. What would have happened if he hadn't taken the test that day? If Alona hadn't been able to start the car, which had happened a lot that winter? But she knew it wouldn't have changed anything. Fleischman would have volunteered to drive him. And what would have happened if the test had been scheduled for a different day? It was hard to get an appointment, and at first all they could get was April, but she'd insisted, forcing Shimshon to pull strings in the health fund to move that appointment up. "So we can get it over with." She chillingly remembered scolding him when he asked what difference it would make to wait another two months? "No," she'd said, "let's get it over with. It's not a good idea to put it off." And he did what he always did: he gave in to her, called the regional manager of the health fund, whom he knew from his old job, and the guy got him that damned February appointment.

Last summer she thought she was going to die. She felt weak and heavy, especially in her legs, which were like two iron rods. There was something wrong with her blood vessels. Edema. And she was overweight and had high blood pressure. And her age, of course. The doctors had all sorts of theories, but at seventy-eight they no longer gave diagnoses. What for? They just sent the patient home with all sorts of philosophical adages. And her legs—her entire existence was now emptied into them.

Alona, who had finally had an alarm installed, thank God, called to ask Nechama if she needed any groceries. "There's veal on sale at the supermarket; you like that. Should I buy you a few cutlets, so you'll have them in the freezer?" Nechama said no, she didn't need anything, and since when did she like veal, anyway?

She knew that what bothered her daughter more than anything, more than the legs, more than her suspicious health, was that her appetite had almost completely disappeared. She'd given her such a look on Rosh Hashanah when she'd left her plate almost full. Even Roni, her adopted granddaughter or step-granddaughter—she never knew exactly what to call her, so she thought of the girl as her oldest grandchild— Roni, who never interfered and seemed not to notice what was going on around her, said, "I'm a little worried, Nechama."

"What are you worried about? What does a girl your age have to be worried about?"

"Oh, really, Nechama, about you! About the fact that you're starving yourself. I mean, what is this? Are you, like, going anorexic now, too? What are you, fifteen? It's not like you, Nechama, it really isn't."

Even though she neither expected nor wanted Roni to call her *Grandma*, something about *Nechama* stung that time, as if this child had somehow been granted authority and was collaborating with Alona. She knew they were truly concerned for her well-being, but still their concern contained condescension.

The little one too, Maya, who didn't miss a thing, who was so alert and sharp that Alona said it was frightening sometimes—but what exactly was frightening about it? Nechama couldn't understand. "You should be happy that you have an intelligent girl. Why should that frighten you?" The problem was that parents today made mountains out of molehills, as if every child was a case, not a child, as if everything that was fine actually signified a problem. And she didn't need to be told about *cases*. She knew all too well what cases were; she'd spent thirty years working with the most difficult ones. But Maya asked her on Rosh Hashanah, when they finished clearing the dishes from the table, if she wasn't eating because she didn't like the food or because she wasn't hungry. "The food was excellent, but a little heavy for my age," she had answered, and the girl said, "You're right, Grandma, it's heavy for my age, too." Then she went to watch TV in the living room. And in fact, who if not a five-year-old girl would automatically take her side? Without asking questions, without condescending, without any pretenses of understanding the first thing about old age and how it worked, as if she were some newfangled electrical appliance that would be easier to operate if you could just decipher its mechanism.

Easier to operate. For example, to get up from that sagging couch of Alona and Mark's without Mark jumping up to help her. Or the daily walk from her home to the grocery store. All the utility poles in Eden were marked with her fingerprints. It took twenty minutes each way. Or eating. It's not that she didn't want to. She did have an appetite, but from the moment she made something, like a hard-boiled egg or a small salad with tuna fish, or the tomato soup she used to love, from the moment she piled something onto her fork until the second she raised it to her lips, something went wrong, as if the food's journey to her mouth also took twenty damn minutes, an infinite and exhausting length of time, during which the food became a foreign body that hurt her tongue or burned it or dried it—something she could not swallow.

She liked veal, of course she did, but lately a little rebellion against Alona had been bubbling up inside her. It reminded her a bit of her own rebellion against her parents more than fifty years ago, which had entailed spite and denial. Not long ago she'd been thinking about her sixteenth birthday party and the huge present her parents had given her. When she'd removed the gift wrap, she'd glared at them both with a betrayed look and said, "Since when do I like to read?" There were ten classic books: *The Brothers Karamazov, Crime and Punishment, War and Peace, Magic Mountain*, and some others she'd asked for. She never forgot the look on their faces when she left the pile of books on the kitchen table and retreated angrily into her room, repeating, as if in disbelief, "*Books?*" Her mother's jilted look, and the anger buried in her father's eyes. On her next birthday they'd given her a tailor-made dress, and she'd said, "Next time give me books. Books are what I like most."

And she did like to read; it was her great love, which Alona had obviously inherited. But she had enjoyed her newfound capacity to cause pain and to confuse, just like adults sometimes did to little children when they wanted to have fun. She herself did it sometimes with her grandchildren. "Is that really your tractor?" she'd tease Ido when he held up a toy for her. "You didn't take it from someone?" And she'd watch how the enthusiastic nod suddenly turned into a look of fear and bewilderment. She tried it with Maya, too, who had a wonderful sense of humor. With her you could really joke around. "Are you sure you're Maya? You're not somebody else?"

And the girl would answer, "I'm sure, Grandma. And you? Maybe you're somebody else?"

Finally Alona told her to stop. "It's abuse," she said shamelessly. "Stop abusing them, Mom." How easy it was to use words these days.

So now she was doing it again, just like when she was a girl. She was confusing Alona. Her legs might be heavy but she was still kicking. An adolescent old lady, that's how she sometimes thought of herself. She hoped Alona would insist on the veal and buy her a few cuts after all. The Alona from before the children, Alona from just a few years ago, would have done that. She would have imposed her own will upon her mother, even suggesting they eat together: she could fry the cutlets in two seconds. She'd quickly take an egg out of the fridge, check the expiration date, ask where the bread crumbs were, and without waiting for an answer she'd find them in the drawer where she kept the spices, all of which, without exception, were expired, but who used them anyway? But *this* Alona, the Alona who belonged to Maya and Ido, couldn't be bothered with that stuff anymore. "Then I won't get any if you don't want them. If you change your mind, call my cell."

After she hung up the phone, Nechama went into the kitchen. All the talk about veal had made her hungry, but when she opened the freezer and took out two slices of low-calorie bread and put them in the toaster, her appetite disappeared and she felt the indi-nausea take over again. That's what Ido called it: "Grandma, why aren't you eating? Do you have indi-nausea?" How often had he heard her tell Alona she couldn't eat because she had indigestion and nausea? That boy was such a sweet, innocent thing. A little like his father, who was naïve, a worrier, and liked to feed everyone, just like a Jewish mother. He was a softie, a good-looking softie. It didn't surprise her at all that after years of being single, years in which who knew what she did and what she went through in Tel Aviv, her daughter had fallen in love with a short, compact man with a baby face, like Shimshon and, also like him, weak.

But they weren't together anymore, so it was irrelevant to think of him as her daughter's husband. Although maybe they *were* together, because since they'd separated it seemed like he spent more time there than he had when they were together. And Alona seemed less angry, even fonder of him. She wondered if they had relations—but she quickly banished the thought from her mind. It was none of her business; a mother should not preoccupy herself with such thoughts about her daughter. Alona thought so too, and thank God for her discreetness. In her heart she always thanked Alona for never letting her in on her love life, even when she was unhappy. Back when she lived in Tel Aviv, every time she visited Eden she brought an imaginary backpack full of urban sorrow and a tired sort of cynicism, and perhaps she wished to unload it at her mother's. Perhaps, but Nechama wouldn't let her.

As soon as she arrived, Alona would say something about how messy the house looked. "Won't you get a cleaning lady? Once every two weeks?" From the moment she walked into the house she had happily grown up in, she busied herself with endless little chores, nonsensical things that no one asked her to do. She took expired dairy products from the fridge, threw away moldy, yellowing cucumbers and tomatoes from the vegetable drawer with a silent expression of disgust, then rolled up her sleeves and washed the dishes in the sink. And it's not like there were that many! Maybe one bowl and one cup. She'd ask where the bleach was, even though she knew; it was not a question but a scolding. She'd take the bottle out from its regular place under the sink, hurry to the bathroom, and pour at least half a bottle into the toilet bowl.

It was never clear if all these actions were her way of disinfecting the house for her biweekly visit or if she did it to avoid talking about what she had been through in those two weeks. When she finished cleaning they would sit at the kitchen table—"I can't understand how the three of us ate around such a small table," she had said once; "wasn't it crowded?"—sit quietly and each look in a different direction. Every so often their looks would happen to cross, like spotlights meeting in the sky. "Everything's the same as usual," she'd say, and offer some anecdote from her job at a small subversive publisher, as she described it. Nechama never dared to ask what was new in *that area*, as Alona called it, when she said, "I don't want to talk about that area," and it was obvious that there *was* nothing new.

Once, in a moment of candor or perhaps desperation, Alona announced that if she didn't find anyone by thirty-five, she was going to have a child with a gay friend or from the sperm bank. Nechama asked if there was such a gay friend in the picture, and Alona said, "The picture is full of gays, Mom," and she wondered how it was possible that there were so many homosexual friends who wanted to have a child with her daughter, but not a single heterosexual man. But of course she didn't say anything. Alona was thirty then, and anything could happen in five years. And it did.

The fact was that she herself had only married at thirty, relatively late for her generation. When she was in her twenties she had a boy-friend, Shmulik Dorfman, who loved her and wanted to get married, but Shmulik, who was an engineer, made it clear that he did not want Nechama to work after they married. He thought she should stay home with the children, when they had them, and he hoped there would be at least four. At the last minute, when they were about to set a date for the wedding, she changed her mind and broke his heart before he could ruin her life. When she told her daughter that story, Alona smiled and said, "You were at the forefront of feminism, Mom," and Nechama said she guessed she was.

Shortly afterward, she met Shimshon Pressler at a Purim party at her friend's house. He was dressed up as a tiger, she told Alona, which made her laugh and also embarrassed her a little. "Dad? A tiger?"

"Yes, yes. You should have seen his tail! And he was a big liberal, or else he just didn't care. Either way, he was very encouraging of my career, and he agreed to move here." Since the conversation about the child and the homosexuals, she hadn't said anything, and Alona's visits, although she looked forward to them, gradually grew as heavy as mud, with all the cleaning and the silences. It occurred to her now that she might secretly have made a pact with her daughter: You save me the burden of your bachelorhood, and I'll save you the burden of my old age. A pact that she now, as it turned out, was unable to keep.

Nor did she want to. She was only a little sorry now, like Shimshon had been, that there were no more children in the picture, because it really wasn't fair to put everything on Alona. But on the other hand, who else could she put it on? And it was a good thing she had a daugh-ter, because a son would have run away. A son wouldn't sit drinking coffee with her in the kitchen but would busy himself with repairs. In fact, if she had had a son, he probably would have turned out like Shimshon, weak and soft and domestic, a guy who couldn't hammer a nail into the wall but whose meatballs were unrivaled.

Like Mark. But Mark fixed things and built furniture, as well. When she first met him she saw a modern, improved, and more handsome version of Shimshon. After he moved to Eden to live with Alona, he gradually fixed all the broken things in Nechama's house, without making a big deal out of it and without insulting her: Mark, who was gregarious for a man, emerged as a quiet and reliable handyman. He did everything himself: replaced the faucets, fixed the bookshelves, patched up the torn screens. Only with the broken floor tiles—"That little valley you have in the living room," he said warmly—had he needed help, so he'd brought Ali and one of his sons to replace all the tiles in the living room. She remembered that week now; when was it? Five years ago. The house was abuzz with people: Mark and Ali and the son. They worked quietly and you practically had to force them to take a coffee break. Alona, who was at the end of her pregnancy with Maya and looked wonderful, was calmer than she'd ever been. Roni was there too, just a little girl from America who clung to her father, not like today. It hurt to see how much she couldn't stand him now. Perhaps that was natural, but it still hurt. That week in early winter when they'd replaced the living room floor seemed like an important milestone now, perhaps because everything had changed unrecognizably since then—the situation in the country, and Alona, who had a baby and then another, both of whom had pushed Nechama and her needs aside. It was natural, of course, but it still hurt. She couldn't help but miss that period a little.

And now this story about Ali, the rumors. It was all they talked about at the grocery store, which was patronized mainly by the elderly, who had turned it into a sort of community center. The information changed every day, but it was always very juicy and completely unreliable. The Arab couldn't have done what they said he did to that little boy. Some claimed it wasn't rape but indecent assault, but what difference did it make? The boy's life was ruined, and so were his poor parents, whom Nechama didn't know; she didn't know the new families in Eden. Almost every morning a new and chilling version of what had happened to the boy was recounted in the grocery store. Rivka, the old spinster who had inherited the store from her parents, lived in Ra'anana, but she came every morning to open up. Rivka said she'd heard the boy's underwear had disappeared.

"Disappeared? How could that be?" Nechama asked.

"Disappeared. The boy came inside wearing his pants, and when the mother showered him that evening and asked where his underwear was, he said he lost it. And it didn't even strike her as odd, you know? Surely she should have realized right then and there that something had happened to him, the poor thing. Maybe they could have still found the criminal. Maybe there was still evidence on the ground. What would you think if your girl came home without her underwear?"

And Nechama thought: Nothing. She wouldn't have thought anything. And she felt like a bad parent who couldn't see the signs.

But it wasn't Ali. It couldn't be. Not the nice, polite man who had knelt on this very floor for a whole week, together with his quiet son. The man who had worked here for years, who was a household member all over Eden. Who had once brought her—and she couldn't remember why—a huge jug of olive oil from his village, which she gave to Alona because she didn't use it. Alona, who never missed a chance to educate, had said, "If you used olive oil, your cholesterol would go down." But she didn't like the smell, and Alona took the oil and mentioned how delicious it was every time they spoke on the phone for weeks. She said it was miles above any of the boutique oils Mark brought from Italy, and Nechama thought the whole thing was more of a political statement than a culinary assertion, as if here, too, was a hidden reprimand: not only was she not clean enough, not only did she not try to lower her cholesterol, but now she wasn't left-wing enough either, which was not true—as evidenced by the fact that she could not conceive of Ali having done this terrible thing to that boy just because he was an Arab.

The Thai, maybe, but not Ali. The Thai man was a little odd, and she'd even been bold enough to tell Rivka that she thought it might be him, if anyone. "What's his name?" asked Reuven Brochstein, who was in the grocery that morning, and then he answered his own question: "Bobo. That's his name. And it's not him. It's the Arab. A hundred percent." He said he knew Ali—after all, he was his boss—and added that he was considering firing him, even though they hadn't proved anything yet.

Rivka, who had never been fond of Reuven—she said he was a big

miser, always double-checking the receipts and finding discrepancies—
said, "So, why don't you fire him then?"

And Reuven replied, "I can't. He'll kill me."

When the toaster popped, Nechama removed the two slices and
threw them in the trash. She opened the fridge, took out a yogurt, and
sat down at the table to eat. At first she enjoyed the tart flavor, but she
put down her teaspoon before she was even halfway through, and suddenly felt an urgent need to get that veal. She knew what to tell Alona.
She covered the yogurt cup, put it back in the fridge, and dialed Alona's
cell phone. "Are you at the supermarket?"

"Yes," Alona replied.

Nechama thought she sounded impatient; why was she so impatient
all the time? She thought she could hear a female voice in the background. "What is that? Are you talking to someone?"

"No, Mom, it's the loudspeaker."

"What are they saying?" she asked, aware of the flattery in her voice.

"Nothing. Some sale or something. I wasn't listening. So what's up?
What did you want?"

Nechama asked if by any chance Alona had her health fund card,
from that time she took her to the bone density test. "I can't find it, so I
thought maybe we left it in your wallet, because you handed it to the
receptionist, remember?"

"Hang on, I'll have a look."

"I'm waiting." She listened alertly to the distant voices coming from
the phone.

"No, I don't have it. Did you look for it properly?"

"Yes." It wasn't the first time she'd lied to her daughter, and certainly wouldn't be the last. The card was in its place, in her wallet.

"Then I'll call the health fund and ask them to order you a new one.
It's not good that you keep losing things."

"No, don't call yet. I'll do one more search. If I can't find it, I'll tell
you." What was she talking about anyway? She hadn't lost anything
recently. She grew tired standing by the window and dragged herself
over to sit at the table. "What supermarket are you at? The Hyper?"

"No, there's a new Mega here."

"Oh, Mega. They have good things there, lots of sales." She waited
for her daughter to say something about the veal, but Alona said she

had to get off the phone; it was difficult to talk while she pushed the trolley, and she was in a hurry. She still had to go to the drugstore before she picked up the kids. "Do you need anything from SuperPharm?"

"No."

Nechama remembered what her mother had said when she'd rejected that birthday gift: "Then next time we'll give you some money and you can buy whatever you want." She read all the books afterward, secretly, in two months. More than sixty years had gone by, but still, every time she thought back to that day, a sense of remorse singed her chest. And failure, too, because she had promised herself then, as a girl, that if she ever had a daughter she would not allow her to rebel as she had rebelled against her own parents, or at least she would be impervious to the unjustified insults this future daughter might throw at her. And now, when Alona was about to hang up and keep doing her shopping, unaware—or perhaps she was aware? Of course she was; how could she not be?—of the distress signals Nechama was trying to broadcast, of the mute pleading for those cutlets, which had become, like everything else, urgent and principled, she asked herself whether she'd learned nothing her whole life. When she hung up, she realized: not a thing.

DAFNA

Not that she wanted to die. Not at all. Not badly enough to do anything about it. The desire to die was set aside for isolated, focused moments, and it never spilled over into what could be called—she hated the expression but couldn't come up with a better one—the day-to-day. No, her day-to-day was booby-trapped in a different, nonsuicidal way, full of little torture devices. Since the failure in May, it was enough to catch sight of a pregnant woman on the street or in a café, or even to hear about a stranger who was pregnant, to stun her with a brief paralysis, after which she would rouse and go about her business as if nothing had happened, but more bitterly. She was angry at herself for that bitterness because it was clear that humanity could not be expected to stop procreating just so one woman could have the chance to bring a child into the world, and even—she knew this was crazy but it's how she felt recently—just to get pregnant and miscarry. Because that was the thing now, the pregnancy, not the birth itself. The boy or girl who was supposed to be waiting at the end of the road had grown so distant now as to be an invisible, insignificant dot.

She had no expectations from this morning's ultrasound. She'd already suffered the blow two days ago, when she'd arrived for the test after five days of injections, six ampoules a day, and Professor Ferber had stared at the screen as he wagged the transducer inside her, tracking down hidden follicles, and said, "Only two follicles, Dafnaleh? That's all you could make for us this month?" He pulled out the transducer as if he, too, were suddenly sick of her, the old hen.

When she got dressed and sat down at his desk, he suggested, without looking up from her file, that they cancel the test tube fertilization that month and do an insemination. "It would be a pity to go through the anesthesia and raise expectations. And a pity to waste the health fund coverage."

But she said, "No, absolutely not. We'll work with these two and that's it."

The doctor said, "All right, if that's what you want," and asked her to come for another ultrasound on Tuesday the sixteenth. He said the retrieval would probably be on the eighteenth. She walked out past the women in the waiting room, and instead of taking the elevator she went down the stairs. When she reached the ground floor she burst into tears.

She sat on the bottom step, digging through her purse to seem busy and avoid the looks of passersby. She sat that way for several minutes with tears streaming down her face, wiping her cheeks with her hand, knowing that Ferber was right, this IVF was unnecessary and wasteful, and worse, that something terrible had happened to her, because her body had stopped responding to the injections. She had never had fewer than four follicles, and now there were only two. It was her body's attempt to do what she herself could not: give up. Call it quits. Finally phone one of the adoption agencies whose numbers were in Eli's Palm Pilot.

She went out into the parking lot, sat down in her car, put her cell phone in the hands-free device, and started the engine. She didn't even call to tell Eli. For the first time in all these years, she did not hurry to phone him after the ultrasound to report how many follicles she'd had. Something in her did not want to hear him trying to conjure up consolation, when she knew that deep inside, or in fact not deep at all, because it had already bubbled to the surface, there was a different voice, one that asked when she would release him from this punishment.

But it wasn't a punishment. Everything else was, but not the fertility treatments. Last week's demonstration, for example, was a huge punishment. She'd spent weeks preparing, and in the end only a few hundred people had turned up in Rabin Square instead of the thousands they'd expected. Of course, people no longer believed in peace, and she

could understand them. She didn't think it had much of a chance herself, or that it was even relevant anymore. Peace was a concept that
might have been right for the nineties. But still, she believed that CUSP
was important, so she pressed on, enlisting support from the press, organizing petitions and demonstrations, getting Gabi onto talk shows,
watching him sweat and argue impassionedly as he sat on panels with
politicians, settlers, generals, and economists and swapped jokes with
entertainers or authors filling the entertainer slot. Sometimes he came
to the studio with the requisite backup: a single mother, a handicapped
person, or an elderly man who sat beside him, blinded by the lights.

And now she was stuck with Gabi's new initiative: Swap-Meet. He
was very proud of the name he'd come up with for his new project, in
which underprivileged Israelis and Palestinians were supposed to offer
items they no longer needed in return for other ones. A sort of virtual
secondhand store, as Gabi envisioned it, mediated by CUSP. He even set
up a toll-free number, and good-naturedly took on the media's bemused
mockery. "Are you crazy?" laughed one talk-show host, "I mean, it's a
noble idea, there's no question about that, but wouldn't it be more reasonable for the rich to donate to the poor than for the poor to donate
to the poor? Because, just between us, Gabi, what do the poor have to
offer?"

That was exactly what Gabi had been waiting for. "Everything!" he
told the host, and repeated to other journalists who took an interest in
CUSP's Swap-Meet initiative. "*Everything*!" he emphasized. "Because
we're not talking about a material project. Not at all. The point is not
whether a Palestinian family gets a used TV or an Israeli family gets a
Sony Play Station. The point is that underprivileged classes on both
sides get closer to each other, *talk* to each other, understand that each
side has something to give, not just to take. And then maybe a sort of
dialogue will emerge, a sort of understanding, a sort of identification.
And a recognition that salvation will not come from above but from
below."

The interviewer wouldn't give in: "But poor people can't afford to
give away their old stuff. They need donations!"

"You'll see!" Gabi retorted. "We will mediate; Israelis and Palestinians will call us and tell us what they need and what they have to give—
and by the way, it doesn't have to be material things. You can also offer

services, each according to his abilities, and we'll arrange for everyone to get what they need."

But only one young man called. His name was Adel, he said—or rather whispered, as Dafna recalled from the hesitant, secretive phone call—and he lived in a village near Nablus; he refused to give an exact address. He asked for a Power Ranger doll for his son, Munir, and in return he offered his services as a floor tiler. Apart from Adel, no one from the Palestinian side called.

"We'll get back to you," Dafna told him. "We'll see what offers we get and call you back." But Adel refused to leave a phone number. He sounded disappointed and betrayed, as if he had imagined a decked-out Israeli office with crates full of unwrapped Power Rangers, one of which would be sent by courier straight to his village, rather than a century-old ruin with a toilet that you couldn't throw toilet paper in because the plumbing couldn't handle it, a twenty-one-year-old secretary who spent most of her time texting her boyfriend, a CEO who was bringing peace to the Middle East while scarfing down salami sandwiches, and an infertile spokeswoman. That was not what Adel had pictured. Dafna asked him to call back in a few days; maybe something would turn up. He said okay and hung up.

But the Israelis called en masse, responding to the widespread ad campaign launched by CUSP: radio jingles, TV spots, and billboards with the heading SWAP-MEET above a photograph of an Israeli child and a Palestinian child sitting on the floor facing each other, each holding a toy behind his back. During the first week the line was flooded with calls from Israelis who said they'd seen the television ad, or the poster, and thought it was wonderful and best of luck.

The poster design was a nightmare. The Israeli child was easy; they purposely chose a fair-haired boy. But the Palestinian? They had trouble finding a model and spent days arguing about the concept. The graphic designer suggested using a dark-skinned boy, maybe a Yemenite, and dressing him in Palestinian-looking clothes.

Dafna was outraged. "What do you mean, Palestinian clothes? Define Palestinian clothes!" Oh, you know, he said, and she said, "No, I don't," even though she did. The Yemenite boy seemed like a bad idea, not just because it smacked of racism, as she told the designer, but because, if they were being honest, it wouldn't be completely accurate to present a fair-skinned child as underprivileged. "It's not realistic to use an Ashkenazi and a Palestinian," she said.

"Once, maybe," the graphic artist said, "but today it is. Think about the Russians." She said that was a stereotype, and you couldn't define the two peoples by two colors. He said you could, and it worked better in photographs that way. If there were two dark kids on the poster, the public wouldn't know what they were talking about and the message wouldn't get through. "Photographically, we have to have contrast," he explained, and offered his five-year-old son as a model. When he showed Dafna some Polaroids of the boy, whose name was Bar, she looked at his lovely face and told the designer that on second thought maybe they should drop the whole kids idea. Maybe it was better to show two men or two women. He said she was crazy: "Why on earth would you use grown-ups? Kids are the most effective, and you know it. There's no debate here, Dafna. Kids, period."

Eventually they cast a little boy from Bar's kindergarten in the Palestinian role. He was the son of foreign workers from Chile, dark-skinned but not too much. His name was Emmanuel, and the designer said he had that Palestinian look. Dafna was forced to agree. As a compromise, they dressed both kids in similar clothes: dark flannel pants and solid T-shirts, orange for Bar and light green for Emmanuel.

One thousand seven hundred and forty calls came in during the first week of the campaign, all from Israelis. Dafna and the secretary could barely keep up, and Gabi was busy talking to journalists. Most people asked for electronics and offered housewares and clothes. There were Russian immigrants with more generous offers, like rugs and pianos. Many asked for computers for their kids, DVD players and Play Stations. Since winter was nearing, there were a lot of requests for heaters, except that no one offered heaters or computers or DVD players, and CUSP had trouble mediating.

Hundreds of forms detailing the callers' names, offers, and requests were placed on Dafna's desk. At first each form looked fresh and clean, full of childish hopefulness, but cumulatively they began to resemble a heap of despair. A month into Swap-Meet, the Palestinian question had been all but forgotten, and she felt like a rag-and-bones man pushing a virtual horse and cart through the streets of big cities and development towns and moshavim.

One evening, when she sat with Gabi in the office and he wondered why the Palestinians weren't calling, she said, "Maybe they don't know about us."

He said, "They know, trust me, they know."

"But how?" she insisted.

"Through the grapevine. It goes through the grapevine. They're just afraid to call. They don't believe a word we say anymore, and rightly so." She reminded him of Adel, the Palestinian sampling, and Gabi enthused. "Does he have an entry permit? I'll get him a floor-tiling job tomorrow. Tomorrow!" She said she hadn't asked, but he called every week to ask if there was a Power Ranger, and there never was. Gabi said, "So let's get one for him! We have to do this, do you understand? It's one thing to disappoint the Israelis, but one poor Palestinian calls and we can't help him out?" His eyes lit up and he started pacing the room. "It's genius, genius! We'll make this Adel into a star. He'll be our star, Dafna, you'll see. We'll get him that doll, we'll get him ten of them, so he can give them out to all the kids in his village. And we'll get him a job, and we'll put him on TV and the radio, and we'll organize a cover story in the *Maariv* supplement. I can already see the headline! Can you guess?" She shook her head. "PALESTINIAN ACTION FIGURE! It's genius, don't you think? Stop by Toys"R"Us tomorrow, can you do that? I won't have time. Buy him the fanciest Power Ranger they have and I'll pay you back."

She kept on with CUSP just like she kept on with the treatments, she realized now as she waited at the light on Nachmani Street to cross Rothschild going west. She decided not to call Eli. He could get hold of her if he wanted to. The day before yesterday she'd told him about the two follicles and he hadn't really reacted, just said he was sorry. And this morning, just before she left, he'd come into the bathroom while she was putting on her makeup and gently, almost fearfully, placed his hands on her hips and softly kissed her cheek.

"I forgot to wish you good luck for today."

She replied, "Oh, thanks, but I'm not really counting on it."

He said, "I know, me neither," and for a moment it seemed like he wanted to linger, to have a conversation. She said she had to run, she wanted to get to the ultrasound early, otherwise she'd be stuck there for hours. He said, "Go on, then, and let me know what happens." She nodded, gave one last glance in the mirror, grabbed her purse from the kitchen table, and left. Eli turned on the alarm and locked the door behind them. Before getting into his SUV, which was parked next to her Peugeot in the driveway, he went over to her car and asked about the engine noise she'd heard a few days earlier.

She said, "It's nothing, it went away," and he said okay, got into his Toyota, and backed out of the drive, waving at her.

When she turned the engine on, she heard the strange chirping sound again, and for a moment she wanted to honk at Eli to stop and have a look, but she decided not to. She pulled out of the driveway and followed the Toyota. She stopped behind him at the intersection and thought that these were the moments when married life was intolerable. The moments when the attempt to speak the truth faltered along a path of little lies. And it made her sad. It saddened her most of all.

No, she wouldn't call him. She knew the ultrasound results would be an excuse for him to try and talk her out of the IVF this month. She knew he still hadn't found a solution for the eighteenth, even though he hadn't said anything. He had a crazy month at the office, with Zvika's reserve duty and a case he was working on around the clock. Yesterday he'd come home at 2 A.M. She'd heard him come in, and what was strange, she thought, was that even if he was cheating on her, which she knew he wasn't, she didn't really care.

Six months ago she'd suggested they see someone. Not therapy, she'd stressed, but counseling. She knew the word *therapy* would deter him. She'd brought it up after their fourth IVF, the one she was convinced would work because it had happened around the time of her thirty-seventh birthday. She never made a big deal out of birthdays, and in fact she always forbade Eli to throw her a party. But this time she'd allowed herself to fall into the trap of symbolism and believe in the power of dates and coincidences, because nothing else worked anyway, so why not? And that's why the disappointment had been so great, so shaking and insulting; for the first time in her life she hadn't been cynical, and during that two-week wait for the pregnancy test she'd felt calmer than usual, less tense, less hating of all those who told her to be positive because it had an effect. And then, stripped bare of her usual pessimism, she'd turned up for the blood test on the arranged date.

"You look good," said the nurse.

"Really?" Dafna said. "What do you mean? Is something different about me?"

The nurse said, "I don't know, maybe something in your skin. Did you have a facial? Your skin looks really great, kind of glowing."

When she finished the blood test and went into the bathroom, she examined her face in the fluorescent light, looking for signs of the pregnancy glow the nurse had hinted at, because of course that's what she'd meant. And yes, she thought she could see it, something soft and placated, something that definitely hadn't been there before.

She kept examining her face in the mirror on the way to the office, encouraged by the fact that even sunlight could not erase the gleam; it was not some sort of fluorescent illusion. She could see it plainly: her face was glowing. Later, in the ancient, dim toilet at the office, she even dared to calculate her estimated due date: mid-January. It would be wonderful to go through the last months of pregnancy in winter, when it wasn't too hot. But then she panicked. Thinking about dates was an old game, filed away in the archives of those first times she had tried to get pregnant. She hadn't done it for four years, so why now? How much hidden power could you attribute to a birthday and a glowing face?

But it wasn't just the skin. Toward noon she began to feel nauseated. She knew that even if she was pregnant it was too early, but Avi's Orit had told her that two days after her four embryos had been implanted, one of whom was Michael today, she'd started feeling terribly nauseated. When the girl with the sandwiches came at lunchtime and asked if she wanted her usual, an herbed omelet, Dafna looked at the basket and said, "No, not today, I don't feel like it."

The girl asked, "Something else, then?" Delighting in the nausea provoked by the sight of those sandwiches, Dafna said she'd pass. The girl said, "Have a good day, then," and placed Gabi's regular salami sandwich on his desk.

She hung around the office until two that afternoon, with the pregnancy and the glow and the nausea. She wrote a few press releases and phoned the printer, who was late again with the invitations for the seminar CUSP was organizing in Sderot. She found herself speaking to him quietly, not angrily, because it was all secondary now and even slightly amusing, in a positive, *proportional* way. That was the term that accompanied her during those hours when magic and anxiety fought it out inside her, frothing up the waters around her embryo. She knew it was as big as a grain of rice and had no water around it, but still, there was such relief in those proportions, as if someone had fitted an oxygen mask on her face after years of difficulty breathing. She was alone in the office that day. Dikla, the secretary, was on her day off, and Gabi had called to say he was going to Jerusalem to meet a foreign businessman who had promised to make a large contribution to CUSP. She was completely alone, pregnant and secretive, disgusted by the unclaimed salami sandwich, debating whether or not to throw it in the trash.

She briefly considered calling Eli to ask if he felt like having a baby boy or a girl in winter. She knew it was a boy and was oddly disappointed. A little boy. Obviously Eli's genes would be more dominant, and besides, it was better not to have a redhead in this Israeli sun. A boy with dark brown hair, almost black maybe. Yonatan, she thought. But she didn't want to call Eli. No; for now this pregnancy was hers alone. If anyone else knew, even Yonatan's father, it would topple the balance in the cosmic-mathematical equation on which that grain of sugar was now resting. She couldn't believe she was thinking in these terms, but how enormously enjoyable it was to believe! She almost understood those born-again religious types of whom she was always so derisive.

No, she wouldn't call until she heard from the nurse, and even then she'd hold out a little longer. She knew Eli was busy all day in court with the Arbel case. It was a big day for him too, and he would probably forget to call her for the results; she hoped he would, she hoped he'd let her keep her pregnancy secret for another few hours, until he got home and found her in the garden, which reminded her that they'd have to build a wall around the fish pond. She'd once read somewhere that a child could drown in even an inch of water. He would find her sitting in an armchair, sipping herbal tea, her hand on her belly, and maybe she'd tease him a little. *You forgot to call*, she'd say with a sour face, and he'd apologize and say he'd had a crazy day with the Arbel case. *So? Negative?* he'd ask, because her face would not disclose anything positive. And she'd say, *There's no Alma.* When he came closer to give her the obligatory hug, she'd grasp his hand—how long it had been since they'd held hands?—and say, *But there's a Yonatan.*

She was so certain about this pregnancy that she didn't even call the nurse exactly at two. She was busy having a friendly phone conversation with a journalist she couldn't stand, although today she thought the woman wasn't actually all that bad. She told Dafna that her son was sick and hadn't been to kindergarten for a week, some crazy virus with diarrhea and vomiting, and she was afraid the little one would get it too, which was all she needed.

"Yes," Dafna said, "that would be a drag." She asked what she was doing about it, how she prevented infection: "I heard they have an echinacea formula for kids. They say Vitamin C is good for prevention, too."

The journalist replied, "Don't make me laugh. Those things can't stand up to us."

Dafna said she had to go, she had another call; "I hope you feel better soon, all of you." When she answered her phone, she was slightly surprised to hear the nurse, who sighed and said, "Sorry, Dafna. It's negative."

When she told Eli she wanted them to see someone, he listened and nodded, and she knew the nod was a sort of refusal, and then their guests arrived—they were having people over to celebrate Eli's victory in the Arbel case—and when they left she didn't bring it up again. It seemed distant now, that evening in the backyard when she had told Eli they needed help. She had watched him standing by their state-of-the-art grill, turning over the lamb chops and steaks, urging their neighbors, Shuki and Iris, to pile more and more food on their plates. They had brought their kid with them; Iris apologized for not being able to find a babysitter. "It's really hard here on the moshav. There's not much to choose from," she said, but Dafna said it was fine, it was a last-minute invitation anyway. The boy, Yaniv, came equipped with video tapes, and Iris asked if he could sit and watch them in the living room. Dafna said sure and asked if she could give him some pretzels or something. Iris said, "Okay, but just a little." Dafna filled a plastic bowl with pretzel sticks for him, and told him not to be shy if he wanted more. His mother said, "Don't leave crumbs," and the boy said okay, without taking his eyes off the screen. He sat there all evening, watching his tapes, and every so often he came out to the yard with his doll and clung to his mother's leg or sat down by the fish pond and dipped his finger in the water. Dafna could see Eli biting his tongue. Just before midnight, when she went inside to get something from the kitchen, she found the boy asleep, curled in a ball, his bare feet in the plastic bowl and the pretzels scattered all over the couch. She felt a twinge of compassion, and now, when she remembered that evening, she shuddered; it was shortly after that, maybe a month or two, that the boy was raped.

She started her usual rounds in search of parking. Down Nachmani, onto Mazeh, up Ahad Ha'Am, left down Balfour to Melchet, left again, and down Nachmani again. She'd had to pee even when she left the ultrasound, but she'd been in a hurry to get away. She circled the block of Ahad Ha'Am for the third time, debating whether to pay for the lot on the corner. Gabi had promised to pay her back—he himself took taxis everywhere—but her receipts were still sitting in a big envelope marked DAFNA—EXPENSES on his desk, and in fact since she'd started working with him, two years ago, she hadn't had a single reimbursement.

It made Eli furious. "I don't treat my employees like that, and I'm not willing to let an employer treat my wife like that," he said. When she replied that in this context she was not his wife, and that he should stop thinking about her as his wife, he said he couldn't, and she said he was patronizing and to do her a favor and not get annoyed on her behalf, because she was perfectly capable of doing that herself.

But that evening, when she stood on the patio, leaning against the wall, and watched him huddle with Zvika and then chitchat with Shuki and Iris, she felt as if she needed a patron. Urgently. That was probably what spurred her demand, which surprised her own self, that they go to counseling. Protection—that's what she wanted from him now. Not sex, not understanding or consideration, but protection in the old-fashioned sense, in the mafioso sense. For example, she wanted him to stand by her side at the ultrasound, and when Ferber made some comment about her meager production, to grab him by the elbow and say, "Don't you dare talk to my wife like that, you piece of shit, or I'll beat the crap out of you."

Because in the treatment room she wasn't anyone's wife. She wasn't a woman at all, but a sort of prehistoric creature with trouble multiplying. A little dinosaur with faulty ovaries or a crooked womb. A dinosaur on the verge of extinction, whose body contained clusters of eggs that were slow and rotten. Her bladder was about to explode now, and she squirmed up and down in the driver's seat. She could still feel the burning sensation from the transducer that had moved around inside her an hour ago. She was angry at Gabi, who hadn't made any effort to get a parking space for her, and withheld reimbursements for all her parking expenses and the meetings with journalists in cafés, which she insisted on paying for, although she didn't dare tell Eli about those. Fuck if she was going to go to Toys"R"Us to buy the Power Ranger for Adel. Gabi would never pay her back.

And suddenly she thought she would tell Eli. She would find the right time this evening to inform him that her boss, whom he despised anyway, owed her eight hundred and thirty shekels. It was no big deal, she'd say, she was sure he'd pay her back sometime, wouldn't he? It wasn't possible that he wouldn't, was it? What do you think? she'd say, and then she'd watch Eli walk right into the trap, a pit covered with branches and leaves. She'd look at him plunge into that pit as he shouted out something like, "I can't believe it! Why didn't you tell me? How did you let it build up like that, Dafna? How?" And he'd quickly dial Gabi's number—he had it in his cell phone memory—without even asking her permission. He would represent her as if she were a client, like a lawyer, like a husband.

Trying to distract herself from the pressure on her bladder, she looked forward impatiently to the evening, to the confession, to Eli's slippered foot stepping on the bed of branches and leaves and falling right through.

"I can't understand you," he'd say, "I just can't understand you." And she'd say *Exactly*. He'd ask what she meant, and she'd say she meant exactly what she'd said: he didn't understand her—and let's be honest, Eli, you've never really tried.

He would ask—and this might be the point at which he looked around and realized he'd been trapped—where she was going with this and what she wanted. She would reply that she wasn't going anywhere, and that what she wanted was for them to recognize that they'd never loved each other, not really, not seriously, that the marriage had been a sort of scientific experiment, a hybridization between two creatures, mammal and insect, say, or rodent and bird. An experiment that had failed, of course, as evidenced by their inability to procreate. He'd say, "Bullshit, Dafna. What does that have to do with anything? I really loved you, and I still do." Then he'd whisper, "And so do you. So do you. I know it." And he'd sit there at the bottom of the pit with his knees folded up against his chest and his hands digging into the walls, ripping out roots, and he'd explain that the fertility treatments were to blame for everything. She was exhausted, that was clear, and desperate, and he understood that, and yes, it probably had taken its toll on their relationship, which was now slightly damaged. It was just scratched.

She'd stand above him, arms crossed over her chest, pushing clods of earth into the pit with her toes, and say, "No, this is not a scratch or a surface wound." Maybe she was exhausted and desperate, but something inside her had become lucid. A haze had lifted over the past seven years, and she could see it clearly now: she didn't love him.

How strange it was that not loving was so simple. Far simpler than loving. As she continued to drive around in circles she realized that her clarity did not even contain the pain it rightly should have, the pain that should have surrounded it like a halo of momentous recognition. On the contrary: there was something trivial about it, like solving a mathematical problem. It was just something you had to prove, like the formulas she remembered from high school math. Something you could draw a line under, something straight and dry and pleasant.

Something familiar, she thought, and knew she wouldn't tell Eli anything about the money Gabi owed her. What for? She had a sense of déjà vu, as if she'd already heard herself saying these same words before: "I don't love him, not really." She'd said them long ago, before they were married, but her tone then had been more dismissive. What she'd probably said back then was, "I'm not in love with him." Yes, that's what she'd said, because she had believed there was no such thing as falling in love. There was only love, and it was quiet, essential, and boring, but so what? And she'd told herself that Eli was not a man you fell in love with but a man you learned to love.

She needed to pee so badly that she decided to park in the lot on Ahad Ha'Am. When she saw the FULL sign, she burst into tears and turned left without giving right of way to the cars coming down Ahad Ha'Am. A taxi honked at her furiously, and she decided to try the lot she'd once seen on Rothschild. When she stopped at a light she was startled by a

rap on the window. Someone motioned for her to roll down her window, and she pressed the button.

"Didn't you see what you did?" the man hissed, and she realized it
was the cabby she'd cut off. Before she could apologize, before she
could tell him she hadn't been paying attention and she was sorry, the
forty-ish driver gave her a contemptuous glare, snickered, and spat out,
"Bitch!" The light changed to green and she drove away quickly.

PART THREE

MARK

Why had they named him Popeye? Yesterday he'd tried to remember but couldn't, and he'd asked Roni, who gave him a strange, pitiful look, as if his interest in family trivia were another sure sign of his old age. "I have no idea," she said and went back to her book. And another thing: lately it seemed like every time he talked to her he was disturbing her in the middle of something, even when she wasn't doing anything. When he casually asked what she was reading, his distress bursting from every pore, she replied, "A book."

"Yes, but which one?" and he went closer to the couch where she was sitting in her usual cross-legged position, her back erect—how could she read like that? To him it seemed uncomfortable, like yoga. When he saw the title, *Past Perfect*, he told her it was one of Alona's favorite books.

"Great," she said.

"But I haven't read it," he said apologetically. "I always wanted to."

"But it never worked out," she muttered, without taking her eyes off the page.

He retreated. "I think I'll take him to the vet tomorrow. Something's not right."

"Do whatever you want, Dad. You don't care what I think anyway."

He walked into the kitchen and wanted to say that he had no idea what she thought, what she really thought. He wanted her to sum up the past four years of her thoughts, maybe more. He wanted her boiling lava of adolescence to coalesce into a comprehensible form, something that would remind him of himself. He asked if she wanted coffee; he was making a fresh pot.

"Since when do I drink coffee?" she scolded.

"Sometimes you do, don't you?"

"No. Never."

He heard her open the door to the yard and hurried into the living room. "Are you going out to smoke again? You just had a cigarette."

"That was two hours ago," she said, throwing his senility at him as a way to excuse her smoking, which he thought was getting much too frequent. He made an espresso and took it out to the yard and looked at Roni sitting on the lawn, her book in one hand and a cigarette in the other. He suddenly realized he'd already seen her reading that book, a long time ago, last winter, and that in fact he kept seeing her with *Past Perfect*. He wondered if the novel had somehow become a part of her, representing something secret in her personality, some motto or sense of anguish, and he realized he had to read it now. In a couple of days, when he picked the kids up from Alona, he'd ask her for a copy; he didn't dare ask Roni. But then it occurred to him that Roni must have taken the book from Alona and he should probably buy his own.

He was sitting in a traffic jam at the Kibbutz Galuyot exit, waiting to turn right toward south Tel Aviv. He had errands to run, and although he'd planned to get up at six and leave early to avoid the traffic, he hadn't been able to wake up and had only left home at eight. He made a mental map of the streets he had to cover this morning: Salameh, Herzl, Ha'aliya. He couldn't remember if he'd seen a bookstore in that area. There was a Steimatsky on Allenby, but it would be crazy to drive there just for a book. He drove slowly along Kibbutz Galuyot and felt his gut wrench as he remembered yesterday again, and Roni, and the fight.

"How can you read like that?" he asked jokingly, sitting down on one of the old loungers left by the owners. His daughter's straight back was turned to him, and she didn't answer. "You need another hand to turn the pages," he went on, hating himself: he sounded bothersome, a dirty old man hitting on a little girl, making all sorts of friendly comments, nagging.

"I don't need another hand, I need some quiet." She put her cigarette out in the ashtray, stood up quickly, and was about to go inside, but he stopped her physically, grabbing her arm—how long had it been since he'd touched her? Years, he thought. Not since she was a little girl. He knew that couldn't be right, because obviously he'd hugged and kissed her more recently, although he couldn't remember exactly when or under what circumstances: birthdays, his and hers; before and after trips abroad, his and hers. Still, he felt as if he hadn't touched her for ages, so even though he did not like the violence in that arm-grabbing, there was something pleasant about it: her skin, the muscles tensing under his touch.

"What's the matter with you?" she asked, staring at him with his ex-wife's eyes. "What's going on with you lately? Is something bothering you? You're acting a little weird, Dad, you know?"

"Me?" A hoarse laugh escaped his throat. "*I'm* acting weird?"

He could feel the big fight, the one they'd never had, the fight that had been simmering for years like a slow, spicy stew, "the fight you've never had with your daughter because you're a coward," Alona had said. He could feel it landing with a thud at their feet and begging to be fought, begging them to get it over with already. He almost wanted to say to this girl, whose mother's eyes were now piercing holes in him, Let's fight, Roni. But he said, "If you really want to know what's bothering me, I'll tell you." He watched her gaze change from hatred to surprise. She hadn't expected him to answer her at all. "It bothers me that for a long time now I have had no idea what's going on with you."

"There's nothing going on with me," she said, trying to divert the missile.

"Yes, there is, and you know it."

Her nights, for example. He had no idea what she did at night. He said he knew from Alona that last week she'd come home at 2 A.M. When was that, Monday? And there were other times, he couldn't remember when, but there were.

"So she's snitching on me about when I get home?" Roni hissed.

"No, she's not snitching, but I ask, so she tells me."

"Oh, you ask. So you don't trust me."

He said he did trust her, of course he did, but he asked because he wanted to know, because it interested him, because he was still her father, after all.

She said she knew that: he didn't miss an opportunity to remind her.

"And besides, these moods, and the mysteriousness, and the lies, Roni, that's what drives me crazy. If you want to go out partying, go ahead, no one's going to stop you; just don't lie." Before she could even deny it, he said, "Yes, you do lie. Because you can't be hanging out with your girlfriends until 2 A.M. And by the way, I don't know exactly who these friends are who you're spending time in Tel Aviv with. Shiri? Is Shiri allowed to hang out in Tel Aviv until the early hours of the morning? And how do you get home, Roni? Do you hitchhike?"

"No, Dad, I don't hitchhike."

But he wasn't listening. The hitchhiking was a distraction, a footnote; he wanted to get to the real thing: drugs. He knew that was it, but he couldn't say it. He knew he would not be able to withstand her stunned, betrayed look, a look that was gathering steam for something, he didn't know what, but something dangerous. He had no doubt about it. She was smoking weed, he'd already drawn that out of her last summer. He tried to be as liberal as possible. The cigarettes, for example. He didn't know any other parents who let their kids smoke at home, right in front of their faces, from age fifteen—fourteen really. He remembered the first time she'd nonchalantly pulled out a cigarette in front of him, two and a half years ago, shortly before the separation from Alona, after a family dinner in the backyard.

What had outraged him even more was that Alona had bummed a cigarette from his daughter's pack, which sat on the table like a deck of cards. Later, in bed, he said to his wife, "You knew? You knew she smoked?"

"She doesn't really smoke, just here and there."

"But she has her own pack!"

"Let it go. You can't do anything about it and you shouldn't pressure her. Why should she have to hide?" Alona told him she'd hidden her smoking from her parents for years and hated them for it. Although, she added, she hated them in general, even though you couldn't ever hate her dad, which was exactly the problem.

"Yes, but do you really think I should let a fourteen-year-old girl smoke at home?"

"Yes."

"We'll see. I have to think about it." But he knew he didn't want to be that kind of parent, the kind who sets limits and forbids things and provokes hatred. He wanted to be an open, tolerant, beloved parent. Not out of some philosophy, but because he wanted to prevent a greater disaster, like drugs or God knows what. But now he regretted his liberalism, because the fact was that it had led exactly to what he'd been trying to avoid. Strange, he thought, how he'd never hated his own parents. Not really. He'd never hated anyone, in fact, which had always seemed like a good thing. But now, with the sparks of his daughter's hatred flying around him, leaving miniature burn marks on his skin, he thought maybe he'd been wrong, and that by never hating anyone, especially not his parents, he had lost out on something, not developed properly, and become crippled.

He let go of Roni's arm and sighed, and although he sounded old again he no longer cared. He didn't want to be her friend now. He couldn't be her friend if he was going to save her from drugs. And of course that's what it was. There was no doubt. Despite Alona's efforts to reassure him—"It's not drugs; Roni's not a girl who does drugs"—he couldn't find any other explanation for her disappearances, and the secrecy, and the crazy moods. It wasn't just adolescent moodiness, it was something else, something deeper and darker, maybe chemical. He didn't want to know, he thought now as he watched her sit down on the lawn again and pull another cigarette out to make him angry. He didn't want to know but he had to.

"I'm worried about you," he said, trying a different approach. "I'm just worried."

She turned to look at him and her face was streaked with tears. How long had it been since he'd seen her cry? Maybe three years. The sobbing attacks of twelve and thirteen had disappeared long ago, replaced by a quiet hostility, and now that he saw her crying, he missed those tears, the way she used to shut herself up in her room, the big fights. Because then at least she had communicated with him honestly. It was like a cheap melodrama, but it was still communication.

She wiped her tears away with her sleeve; she was wearing one of those big, faded, long-sleeved shirts she loved so much, which did not flatter her. And she had such a nice body. "Do me a favor, don't worry about me, okay? If you really love me then don't worry about me. That's all. That's all I ask. It's not a lot."

"It is a lot, and I can't."

"Then that's your problem," she said, and sniveled.

"No." He gave in to the moderate tone that his voice had suddenly taken on. "It's not my problem, it's our problem."

"Why? Are we married?"

"Yes. In some sense we are."

"Then let's get divorced. You're used to that, aren't you? Let's get divorced already."

He looked away to the fruit trees that bordered the yard: red guava, peach, two avocado trees whose leaves had inexplicably blackened, and a few spindly citrus, all victims of his neglect. He always forgot to water then. Roni suddenly got up and looked at him, her eyes dry and her face red. Alona was right, he thought, the girl has amazing skin. He'd never understood why Alona had envied her skin but now he got it. It not only glowed, it spoke. That skin spoke in a language he no longer understood, the eager language of children. She took two steps toward him, looked at him from above, and said, "I just want to tell you one thing, Dad. A piece of friendly advice, okay?"

"Okay," he said, encouraged by her change of tone, by the warmth that perhaps signaled a breakthrough.

"With me you've blown your chance. But with Maya and Ido you may still have a shot, so don't ruin it." She turned and went inside, and although she didn't shut the big glass door behind her, he felt as if it had shattered, as if the dozens of little square panes of glass had cracked into shards and crashed like a huge waterfall on the stone floor.

He began his search for a parking spot. He wanted to drop by the chefs' supply store to look at some pasta makers. His two manual machines could no longer handle the workload, and they were generally annoying. He'd read an article about pasta machines in an American magazine and wanted to find out which brands were exported to Israel. He also planned to stop at the spice store and also the cheese shop, to check out their Parmigiano Reggiano. The stock he'd brought from Italy was almost finished, and although he was suspicious of the cheeses they sent to Israel, he had no choice. He couldn't afford another trip in the next few months, now that the Trattoria was full.

Once a month he spent a morning in south Tel Aviv, and he both loved and hated these times. He hated them because life in Eden had taken him away from the crowds and the dirt and the noise, and the search for parking, a procedure he had never excelled at. But he also loved and looked forward to these monthly excursions because they made him forget Eden and his life as a bourgeois imposter—perhaps no longer an imposter, he thought with some alarm. It scared him to think about his life as the owner of a restaurant that had started out as a fantasy and turned into a promising reality, if also a nightmarish one: he would need at least another two years, two good years, to pay back his brothers and the bank, which he would, of course. He found himself distractedly pulling into a lot that charged twenty shekels an hour.

When he left the lot and started walking to the chefs' store, he tried to shake off the crumbs of distress that had stuck to him on the way there, telling himself that the parking question was settled—so what if Alona would never park in a paid lot, on principle, instead spending hours looking for parking on the side streets, if only to prove that she could?—now he could really enjoy this free, early autumn morning of rambling. He liked rambling. Or not rambling so much as walking. Walking quickly from one point to the next, like in Eden, from home to the restaurant, from home to the pool, through the field and the woods and the dirt paths. Rambling was something completely different, brave and amorphous, not for him.

Alona was a pro at rambling, as were Jane and Roni. You could drop the three of them from a helicopter into the heart of a labyrinthine foreign city, and like three windup dolls they would start to wander around in a trance. Would they each head in a different direction? He amused himself with this little riddle. Alona would head to the bookstores and cafés. Jane—although he had to admit he no longer knew her that well, not the middle-aged Jane—to the galleries and museums and New Age stores with their crystals and candles and beads. And Roni—where would Roni go?

He remembered yesterday again, how he'd kept sitting on the lounger for a long time after Roni had gone inside, until he heard the front door slam shut. Then he hurried in and found a note on the kitchen table in her wild handwriting: *Gone to Shiri to study for a history test.* He'd thought of calling her to demand that she come back immediately, because they hadn't finished fighting. It's not that he wanted to fight but

he felt it was his duty as a parent to iron out this issue. *Iron out*: another
term used by parents, he thought now, as he stood outside the chefs'
supply store and discovered it only opened at ten; he had half an hour
to kill. But he hadn't done anything. Nothing. When she came home in
the evening, he asked if she'd had dinner. He was making lasagna. She
said she'd already eaten and went to her room. A few minutes later she
emerged and said she would spend the night at Alona's. "But why?"
Mark asked. She usually slept at his place on the nights when he didn't
have the kids and the restaurant was closed, so as not to leave him completely alone; it was their unspoken agreement. "Is it because you're
mad at me?" he asked as she stood facing him, her backpack slung over
her shoulder. "Are you doing it out of spite?" He hated himself for the
pleading tone.

"No, it's not spite. I just don't feel like being here tonight. I want to
be with myself."

"You can be with yourself here. I won't get in your way." He could
feel every word digging him another inch deeper into the pit.

"Look, Dad, what do you want from me? Do you want me to stay?"

He wanted to say, *Yes, stay*, but he said, "No, if you feel like going
to Alona's, then go. Do you want a ride?"

She smiled. Since when did he give her a ride two blocks over to
Alona's? "It's a two-minute walk, come on."

"Okay."

They both looked at Popeye, who had sat down between them,
waiting.

"You're staying here, my poor thing," she said, and for a moment
Mark felt as if she were talking to him. "You can't come with me, okay,
sweetie pie?"

The dog whimpered and Roni petted him, and suddenly his head
started rocking back and forth and he made a gargling sound.

"Oh, no, not again," Mark said.

"Wait, maybe it's nothing."

But the dog vomited on the floor, as he had done yesterday and the
day before, as he had done almost every day for the past two weeks.

"He must have had too much to eat," Roni said. She put her backpack
on the floor and brought some paper towels from the kitchen to clean up
the yellowish puddle, trying to eliminate the evidence of his disease. But

Mark knew Popeye hadn't eaten too much, because the dog had spent the day by his side, like a shadow or an elderly charge, and in fact he'd barely eaten a thing. In the morning, when Roni was at school, he'd vomited twice on the deck outside the Trattoria, but Mark hadn't told her.

Now he debated whether to wait outside the store or pop over to the spice shop and come back later. It annoyed him that a store in the south of the city allowed itself to act like some boutique in the northern suburbs and only open at ten. He wished there were a café nearby, where he could spend the next twenty-five minutes, or a bench or a fence to sit on. The spice and cheese shops were a ten-minute walk away, but he was too lazy to go and come back and decided to wait in the doorway. His sense of freedom, which had been deficient in any case, went completely haywire when he remembered that he had to take Popeye to the vet in the afternoon. If he didn't go today he would have to put it off until next week, since the vet wouldn't be at work tomorrow, and the day after that he had the kids. He had to go today, which meant he had to finish all his errands by two, at the latest, so he could get back and pick up the dog before four. Popeye. Why had they even called him Popeye?

Jane would remember, he was sure, but he didn't want to phone just to ask her that. He'd wait for their monthly conversation, in a couple of weeks. He might also tell her about the big fight with Roni, even though it hadn't really materialized. Or had it? It didn't really make any difference anymore, because her final words wouldn't let him go. They had cast a spell on him. He didn't know which part troubled him more, *With me you've blown your chance* or *With Maya and Ido you still have a shot, so don't ruin it.* They were both equally menacing.

At night, before going to sleep, he hadn't been able to resist calling Alona to ask how Roni was. He told her they'd had a little fight. Alona said she was fine, she'd gone to sleep early and they'd actually had a fun evening with the kids. "She's great with them, you know?" Mark said he did, and Alona told him that Roni had built a tent for the children in the living room: "An awesome tent, not like the ones I build them. She really put her heart into it. And the three of them sat in the tent until ten, and she read them stories."

"Sounds nice."

"You should see the living room, it looks like a Bedouin encampment. The kids made me swear I wouldn't take it apart *ever*."

"What did you say?" he asked, feeling a bit like a parasite attaching itself to the fur of a large family beast, his family, two blocks away, in a nicer, smaller house, one much happier than his own.

"I said okay; what could I say? I'll leave it for a couple of days until they get sick of it. So, you finally fought?"

"A little." He was afraid to disappoint her, so he changed the topic and asked how Ido was. He thought the boy had been acting a little strange since the break-in, quieter than usual, frightened.

"He seems fine. I don't know." Then she said she was tired, it was already midnight. "Are you going to sleep?"

"Soon."

They hung up and he got into bed and felt a little calmer. Ido was fine, Roni was fine. But he was angry: How could she have spent such a pleasant evening after their tempestuous, crushing afternoon? Yes, that's what it had been. Because after she'd left he'd found himself roaming the house, walking from room to room without daring to touch anything, just sniffing around like a dog, searching for something. Popeye had padded along behind him for a while, until Mark went out to the yard and sat down on the lounger again. A criminal always returns to the scene of the crime, but he felt like a rape victim returning to the scene of his assault. She *had* battered him, he thought, with that vicious line. He tried to distract himself by thinking about other things, like the lasagna, which he could bake or just keep in the fridge, and the computer system he might need to get for his watering system. A thousand shekels and he could have a flourishing yard and a clear conscience.

Brutus and Olive came back from their nocturnal foray through the fields and rubbed up against each other and against his legs. Then they went over to their big water dish, drank thirstily, and sprawled out on the stone floor, far from him and from the sick Labrador resting his snout on Mark's thigh. He sat like that for a long time, staring at the place on the lawn where his daughter had sat, and thought that if life were a science-fiction movie the lawn would have turned yellow in that exact spot, or maybe it would have suddenly glowed and fluoresced, millions of fireflies flying above it. He sat there until he grew too cold and too sad, and then he went inside, waited for Popeye to follow him, and left the other two dogs outside. He put his mug in the sink and the lasagna in the fridge.

He'd made it for Roni. It was her favorite dish, or at least it used to be. He had no idea what she liked now. When she'd gone to Shiri's in the afternoon, leaving him with the note, he'd decided to mend the damages of the fight that had or had not been fought—it didn't matter anymore—with a spinach and mushroom lasagna. The cooking passed the time until she came home to puncture his fantasy of a father-daughter reconciliation dinner by announcing that she was going to Alona's. That she wanted to be with herself.

He glanced at the clock. Ten minutes to ten. He leaned on the building wall, tired of holding his face up to the window in search of pasta machines and remembered what Alona had told him roughly a year ago, when Roni started disappearing at nights and he said it was driving him crazy and he didn't know what to do. "She's playing power games with me, Alona. She's doing this to me on purpose."

"You treat her like she's a spouse, another woman in your life, another woman who hurts you, who doesn't understand you and doesn't want to be in a symbiotic relationship with you. That's how you talk about her. Not like a daughter."

He had strongly protested at the time, but over the last year, especially this morning, he felt that she might be right, as usual. And that was also part of the thing, the separation. He didn't want a woman who was always right. He wanted someone who made mistakes. "A human woman," he'd hurled at her once when they'd fought, and she'd shot right back: "A woman who's right is human, too." She was right: with women, all the women in his life, he only knew how to speak one language, a sort of Esperanto of his love life, the language of hurt. When he told Roni yesterday that he was worried about her, even when he tried to set parental limits—but how unskillfully, he realized now with self-derision—even then it was obvious that he saw her as the strong one, as the one who had to do something to mend things. Not him.

He was shaken out of his reflections by a young man who walked up to him and said, "May I?" and held up a ring of keys. Apparently Mark had been leaning on the front door. When the young man opened it, he said, "Good morning, sorry for the wait," even though it was exactly ten. Mark said he wasn't waiting long and walked into the store, which looked completely different from the inside: smaller, the stock less promising than it had seemed through the glass. He was overcome again by the fearsadness that had accompanied him these last few weeks, quiet and loyal, like Popeye, like the symptom of a possible illness that might be terminal and was surfacing day by day as not merely a possibility but a fact.

He looked at the pasta machines and listened to the clerk's explanations. He was very courteous and seemed trustworthy when he recommended the simpler, cheaper model. But Mark had lost interest in the machines and was impatient to be on his way to the spice shop, where at least he knew exactly what he wanted. He thanked the sales clerk and asked if there was a catalog he could take. The clerk went over to the table in the back of the store and took a brochure out of the drawer. Mark thanked him, folded the brochure, and shoved it in the back pocket of his pants, the ones Roni had bought him for his birthday last year. This past birthday, which they'd celebrated three weeks ago with a dinner at Alona's, she hadn't given him anything. She said she hadn't had time because the gift she was planning was slightly complicated, and she promised he'd have it within a week, at most. He said she didn't need to get him anything, and she said, "No way, of course I do, you're my dad!" Now it seemed to him that even that statement had concealed a meanness. But three weeks had gone by; she must have forgotten.

This morning, when he'd been about to put on the jeans he'd worn yesterday, he changed his mind and reached into the bottom of the closet for the bag with the pants Roni had bought him last year. They were too long and he'd been meaning to get them altered all year. Every so often Roni would scold him for taking so long to get them fixed, insinuating that maybe he didn't like them. He said he loved them, but every time he went to Tel Aviv he forgot to take them. "Then put them in the car," she suggested, and he said that was a good idea, but he forgot again. She really had chosen a pair that was just his taste: faded-blue cargo pants, kibbutz style, in soft, prewashed cotton. Yet they'd sat in his closet for a whole year, folded in the bag. But this morning, when he got dressed, he stood in the room in his underwear, held the new pants up against his body, looked at himself in the mirror, and thought that although they were definitely too long he wanted to wear them. It felt almost urgent that he wear them, as if yesterday's fight and her abandonment and worse—her sitting in the tent with her little brother and sister, hiding from him, retreating into a new childhood of her own invention—all these aroused in him a desire to be close to her, physically. Not to make peace, because he wasn't angry at her—she was the one who was angry—but because he didn't want to part with her, and he knew that when he saw her this afternoon they would be separated, like Alona and him but much more. He put the pants on and folded the cuffs up twice, and although he looked a little ridiculous and childish, he walked out of the house wearing his gift, wearing something she had or had not deliberated over in a store—and if he knew her, she hadn't at all. He was wearing his daughter, just a little. The daughter who maybe hadn't hated him, at least for that one moment when she'd picked out these pants.

He went to the cheese shop, where he ended up buying ten pounds of Parmigiano Reggiano at an exorbitant forty-two dollars a pound, and his mood began to improve. A haze seemed to lift and he could breathe easier, and he told himself that if he knew his daughter, she'd long ago forgotten about yesterday; for her the whole incident had been just a nuisance, not anything fateful. It occurred to him that maybe he should learn to approach it that way too, as a passing unpleasantness. Ma'ayan, Alona's close friend, used to phone almost every day to report on some catastrophic fight with her older daughter when she was seventeen, and now with the younger one, at thirteen. He used to feel sorry for her and think how lucky he was not to have these problems with Roni, with whom he had a relationship of mutual respect, freedom, and understanding. But now he envied Ma'ayan. He envied all those who took it lightly, blaming the kids and not themselves.

Perhaps that was what he should do, he thought, as he walked back to the car. Perhaps he should learn to take things lightly, otherwise how would he survive? He remembered one particularly annoying conversation with Ma'ayan. He could never stand her, and couldn't understand what Alona saw in her. She was too simple for Alona. "Yes, she's uncomplicated, and that's exactly what I like about her," Alona explained. He'd once cooked dinner for Ma'ayan's fortieth birthday, three years ago, and that evening they had a big argument about Ido's sleeping problems.

Ido was eight or nine months old at the time and refused to fall asleep in his crib, so they had to put him to sleep in their arms and then carefully lower him into the crib. As he walked down Herzl Street and thought back to that time, he could almost feel baby Ido's body in his hands, with his doll-like limbs, which despite their sleepy softness became suspiciously tense the moment they bent to lay him down. It was a sort of threat, a rigid message that the babyish body was trying to transmit to his parents: you can't put one over on me. And he would wake up every hour or two, screaming, and refuse to fall asleep again until he was taken out of his prison and carried around, insulted and righteous, his eyes wide open in a troubled, suspicious gaze, until exhaustion defeated him and he fell asleep again. Then they'd carefully put him back in his crib and he'd wake up again, and the whole thing would start over.

Alona was close to her breaking point. It had been different with Maya. She'd stopped breast-feeding at five months, and there was a one-week weaning crisis, and then Maya would fall asleep easily in her crib and sleep the whole night through. Roni had been like that too, although when she moved to the States with her mother they had a difficult year, with nightmares. But Jane, unlike Alona, did not view sleepless nights as armed robbery. With Ido, Alona crumbled, and to Mark's chagrin she asked Ma'ayan for advice. "Save us!" she said to her during that dinner. "We'll do anything!"

Ma'ayan, who had four children and was considered a supreme authority in their household, at least by Alona, suggested a method that would solve the problem in a few days. "If you can tolerate it," she added mysteriously, and exchanged a look with Lior, her husband, who sighed, scoffed, and said, "They won't, Ma'ayan, come on. They're not built for that." Then Ma'ayan laid out the main tenets of the five-minute method: "You put him in bed awake, never when he's already asleep. You say 'Good night, sweetie, Mommy and Daddy are in the other room,' you give him a kiss, and you walk out. He screams, of course, but you don't go into his room. You sit with a watch and time five minutes—and it's hard, I'm warning you. Those five minutes are an eternity when the kid is screaming in the other room. But you don't go back in until exactly five minutes have passed, and then you go in and say calmly—you have to fake it but there's no other way—'Sweetie, you have to go to sleep now. Mommy and Daddy also have to go to sleep. Good night.' And again, five minutes."

"And all that time he's screaming?" Alona asked.

"For the first week, probably, yes," Ma'ayan replied indifferently.

"With Sivan it took a week. With Adi—how long, Lior? A little longer. Maybe ten days. And with the boys it was a piece of cake. Trust me: if you're consistent, your problem is solved in two weeks, tops."

Alona said she would try, but Mark protested. "What are you talking about? That's not educating, that's training. Breaking. How can you do something like that to a child? It leaves scars for life."

Ma'ayan laughed and asked if he thought her kids were scarred.

He thought about her four children, who seemed normal and happy, and said, "Not all scars are visible."

"Be my guest then, Mark. Don't sleep for two years."

Alona insisted. "No, no, we'll try it. We'll try it tonight, after you leave."

The moment she said that, as if he'd heard the conversation, Ido woke up screaming. Ma'ayan said, "Well, do it now. What do you say? Try it now while Lior and I are here to give you support."

Mark said they didn't need support, and Alona said, "Yes, we do." When she saw him get up and head to the kids' room, she said, "Come on, don't go in there. Mark, don't go." But he walked defiantly to the room and came back to the dinner table with Ido in his arms, ignoring Ma'ayan's preaching about how they were making a mistake.

After they left, he said, "I'm shocked by your friend's behavior."

"Shocked?" Alona said. She threatened that from now on he would get up at night and only he, because if he wasn't willing at least to give the method a chance, she saw herself absolved of having to get up. As if by the wave of a magic wand, Ido woke up again. "There you go," Alona said, and withdrew to the bedroom. Without answering, he went to the kids' room, picked up Ido, and sat with him on the living room couch for a long time, even after he'd fallen asleep, looking at his almost-tranquil face, stroking his chubby thighs. Ido's hands were clenched into tiny fists that said, *I'm not letting go even when I'm asleep*, and Mark felt as if he were entering a secret pact with the child against the world, against Ma'ayan and Lior and against Alona, who didn't understand them. *We'll show them*, he thought, and almost fell asleep himself. He put the baby back in his crib and got into bed. Alona was sleeping deeply, so tired she'd fallen asleep on her back with her arms to the sides, legs spread, mouth slightly agape, like the caricature of an exhausted mother. Mark fell asleep with surprising ease, considering how angry he still was. Before he'd had kids he was incapable of falling asleep when he was in a bad mood.

When Ido woke up again, at four in the morning, he waited a minute to see if Alona would get up. "Mark," she muttered and rolled over onto her stomach. He got up.

He kept it up for two days and then announced that as far as he was concerned she could start using Ma'ayan's Nazi method, but he wasn't going to be a part of it. He was absolutely unwilling to sit there with a stopwatch while the kid screamed. "What if he wakes up Maya? What about Maya? Did you think about her? And Roni? She has to get up for school, you know." Alona said Maya wouldn't wake up, and Roni slept with her door closed anyway, and it wouldn't be the end of the world if she didn't sleep well for a few nights.

For the next three nights, Alona tried the method. She sat outside and chain-smoked, staring at the hands on the watch. Mark would walk by, carry a plate or a glass to the sink, pace back and forth on the lawn, or pretend to read the paper and wait for the five minutes to be up. Then he'd hear Alona go into the room and order the boy, in a tone whose sweetness sounded explosive, "Sleep, Ido. Go to sleep, sweetie. Mommy and Daddy are in the other room." She'd leave, and after a moment of silence the screams would come, and again Alona would sit with the watch. But he didn't say a word. He let her stew in her own nightly juices of desperation and exhaustion. "I can't take it," she cried on the phone to Ma'ayan, "It's heartbreaking. And Mark isn't cooperating." Not only was he not angry at her for blaming him, he was happy to give her the excuse she needed to stop this cruelty. Ido made their lives miserable for another six months, until he learned how to fall asleep on his own and stopped waking up at night, just like that, without any method.

It was strange to miss that terrible period now, which in retrospect did not seem so terrible after all. Those white nights had enveloped Alona and him in an intimacy that, granted, had contained some hostility, but today the hostility was gone while the intimacy had morphed into something businesslike, practiced, and painfully friendly.

They still argued about everything to do with the children. Like Ido, for example. Mark thought the boy had recently experienced an intellectual growth spurt. In the past few weeks he had asked lots of questions; everything interested him, good and bad, right and wrong, and he wanted definitions, like, what is a thief? Why is stealing bad? And what happens to someone who steals? Does he get punished? Do they kill him? All this must have been because of the burglary.

A few days ago Mark had spent the afternoon alone with Ido. Maya was playing with a friend from kindergarten, and Mark took Ido to the restaurant to wait for his produce supplier. They sat outside on the deck. Ido was wearing his sweatshirt. Last year, they'd had to fight with him to put away his summer clothes and switch to winter clothes, but this year he'd shown remarkable maturity and had even asked Mark to put on his sweatshirt, " 'Cause it's a little cold outside, Dad, isn't it? Aren't you cold?"

He made Ido some hot chocolate with whipped cream and put a slice of tiramisu on a plate for him. "Try it," he said, even though he knew Ido found the coffee flavor bitter. "Try it, maybe you'll like it now."

Ido shoveled a teaspoon of cake into his mouth and nodded gravely. "It's tasty, Dad. I like it now. You were right." But he put the spoon down and did not eat any more.

"So you don't really like it, hey?" Mark said, and caressed the boy's soft, velvety hair.

"I like it, but I don't think I'm hungry now."

Mark said, "Well, maybe you'll be hungry later."

Ido nodded very seriously and said, "Yes, I think I'll be hungry later."

They sat waiting for the supplier and Ido asked if he was a good man or a bad man. "A good man. Why do you ask?" Mark replied.

"Because once you said he was a thief."

"Oh, that was just a joke." He looked at his son huddled in his sweatshirt, which was a little too big, looking up at the sky, and wanted to ask him what he was thinking about. If it was hard to keep quiet with adults, he thought, keeping quiet with children was almost impossible. It was as if you were abandoning them to their loneliness. "What are you thinking about?"

"I'm thinking about the thieves."

"Oh, them again?"

"Yes. I think maybe they're not bad men. Maybe they came into our house and stole Mommy's car to save someone."

"To save someone?" Mark asked in a bemused tone.

"Yes." Ido's eyes lit up. "Maybe they needed the car to save their child, maybe he was sick and they had to take him to the hospital."

"Then why didn't they call an ambulance?"

"I don't know."

"Maybe they did but it didn't come. Or maybe the ambulance had a flat tire."

"Yes. That's what happened. The ambulance drove over a nail, like you did once, and we had a flat tire."

"So they took Mommy's car to save their child." Alona would have been psychoanalyzing the conversation, but not him. He was just planning to enjoy it, to get as excited as his son was. "So why did they pick Mommy's car?"

Ido contemplated for a moment. "Because they saw there were toys in it, and they thought their child would be happy to have toys on the way to the hospital, so he wouldn't get bored."

"Oh, that's a good idea. I hadn't thought of that."

"Yes," Ido said, flattered. "I thought of that."

Mark looked at the boy's profile lit up in pink, the setting sun's rays playing like fingers in his black hair. He asked Ido if he wasn't mad at the men for coming into their house like that and stealing their car.

"I'm not mad. But Mommy is. And Maya is too, a little. Are you mad?"

"A little. I'm a little mad. I think what they did was wrong. You have to ask permission. Maybe if they'd knocked on the door and asked permission from Mommy, she would have let them have the car, on condition they brought it back. What do you think?"

"No, she wouldn't let them." Ido shook his head heavily. "She won't let me have things I ask for either."

"Really? Like what?"

"All kinds." His voice suddenly turned quiet.

"Come on, like what? Tell me. Maybe I can ask her and she'll agree."

But Ido shrugged his shoulders and whispered that he didn't remember. He picked up the teaspoon and took some more cake. He touched the spoon to the tip of his tongue and said, "I don't like it."

• • •

In the evening, after he put the kids to bed, Mark called Alona to report
on how they'd spent the afternoon, as he always did. She was on another
call for a long time, and he wondered who she was talking to this late—
probably Ma'ayan. When he finally got through, he told her with
amusement about his conversation with Ido. "Look how grown up he's
become all of a sudden, hasn't he? And he's so cute, trying to find excuses
for the thieves as if he just can't tolerate the idea that there's evil in the
world."

But Alona didn't find it amusing. She was in a bad mood. The writer
Uri Breutner was driving her crazy, getting under her skin like a parasite, she said; that's why she'd been on the other line. "For an hour and
forty minutes, Mark! And I don't like this whole thing with Ido. It seems
a little odd to me."

"What's odd about it?"

"I don't know, and I can't deal with it now; Uri is driving me up the
wall. He has no boundaries, that guy."

"What is it now?"

"He stopped going to therapy because he claims he can't afford it.
So apparently he's decided to use me as a replacement. He has issues
with his ex. They got back together, and this weekend he's moving in
with her in Ramat Ha'Hayal, and he's a little hysterical about it. But
forget that, Mark, it's not interesting."

"I feel like punching him."

"Yeah, me too."

"When is this fucking book coming out already?"

"In two months, and we still don't have a title."

He tried to cheer her up. "Two months from now, you'll be free."

"Yeah, right. That's when my troubles will really start. There'll be
reviews, and publicity, and if I know him he'll probably call me every five
minutes to find out how many books have sold. I'm stuck with him for at
least another year. He's a desperate puppy, but what can I do, he's brilliant." Then her voice grew quiet and serious. "Mark, I'm really cracking.
It's like I have a third child, you know?"

"But much less cute."

"Much, *much* less cute."

Mark thought she was about to cry. Alona almost never cried. "And
you love him much less."

"I hate him."

He waited for the tears. He hoped for the tears, so he could cheer her up, but instead of a snivel and a cracking voice, he heard a large, whalelike yawn. "I'm beat," she said.

Before they hung up she said she wanted to talk to him about Ido. Something was going on with him lately and she wasn't sure what. Mark protested, trying not to annoy her too much, and said he thought Ido was fantastic lately, that he was growing up. "He didn't even argue when I put his sweatshirt on, you know? He suggested it himself."

"Really? Well, then, that just proves what I was saying."

Mark put his shopping in the trunk and considered a trip to the fabric store someone had once told him about, which was supposed to be around here, on Herzl Street. He could buy new tablecloths for the restaurant to replace the red-and-white checkered ones. But he didn't know exactly where the store was and the tablecloths he had now were cool, according to Roni. "Retro," she'd called them.

When he'd asked what was retro about them, she said she wasn't sure; they reminded her of something but she didn't know exactly what, maybe something from a previous life, another incarnation. He asked since when she believed in reincarnation: "Don't tell me you're becoming like your mom."

"I'm not," she replied, "I don't believe in this incarnation either," and the fearsadness came back again, landing like a hairy beast on his shoulder. Obviously she was joking, she hadn't really meant it, but now he thought maybe he was missing something, some hidden but important element, that maybe he really was a very bad parent, negligent.

When he started the car he promised himself that today, after he got home from the vet, he would confront her, really confront her, sit her down to eat the lasagna and find out what she meant when she'd said he'd lost his chance with her. "What did you mean, Roni?" he'd ask. No, he swore now: he wouldn't ask—he would demand to know exactly what she'd meant.

RONI

You crack me like a code.
   A secret code.
   And I am hard to crack, and soft, and I am what?
   And who?
   And you?
   How will I crack you?

Bella, the math teacher, looked at her and smiled. Roni no longer had to pretend to be concentrating on the material or copying exercises into her notebook, because she didn't have a notebook, and Bella knew it. They'd already had the talk last year, in the tenth grade. Ziva, the principal, Bella, her dad, and herself had sat in Ziva's office, which always smelled like dust and tea, on a very rainy evening. There was a small space heater by the principal's feet. She'd invited them to discuss Roni's huge deficiency in math, which had started in the States in elementary school and had followed her to Israel. They simply had to do something about it, because otherwise she wouldn't be able to take her matriculation exams, not even at the minimal level.

"I was also bad at math," her dad said. He always did that kind of thing, made all sorts of stupid comments because he hated silences. "She probably inherited it from me. And truth be told, from her mother, too. Isn't that so, Roni?" He had a zit on the right side of his forehead. "Mom can't add or subtract without a calculator."

"Or even with one," Roni said. He laughed, and Ziva and Bella laughed, and they seemed to be laughing at the zit and it embarrassed her. It was one thing to go to the principal's office with her dad—it wasn't the first time, they'd had a million talks like these. But that pimple! Since when did men in their forties get zits?

"Anyway," Ziva said, and glanced at Bella. It was precisely because she was always so nice and considerate that Roni couldn't stand the math teacher, who seemed like she was trying to be a bit of a mother to her, a substitute for the spaced-out, bad-at-math mother who had just let her leave, who had abandoned her, which was obviously what all the teachers and the principal thought, because otherwise how could you explain the way they were so considerate of her in a school that was relatively strict, where at least five students got thrown out almost every year? She was hoping they'd kick her out too, because she could work during the days and get a GED in the evenings, and she'd be free and she could make enough money to get a car and live with roommates in an apartment in Tel Aviv, near him.

But no. Everyone was considerate of her. All the time. "They love you, Roni," her dad said smugly whenever they left those talks, which always ended with, "So let's see how we can meet you halfway, Roni. Help us meet you halfway, okay?" But she didn't want them to love her, she didn't need their faked love, certainly not now that she had real love, crazy love, love that Ziva and Bella and her father had obviously never experienced—that they just weren't built for.

This particular meeting ended with Bella and Ziva recommending that she get a math tutor and handing her a list with phone numbers of three *wonderful* tutors with *proven* success, one of whom even lived near Eden. That evening, after she got home with her dad, she went to see Uri.

She'd arranged ahead of time to get a ride with Erez, Eilon's older brother, who worked as a security guard at a restaurant in central Tel Aviv. She told her father she was going to a party for a friend in the twelfth grade who was starting his army service, and he asked since when did she have friends in the twelfth grade? "I thought you didn't like the guys from school. When are you coming home? And who else is going?"

When she finally got to Uri's it was pouring, which made her happy:

it had been raining the first time. She told him about the talk with the principal. "Apparently I have unfulfilled potential," she said.

He peeled off her jacket and sweatshirt. "I have unfulfilled potential, too. Feel it." And they had one of their most amazing nights together, doing it three times, until the whole day seemed to melt away: school, the principal's office, her father (who had phoned one of the tutors from the list on their way home, but he wasn't available, thank God); it was all erased as if each time wiped out a few hours, maybe days, maybe years. Afterward, on the way home, she sat huddled on the cold back seat of the bus, which she'd almost missed because Uri kept pulling her back in for another kiss every time she tried to walk out the door.

"It's already eleven-twenty," she'd said, trying to leave.

"I don't believe it—look! I have another hard-on! What did you do?" She'd never felt the way she felt at that moment by the door. It was as if she'd acquired superhuman strength, as if in an instant she'd become the person she'd always wanted to be. Uri said, "Don't leave me like this. But you have to run, I know." He added, "I'll walk you to a cab," because he always did, and he was about to pull his clothes on and go downstairs with her but she unzipped her pants and pulled them down and grabbed Uri, who was in his underwear, and they did it while she leaned against the wall, like in *Last Tango* but without the alienation. In fact, it was the first time he told her, when he was inside her, with her legs wrapped around his waist, that he loved her.

"I love you so much," he said, and only when she heard him say those words did she realize how much she'd wanted to hear them, even though it wasn't the first time; Eilon had said it a lot. Eilon had cried when she broke up with him and said, "But I love you!" For her, that didn't count, and there was something demanding in his *but*, something whiny that disgusted and frightened her. That dependency was so unmasculine, like a puppy. But when Uri said it, repeating it over and over again until he came—and she thought she might have come too, or at least been as close as she'd ever been—it was completely different. Afterward they ran down the stairs together and he hailed a cab on Yehuda Halevy Street and gave the driver twenty shekels and told him, "Book it to the Central Bus Station. She has to get the last bus." He kissed her and pushed her into the cab, and the driver took her to the main entrance. With four minutes to go, she raced like a madwoman to the platform, feeling the semen dripping down her thigh, and as she sat in the bus she knew that if she were ever asked to choose the happiest moment in her life, that would be it. For sure.

Now she looked at Bella, who smiled understandingly. Since their talk last winter, nothing had progressed. On the contrary. After her father tried to get hold of a tutor a few times, unsuccessfully, she told him quietly, with convincing tenderness, a tenderness that was a luxury she could afford back then, because of Uri, that there was no point spending all that money on private lessons when she was obviously so far behind that nothing could help. He asked what she proposed doing, and she said she would just try and get through the matriculation exam somehow, do the minimum two credits, maybe she'd pass, and if not she'd have a couple of years before she wanted to go to college anyway, so she could improve her grades by taking private lessons or a course, and there'd be less pressure. He said that sounded reasonable, and she thought how easy it was to dupe him, how easy it was to dupe everyone. Her father called the principal to inform her of the decision, and she was unenthusiastic but she said, "Okay, I can accept that. But she has to make some sort of effort. She has to try." Her father agreed, and Ziva took the opportunity to suggest that he also talk to Roni about PE class, which she always found an excuse to get out of. When he approached her, she told him she hated PE and it was unnecessary. He said okay, and that was it. Amazing.

Now that Bella had stopped looking at her, she turned to the poem in her brown notebook that she'd written that morning in history class, for Eli, although maybe it wasn't a poem but the beginning of something, perhaps a short story.

Their meeting last week had been a little odd. It seemed to her like he couldn't be bothered with her, and truthfully she had been in a strange mood, too. She didn't really want to sleep with him, she wanted them to do something else, something couples did, even though she knew they weren't a couple and never would be, and she didn't want them to be. Maybe a trip somewhere. She had thought of Jerusalem because it had always struck her as mysterious and sad. But things had gotten a little out of hand, with the hotel being full, and although they had time and she wanted them to get out of the car and walk around a bit, Eli decided they were going home, and he drove through the Jerusalem Forest, which was a little scary. As the Toyota crawled through the narrow paths, she thought it might have been a mistake to insist on something different and schlep all the way to Jerusalem. She felt increasingly nervous, as if she'd hitched a ride with someone who had suddenly driven off the road and was going to rape her. Here it is, she thought. Here is the ride that everyone kept warning her about. She wasn't afraid of rape, because obviously Eli couldn't rape her; you can't exactly rape your lover. Although, in fact, maybe you can. They'd played that game a few times, pretending he was raping her, or she him. Once, when her dad was overseas and they did it at home, she tied Eli's hands behind his back with her stockings and rode him, and before he came she untied him and said, "Now me. Tie me up." He said they shouldn't, he was dying to try it but he was afraid of what might come out of him, what sort of monster might emerge, so he just came as usual, shouting her name. But in the forest it was different, not a game but completely true. In the forest it was like he wasn't fucking her at all, or anyone else. In the forest she felt as if he wasn't fucking someone but something.

It was okay. Painful but okay. A little strange but tolerable. And it was over pretty quickly, for Eli, who sometimes took hours to come. Hours! Not like Eilon, who came in a second and immediately wanted more. And not like Uri: she never really noticed how long it took him because she felt so good with him. And Yossi. Yossi held the world record in quick orgasms. But not Eli, no. Sometimes he took so long she couldn't stand it anymore, and sometimes she got bored. He liked to change positions in the middle, and sometimes he would say, "Feel like a cigarette? Light one," and while she smoked he'd go on, and the truth was that it was kind of cool to sit on him and smoke while they did it. But in the forest it was over in a minute and she was prepared to forget the whole thing and convince herself that technically it might really have been a bit like a rape, even though it wasn't. But then why did he have to go and call her a whore?

It wasn't insulting so much as it was scary. It took a few days for it to sink in that he'd actually said that, and the unpleasantness had only just started to trickle down, like an insect bite that swells slowly or a dry bruise that spreads and blackens the skin. When she woke up the next morning, even before opening her eyes, she could feel the burning around her anus and his words echoing like a morning greeting: *whore, whore*. At first she told herself it was cool; he was so hot for her he didn't know what he was saying and lost control. But that didn't take. She couldn't shake the feeling that something had happened, something bad.

He hadn't even tried to help her come, nothing, he just came and shouted, "Whore!" and pulled out, and it was quiet for a few minutes, as if nature itself was shocked. She felt the weight of his body lift off her and heard his zipper, and then the door opened and branches crackled beneath his shoes when he got out of the car—the sound was amplified in the silence of the forest, in the silence of the humiliation—and with her cheek crushed against the upholstery, which still smelled new because no one ever sat in the backseat, she heard him say, "Are you okay?" She said yes, still waiting for something, something that would be a fitting end to this, a different ending, and then she heard him say, "Come on, then, it's really late." In slow motion she got up on her elbows and knees, pulled up her underwear and pants, and sat down on the front seat, stunned.

They drove silently all the way to the highway. Eli turned the radio on and then off again, as if he realized it wasn't appropriate. She took her book out of her backpack, not that she was planning to read it in the dark. He asked what it was and she said, "*Past Perfect*."

"Don't know it. Any good?"

Something in her contracted. She knew he wasn't exactly a genius, but to ask if *Past Perfect* was any good? "Very," she said.

He asked what it was about, and she said it was impossible to describe, and he said, "Oh, one of *those* books. I probably wouldn't like it then. I need a plot."

But still, not to educate him—that wasn't the purpose, but maybe she wanted to restore some magic that had evaporated from the evening— she opened the book in the dark to the first page and read the first line, which she would have memorized if it wasn't endless. "Listen," she said. "Are you listening?"

"I'm all ears."

At the age of forty-two, shortly after Sukkoth, Meir was gripped by the fear of death—a fear that took hold of him as soon as he had

acknowledged the fact that death was a real and integral part of his life,
which had already passed its peak—

Eli cut her off. "Whoa, it's about me! I'll be forty-two soon, too."
She ignored him and continued:

—that he was moving swiftly and surely toward it on a route that
allowed for no digressions, and that the distance between them—which
had seemed almost infinite during the Sukkoth holiday, let alone the
summer, which now seemed no more than a distant dream—was growing
shorter all the time, so that he could envisage it without difficulty and
measure it out in ordinary, everyday terms, such as—

"Sounds a little tedious, doesn't it? Kind of repetitive."
She shut the book and shook her head, suddenly sadder than she'd
ever been with him, maybe because it was a new sadness, different from
any kind she knew. She considered herself proficient in all possible
types of sadness, but this was something different.
Eli seemed to sense something crumbling between them like a clod
of dry earth. "What's the hero's name? Yair?"
She whispered, "Meir. It doesn't really matter."
"It does matter, sure it does. Obviously a writer picks a name with
meaning, doesn't he? Isn't that so?"
She shook her head again. This was horrible torture, worse than the
sex. That had been stinging and sharp and very short, but this pain was
different: dull and guttural. She said no, she didn't think the protago-
nist's name was important, that wasn't the thing. He asked what was
the thing, and she wondered if there was any benefit to feeling smarter
than the man she was sleeping with. She'd felt that way with Eilon, but
he didn't count. And with Yossi too, but Yossi was a mistake that would
soon be over. But Eli, what about him?
"Go on, I'm waiting for an answer." His voice sounded suddenly
pestering, higher than usual.
"Let's drop it. I don't feel like talking now."
"I tired you out, hey?"
She nodded in the dark and heard that *hey?* again, like the grunt of
a horny animal.

When she remained silent he insisted. "At least tell me what's so special about this book. Maybe I'll give it a chance, you know? Maybe I'll try and read it after all."

She wanted to tell him not to try, he wouldn't get it. But it was terrible even to think that way, because what was she doing sleeping with a guy like this? And maybe even falling in love a little—otherwise how could you explain the poems in her notebook? She didn't write for people who weren't important. It never occurred to her to write for Yossi. And so she said, "Death. That's what's interesting about it. Death."

"What do you mean? I really want to know."

He sounded different, and she was willing to forgive him. Maybe she'd pegged him wrong; maybe he did have the necessary depth—but for what? Necessary for what? She said that even though the book was about a forty-two-year-old man, she completely identified with every word, every sensation. "Don't you think about death sometimes? About your death?"

There was a snort of laughter, followed by silence. "Oy, Roni, Roni." She asked why he was mocking her, and he said he wasn't, he'd just remembered how old she was. She asked why he was thinking about that now, and he said, "Never mind, forget it. I didn't say anything. Let's talk about death."

She told him she thought about it a lot recently: why we die, and how, and whether every person's death is already planned from the moment they're born. It seemed amazing to her, this thing. He asked what she meant, and she said, "Death. And that really, when you say someone died before their time, it's ridiculous." He asked why it was ridiculous, and she said that no one really knows when anyone is supposed to die, and why do we automatically assume that everyone's supposed to die when they're a hundred, when maybe it was preordained for someone to die at twenty? You can't say that anyone dies before their time.

"Children, too?" he asked, and gave her a curious look.

"Yes. Children, too."

"I don't know, Roni. I don't know if you're right. I've never thought about these things, death and all that."

"Really?" She honestly found it hard to believe. She thought about it a lot. All the time, in fact. Not in the context of suicide, not at all, she thought about it the same way she thought about love, without fear. And just as it was clear to her that every person had their death, which may have been determined at the moment they were born, she also knew that each person had a love that was destined for them, and whenever someone was born they were given these items, love and death, like they hand out equipment to soldiers at the induction center, except without any dates. And she had received her love, early and unexpectedly. It was her love and she had to protect it, because just like you only die once, it could be that you only love once. Really love.

Eli put his hand on her thigh and asked why she was so quiet.

"No reason. I'm just a little tired."

"I wore you out!" he repeated proudly. Such a baby.

"No, I'm just tired."

He asked if she'd had a rough day, if school was hard. "Poor girl, the teachers torture you in the morning and I torture you at night. What a rough life you have." She thought he was mocking her again, and when he shoved his fist between her thighs and said, "Do you know you have the loveliest pussy in the world?" she still said nothing. Then he added, "And the truth is that I kind of neglected it today. But I'll make it up to you, big time, I promise."

She thought about Uri, and wondered what he was doing now. She knew he was awake; he never went to sleep before 3 or 4 A.M. She hadn't seen him for seven months, and she had so much to tell him: how she'd changed, how she was no longer the baby he thought she was when they were together, which may have been true at the time but not anymore. And maybe after he got to know her again—her whole body seemed to tremble inside when she imagined what it would be like for him to meet the person she was now, what it would be like for who she was now to meet him again, and how after the meeting, which would be just like in the movies, stormy and a little kitschy, they would fall into the routine of a couple that had gone through a crisis and separated and got back together again and knew that this was it, this was forever. He would be in his apartment on Nachmani, she would live with roommates nearby, on one of those streets like Mazeh or Balfour or Melchet. He would write and she would wait tables, and maybe she wouldn't do her army service; her dad wouldn't have any problem if she decided to get an exemption, and her mother definitely wouldn't, she would be thrilled;

and suddenly, oddly, she missed her mother, now of all times, in the car, which always smelled of air freshener, with Eli, whose fingers were playing in her underwear, and instead of feeling bummed out at the thought of going to the States in a month, at Hanukah, she suddenly looked forward to it. She promised herself that she would try and mend what had gone wrong between them, what she herself, with her own two horrible hands, had ruined.

She pressed her thighs together and said she wasn't in the mood. "I'm tired, okay?"

He leaned back. "Death. It's an interesting topic."

She couldn't wait for the drive to be over.

Class was almost finished and she looked up from her notebook and turned her head to glance at Shiri, who sat at the desk to her right. She also looked unfocused, even though she was sitting up straight and staring at the blackboard. She was very pale, her lips were coated with a thin layer that looked like whitewash, and Roni knew she'd thrown up before class. On the bus she'd offered her a croissant her father had baked, and at first Shiri had refused, but she kept watching Roni eat. "Come on already, just take one! They're so small," Roni said. Shiri reached into the greasy bag and pulled out a croissant, which she finished off with tiny little bites. When they got to school she said, "I'll see you in class," and Roni knew she was running to the bathroom to vomit.

At the end of ninth grade, when it had just started and they were still attached at the hip, Roni found it a little hurtful that Shiri hid her anorexia from her; they even had a big falling out when Roni decided to confront her and ask what the deal with the vomiting was. Since Shiri was thin to begin with, it took people awhile to notice that she'd lost even more weight, but Shiri wouldn't talk about it. On the other hand, she didn't go to much trouble to hide it. Roni heard her a million times choking and flushing the toilet, and when she came back you could see it on her lips and around her mouth.

One morning after she'd overslept at Shiri's and missed the bus, as usual, Dalia Silver was waiting for her in the kitchen, all scary smiles. She said Shiri had made the bus. "But as you know, Shiri's an early riser.

She has a turbo engine, that girl." Dalia said she'd taken the day off because the carpenters were coming to take measurements for the new kitchen.

Roni asked, "You're redoing the kitchen? But your kitchen is so nice!" Dalia said it was nice but old, and asked Roni if she wanted something to eat. There was some artisanal bread she'd bought yesterday, and wonderful cheeses that Avner had brought back from his trip abroad last week. Roni said she didn't feel like anything; she wasn't hungry in the mornings.

Dalia leaned on the counter, took a deep breath, and asked, "Speaking of food, do you happen to know if Shiri is anorexic?"

Roni was slightly shocked. For some reason she'd assumed Shiri's parents knew. How could you not know something like that about your own child? A blind man could see it. And what was she supposed to say now? She replied, "I don't think so."

Dalia, who on the one hand obviously knew she was being lied to, but on the other hand was relieved, said, "You know, it's funny the things parents worry about today. When I was Shiri's age my mother once gave me a talk. I can still remember the embarrassment. She said something was bothering her, she had to know, she would only ask me once, it was her duty. I remember every word she said. 'It's my duty as a mother,' she said. 'Are you still a virgin?'" She let out a wild and completely uncharacteristic laugh, then looked down at the floor and, as if having noticed an invisible spot of dirt, leaned down and picked something up and threw it in the sink. "Oh, it was so embarrassing."

Roni thought there was something repulsive about the whole situation. Why did mothers, hers and others, always trap her in these cages of intimacy, like they had an urgent need to confess, to be little girls?

"So I said, 'Of course I'm still a virgin, Mom, and I'm surprised at you for even thinking otherwise.' And that was the end of that."

Then, fortunately, the phone rang, and Dalia answered it and got into an argument with the carpenter, who wanted to postpone until the next day. Roni took advantage of the opportunity to grab her backpack and motion to Dalia that she was leaving.

She debated for weeks whether to tell Shiri about the conversation, and eventually she told her one afternoon on the bus home. Shiri said angrily, "That's just like her. That is so like her."

Roni unexpectedly found herself defending Dalia. "Look, she's your mom. She cares about you."

"She cares about herself. And since when do you care about my mom? Do you care about your own?"

She tried a different approach. "Forget your mom, that's not what matters. Why are you destroying your body?" She was trying to be tender and friendly.

"You have no right to talk. Why are *you* destroying your body? Why do you smoke?" Then she said, "Stop it, let's not talk about it, okay? I really don't want to talk about it."

Since Roni was at the height of her relationship with Uri at the time, she decided that was just fine, because she had her secrets, too, and maybe it was for the best, and anyway they'd been in the process of drifting apart for a long time and Shiri obviously needed her more than she needed Shiri.

The class was almost over and she gave one last glance at her notebook, at the poem or whatever it was that she'd written for Eli, and wondered whether to show it to him. It would be like showing someone who's seen you naked dozens of times a small, hidden detail, but an important one, one that might help him understand something about her, about them, something that would give their relationship another dimension, a more literary or cinematic one. Because he didn't know her at all. He didn't know who she really was, what kind of soul she had, and how complex she was, and complicated. She knew he didn't really like literature, didn't really like words, but that was exactly why she had to show him, she had to.

She decided that next time they met it wouldn't be for sex. Next time they met it would be different. Maybe she'd suggest that they meet in the café near his office and talk. She'd ask him all kinds of questions, things she'd never asked before, and she would insist that he tell her about himself, who he was and what he was and where he'd come from, and what his dreams were, and his nightmares, what he liked to eat, for example, and what he was most afraid of. And then he'd probably ask her the same questions, and she would show him the piece from her notebook, and he would suddenly understand, and everything between them after that would be completely different. Even his *wow* would be different, because he used that word too often, like it was something involuntary, a tic—when he came he said *wow*, and when she touched him he said *wow*, and when she undressed he said *wow*. It was always *wow*, and in the first few months that was enough, but now she wanted to take the *wow* to other places, deep and secret places. She wanted him, for example, to read the piece she'd written and say *wow*. Maybe she'd also show him the things she'd written for Uri, so he could say *wow, wow, wow*, with the amazement and fear of someone who suddenly realizes that the woman he is sleeping with, the woman he has called, perhaps mistakenly, inadvertently, a whore, was not at all the woman he'd thought she was, and more than that—that the woman he'd always thought was too little for him was actually a few sizes too large.

ALONA

The boy was depressed. It had been over three weeks, and even though he was only three and a half years old, she didn't think there was any need to come up with a better, more age-appropriate word, like *crisis* or *anxiety*. She knew it: Ido was depressed. The depression had settled on him like a coat several sizes too large, and he was swimming around in it like a little fish—like Nemo, she thought back, with a pang of guilt. That Saturday at the end of summer, when she'd taken the kids to the movies, the darkness of the auditorium had excited Ido as much as the film itself. When the lights went out he'd whispered, "I'm not scared." Then he'd fallen in love with the stripy orange fish who lost his mother even before he was born and was left with his hysterical father.

During the first half of the movie, Ido sat alertly on the edge of his seat, his hand in the popcorn box, too fascinated to eat. Maya, on Alona's other side, swung her feet and kicked the seat in front of her and sighed. "I'm bored. This movie stinks." But then the sharks arrived, frothing up the screen, and Maya started to laugh and clap her hands, while Ido shrank back as if in shock. He burst into tears and demanded to leave the theater. "Why now?" Maya protested.

Alona grabbed her arm and said, "Now." She dragged the two kids outside. Ido kept whimpering, even when she bought them ice cream, and only at home, when she showered him, did he calm down and ask if those were the same sharks who had eaten Nemo's mother and unhatched brothers. Alona said she didn't know, but he insisted that she tell him, and since it was one of those moments when a child needs a firm answer rather than the truth, she said, "I don't think so. Those were different sharks." He looked at her, encouraged, and let go of his penis, which he tended to finger nervously when he was bored or scared. He asked if a shark could eat a boy, too. At first she wanted to say no, of course not, but at this point the truth seemed important, lifesaving; what if he encountered a shark one day? So she said, "Yes."

"And mommies, too?"

"Yes, mommies, too."

"But not Dad," he asserted with a whisper, and his fingers took hold of his penis again, absentmindedly fondling it.

"Where we live there aren't any sharks, not like those ones."

"But what if we go to where Nemo lives one day?"

"We won't go anywhere like that, don't worry, okay?"

Ido nodded seriously and gratefully.

She soaped his thighs and tummy, gently moving his fingers away from his penis. Ma'ayan had told her it was normal. "All boys do it, it's not masturbation, and even if it is, just don't worry about it. Pretend you don't see it, and don't make a big deal out of it."

Ido, who had calmed down now, turned his back to her, picked up the big water pistol, and started to shoot at the tiles. "I'm killing them! Look, I've killed them all!"

She asked who he was killing.

"The sharks," he replied, and sprayed water all over. Then he mumbled, "But I think there are more. Lots more. Fill it up with more water for me, Mommy, fill it all the way up."

She filled the pistol and went to get a towel and asked him not to spray the floor. In the bedroom she found Maya lying on her stomach on the big bed, her head covered with a pillow. When Alona asked what she was doing, Maya peeked out from under the pillow with a tear-streaked face. "I wanted to see the end of the movie!" she wailed. "Because of you I didn't see it!"

"But you were bored the whole time, don't you remember?"

"I wasn't bored."

"Then I'm sorry, but we had no choice. We had to leave and that's that."

"Then I want Dad to take me to Nemo. I want Dad to take me on my own!"

"Okay, he'll take you."

"Now!"

"You know that's impossible."

"Then when?"

"We'll see. I'll talk to him."

"You won't!" Maya shouted. "You'll forget, you always forget!"

"You'll remind me then, Maya, okay?"

"Call him now! Now!"

"He's not home now."

"He is! You're lying! He is at home!" Maya screamed.

"I'm not lying," she said, giving her voice a sugary tone of patience, and asked Maya to stop shouting and go brush her teeth and pick out a book. "I'll be there in a minute."

Her daughter looked at her and said, "You're horrible."

When she went to get Ido out of the bathtub, he was standing with his back to her, screaming at the tiles: "I killed you!" She thought of how the children had introduced a soap-operatic pitch of drama into her life, an endless burst of exclamation marks, a deafening volume that was so different from the murmuring quiet in which she'd lived previously. Her life before the children had been one long sentence dotted with commas, making its curly way along without any exclamation points or periods, like a sentence written by Yaakov Shabtai, who used to be her favorite author. He still was, even though she no longer felt that her life was a syntax of wanderings. On the contrary: even when she tried very hard, she could not reconstruct the long hours of staring into space, of daydreaming.

"I had too much time to myself," she told Mark when they met, when she was trying to explain what she thought the essential difference was between someone who had spent most of her life alone, first as a child and then as an adult, and someone for whom time spent alone was predefined by the time he spent with others. "It does something to you. Something fundamental, not related to loneliness or sadness or longing. Something different, more complex."

But she could not define what this complex thing was, and it infuriated Mark, who claimed there was no such thing; anyone could change if they wanted to. "But you," he observed, almost every time they fought, "just don't want to."

One thing in particular Mark found it difficult to forgive her for: the children, rather than he, had discovered her emotional G-spot. They'd "factorized" her, as she said, and then they'd put her back together again. But they'd rewired her control panel so that the old wires were crossed, creating dangerous contacts. And they'd stripped the insulation from the wires with a penknife, and now every emotion was a spark that set fire to the whole system. That was what happened when she looked in the children's faces, for example, especially when they weren't aware of her gaze. Those moments when they were alone, like when she came to pick them up from kindergarten and spotted Maya sitting at a desk, painting, squeezed in among the other children. Or Ido on a chair in the doll area, playing with a toy. As soon as that happened, she could hear the crackling explosions in herself, the electric *tssss of* massive, hulking, impatient emotions shoving one another into a narrow tunnel in the wall, one dense second of compassion, fear, tenderness, longing, happiness, and guilt. When they noticed her, when their looks met hers, the switch flipped and the light went on, and Maya and Ido stopped being pure arousers of emotion and turned once again into her children: running toward her, hugging, crying, arguing, demanding. Ido had a recent habit of welcoming her with kicks, and Maya, as soon as she'd said, "I missed you, Mom, I missed you so much," would break away and hurry off to make arrangements with her friends.

And now Ido and his depression. At first she attributed it to the break-in and to her own negligence: he had heard her telling Ma'ayan on the phone that there were three men, probably Palestinians, and maybe he'd heard her say, "We could have all died." At first she hadn't thought it unusual for him to respond this way. Maya was upset, too, and wanted to know all the details: Who were these people, and where did they live, and why did they come, and what did they take, and why only the camera, and what would they do with it? Ido grew quiet and ponderous, but she didn't think much of that either. He was always less excitable than his sister, less rebellious. He wanted to be liked and avoided conflict. He was a bit like his father, she thought: cowardly. But she scolded herself for thinking that—why turn an agreeable temperament into a problem?

In the first few days after the burglary, Ido's behavior had seemed normal. But unlike Maya, who forgot about the whole thing within a week, Ido kept walking around the house lost in thought, his head bowed, carrying his toolbox. Every time she asked what was wrong, if something had happened at preschool or if he was sad, he shrugged his shoulders and bowed his head even lower. But he also gave her a sideways glance, as if waiting—but for what? At nights he woke up crying, two or three times, and when she went to him she found him wide awake and sitting up in bed, not half asleep like he used to be. Over and over again, every night, for three weeks, he repeated his question: What happens to people who steal?

Out of a vague sense of guilt—if they'd had an alarm system all this might have been avoided, and how much could she really blame Mark?— she enlisted true patience every night, the kind she'd never had before. She sat on his bed, hugged him, and told him that people who steal are usually punished. That the police catch the thieves, and a judge decides if they should go to prison to learn a lesson so they won't steal again. But she was surprised to discover that her answer not only did not reassure him but magnified his fears. "All of them?" he asked. "They catch and punish all of them?"

"Not all of them, but you don't need to be scared, because those thieves won't come here anymore."

He said he wasn't scared, those thieves didn't scare him at all, because he knew they hadn't done it for bad reasons. He thought they needed the car for something.

"For what?"

Ido explained that they had a sick boy and they had to take him to the hospital so he wouldn't die.

"You're such a smart boy," she said. He smiled a contemplative smile and she kissed his forehead and laid him down and said, "Call me if you're frightened again." He nodded into the pillow and put a pacifier in his mouth. She went back to bed satisfied: she was implementing that statement Ma'ayan had once made, which had sounded like a quote from a women's magazine: "Only a mother knows how to reassure her child." Curling up into a sleeping position in bed, she told herself she was finally successful at being *the* mother.

But why this sudden interest in death? Where had he come up with the sick child who had to go to the hospital? A response to the situation, she thought. And although she knew it was excessive to attribute that kind of comprehension to a little boy, she thought about those Saturdays when he used to come up to her while she read the paper, stand beside her, and look at the pictures of Palestinian families, portraits of injured children. Once he asked who the children were, and she said, "Just children." What else could she say? "Just children the newspaper wrote about."

"Why, because they're Arabs?"

"Yes," she replied, and that seemed to satisfy him.

But later, in the middle of dinner, he asked, "What are Arabs?"

"People."

"Like us?"

"Yes, exactly like us," she replied proudly. But a better mother would have quickly shut the newspaper. And besides, was she seriously trying to give her kids a class in Politics 101? One of the preschool mothers had warned her about Nemo. She'd said it was a scary movie and they shouldn't go, but Alona had discounted her words—a right-winger whose little girl came to preschool every morning with a huge bag of junk-food snacks and another little bag with Gummy Bears full of food coloring.

She stood in the doorway of the children's room, debating whether to switch on the heater. Although it wasn't cold enough to use the wood-burning stove yet, there was an early winter chill in the air, and the children, as they did every time the seasons changed, refused to use their comforters, the same ones they would refuse to part with six months later.

She looked at them sleeping. Maya, as usual, was sprawled on her back, her arms and legs askew, a position that always amused Alona but also touched her. Ido was on his stomach with his bottom hoisted up and his face turned to one side. He had a troubled expression, even in sleep. The pacifier lay on the pillow next to him in a circle of saliva, and suddenly she knew for sure: he was depressed.

It occurred to her that maybe it wasn't just the past three weeks. Maybe it had always been this way, and the boy had been born depressive. When she went out to smoke her last nightly cigarette, she started to replay all sorts of little events that she threaded together like beads on a string, and what came out in the end was a black and melancholy necklace.

Like the thing with the drawing. Every day Maya brought home an impressive portfolio of art, which she would spread out on the floor. She'd explain at length what every picture was, what she'd been trying to do, what had come out, and what the teacher had said—sweeping compliments—and wait for Alona's pronouncement. "Amazing, Maya, I can't believe it! Did you really make these pictures? All on your own?" Maya would nod impatiently and then think out loud about where to hang the new works. The fridge was full, and so was the bulletin board in the study.

Ido would monitor her silently and watch her tape the pictures to the bedroom walls. He also came home almost every day with a full bag, and when Alona asked to see what he'd made, he would shrug his shoulders, claim he hadn't made anything, and go about his business: imaginary repairs around the house that he did with his and Mark's tools. At night, after putting them to bed, she would remember the bag thrown in the entrance by the shoes, and she would pull out the pages: the usual scribbles of a three-year-old, nothing attesting to any particular talent. But now, sitting outside smoking, she wondered if his jealousy of Maya was actually something else, a basic existential sense of failure. But why?

She felt a chill run through her body and admonished herself for these thoughts. Mark had once said that the real price the children would pay one day would not be for their weaknesses but for her interpretations. She knew he was right but she couldn't shake the thought that Ido would suffer in life, suffer terribly, and in fact he already was, because something in his structure would magnetize all the particles of sorrow in the world to him. It was a mistake to think of Maya as tempestuous and Ido as calm. How had she ever fallen into that trap? It was clear to her now that a tornado was brewing inside her son. When she put out her cigarette, tears came to her eyes as she remembered how she'd been making herself a cup of coffee in the kitchen a few days ago. When she'd taken the milk out of the fridge she'd noticed a new piece of paper on the door, overlapping the others. It was a scribble in blue marker, with a caption handwritten by a teacher in print letters: "Ido S." There were two other Idos in his class. And that suddenly pained her: Why had they given him such a common name? Maybe that was her fault, too, that her son thought of himself as just another Ido. She had stood looking at the paper her son had secretly hung on the fridge door, carefully attaching a fruit-shaped magnet to each corner, and she'd wanted to rush over to the preschool and rescue the child from his loneliness, or at least sit by his side while he drew and express real exclamation, not consolation or encouragement. "You're an artist, chickie! You're a real artist!" she'd say. And maybe she'd just use his name, so it would sound more real.

She went inside, shut the door to the yard and locked it, and walked over to the alarm panel. She wondered if she would remember to tell Ido these things when he got back from school. Because that was part of the problem too, the forgetting. She could no longer remember when she'd become so forgetful, when forgetting had become a way of life. In the past she used to torment herself day and night if something was bothering her, but now she could start her day with a huge burden—Ido, Maya, her mother, work, or something else—and before she could even promise to deal with it later, when she had time, the matter would be forgotten, melted away. And so she found herself flooded with guilt at least once a day, usually at night, like now, and even that guilt, just like whatever had caused it in the first place, would be forgotten as soon as she fell asleep.

That was how she had ended up with a three-and-a-half-year-old boy who was suffering from a deep depression, and it might be too late to do anything about it. Perhaps the depression was clinical. Perhaps there was a gene in her family. Her father, she thought, although maybe it was her mother. Ever since she'd fallen, five years ago, her mother had never quite recovered. Her broken hands had healed but something in her had remained unstable, unforgiving, as if the tumble outside the grocery store was the first in a chain of events. It reminded Alona of chaos theory, with that butterfly flapping its wings, or whatever it was. A steel marble falling into a toy maze and moving down the tracks until it finally landed on the bottom. If she tried hard, she could hear its journey, the sliding and banging, the *tick-tick-tick*, and maybe the bell it activated when it landed. But she didn't want to hear that. No. It was just like the CT and bone-density images her mother got every so often, which embarrassed her, as if she had seen something more frightening than nudity: her mother from the inside. That's what her brain looks like, this is how her bones are built. Like seeing the soul itself, the fibers of the fabric. And who wants to see their parents' souls?

But maybe, as usual, she was making too much of it. How easy it was to confuse old age with depression, just like people automatically assumed that childhood was a synonym for happiness. Perhaps her mother was not depressed but just living her life. Although even that phrase sounded despondent now.

Alona had always wondered what she would be like when she grew old, and what old age looked like from the inside. She knew that whatever she thought would be not be right, not completely, and that whatever she imagined would not come to be—which might be why she always imagined the worst, to protect herself. She knew that to try and see herself as an old woman now, at forty, was no different than seeing herself at forty when she was ten, hiding behind the towel in the women's changing rooms at the pool, quickly getting dressed and staring at the older women who walked around naked with no shame. The sight of their bodies alarmed her—the big, droopy breasts, the tummies, some of which were scarred, folding over furry private parts, and bottoms that looked like they were trying to say something, something impudent or sad. How old those women had seemed to her then; they were probably in their thirties or forties—like she was today, she who still stole glances in the changing rooms while Ido and Maya darted around her in their childish nakedness. While she dried them and dressed them and slid into a large tank top and shorts—she only took off her damp swimsuit later, at home—her gaze wandered to the other women, mainly the elderly ones, and she still experienced that same curious astonishment at the sight of their bodies, wondering, as she had thirty years ago, how they could be so unembarrassed while she, whose body today looked like theirs, was still ashamed, avoiding any exposure of her body in their presence. And now that body of hers longed to get laid.

She'd been pining for Mark for weeks, infuriated by the way he ignored her, by the possibility that maybe—but this couldn't be true—he was no longer attracted to her. After all, it had been two years, and maybe he had someone. But that couldn't be. He would have told her. Of that, at least, she was sure. It was one thing for him not to want to sleep with her, but not to tell her about sex with other women? No way.

The break-in had shaken them up a little, obviously, but instead of extinguishing her feelings for Mark, or at least taking her mind off it for a while, it seemed to have done exactly the opposite. And Mark had seemed troubled recently. He was going through something. When she asked, he shook her off, almost physically, with a shrug of the shoulders that reminded her of Ido, a sort of don't-know or don't-want-to or both. It was strange that his response, which was neither denial nor confirmation, no longer aroused in her the old anger at his ability to repress or escape—all the principles she'd so insisted on before they broke up. But who was she kidding? They were more together now than they'd ever been. And in fact she slightly envied him for his basic joyfulness, the kind that was not subject to daily negotiation. She envied the way he moved through the world: an endless Shabtai sentence but an optimistic one. She envied him because even though she had changed since the children were born, and she did sometimes experience true joy, even happiness, the very word frightened her because the happiness had been tagged by a terrible anxiety, like a price tag.

Yesterday she'd tried to explain to Uri Breutner what it meant to be a parent.

"I trust you," he'd said, " 'cause you won't try to prettify it. So tell me what to expect. Will it change me, d'you think? I mean, I want it to change me, but I'm not sure how I want to change." He fiddled with the lighter she'd put on the table. Zohar was sixteen weeks pregnant, with a boy. And it turned out that a large part of his hysterical state for the past few weeks was because of the pregnancy, not the book. "But I couldn't tell you until now, I'm sorry. She made me swear not to tell until the comprehensive ultrasound, but now we're telling everyone."

They were sitting in a café on Yehuda Halevy, where they used to meet when he'd lived on Nachmani. Uri had insisted they meet there, even though she'd suggested other places, where it was easier to find parking. "No, I'm into a nostalgic worshipping of my previous life," he'd explained.

"Okay, but you're a baby, you know that?"

"I know. It's part of my charm, isn't it?" He sounded calmer now that he'd unburdened himself of the pregnancy secret.

"You know? Maybe we should call your book *Baby*. I'm serious. It seems appropriate, doesn't it? Because the male character is incredibly babyish."

"Yes, but it's not a good idea. It would be confusing. The readers might think there's a real baby in the book."

"And how ironic that now there actually is."

"Witty. You're witty. I love you."

On the way to the café she thought about that conversation and the way he'd said, "Witty. I love you." An ancient insult, which she thought had long ago crumbled into dust, re-formed itself inside her. In her twenties she had been proud of the fact that she wasn't the type of woman whom men wanted to marry. Men worshipped her and were in awe of her, they were fascinated by her and desperately wanted her, but in a fleeting way. They never fell in love with her. And in her thirties that fact made her desperate.

"Whoa!" he said, after the coffee arrived. He smoothed his pony-tailed hair back with his hand. "I'm going to have a child, do you get that? I'm a baby about to have a baby. What do you think about that? Go on, Alona, say something. I trust you. Say something brilliant."

She wanted to say something profound and reassuring, something brilliant, like he'd asked, but she looked at him leaning back in his chair playing with her lighter, his gaze following passersby, his foot bouncing on the sidewalk, until he finally pulled a cigarette out of her pack and lit it, and she suddenly had the urge to get up and slap him on his pale blond-stubbled cheek. Drama, she thought. What fun. She would never have seriously considered doing something like that, and it made her happy because she realized that even today, after Mark and the kids, she was still not immune to the Uri Breutners of the world.

Take her late twenties, for example. She'd been at the beginning of her career as an editor at Subtext. Every day she went home to her apartment on King Solomon Street with two or three manuscripts by authors who had been rejected by the larger publishers. She'd had a sense of mission about it. She was the person who would comb that pile of rejected manuscripts for the ones that had gotten past older and wearier editors. The ones that were too strange or too raw or too desperate for them, the ones that deserved to be discovered. Whenever she phoned the writers of these manuscripts, she was flattered by the excitement in their voices, but also a little startled. She would ask them to meet with her to discuss their book and see if they could work together, and every so often she fell in love with one of those young writers and had a quick affair. Most of them were her own age or even older, but somehow her status as editor made them seem younger. She was twenty-eight but felt old.

She looked at Uri and wondered what had happened to Eyal, one of those young writers, with whom the affair had been particularly awkward. She'd had the impression that he was expecting her to accept his manuscript in return. "I'm trusting you to do what you can," he'd told her, and she'd said she would. The publisher had ultimately rejected his short story collection, which another editor had said was immature and needed more work. They stopped seeing each other even before the rejection, at her initiative. And now here was Uri with his "I trust you, Alona." It embarrassed her a little, and then her cell phone rang, and "MARK CELL" flashed across the screen. Before she answered, it occurred to her that the man who had rescued her from the Uri Breutners of the world was rescuing her again. "It's Mark," she told Uri.

"Are you getting it?" he asked, as if he were a partner to the secret.

"I have to," she said, and picked up the phone.

"Where are you?" Mark asked.

She said she was in a meeting with Uri.

"Oh, is he bugging you?"

"A little."

Mark said he'd almost gone to Tel Aviv that morning. "It's too bad, I could have met the phenom."

"It really is a pity."

They exchanged a few words about the afternoon plans. He was supposed to pick the kids up but the restaurant stove wasn't working and someone was coming at four to fix it. He asked if she could pick them up and he'd come later. "I'm sorry, I just have to get it working. They say it's going to be cold this weekend."

"It's fine, no problem. So we'll talk later?"

He said yes, and maybe she could bring Ido to see the man fixing the stove. "He likes that kind of stuff."

She said she'd see.

"Okay, I hope you survive the meeting. Don't let him get on your nerves, okay?"

"Too late for that."

He laughed and they hung up.

"Something important?" Uri asked. In the two minutes she'd been on the phone he'd covered his napkin with childish doodles of houses with red-tiled roofs and chimneys.

"Yes," she said.

"Look what I drew!" He smiled.

She took the napkin and looked at the drawings. "My son does better than this."

Now she got into bed and thought about the fact that maybe she had been so busy defining Mark that she'd completely missed him. Mark never stood on his own. He was always relative to others: less hurtful, more trustworthy, less complicated, more loving but never loved himself, unconnected, untainted. She knew that was how the world worked—unless you chose, like Ma'ayan, to spend your life with the first person you fell in love with—and no couple was immune to these things. Still, she realized now that it was not Mark she'd hurt but herself, robbing herself of the experience of falling in love that she must have had, she couldn't not have had, but she was too busy giving it names and examining its validity to allow it to change her or, at least, reassure her that she didn't need to change.

Ido started crying and she hurried to the room and sat next to him and took him in her arms. But tonight, unlike other nights, he pushed her away, crawled back to the wall, sat cross-legged on his pillow, and said he wanted to talk to Dad. "Let's call him now."

"Now? It's late. We can't call now, Ido. Go back to sleep and we'll talk to him tomorrow."

"No!" the boy wailed. "I have to talk to him now, it's important!"

"What do you need to talk to him about?"

"About the new camera he's getting us. Did he already buy it?"

She said she didn't know, she didn't think so. "But why does that matter now, chickie? Talk to him tomorrow."

"I can't tomorrow," Ido said, and started beating his fists on the pillow. Maya sighed in her sleep, and Alona tried to embrace him again. "I have to tell Dad something, please! I have to talk to him now!"

She glanced at the clock: quarter past twelve. Mark was probably still awake, but it was crazy to call him now. If she gave in once, who knew what might happen. The boy would wake up every night with peculiar requests. "We're not calling Dad now," she said, and Ido burst into tears again. Not demanding sobs but desperate ones. She remembered the note she'd stuck to the computer screen that morning weeks ago, a moment before discovering that the car was gone. It was the last note, because she'd quit the habit since then. It had said, SURRENDER TO THE MOMENT. She said, "Okay, Ido, if it's important to you, we'll call him, but only this one time, okay?"

He nodded quickly. "I promise, only this time!"

He leaped off the bed and ran to the living room, and stood next to her while she dialed. She felt his heavy breaths on her thigh, and stroked his head, which was warm and damp with sweat as usual. "Did I wake you?" she asked when she heard Mark's sleepy voice.

"Kind of. What time is it? What's wrong?"

"Ido is hysterical. He woke up and wants to talk to you."

"Is he next to you?"

"Yes, but make it short, okay?"

"This isn't like you, Alona."

"What do you mean?" she asked impatiently, regretting the whole adventure. It was obvious she'd made a mistake, from now on the kids would wake up at all kinds of strange hours and demand to call their father; maybe this whole thing was actually connected to the breakup, not the break-in.

"It's unlike you to agree. I'm really pleased with you."

She felt angry: he was condescending, preaching to her in the middle of the night, like that time with the five-minute method. But then an odd tranquillity came over her, a happiness. No one knew her like he did. It amused her to think that she had once hoped for a different kind of knowing, a deeper kind, like knowing a literary text, and she had felt a little girl's fury when she'd discovered that no one could know her that way. While Mark—what was Mark? Mark was just a reader, and that *just*, which used to be insulting, was now everything. With her son brushing up against her restlessly, lifting his hand up to grab the phone, and on the other end of the line her husband—and he was still her husband, after all—sleepy but happy to have been woken, ready to put on his fatherhood hat at any moment and really never taking it off, she realized that these moments, the nighttime disturbances, should be treasured like random but very real Polaroids of the family. "Here's Daddy," she said, and handed Ido the phone.

He turned his back to her, grasped the phone, tilted his head to one side, and paced back and forth across the room like she herself did. She smiled to herself and went to put the kettle on. She filled a bottle with milk to make hot chocolate for Ido, an unexpected nighttime treat; she no longer cared how much it would cost and what would happen when Maya found out the next day. She heard Ido interrogating his father about the new camera, and of course it didn't occur to Mark to ask why he'd suddenly thought of it in the middle of the night. That was why she loved him. That, too.

Ido finished talking to his dad and looked suddenly calm. "Dad said he hasn't bought the camera yet. He said he'll take me, we'll go together!" He started walking to the bedroom, and she waved the bottle she'd warmed up for him. "Want some hot chocolate?" Surprised and almost fearful, he approached her. She caressed his head and said, "Let's sit on the couch for a while. I'll have tea and you'll have hot chocolate. Would you like that?"

He nodded and sat down next to her. He placed his bottle on the table next to her mug of tea and leaned his head against her chest, and she thought, The moment is surrendering to us.

ELI

And now this guy is trying to be his friend and he doesn't know what to do. They met about a month ago in line for the car wash, and it turned out they both lived in Eden and he owned the Trattoria and, horrifyingly, was her father. It was embarrassing on a level that can barely be described, to sit there with him on the bench outside the car wash, both slightly hunched over, each watching his car. The guy, her father, asked Eli if he was pleased with his car, and they spent a few minutes talking about how half the country was driving SUVs now. In a moment of candor, or maybe because of the crushing awkwardness, Eli told him about Dafna, who loathed SUVs on principle, and the guy said, "My wife would shoot me too if I even brought up the idea. I mean, my exwife. Actually she's not my ex, 'cause we're still married."

Eli responded, "Then just say *my wife*. Legally, you still can." The guy looked thrilled to have been given this permission, as if the question had been bothering him for a long time. He said that his wife, Alona, absolutely hated SUVs. "Mine too, Dafna too," Eli said, and the conversation about cars momentarily distracted him from the fact that this man sitting next to him, practically touching him, staring at his beat-up Hyundai with his hands between his knees, was Roni's father.

He looked a lot like her. He had the same soft profile that Eli liked to gaze at in the darkness of the car: small nose, rounded chin, cheek like a pillow of velvet. And the lips. It horrified him.

The conversation somehow moved on to gardening, although he couldn't remember how. Maybe they'd wondered when it would finally rain. Her father said he was praying for a rainy year, so he wouldn't have to water his garden at the house he was renting.

"Where is it?" Eli asked. "Oh, yeah, I know that house. Next to the Rosenbergs' mansion," he said, when the guy explained.

"Yes, they're my neighbors, but I've never seen them even once."

"Well, that's why we live here, isn't it? So we don't have to see our neighbors."

The Mark guy agreed, and then Eli suggested that he install a computer system.

"A computer? What for?"

"For the sprinklers."

"Oh, yeah," Mark said, and told him that in his old house, where his wife and children lived, there was an automatic sprinkler, but it was broken.

Eli warmly recommended a simple one, like his, which he could get for about fifteen hundred shekels, maybe less. "And you should get a gardener, too. Even once a month, to do the dirty work. We have one. I can ask if he has time."

"Who is it, that Thai man?"

"Bobo," Eli said, and asked if he'd heard about the boy, and this space cadet Mark, God knows where he was living, said no. So Eli told him the story and said they suspected Bobo, and Ali, too, the maintenance guy.

Mark said that if they ever considered instituting the death penalty in Israel, it should be for that. Only that.

"For what?" Eli asked.

"Pedophiles."

"Oh, yeah, I totally agree," he said, and was relieved to see his car was done. He rushed over to tip the car-wash guy. "Okay, then, nice meeting you. And don't forget, get an automatic sprinkler. Believe me, it'll change your life." In a moment of stupidity, an idiotic moment of what, penance? he pulled out a business card from his shirt pocket and said, "Call me if you need more information."

He regretted it immediately. What was he doing, giving this man a business card? He spent several days fearing the phone call, but he didn't hear anything, and eventually he forgot about it. But this morning, four weeks after that day, right in the middle of a meeting with clients, the phone rang and Liat said it was Mark Segal. For a minute he couldn't think who that was. "Just a minute, I'll check," Liat said. Then her voice came back on the speakerphone: "Your neighbor from the moshav." Eli said, "Oh," and wondered whether to ask him to leave a message. But he had the secretary put him through, and he picked up the phone and motioned an apology to the people in his office. "Hi, Mark," he said genially.

"Am I disturbing you?" Mark asked. On the phone he sounded even younger than he looked.

"I'm in the middle of a meeting, but it's okay, go ahead. What's up?"

"You remember how we talked about the automatic sprinkler?"

Eli said he did, and Mark asked if he could recommend a specific model because he was considering finally buying one, maybe even today. He said his heart was breaking over those poor trees. Yesterday he'd examined each one, and the situation was really not good. "So I thought I'd ask you which one I should get. You're more of an expert than me."

"Not exactly an expert, but I can recommend the one I have."

"Because I'm clueless about these things," her father went on. "You could sell me anything, I'm a sucker."

Something tugged at Eli's heart, and he said, "Look, I can't remember the exact name right now, but give me your number and I'll get back to you later, when I get home." He took down Mark's cell phone number.

All day the paper with the number lay on his desk right in front of his eyes, and much as he tried not to think about it, he could not avoid the feeling that he was in trouble, big trouble, and he feared the moment when he got home and found the information and called Mark's cell. What if she picked up? But he quickly reassured himself. Why would she answer her dad's phone? She barely answered her own. Still, he hoped that when he did phone, he would get voice mail and could just leave the details and be done with it. Because it occurred to him that the guy might not be calling about the sprinkler but because he knew, and he was now going to persecute Eli in some twisted way. That he'd play this I-need-your-advice game with him, you're such an expert, please recommend a sprinkler for me, what should I get, how much does it cost, where do I buy it, and, by the way, I know you're fucking my daughter.

When the meeting ended and he sat wondering whether to go out for lunch or order in, he realized that was impossible. Mark looked innocent, innocent for real. But instead of finding this thought reassuring, it saddened him and made him feel even more of a louse than he really was. And he wasn't. Because the thing with Roni was much deeper, much less dirty, than someone from the outside might think. And anyway, he hadn't really had much of a choice, had he? What could he have done? A beautiful girl hops into his car in the middle of the night, sits next to him, all melancholia and teenage angst, and all of a sudden, totally out of the blue (except not totally—after all, he had turned up the volume on the radio, wanting to impress her with his state-of-the-art sound system, wanting to be young), had declared that she simply had to have a beer. What could he have done, ignore her?

Maybe yes, he thought now. Maybe if he had children he would have seen it differently, would have hurried back to his kids sleeping in their beds, hurried away from the dangerous girl who'd jumped into his car. But he'd said, "No problem, we'll get you a beer. There's an all-night grocery store by the gas station." He'd been there a million times, for milk or snacks or whatever, but never for beer.

It was obvious that he was hitting on her. Not that he planned on anything happening, not at all, but he had definitely wanted to pick up the gauntlet and play the game. He'd had a long day at the office and there was something refreshing in this little beer adventure in the middle of the night, so why not?

They drove to the gas station and she waited in the car with the radio on at full volume. He liked the vulgarity of it all, like they were Bonnie and Clyde robbing the gas station. He came back with two cold beers and she said, "So where should we drink them?"

"Excellent question. I don't feel like getting stopped by a cop for drunk driving. We could sit there"—he pointed at the grocery store—"they have some tables."

"It's gross in there, isn't it?"

"Maybe a little." He handed her his open bottle to hold. "We'll find somewhere." He drove back toward the moshav and glanced at her sipping her beer, with his bottle propped between her legs.

"We could go to the orchards," she said, and when she navigated him to a hidden path on the side of the road that he'd never noticed before, it seemed natural to him that a girl who'd grown up on the moshav would know every crevice. "Keep driving until you can't go any farther and then stop," she told him.

"Give me a swig," he said, maybe because he felt tense, maybe because he understood.

She pointed into the dark and said, "See there? Where the eucalyptus is? That's my dad's restaurant."

"Oh, that's your dad? We keep meaning to try it, my wife and I." He felt a bit dumb for working in this piece of information, just so she'd know he was married, as if she didn't already.

"You should go, it's an awesome place, and I wait tables there, so you'll have awesome service." They drove on, the SUV bouncing on the dirt path that grew more and more rocky, until she said, "This is it, you can't go any farther, it's all rocks."

"I could do it with the four-wheel drive," he boasted, but he stopped and turned off the engine, leaving the key half-turned in the ignition so they could keep listening to music.

"I was at a crappy party. I hate myself for always going to those parties," Roni said.

Eli's voice came out a little odd, a little perverted, when he said, "Could you possibly have anything to hate yourself for? I don't think so."

She said she did, lots of things, and gave him a look that seemed slutty. But what if it wasn't? he thought now. What if he'd been wrong? What if it wasn't that but something different? A desperate girl's cry for help, for a listening ear? But what could he have done when she suddenly lunged at him and pressed her lips against his? What could he have done?

And then she said, "I want you to fuck me." That's what she said. He remembered the exact words; he'd never forget them. Those words had totally stunned him. There was something horrifying about it, but it flicked his dick into a massive hard-on. What could he do? And so, in the blink of an eye, he turned from a pseudo-yuppie workaholic and decent husband, a geeky Jerusalemite, into a piece of shit. A louse. A pedophile.

He decided to go downstairs for a bite to eat, to get some fresh air, to get away from the white piece of paper that stared right back at him. Yesterday he'd phoned Roni to find out how she was doing. They hadn't met since their trip to Jerusalem a couple of weeks ago, and she sounded really cold on the phone. Not just unfocused or busy, like she usually was, but cold.

"I want to be with myself for a while," she said, with an infuriating little question mark at the end. "Maybe it's the winter. What an amazing storm yesterday! I thought about you, I thought of calling, with the rain and all that. I really wanted to hug you in the rain."

"Then why didn't you call?" he asked, and she said she didn't know, the rain had made her sad. "Well then," he said, sounding like a grandfather, "that's exactly why you should have done it." She said she didn't know, she felt like taking a little break, just for a while, nothing permanent, not breaking up or anything. He said, "Oh."

That's all he could get out: Oh.

He couldn't tell her that he hadn't called to set up a date but to talk. Yesterday was the eighteenth, and he spent it with Dafna, who'd had a bad response to the anesthesia for the first time and had been vomiting steadily. He'd played at nurse the whole day, hadn't even gone to the office but driven straight home with her, gallantly refraining from saying what she was obviously thinking: To go through all this for one egg? *One?* When this month they could have done it naturally? She'd responded indifferently when he'd told her he'd been able to get a postponement from the judge. Even when she stopped throwing up and finally got out of bed, she looked crushed, lifeless. And all that for one egg that didn't have a chance anyway. They hadn't even been able to extract the second one, for some reason, and when Dafna fell asleep in the afternoon, after they got home from the hospital, he felt like he needed a listening ear. He hadn't taken into account that such a young ear would not be right, but who else could he talk to? Now he realized that maybe that was the problem: she'd sensed his distress, she'd felt he needed her, and she was frightened, or disgusted, or God knows what, but she'd decided she wasn't into it anymore. What did she need some middle-aged guy with problems for?

That's what had happened, he decided, and he promised himself that from now on, once things settled down, after she spent some time with herself—she and her high school expressions—and they went back to their usual steamy encounters like last winter—he almost got an erection just thinking about last winter, about their first few times in February, in the SUV—he would avoid talking about himself and what he was really going through at all costs. She was right: she didn't need these hassles at her age. He would focus on what he knew best, on what she expected him to do: fuck her. Just like it should be. Without all this background noise.

It was lucky that one egg had even been fertilized. This morning Dafna had called to let him know, and she hadn't sounded happy but businesslike, informing him because she had to, like you notify someone of a ceremony or a meeting or a funeral. "It was fertilized, and they'll implant it in two days, but you don't have to come with me. You know, it's no big deal."

"I know," he said. "We'll see. I'm not sure what kind of day I have in two days."

When they hung up, he stared at his desk for a few minutes, examining the dark wood. He'd spent weeks choosing the desk. To him it was not just a desk, and not a status symbol either, but something else. A toy, like his SUV, maybe. Or not a toy but compensation. But for what? That wasn't clear. Ultimately he wasn't all that happy with the choice. "You chose a shit-brown color," Zvika said. "It's respectable, but it's shit-brown." At first Eli had protested, but Zvika was right, and there was nothing he could do, and so for three years he'd been sitting at a desk that reminded him of shit. Luxurious and impressive shit, but still shit, and he didn't have the guts to replace it.

He thought about how the morning had begun, the distress that had landed on him before lunch. First Mark with the sprinkler system, and then Dafna with the news about the egg, and it seemed to him as if both of them, Dafna and Mark, wanted something from him but he didn't know what. Like they were calling him to say something completely different from what they actually said, something more profound and convoluted and extremely scary.

He wanted to put off going home for as long as he could, to put off calling Mark Segal, so he decided to stay and go over Shabtai's papers. He'd been postponing it for ages, and his brother hadn't said a word because he was afraid of him, he needed him. Eli pulled the file out of the bottom of a pile on his desk and started reading, but he couldn't concentrate. Liat came in and said it was five-fifteen and asked if she could leave. He said, "Sure." Officially she worked from eight to four-thirty, but she never went home until he said, *That's it for today, you're free to go.* Today he'd gotten carried away and forgotten. "I'm sorry, I didn't notice the time," he said, and she said it was okay. She was a sweet girl, Liat. Not the sharpest tool in the shed, but absolutely fine. He and Zvika were lucky to have found her, after a series of terrible secretaries. She was twenty-four and getting married in the spring, and he was suddenly afraid to lose her, too. She would obviously get pregnant right away and then the trouble would start. Absences. Maternity leave. He hated being alone in the office. Hated Zvika's reserve duty, hated Liat, who was in such a rush to get married, and he was absolutely unable to concentrate on Shabtai's documents, which had been waiting patiently for two months.

He got up and walked over to the window and looked out at Ayalon Highway, which was jammed up with traffic, car headlights coloring the dusk. He thought he might call Dafna and ask if he should bring home sushi or something, or arrange some entertainment for the evening, whatever she felt like. Or maybe she wanted to go out for dinner? There was a new place on Montefiori Street he'd been wanting to try for ages: Brazilian or Cuban, he couldn't remember. But he knew she'd say she didn't feel like driving all the way back to Tel Aviv now, and he should have said something earlier, so she wouldn't have driven home. But why did he have to be the one to suggest dinner? Why not her? Anyway, why would they want to go out to a restaurant on a night like this, when they were both on edge before the implantation? It was better to go to sleep early and not pretend that everything was okay and they were happy.

Although, he thought, they weren't unhappy either. Not really. And things could have been even better if she would just finally drop the IVF business and agree to adopt. A little Ukrainian baby girl, or a boy, he didn't care which and he didn't care where from, and as far as he was concerned they could get two. Why not? Yesterday morning, in Room 4, he hadn't been able to resist fantasizing about Roni, even though he'd promised himself he wouldn't. He just could not conjure up any other image, and he knew Dafna had already gone in for the extraction and they were waiting for him. When he gave in and told himself to just go ahead with it, closed his eyes, and started to masturbate, the wrong slide jumped up in his vision: that time in the forest, maybe because it was the freshest memory, but that wasn't the picture he wanted, and it scared him. He wasn't sure what had happened there, and in the intervening two weeks he'd tried not to think about it; what was there to think about? Just an unsuccessful, grating, tense evening. But that wasn't all, because even though he hated himself for having hurt her, knowingly, for having ripped her apart, someone inside him not only forgave him for it but also enjoyed what had happened there. That someone was slightly horrified by the words and ashamed to say them out loud, but they tickled him, they sent electric pulses coursing through his blood and into the fist that encircled his dick, and he quickly positioned the plastic cup, and a second before overshooting—the words flashed before his eyes: *a second before I fucked her in the ass*—he ejaculated into the cup, groaning loudly, almost screaming her name. But this time, right after he came, he was enveloped by a terrible sadness.

And then there was Dafna, who woke up from the anesthetic and started to vomit, and since she'd been fasting there was nothing to throw up, just dry heaves. The nurses said it was normal, it happened, sometimes people responded badly to the anesthetic, and it did ease up after a few hours. When she recovered, they let her go home, but then it started again, and he had to stop twice at the side of the road and stand next to her while she doubled over and tried to vomit, but nothing came out. One time he put his hand on her shoulder to comfort her and she shook him off and asked him to wait in the car. He went back and sat behind the wheel and watched her clutching a utility pole, hunched over, and the sight of her large back, with his tailored black jacket that she wore because she was cold, reminded him of a wounded crow. She got back in the car and leaned her head back and closed her eyes and said, "That's it. Let's not stop anymore, I have nothing to throw up." He said okay, and they got home and he helped her into bed. As he removed the jacket, he felt her shoulders shaking him off again. He made her some herbal tea and said she should eat something, she'd been fasting for almost twenty-four hours. She said she didn't feel like anything, maybe later; she just wanted to sleep. Still, he spread some butter on a few crackers and took them on a tray into the bedroom, but she'd already fallen asleep, lying on her side on top of the comforter, her knees hunched up against her stomach. Like a fetus that had had the possibility of another fetus extracted from it that morning.

He put the tray on the dresser and brought in the wool blanket she sometimes used when she was watching TV. He spread it over her and spent the rest of the afternoon walking restlessly around the house, checking on her every so often. Even the phone didn't wake her, and Dafna usually awoke from the slightest sound. It was her boss, Gabi, who didn't even know she'd had an extraction today. He said, "Oh, no kidding. She didn't tell me. Or maybe I forgot. Well, I hope she feels better. And tell her to call when she can, because Adel—yes, she'll know who it is—is trying to get hold of her urgently."

Who was Adel? Eli wondered. Although he knew she worked with Arabs, and she'd told him about CUSP's latest project, the name bothered him. Who was this Adel and what was so urgent? He knew so little about her, he realized. There was so little he wanted to know. And now this Adel.

He went out to the yard and decided to clean out the fish pond. The rain from a few days ago had blown leaves and earth into the water, and you could barely see the fish. When he turned on the underwater bulbs the light was a murky blue, stuck in one place as if unable to diffuse. He picked up the net and started fishing out rotting leaves. The fish scattered in a panic, seeking shelter in the corners of the pond, and then he saw two dead goldfish floating on the surface. Every so often he had to remove a dead fish from the pond, but two was odd. He wondered if the water was polluted, if the fish were sick, or if it was just a coincidence. Maybe the rain and the silt were responsible for their death. He fished out one orange corpse in the net and placed it on the rockery, then the second one, and looked into the cloudy eyes of the two bloated fish, their color slightly faded. He wondered if he should consult with someone or just wait and see if any more died. He went inside to put a sweater on, it was getting very cold, and looked in on Dafna, who was curled up under the wool blanket with her lips parted, her red hair spread over the pillow. He picked up his jacket and took his cigarettes out of the drawer in the large dresser in the foyer. He went outside and lit one, sat down on the rockery, smoked, and looked at the dead fish.

Without knowing why, he went back inside, got his cell phone, came outside and dialed her number. "Roni?" he said, and asked if he was disturbing her.

"No, not at all. Well, kind of." She was in the middle of writing.

He asked what she was writing, but he quickly realized that it didn't interest him. In fact it annoyed him that he had to take an interest in her high school nonsense.

"Nothing, you know, just thoughts."

He asked what thoughts. He knew he sounded too horny—this was not what he wanted, after all. But what did he want?

"All kinds."

He could hear her taking a drag on a cigarette and asked if she was smoking.

"Yeah, I'm in the backyard."

"I'm in the yard too, smoking."

"So what's going on?"

He told her about the extraction, about Dafna, and about his awful day.

"Wow, sounds terrible. How is she now?"

He said she was asleep, he'd just gone out for a smoke and to phone her.

"You sound sad," Roni said.

"No, just tired. Well, maybe a little. It's a rough thing, these treatments." He couldn't stop staring at the fishes.

"I know. Actually, I don't know."

And all of a sudden a pathetic little speech poured out of him, about why Dafna was even doing it, and what sort of endurance she must have, and for what? For one egg?

Roni said, "But maybe that one is *the* one, no? Maybe it's your child. Think about it that way."

"Last time they implanted three embryos, Roni. Three. And nothing came of it."

"Oh. I didn't know."

Then there was a pause, and he asked, "So what are you up to now?" He didn't want it to sound like an invitation to get together.

"Nothing. I told you, just writing a little. I think I'll go to bed afterward." And then she hit him with it. "Listen," she said. "Listen, Eli, I've been thinking. . . ."

"About what? What have you been thinking about?"

"All kinds of things. About me, about us."

"And what have you come up with?" he asked, automatically anticipating dirty talk, anticipating it like you anticipate a compliment or comfort.

"I was thinking maybe we shouldn't see each other for a while." Then she explained that she had to be with herself a little, and it wasn't him, it really wasn't.

"Of course it's me. I understand."

She said no, it wasn't him, it was just about her, and it wasn't a breakup.

"What is it then?"

"I don't know," she said, as usual.

"Two of my fish died," he said, wanting urgently to change the topic, or perhaps wanting her to feel a little sorry for him. "I just found two dead goldfish in the pond."

"Really?" She asked if he was going to give them a funeral.

"I don't think so. It's just fish."

"But you're a little sad that they died, aren't you?"

"No, not at all. So I gather you don't want to see me, is that what you're saying?"

She said she wasn't really sure if that was what she was saying, but maybe yes, just for a while, temporarily.

"That's too bad," he said.

She told him he shouldn't be so sad.

"I'm not sad, I just think it's a pity." He asked if it had anything to do with their trip to Jerusalem.

"No, not at all."

"Are you sure? Because I think I was a bit of an asshole. I don't know what happened to me, Roni."

"No big deal. That has nothing to do with it."

"I'll miss you."

"It's just for a while, so there's nothing to miss. But I'll miss you too, okay? Let's agree that I'll miss you, too?"

Baby, he thought. Annoying baby. "Okay, let's agree that you'll miss me, too."

"And let's agree that when I miss you so badly that I can't take it anymore, I'll call you."

"Okay. When do you think that will happen?"

"I don't know. That's what's so cool about it, isn't it? That I don't know."

He absentmindedly started to push the fish corpses around with a stick. He flipped them over as if they were on a grill. "I think it's too bad, but if that's what you want. . . ."

"It's for the best, I think."

He tossed the stick on the ground and suddenly felt exhausted. These childish conversations, which used to turn him on so much, which used to be their foreplay, not only exhausted him now but sounded like a foreign language he could no longer understand. As if all these months he'd been chattering away in some exotic dialect and now he'd forgotten how to speak it.

Roni said, "You sound bummed out, sweet pea."

"Okay, Roni, let's cut this short, 'cause I have to go check on Dafna. I gather the bottom line is you want to break up."

"No, you're not getting me. I just want some time for myself," she repeated, and told him again that she was sad, maybe because of the rain.

"You think about things, then, and if you come to any conclusions, call me, okay? I'm here."

"Okay. And kisses, you know where."

"Okay," he said again, and hung up.

He was suddenly desperate for Dafna to wake up. He roamed the house for another hour or so, looking in on her every so often, but instead of trying to keep quiet he deliberately opened and shut the closet doors and flushed the toilet. When she finally woke up, just before eight, she looked better and said she was starving. He said, "Great, I'll make something. I waited for you for dinner." She said she would make something, and tried to get up, but he said, "No way! Let me pamper you a little." The word *pamper* sounded grating, out of place, arousing memories from a different context. He used to use that word a lot in bed: *let me pamper you*, even though she'd told him several times she couldn't stand it.

Now she said, "All right," and asked what time it was.

He said, "Eight. Do you feel like pasta?" She shook her head. "*Shakshuka?*" he asked; it was his specialty, the only dish he excelled at.

"Yes, *shakshuka*. But go easy on the hot peppers."

He went into the kitchen and took some eggs out of the fridge, and heard Dafna say she was going to take a shower and he should defrost some pitas. He took the bag out of the freezer and placed it on the counter, chopped an onion, and tossed it into a frying pan. The phone rang and he picked it up. Irit wanted to know what was going on and how it went today, and said Dafna had promised to call right after the extraction but she hadn't. She knew Dafna hated to be pestered so she'd waited, but still, any news? He told her it had been traumatic, she'd had a bad response to the anesthetic, and in the end they'd only been able to extract one egg. Irit said Dafna must be beat, and he said yes, and she was in the shower. "Have her call me later, then," Irit said. He asked how the kids were, and she said, "Fine. Crazy, as usual, but sweet," and he agreed, and they hung up. He turned the heat down under the frying pan, added tomato paste and spices, easy on the chili, and broke the eggs into the pan and covered it.

Dafna asked who called, and he said, "Your sister. She wanted to know how it went."

Dafna yelled, "What? I couldn't hear you."

He went to the bathroom and opened the door. "Irit," he said.

Dafna was sitting on the edge of the bathtub, naked, with a towel wrapped around her hair. She looked like a sculpture made of pale, veiny marble.

"Hey, who's Adel?" Eli asked. He told her Gabi had called for her and said someone named Adel needed her urgently.

"Urgently?" She asked him to hand her the big towel from the hook on the door.

He gave her the towel and she swiftly wrapped it around her body, and it suddenly occurred to him that she was embarrassed to get up, embarrassed to be seen standing nude, and his heart sank again. "So who's this Adel?" he asked again, and walked over to the steamed-up mirror. He wiped it with his fist and looked at his face.

Dafna got up and tightened the edges of the towel around her chest. Then she removed the towel from her head and shook out her hair, which emitted a scent that reminded him of something distant. "He's from that project, Swap-Meet. He's the only Palestinian who ever called, and he wants a Power Ranger for his kid."

Eli giggled. "A Power Ranger? That's what's going to make his life better?"

"Apparently." Dafna explained that she was supposed to buy him one this week but she hadn't had time.

"But that's cheating! It's supposed to be people trading things, isn't it?"

"Yes, but since he's the only Palestinian who called, Gabi decided to turn him into his protégé. He'll do anything not to disappoint him. He has plans to make him a star."

That wonderful smell tickled his nostrils again. "What is that? What's that scent?"

"Shampoo."

"It smells familiar, but that's not your usual shampoo, is it?"

She said no, she'd switched, it was just a cheap shampoo she used to use years ago.

He looked at the bottle and said, "You used this when we met, didn't you?"

"Wow, what a good memory!"

He suddenly felt like ripping the towel off her body—the shampoo, Adel, the nakedness, all the things he didn't know about her. "I found two dead fish in the pond," he said.

"Really? How did they die?"

He said he had no idea and then remembered the *shakshuka* and hurried to the kitchen. He lifted up the lid and looked at the eggs hardening, two eyes with yellow cataract-ridden pupils inside a bubbling red swamp. He went back to the bathroom.

Dafna had already gone into the bedroom and was sitting on the edge of the bed. "I feel a little dizzy," she said, and lay down on her back. She looked like a mummy in that towel. "I wish I had his phone number."

"Whose?" he asked, and sat down next to her.

"Adel's. He wouldn't give it to me. We've been torturing him for a month now with this doll. I'm buying it tomorrow. Did anyone else call?"

"Irit."

"Yes, you told me."

He asked if she was still dizzy. The *shakshuka* was almost ready.

"No, I'm just very weak. So what do you think happened to your poor fish?"

And those words, *your poor fish*, sent a shiver of self-pity through his body. But there was also sadness for them both and nostalgia for the days when they told each other absolutely everything. Except maybe they never did tell each other everything.

"Could a cat have killed them?" she asked.

He said he didn't think so, a cat would have eaten them. He thought it was a disease, or old age, or the rain. Almost inadvertently he put his hand on the towel, on her stomach. "Or maybe it's my fault. I haven't been cleaning the pond out, and there's loads of crud built up in there."

"I don't think you can die of crud."

"Fish can, I guess."

"Lousy pets. It's really not worth it."

"Yes, it is. They don't need any attention, they don't need love, they don't need anything."

She turned over to her side, possibly to push away his hand, which was making circles on the towel, and said, "Turns out that's wrong."

His heart sank again, not because she was right about the fish—he couldn't care less about them, and the truth is he'd be happy if they all dropped dead and he could give up the pond and plant something there instead, like a tree. His heart sank because this conversation about nothing, about everything, reminded him of how much he missed the old Dafna. Except he realized now that there was no old Dafna but only one Dafna, and it was childish to invent a new one, an IVF Dafna, a stubborn, obsessive Dafna. There was no such woman, just like he himself hadn't really changed. It didn't matter what he told himself, and it didn't matter how many times he fucked that girl, whom he shouldn't be angry with, because she was growing up—although perhaps because of him she was growing up faster than she should—while he was just going backward, feeling more and more like a child who needed protection. "I thought Power Rangers were out, aren't they? Your sister's kids used to have them," he said.

"Maybe the Palestinians have a delayed sense of what's in and what's out." She sighed. "That sounds awful."

"What does?"

She sat up. "It sounds condescending, what I said, doesn't it?"

"So condescend. What do you care? I'm the only one listening."

"What's up with the *shakshuka*?" she asked.

He leaped off the bed and hurried to the kitchen. The bubbling eggs had almost completely dried up, exposing a charred bottom. He turned off the heat and took the pan off the stove.

"Is it burnt?" Dafna asked, appearing in the kitchen in a long T-shirt and underwear. How long had it been since she'd walked around in her underwear?

"Almost, but I think it's still edible."

She opened the lid and pronounced, "Edible." She took two pitas out of the bag and put them in the microwave. They sat down at the table and Dafna ate ravenously, soaking up the sauce with pieces of pita.

"You like it?" he asked.

"It's great. You're a champion at this. And it's just what I wanted now." When her plate was empty he offered her his portion, and she said, "Okay, I really am starved. But what about you?" He said he wasn't that hungry, he'd had something at the hospital. "Really?" she asked. "When? I didn't notice."

"You didn't notice anything, you were out of it." In fact he hadn't eaten at the hospital, and he was very hungry, but he wanted to give up something for her, to be generous. As he watched her gobble down the half portion he'd slid onto her plate, he said, "So what do you think? Will there be a fertilization?"

She said she really didn't feel like talking about that now. "Either there will or there won't." She didn't want to think about it. He asked if she really could put it out of her mind and she said, "Of course not." She asked what was on TV. He said he'd check and got up to find the newspaper, but she said, "Never mind, leave it. Sit with me for a while."

Sit with me for a while. It had been so long since she'd made such a simple, heart-wrenching request of him. Run around doing errands, yes. Buy medication, argue with the health fund, go grocery shopping, fix the car—he wondered what had happened with that noise the car was making, but didn't ask—but *sit with me for a while* was new. Or, rather, very old. Something rummaged from their shared attic, even though she'd never asked him for anything as simple as that, anything as frighteningly simple.

"I'll sit with you for as long as you want," he said tenderly.

She looked up from her plate and gazed at him for a moment, or maybe tried to capture with her eyes the shape of that strange sentence. "So what happened with the fish? Did you throw them out?"

"Not yet, there's no hurry. They're already dead."

She smiled. "But they'll start to stink, won't they?"

"Some cat or dog will probably take care of them." He got up and took his plate to the sink, and when he went back to the table he wanted to hug her. He put a hand on her shoulder and immediately felt that spring tighten, but he left his hand there, like a soft but heavy cloud. She dropped her fork to the plate and placed her hand on his.

Now he closed Shabtai's file and stood by the window again, looking down at Ayalon Highway, which was still jammed up. He wondered whether to spend another hour or so in the office until the traffic eased up. He hated being one of the thousands making their way home at the same time.

He sat down in his chair again, leaned back, and looked at his desk, which in the halogen light looked even more like shit. Glowing shit. He got up and walked out of the office, locked the door behind him, and took the elevator down to the parking lot. He walked quickly to his SUV, which welcomed him with a cheerful beep, as if to say, *I've been waiting for you here all day in the dark, and I missed you terribly*. He sat down behind the wheel and started the engine, and as soon as he drove onto the street and the light blinked on the hands-free unit to signal that he had good reception, he phoned home and told Dafna it was okay for two days from now. It was fine; he'd go with her to the implantation. He was free.

REUVEN

At night he dreamed that Lake Kinneret was full to the brim. There were no red lines signaling a water shortage. Not an upper line or a lower line, just a wonderful, deep, glistening lake. When he woke up, even before opening his eyes, something in him rejoiced and his heart overflowed, just like the Kinneret, which in his dream had looked like one of the lakes he'd seen in Scotland, on the package tour Rina had convinced him to take last summer.

From the moment she booked the tickets, he regretted agreeing to the trip. He hated traveling and was afraid of flying, and he thought the package tour she'd found was a swindle. He phoned the travel agent and claimed she'd lied when she'd told his wife it was all-inclusive. "My wife doesn't fully understand about finances," he explained, and argued that she'd made the booking of her own accord. "Yes, of course she needs her husband's approval," he said, at the impudent travel agent's gibe—*I didn't know Mrs. Brochstein needed her husband's permission.* Every little bimbo is a feminist these days, he thought to himself. "And not only does the price not include everything," he yelled into the phone, smelling his saliva that sprayed into the little holes in the mouthpiece, "it doesn't include anything! Nothing at all! Not airport taxes, not transportation from the airport to the hotel, and what kind of hotel is it anyway? I'm not so sure." He threatened to have his son look the hotel up on the Internet when he got home from the army in the evening, and asked her to spell out the name for him, "and then we'll see if it really is a four-star like you say."

The agent surprised him by saying softly, "Mr. Brochstein, would you like to cancel? Because you can, but you'll forfeit the registration fee."

"Why would I cancel?" he retorted. "You're completely misunderstanding me."

He didn't want to cancel, he wanted to argue. But this impertinent agent—and he could teach her a thing or two about customer service: he dealt with people all the time in his job; every day he held court for all kinds of tricksters who wanted business licenses, and most of them he rejected outright, sent them away with a warning that he'd instruct the inspectors to keep a close eye on them and make sure some illegal business didn't happen to pop up within the Pardesim Regional Council's jurisdiction—this little bimbo wouldn't give him the time of day.

He didn't want to cancel, and not because of the registration fee but because of Rina. She hadn't been feeling well lately, all kinds of female troubles, aches and bleeding. She wanted to talk about it, he knew that. After all, who would she talk to if not him? She had almost no girlfriends. But he wouldn't let her. It wasn't any of his business. He told her to go and see a doctor, and not her regular gynecologist at the health fund, that old Russian man who shouldn't even be allowed to work there, but a real specialist. They were entitled to a specialist's opinion three times a year; he'd asked about it. "So go, don't put it off anymore," he told her, and she said she'd go after the trip. Ten days in Scotland. Why Scotland? He couldn't understand that but he didn't argue, because for him any destination was just the same as any other, arousing the same melancholy. He hadn't enjoyed their last package tour either, which they'd done six years ago with Dudi, for his bar mitzvah: Classical Europe. So what did he care? If she wanted Scotland, then Scotland it was. It could just as well be Ireland, Greenland, or Iceland, just as long as he didn't break his wife's heart. She seemed to be aging twice as fast as he was, and not just because of the aches and pains but generally, in the way she looked. Nothing seemed to be quite in its place. Bags under the eyes, flabby arms, a protrusion in the back of the neck that looked like the start of a hunchback, God forbid. And she was sprouting a little potbelly. Her legs looked too short and her arms looked huge, and her behind, which had always been flat, was completely swallowed

up in the general defective picture. Like Humpty Dumpty. He thought
back to the only story Dudi had liked when he was little. He used to ask
over and over again to hear about how Humpty Dumpty fell off a wall
and shattered into pieces. Reuven had kept his promise and tried to
enjoy himself on the trip, but he hated it.

He couldn't remember the details of his dream, like how he even
wound up at the Kinneret or what he was doing there, but he knew he
was on his own. It was strange that he'd even dreamed at all. He hadn't
had any dreams for a long time, or at least he couldn't remember them.
When he was younger he had dreams every night, full of people he
argued or fought with, wild scenes with lots of shouting. Sometimes he
shouted out in his sleep and Rina would wake him and he'd fall asleep
again, angry at her for cutting off a dream argument. He'd fall right back
into an urgent sleep and a new dream, or a continuation of the previous
one, and he would keep on arguing, but quietly.

Only after he opened his eyes, sat up in bed, and looked around did
he remember: he was on his own today. And on the news they'd said it
would rain, which probably explained the dream. Rina had gone to visit
her brother in Holon yesterday, and since she'd finally scheduled an
appointment with a gynecologist in Tel Aviv, she'd spent the night there
and was only coming back this evening. He remembered how he'd fought
with her yesterday when he took her to the bus stop. She said she would
take advantage of the opportunity to walk around Carmel Market a
little. They had a stand that sold underpants and bras, some brand she
liked, and she couldn't find them anywhere else.

"Are you crazy?" he said. "There's a terrorist alert. They said on the
news they had concrete warnings."

"But there hasn't been an attack for ages, except in the Territories."

"That's exactly why there's going to be one, because there hasn't
been anything for ages."

"Oh, come on. You can't live in fear the whole time." She had mocked
him when he claimed Ali was trying to kill him with poisoned sesame
bread. "It's not poisoned, it's just not fresh, or maybe dirty," she'd said,
"maybe someone touched it with dirty hands, or someone had a stomach bug."

"You're wrong, you're naïve," he had said, because the idea that he
might have picked up a bug from an Arab who hadn't washed his hands

after wiping his ass seemed even more horrendous than the notion of an intentional poisoning.

The bag Rina took out of the trunk was so huge it looked like she was going on a long vacation rather than to visit her vegetable brother in a state hospital in Holon. The Ministry of Health was threatening to close it down because of budget cuts, and maybe that would be for the best. Reuven had only visited him once with Rina, a few years ago, and he'd been horrified.

"Rubi," she repeated, "you can't live in fear like this the whole time. You have to live a little."

He mumbled something belittling and drove away. Even that woman, Alona, had agreed with him about the fear when they'd talked about it two weeks ago, when her car was stolen.

She'd rung the doorbell that morning, and he'd opened the door and found her standing there barefoot, wearing shorts and a long tank top, probably her husband's, with no bra. She said someone had broken in and stolen her car and locked them in the house, and she had to take the kids to preschool. No, she hadn't called the police yet, she wanted to drop the kids off first, she didn't want them to be at home when the police came so they wouldn't get scared. She was very sorry to bother him.

"It's no bother at all," he said.

She said the kids were alone, watching TV, and she'd come to ask if he could give them a ride to preschool. It wasn't far, just in Ganei Zur.

"Of course, it's no trouble at all," he said, and forgot about his aching stomach for a moment, and how he'd almost passed out in the bathroom.

Then Rina appeared and asked what had happened. When he told her and said he was going out, she said, "But Rubi, what about . . . you know. What about your stomach?"

He shushed her, embarrassed and angry, and Alona said she was sorry again, didn't he feel well? She could ask another neighbor; everyone's cars were still here.

"Absolutely not. I'll drive you." And to Rina, who stood close behind him, he said, "I'm fine. It's better." Only then did he notice that he wasn't dressed yet, and that his neighbor, who even in her state of panic still looked extremely attractive, was seeing him in the kind of pajamas he

knew no one wore anymore, certainly not the kind of men she would
have any interest in, only *alte kockers*.

Alona said, "Thanks, I'll get the kids organized and we'll be outside
in five minutes."

"You're welcome, it's no trouble," and he hurried to the bedroom to
get dressed, with Rina right behind him, asking if he really thought this
was a good idea, and why wasn't that woman phoning her husband?
He lived right there, after all. "You've had four bowel movements, Rubi,
maybe you'll have more." Without looking at her—he knew that if he
did he would disclose more than he himself knew—he said he was fine;
it was only a short drive. But as he buttoned up his favorite top, a soft
pale blue cotton shirt that often received compliments, even from Ali,
the murderer, who said he looked not a day over thirty in it, he thought
maybe Rina was right. What would happen if he had an urgent need to
relieve himself again? Still, fifteen minutes ago it had been clear to him
that he'd gotten out everything there was to get out. He tied his shoelaces and noticed he was wearing yesterday's brown socks, which did
not match the blue shirt, and he hurried to the closet to find a different
pair. Rina asked, "What's the problem, Rubi? Why are you changing
your socks?"

"I wore these yesterday."

"So what?" she said, and then, as if finally understanding something,
she sighed and walked down the hallway to the kitchen, and he heard
her washing the breakfast dishes. Then she came back, caught him looking at himself in the full-length mirror attached to the closet door, and
said the woman and her kids were already waiting on the street and Mr.
Peacock had better hurry up.

When he sat down behind the wheel, after insisting that the children
should be strapped in, even though Alona said there was no need for
such a short drive, he remembered that he hadn't yet decided if he was
going to work or not. After all, he was sick. He decided to see how
things developed. He'd drop the kids off and drive Alona home, and
obviously he'd wait with her until the police got there. She looked
upset. Her hair, which was never neat, and that was really a shame, was
flattened against one side of her head, probably the side she'd slept on.
The children also looked neglected. The girl had all kinds of barrettes
and ponytail holders hanging from her hair like insects, and the boy

looked like a little hedgehog, with his spiky black hair. The sight of him tugged at Reuven's heart for a moment, especially when the hedgehog started to whimper that he was thirsty. It didn't help when his mother tried to comfort him and said she'd ask the teacher to make him some chocolate milk. "But they don't have chocolate milk there!" he wailed.

"Yes, they do, of course they do," Alona said.

The little girl said quietly, "They don't."

The boy climbed onto his mother's lap and put his head on her chest. They were sitting in the middle and blocking his visibility, and Reuven wanted to ask them to move, but he just asked the girl to sit still and not lean on the front seat, because if he stopped suddenly she'd fly out the window. Her mother said, "Yes, Maya, Rubi is right." Since when did she call him Rubi? How did she even know that was his nickname? But then he remembered the note he'd left when he gave her back the five shekels from the supermarket.

"I won't fly out," the girl said, and kept sitting with her head sticking through the two front seats. "People don't fly. Only birds and planes and butterflies."

Alona said, "Oh, come on, Maya, stop being a smarty-pants."

The boy cried louder. "I'm thirsty, I didn't get any chocolate milk!"

"Me neither," the girl grumbled, and she started whining, too.

"Maya, stop it. This isn't a regular morning. We're in a big hurry today."

The boy asked, "But where's our car? Why aren't we going in our car?"

Maya said, "Someone took it, right, Mom? They stole our car."

Ido asked, "Really, Mom?"

"Yes."

The boy got off her lap and put his face up against the back window and said, "There they are—the thieves!" and for a moment everyone turned their heads back, but they couldn't see anything.

"Where?" the girl asked, curious.

"There! Behind the trees!"

Alona sighed, and Rubi's eyes met hers in the window, and she smiled, and he did, too: Children! Oh, the children! So wonderful, but such hard work. He was impatient to get rid of them and go back to Eden, and it suddenly occurred to him that Rina was right; why hadn't Alona called her husband? It was strange and slightly unusual, but he didn't want to think about it too much. No, because she had come to him. It was his door she'd knocked on.

He drove into Ganei Zur, stopped outside the preschool and kindergarten, and watched Alona quickly walk her children to the door. With some awkwardness, but also a little nostalgia, he remembered that morning when she'd come to the council to settle a debt, and the embarrassing business in the bathroom.

He'd hardly thought about her since. Sometimes he would look through the kitchen window when she got in and out of the car, but they hadn't run into each other since that day. The pool had been closed for six weeks, and he hadn't seen her at the supermarket, and then this morning these unfortunate circumstances had thrown her right into his arms. It was as if a cannon had shot her from her house to his, he thought, and complimented himself for the creative metaphor. Sometimes he could be poetic, even though he didn't like to read, and movies didn't do it for him either, nor did museums. How he had suffered on that trip to Europe, while Rina and Dudi dragged him from one museum to the next. Dudi had seemed very interested, for a boy of his age. He'd stood quietly looking at the paintings, listening to explanations in English. Even though he wasn't the artistic type, Reuven had these sort of magical moments when even he was touched by inspiration.

But then something started to go wrong. The pleasant scenes of young parents walking from the parking lot to the gate with their children, and the thought of the moment when Alona would come back to the car—all this was suddenly interrupted by a rumbling sound from his stomach, as if an engine had started to run. He knew the anxiety would only make things worse, but still his forehead started to pour with sweat and he quickly turned on the engine so he could put the air-conditioning on, even though he never used the air when the car was standing still. It was a waste of gas and it caused air pollution. Still, he turned it all the way up and tried to distract himself from his aching gut by fiddling with buttons and adjusting the air vents. He thought perhaps he should get out, walk over to the guard, explain that he was waiting for a mother, Alona—what was her last name? Segal. Good thing he remembered—and casually ask if there happened to be a bathroom nearby. But what if he was directed to the bathroom in one of the preschools? It might even be the hedgehog boy's preschool, and then she'd see him. No, he could hold it in. His intestines were obviously empty and this was just some phantom urge that would pass when the woman came back and they started to chat. It was a little much of her to make him wait here all this time; it had already been fifteen minutes. How long did it take to say goodbye to a child?

When she finally came hurrying down the path, faltering in her flip-flops, her large breasts bouncing up and down as she ran, she got quickly into the car and apologized profusely. "I'm sorry, he made a scene. Hysterics, don't ask."

He pulled out of the parking spot. "That's okay. It happens with kids. You have to be patient."

She said the car was cold, and he asked if he should turn off the air, but she said, "No, it's actually nice." He liked that she felt nice, and she said, "It's a bit chilly outside, in fact. I think winter is here. Yesterday was still quite warm, wasn't it?"

He said it was, and looked at her bare thighs, chubby thighs that stuck to each other, with spider veins on the sides, but that didn't bother him.

"It's funny how winter always arrives suddenly," she said. "Like we don't really have transitional seasons."

"That's true. But if you're cold I can turn off the air. I see you're wearing shorts."

She looked at her legs and rubbed her arms, as if only just noticing that she was practically naked. "I didn't have time to get dressed this morning, I was in such a hurry with the kids. But don't turn it off. It's nice with the air on. I was running, so I'm hot."

"But you'll tell me if you get cold?"

"Yes."

"Promise?" His voice changed suddenly, dropped an octave or two, but it still sounded screechy, not like the voice of the man she would want to be with this morning. Too much like the old man she'd seen in his pajamas only a few minutes ago.

Why was he so attracted to her? After that incident last summer he'd been angry, even though he knew it wasn't her fault. After all, he wasn't a baby, he knew it took two to tango and all that. Still, every time he saw her through the kitchen window, he felt a bitterness frothing up his blood. But the anger would melt away when he saw her lean into the car to strap the children into their seats, then sit down behind the wheel and drive away. The anger would make way for this elusive passion, which was almost irrelevant to his life yet still very precious, and when the outline of her body remained in the spot she'd stood in long after she was gone, he would realize that the protrusions were what had won him over. Everything protruded with her. Not just her breasts, but her thighs and ass and stomach. Even her ankles looked chubby, and her cheeks, which reminded him of a squirrel. They were puffed out, perhaps because her lips pouted in a slightly childish expression. Her daughter had that too, but with the woman it was something else, something between insulted and contemplative, and it gave her face a look that was seductive and just a little—he found it hard to think this about her, but there was no escaping it—a little sluttish.

She sat with her hands between her thighs, and he asked again if she was cold.

"No. Well, maybe a little. Could you turn it down a bit? I'm sorry."

"Don't be sorry, I'll turn it off. I'm a little cold, too."

He never turned the air on in November, on principle, even on warm days. He had endless arguments about it with Rina, who was always hot, even though she'd been done with the menopause thing more than ten years ago. Ever since then she was always hot, and she would beg him to turn the air on: "Just a little! What do you care?" But he would never turn the air on in winter. She'd say, "What winter are you talking about? Does this feel like winter? It's hot!" Now, with the air turned on all the way in November and the window open and the gas wasting, he wondered whether he didn't enjoy tormenting his wife a little, seeing her stew in her menopause juices.

Waking up from his dream now, he noticed that this morning really was cold. How disappointed he had been last winter. He had naïvely believed that the generous amounts of rain would fill the Kinneret, but in fact the water level had stayed under the red line. He sat on the edge of the bed and wiggled his toes, listening to the trickle of rain. He berated himself for forgetting to tell Rina that they'd predicted rain for today. That could have been his winning argument: Who wanted to walk

around the market in the rain? She probably didn't know it was supposed to rain. He liked the way she treated him like a general inquiries
service, asking what the weather would be, what they'd said on the
news, adopting his political views out of laziness and perhaps slight
stupidity.

He went into the kitchen and poured one glass of water into the
electric kettle. Rina always boiled a full kettle, which drove him crazy.
While he waited for the water to boil, he looked out onto the street and
saw Alona walk through the gate with the children, who were holding
umbrellas over their heads and all you could see was their feet in rubber
boots. She didn't have an umbrella, and she was wearing one of her old
track suits. She tried to pull the umbrella out of the girl's hand, but she
refused to let go. They stood arguing for a few minutes until suddenly
Alona abandoned the girl and hurried to the boy, who was running
down the street, splashing through the gutter in his boots. She held his
hand and pulled him to the car, where the girl still stood under her
umbrella. Alona picked up the boy, and his umbrella pressed against
her cheek. Reuven couldn't hear anything, and didn't want to draw her
attention by opening the window, but he assumed the child was protest-
ing, because he was kicking his feet and one of his boots fell to the
ground. She shut the boy's umbrella and put him in his seat and strapped
him in—now her behind was facing Reuven—and then she went back
to the girl and said something, waving her hand angrily, and the girl
threw her umbrella on the sidewalk and crawled into the car. After strap-
ping her in, the woman picked up the umbrella and shut it, tossed it
onto the front seat, and sat down behind the wheel. But she quickly got
out again and ran back for the boot. She got into the car again, brushed
her wet hair off her face, started the engine, and drove off.

He made himself a cup of instant coffee and sat down at the table,
wishing he had the newspaper. He always refused to subscribe, explaining to Rina that it was a con. Yes, it was cheaper, but only assuming a
person really bought the paper every single day. He knew he was wrong,
but he left it at that, and today he regretted it, because suddenly, perhaps
because he hadn't been alone for a long time, he felt slightly lonely and
disoriented.

Dudi wasn't home today either; he had guard duty on the army base
again. Reuven remembered the big fight they'd had on Saturday, about

the showers. "How many showers do you need?" he'd yelled at Dudi. "Isn't once a day enough? What are you, a girl? And fresh towels every time, like you're in a hotel! How dirty could you possibly get, sitting at your Internet all day? Anyone would think you worked the land or something."

He'd stood there in the hallway facing his son, who wore only gym shorts, his chest bare and covered with curly hair like Reuven's own used to be, and a sour, warm scent coming from his skin. Dudi was a head taller than him. When he'd enlisted, he'd measured in at six-one, and he seemed to have grown even more since then. Reuven stood facing his giant son and asked him, for the third time that day, why he had to take another shower. Why waste all that water? And if he had to, why take a new towel every time? The boy stared beyond him at the wall and said, "What can I do for you, Dad? Do you have a problem?"

"Nothing. I don't need you to do anything for me. I just want you to show some consideration for us, for the situation. Show some consideration for the Kinneret."

"You can shove the Kinneret up your ass!" the boy spat out.

Reuven almost slapped him. There was a time when he would have slapped him for less. But he just said, "This is the last time you're taking a shower today. Really, Dudi, I'm forewarning you."

The boy had turned his huge pimply back to him and said, "Wow, Dad, such language! *Forewarning!*" He locked himself in the bathroom for ages, as usual, wasting all forty gallons that the tank contained, and then he shut himself up in his bedroom for hours upon hours, emerging only to eat dinner.

Reuven sipped his coffee slowly, drawing out the time even though he had business to take care of that morning, and a meeting with the deputy council chair at nine. He had to be at the meeting because the deputy chair, a thirty-year-old kid, was proposing a lenient stance toward people who had recently requested business licenses in the region. He said it was "because of the situation," and that ultimately the council would profit from high taxes on these businesses. Reuven firmly objected, for idealistic reasons, because what would become of the character of all these little towns and villages if they ended up turning into a commerce and industry region? Today some bored housewife opens a bakery in her front yard, and tomorrow—what will happen tomorrow?

"Exactly. What about tomorrow?" the deputy chair had recently retorted. "You tell me, what do *you* want to have here tomorrow?"

Reuven wasn't sure what to answer, so he said, "Tomorrow we'll be a mall. We'll be Dizengoff Center, that's what we'll be."

And the deputy chair said, "Yeah, so? What's so bad about that?" Reuven knew in the depths of his heart that his motives were not environmental but petty. Still, he felt that even this pettiness was a type of idealism, in a back-asswards kind of way, as he'd heard his son say about all sorts of things. He didn't quite understand the meaning of the idiom, but it seemed apt.

He had to make his voice heard at the meeting this morning, but still he did not hurry. Something about the empty house was pleasant, even though he felt slightly lost. He sat down at the kitchen table and debated whether to eat toast again for breakfast, as he had every morning since the food poisoning had almost killed him. For two weeks he'd been treating Ali coolly and suspiciously, and Ali, who had always been a sycophant, was groveling even more. "What's wrong, Reuven?" he kept asking. "Don't you feel well? Still have the stomachache?" He offered all sorts of witch doctor medicines from his village, and one day he was impudent and stupid enough to bring Reuven a jar full of dried herbs. "It's good for the stomach. Make some tea from this and you'll feel better," he said. Reuven thought, Yeah, right. He couldn't pull it off the first time, so now he's delivering the poison just like that, neat. He took the jar and thanked him, and the Arab said, "Drink some now, I'll make it for you." Reuven, almost begging, said not now and put the jar in his bag. It occurred to him that he should take the herbs to a lab so he could get some clear-cut evidence, thereby not only saving his own life but becoming a national hero. He had walked around with the jar in his bag for a week, and yesterday he had flushed the herbs down the toilet.

That day in the car, he'd said to Alona, "It's Arabs. They broke into your house." He remembered how she'd smiled weakly, politely, the smile of a leftie who would not bite the hand of the old right-winger driving her home to wait for the police. "I know you people don't like to hear this kind of talk, but I guarantee you that it was Arabs."

"Maybe, we'll see. And what do you mean by 'you people'?"

She smiled again, bitterly this time, he thought, and for a moment he regretted having ruined the friendly, even romantic atmosphere. "You know, the bleeding hearts."

"Oh, the bleeding hearts. Well, yes, that's definitely me. I fit the description."

"Although, you happen to be a lovely looking bleeding heart," he said, and blushed.

"Oh, Rubi, thank you. Just for that it was worth being burgled."

"You're welcome, it's the truth. I only speak the truth." He shifted uncomfortably in his seat. His stomach hadn't stopped bothering him since they left Ganei Zur, and now they were stuck in a bad traffic jam at Bustanim Intersection. "Maybe you should call the police from your cell phone, at least to let them know. Sometimes it takes them a few hours to come."

She said that was an excellent idea and dug through her bag. "Shit."

"What?"

She said she'd left her cell in the car yesterday. "Fuck! What am I going to do without my cell?" She asked if he had one, and he said he didn't. She laughed. "Are you serious?"

"Absolutely. They're a waste of money. It's one big fraud." She said he must be an endangered species, and he smiled. He liked the idea of being an endangered species. He would have liked anything she said about him, if not for his stomach, whose quiet threats were about to become an ultimatum. There was no way around it. They were stuck in a long procession of cars crawling toward the light, and he was going to have to stop somewhere. But where?

Now, standing by the kitchen window, looking out at the drizzle that had become a downpour, he remembered the panic that had struck him in the car, which seemed to have been standing still for ages, although they were moving very slightly. Every inch filled him with hope that soon the traffic would start to flow. But why would it, when the cause of the jam was a short light? He'd been hearing complaints about it for years, but until that morning it had never concerned him. In fact he'd always smiled somewhat smugly when he'd driven to the council offices, zooming past the row of cars stuck in the opposite direction. "Is it always like this?" he asked Alona, who also seemed restless, but for less critical reasons.

She nodded. "This morning it's a bit worse than usual. What day is it today—Thursday? There shouldn't be any reason. On Sundays it's sometimes awful, but what's going on today?"

Her voice sounded distant, speaking to him from outside the bubble that was about to burst in his stomach. He had to stop, there was no way around it, but where? Then he noticed a gas station about two hundred yards up ahead, and glanced at the gas gauge. The tank was almost full— how would he excuse this stop when she was in such a hurry? Then he had an idea. "Maybe we could stop here at the station for a minute and you can call the police. I have a phone card if you need one. And anyway I think it will be a free call."

"No, we shouldn't stop now. We could be stuck in this traffic forever. What if the police get there and I'm not home? It's not a good idea, Rubi. Let's just keep going."

Rubi. His nickname had never caused him so much pain. The cursed light was still far away, but the station was close. "Listen, I have to run to the bathroom for a minute. I'm stopping here for a second."

"Sure, no problem."

"Should I get you something to drink? Coffee?"

She refused and sighed. "What a crazy morning."

He went into the station and she stretched out in her seat, exposing armpits dotted with black stubble, and the edges of her full breasts. He was relieved she hadn't asked for anything, because he knew the gas station charged exorbitant prices.

When he got to the bathroom he hurried inside and shut himself in a stall. The stall was filthy, the walls smeared with excrement. What do people do in here? he wondered. He could not fathom how excrement had come to be spread on the walls. He pulled his pants down and hovered over the toilet, careful not to touch it. His thighs shook from the effort, and for a moment he almost forgot and leaned his hand on the wall for support. He quickly buried both hands between his legs and strained, but nothing happened. The spasm had passed. He stood that way for a few more moments, but his intestines were empty. He felt relieved. Now he could continue the drive, and if his stomach threatened again he would ignore it without fear. That's what he'd do. He pulled up his pants and hurried back to the car, glancing at his watch: he hadn't spent more than five minutes in the bathroom. She'd think he'd just gone to pee, so nothing was ruined.

When they got to Eden, he pulled up outside her house and offered to come in and wait for the police with her. At first she protested: "No, there's no need. I'm fine now." It occurred to him that she was sick of him, that the hour and a half they'd spent together had been enough for her to determine decisively that she had no interest in him, no interest of any kind.

He pretended to be hurt. "How can I leave? Come on, take advantage of me, I'm free, you shouldn't be alone now." He remembered that he had to call the office and tell them he wouldn't be in. It was eight-thirty and they were probably wondering where he was.

"If you insist," she said.

"I do."

He hadn't been in this house for a long time. Two years exactly, since that first winter, which he remembered longingly as if some great opportunity had been missed, as if he'd been banished from the Garden of Eden. Nothing had changed, he thought when he followed her inside and looked around. It was chaos: toys and clothes strewn everywhere. "I'll just call the police and then make us some coffee," she said.

"There's plenty of time, don't rush," he called out.

Again he heard her say, "Shit!"

"What happened?" He hurried over and saw her plugging the phone into the wall outlet.

"It was disconnected," she explained as she dialed. "The kids always play with the phone." She hopped from one leg to the other. "Man, I can't believe it takes them this long to answer. I'm dying to pee, I've been holding it in since Ganei Zur."

He blushed and asked why she hadn't gone at the gas station, surprised by the ease with which they were even having this conversation. Someone must have finally answered the phone and she reported the burglary. When she hung up she said they promised to be there in half an hour; they had a vehicle in the area.

"There must have been another break-in," he said authoritatively.

She hurried down the hallway. "I'll be right with you!"

"Take your time."

When she came back she was wearing different clothes, jeans and a long-sleeved T-shirt. "It got a little chilly, didn't it?" she said, as she went to fill the kettle.

He wondered if she'd got dressed because of him, if she'd suddenly become aware of her almost nakedness, of the fact that they were alone in this house, and who knew how long it would be before the police came. They could be waiting here for hours. Hours. The thought flooded him with joy, and then it occurred to him that Rina must have seen his car parked outside and would be wondering what he was doing. He asked if he could use the phone briefly, for a local call.

She laughed. "There's no such thing anymore."

"What do you mean?" he asked, embarrassed.

"It doesn't matter where you're calling. All the area codes are the same rate now."

"That's true, I forgot." He dialed home and told his wife dryly that he was waiting with Alona for the police.

Rina said, "Osnat from the office called and I told her you weren't feeling well and you wouldn't be in today. Will you be there for long?"

"We'll see, I'm not sure. We'll see how long they make us wait." He spoke as if this was a shared predicament, a couple's predicament.

"And how's the stomach?"

He told her it was fine and hung up. Then he noticed a painting in the hallway leading to the bedrooms that hadn't been there two years ago. It was a frame drawn in black crayon, with kids' scribbles in the middle. "What's that?" he asked.

"That's the children's wall." She told him that since they used to scribble on the walls and kept fighting about it, she decided this summer to permit some legitimate artistic expression and allotted them that whole wall, which was now the only one they were allowed to draw on. They could use markers, crayons, chalk, whatever they wanted. They could even smear their chocolate puddings on that wall.

"You don't say! What a nice idea!" He was horrified. He asked how long she was planning to keep it that way.

She called out from the kitchen, "Probably forever. Or at least until they grow up. And that too, between you and me, is a kind of forever." She came and stood next to him with a jar of instant coffee.

He smiled and said, "I like the way you talk."

"How do I talk?"

"You know, like a writer."

"Thanks for the compliment, but I'm an editor, not a writer."

He said he knew that, she'd told him what she did for a living.

"When?" she asked, as if she didn't remember.

"Oh, really, Alona," he scolded, his eyes fixed on the scribbled wall. "I'm surprised at you. You told me lots of things about yourself."

"Oh, no, really? I'm sorry. I must be going senile. Old age, you know."

"Old age? You? You're a spring chicken."

She went back to the kitchen and said, "It really was worthwhile to be broken into. I haven't heard so many compliments in one morning for ages."

When she asked if he took sugar, he felt briefly insulted again: he'd had dozens of cups of coffee here that winter. "One level teaspoon and a little milk," he said.

Before they could even sit down, the police arrived. One older officer and one young one. Reuven said, "I'm the neighbor. Reuven Brochstein. I've been waiting here with the lady. I'm from the council," he added, as if that were an important fact that gave him some official status.

Alona said, "I really appreciate it, Rubi. You can go now, I'm sorry to have bothered you."

"Are you sure?" He wanted to complain that he hadn't had his coffee yet, but he didn't dare.

"You really saved me. Thanks," she said, and disappeared with the officers into the laundry room, which is where the burglars had apparently entered. He left the house, crossed the street, and went back home.

Perhaps under the influence of the dream, which had put him in an optimistic, generous mood, he decided this morning to pluck up the courage to deviate from the toast regime and made himself an omelet. After eating it and putting the frying pan and plate in the sink, he went to the bathroom and decided to shave, even though he normally shaved in the evenings. But he couldn't find his favorite razor blade, the one Dudi also liked. At first it flattered him that they were so similar: Dudi, just like him, did not like to use an electric shaver. But every so often he would take Reuven's razor and not put it back. Then in the evening, when he wanted to shave, he'd have to knock on Dudi's door and ask if he happened to have taken it, and why did he always forget to put it back. Dudi would mumble, "Okay," and take the razor out of the toiletry

kit he sometimes took when he had to spend Shabbat on the base. He'd
hand over the razor and sit back down at his computer.

"All day long at the computer," Reuven grumbled every so often.
"You'll end up with an ass like a tractor wheel," he said once.

His son turned to face him for a change, and said, "When was the
last time you saw a tractor, Dad?" His words shot an arrow straight into
an old wound that Reuven thought had already healed and had left no
scar. He had the urge to slap his son, but he didn't touch him. Ever since
Dudi had grown taller than him, shortly after his bar mitzvah, Reuven
had started to fear him. But not because of his size—rather, because of
his quiet way.

He went into Dudi's room and found his toiletry kit on the computer
desk. He took the razor out, and as he was about to leave the room he
noticed a large brown envelope peeking out from under the keyboard.
Without knowing why, he pulled it out. Before he'd even opened it, he
felt a chill. He hadn't been in this room for years. Not really. He always
stood in the doorway, exchanging a few words with his son, calling him
for dinner, asking him questions that Dudi would answer without even
bothering to turn around. He conducted brief conversations with his
son's large back. The back was like a screen dividing the computer and
that goddamn Internet from the door.

Reuven felt like a burglar, but a burglar with a license: after all, the
boy had taken his razor and forgotten to put it back, and it was a good
thing he hadn't taken his toiletries to the army yesterday. He carefully
opened the envelope, glanced inside, and pulled out a stack of pictures.

It took him awhile to comprehend what he was seeing. There were
about twenty photographs of children, all boys, mostly five or six years
old, and a few who looked twelve or thirteen. They were all blond
except for one black boy with frizzy hair and one who looked Asian.
They were naked, standing facing the camera. But one picture showed
a boy sitting on a chair, wrapped in a sort of sack that had a rope tied
around it, and his eyes were blindfolded.

He lingered on that picture, turning it from side to side, and then he
noticed a man's arm and hand resting on the tied-up boy's shoulder. He
looked again at the other pictures of naked boys in various positions.
Most of them were just standing straight up with their hands alongside
their bodies. There was one boy, who looked like the youngest, who

had his hands around his penis. It was so small that it was hard to make out between his fingers. That boy was the only one whose image became burned in Reuven's memory, and he kept seeing the face long afterward, for days and nights. It was not because he was holding his penis like that, and not because he was the youngest, but because, unlike the others, whose eyes were empty and frozen and expressed a peculiar indifference, this boy looked terrified.

Reuven wasn't sure how long he stood there like that, holding the photographs. Eventually he put them back in the envelope and placed it exactly where he'd found it, under the keyboard. He took his razor and went into the bathroom and lathered his face, but then he just stood looking at the mirror. Later, in his office, it seemed to him that he'd been trapped in some kind of air pocket of time for hours, standing with a foam-covered face by the mirror, his legs trembling slightly. But he knew that in reality—the normal, usual reality that he no longer knew how to find his way back to—only thirty minutes or so must have passed, because he did shave, and he did make it to the meeting in time, and he even had time to go past the office and pick up a document he needed and take a piss. He'd stood in the little bathroom attached to his office and peed for a long time, his eyes fixated on the stream of urine coming out of his body like a surprising well. He always peed in short staccato bursts. Then he'd gone to the meeting, and it was the first meeting in years where he hadn't opened his mouth. The deputy council chair, with whom Reuven had always shared a mutual hostil- ity, had even commented, asking if Reuven felt all right, because he was so quiet.

Later, when he sat in his office, he thought back to that urination. Of all the events that morning, that was what stuck in his mind. He'd peed for maybe three minutes, no more, but how could it be? For years he'd been peeing in a stutter. What had happened this morning? What was it? He'd peed like a horse, like he was eighteen again. And then he understood: it was the fear. The fear had made him pee like that. He felt pressure at the bottom of his stomach. Maybe he needed to pee again. He got up and went into the bathroom, unzipped his fly, and took out his penis, and in front of his eyes he saw the picture of that little boy with his tiny organ glimpsed through his fingers. This time nothing came out, just a few drops, but he felt nauseated, and not the kind of

nausea that slowly climbs up your throat like when he had that diarrhea two weeks ago. This was something sudden, like suffocating, as if
someone—maybe the man whose hand was in the picture of the tied-up
boy—had tightened his fingers around Reuven's throat and was pressing hard. Or worse, he thought, as he quickly zipped up and flushed: it
was as if he himself had been forced to do what the boys in the photos,
even that little one, had probably done—had *certainly* done—before or
after being photographed. A second before he vomited, missing the toilet
by a couple of inches and soiling the PVC floor and the molding with
sprays of instant coffee and pieces of omelet, he felt a huge, horselike
penis shoving its way into his mouth and filling his throat.

PART FOUR

MARK

He found them in the morning, out in the backyard. They were lying on their sides, their legs sticking forward as though clutching at the earth with their claws, and although he knew dead dogs sometimes looked alert, the deathly rigidity gave them a look of mid-escape. Their half-open eyes looked tranquil, even though it was clear they had died in agony.

When he'd walked to the back door after getting up, Popeye had struggled up from his bed, stood next to him, and glued his nose to the glass door, waiting for it to be opened so he could go outside and pee on the lawn, crouched like a female. Strangely, the first thought that came into Mark's mind when he saw the mixed German shepherd and the pinscher sprawled a few yards apart from each other, their water dish upturned between them, was that it was lucky the kids hadn't slept at his place that night. Very lucky. Not just the little ones, but Roni, too. She'd gone to see a friend in Tel Aviv the night before. They were going to a demonstration against the separation wall, she'd said. "A new friend," she'd quickly responded to his unasked question. Someone she'd met at a party a few weeks ago. "And if you really want to rehabilitate our relationship," she cautioned him before he could say anything, "then I suggest you stop interrogating me. Just trust me for once. Can you do that?"

"Okay, I'll try," he'd said. But trusting her was the last thing he wanted to do. He was sick of trusting her, and besides, since when did she go to demonstrations? "I didn't know you were against the wall," he said.

She gave him a contemptuous look. "Aren't you?"

"Of course," he mumbled. "Of course I am, but I don't go to demonstrations."

"I know, you can't be bothered. But I can. You should be happy that someone is representing you."

"I guess so." He asked where this demonstration was, anyway.

She said she wasn't sure. She thought it was in Tel Aviv.

"Not in the Territories?"

"No, I don't think so."

"Because you're not going there. Promise?"

"I promise."

He didn't believe her. Why should he? From now on, he decided, he would never believe her. On principle, he would suspect her. Always.

He thought about all those people like Ma'ayan, who claimed children needed limits. Not just limits but strict ones, because that was the biggest problem today. It was all because there were no limits. He always belittled those people, yet how badly he'd needed them yesterday afternoon when Roni had come into the restaurant with her backpack on her shoulder, drunk a glass of water from the tap, wiped her mouth on the back of her hand, and said, "Okay, I'm off. See you tomorrow."

"Where to?" he asked, as if he didn't know. As if his question would change her plans.

"Come on, Dad, I already told you. Don't you remember? I told you I was going to Sivan's today, you know, for the demonstration?"

When he asked how she was getting to school tomorrow, she said her first period was PE, so she'd get there late, on the bus. She'd already checked the schedule and there was a bus from Tel Aviv at nine.

When he tried to say something like *But Roni* or *no*—a firm *no*, something rigid and delimiting—she quickly kissed him on his cheek, which she hadn't done for years—in fact, had never done it like that, on his cheek, as if she were older than he was, and said, "Yesterday you promised not to interrogate me." He nodded. "I'll be on my cell if you need me. I have to run; there's a bus in five minutes." She turned her back to him and ran down the front steps and up the dirt path. As he watched her run through the fields, she looked like a doe or a fawn. Brutus and Olive had galloped behind her, and she reached the main road and turned into a tiny dot and eventually disappeared.

He kept standing under the vine canopy for a long time, staring, shading his eyes with his hand, even though the sky was cloudy, even though he knew she was already on the bus. He'd seen it come from the east and stop at the station, and he hoped she'd made it. He kept standing like that, sweating, despite the cool air and the small, sharp raindrops the wind slammed into his face, until he heard the heavy breathing of the dogs, who had returned without his noticing. They sprawled at his feet, and he leaned down and caressed them. Strange, he thought now, because unlike he did often with Popeye, he almost never petted these dogs. They were a small background ensemble, living props, and how odd that just yesterday he'd petted them for a long time and they'd whimpered gratefully, or perhaps out of some prophetic sorrow.

Now he looked at the two poisoned dogs—they had obviously been poisoned—lately there'd been rumors around Eden about dog poisonings; the local council claimed it must be a private individual, perhaps someone from Eden or a nearby moshav, and instructed anyone whose dog had been poisoned to call the police. He'd already heard about the grocery store owner's boxer, who spent most of his time dozing behind the counter at her feet and no one could figure out how he'd even got to the poison. He knew the danger was out there, concrete, but it hadn't bothered him enough to do anything about it. And what could he have done? Olive and Brutus couldn't be tied up. Those dogs had never seen a leash in their life. He'd considered keeping them inside at night, but he kept forgetting, and now they had fallen victims to this crazy poisoner. He'd heard someone at the pool conjecturing that it was a Satanic cult or that it had something to do with the sexual assault of that boy. There had to be a connection. Alona told him a few days ago that her annoying neighbor, Brochstein, had told her one morning that they suspected the Thai. After all, it was well known that they ate dogs. She'd responded, "Why would they poison them if they're going to eat them?"

Mark couldn't stand that Brochstein, and didn't know how Alona could. "What did he say?" he asked.

"He said anything was possible," Alona replied, and said they also suspected that Arab.

"That Arab, that poor Arab," Alona had said yesterday. She'd been infuriated by it right from the beginning, when the incident with the boy came out. "You know what?" she said, "I feel like inviting this so-called *that Arab* over for dinner, so you can cook him a gourmet meal and we can both apologize to him, on behalf of everyone."

"You're kidding," Mark said.

"Yes, but not really. The police took him in for questioning, and who knows what they did to him there? Why didn't they question us? You or I could be dangerous sex criminals, but of course they wouldn't take us in for questioning. And that boy's neighbors, the lawyer and his wife—will they bring them in? No. But why not pick up the Thai and the Arab for a little interrogation? It's natural, right?"

He was driving her to pick up her car, which was in the shop for its 10,000-mile service. He gave her a desperate and bemused look and said, "Aloncha"—he hadn't called her that for ages—"I have a confession. I'm sick of being a leftie." When she stared at him in astonishment, he went on. "It's just too high maintenance to keep holding on to these enlightened opinions; I don't have the strength for it. I'm tired, I'm old, I have too many things going on to invest the proper effort in my leftie-ness. You know?"

This drove her up the wall, of course. He'd done it intentionally, to annoy her, to flirt with her, because they hadn't flirted for a long time. She attacked him, which was exactly what he wanted. If she was never going to sleep with him, then at least have a verbal romp.

"Tell me, have you completely lost your mind?" she said.

"Maybe." He said this quietly, seductively.

He didn't even try to disguise the little smile that came to his lips when she said, "I feel like getting out right now and hitchhiking. I don't care if I get raped, as long as I don't have to listen to your ridiculous crap. And you're driving fifteen miles an hour. We'll never get there." She lit a cigarette. "This is your fortieth birthday crisis. That's what it is. It's just hitting you a bit late. So now you're going to be a right-winger, that's the deal?"

"No," he said calmly, putting his arm on her seat back. "You're mis-understanding me, as usual. I don't want to be right-wing *or* left-wing."

"Then what do you want to be?"

"Nothing. Just me. That's what I want to be."

She let out a scornful huff. "Oh, come on! Are you sixteen? You want to be *you*? What is *you*? Can you explain that to me?"

"I don't know. I really don't know, honey."

"Don't call me honey!" she screamed. "Honey is what you call me when you're angry at me or when you want to get laid!"

He turned to look at the road and said, "Both, I guess."

"Both what?" Her voice plunged into a curious whisper.

"Both."

And then she dropped the bomb. She always beat him, but for once he was happy to be the loser. Looking straight ahead, she put out her cigarette in his clean ashtray and said, "Okay. When, then?"

And they arranged to meet that evening.

Alona suggested getting a babysitter and coming to his place. She hadn't been in his rental house for a long time. "I want to see how you live," she explained. He said that would work out well, because Roni was going to a demonstration in Tel Aviv and would be back late—he still didn't know she was planning to stay the night.

And his wife, his ex, his lover, the woman he was arranging to have sex with that night, said, "Great. But since when is Roni a political activist?"

"Since today, apparently. But I don't believe she's going to a demonstration."

"Oh, come on. Enough with that, okay?"

"You're right."

Before she got out at the garage she debated whether to get Yonat or Neta to babysit. Mark said he'd rather she call Neta, the older of the two, but Alona said the kids preferred Yonat.

"She's fourteen!" he protested.

"But I'll only be two minutes away. So should I book her for an hour and a half? Two?" She giggled.

"More than that, I hope."

Then he drove back to the restaurant, even though he didn't have anything to do there on a Tuesday, which was always his day off, the bridge between post-weekend cleanup and preparations for the upcoming weekend. Still, he preferred to go there rather than home, because he knew that at home he'd wander around restlessly, maybe even have the urge to clean and tidy up. At home he ran the risk of sending himself into a state of paralysis, because in a few hours he would sleep with his wife, and soon this new mantra replaced *my daughter is lying to me*, piercing his anxiety like a woodpecker perforates a tree trunk until it splits in two. When he got back to the restaurant and sat down outside, suddenly exhausted, he began to think about how strange it was, and how improbable, that this had happened just like that, so easily, after two years, when he was already convinced he would never sleep with her again.

And now he was no longer sure he wanted to. He desired her, yes. There was no argument about that. But as he sat looking out at the view—and a few hours later, when Roni left, he would do it again, so that in fact he ended up spending most of his day staring out at those fields—when he looked at the view he thought about how a two-year fantasy was now becoming reality. With insulting and exciting efficiency his wife had set up an appointment for sex, as if it were with a hair salon or a doctor. He hadn't bothered to find out if this would be a one-off thing or if they were going back to having regular sex. "Eight-thirty or nine," she'd said. "I'll put them to bed and come over." He wondered if he was supposed to make any preparations, like cook something or buy some beer. For years she'd claimed the pregnancies had ruined her ability to drink, but maybe she'd feel like it tonight; there was no way of knowing. And maybe he didn't know her at all, as she'd claimed angrily before the separation. He'd fought with her about that. "Of course I know you. How could I live with you for three years and not know you? Don't flatter yourself, you're not immune to being known." But now he thought she was right. He *didn't* know her. He didn't know anyone, not really. Even with Maya he was lately getting that sneaking, familiar, not-knowing feeling. She was an independent entity, opinionated and tempestuous like her mother, and slightly mysterious, even though she was only four.

Roni was also a riddle. She had been long before adolescence. And added to that there'd been the geographical distance, and the fact that she'd grown up with her mother. But he knew that ultimately it was not the ocean but himself that had separated him from his oldest child. Alona was right; he was charming and kind and a wonderful father, but still he was sixteen, a child. "And a child," she always said—and this infuriated him, because she was the first to admit that most of the time she was lost, too, but she acknowledged the shortcoming as if it were an accomplishment—"a child can't really know his parents or the other adults around him, and certainly not other children. You're a child. You give like a child and you take like a child."

When he got back from the supermarket in the afternoon—he couldn't remember when he'd left the Trattoria to drive to the store—he quickly unpacked the shopping, still lost in the trance that had taken him to the mall in the first place. He'd purchased three jars of supposedly homemade jelly, which had attracted him because of their exotic ingredients and because Alona had a weakness for jelly. When they'd lived together in Tel Aviv, she'd tried to make jelly a few times, unsuccessfully. He'd also picked up some imported cheeses and two bottles of Belgian beer, which he'd decided to buy after all—or, rather, had not decided; during the two hours he'd spent in the mall, his legs seemed to have carried him along with a mind of their own.

He made room in the fridge for the triple-layer chocolate cheesecake, which had cost him sixty dollars (only when he'd placed it on the seat next to him in its cardboard box had he remembered that Alona was on a diet; he wondered if she would break it tonight, if tonight was sufficiently important or celebratory, because there was something chilling in the way she'd said, "Okay. When, then?"), and as he pushed aside the regular fridge inhabitants to make room for the cake, he was no longer certain he wanted to sleep with her. Or needed to. Or could.

Now he stood between the two dead dogs, looking from one to the other. Popeye came over to sniff them, like a doctor pronouncing their death, then padded back inside and lay down on his bed, rested his head on his paws, and let out his usual sigh. Mark tried to read it. What was the old dog saying? What was his diagnosis? But Popeye closed his eyes and fell asleep. Mark was about to phone the police, but he went outside again, with the phone in his hand, and wondered what the police would do. Nothing—so why bother? Lawless country, he thought, but the expression sounded meaningless, vapid, even slightly comical. He finally got up the courage to get near Olive, whose compact corpse looked less threatening than Brutus's. He held his nose up to her mouth, thinking there might be an odor of poisonous chemicals, but there was nothing, not even the scent of death that he feared so much. He realized the dogs might have only just died, a few moments ago, and that perhaps if he'd woken up half an hour earlier he would have found them in the throes of death. He touched the bitch's head lightly. Still warm. But maybe that was just the fur. A person would have gone cold faster. He was happy he'd gotten up late this morning.

The sex with Alona had exhausted him even before it began. She didn't arrive until ten-thirty. "The kids wouldn't fall asleep. It's like they knew something was going on," she said, and sat down cross-legged on the couch.

For a second she reminded him of Roni, and he wondered what she was doing now, and remembered that he'd meant to watch the news to see if there really was a demonstration. He'd been so busy preparing— he'd doused both toilets with bleach and then taken a long shower— that he'd forgotten to turn on the TV. Now he wanted to call her, to hear her voice but mainly to interrupt her in the middle of whatever she was doing.

Alona jumped up off the couch and said, "Don't you ever clean this place? There's dog hair everywhere." She went over to Popeye and rubbed his head. "I missed you, Popolo." She asked where the other dogs were.

"Outside." He asked if she wanted a beer; he'd picked up something Belgian. She said no and seemed distracted, or maybe just trying to hide her excitement. That's what he hoped, because his own knees had been shaking when he'd heard her car door slam and had opened the front door wide and welcomed her with a light touch on her cheek and said, "Hi."

No, she wasn't drinking. "You know I can't."

"But why don't you try?"

She sat down on the couch again and tried to brush the fur off with her hand. "We have to take Ido to a psychologist. That's it. I've said it. I won't say it again, I know it annoys you, but I want you to think about it."

"I'm pouring some wine. Are you sure you don't want a drink?"

"No, maybe water. But don't avoid the topic, okay? At least answer me." She followed him into the kitchen and opened the fridge and looked at the cake box. "What's that?"

"A surprise."

She held up the lid. "Wow! You really put a lot of effort into this. Did you make it?"

"No, I didn't have time. I bought it at Kochav."

"Kochav!" She let out a whistle of admiration. "How much did it cost, a million shekels?"

"Just under. D'you want some?"

"Sure." She took the box out of the fridge and set it on the table. She asked where the dishes were, and he took out two cake plates. "Where are these from? They're lovely. New?"

"What's with you? You know these. They're from your mom. She gave them to you and you didn't want them."

"You're right, I forgot." She sat down at the table and put a large forkful of cake in her mouth. "Amazing," she moaned.

"I remembered this was your favorite cake."

"Mmmm. . . . But when I'm dieting every cake is my favorite cake. At night I dream about packaged Elite pound cake. Give me another slice. And you know what? Crack open a beer for me after all."

When he gave her the bottle she said, "Whoa, fancy!" and just as he was about to press his lips to hers, not because he wanted to kiss her but because he wanted to get it over with, to start so that it could be finished and everything could go back to the way it was, she sighed and said, "Don't avoid me, Mark. We have to do something. Ido is depressed."

But if there was one person Mark did know, a branch grown from within him, straight from his body, from his mind, it was his son. "He's not depressed," he said softly, trying to temper the anger that simmered in him when he heard that word *depressed*, as if she were trying to fit the kid into a tuxedo. "On the contrary, Alona, he's flourishing. You just can't see it."

He sat down opposite her and took a slice of cake, even though he wasn't hungry. His day of staring into space and making strange purchases had exhausted him, and now he felt a chill all over his body, as if he were coming down with the flu. It felt like he had a fever, and his throat was burning. He took a sip of wine. "Enough with this already, okay?"

"Enough with what?"

"With how every time something good happens, it scares you. It's like you'd rather live with possible bad than with certain good."

It wasn't the first time he'd said this. She'd heard these words and similar ones endless times, but this evening his observation, which she usually slashed with imaginary swords and diced into tiny pieces even before he'd finished uttering it, seemed to be comforting her.

She scraped the bottom of the plate with her fork, plowing furrows in the chocolate mud, and looked very contemplative, submissive even, when she said, "Maybe. But I would put it differently: not possible bad but certain bad. For me, it's the good that is possible."

"Okay, it doesn't matter. It doesn't matter how you put it, it's the same thing."

After a long pause, she said, "Maybe. I hope so. I hope you're right, because to me he looks like he's suffering terribly, like he's really depressed, and I don't think I'm saying this because I'm afraid that one day in the future he'll be unhappy and if I say it now it won't happen, like by being so afraid I can protect him. I don't think that's what I think. I don't know, maybe."

"Alona, Ido is fine. You can trust me about Ido, I know him."

She sighed and looked around, examining the kitchen as if seeing it for the first time. "I hope so."

"No, Alona, I'm right. Trust me. Could you just trust me for once?" The words sounded familiar, and he smiled.

"Why are you smiling?"

He told her that earlier that day Roni had said the same exact thing to him before leaving. She'd asked him to trust her if he wanted to reha-bilitate their relationship.

"*Rehabilitate your relationship*?" Alona hiccupped and apologized. "You see, two sips and I'm drunk. Is that really what she said?"

"Yeah. Funny, isn't it?" He expected her to get annoyed and ask what was funny about it, and why he couldn't pick up on the distress signals.

But she said, "Yes, a little."

"Really? Or am I just ignoring something important here?"

"No, you're not ignoring anything. It's sweet, what she said. And encouraging, because you haven't talked about your relationship for a long time, and now you're talking, right?"

He got up and went over to her. "And what about *our* relationship? Didn't we arrange to have sex?" He didn't know why he'd said that. What would be so bad if they spent the next couple of hours talking? He wasn't feeling well anyway. He had all the symptoms of flu. "Tell me if I feel hot," he said.

She put her hand on his forehead. "Not really." Then she told him she'd shaved her legs in his honor, and she was still red and bumpy. "Maybe it was a mistake," she said, and rolled up her pants, exposing pale, spotty legs.

"It's fine. And you didn't have to shave your legs for me."

"Do you think we're ever going to get to bed tonight?" she asked, and lit a cigarette.

He quickly brought in Roni's ashtray from the yard. Before putting it on the table he emptied it into the trash. "Look how much she smokes," he grumbled, and started counting the butts.

"Mark, stop it. You're counting cigarette butts?"

"She's made me sick." He plunked down on the chair opposite her.

His wife grimaced. "Oh, Mark, that's cheap. Now you're a right-winger *and* an overbearing, long-suffering father?"

"Yes, I know. And yes, I think we will get to bed tonight. If you feel like it, I mean."

"Yes, of course I feel like it." She looked at her watch and said, "Wow, it's late. Are you even into it? You said you weren't feeling well."

"Sure."

"Soon, then." She sighed again.

"What?"

"Nothing."

"Stop it. I know something's bothering you."

"No, nothing, you'll get mad."

"I won't."

"Do you really think Ido is fine? Do you really think I'm overreacting?"

"I'm positive, Alona. Ido is absolutely fine, and you're really overreacting."

"Good. That's what I wanted to hear. Thanks."

And instead of asking what was going on, what was *really* going on—because why wasn't she fighting him? Since when did she ask him to reassure her? Since when did she believe him and thank him?—he got up and stood behind her chair, leaned over and folded his arms around her shoulders, kissed her ear, and whispered, "It's going to be fine, Aloncha." It suddenly occurred to him that this would be the first time they slept together and then went to separate houses. Even that first night in Ein Kerem, they hadn't done that.

"Maybe you're right, and I'm just afraid of the good. But it's better to worry than to suddenly get slammed. If you don't think things are good, no one can take that away from you, right?"

"No. You can't protect yourself, you know that. So why not enjoy it while you can?"

"Since when did you get so mature?"

"What do you mean? I always was." But he knew that wasn't true. He knew that only now, in this strange and graceful moment, a sudden maturity had come to him, perhaps temporarily, and it was flickering against the sweet childishness—he almost suspected its authenticity, but decided to believe it—against the wonderful neediness of his wife, and as far as he was concerned it could go on this way; they could give up on the sex and continue with exactly this. It was better than sex, although he could not quite describe this new thing that excited him. Was it possible that this was how it had always been? That the Alona he thought he loved, the Alona he thought he'd broken up with, had in fact always been the woman who came for sex but asked for comfort?

She leaned her head against his stomach, perhaps probing for his erection, perhaps just clinging fondly. But Alona wasn't a clinger. She said she was in a strange, melancholy mood, and she wasn't sure why.

"You see," he said, kissing her forehead, "you're the one who's depressed, not Ido."

"Maybe," she said. He wanted to tell her about his fearsadness, to tell her he had also been walking around with a strange beast on his shoulder, something in between distress and terror, something quiet and furry and irritable. Although, oddly, he hadn't felt it today. Perhaps because today was too outlandish to enable the fearsadness to envelop him. There was something pleasant about this tiredness—or perhaps it was the flu—and the excitement that came and went like a shiver. "You seem a bit depressed too, lately," she said, reading him, as usual.

"Yeah, a little. It's nothing serious. I'll get through it."

"Are you sure?"

"No."

"I guess we all need to go into therapy."

He put his hands on her breasts, sensing her surprise, even though she knew this was what he would do—how could she not? He always started by hugging her from behind, crossing his arms around her, kissing her neck and then her breasts.

"I don't need a psychologist," he said, and felt the beginning of a hard-on after all, despite the word *psychologist*, which always scared him a little. "I need God."

She sighed as his fingers recalled her favorite maneuver, a slow walk along her collarbone. "Since when do you believe in God?"

He fluttered his tongue over her earlobe, hoping she still liked that— why would her tastes have changed if she hadn't slept with anyone for two years? "Since today."

Now he shut the back door, leaving the dead dogs where they were. It occurred to him that he would have to get rid of the bodies. What did one do in such a case? He thought of phoning that Arab. Alona would have killed him if she knew those two words had appeared so naturally in his mind. Or maybe he should call the council. Would they send anyone?

He contemplated calling Alona, even though he knew she had a busy morning. She had to go to Tel Aviv again to meet Uri Breutner and the graphic designer who was doing the book cover. In bed, after last night's strange coupling—now he realized he didn't want to think about it at all; no, he wouldn't think about it, he would erase it—she'd told him that Breutner was driving the designer mad. "He has this concept for the cover," she'd said, sitting up in bed and pulling the sheet up over her breasts, "something white with a black frame, like a death notice, but with his name and the book's name in the middle. Oh, and by the way, we found a title: *Baby*."

"Baby?"

"It started as a joke, but then we got into it, and it works. And his girlfriend's pregnant, so he thought it seemed symbolic. Maybe it will bring good luck for the book."

"Or bad luck for the baby," Mark said, and got up angrily.

Unlike Alona, he'd never had a problem with his nudity. He walked around the room, opened the window, and put his head out. "The rain's stopped."

"Yes, but they said it would pour tomorrow."

He went into the kitchen to get the rest of his wine, and she asked him to bring the cigarettes and ashtray. In the kitchen, he wondered if they should talk about it, about what had happened to them just a few moments earlier. He went back into the bedroom, and when he sat down on the edge of the bed, she said, "You're still cute, you know?"

"But you've seen me in the pool. Why do you sound so surprised?"

She said she hadn't seen his ass for a long time, and he was so lucky that nothing in his body had changed.

"Yours hasn't either," he said, which was a lie. Something had changed. Something about her body was absolutely forty, but he couldn't put his finger on it. Something internal, perhaps. A temperature, or something in her tissue.

"It was bound to be a disaster, wasn't it?"

He turned to her. "What do you mean?"

She leaned back on the pillows and pulled the sheet up to her shoulders. "We both pinned too many hopes on this. There was no chance we would enjoy it." And before he could say he *had* enjoyed it, she said, "And don't tell me you *did* enjoy it." He wondered how she could not have enjoyed it when she'd come three times. Then she went on, as if talking to herself. "It's a good thing we're married, that we're not a new couple or anything like that, 'cause otherwise we'd be really bummed out about it, you know?"

But he *was* bummed out. He felt bad. Not that he had a problem with quickies—on the contrary, in the past they'd used every opportunity for a quickie. But this time it had been urgent, for both of them; why blame only her? Still, he felt as if she had raped him. And because of the urgency, or at least he hoped that was why, it had also been somehow very businesslike, almost calculated, despite her passion, despite the fact that she seemed to have lost control, to be crumbling beneath him, that his wife had turned into a shrapnel grenade of orgasms. He couldn't understand how she'd come three times in less than half an hour, and instead of being flattered he was hurt. It was if he hadn't been the one directly responsible for her orgasms, he thought, as he watched her smoking and pondering in his bed, her eyes intent on the open window. It was as if she'd been there completely alone.

He'd climaxed quickly, almost immediately, like a sixteen-year-old boy. A second before, he'd remembered to ask if she'd put her diaphragm in, and she'd said, "Of course." And it wasn't that he was counting orgasms, but hers had seemed more powerful, more real. But now, as he stood in the living room deliberating over whether to call her, looking out at the dogs and the darkening sky that had taken on a stainless-steel shade, one frightening and accurate word came to his mind: autistic.

Their sex, he thought, was the shattering of the illusion that had preceded it: that Alona needed him, that she was different, that he was different, that anything at all was different. Because obviously it wasn't. As far as she was concerned, you could have put a Mark-shaped dummy in bed with her. Or not necessarily a Mark-shaped one. You could have just done away with the dummy and she still would have come three times.

She'd put her cigarette out and got dressed and said, "Poor Yonat. I told her twelve at the latest. What time is it?"

"Twelve."

"Oh, it's okay then. No big deal. I told her I was at your place. I wonder if she suspects anything." She smiled to herself.

"She's fourteen, Alona, what could she suspect?" For a moment he hated her, his forty-year-old lover who was trying to force a sense of cheap drama into her life, as if three orgasms weren't dramatic enough.

He dialed her number after all, to tell her about the dogs. He wanted her to tell the kids—he was bad at that kind of thing. But he knew he was calling to hear her voice, the morning-after voice. That expression had never had any significance for him, because for him the morning after was always the beginning of a long relationship. This morning he felt the words' menacing power, but Alona was unavailable. It was nine-thirty. She was probably on her way to Tel Aviv, or maybe she was already there, sitting with that little asshole at the graphic designer's. But it was unlike her to turn off her cell. She'd never done that since the kids were born.

The sky was completely black now, and despite the time it looked as if night had come again and the day was over even before it had begun, as if someone had changed their mind and was trying to erase this day from the calendar. He tried to remember the date. It was November twenty-sixth. And since he hadn't had his coffee yet, or brushed his teeth or washed his face, he decided to deal with the bodies later, when he was fresher and more awake. By that time maybe he'd be able to get hold of Alona, who might not know what to do, but at least her voice would balance him out and banish the fearsadness that had suddenly landed on his shoulder again, like a trained falcon. That was the image he'd been trying to come up with. This thing wasn't furry at all. No, there was nothing soft or sweet about it. This thing, he now felt clearly, had talons.

He brushed his teeth and washed his face and then stood leaning against the bedroom doorway and looked at the bed in which he had slept alone. It looked different this morning, not his, and it did not have the traditional after-sex warmth. But what had happened last night was undoubtedly a kind of first. He called Alona again and she still wasn't available, and he was desperate to hear her voice now, the one he'd heard say last night, when he'd walked her to the car, "I don't see any reason why we shouldn't do this again. If you want to, I mean. Here and there, or soon, or regularly, or whatever you feel like." Astonished, he'd wanted to ask what that meant. Did it mean that—what? What *did* it mean? And why play games? Why not say outright what she wanted?

When she started the engine, he leaned inside and kissed her cheek, and she said, reading him again, "I don't really know what I want." He said he didn't either, and she said she didn't want things to be weird between them now. "That's the most important thing. That it doesn't get awkward and weird." And he said she was obviously right.

But it *was* awkward and weird, and he wanted to talk to her about that, although he knew that even if he got hold of her, she wouldn't be available for that kind of conversation. It wasn't for the phone, and actually it wasn't for face-to-face either. No, he thought as he turned on the espresso machine, that was a conversation they could never have. It would just have to play out on its own, not face-to-face but life-to-life, and maybe it should not be had at all; maybe they should let their hearts be quiet for a while.

Yes, life-to-life. Because maybe she was right, and there really was no such thing as a shared life. Yesterday had proved it: he'd never felt so lonely. Except there was that one time they'd slept together about two years ago, a few weeks after they'd separated, and that time he'd burst into tears, right after, or during, he couldn't remember now, but he remembered being hurt—it seemed silly now—when she told him she'd put her diaphragm in before she came over because she knew they were going to have sex. That wasn't what had made him cry. He'd cried because he'd realized then—how stupid that the diaphragm thing made him understand this, but that's what happened—he'd realized that the separation was justified, that Alona was right, that they were in different places, and that she didn't need him, not really.

He stood by the fridge and sipped his coffee. To go outside and drink it in the yard, as he always did, would be sacrilegious, an espresso with his dead dogs. His eyes fell on the piece of paper that had hung on the fridge for two years, an information sheet distributed to everyone's mailbox with useful phone numbers. He'd never bothered to look at it, yet he'd affixed it to the fridge with a magnet. Among the phone numbers of the council office, the fire department, the police, and the ambulance service, he noticed the cell phone of that Arab. ALI MAINTENANCE, it said, as if Maintenance were his last name. But he didn't have the courage to call. Why bother Ali with this? He wasn't sure if clearing dead dogs from private yards was part of his job description. But as he kept staring at the page and sipping his coffee, it occurred to him that had the paper said Benny Maintenance, he wouldn't have hesitated to call, describe the situation, and let Benny decide whether or not he wanted to come. Whereas Ali would probably come without asking any questions, if only to keep out of trouble and not give another resident the chance to grumble about him. He realized that in fact, because of some warped leftie stance, he was denying himself his basic right as a resident. He knew that the residents paid for Ali's salary out of their own pockets, so why shouldn't he call?

He quickly dialed the number, hoping Ali would be unavailable, thereby exempting him from this ridiculous dilemma, which was growing larger from one moment to the next. But the Arab picked up immediately.

"Oh, yes, I know you. You're the one with the restaurant, right?"

Mark was surprised. "Yes. How did you know?"

"Of course I know. I know everyone here."

"I don't think we've met, have we?" He wondered what all this small talk was about.

"We met. I did the floor tiles for your mother-in-law."

"Oh, yeah. Listen, Ali"—he said *Ali* as if he were saying *Benny*; his voice sounding so natural, but aware of the particles of lead that weighed down that word—"Ali, I wanted to ask your advice. Maybe you can help me." He told him about the dogs.

Ali clicked his tongue. "Bastards. May God strike whoever does a thing like that. It's already six dogs in one week."

"Six?"

Ali told him they'd found two more the day before. "Beautiful dogs. One Siberian husky and the other a Great Pyrenees. Are yours pure-bred?"

"No. Mixed breed."

"Poor things. Okay, well, I'll be there in half an hour. I'll take them in the truck to Hiriya."

"Oh, so that's what people do? Throw them in the dump in Hiriya? Is that allowed?" Something told him to stop talking, stop asking questions, not give Ali the chance to change his mind, but he was so grateful that he couldn't stop chattering.

"Sure it's allowed."

"Okay, I'll be here." Thunder ripped through the sky, and he couldn't help asking if he should cover the bodies.

"Why?"

"Because of the rain. So they don't get wet."

"It's okay, it won't do any damage," Ali said, and they hung up.

Mark dragged the large armchair that Roni liked over to the back door, sat down, and looked outside. How simple it had been. One phone call had solved the whole problem, extricated him from making endless circles inside his own inner maze. Maybe he'd been wrong about the sex, too, and what had happened last night could be viewed differently, not as a shattered illusion but as proof of a new reality. Because what was neediness if not three orgasms? Three orgasms of hunger, a direct continuation of the tenderness she'd brought with her when she'd arrived, a continuation of *Tell me it will work out, Mark,* and *Yes, I agree, maybe you're right, Mark,* and *Yes, I trust you, yes.*

He started to really cheer up when he saw her naked body in his mind's eye—and she *had* put on a little weight the last couple of years. Yesterday he'd finally understood what she meant when she grumbled that her lower abdomen had turned to jelly. He smiled to himself as he remembered. I bet you're so grossed out by it that you don't want me, she'd said. Of course I want you, he'd replied, and started to kiss her body, lingering on her stomach for a long time. And now the ease he felt as he sat drinking his espresso and watching the storm was invaded by a small, petty thought: was it possible that she'd suggested they keep doing it, and maybe they'd get back together—true, the words *get back together* had not been uttered, but still—was it possible that she'd said-not-said that only because she didn't have the courage to undress in front of another man? She herself had said later, between the second and third orgasms, if he remembered correctly—but stop keeping records, he scolded himself—she had lain on her stomach and leaned on her elbows and said, "There's something fun about how we know each other, and that you saw me during two childbirths, that you know all my gross stuff."

"Yes."

"Because you know what? Even though I'm so horny and all that, I don't think I would ever sleep with another man. I'd be too embarrassed."

"Like hell you wouldn't. You'd spend the rest of your life without sex? I don't think so!"

"I'd probably miss it less after, say, five or six years, don't you think? I don't think it's like swimming or riding a bike. I think you do forget how to do it."

"Maybe your head does but your body doesn't."

"Well, look at us now—my body did almost forget. But you rescued me. Thank you, thank you, thank you!"

"Are you crazy?"

"Thank you," she repeated, and started rubbing herself against his leg.

At first he thought she was joking, and he shook his leg under her and said, "I'm always happy to help out." But then he heard her breathing grow heavier, and she stopped speaking and kept rubbing against him for one more minute, less even, and his leg froze under her and she came again, and it reminded him—he hated himself for even thinking this—of those dogs who hump people's legs.

So much hunger, he thought now. So much hunger. He flicked the thought of the dogs out of his mind, not wanting to defile his wife's honor, their joint honor. He was restless to sate her hunger again, to let her body remember again and again. He dialed her number but she still wasn't available, and now he was no longer angry at her but sympathetic. She must be stuck in some horrible meeting, and then she'd have to drive home in this squall. He was impatient to get hold of her, so she could tell him about the fight with Breutner and what they'd ended up agreeing on, and he'd tell her about the dogs and about his brilliant idea of calling Ali, and what should they tell the kids, the truth? She'd say, Of course not. We'll tell them they ran away. And he'd insist. We have to tell Roni the truth, of course. And she'd say, Of course. She's too old for us to lie to.

Now, almost completely relaxed, a thought pierced this fragile tranquillity: she's old enough to lie to us. He glanced at his watch: ten after ten. She should be in school by now. He wanted to call her and say a casual good morning, and how's it going and how was the demonstration. But he heard a knock at the door and hurried to open it.

A huge man, almost a giant, stood in the doorway, wearing a military parka spotted with water, raindrops glistening on his gray mane of hair. Mark held out his hand, and Ali quickly wiped his wet hand on his cargo pants, which were also olive green, and it suddenly looked as if the Arab were actually a soldier on reserve duty. He gave Mark a short and bone-crushingly firm handshake. Then he looked down, apparently searching for a doormat, and pointed to his muddy black rubber boots. Mark said, "Never mind, it's okay, come in."

"No, I can't walk in like this. Do you have a towel, maybe? Or a rag?"

"It's okay."

"No, not like this."

"Okay, I'll get something," Mark said, and he hurried to fetch a rag from the broom closet and spread it out in the entrance. Like a red carpet, he thought. Or the opposite of a red carpet.

Ali wiped his boots thoroughly, then walked inside and asked where the dogs were, as if expecting to find them in the living room. Mark led him to the back door. Before he opened it he asked whether Ali wouldn't prefer to wait until the rain eased up. "No," Ali said, "they said it would be like this all day."

"Oh, really?" Mark replied, as if he hadn't known. "Then I'll get an umbrella."

But Ali had already opened the door and gone out, and Mark followed him, the rain coming down hard on their heads.

"Such a shame," Ali said, clucking his tongue. Mark couldn't tell if his look was one of commiseration or accusation. "Not purebred, but still, it's a crying shame. How long have you had them?" The rain did not seem to bother him at all, as if he were used to standing that way, indifferent to the weather, like a horse.

"That one, the big one, Brutus—"

"Brutus?" Ali looked at him questioningly. "Like Butrus?"

Mark smiled. "Yes, like Boutros-Ghali, but not named after him, of course. We've had him for six years, since he was a puppy. And the other one, Olive"—he waited for Ali to respond to the name, but Ali said nothing—"she arrived about six months later."

Ali stood over the dogs and clucked his tongue. Then he pulled himself together and said, "Okay, let's do it. I'll take them to the truck."

"I'll help you," Mark said quickly, suddenly embarrassed. After all, he could have taken the dogs away on his own, he suddenly realized. What kind of a man makes a big fuss over two dead dogs?

"Okay. You take the little one, I'll take the big one."

Mark hurried over to Olive and picked her up in his arms. She was heavier than he'd expected. He backed into the living room, water dripping from his hair and from the dog's fur. He looked at Ali, who got down on one knee next to Brutus and stayed that way for a moment, as if eulogizing him, until with one swift motion he swung the dog up in his arms. When he came into the living room, Popeye padded over, and Ali, who hadn't noticed the fur statue on its bed of pillows, looked surprised. "Wait, is this another one?"

Mark, absentmindedly stroking the pinscher's wet fur, said, "Yes, this is Popeye. He's old."

"But how come he isn't also dead?"

"Oh, he almost never goes outside. He can barely walk."

"Bless him," Ali said, and took a few broad strides to the door. The German shepherd's head drooped over his right arm and the rigid legs stuck straight up. "Okay then, let's load them on the truck."

Mark nodded, followed him outside, and stood behind him as he moved Brutus into the open bed of an old Mitsubishi.

"Give him to me," Ali said.

Mark wanted to correct him about the dog's gender, but what difference did it make now? He handed Olive to Ali, who held her with one hand like you hold a mouse or a rabbit, and put her down next to Brutus. He rubbed his hands together.

Mark said, "Okay, come in and wash your hands."

Ali nodded, and they walked inside. Mark led him to the bathroom and pointed to the sink and the liquid soap, and said, "I'll get you a clean towel."

Before Ali could protest, he took a hand towel off the shelf above the toilet, and while Ali thoroughly washed his hands, he suddenly became aware of this room, of the pile of laundry he'd been planning to do, of the bathtub full of toys. Unlike Alona, he never bothered to clear the toys out when he showered.

He looked at Ali drying his hands on the towel, and their eyes met in the mirror, and he suddenly wanted to apologize but he didn't know what for, so he said, "I'll wash too, and then we can have some coffee. Do you have time?"

Ali hesitated for a moment and then said, "Yes, all right. Turkish, two sugars."

"I don't think I have any Turkish coffee, but I can make you an espresso." There, he'd found something to apologize for.

"Espresso is fine. But make it strong."

Mark was happy he had a good machine, because he didn't want the maintenance guy thinking he didn't know how to make a decent cup of coffee.

He suggested that Ali take off his wet coat, but Ali said he was okay, and only then did Mark notice that he himself was drenched. His sweatshirt was soaked, and his wet jeans clung to his thighs. He wanted to change, but he thought it would be weird and embarrassing to disappear into the bedroom. He leaned on the counter and looked at Ali, who pulled a pack of Marlboros from his coat pocket and asked, "Okay if I smoke?"

"Sure, I'll get you an ashtray." He remembered it was in the bedroom, so he would have to leave his post after all. He quickly went to get the ashtray. It had three butts in it, two of which, he noticed, had shadows of pink lipstick dotted with silver glitter. How had he not noticed that yesterday, when she'd arrived? She used lipstick so rarely.

When he went back to the kitchen he found Ali inspecting the espresso machine, an unlit cigarette dangling from his lips. Mark asked if he needed a light. "I have one," Ali said, and took out a lighter from his pocket.

He suggested they open a window, so the house wouldn't smell, but Mark said, "It's okay, it doesn't bother me. My wife smokes, too."

Ali sat down in his chair. "Your wife? I thought you got divorced."

"Jeez, you really do know everything about everyone here, huh?"

Ali nodded.

"We're not divorced. Separated."

"That's a shame. You have two little children, bless them."

"Bless them," Mark said, and wanted to tell Ali that they were probably getting back together. But he didn't, not because he had no basis for saying it but because he was afraid that saying the words out loud would sabotage some mysterious cosmic plan being woven around him at this very moment. He sighed. "Yes, we have two little children, Maya and Ido." But why was he telling him their names?

"And you have an older daughter, right?"

"Yes."

"But that's not from your wife."

"No. Roni's mother lives in the States."

Ali looked around, examining the kitchen. "I know her. Nice girl. I see her a lot around the moshav, hitching rides."

"Really? She hitchhikes?" Mark said, as if he didn't know. He grimaced with an exaggerated look of dissatisfaction.

The Arab nodded again, without looking at him. "Yep, I see her sometimes. I saw her at night once, too, at the intersection. I was working late on a job. Very nice girl. Beautiful, really beautiful."

"Thanks." He felt as though the Arab was torturing him a little. Why else would he tell him so laconically that he'd seen his daughter hitchhiking at night? But maybe he was just making too much out of it. Maybe Ali didn't see anything wrong with a girl hitchhiking at night. It wasn't like he'd seen her on some random road. It was just here, at the entrance to Eden. "How many children do you have?" he asked.

Ali coughed, a loud, damp cough, and quickly swallowed his phlegm like a frog downing a fly. "Six children and six grandchildren, bless them."

"But you're so young!" Mark said, putting the sugar bowl on the table and wondering if there were any croissants left in the freezer.

"Me? I'm fifty-five."

"Young. I'm forty-four. It was my birthday not long ago."

"Congratulations."

He again had the suspicion that the Arab was mocking him, looking down on him, on this yuppie with his espresso machine and the messy bathroom and the daughter who hitchhiked at night.

"Yes. To tell you the truth, I had a bit of a crisis." He knew he should stop chattering, that every additional word was a nail in the coffin of his inferiority, but he urgently needed to befriend this Ali, who took small sips of espresso and didn't say a word. It was hard to tell if he was enjoying the coffee or forcing it down. And if not befriend him, then at least crack him.

But what was there to crack? he wondered, as he frothed the milk for his cappuccino, which also seemed like the wrong choice, too feminine. After all, this was a maintenance man, a simple, uncomplicated guy who had come to help Mark as part of his job, either out of the goodness of his heart or simply because he was an Arab and therefore didn't have much of a choice. But enough with the interpretations. Just let this guy drink his coffee and leave. Take the dogs and be gone. Only then did it occur to him that he would never see Brutus and Olive again, and his heart sank, not because he knew he would miss them, but because he realized he'd taken them for granted. They were just two deputies to Popeye, his senior dog. He asked Ali if he had a dog.

"Yes, of course. Three of them. But outside, not in the house."

"Oh, right. It's an impure animal in Islam, isn't it?"

"Yes, impure. You're not allowed to touch them."

He felt like the man was reprimanding him again, wagging an invisible but very clear finger that said, *This is how you live, mister, like this?*

With no Turkish coffee? With all this impurity? He said, "I'm sorry, maybe you're not allowed to handle dogs, even if they're dead, no?"

"It's okay. It's my job, so it's okay."

Mark was impatient for Ali to finish his coffee and leave, and he decided not to offer him any food so as not to encourage him to stay, even though a moment ago, when he'd wondered if there were any croissants, he'd remembered the cake in the fridge, which was missing only the three slices he and Alona had eaten. No, he wouldn't offer Ali the cake. Why let things get complicated? A cake like that demanded explanations. He glanced at the glass jar on the windowsill, which contained a few butter and almond cookies that he served at the restaurant with coffee. But no, he would absolutely not encourage Ali to sit here any longer than necessary. Ali took another sip and put his cup on the table and leaned back, and Mark thought he was about to get up, but he took out his cigarettes and lit another one, exhaling and staring at some invisible spot, contemplative, not in a hurry to get anywhere.

"We have a welder in our village who makes those windows," he said, and jutted his chin toward the large square comprised of little panes in the kitchen. "Used to make them for the whole country. Even Ramat Aviv, Savyon, all those fancy suburbs."

"Oh, really?"

"Yes. But now he's home, not working, poor guy. They won't give him working papers."

Mark sat down, bored and anxious. "It breaks your heart to think of all those professionals, doesn't it?"

Ali nodded heavily again. "Who does the work here, do you know?"

"I have no idea. I'm only renting. But in our house, where my wife lives, we had two welders from Tel Aviv."

"Jews," Ali determined.

"Yes," Mark said, hating himself for the apologetic tone. "But they were excellent. And very affordable, if I remember correctly."

The Arab's nod turned into a shake. "It's a shame." He sighed. "My guy would have done work ten times better for you at half the price."

"Maybe so, but we were very happy with them. And compared to some others they gave us a good price."

"They do shitty work, I know the windows in your house. I bet you have leaks all over the place in winter."

Mark wanted to protest, but Ali was right. Even the first winter they'd lived there, they'd discovered annoying leaks in almost all the windows. "We're actually quite happy," he said softly.

"It's a shame. He does excellent work, my neighbor. For him it's an art. He's the one who invented these windows anyway, and then everyone copied him and now he's sitting at home for two years already. They say he's a security risk, I don't know why; maybe because he's young. Me, I'm lucky I'm old. If he came here he'd cry. He'd take one look at the shitty work the Tel Aviv welders did, and he'd cry."

"So you're saying with you it's the opposite than with us? It's better to be an old Palestinian than a young Palestinian?" Mark quipped, but he suddenly panicked. What if his joke was interpreted as an insult? As condescending?

But Ali looked pleased. He nodded gravely. "Yes, the opposite than with you."

There was a long silence as each man pondered. They turned their heads to the window periodically, when lightning or thunder violated the silence, and it seemed as if the unemployed welder's spirit hovered in the kitchen and it was he, rather than the wind, who was rattling the glass panes, like a prisoner clanging his bars. The house darkened abruptly, and Mark got up and turned on the kitchen light. The bare bulb hanging from the ceiling shed a yellow light that suddenly looked scary, as if Ali and he were sitting in an interrogation room. But it was unclear who was the interrogator and who the subject, and he hoped with all his heart that something would happen, that the phone would ring, that someone would knock on the door, that something would shake Ali out of his reverie and remind him that he had to go. Because it suddenly seemed to Mark that the Arab had settled here in his kitchen and had no intention of leaving. That in return for the small service he'd performed, he was now demanding a price. It wasn't clear what this price was, but obviously coffee and small talk wouldn't do it.

It occurred to Mark that Ali was expecting a tip. He hoped he had a fifty-shekel note, because twenty seemed too little and a hundred was out of the question. But Ali stood up and said, "Come and see." He pointed at the back door, and Mark thought he was about to show him a flaw in the welding work, but Ali hurried to the door and opened it and walked out, indifferent again to the downpour, and said, "You could put together a beautiful garden here. Why have you let it go? Look, all your trees, all the fruit, it's all dead. Nothing."

"They're not mine," Mark said, and this time he refused to go out into the rain. He stood behind the glass door. "The trees aren't mine. I'm just a tenant."

Ali looked at him in astonishment, or perhaps contempt.

Mark no longer cared, he just wanted Ali to leave.

"But isn't it a shame?" asked the giant man, standing with his back to Mark. "This is fruit trees. Here." He pointed at the lemon tree. "One tree of mine like this gave a hundred pounds of fruit last year. And this one"—he pointed to his right—"this is peach, you know? White peach. Probably didn't even give you one fruit this summer, right?"

Mark nodded.

"That's 'cause you don't water. And here"—he pointed to the skeleton of another tree—"that's an apricot. Dead."

Mark was about to tell him about the automatic sprinkler he was planning to buy, but he kept quiet, looking at the maintenance man's back as he stood in the rain clucking his tongue. Mark could tell he was growing more furious by the minute.

"I have over seven acres of olive trees, and I take care of each one personally, like it's my child. No computerized sprinkler, no irrigation, no nothing. Just with my hands." He turned to face Mark. "You have wonderful land here." If not for the rain, one might have thought he was crying. "All you need to do is water and give them a little attention, and that's it. Isn't it a shame, Mr. Segal?"

Mark felt a chill run down his spine. Ali even knew his last name? He couldn't remember having said it on the phone. He pulled himself together and said, "It really is a shame. Can you recommend a gardener?"

"You don't need a gardener, that's what I'm trying to tell you. It's a waste of money. You just need to water and give them a little attention, that's it." He came inside and closed the door. "You see? Doesn't shut properly. Feel it, feel it." He reached for Mark's hand, but Mark pulled back. "Touch it, touch the handle." Mark wanted to scream *No! I don't want to!* But he smiled and walked over to the door and put his hand on the handle.

"Push," said the Arab. "See how it doesn't go up properly? Don't you get water coming in here? Sure you do," he said, without waiting for the answer. He moved Mark away from the door with his large body, without touching him, and ran one of his huge fingers over the frame. "See?" He held his finger up in front of Mark's eyes. "See the drop here?"

"Okay, I'll talk to the landlords. I think they're overseas now."

The Arab scoffed. "This is shit work you got here. I told you." He zipped up his parka sharply, and Mark breathed a sigh of relief. He was leaving. "And I want to show you one more thing. Can I?"

"Well, I'm in a bit of a hurry, I'm getting a delivery at the restaurant."

"Just one minute," Ali said, and without waiting for an answer he walked down the hallway to the bedrooms and bathroom. Mark hurried after him, feeling like a wild animal whose territory has been invaded by a bear, and Ali went into the bathroom and turned on the faucet in the sink. "Look. Come and see." He beckoned Mark with his finger, and Mark stood by the sink, looking at the flow of water. "No, not here. Look here." He pointed to the tap.

"What?"

"Look!" Ali said ceremoniously, and ran his large finger along the handle. "It drips!"

Mark squinted. It was hard to see the drop in the dark room.

"Turn it on, turn on the light," Ali said.

"There's no need, I believe you."

"No, don't believe me!" the Arab protested. "Look with your own eyes. Turn it on."

Mark flipped the switch, and for a moment he had the comforting, childish thought that he was flipping a switch that would detonate a bomb and everything would explode and disappear. That was what he used to imagine as a child, when he found himself trapped, when his parents got mad at him or friends made fun of him. Or in math class, which he struggled with. He would imagine that he could press a secret button whenever he wanted to, whenever he got sick of things, and everything would blow up.

The room filled with light, and in the big mirror he saw his own and Ali's profiles. When Ali held his finger out, he briefly thought he was trying to gouge out his eye. "See?" Ali asked. Mark couldn't see anything except the giant finger that made him blink. The finger was so close to his nose that he could smell it.

"Yes, I see. I really should call the landlords."

Ali wiped his finger off thoroughly on the towel he'd used earlier, as if he were trying to remove something filthy. As he walked back down the hallway, Mark behind him, he turned to look at the bedroom. The door was open, inviting a glimpse into another failure. Then he glanced at the children's rooms, where there was always chaos, where the windows also leaked. He sighed, stood by the front door, and thrust his hand into his coat pocket. Mark was afraid he was about to take out another cigarette, but Ali reached for a huge bunch of keys, like a warden's, and said, "Well, I'm taking them to Hiriya then."

"Okay. Thank you so much, really."

Ali nodded. He lingered in the entrance for one more minute, looking around at the neglected house, which could have been paradise if someone else had lived there—like him, for example.

Mark quickly opened the door and Ali walked out. "Thanks again."

"Goodbye," Ali said.

"Goodbye." Mark closed the door and watched from the kitchen window as the maintenance guy glanced at the back of his truck and then sat down behind the wheel, started the engine, and drove away.

RONI

A woman of about thirty opened the door, and at first Roni was star-tled. He hadn't liked talking about Zohar and she'd never asked, afraid her interest might give away her sense of inferiority. A woman secure in her man's love, she told herself, shouldn't take an interest in his former lovers. But he had once let slip that she was short and full-figured with curly hair, and that described this woman. But the woman told Roni that Uri hadn't lived there for two months. She didn't know where he'd moved; they didn't really know each other; she was just the ten-ant. She'd heard about the apartment from a friend of Uri's girlfriend. "If you want, I can call him. Should I? He might know where Uri is. He told me, actually, but I can't remember, sorry. Maybe Ramat Gan? No, that wasn't it. Ramat Efal, I think. He moved in with his girl-friend somewhere."

"With Zohar?" Roni asked.

"Yes, Zohar."

Perhaps because Roni looked so stunned and let her backpack drop from her shoulder, not knowing what to say, and because her eyes welled up—it was uncharacteristic for her to cry, but it was happening— the woman asked if she was okay and said she could come in for a drink. Roni followed her down the long hallway to the kitchen, which looked different, and the woman asked if she wanted water or juice.

"Water," Roni said.

"You can sit down if you'd like," the woman told her, so she sat on a light-blue wooden chair that looked nothing like the folding chairs that had been in this kitchen last winter.

"I'm Na'ama," the woman said.

"Roni."

"To tell you the truth? I can't believe I even let a stranger into my home. It's unlike me, I'm totally paranoid. But you look harmless, and you were crying and everything, so I guess I thought you couldn't be a serial killer or a rapist, right?" Roni tried to smile but couldn't pull it off, and Na'ama said, "Well, I can see you still need time to recover, so I won't bother you. Drink your water." But she couldn't help talking, so she told Roni that she didn't really know Uri. "Are you a friend of his? Carlos told me about the apartment. Do you know Carlos? He plays bass in a band, and I write lyrics for them sometimes? And I'm working on a novel now, too."

"Really?" Roni asked. She no longer cared if Na'ama saw her crying, so she looked up at her.

"Uri writes, too, doesn't he?"

Roni nodded and said his book was coming out soon.

"Are you serious? Wow! I'm jealous. Where's it coming out, do you know?" She got up and took a pack of cigarettes from the shelf above the counter.

Roni noticed that the kitchen cabinets had been freshly painted in shades of pistachio green and light blue, like the chair. "Subtext," she said.

"That's a great publisher. Maybe I'll send them my book when it's finished."

Without knowing why—perhaps to repay her for her hospitality, perhaps to draw out the conversation so she wouldn't have to get up and go out into the street, which seemed impossible—she said, "My dad's wife is their senior editor."

"Really? Then it's a stroke of luck that I opened the door for you. You see? It's all from God. Even though I don't believe in him."

"Me neither."

"I believe in fate."

"Me, too."

"How old are you, anyway? You look really young."

"Sixteen and ten months."

"You're so funny. Just say seventeen!"

"Then seventeen. And you?"

"Thirty-three and two months," Na'ama said. Then she said, "You remember what this kitchen used to look like. You've been here before, right?"

Roni nodded, a heavy, doll-like nod.

"Listen, he left this apartment in shocking condition. Sanitation-wise? I don't know how that guy lived here. Do you know there were fleas? Did he have a dog?"

Roni shook her head.

"You have no idea what I went through when I moved in." Na'ama blew her cigarette smoke out the window, into the inner courtyard that separated the building from the one behind it. The yard was full of gas cylinders, planks of wood, and piles of damp cardboard boxes. A flash of light came on, like a fluorescent, flooding Roni's brain. If she could have, she would have closed her eyes to focus on the picture: she and Uri in this kitchen, the different one, nine months ago, a million years ago. She standing by the little gas cooker that was balanced on a shelf beneath that window—her eyes now traced the path of the gas pipe along the wall to its source at a new, clean outlet, not like the sticky, brown one that used to be there; the oven also looked new—and in the picture she stands stirring tomato soup from a packet, wearing her box-ers and his blue sweatshirt. They were hungry after sex and the joint they'd smoked, beset by intense munchies, but the fridge was empty. She had suggested they go out or order in, but there wasn't enough time, she had to get the bus, so he dug through the cabinets until he found the packet of soup and said—now a sound track came into the picture—"I bet you've never had packet soup. With a restaurateur dad it's probably forbidden in your home." He'd said it contemptuously, she now realized.

She'd replied, "Actually I grew up on canned soup—don't forget my mom." That's what she said, and he stood close behind her and said, "Turn the gas down, so it doesn't boil over," and he pulled her under-wear down. She said, Again? and he said, "Again and again and again; look what you're doing to me." She turned to him, wanting to see the mouth that had produced those wonderful words, but he said, "Don't turn around," and they did it like that, with her face to the window, but it wasn't this same window, it couldn't have been: this window was painted in a soft cream shade, and above it, rolled up like a little sleeping bag, was a light bamboo blind. That window's paint was cracked and peeling, and the glass was covered with a layer of grease, and she'd opened it despite the cold, and he'd said, "Are you crazy?" and she'd looked out into the courtyard and hadn't known that it was what she'd always remember: the rusty, damp scene, the cats huddled by the gas cylinders, looking up at her, or so she thought. Because it was their last time, their absolute last.

She watched Na'ama flick her cigarette ash out into the courtyard.

When she'd called the day after, to say it was amazing last night, to say she missed him, to say she felt like skipping school the next day and coming over, he said, "Listen." Now she heard that *listen* as if for the first time, as if she hadn't replayed it over and over again for nine months like a record, like a trauma. "Listen. We have to talk. If you want to come tomorrow, that's fine, but let's meet at a café and talk, okay?" She asked why not in the apartment, and he said, "Just because. I'd rather meet at a café."

Now she looked at Na'ama standing by the window and thought perhaps the clues had been hidden there, in those terrible ten or fifteen minutes in the kitchen, because that's what it had been, terrible. He'd said the usual *I love you, I love you so much*, but there had been something else, something different, new, a violence that could no longer be mistaken for passion. It was similar to what had happened the last time with Eli, in the forest. But not really similar; it couldn't be. Eli was Eli and Uri was something else. Uri really loved her.

Still, there had been violence. Not that he'd hurt her or humiliated her. No, it wasn't that, not like with Eli. But something in his body had said the opposite of *I love you*. There had been a moment when she'd thought he wanted to throw her out the window. That all his movements inside her were gaining momentum to fling her out, and although she knew it was impossible—there was no way he could do that, he was just carried away with love and lust for her—she was flooded with fear at the thought that someone could even want to do something like that to her, to see her plunge three stories down and shatter. Her body hardened, protecting itself from the possibility, and she waited for him to ask what was wrong, if he'd hurt her, because he always asked, he was so attentive to her every muscle, to the smallest change in her position, to her breaths. But he didn't ask. Maybe she should have said something, but what?

What do you say when you feel like someone doesn't want to sleep with you but to throw you out the window?

Na'ama told her that the day she moved in, she'd started itching like crazy. "At first I didn't know what it was. I thought I was allergic to something. But in the morning I woke up with a band of red bites around my waist. Like someone had drawn a line? You wouldn't believe it; the whole house was full of fleas! It was unreal, what was going on here. I don't understand how anyone could live like that. I mean, it's one thing to be a slob, but this was inhuman. If I'd known what shape the apartment was in, I'd never have taken it, I swear, because I saw much nicer places. But Carlos told me about this apartment, he said a friend of a good friend of his, the one who'd designed one of their CD covers, needed to get out of his lease urgently and was looking for a replacement, and he was willing to cover half a month's rent. So I said, awesome. The apartment looked cute." She tossed her cigarette out into the courtyard and immediately said, "Oops. I forgot about the gas cylinders. I hope we don't blow up." She sat down again. "So, your dad's wife—what's her taste in books?" Without waiting for an answer, she went on. "Because my writing is a little experimental, you know what I mean? Wait, do you even read?"

Roni nodded. She felt very tired.

"I don't like the books people write these days. Everyone's all like bourgeois? Old? They're all writing about Tel Aviv like it's so hot. But maybe she won't like what I write; there's no story, you know? Like, not in the acceptable sense? It's like vignettes, you know?"

Roni wanted to warn her that indeed Alona wouldn't like it; she had no patience for that kind of writing, but she kept quiet and stared out the window that Na'ama had shut and wondered what would happen to that cigarette if it had landed too close to a gas cylinder.

"Well, never mind, I still have to work on it anyway. But would you mind giving me your number? And when I have something to show I'll call, and maybe you can hook us up? You could just say you know me and all that?"

Roni said, "Sure," and it seemed like the first word she had uttered for years. "Sure. No problem."

Na'ama stood up. "I'm going to get my diary."

Roni got up and followed her to the bedroom. Na'ama went over to her desk, which had a computer and fax machine on it. The desk was exactly where his had been, up against the window that faced the street and so was usually closed, but like Uri had said once, it was still a window, so you put a desk under it. When Na'ama saw her standing there she apologized for the mess, even though the room was tidy. The window was wide open despite the rain, and the light filtered through a blind like the one in the kitchen, painting the room in an orangey yellow, like the color of the floor tiles. The room smelled like perfume, or incense, something warm and spicy. Another scent, clean and babyish, suddenly mingled with it when Roni stepped into the room. Searching for the smell's source, she noticed a pile of clothes on the bed—which Na'ama had positioned on the opposite side of where Uri had it, making the room look bigger. Roni smiled to herself and remembered how once, right at the beginning, she'd suggested he move the bed to where it was now, and he'd said, "Are you crazy? You can't have your feet facing the door. That's how they take dead people out of a room." She'd quickly dropped the idea and abandoned her attempts to be that sort of couple—the kind where she could give him advice and interfere with his interior design and buy him things. But one day she couldn't resist and brought him a gray T-shirt made of soft fabric that she'd found at a factory seconds store where she'd gone with Shiri once. Since she didn't want the shirt to give away the fact that it was a gift, she didn't wrap it but just pulled it out of a plain plastic bag, the kind you get at the supermarket. He thanked her profusely and said it was a great shirt, just his taste, and asked where she'd bought it and how much it had cost. He wanted to pay her back, and he tried it on, but only because she insisted, and then he suddenly got into a strange mood. He took the shirt off and said, "Look, Roni, it's nice that you thought of me, and I love the shirt, but I'd rather you not buy me any more presents." She said it wasn't a present, and he said, "Whatever, just don't buy me anything, okay? It stresses me out a bit." She said okay, and restrained herself, even though during that winter she saw dozens of things she thought would look good on him, and even though she didn't really understand why it was wrong to give him gifts. When she was Eilon's girlfriend she'd bought him a sweatshirt for his birthday and he hadn't taken it off to this day.

Na'ama took down her phone number and they sat down in the kitchen again. A sudden flash of lightning lit up the apartment, followed by a bolt of thunder. "Wow, this is some storm!" Na'ama said, and Roni nodded. Na'ama asked if she had an umbrella, and she shook her head. "How will you go outside, then? You can't go out without an umbrella." It seemed as though she was sick of her and wanted her to leave, so Roni stood up and slung her backpack over her shoulder. But Na'ama said, "Wait, you can't go out like this."

"It's okay, I have to be somewhere."

"Okay, but I'm fine if you want to stay here awhile longer. Even though, I don't know, they said it would be like this all day, didn't they?"

Roni walked to the front door and Na'ama opened it—now she noticed that it had also been painted, and a new deadbolt had replaced the old lock. "So you don't want me to call Carlos? Maybe he has the new number."

"No, no, I'll call," Roni said, even though she had no intention of doing so. But as she started down the steps an internal lightning flashed in her mind, and before Na'ama shut the door she turned back and said, "You know what? Do you have Carlos's number? I don't think I have it."

Seeming relieved that she would not have to send her guest out into the storm empty-handed, Na'ama said, "Sure, hang on a sec. I'll write it down for you." She disappeared into the apartment and came back with a pink note. "It's his cell. I don't have his home number, but he's never home anyway."

Roni took the note and buried it in her backpack's side pocket and said thanks.

"You're welcome, really. Are you sure you're all right?"

Roni nodded.

"I didn't even ask why you were crying."

Roni smiled. "Forget it, it doesn't matter, but thanks, really, and good luck with the book." She skipped down the steps.

Outside it was already dark, and even though it was early it seemed very late. Her legs automatically carried her toward Rothschild to get back to the Central Bus Station. But when a number 5 pulled up she kept standing at the stop, and she did not get on the next one either, or the next one. She suddenly felt that she had no idea what she was supposed to do now, because everything had been planned down to the last detail. She'd been anticipating this day for nine months, just waiting for the right moment, for a lucid instant of knowledge. It wasn't a question of courage but of clarity, of being able suddenly to see all the details after the journey to Tel Aviv in the afternoon—she even knew what she would do if he wasn't home: she would wait at their café until she saw him, and that might be the moment when she really got excited, and her knees might tremble as she walked up the steps to his apartment, the apartment that was theirs for a few months. In the morning, when they said on the weather forecast that there would be a storm today and it would worsen tomorrow, she was filled with excitement and gratitude: perfect, she thought. Just like their first meeting. And as she made her way from the Trattoria to the bus stop and it started to rain, just a soft, prickly drizzle, she told herself that later, when they were together, the thunder and lightning would probably start, and then the downpour, and what could be more perfect than that? And indeed, it had started to pour five minutes ago, when she was in the apartment that was no longer his, and what should she do now?

She'd thought of everything these past few months—everything except Zohar, who was not a possibility or a threat. Zohar was the past. That was the order of things: first Zohar, then her. So it was clear that after their time-out it was *her* he was supposed to miss, not Zohar. The breakup with Zohar was ancient history that had been chewed over and digested and vomited into a novel. Zohar was a character in the novel, not someone you moved in with out of town. And it was strange, because he'd always said he would never leave Tel Aviv, there was no way he could survive in the suburbs for more than two days, and she'd agreed. She'd agreed so vehemently that in the past year her life on Eden seemed to have become intolerable. She saw everything through his eyes, the eyes of an urbanite who despised the tedium charged by the countryside in return for the quiet and the fresh air—who needed air? Who needed quality of life? Quality of life was an advertising slogan for the bourgeoisie who were trying to compensate for the terrible vapidity of their lives. Uri wasn't like that, and neither was she. He always mocked Eden, teasing her about the name at almost every opportunity. "Doesn't it sound like a joke to you?" he'd ask, and she'd quickly agree: a bad joke.

She headed south on Rothschild, preferring to walk to the station instead of taking a bus. That way, there was always the chance that something would happen, something that would change everything. She was hungry. She hadn't eaten anything since last night's dinner; she hadn't taken her usual sandwich to school: low-calorie bread, which was what Alona always had, with hummus and tomato. The excitement had been food enough, and her stomach had been full, but suddenly the hunger was almost painful, and she had a strange craving for soup. Funny, she thought, as she kept going south, she'd never liked soup. In summer she would sometimes taste some of her father's dishes at the restaurant, like gazpacho or cold zucchini and mint soup. But in winter, when he cooked up his strange, heavy stews and begged her, "Just taste some, why not?" she always refused, brushing off the thick soups as one brushes off a fake forced homeliness, smiling secretly at Maya and Ido, who joined her in this categorical refusal. But now she wanted just that kind of soup: something thick and full of content, something with chickpeas and big chunks of vegetables. She had enough money, and she passed a few restaurants and cafés. The soft light seeping out from their windows onto the wet street looked tempting, but she kept walking and came to the end of Rothschild and turned right onto Allenby. Maybe she would take the bus to the central station after all and get home in time for a real dinner—not that such a thing existed at Alona's, but she could call her father and tell him the demonstration had been canceled because of the weather and that she was on her way home. And she'd ask if he happened to have any soup, because she really felt like some, knowing that by the time she got home he'd have time to put something together. He'd be thrilled that she even asked, that she even wanted anything from him. She could picture him darting around the kitchen, maybe making a quick run to the Trattoria for ingredients, putting on his funny apron with the picture of a piglet eating spaghetti, and cooking her up some soup—*the* soup. She had a sudden urge to write it down: he's cooking me *the* soup. Her craving for soup was superseded by something more urgent: the notebook. She had to sit down somewhere and write a few lines, but these cafés didn't look right for sitting alone with her thoughts, so she turned west, knowing there would be no more cafés but suddenly wanting to be close to the sea, to see it frothing, like her, like in the movies. She remembered the scene from *Last Tango in Paris*, when Maria Schneider and Marlon Brando get wet in the rain and go up in that strange elevator to the apartment, and she lifts up her dress and shows him her naked body, and then the bath, and then that strange, exciting scene—Shiri had burst out laughing in this bit, too—when he clips her nails and forces her to put her finger up his anus. Why? she'd wondered at the time, ignoring Shiri, who said, "Let's turn it off, come on, this is gross." Why had he done that? She hadn't understood, but now that she reached the sea, and it was grayish-brown and stormy, almost European, she thought she knew: for him, pain was redemption. Just like for her.

The rain let up and turned to a drizzle, just as it had earlier, when she'd run from the Trattoria to the bus stop to catch the bus to Tel Aviv. Brutus and Olive had chased her, rubbing up against her legs every so often. Olive barked sharply, as if to confirm the plans, the tags on Brutus's thick collar clanged, and everything was so celebratory, the gray turning darker in preparation for the storm, the wind whipping her face, the bus she almost missed—it had already pulled away when she stood on the other side of the road, waiting for a break in traffic so she could cross, waving at the driver with her arms. He waited for her, and when she got on she said, "Thank you, thank you, thank you." She knew without having to look back that her father was still standing on the front deck, that he suspected her, because this time she had probably gone too far with her story about the demonstration and the new friend Sivan—where had she even come up with that name? She knew he didn't believe her but that he was afraid to ask, afraid of her, and she knew he'd probably call Alona, as usual, and Alona would reassure him and say he was overreacting and he should give the girl some freedom and just trust her.

The whole way to Tel Aviv she thought about what she would be like as a mother, and about the daughter she would have. She very much wanted a girl, but not now, of course. Not for another ten years, at least. She tried to imagine what kind of parents they would be, she and Uri, and although she was unable to really picture it, picture them, especially herself, as parents, she knew they would be amazing, and that their child—preferably a girl—would grow up free, and Roni would understand her and know how to look deep into her soul. She would be the perfect mother, she knew it, if only because her own parents were so defective.

She and Uri would name their daughter Anna, or Naomi, or Rachel. Something simple and unsophisticated. Something that would light up the girl from the inside like a bulb with warm colors, like the light she used to have in her room in Ein Kerem when she was little. It had shone from a parchment lampshade her mother had bought at an Indian reservation. What was the illustration, was it deer? Horses? She couldn't remember, but she remembered the light: something magical, like in a theater. What had happened to that lampshade? She hadn't taken it to the States, it had stayed in the house in Ein Kerem, and when she'd moved in with her father and Alona it was gone, like many other things from that room.

When she got to the promenade her cell phone rang. She was sure it would be her dad, with some excuse to check up on her, and she knew it was better to pick up and get it over with, otherwise he'd be after her all evening. But when she took the phone out of her bag she saw Shiri's number flashing on the screen. Why was Shiri calling her now? she thought irritably. When was she going to realize they hadn't really been friends for ages? She ignored the ring and sat down on the damp sand. Her clothes were soaked anyway. She lit a cigarette and glanced at the clock on the phone: it was eight. She still had time, the last bus was at midnight. She knew the bus schedule by heart and hoped they hadn't changed it since last winter; that hurt suddenly, that bus schedule; it used to be her enemy but now she missed it.

Her wet clothes were freezing. The denim jacket was like a shroud, rigid and chilling. She'd searched for something like this since the breakup, something like the jacket Uri had loaned her a few times when they'd gone out for coffee. His was old and faded, hip length, and she hadn't been able to find one anywhere. She was almost tempted to ask her mother to buy her one and send it, but she knew she'd buy something not quite right, forget an important detail, fake it, and then say, "I couldn't find exactly what you wanted so I got something similar," and she wouldn't understand why Roni was annoyed.

In the fall, Alona had taken her winter clothes down from the top shelf in the closet and had laid this jacket out on the bed. When Roni came into the room and saw it, she commented on how much she liked it. Alona said she used to wear it to death, but it was too small now. "Every winter I delude myself into thinking it will fit, but it's not just a question of a pound or two, it's my whole build. Do you want it?" she asked. Roni tried the jacket on and it fit perfectly.

But now the jacket was a frozen trap. She got up and made her way back to Allenby, turned onto Sheinkin, and decided to go into one of the cafés after all, for a hot drink. When she sat down in the first place she came across, which was very crowded, she asked the waitress what kind of soup they had. The waitress said, "Sweet potato and lentil. The lentil is out of this world, would you like it?"

Roni said no thanks, and ordered a hot chocolate. She looked around at the people chattering, drinking, gobbling food, and they all looked indifferent to the sadness that had followed her into this place, seeking refuge from the cold. She had only just begun to feel it physically, like the wet jacket that she took off and hung on the back of her chair, hoping it would dry off a little before she left, knowing it wouldn't.

Her phone rang: Shiri again, not her father. It was funny how he was resisting the urge to call, to find out where she was and what she was doing. Coward, she thought. But the notion no longer had the satisfaction it used to. On the contrary: it scared her to think that he was afraid of her and wasn't even looking for an excuse to call, like to ask if she knew where the remote control was, or to make sure she remembered she'd agreed to work this weekend; the restaurant would be crowded or something—anything to force her to say she was coming home, the demonstration was canceled, she'd be home in an hour or two and would call from the intersection for him to pick her up.

She listened to Shiri's message. Shiri said she had to talk to her urgently. It was obviously something about Idan, her new boyfriend, with whom, after much deliberation, she'd lost her virginity. It amused Roni to think about Shiri having sex, about Shiri tormenting herself over her silly little love troubles, and over Idan, with his soul patch and long sideburns, and his thick-rimmed glasses, and the asthma, which enchanted Shiri as if she were dating a consumptive on his deathbed.

How happy she was to think she had been spared all that, boys like Idan and Eilon, those excitable lapdogs. How lucky that she had found the love of her life so quickly, and so had he. How many times had he told her that? "It hurts how much I love you, Roni, it hurts my whole body. Here, feel it. Here, and here, and here." And he would take her hand and run it over his body. Not like Eli, to say nothing of Yossi, whose piggish face appeared before her as she stared into her mug of cocoa. A piece of Flake bar slowly melted into the hot liquid.

Yesterday in her driving lesson, she'd asked Yossi if she was ready to take the test yet. She'd already had over forty lessons. And after all, he'd told her she was an amazing driver. But he said she shouldn't take it yet and suggested they do another four or five lessons. "It would be a shame, doll. It would be too bad if you didn't pass the first test." She said okay, and he asked, "What's the problem? Your dad won't pay anymore?" She said no, of course not, and remembered how her father had asked not long ago if this driving business wasn't becoming interminable. He asked how many lessons she'd taken—not that he was counting, but it seemed like a million. She said she hadn't taken that many, the average amount, she thought, and he said okay and wrote a check.

Yesterday, when she got into Yossi's car, she decided she wouldn't sleep with him. She'd tell him she had her period or something, because she wanted to be ready for today, clean. When the lesson was over and Yossi switched places with her and was about to drive onto the dirt road, she said, "Not today, I have my period." Without looking at her he said, "Don't worry about it," and kept driving. She said nothing— why didn't she say anything? They got to their regular spot, a small clearing among the grapefruit trees, and when he stopped and they both got out to move to the backseat, she noticed that the area looked slightly different, as if someone else had been there. There were all sorts of signs: a crushed pack of Marlboros, a can of Coke, and a condom hanging from a low branch.

Yossi, who also noticed it, giggled and said, "Someone stole our spot, hey?" He peeled off his sweater and tossed it onto the driver's seat, lay down in the back, unbuckled his belt and unzipped his pants and said, "Are you coming?" But she kept standing outside the car. Yossi said, "Can you believe this? Soon they'll be charging people to park here." He laughed and coughed a deep, moist cough. "Let's go, your friend has a lesson in ten minutes," he said, and she thought about Shiri, who had already failed three driving tests and blamed Yossi for it. "Lousy teacher," she'd said, and asked Roni if she didn't notice that his car always reeked.

"Roni?" Yossi was calling her again. His nose was stuffed up. "You don't want your girlfriend waiting outside, do you? That girl's so thin the wind will blow her away."

She looked at the crushed pack of cigarettes and the soda can, and at the condom hanging from the branch like a plant pod, and was overcome with panic and disgust.

"Roni, doll," he called again in his nasal voice, and she got in on the other side of the car and sat on his legs. "So, you have your period?" he asked. She nodded and said she had cramps, and he asked if she felt like blowing him. He really needed it now, he had to unload, otherwise he had no idea how he'd get through a lesson with her annoying girlfriend. "Does she even have a boyfriend?"

Roni said, "No. Yes. Actually, I don't know," and she looked at her driving teacher's hand rubbing his dick.

"I'm saving you some of the work," he said, when he saw her watching. "Here you go. Your turn." He slid his ass down the seat until he was close to her. His little penis waited like an exclamation point at the end of a very insignificant sentence.

And she couldn't do it. For the first time in her life, she couldn't. But she had to, because they were already here, and how could she change her mind now? Since she knew Yossi came fast, not like Eli, who took a long, long time, or Uri, who she never wanted to come, she decided to rise to the occasion—that's how she thought of it—and help this pathetic man sprawled on the backseat, his head leaning on the door, breathing through his stuffed nose. A white undershirt was stretched over his potbelly like a doll's clothing, above his little erect penis. He opened his eyes, which had been closed in anticipation, and asked, "What's going on, doll? Did you fall asleep?" She smiled, and he glanced at his watch and said, "Crap, let's hurry this up, okay?" She bowed her head and started to suck on him.

Her phone rang again and Shiri's number flashed, desperately, and she decided to answer it just to get it over with, but also because she felt slightly lonely, far away, not a few miles but a few thousand miles away from the place she'd left only that afternoon, but had actually left long ago, when she'd met him, maybe before, and now she could no longer go back—how could she?

She leaned back in her chair, her back touching the wet jacket, and
let Shiri scold her: "I've been trying to get you for hours." Roni said she
hadn't heard the phone ring, and Shiri said, "Listen, something terrible
happened. Our condom tore. What am I going to do?" She whimpered,
and wondered whether to get the morning-after pill.

Roni lit a cigarette and told Shiri not to worry. "You don't get pregnant that quickly. When did you notice that it happened?" Shiri stam-
mered, "I don't know. Afterward, you know. Oh, God, we're such
idiots! I'll die if I'm pregnant, Roni, I'll die!" She said her period had
just finished three days ago, so maybe it was okay, "What do you think?
But still, you know? Should I go to a pharmacy? Idan promised he'd
drive me to SuperPharm; he's picking me up soon. Oh, God! He's such a
retard. How did he not notice?" Thankfully, Shiri had another call. "It's
him," she said, "I have to go, he's waiting outside." She promised to call
Roni later with an update, "But be available, okay? Promise me you'll be
available." Roni promised, and when she hung up she decided to quickly
call her dad before she could change her mind. She hit the first number
in the memory and looked at the screen: *Dad-home. Dialing.* But the
answering machine picked up, and Maya's voice said, "Hi! This is Roni,
Maya, Ido, and Mark's house. We're not home. Leave us a message." She
hung up and wondered whether to call the restaurant, even though it
didn't seem likely that he would be there tonight. She dialed the third
number in the memory; the second was Alona, and the fourth was Uri.
There was no answer at the Trattoria either, or on his cell.

The waitress came over and asked if she wanted anything else. "We
have other things besides soup. There's amazing quiches, if you feel like
that." Roni said no and asked for the check, and kept staring at her cell
phone that sat on the table next to an ashtray, cigarettes, and a lighter.
Then she remembered that she'd wanted to read her notebook, and she
took it out of the backpack. It was a bit damp around the edges, and
she started to flip through the pages until she got to the letter she'd
started writing him a few weeks ago, the letter that was different from
all the others because she had planned to finish it in his arms.

When will we be together again?

Yesterday I listened on my discman to the Mozart Requiem you said
you liked. I even bought the same recording you have. I lay in bed and

*listened on my headphones. It was amazing. The whole time I could see
us sitting together in the bathtub and soaping ourselves, and there was
lots of hot water (remember how your hot water always runs out? I
wonder if your landlord got you a new heater).*

*Actually, we spend the whole day in the bath. Of course there's a
stereo system in the bathroom. The water has a sharp, soft scent, like
fresh grass and flowers. And when we get out of the water we are so
beautiful, scrubbed and shiny, and then we sit around relaxing, and
it's evening, and we have a good meal, lounge around, then ask some
people over. Oh, and it's raining, of course. That's the most important
thing.*

*My sweet, what are you doing now? I miss you. I so want to be
close to people who are close to you, but other than Alona I don't know
anyone, and with Alona I don't know; it hurts me to know that she sees
you, or at least talks to you, and I don't.*

*I feel like I'm going mad. Not because of you, because of everything.
I don't know what I think anymore. I hate something so badly and I
don't know what it is. And I love something so badly, too. You.*

*I want you so much. I feel so tired. Not sad, but heavy. And I love
you so much.*

How can I be sad when I have you?

The waitress brought the check and Roni put a twenty-shekel note
in the dish, then took the pink note with Carlos's number from her bag.
Without knowing what she would say if he answered, she dialed the
number. A sleepy-sounding man picked up, and in the background she
could hear deafening music.

"Carlos?"

"Yes. Hi. Who's this?"

"Roni, a friend of Uri Breutner." When he didn't respond, she added,
"Uri, Zohar's boyfriend."

"Oh, yeah. How are you doing?"

"Okay. I'm looking for Uri. The tenant in his apartment, Na'ama,
said they moved out of town—"

"To Ramat Ha'Hayal. Where you can hear the 'burbs chirping."

"What? I can't hear you, there's tons of noise."

"We're in rehearsals, we have a gig tonight. Do you want to come?

You should come, it'll be cool. I'll put your name on the list. What did you say your name was?"

"Roni." Her heart was pounding.

"Romy?"

"No, Roni!" she shouted.

"Okay, I got it. They're waiting for me, I have to go."

"But do you have their number? Uri's?"

"Yes, hang on, it's in my phone." He disappeared for a minute and then came back. "Are you writing?"

She pulled out a pen from the notebook and wrote the number on the other side of the pink note and asked what time the gig was.

"Eleven. You should come, Romy, I'm leaving your name on the list. And bring your friends." He told her the name of the club, and she thought he might have blown her a cellular kiss, and then he hung up.

Since she'd already paid the check and left a tip, she couldn't keep sitting there, even though she suddenly felt weak and ravenous. It would be embarrassing to change her mind now and ask for a menu. She looked at the waitress carrying a tray with two bowls of lentil soup to the table next to her, and wished she'd ordered some. "Is everything okay?" the waitress asked when she saw her staring. She nodded quickly and got up, put on her coat, which was just as wet as it had been an hour ago, and left.

At least it wasn't raining now, even though the sky was covered with a new layer of clouds. The street was bustling, full of life, defiant like the café. She walked back to Rothschild, as if it had a magnetic pull on her, a combination of adventure and shelter. When she crossed Rothschild and looked at the number 5 bus on the corner, she knew that tonight she would not go back to the Central Bus Station. There was no reason to think about it anymore or try and get hold of her dad, and although she did not know exactly where she would go and what she would do or where she would sleep, she knew she would not be going home tonight. The decision, if it even was a decision—she didn't feel as if she'd decided but more like she was on a raft drifting down a frothy river that she could not get off, not now, not yet—the decision calmed her.

She walked faster and found herself standing at his building again, and she looked up at the third floor, where a soft light seeped through the bamboo blinds on Na'ama's bedroom window. When he had lived there, there'd been old metal blinds that were always closed, so no light had seeped through that window at night. But now it looked like a lighthouse. Should I go up again? she thought. Knock on the door and make up some excuse? But what could she say? Anything would sound crazy and desperate and would scare Na'ama, make her feel like she'd gotten mixed up in something, and that she'd made a mistake to let Roni in before.

She had another hour at least before the show. Carlos hadn't told her how to get to the club, and she sat down on the low fence outside his building, the fence she'd sat on several times last winter, waiting. Uri had never been one for punctuality, and he'd often been late, always out of breath and apologetic when he arrived. "I feel bad for every minute with you that gets wasted," he'd say. "I'm such a shit for making you wait. I'm sorry." And then they'd quickly skip up the stairs to his apartment.

She took her cell phone out, dialed directory service, and asked for the phone number and address of the club, but the address meant nothing to her. She didn't want to phone the place, or Carlos, to ask where it was, because that would sound kind of desperate and childish. She'd find it. She had enough money for a cab, and the driver would know where to go. As far as she was concerned, she could just keep sitting on the fence, smoking, killing time. But then she wondered what she would do if Na'ama came out and saw her, and she got up quickly and turned back toward Rothschild—the avenue was a suture between everything that had been and everything that would be.

Her phone rang again. Shiri. But she didn't want to answer so she turned it off. She hailed a cab, even though it was still too early, but she wanted to get away from this place. When she gave the driver the name and address of the club, he nodded silently and drove south on Rothschild, then turned onto Florentin. She looked out at the deserted streets. Where were they going? The cab stopped on a side street that wound its way past closed woodworking shops, and the driver pointed to a two-story industrial building. "It's upstairs over there, but I think it's still closed." She said that was all right, here was fine. She paid him and got out of the cab, and asked what time it was. The driver glanced at the dashboard clock and told her, "Ten past ten," and since the club was at the end of a dead-end street, he maneuvered his car around and drove away.

She looked up at the second floor. There were no windows, only a sliding iron door, which she now noticed was slightly open. When she started to walk up the concrete steps she could hear the sounds of an electric guitar, and she turned back; what would Carlos think if she was the first one there? It was better to keep wandering, kill another half an hour, even an hour. But when she looked around she was frightened by the empty, abandoned street, which looked mute and frozen, as if it were scaring itself.

She remembered how she used to be embarrassed every time she went out with her mother to a gallery show or dinner with her artist friends, because her mother always showed up on time. When Roni complained and said, "I don't want to be the first ones there, it's embarrassing and desperate, Mom," her mother just looked at her with infuriating calmness.

"What's desperate is to not be yourself, and I am punctual." Roni said in a condescending tone that she was not punctual, she was restless, and Jane replied, "So I'm restless, so what? Hiding it costs me more than going with it."

It dawned on her now that she had inherited the restlessness, the punctuality. It had been pointless to get angry at Uri all those times he was late, sometimes even by an hour or two, when she used to sit on the fence wondering how he could waste their precious, sacred time together. She now understood it wasn't his fault but hers. She was always on time or a little early; maybe he thought she was too desperate, and that's why he broke up with her: he didn't want a desperate girlfriend. It disgusted her, too, just like Eilon's desperation. He had called it being in love, but she didn't think of it that way, and now, seeing herself through Uri's eyes, she realized what she'd done wrong and what she had to fix.

The fragments of her shattered plan coalesced into something new, something sharp and full of light, and she started walking quickly down the windy road, passing shuttered workshops, suddenly unafraid. She would call him—maybe even tonight, because he never went to sleep before two or three—and tell him she was in Tel Aviv and wanted to meet for coffee in the morning; she had the day off school—no, she shouldn't mention school—and when they met she'd tell him every-thing, but differently. She'd tell him she was having lots of doubts and wanted advice about someone she'd been dating for a while, an older man, a lawyer, "Older than you, yes, forty-something. But he's married," and yes, she knew it was wrong.

Naughty you, he'd quip, but he'd be curious, and he'd realize that something had happened to her since their breakup, something intrigu-ing, seductive. She'd try to sound indifferent and tell him she didn't know what to do about this Eli because he was really in love with her and kept bugging her and wanting to see her, and she was a little sick of him, of how desperate he was. You know what I mean? she'd say. Just like Maria Schneider, who also had a boyfriend in the movie who really wanted her. And he'd say, Yes, I know exactly what you mean.

He'd probably tell her about Zohar, that they were back together, and he'd say it awkwardly, almost apologetically. I'm a sissy, right? I never told you much about her. And she'd say she thought she knew her anyway, she knew the type: After all, how can anyone read your book—and by the way, have you found a title?—without knowing her a little? She knew so many girls like that, she'd say—except she couldn't say *girls*, it was better to say *women*—she knew a lot of women like that, who only cared about commitment and exclusivity: They don't really understand what's important, do they? They don't understand that the moment is more important than anything. And he'd say yes and won-der what had happened to her. How had she changed so much? She'd tell him that was exactly the problem with this Eli guy she was seeing; he wanted exclusivity. Can you believe that? She wasn't into being exclusive with anyone right now!

She would stress the *anyone*, she thought, as she sped up and turned off the narrow street onto a very wide main road. SALAMEH, the sign said. She stood at the intersection, not knowing whether to cross but knowing she had to keep walking. Then she noticed a convenience store across the street and remembered that she was almost out of cigarettes, so she went over quickly and bought herself a pack and a bag of Bamba.

She started gobbling down the snacks, as she walked back, and told herself again it was crucial to emphasize to Uri that she wasn't inter-ested in a serious relationship with anyone now. There's plenty of time for that, right? she'd say. So, what should she do about this Eli, brush him off? Because the sex, she would tell him, was really amazing. A little violent, you know? But good. And he'd say, Oh, really? And she'd sigh and say yes, that's why it was such a dilemma. If he could just settle for that, you know? But he wants a relationship, with love and everything. He's even talking about leaving his wife, and I'm *so* not into that right now. Totally not.

He'd look at her and say, You've changed, you know? And he'd sound ponderous and nostalgic, and curious to rediscover her—or not rediscover her so much as discover the *new* her. And then he'd understand; he'd have no choice but to understand that he'd made a terrible mistake by going back to Zohar, to the *cage of couplehood*, as he called it in the book, when right in front of him sat a different, amazing possibility. She'd tell him she was taking her driving test in two months, and she was going to pass the first time; her teacher had promised. Oh, and you know what else? I'm leaving home. And she'd tell him how she was going to rent an apartment; she'd even been reading the classifieds. "I was actually thinking about your area. Nachmani, Balfour, those streets, you know. Something with roommates, at least at first, until I find a job. Do you know of anything?"

She walked down the street parallel to the club and turned fearlessly into an alleyway, the new plan having made her practically immortal. It wouldn't really be a lie, she thought, because she *had* brushed off Eli a few days ago—she now understood that that's what she'd done: she'd broken up with him. And it was at least a half-truth to say he wanted more from her than she wanted from him. It was also true that she wasn't into commitment, because in her fantasies she saw Uri and herself reuniting in bed, without talking about the past or the future.

How's life in the countryside? she'd ask. Ramat Ha'Hayal, you said? He'd tell her it wasn't exactly the countryside and it was shitty, really shitty, and he hated it. I can so relate to that, she'd say, and they'd look out at the rain—she could see a storm brewing in the sky now—because Uri, just like her, always said rain made him horny and lonely, and tomorrow the two of them would sit and gaze at the sheets of rain coming down outside the café window, and when they said goodbye—she had to remember to be the first one to leave—he'd ask if she still had the same number, and she'd say, Yes. It was really fun to see you, you know? And he'd look at her sadly and say, For me, too, and she'd know that it wasn't the end but the beginning, that the encounter had sowed the seeds of restlessness in him; it was only a question of a day or two, a week at most, until he called and asked to get together again. Standing at the foot of the concrete steps to the club, she realized she should come up with a place for them to meet, like an apartment. But where? Maybe she should leave that up to him.

Since she'd killed almost an hour walking around, she realized it was too late to call him tonight. After all, he did live with someone, and it might seem suspicious. She decided to put off the call until the first thing next morning. She was no longer worried about where she would sleep and what would happen. She was happy to keep roaming the streets until morning. The show would probably run until two or three, and then anything could happen.

She climbed the steps and saw that the iron door was open and a young woman was standing in the doorway with a list. "Roni," she said, and the woman looked for her name. "Carlos put my name on the list."

The woman said, "I can't find it."

Roni smiled. "Try Romy."

The woman looked again and said, "Yes, Romy. Go in."

The club was tiny and already packed with people, some of whom sat around little tables close to the stage. Most were crowded around the bar. Three men and one woman stood on stage, and Roni walked up to one of the guitarists and asked, "Carlos?" He jutted his chin at a man leaning over an amplifier, tuning buttons. "Carlos?" she said, and the man looked at her. "I'm Roni." When she saw the questioning look on his face, she said, "We talked on the phone before. You put my name on the list."

"Oh, yeah," he said. "Awesome that you came. Did you bring your friends?" She shook her head and he said, "Super. Okay. Sit down, make yourself at home. Do you want a drink?" She said yes, and pulled her wallet out of her backpack, but he said, "That's okay. What do you want?" She asked for a beer.

She sat down at a small table up against the left side of the stage and waited for Carlos. He came back from the bar with a bottle of Tuborg for her and one for himself and jumped back onto the stage. "Later?" he said. She nodded and sipped her beer, and thought how brilliant it was to have eaten that Bamba earlier, so she wouldn't be drinking on an empty stomach. That was something her mother had taught her; every time they went out to those awkward events she made sure to eat at least a few crackers before she got glasses of wine or punch for the two of them. Roni suddenly felt a small pang of nostalgia—not for those parties, which she hated, and not for her mother, but for that contempt she used to feel toward her, which had slightly dissipated this past year. Why didn't she feel it anymore? Did that mean she'd grown up? She remembered what Alona had once said about anger giving way to sadness. But what happens to the contempt? she wondered. Does it also crumble and turn into nostalgia?

She looked at Carlos tuning his guitar. He was older, thirty-five at least, and looked like a regular balding guy, wearing brown corduroys, a thick black sweater, and an old pair of Nikes. When he looked at the audience every so often, his eyes met hers and he smiled a slightly crooked smile, embarrassed, as if he too had found himself here by accident and didn't belong, being too old and too tired. If she wasn't already in love, she thought, she could have fallen in love with him.

He jumped off the stage again, walked over, and asked if everything was okay. He said they were going on in five minutes. "I hope you're not bummed out about being here on your own. I thought you'd bring some friends." She said no, not at all, it's really nice, and he said, "Okay, we'll talk later then?" as if he were claiming patronage, as if they'd arranged to meet and talk, and he hadn't just invited some strange girl to his gig. It flattered her: she really had changed, and she was projecting something different, not so childish, not so desperate. She must be coming off like someone whom a guy of at least thirty-five would be interested in.

The lead singer walked up to the microphone, and the *good evening* she whispered sounded secretive and seductive, like she was saying it to herself or maybe to someone in the audience, a boyfriend or lover. Then she let out a screech, and since Roni was sitting right by the speaker, she felt as if the sound had split her body open. The singer smiled and whispered, "That's a tribute to Patti Smith. Hey, Patti!" The audience laughed, and although Roni didn't know who Patti Smith was, she assumed she was a singer, and she also smiled. The singer said, "I'm a star," and the audience laughed again, and the singer said, "I mean, my name is Star. That's what my mom and dad named me, would you believe it?"

The crowd yelled out, "We believe it!"

"Because my parents were groovy, you know, the sixties and all that." She held the microphone close to her lips, almost licking it. "Totally awesome parents. Hi, Mom and Dad!" Roni turned her head back to spot the singer's parents, but when the crowd burst into laughter she realized this must be Star's regular opening banter, which her fans already knew by heart.

"Just kidding!" Star said. "They're not here. And that's a good thing, isn't it?" The crowd shouted back, "Yes!"

Roni tried to guess Star's age. Twenty-something, she thought. Around twenty-five. She was very thin, even thinner than Shiri, and her long black hair looked dirty and greasy. She wore heavy eye makeup, and she had on a midriff blouse and a miniskirt.

"So I'd like to dedicate the first song to Mom and Dad. It's our cover of 'Because the Night' by Patti-the-Goddess Smith!"

The crowd whistled and clapped, and Roni joined in, applauding eagerly. Only now, like a bruise that starts to hurt long after the blow, did she begin to the feel the effect of the last few hours. Although she was used to being alone and liked solitude, even worshipped it slightly, this afternoon and evening had been an overdose that almost made her withdraw instead of progress. There had even been a moment in the taxi, when the warm air coming through the vents had cradled her and almost put her to sleep, when she'd thought of calling her mother collect and maybe, for once, letting her be what she'd always wanted to be: her friend.

She felt she urgently needed a friend, and it was too bad she'd wasted four precious years on Shiri instead of looking for someone else, someone older, deep and complicated, like her, even though she didn't really know any girls like that and didn't think they even existed. Someone like Alona, but younger, because Alona, it had to be said, was a little extinguished on the inside, and although she was sweet and funny and brilliant, she had no fire, only the glowing embers of what used to be, and embers weren't enough. She needed someone like Na'ama or like Star, who was practically making love to the microphone as she sang. The song was amazing. She wondered if Uri knew it. Maybe tomorrow, before they met, she'd buy the CD, so she'd have it for later, so she'd have it in her backpack like a secret code when they sat in the café.

When the song ended and Star kept standing there with her eyes closed, cupping the microphone with both hands, Roni applauded enthusiastically and felt tears wetting her cheeks—tears of happiness at having found this love that made her body crack from the inside. She was a little sorry she hadn't called him this evening. They might have been able to meet, even now. But no, that would have sounded desperate. Tomorrow was better. The band started playing their original songs, which weren't nearly as good as the cover, and it occurred to her that there was something apt about being alone tonight, as if she were at the end of a voyage, having reached a site of purification, of intention, of erasing everything that had come before. She was shedding her last traces of innocence, happy to be rid of them forever. Really, Uri might have been right when he used to tease her sometimes and say, "You're naïve. You have no idea how naïve. And that's why I love you."

But now he'd love her differently. Then she quickly corrected herself: she didn't want love. She just wanted to be with him. She wasn't naïve anymore.

At around one-thirty the gig ended. Star got off the stage and perched on the lap of a man sitting at a nearby table, and they started kissing deeply. Roni couldn't stop watching them. They were so beautiful together, kissing as if it were a verse in the song. Star turned her face aside briefly and their eyes met, and Star gave her a little smile, like she knew Roni also had that kind of love, and that soon, in a couple of days, maybe a week, she would also be sitting on her lover's lap.

Meanwhile she stayed at her table, watching Carlos and the other musicians pack up their gear. Carlos noticed her and came up to the edge of the stage and squatted down. "So? Did you like it?" he asked.

"I really, really liked it. You're great, really great." He thanked her, got up, and went back to rolling up electrical cables. She wondered if he might have forgotten that they'd arranged to talk.

The club emptied out while Carlos went in and out of a door behind the stage, lugging equipment. Every so often he looked at her and smiled, and she kept sitting there, watching the barman collecting glasses and ashtrays from the tables, and Star and her boyfriend, who kept making out at their table. Carlos got off the stage and asked if she was waiting for someone, and she said she wasn't. He asked if she was from around there, and she said no, and she asked if he knew somewhere in the area that would be open now, because she was starved and was dying for some soup. He said, "Yeah, sure," and said he was also going to get something to eat, and she could join him. She said that would be great, and he told her to wait a few minutes while he finished loading the gear. She nodded: of course she would wait. To emphasize her intention, she lit a cigarette.

Carlos and the other guys dragged the last crates out, the barman disappeared, and Roni suddenly felt like writing in her notebook, to document everything she'd been through these last few hours. She already had a few lines in her head, and she leaned down to her back-pack and then saw out of the corner of her eye that Star and her boy-friend were fucking.

It scared her a bit, that people were having sex right next to her as if she didn't exist, and she was impatient for Carlos to finish with the gear and come back. She took her notebook out and put it carefully on the table. She was afraid to dig around for a pen. She looked aside for a moment, and Star was looking right at her but no longer smiling, just looking at her and at the notebook. She quickly turned away toward the bar, and since she couldn't get up and leave now, or busy herself with writing, she kept sitting like that until Star and her boyfriend got up and walked past her hand in hand and left the club. She started to dig through the backpack for her pen, and when she found it at the bot-tom, the whole writing thing suddenly seemed unnecessary, ridiculous, a silly leftover from that naïveté; she knew now that she was *living* life, and she felt like throwing the stupid notebook right there in the trash can that must be behind the bar.

Then Carlos came back, rubbing his hands. "It's super cold," he said, and got his jacket from behind the bar. "Shall we? You wanted soup, right?" he asked. She said yes. He asked if she minded walking a bit, and she said no, of course not, even though she did. They walked quickly, their arms touching occasionally. Her backpack was heavy and bulky, and suddenly very noisy. The items inside it clanged against one another as she walked.

"So how old did you say you were?" he asked, when they sat down in a charming little place. It was completely empty except for the woman tending bar, who greeted Carlos with a hug. Even before he said any-thing, she put a little glass of vodka out on the table in front of him.

"Nineteen," Roni said.

"Soldier?"

She said yes, she was on leave now; she served up north.

"Good stuff. So where do you know Zohar from?"

She said she didn't really know Zohar, she was a friend of Uri's.

"Oh, right," Carlos said, and downed the vodka in one gulp. "Want some?" he asked, when he saw her looking at the glass. She said yes, and he called the waitress and asked for a glass for Roni and another for him. Then he asked if there was soup today, and the waitress said there was goulash. Carlos stroked her back and asked, "What's up?" and she said everything was okay. She brought them two bowls of soup and went back to the bar. Carlos asked Roni if she liked the soup and she said yes, even though it was disappointingly thin and tasteless, with tiny bits of meat floating around. It was nothing like the goulash her father made.

When she sipped the frozen vodka she felt heat spread through her stomach, compensating a little for the soup. She wasn't used to drinking. Once in a while she had a beer, and one was enough to mess her up. Carlos asked how she knew Uri, and she said, "My dad's wife is editing his book."

"Oh, yeah, he *is* publishing a book. I have to tell you something"—he leaned over to her—"but don't tell anyone; I mean it."

"I won't," she said, already light-headed from the vodka.

"Want another one?" he asked, pointing at her glass, which was not yet empty.

"Yeah, why not? I like it."

Carlos smiled, and to prove that she was serious, she emptied the rest of the glass. He blew cigarette smoke out. "Didush! Bring us two more shots." Then he leaned back to Roni and said, "I can't stand him."

"Who?" she asked.

"Uri. I just don't get what Zohar is doing with him. She's a terrific person, Zohar, and I'm telling you, I have no clue what she's doing with that loser."

She asked why he couldn't stand Uri. Her voice sounded very distant and cheerful, not her own.

"The guy is such a windbag, I've never seen anything like it. To tell you the truth, he's not so keen on me either. I had a thing with Zohar once, a long fling, so maybe he's a bit jealous; we try not to bump into each other too often. But honestly? I feel bad for Zohar."

Without noticing, she'd almost finished her second shot, and she felt pleasantly dizzy. Beer knocked her down like a weight, but the vodka did something else, something that reminded her of a hug, like the sleepy hugs with Uri, when they tried not to fall asleep because of the damn bus she always had to get, the bus—she realized happily—that was completely irrelevant tonight.

"Another?" Carlos asked when he saw she'd finished her second, and without waiting for an answer he signaled to the waitress. "You can hold your liquor, for a girl," he said, and she felt proud. "So, did you find him in the end? Was he at home?"

She said she hadn't had time to call yet, maybe tomorrow.

"I'm sorry if I hurt your feelings or anything. I probably shouldn't diss your friend like that. Who did you say was editing his book—your mom?"

"My dad's wife," she said.

Carlos hiccupped and covered his mouth and apologized. "Man, I'm kind of drunk. Aren't you?"

She shook her head. She wasn't drunk at all. On the contrary: she felt an animalistic alertness.

Carlos sighed and yawned. "I mean, I'm happy for her, you know. She really wanted a baby. But to be stuck with that idiot for the rest of her life?" And then something sharp, like a whistle in her ear, split her open as Carlos emptied his glass and hiccupped again. This time he didn't apologize. "Don't get me wrong, really, I'm on her side, but to be honest? I think the pregnancy kind of spun her brain around."

But Roni was the one whose brain was spinning, making a U-turn inside her head but not knowing where to turn next, and the pleasant dizziness turned into a tidal wave, a sober man trying to squeeze his way through a drunken crowd. She sat quietly and looked at Carlos, who stared sadly at the table and slid her lighter back and forth.

He yawned again. "What time is it, anyway?"

She pulled her cell phone out. "Five to three."

"I'm beat. Should we get going?"

She said, "Yes, let's get going," but she couldn't stand up. Carlos put a few bills on the table and asked where she needed to go, and she said,

"I don't know." She could see his lips moving, he must have been asking something, but she couldn't hear the words. The whistle in her head had become a breeze, a murmur, something that sounded like the inside of a seashell. She thought it might be possible that she was drunk; she'd never really been drunk before but here it was, this must be it. Carlos put his hand on her arm and shook it, and she saw his lips move again, and she asked, "What?" and a giggle escaped her lips. He said, "Don't you have anywhere to sleep?" This time she heard the words, and she said, "I don't know."

He got up and grasped her arm and said, "You're trashed, Romy," and she no longer cared that he called her that. The sudden motion made her giddy, and he asked if she needed the bathroom. She shook her head, and said, "Bye," and gave him a slow wave that, she thought, continued when she walked out into the street ahead of him. The sudden cold air slapped her cheeks, trying to wake her, but her eyes drooped shut and she sat down on the sidewalk outside the door, put her head on her knees, and imagined herself on a ship. The asphalt swelled up and down beneath her, and when she looked up she saw Carlos's shoes and the brown corduroy, and she threw up.

Then she heard whispering, and a woman's voice, and Carlos's voice, and she opened her eyes and looked aside and saw him wiping his shoes off with a rag. She heard the woman, Didush, whispering, but she couldn't make out what she was saying. Then Carlos said, "Fuck, Didush. Get me some water, okay?" and she heard Didush say, "Where does she live? Did you ask her?"

"I don't know." Carlos replied. "Where do you live?"

Didush's face suddenly appeared before her eyes, and now, of all times, as another wave of vomit made its way up her throat, she noticed that Didush was very pretty, stunning even, and she couldn't answer, but this time she turned her head away and threw up on the sidewalk, and as her head rocked above the puddle of vomit, and a strand of saliva hung from her chin, she heard Didush say, "We can't leave her like this, Carlos."

Carlos said, "I know. I know, okay? Wait, let's see how she's doing. . . . How are you doing?" he asked. He sounded angry, and she wanted to say that everything was fine, she was going home now, but she couldn't speak.

Didush said, "I have to close up, will you manage?"

He said, "Yeah, I guess I'll have to. Fuck, I'll take her to my place. I can't believe I got into this mess." She saw their legs growing farther away; then she heard Carlos's deep voice: "Never mind, I'll take her."

Didush came back and her beautiful face appeared before Roni's half-open eyes again, and then it occurred to her that she herself was ugly now, very ugly and frightening, and she wanted to burst into tears because of this ugliness, but the tears were waiting on a faraway desert island, and she was still rocking around on this boat, on the asphalt. Didush opened her backpack and rummaged through it. She took out the notebook and flipped a few pages, and that filled Roni with sudden optimism, to think that Didush was reading her writing. But the beautiful woman put the notebook back in the bag and dug through it again. She pulled out Roni's old leather wallet, which Nechama had bought her for her bat mitzvah, said, "Here! I got it!" and took out the new ID card, which had only been issued six months ago.

Roni put her head on her knees as if awaiting a verdict. Out of the corner of her eye she saw Carlos's shoes again and heard him say, "I guess she lives on some moshav. Where is Eden? Is your dad named Mark? Mark Segal?"

She nodded into her arms, and at the mention of her father's name the tears suddenly started to stream down her cheeks.

"Give me your cell phone," the bartender said, "we'll call Information."

At that, something propelled her and she managed to stand up on her feet and burst into tears. "Don't call, okay? I'm leaving, I'll be fine. Don't call!"

They both looked at her, alarmed, and Didush stood closer to Carlos and showed him the ID: "Look, she's sixteen."

"Oh, I don't believe this!" Carlos said. "Okay, Didush, put it away. She can stay at my place; it's okay. Come on, put it away. I'll call her parents tomorrow. It's almost morning, forget it now. It'll be okay."

Grateful, she sat down on the sidewalk again and leaned against the building. The cold felt good, even though she was shivering. Carlos asked if she thought she could walk two blocks; it was only five minutes away. She nodded, and he pulled her hand and lifted her up and propped her body against his. He put her backpack over his shoulder and walked her, at first quickly, but after she stopped and threw up again between two parked cars he slowed down the pace. They reached a dark building and she heard him take his keys out of his pocket and say, "It's lucky I live nearby." *Lucky*, she thought, and the word played in her mind over and over again, musical and bothersome, and then they walked up a few stairs and Carlos opened the door.

A little dog jumped up and down to welcome them. Roni wasn't sure if it was a puppy or a small breed, but she was so happy to see a dog that for a moment the clouds of drunkenness and the waves of nausea dissipated, and she heard her voice crackle like a dry twig. "Is he yours?"

"Yeah, that's Bongo."

She heard that strange voice of hers again. "Is he a puppy?"

"In his soul, yes. In reality he's more than ten years old. Do you want to throw up again? Do you need the bathroom?"

She shook her head and looked at the dog sniffing Carlos's shoes. He walked her into the living room and turned the light on and laid her down on the couch. He asked if she wanted tea or water, and she mumbled, "No; no, thanks," and lay on her stomach, her hand stroking the dog, who sat at the foot of the couch.

"Do you want to take a shower?" Carlos asked. "I can give you some clothes to sleep in." She said no. "I don't think there's any hot water anyway," he said, and she remembered Uri, and suddenly it seemed as if she was actually there, in the apartment on Nachmani, the pre-Na'ama apartment, with the scratchy couch and the darkness and the damp smell mixed with something masculine and dusty and lonely. Carlos said he was going to wash off quickly, he was really sweaty, and he'd be right back. She nodded and heard the dog's paws clicking on the floor and his tags clinking as he ran after Carlos. She shut her eyes tight, trying to subdue a new wave of nausea, and heard Brutus's and Olive's tags as they ran after her down the dirt path, stopping only when she got to the main road, knowing they were forbidden to continue. That was where they made a U-turn and went back to the restaurant, to her dad, her dad, her daddy.

She threw up on the floor, and Carlos came in wearing sweatpants and no shirt and said, "Again, huh?" He sat down next to her and put his hand on the back of her neck. "Are you okay?" She shook her head.

"Can I get you something?" She shook her head, felt another spasm, and threw up again, and Carlos tried to get her up on her feet. "I'll take you to the bathroom, come on," he said, and dragged her to the bathroom. He wet a towel and wiped her forehead and said, "Are you okay?" She shook her head and leaned over the toilet, but nothing came out. She just seemed to be vomiting air now, and words, and ideas. All her plans were being vomited out.

"I think you need some sleep now," Carlos said. "Okay? Come on, sleep in my bed, I'll sleep in the living room." He walked her to the bedroom, which was dark except for a reading lamp that shone a yellow light on the bed, and the room was stuffy and smelled of cigarette smoke. Carlos said, "Look, I hate to say it, but you threw up on your clothes. Let me give you a shirt to wear." She was about to tell him there was no need, but Carlos said, "Don't worry, I won't look, okay?" He pulled up the thin knit top she was wearing, the tight black top that Uri liked, and said, "I'm not looking, okay? I swear. I'm just going to put a sweatshirt on you, okay?" She nodded, while a terrible sound grated in her head like a ball bearing. He sat her down and took off the top and said, "Hang on, I'll get you a sweatshirt." She heard a closet door open with a creak, the same familiar and beloved creak she had heard so many times last winter, when Uri used to get dressed or look for a sweatshirt or something for her, like now, just like now.

"I don't want you to get cold," Carlos whispered, when he sat down on the bed and handed her a sweatshirt. He waited for her to put it on but she didn't move. She kept sitting there, her chin slightly drooping, shivering, feeling the cold scratching her nipples, and then the rough warmth of Carlos's skin as he slipped the opening over her head and carefully, as if he were handling a doll, pulled her arms through the sleeves. His fingers fluttered briefly over her breasts and he said, "Sorry, that wasn't on purpose. Try and help me a bit, okay? Put your arm up." When she couldn't do it, he sighed. "Jesus, you're really trashed." She leaned her head on his chest and he laughed. "Come on, let's put the sweatshirt on. You're freezing, your whole body is shivering." She wondered what he thought, if he thought she was ugly, like before, on the sidewalk. He said, "It's my fault. I could tell you knew how to drink, but I shouldn't have let you have so much. Fuck! Come on, Romy, help me with your arm. One more sleeve and we're done." She lifted her right arm mechanically and he said, "No, I've already done that one." She lifted the other, and the whole time she burrowed her forehead into his chest, and the nausea was gone, and something else came instead, like the sadness that replaces anger, like the nostalgia that follows contempt: love.

That's what she felt now, warm, fluid love, something she hadn't ever known before and hadn't realized existed. Not that rocking, dismantling thing she'd had with Uri but something else, a tranquil synonym, a different word. She felt like a crucified Jesus, or a scarecrow, as she sat there with her arms stretched up and to the sides, as if she were about to take off. Her head nested in Carlos's bare chest, her breasts drooped, swaying slightly, and she heard Carlos laugh: "Oh, come on already!"

She quickly squirmed out of the half sweatshirt he'd just managed to get on her and wrapped her arms around his neck, clinging to him as hard as she could. How different this was from anything she'd known. Not the soft, cool spring that was Eilon's chest, not the warm, nervous thicket of Eli's. She had never hugged Yossi, thank God, but it was completely different from Uri, who had a sunken chest and a slightly protruding stomach, like a boy. No, Carlos was different. Slightly bearlike and limp and pleasant, something from long ago, like a stuffed animal, something you could fall asleep on, or love, love terribly. She heard him whisper, "Romy, stop, you're drunk." She didn't have the strength to correct him: Roni, not Romy. And in fact, why shouldn't she be Romy? Maybe she should invent a new identity for herself, because her own was ruined, erased in a moment. "Kiddo, you're really drunk. Come on, lie down, forget the sweatshirt, I'll get you a blanket." He laid her down on her back, but she pulled him on top of her, feeling his chest crushing her breasts and his lips yelling, "Stop it! Stop it!" and again, "Romy, stop it! I'm not into this." He covered her and said, "I don't know who you are, I don't know what your problem is, but get some sleep and everything will be fine, all right? You'll feel better tomorrow."

And suddenly it was tomorrow. She wasn't sure how long she'd slept, but she woke up hearing thunder and sat straight up in bed and looked at the room, which was both strange and familiar. The floor tiles were speckled with orange and brown, and her black knit top lay there like a kitten, and a little black-and-white dog stood in the doorway, wagged its tail, sneezed, then disappeared. She looked for her backpack but couldn't see it, and she bent over and picked up her top, which was stained and damp and smelled like vomit, and she put it on and got out of bed. When she stood up, she felt her head pounding; hammers clobbered her temples as she walked down the hallway to the living room. Carlos was asleep on the couch under a blanket, with one bare foot hanging off to the side. The skin on his heel was red and rough. She saw her backpack on the floor and pulled out her cell phone. It was 10:30 A.M., even though it felt early, as if the sun hadn't risen yet. Outside she heard rain and thunder, and she hurried to the bathroom with her backpack, turned on the tap, and drank. Then she sat down on the toilet and peed but did not flush, afraid to wake Carlos, who now seemed not human at all but just a stop on a journey that had yet to end.

Her stomach felt like a piece of clothing turned inside out. She was starved and decided to leave quickly and find a café where she could phone Uri. Because suddenly, as she washed her face and wished she had some perfume with her, she realized that there were different ways to approach what Carlos had told her about Zohar being pregnant: insanely, as she had done last night, or with devastating, deadening despair, or with logic. Level-headedness. Calmness and maturity.

The thought of hot chocolate and breakfast cheered her up. She took out her notebook—her past—and tore out a blank page and wrote a note:

> Thanks from the bottom of my heart for what you did for me. You saved me. Thank you. Sorry for the mess. Roni (Romy).

She put the note on the coffee table, patted the dog's head, turned the key in the front door, went out, and shut the door behind her, hoping her host would not be angry at her for leaving him asleep in an unlocked apartment. But she knew he wouldn't.

Calmness and level-headedness. Those words caressed her as she walked up Carlos's street. She was heartened by the sounds of sawing from the carpenter shops, as if life were back on track. The rain was no problem; in the past twenty-four hours it had become a part of her. But the sadness started to sneak in again, shyly, as if it were standing in the doorway, clearing its throat and mumbling, *Excuse me, but I'm here, too*. And she told herself, *No. No way*.

The alcohol is what had made things seem so bleak, the things Carlos had told her about Zohar and about Uri. She was absolutely unable to think of them as Uri-and-Zohar, which sounded almost terminal. Okay, so she was pregnant, so what? Maybe he'd just made a baby for her, like she wanted. She thought back to that chapter in his novel where the woman, Zohar—and obviously it was Zohar, even though in the novel she was called Tamar—begs the man to at least give her a child before he leaves: she doesn't need anything from him, she doesn't want anything, "Just get me pregnant and go to hell."

Roni remembered that sentence, which she hadn't entirely understood but had still been impressed by. When she'd said to Uri, "That's a great line, really powerful," and he'd answered, "I know, you wouldn't believe how many times I've heard it," she'd kissed him—he'd looked so depressed—and said, "But you'll never hear it from me."

"I know. That's why I love you," he'd said.

As she looked for a café she realized that it was possible to see things differently, less desperately: not only had her new plan not fallen apart, what had happened, this pregnancy, gave it all the more validity, because she sensed that Uri needed her now; his prison cell had grown extremely confining. Maybe he was waiting for her call, expecting it in some unconscious way, expecting it with all his body and soul, and when he heard her voice he would suddenly know that this was it, this was what he'd been waiting for, this was his key. She was his key.

The rain grew harder and she started to run. There were no cafés to be found, and at the end of the street she saw a main road that looked familiar. It was Salameh, she realized, from last night. She'd bought cigarettes and Bamba there before the show. She wondered if she was close to that convenience store; they'd had a few tables inside, where she could sit and make a phone call.

Her phone rang from inside the depths of her bag and she knew it was Shiri, wanting to know why she wasn't at school. She suddenly feared Shiri might call her father to ask where she was, and she'd told him she'd get to school after gym class. She could always say she'd missed the bus and was at the Central Bus Station. That's what she'd say if he called.

But she felt angry at him, at having even to take him into account now; although she remembered that yesterday she'd had all sorts of strange homesick feelings and longings, she was happy that they had passed, because it was a little confusing, a little desperate, and completely childish.

When she reached Salameh she couldn't find the store from last night and assumed it was in a different part of the street. She looked right and left, trying to get her bearings, searching for something that would connect her to last night, as if last night were a book she'd stopped reading and had forgotten to mark her page. Nothing looked familiar. She couldn't even figure out which way Rothschild was. She decided that after they arranged to meet in their café, she would take a cab there. She just hoped he was still home, but she calmed down when she remembered that unless he had an important meeting, he usually didn't leave the house before noon.

He was probably waking up now, she thought, and she kissed his forehead and ran her fingers through his long hair, like she used to do when he fell asleep. She always let him sleep a little after she woke up, and she would sit and watch him. That was a lot, to sit and look at him. A lot, almost everything, and then, when it was late, borderline, she would wake him like you wake a child, like Alona or her father woke Maya and Ido, tenderly, mercifully, but also out of some fear that the sleeping child would be angry. She was a little afraid of Uri, too, afraid because everything last winter had been so fragile, so uncertain. But now she knew it was all about to change.

She really should sit down somewhere and make the call, before he went out. She hoped Zohar wouldn't answer. What would she do if Zohar answered? She decided to risk it. Whatever happened, happened. Then she noticed a convenience store on the other side of the street, but not the one from yesterday. A sign hanging outside read HOT SAHLAB! She knew this was it, this was what she needed now: hot *sahlab* and shelter from the rain. The sign swayed in the wind, playing with her; she noticed that the exclamation point was slanted, as if it were about to fall over, and she suddenly knew that everything was going to be fine. "I'm fine," she remembered her mother telling the waitress in the diner that time, when they had talked about separating, about Roni wanting to go live with her father, wanting a normal life. "I'm fine," she'd said to the waitress when she came to refill her coffee. Roni had been too young to understand how her mother could say "I'm fine" when everything around her was crumbling, but now she knew it was possible. Now she knew that great pain could kill you or redeem you, it just depended on you. "I'm fine," she murmured, a new-old mantra. The Sahlab sign with its crooked exclamation point danced in the wind before her eyes.

NECHAMA

"Mom!" It was strange, but despite the *Mom* it took her a moment to identify the voice on the other end of the line. It didn't sound like Alona, but you could never hear anything properly on those cellular phones anyway. "Mom! It's me, can you hear me?" She started to grumble—no, she couldn't hear her very well, her line wasn't working, someone had to call the phone company—but the girl wouldn't let her speak. "Mom, listen! Something terrible has happened!"

And then she had to sit down before her knees gave in and she collapsed to the floor. She barely made it to the chair, which waited in the distance like an island in a stormy ocean. She asked to hear again how it had happened, as if she hadn't comprehended or really hadn't heard properly. The line was faulty, and it seemed as if the torrent of rain outside was coming from the phone itself. But Alona said she couldn't talk now: "I'll tell you later. Now listen."

She said that at four-thirty a mother from the kindergarten, Hila— yes, Hila, not Gila—would bring the children over to her house, and she'd pick them up later. "Mark's going to stay here all night. . . . Yes, in intensive care, not the ER. You don't have to give them dinner, just make them a sandwich if they're hungry. . . . Yes, low-calorie bread is fine. Enough, I have to go; we'll talk later."

But Nechama had no idea how she would get to *later*. *Later* was distant, or might already have passed, and she felt that not only was her body about to collapse but the chair itself. Its legs were trembling beneath her and starting to splay to the sides, and the silent phone in her hand grew cold and heavy like a stone, and when she stared at it the keypad turned into a medley of numbers and letters and symbols. But how could she faint now, when she was needed? She heard now what she hadn't heard before, because of the excitement and the fear, because of the noise; she heard tears. She clearly heard now that Alona had been crying. *Mom! Something terrible has happened, and I need you to help me!* She couldn't lose her grip on things when all this responsibility was in her hands—those hands that ever since the fall had remained somehow broken, theoretical, a symbol of who she used to be: a woman who had helped so many children and had even been awarded a presidential medal—her daughter was asking for her help. A sense of satisfaction trickled into the blackness of fainting, like a different honey-colored hue.

And what had she said about Roni? Intensive care. Unconscious. What else? Critical? Fatal? No, she hadn't said fatal. She would have remembered that—fatal was not a word you forgot. Maybe she'd said *critical*. She thought back to that day ten years ago. The word fatal had not been uttered then either, only *critical*. But Shimshon was gone anyway.

She panicked: What would she do with the children? She'd never been alone with them. And they were not easy, those kids. They were demanding, especially the girl, who was never happy, always whining like a pussycat. She didn't have any of the things kids liked at home, snacks and chocolate, and that cereal they were always munching. How would she keep them busy until nighttime? Who knew when Alona would be back from Tel Aviv if the situation was so critical? She remembered now: Alona had said Roni was on respiratory support. What if she couldn't handle the task her daughter had given her? What if it was too much for her? But no, she mustn't be an old lady now. She massaged her temples. Now was not the time to be old. She would pull herself together. She would get control of things, resurrect those hands. She would get through the dizziness soon, and then she would get up and go to the grocery store. She had to. Who knew when someone would come to pick up the kids? They might end up having to sleep over. The idea was horrifying, but also somewhat adventurous. Where would they sleep? She didn't even have a spare mattress. If she'd had the key to Alona's house she could have taken them there; it would be easier. It was a pity she didn't have the key, but she'd never needed it—when did she ever go there? Still, someone should have thought of it. Taken her into account. In case of an emergency. Maybe she'd ask Alona if a neighbor had a key, and then she could ask the mother from the kindergarten to drive them there. But she was putting the horse before the cart. The day was still long, even though in recent years all her days seemed long. But obviously this day would be really long. Long and full of life.

First the grocery store. What time was it? Ten past twelve. The store was open until six today, thank God, unless Rivka closed early because of the rain. She should phone and make sure. Even if the store was open, how would she get there? The rain didn't bother her so much as the uphill road, and then coming back downhill, which would be slippery and dangerous. How would she make her way home with an umbrella and bags full of groceries? Maybe she could ask someone to drive her. But who? Maybe she could ask Rivka if there was anyone around who could bring her a few things, not much, just some snacks and maybe ice cream—they liked ice cream—or chocolate—that was always good to have around, because the house was completely empty and not suitable for children.

She remembered how she'd once complained that the children never came to visit her. "Why don't you bring them after school one day?" she'd asked Alona. "They can sit with me for a while, play in the yard. We *have* a yard, you know." She remembered Alona's cynical look, and the way she'd puffed up her cheeks and said, "Sit with you for a while? You mean, and tell you how their day at school was? Apparently you don't know Maya and Ido, Mom. They need constant activities."

"Then I'll give them activities!" she'd replied, and her daughter had let out a venomous laugh—*Mom, this house isn't suitable for kids*—and she knew then, of course she did, she always had, that Alona was not talking about her children but about herself; *she* was the child for whom this house was unsuitable. Never had been and never would be.

At four-twenty the children burst in, dropped their open, wet umbrellas on the floor, and commanded, "TV!" They leaped onto the old couch and sat next to each other, swinging their rubber-booted feet.

The woman who came in behind them, Hila, with a boy of about five and a baby, said, "Man, what a storm!" The boy hurried to join Maya and Ido on the couch, and she said, "Tomer, we're not staying." She gestured for Nechama to follow her into the kitchen. "Have you heard anything from Alona?" When Nechama shook her head, the woman clucked her tongue. "So terrible. How did it happen? Did she get run over?"

"TV!" the kids yelled again from the living room.

Hila said she had to run. "We have a doctor's appointment at five, Omri has an ear infection." She held her lips to the baby's head. "Alona promised to update me, but I don't think she'll remember. I feel so bad for her. And poor Mark! Would you mind calling me if you hear anything? I'll leave you my number." With her free hand she pulled out her diary, ripped out a page and wrote her number on it, then put the paper on the counter under a jar of instant coffee. "Tomer! We're leaving!" But she kept standing there, bouncing the baby on her thigh to get a better grip on him, and said, "Look—I'm shaking." She put her hand on Nechama's arm. "Feel it?" Nechama nodded, even though she didn't. "Okay. Deep breath. Gotta get to the doctor, the traffic's going to be awful." She touched the baby's head again. "He's burning up. Tomer! We're leaving!"

Maya appeared in the kitchen and asked sweetly, "Grandma? Would you mind please turning on the TV for us? We don't know how to turn on your TV." Nechama said yes, of course. "Put it on Hop for us," Maya said, and Nechama panicked: Which channel was that?

Hila asked if she had cable, and she nodded: thank God she did. "I'll turn it on for them," Hila said. She hurried to the living room and turned the television on, and someone dressed up as a bear appeared on the screen.

"Just till the end of the show, Mom," Tomer whimpered.

Hila hurried over to him and grabbed his hand and yanked him off the couch. "We're leaving! Let's go! We're late." She dragged him to the door. "So you have my number, okay?"

Nechama nodded, suddenly confused. The strange voice of the man dressed up as a bear sounded familiar. She asked if the children were thirsty, and they both nodded, their eyes glued to the screen. "Do you want chocolate milk? I bought you some, the kind in plastic bags."

Maya looked at her for a minute, as if she'd only just noticed that her grandmother was standing there, slightly hunched, leaning on the couch. "Mommy doesn't let us have the bags, because it spills."

"It's all right, just be careful," Nechama said.

Maya looked back at the screen. "Ido doesn't know how to be careful."

Ido started kicking at the couch. "I do! She's just saying that, Grandma, I do!"

"All right, I'll get it for you." She headed to the kitchen.

Maya asked, "Grandma, do you have any snacks? Mommy lets us have a snack after kindergarten."

"But just one," Ido added.

His sister dug her elbow into him and whispered, "Why are you telling her that?"

The boy started to cry. "Grandma! She kicked me with her arm!"

"I bought you some Bamba and those potato chips you like."

"Pringles?" Maya asked.

"No, the ones with the shapes."

"Oh," said the girl, disappointed. "That's not potato chips, Grandma, you got confused. That's corn chips." She accentuated the words like a teacher.

Ido said, "We like corn chips, too."

"No we don't!" his sister grumbled.

"I do, Grandma," he said softly.

Maya elbowed him again and whispered, "Why are you lying?"

The boy burst into tears. "She did it again!"

Nechama came back and leaned on the couch. "Mayaleh, please stop hitting him."

Maya twisted her face. "He's sitting too close and he's touching me."

"Then Ido, maybe you could sit on this armchair? You can see better from here, it's my armchair, you'll like it."

"I want it!" Maya jumped onto the chair.

The boy started wailing again. "She took it from me, Grandma! You said I could have your armchair, not her, right?"

And again that feeling, like earlier, when she'd talked to Alona: too much information flowing through too-thin cables. She thought she was going to lose her balance, so she gripped the back of the armchair, leaning on both hands.

Maya flicked her head back and looked at her. "Grandma, I don't like that."

"What?"

"When you press on my back with your hand."

She wanted to say, *I didn't touch you. I was just leaning a little.* But she said nothing, just listened to the bear, who wasn't talking but making grunts and murmurs like an old man.

"Where's the chocolate milk?" Maya asked. "You promised us chocolate milk and two snacks."

"Yes, I'm going to get it." She suggested they take off their muddy boots.

Ido quickly pulled his off and asked where to put them: "By the door?"

She nodded. "Yes, good boy." Maya said she didn't want to take hers off and folded her legs underneath her. What to do now? Nechama wondered. Should she insist? She reminded herself that she was only the babysitter—she liked the word, it was a young word—not an educator. She went back to the kitchen, opened the fridge, and took out two bags of chocolate milk—she'd bought six, not knowing how long the children would be staying—and shook them as she walked back to the living room.

Ido started jumping up and down on the couch: "Yay! Thanks, Grandma! This is my favorite chocolate milk!" Maya reached out a hand without looking at her, and the insult crept into her heart: What sort of behavior was that? But the exhaustion defeated her; it was really not exhaustion but fear. She was simply scared to death of these children.

And then: "Grandma! Can you open them for us?"

"I'll get you a snack and then I'll come and open them for you." Her voice sounded hoarse and grating. She wanted to spare herself another trip to the living room and tried to remember if she used to wait on her daughter like this, but she knew she hadn't. The mileage had been different once, and, like old cars, old parents were stronger, more reliable, less complicated, and they all took the same roads. She took out two packets of corn chips and two of Bamba. Never mind what Alona did or did not allow them. She was making the decisions now. She went back to the living room. Had she been afraid of Alona, too? She couldn't remember. Today she was afraid of her, yes, but had that fear always been there or had it been born in recent years?

Now she no longer walked but padded over to the living room, and Ido got off the couch and looked at her slippered feet and asked, "Why do you walk like that? Like you're falling?"

"My feet are a little tired, sweetheart. In a minute I'll sit down and rest a bit."

Maya turned her head again and looked at Nechama's feet, but her face remained expressionless. She looked back to the screen. "I opened mine on my own," she announced, and sucked from the bag of chocolate milk. "He can't do it on his own." She pointed to her brother, whose face crumpled.

"Yes, I can! I can! Look, Grandma!" He yanked at the bag with his teeth and the chocolate milk sprayed all over the couch and his clothes. Maya burst out laughing and Ido started to cry.

"Never mind, never mind," Nechama said, and hurried over to him, but she slipped and her knee hit the corner of the coffee table.

"*Grand*-ma, what's happening to you today?" Maya scolded, and those satanic eyes flashed a gloating spark—those eyes were exactly like Alona's.

She straightened up slowly. Her hands were trembling. She asked the crying boy if he had a change of clothes, and he shook his head, holding the wet sweater away from his body. "What's in that box?" she asked, and looked at the little toolbox in the entryway.

The boy hurried over to the box and held it close to his chest. "It's just work tools. Can I have another chocolate milk? I didn't spill it on purpose."

"Of course, I'll just get a cloth and wipe up here a bit." But the thought of going back to the kitchen suddenly seemed impossible, as if she'd been asked to walk to another galaxy.

It had been a stupid mistake to go to the grocery store. Suicide. Rivka had suggested that she ask a neighbor for a ride: "Call the Sonenfelds, they're very nice." But she didn't know the Sonenfelds, or the Levins, or any of the others Rivka mentioned. She didn't know anyone on her street. They were all new. And at three, after sitting on the chair for a whole hour, waiting, depleted, as if hooked up to a battery charger, she'd filled with determination and a strange, temporary strength. She had put on her long raincoat—the English coat, she called it—and tied a plastic bag over her head. It was better not to take an umbrella because she would need both hands to steady herself, to lean on a parked car or hold on to a utility pole. When she'd reached the main road, where that malicious hill was waiting, she'd heard the sound of wheels on the wet road behind her and had turned her head and held out a hand, hitching a ride for the first time in her life at the age of seventy-eight. But the car had kept going, and a spray of water had dirtied the hem of the English coat.

Rivka, sitting on a chair behind the counter, stood up quickly when she saw Nechama open the door. She clapped her hands together and said, "*Oy vey*, Nechama!" and quickly pulled a chair out and put it in the entryway, as if knowing that one more step and this elderly woman would collapse to the floor. Nechama sat down obediently and looked at Rivka, who stood above her with her hands on her hips and shook her head from side to side: "*Oy*, Nechama, really. For snacks? So they would have done without snacks—is that the end of the world? Would it kill them?" Then she remembered the phone call: "So, have you heard anything from Alona?" The grocery store lit up with purple lightning, and they waited for the thunder. After it came, Rivka said, "I'll phone Brochstein. He can drive you home with the groceries. What do you say?"

Nechama said nothing. She sat there looking at the floor, at the water dripping from her coat and the bag on her head, and wanted to say, Yes, phone Brochstein. But tears flooded her eyes—how long had it been since she'd cried? Since Shimshon's death, at least. Rivka hurried to the phone, and she stood up heavily and went to the refrigerator, where she found the bags of chocolate milk. They had it in bottles, too, but she liked the bags. They'd had those when Alona was a child. The tears kept flowing unhindered down her cheeks as she stared at the shelves of snacks.

"There's no answer at Brochstein," Rivka said. "Odd. Where would they go in this weather? Maybe the line is down?" Nechama walked up to the counter with her groceries, and Rivka gave her a dubious look. "How will you get home, Nechama? You'll slip. I'm sure someone will be in soon." But they both knew nobody would come. Rivka looked down at the floor and sighed, and Nechama sighed, too.

Now she wiped off the couch with a cloth, her breath wheezing, and smiled at Ido who stood nearby, embarrassed and guilty. And she suddenly knew who that bear's voice reminded her of: Shimshon. She straightened up, took a deep breath, and said, "Well. Should I open the snacks for you?"

"We already opened them." Maya pointed at the bag of corn chips propped between her legs and asked when her mother was coming.

"Later, in the evening. But we're going to have fun together. Do you want to do some drawing? I have paper and pencils." Ido shrugged and Maya said, "Yes," and then Nechama realized she would have to walk again. She sat down on the couch next to Ido, leaned back, and said, "Maybe you'd like to get them, Maya? They're in the drawer next to my bed. Bring them and sit here and do some drawing."

But the girl shrugged her shoulders. "I don't want to. You get them."

"I'll get them!" Ido jumped up. "Can I?"

Nechama nodded. "Yes, that would help me. Good boy."

Maya smiled crookedly. "Why do you call him a good boy? What is he, a dog?"

"Why a dog?"

"Because." She shoved a handful of corn chips into her mouth and stared at the screen again.

When Ido ran into the bedroom, Nechama remembered that when Maya was a year old, she sometimes used to help to feed her. How easy it was to help back then. The tasks were simpler, and it was harder to fail. Every time the baby swallowed her pureed vegetables, Nechama would encourage her: "Good girl, what a good girl!" That's how she fed her, for months, with great success, until one day, after she proudly showed Alona the empty dish, her daughter said, "Mom, I really appreciate you helping out, and Maya obviously loves it when you feed her. But I'd rather you didn't say *good girl*. Because that's not how we talk these days." When she saw the look of shock and insult on her mother's face, she quickly explained. "You don't say to a child, *You're good* or *You're bad*. You just don't say that anymore, Mom."

"Then what do you say?"

Alona had been happy to explain—perhaps a little too happy—that you responded to what the child did, and you said *You did something good* or *You did something bad*, not *You're good; You're bad*.

She promised to try, even though it seemed a bit ridiculous. "After all," she commented, "you were brought up that way."

"Exactly."

"Well, and look how you turned out."

Alona let out a little dragon breath from her nose and said, "Don't go there, Mom. You really don't want to." She made one of her arrogant faces. "Just drop it. Let's agree that what was acceptable once is no longer acceptable. That's all. Let's say it's like the popsicle dilemma." She smiled, and that, as usual, was the end of the discussion.

The popsicle story always shut her up, although the truth is that she'd never understood what was so special about that incident. It happened when Alona was five, in summer, and they went to the grocery store to buy food for Shabbat. Alona asked for a popsicle, Nechama bought her one, and they walked home. It was very hot outside, and they made their way home painfully slowly. Nechama was impatient, she was in a hurry, she was thirsty, but the little girl had all the time in the world. Halfway home Nechama got so thirsty she asked for a bite of the popsicle. Alona shrugged. "Give me a little bite, Alona, Mommy's thirsty."

"No. It's mine."

Her thirst suddenly became intolerable: simple, human thirst. She asked her again: "Give me a little bite."

But again the girl said, "No, it's mine. If you want a popsicle, get your own."

Nechama explained that that was impossible, they couldn't go all the way back to the grocery store, and she didn't want a whole popsicle, just a little bite to quench her thirst.

"No," said Alona stubbornly, so Nechama grabbed the popsicle without thinking, took a bite, and gave it back to her daughter.

"And what happened then," Nechama liked to recount in horror, "is that you threw the popsicle on the sidewalk and stomped on it and screamed that you wanted another one. You threw yourself on the road in a tantrum, and I told you to get up, and you said no."

"And then you said to me, *Bad girl!*" This is the point where Alona would pick up the story.

And Nechama would say, "Yes, so what? You really were a bad girl at that moment. It's a good thing there weren't a lot of cars in those days. You sat in the middle of the road and screamed. What could I do?"

"You hit me on the behind."

"A little slap, not a hit."

Alona claimed that today not only would it not occur to her to slap her children, but she would obviously never take a bite out of her daughter's popsicle without her consent.

"Alona, you're making up whole psychologies out of nonsense. You didn't want to give me a bite, so I took one; what's the big deal?"

But Alona said that was just it. "You only saw yourselves, you were blind to your children." And Nechama thought, *You're also blind, Alona. But in a different way.*

Ido came back with the paper and pencils and put them on the table. "Good boy," she said and stroked his head, and for a moment she enjoyed Maya's scolding look. She smiled at her and said, "You're a good girl, too."

"Don't you have any markers?" Maya asked. "You used to."

"I used to, but you didn't put the caps on, so they dried up." The phone rang. Luckily, she'd left it nearby. "Hello?" She heard Alona's voice: *Mom?* This time she heard her clearly.

The children looked at her. "Mommy?" Maya asked, and Nechama nodded. "Let me talk to her, I want to talk to her."

"Me too!" Ido shouted.

Nechama signaled to them with her hand: one minute. Then she asked, "Any news?"

"No, we're still waiting," Alona said. "The head of neurosurgery is supposed to be here soon. She's still unconscious. It's awful, Mom, it's awful." Nechama asked if they knew what had happened, and Alona said, "A car hit her and she was thrown thirty feet. She was hit really badly on her head. But Mom, don't tell the children for now. Mark spoke with Jane; she's arriving tomorrow morning. I'll pick her up at the airport. Are the kids okay?"

"Fine. I got them chocolate milk and corn chips. And this thing, Alona, that we're talking about—where did it happen?"

She saw the children looking at her curiously and wished she'd phrased her question differently. She was also worried that Alona was about to reprimand her, but Alona just said, "On Salameh, at a pedestrian crossing. Okay, I have to hang up now. I hope I'll be there at around seven or eight. Will you manage? I want to be here with Mark when the neurosurgeon gets here. Mark is a wreck, Mom. He's falling apart. Of course the neurologist has seen her, but they want the department chair to see her too. Okay, Mom, don't tell the kids it's me. . . . Oh, okay, then hand them over for a minute."

The children reported laconically to their mother about what they'd done and asked when she'd be there. Nechama gathered her strength and got up off the couch to make herself a cup of coffee. While she waited for the water to boil she felt her heart racing again, as it had when she'd walked back from the grocery. As she'd started down the hill, her boots had tried to grip the asphalt that was submerged under water, but the fur lining had sealed off her feet, encased them like silkworm pupae, and that's why she hadn't felt the new pothole—or had it always been there?—that lurked right before the turnoff to her street. Her right foot sank into it and twisted, her body was thrown forward, and both hands tried to stop the fall in vain. And it turned out, there was a God up above. It sounded like a joke, but apparently He was protecting her, because as she lay there on the sidewalk, an invisible rope seemed to pull her up, and she quickly got to her knees, not like that other time, when she'd lain on her stomach for ages and the medics had had to get her up on her feet and onto the stretcher. No, this time there was a miracle and she stood right up, as if that supreme power that had pushed her to the ground had changed its mind and said, *No, today you won't be hurt. Not today.*

She looked at Maya sitting on the floor drawing. She didn't look good or bad, just a little girl drawing, and Nechama wanted to go over to her and hug her. But she was too tired and her legs hurt, and when she sat down at the kitchen table and sipped her coffee, she realized that the thick wool trousers she'd put on for her journey were sticking to her knees. There was something damp and sticky beneath the fabric. She carefully pulled up the right pant leg to reveal a swollen knee covered with scrapes and congealed blood. She quickly pulled it down when she saw Ido standing in the kitchen doorway watching, holding his toolbox by the handle.

"Did you come to repair something?" she tried to joke.

He shook his head and looked very glum. "What happened to Roni?"

"Nothing, sweetie." She held the coffee cup to her lips as if to seal off her speech.

But the boy insisted. "But Mommy said she and Daddy took Roni to a doctor in Tel Aviv; that's why we're here, because they had to take her."

"Oh, you're right, I forgot, I'm confused." She rapped her forehead with her finger and smiled. "She did say they went with Roni to the doctor. She wasn't feeling well."

For a moment it seemed he would be satisfied with that answer, but then he said, "Roni's a big girl. She doesn't need two people to take her to the doctor. So why did Daddy and Mommy go? Why both of them?"

She put her cup down and looked at the boy as he waited for an answer, and remembered that Alona at age four had also been full of questions. She'd been all about *why*. But not the reproachful, accusatory *why*, not the score-settling that had started who-knew-when. As a child, it had been a clean and glistening *why*. In the evenings, when Nechama came back from the home after being everybody's mother for ten hours a day, she had to become one girl's mother all over again every evening. Even on the bus from Netanya, on her way home, she would feel discomfort sneak into her heart, perhaps even anxiety. At home Alona would be waiting after a shower and the dinner Shimshon had cooked. He would stretch out the time until Nechama came home, reading two or three stories, to enable her to be a mother for a little and not just a career woman, as he put it, to her chagrin. They would both wait for her, as though the day could not end without her presence, no matter how exhausted and distracted she was. The night-shift supervisor would always call to ask for her advice on some crisis, and they would wait, Shimshon and Alona, as if they were both children. They would wait for her to shower them with something, although she was never quite sure what.

It wasn't that she didn't want to be a mother. Of course she did. How could she not, in those days? Back then not many questions were asked, or no questions at all. Even if someone had asked what she wanted, she wouldn't have known what to say. *Of course I want to be a mother, what sort of question is that?*

But those evenings, and the weekends, were difficult and confusing. The girl seemed to lie in wait all day long with her highway of questions. When Shimshon, who always tried to make things easier, would say,

"Let Mommy rest, Mommy works hard, come and ask me," Alona would protest, "No! Mommy! I want Mommy to talk to me." And she would listen to the girl's flow of speech, amazed each time at the power, the clarity, the wild things that came out. *Who makes the sky? What is electricity? How does the phone work?*

When she told Shimshon she thought the girl was gifted, he scoffed and said, "She's not gifted, she's normal. You just spend all day working with retarded kids." He was right, apparently. Once, in a moment of anger—she couldn't remember what he was angry about now—he said, "It's funny, Nechama, how you perform miracles every day on dozens of sick children, but you have no idea what to do with one healthy girl."

"Grandma?" Ido's bright voice invaded her thoughts. "Why won't you answer me?"

She smiled and rapped her finger on her forehead again. "I really don't know why they took Roni to the doctor. Maybe later Mommy will tell us."

He nodded. "Yes, later."

"Maya draws very nicely, doesn't she?"

He nodded again. "But I don't. I don't know how to draw nicely."

"What are you talking about? Of course you do. Maybe you need to learn some more. Maya is older, she's just had more practice." He asked what practice was, and she said, "Learning. Practice is when you do something over and over again, until in the end it comes out well."

"Does it always work that way?"

She was about to say yes. That's how she would have answered Alona once, to give her hope or to get it over with. But now she thought for a moment and said, "Not always. Sometimes it doesn't work that way." The boy looked miserable, and she said, "But don't be sad."

"I'm allowed. Mommy says I'm allowed to be sad as much as I want."

Nechama smiled. "Really?" Ido nodded quickly, and she said, "Interesting. Mommy tells you interesting things, and good things. You have a good Mommy, Ido, and she loves you very much."

"And Daddy," he whispered.

"Of course." But then the boy burst into bitter, painful tears. She got up quickly, the fabric of her trousers clinging to her knee, and went over and hugged him. "What happened?" He shrugged his shoulders and wriggled out of her embrace and looked at his sister, who had appeared in the kitchen holding a drawing.

"Why is he crying?" Maya asked.

"I don't know, honey. He just started. Maybe he misses Mommy and Daddy."

Maya asked, "Do you, Ido?" She looked worried.

Ido shook his head. "Tell her to go away, Grandma. I don't want her here."

"I don't want to go away! I want to be here."

Nechama said, "Maya, I'd like you to go into the living room for a while. We'll be there soon."

"I don't want to be there by myself. You can't tell me what to do."

"Yes, I can," said Nechama. She put her hand on Maya's shoulder and led her to the living room.

Maya stomped her feet. "It's horrible here in this house! It smells gross! I want to go home."

"I'm sorry that you don't like it in my house, but right now we don't have a choice. You have to stay here until Mommy comes. Here, sit down and do another drawing for me and I'll hang it on the fridge. What do you say?"

The girl made a face but picked up a pencil.

When she went back to the kitchen, Ido had stopped crying and had arranged all his tools on the table. There were rows of plastic screwdrivers, hammers, a real-looking drill, screws and nails in various sizes, and a camera in the middle of the table.

She sat down opposite him, took a last sip of her coffee, now cold, and smiled at him. He gave her a strange, expectant look, and his eyes brimmed over again.

"So, Idoleh, do you miss your parents a little?"

He shook his head, tears streaming down his cheeks.

"Then why are you crying so much? What's wrong?"

He shrugged his shoulders, came over, and climbed onto her lap. Even though it hurt when his little knees crushed her wounded ones, she wrapped her arms around him and stroked his soft hair as he leaned his head against her chest, breathing heavily and rubbing his nose on her sweater. She tried to encourage him:

"What is it? Tell Grandma why you're crying." She heard him mumble something about thieves, and what the police did to them. "Yes, that's true, you're right, you're a clever boy."

He pulled away and started to kick her chair leg and screamed, "I'm a thief!" He ran from the kitchen, and before she could get up—she thought her knees were bleeding again; something warm was dripping down her left leg—Maya came into the kitchen. She looked at Nechama, then at the table, and her eyes opened wide.

"Look! Look, Grandma! There's our camera! How did it get here? Did you find it?" She climbed up on the chair and picked up the camera, but only half of it came up in her hand. "It's broken!" Nechama looked closer and saw that what was left of the camera was a sort of puzzle of camera pieces that the boy had painstakingly assembled. "There's nothing left of it!" Maya said. "Did you break it, Grandma?"

Nechama picked up the pieces and put them on the counter. "Yes, Maya."

"But why did you take it? Mommy will be angry at you."

"It's all right. I'll explain it to her. She'll understand."

"No, she won't. Do you know how long she's been looking for it? She even called the police to ask if they found it! Wow, Grandma, let's call Mommy now. We have to tell her we found the camera!"

"Later. Let's go and see where Ido is."

"He's in your bed," Maya said and hurried to the bedroom, shouting, "Ido! We found Mommy's camera! Grandma had it!"

She walked heavily down the hallway until she got to her room, where she found Maya leaning over her brother, who lay sobbing into the pillow.

Maya looked at her. "He's the one who took the camera, isn't he? You just made it up that it was you. He broke it, right?"

She sat down on the bed with a thud. "Yes, you're right."

Maya looked more curious than angry now, her face clear and lovely. "Why did you lie? Are you protecting Ido? Don't you want Ido to be punished?"

She smiled. "He's not going to be punished. We'll tell Mommy that we found the camera, right, Ido? And we'll explain why you took it. I'm sure you had a good reason."

Ido sat up and rubbed his eyes. "Yes, I had a really good reason."

And then, as if the explanation and the confession were a magic wand, all the sorrow and guilt vanished from his face and he sat cross-legged on the bed and told them how he'd once heard his mother tell her friend Ma'ayan on the phone that her dream was to install a hidden camera in the house—every parent needed that, didn't they?—That way she could learn a few things about herself and maybe be a better mother. Every morning after she dropped the kids off, she would sit down with her coffee and a cigarette and watch the video and learn from it. So he had an idea to make Mommy's dream come true, and he took the camera and decided to hide it somewhere in the house, in a secret place that no one would find. But he had trouble thinking of a good place, and in the end he decided to put it on the fridge, and he climbed up on a chair onto the counter, and in the end he managed to put it up there, but it fell down.

The tears started to stream down his cheeks again, and he mumbled that he'd tried to fix the camera's back door with a hammer and a screwdriver, but then another piece fell off, in the front, with glass. His words became slurred and he was crying almost hysterically.

Nechama gathered him into an embrace, pressed his head to her chest, caressed his hair, and whispered, "Shhh . . . it's okay. . . . I understand."

"I just wanted to fix it," he said in a muffled voice.

"I know, I know."

"I just wanted to fix it," he murmured deep into her sweater, and it seemed as if his voice were coming from inside her chest. "Just to fix it."

ALONA

"Do whatever you want, I don't care." That sentence echoed in her head as she took the elevator down to get Mark some coffee. "Do whatever you want, I don't care," she had heard Maya say in the car.

She had glanced in the rearview mirror. "What did you say?"

"I wasn't talking to you, I was talking to the doll," Maya answered.

"But why are you angry at her?" Ido asked.

"I'm not angry. I was just talking."

Alona turned on the radio for the news, but kept listening to Maya, thinking about the legacy she'd bequeathed to her daughter. When Maya kept chattering with the doll after they got to kindergarten, she almost wanted to say, Let's start fresh. Let's scrub the language clean, purify it.

"Bye, Mom, have a good day!" Maya said, and went off to play with her friends.

Ido held Alona's hand as they walked to his preschool. "I have a secret. I'll whisper it in your ear," he said. She leaned over and he whispered, "Today I'll say goodbye nicely. I won't cry."

She smiled at him. "Really?"

"Yes, I made up my mind."

"Good job! What a grown-up boy!"

But even before they reached the yard, Ido's grip on her hand tightened. "Pick me up," he ordered when they walked in, forgetting his promise.

She picked him up and looked in his eyes. "We're saying goodbye nicely today, right? You promised." He nodded, but his eyes welled up. "Didn't we say you'd be grown-up today?"

He nodded desperately but refused to get down when they got to the big room. The teacher welcomed them cheerfully: "Good morning, I-*do*! Good morning, Ido's *mother*!" Then she changed her voice and asked, "How's it going, Alona?" as if Alona and Ido's mother were two separate entities that had to be addressed in different tones.

Ido buried his head in her neck and started to whimper. "You know what Ido promised today?" Alona said, betraying him.

The teacher, happy to collaborate, asked, "What?"

"That today we're saying goodbye nicely. No tears today."

"What a grown-up boy!" the teacher exclaimed, and gently pulled him away. She carried the sobbing child in her arms and signaled for Alona to leave.

As she had walked out quickly and got into the car, it occurred to her that their entire lexicon was full of misuses and contradictions: grown-up, for example. And boy. Who was the madman who thought of putting those two terms together?

Now she bought a latte and a croissant and went back up to the neurosurgical ICU, missing her children as if it had been days, rather than a mere twelve hours since she'd seen them. She knew she wouldn't be allowed into the ward with food and drink, and in any case no more than one person could be at Roni's bedside, so she asked a nurse to call Mark. When he came out, surprised, forgetting that she'd told him just fifteen minutes ago she was going to get him a drink, she said, "Take this. You have to eat and drink. I'll go in to her now." Without saying a word, he took the paper cup and bag and walked to the waiting room, which had become their second home in the last few hours. Then he stopped and turned around, pulling off the mask that covered his face and mouth, and said, "Jane's on the six-fifteen flight." Alona said she knew, they'd already agreed that Alona would pick her up at the airport. "Jane's on the six-fifteen flight," he repeated, not stating a fact but reciting a line of poetry.

"Mom's coming soon," she told Roni, when she sat down next to the wide, convoluted bed, an empire of instruments and tubes. Although she knew Roni couldn't hear, not only because she was anesthetized but because the masks seemed to dull the words, she said again, "Mom will be here soon," tasting the words trapped in the thin paper fibers.

Muffled whimpers escaped from the lips of the woman sitting to her left. She was in her fifties, and her soldier son had been shot a few days earlier when his roommate had accidentally discharged his gun. Her name was Tzippi, and she'd told Alona that by some miracle the bullet had penetrated the boy's skull without killing him. Something about the angle, she explained over and over again, as if the explanation was the cure, the second miracle, the real one. But his brain has been scratched. They'd removed the bullet but the brain had started bleeding, and during the night edema had set in. The boy had not regained consciousness yet, and the doctors said the situation was very bad. His bleeding was spreading and the edema was getting worse.

"This morning, right after they brought your girl in"—she pointed at Roni's bed—"I saw them bringing her in, poor thing. . . ." She shook her head and explained that her son's condition had deteriorated. The professor who spoke to her an hour ago had said it was life-threatening. The situation was life-threatening. Apparently there was severe brain damage. "But that's what they said when he first came in, isn't it?" she added cheerfully, in between sobs. "That's just what they said, and here he is, still alive, my boy. Still alive." She was a war widow, she said, as if that were an identity or a profession. She'd been sitting at her son's bed for four days and nights. "I haven't been home for four days. I haven't slept or showered or brushed my hair. Nothing. I just change my clothes. My daughter brings them for me. And a bagel here and there, and some fruit. So I won't waste away." She repeated her story over and over again; the details seemed to give her comfort. Because you couldn't just let time slip away without a fight. Perhaps the enumeration of actions not performed during the lost time created a new schedule within the vacuum: all the things you didn't do, all the things that from now on you would never take for granted.

Alona looked at Tzippi, who sobbed into her hands, and thought: And us? We've only been here a few hours. Fresh. We haven't lost anything yet. Our anchors are still deep in the muddy ground of the outside world. We've just set sail, newbies, grabbing onto the railing of this state-of-the-art bed rocking on a stormy sea that wants to swallow up everything we own—the combs, the toothbrushes, the mug we left this morning on the kitchen counter, the leftover coffee grown cold and cloudy. This sea would swallow it all up, especially the little things, like the lipstick she'd quickly applied in the parking lot by the café where she'd waited for Uri for an hour. "Did we say ten?" he asked when he finally arrived. "I thought it was eleven. I'm sorry." And the sea was threatening to erase her anger, and her relief when the meeting ended with a handshake and a friendly hug: "We did it, Alona. It's all thanks to you. What would I do without you? Really, you're such a savior. I love you." The sea was threatening to swallow up those last moments of life, when she'd sat in traffic at one o'clock on her way home, listening to a Crosby, Stills, & Nash song she liked on the radio.

Her mind had wandered to two different places, as if she were walking two dogs, each pulling in the opposite direction. Then her cell phone rang through the hands-free unit. She had the music turned up very loud, and the phone must have been ringing for a while before she happened to notice the screen flashing: MARK-CELL. She quickly turned off the radio, snapping the thin thread that probed lazily in her mind to a time twenty-five years ago, when she was fifteen and heard that song for the first time. But a thicker thread got tangled up and dragged her back to yesterday, to sex with Mark, which had left her body tranquil but her mind discordant. She felt so old, like a real forty-year-old, with a body that no longer needed to be told what to do and a mind that nothing could surprise. A place where passion was used up and an orgasm was as efficient as a reflex.

"Mom's coming later," she repeated, and looked at Roni. Half of her face was hidden by the artificial respiration tubes. A yellow sheet was pulled up over her chest, concealing her naked body. It was hard to make out the body's outline, which seemed to have also been anesthetized. She suddenly wanted to cry with Tzippi, but the nurse came up and whispered that Mark wanted to come in. She stood up and touched the taut yellow sheet with her fingertips.

The nurses had explained that patients were vulnerable to infections, so they had to insist on only one visitor at a time. But she became angry again at this restriction and had decided to ask the department head for special permission: she would promise they'd wear robes and wash their hands and keep their masks on. The nurse had told her at lunchtime: "No chance. You'll have to take turns." Even Tzippi, whom she regarded as an expert, had shaken her head and said, "No way."

Mark waited outside, wearing a new mask. "Go home, it's already eight," he said. "Go and put the kids to bed."

She said, "Yes," but she knew she wouldn't. The kids were fine. She'd talked to her mother not long ago, and she'd sounded cheerful. She said she'd made them scrambled eggs, like they asked for, and some toast, but they hadn't touched the food; they probably weren't hungry after all the snacks. Alona said, "It's okay, Mom."

Then her mother added apologetically, "I gave them chocolate, too. A lot. And chocolate milk. And what about bathing? Do you want me to give them showers?"

Alona said, "No, of course not, Mom!" She said it firmly, and her mother said she'd turned the heater on two hours ago, so they'd have hot water, except they didn't have a change of clothes. Alona said, "No, no, really, there's no need. I'll be there soon, and anyway it's not the end of the world if they don't shower." She'd promised to be there at around eight, but it was eight now, and she had no idea how she was going to leave this place, and leave Mark, who seemed to be getting sucked into the void already, as if on the other side of the two automatic doors, in the hall where Roni and the soldier and two other people lay—an old man who'd had a stroke and a young Arab who'd also been in an accident—as if secret agents were lurking in that room, waiting for the right moment to carry out their kidnapping, and they would take Mark to the place where Tzippi was, the place where you counted skipped showers and sleepless nights and unused combs.

"I can't leave. Maybe I'll call Hila and have her pick up the kids. They can sleep over at her place. I'll stay with you. How are you going to get through the night alone here? You'll go crazy on your own."

"No, Alona, you have to get up at five to pick up Jane. And what about the kids? Will you take them with you?"

"I hadn't thought about that. Oh, God, I really didn't think about that. If the flight lands at six-fifteen, it'll be at least half an hour until she comes out, right?"

"I think so, yes." Mark nodded distractedly.

"So that puts it at, let's say, quarter to seven. Maybe I can ask Hila if I can drop the kids off around six. She gets up early with the baby anyway."

"Fine. I have to go in, okay? Go home."

"Okay. I'll go soon. I'll call Hila first. Go in, and I'll call you before I leave."

She went into the waiting room and nodded at the family of the young Arab: a man and woman who looked in their sixties, three young men, and a young woman. They were sitting around a low table scattered with large bottles of Fanta and Coke and plates of cookies and fruit, whispering among themselves. She sat down on an armchair, put her bag down next to her, and took her phone out to call Hila. She knew Hila would be busy with bath time and bedtime—her older son Tomer always refused to take a shower. Just yesterday they'd discussed it, standing outside Maya's kindergarten exchanging complaints and advice. "When will these battles be over?" Hila had said with a sigh. "I don't have the energy for it anymore."

When she finished making arrangements for the next morning, it occurred to her that it was the first time in her children's lives that either she or Mark weren't with them at this time of day, so they probably perceived as a change of routine or an adventure what was a painful stab for her. She missed them, she missed the domestic dramas that suddenly seemed to have the power to save you from all the real dramas lurking outside. When she put the phone back in her bag, the tears started running down her face. She wasn't sure if she was crying over Roni or over herself, over how fragile she'd become since her children were born.

She wiped her eyes and saw the older Arab woman standing over her holding out a plate of cookies. Then she noticed the woman's hand was trembling, and so were the cookies. Alona took one and thanked her. The woman nodded and said, "Take," as if she hadn't just taken one.

Alona said, "Thanks, but one's enough, I'm on a diet."

The woman smiled, waved dismissively, and said, "No need for diet, you're like this"—she illustrated a stick with her finger—"like a bird."

Alona laughed and said, "Thanks, but that's not true."

When she got up and started walking back to Roni's room, she saw the neurosurgery professor standing by the nurses' station. Even though he'd talked to them just an hour ago, when he'd visited the ward, she felt as if she couldn't go home without asking him something else, although she didn't know what.

Roni had been hit by a car when she'd crossed Salameh Street in south Tel Aviv, at a pedestrian crossing, just before 11 A.M. The driver, a man in his mid-forties who was driving over the speed limit, claimed he hadn't seen her at all. That's what the police officers told them when they came to the hospital that afternoon. He swore she'd suddenly jumped in front of him and that he hadn't been going very quickly— although one of the cops had said it was sixty miles per hour—but he swore on everything he held dear that she had just appeared out of nowhere, like a ghost. The car had thrown her almost thirty feet, and she'd suffered abdominal injuries and, even worse, head injuries. She was brought to the ER unconscious. Mark was at home when they called from the hospital around one. It took them awhile to identify her because her backpack, which was thrown when she was hit, wasn't with her when they brought her to the hospital. The convenience store owner across the street had picked it up and called the police. He and two foreign workers from Romania were the only witnesses to the accident.

When Mark arrived at the hospital, Roni was in surgery. The doctor in the trauma unit had found that one of her pupils was enlarged and suspected a blood clot—"epidural hematoma," he'd explained—between the skull and the brain membranes, and in the passing hours they'd memorized the words like a mantra. She was rushed into surgery to drain the clot and sedated for twenty-four hours. Tomorrow, the deputy chair of neurosurgery had explained, they would stop the sedative and slowly ease up the artificial respiration to see if she could breathe on her own. She would go through a process called *reversal*. Not something they needed to memorize, but still, when she heard the term for the first time she found it difficult to disconnect it from its daily usage and think of it as a process that was supposed to bring Roni back to conscious-ness. At this stage, he told them, they still didn't know if or how she would come out of it. She could wake up with neurological damage. It might be days or months until they found out whether there was brain damage. It could be that she'd wake up and be fine. That happened too, he said. Or she might not wake up at all.

It was this option, the strangest of them all, the one that sounded almost literary, like part of an overly dramatic plot in the debut novels she edited, that she wanted to discuss with the professor. He had emerged in recent hours as an almost fictional character: present, frenetic, but evasive, coming and going, disappearing all the time like the rabbit in *Alice in Wonderland*. Mark had tried to talk to him three times. The first time, when he had just arrived, the professor was hurrying into the operating room and told Mark, "Later." The second time, when he made rounds with his deputy and three residents, he told Mark that his deputy had already explained everything, hadn't he?—and turned to the deputy, who nodded. And the third time, not long ago, they saw him rushing down the hallway, surrounded by the family of the young Arab, who tried to block him without touching him, dancing a strange dance around him until he managed to slip away through the automatic doors, leaving them standing there, a startled, muted mass. Mark had suddenly taken off after him. "I'll get him before he gets to the elevator! Before he goes home. I have to." Alona hurried after him, more to protect him than to hear what the professor said.

They caught up with him a moment before he got in the elevator. "Excuse me, Professor, I have to talk to you for a minute, just a minute, please," Mark said. The man turned to him and thrust his hands in his white coat pockets, waiting, or just wanting his fists to be in a safe place. "Yes, what is it?" he asked, as if it were not obvious what this was about, as if he were being impertinently approached about some esoteric topic.

Alona stood a few feet away, afraid that she would scare the man off if she got closer, that she and Mark would look like the Arab family that only a moment ago had closed in on him in a circle of desperation. As she stood there, her heart pounding, she suddenly became aware of having developed strange survival skills, perhaps even expecting that everything she and Mark had achieved in life would now carry them on wings over the masses storming the professor. But no. Mark threw his hands up in a gesture that might have been questioning and might have been begging, and the professor was swallowed up into the elevator. When she asked what they'd talked about, Mark said, "Forget it. I couldn't understand it. He said he couldn't say, that we'd know more tomorrow." And then he burst into tears. Not the tears of a few hours ago, when she'd met him at the ICU, but a different sort of crying,

which reminded her of Ido in the mornings. It was the sobbing of someone who has been abandoned, who has seen a back turned on him.

But now it turned out the professor hadn't gone home. The white
rabbit had reemerged from his hole and was standing a few feet away
with his back to her, resting his arms on the counter, feet crossed, his
rear end protruding like a bull's-eye target.

She went up to him. "Look, I know people keep harassing you all day
long. I know you're busy. I know you already told us everything you have
to say. But I want to ask you just one thing, and I'm begging you not to
pull out some standard line."

The professor straightened up, took his arms off the counter, and
was about to reflexively stick his hands into his pockets, except that he
wasn't wearing his white coat anymore. Now he really was on his way
out. So he crossed his arms over his chest and said, "Go ahead, please.
What did you want to ask?"

"I wanted to ask you about this reversal. Can you tell me, say, if
there are statistics on her chances? Let's say if her type of injury indi-
cates a good possibility that she'll wake up without any brain damage?
Because that guy, the one lying next to her in the ward? They did that
reversal thing on him, too, two days ago, but he hasn't woken up yet."

"His injury is different."

"But compared to him, let's say, or to the other guy who was hit by
a car, what is her condition?"

"Ms. Segal"—she was amazed that he remembered her name—"I
don't deal with comparisons."

"I know, I know, but listen, my husband and I need something so we
can get through the night. A glimmer of hope."

"You have that."

"We do?"

"There is a glimmer of hope."

"Just a glimmer?" She smiled.

"You asked for a glimmer and I gave you one, okay?"

"Okay. Okay, thanks."

"I understand her mother is arriving from the States tomorrow," he
said, after he'd already turned to leave.

"Yes, I'm picking her up. She's coming in tomorrow, from New
York." She knew these details didn't interest him and that recounting

them was turning her into a nuisance, but she couldn't stop. There was something reassuring in talking about all the rest, the unimportant stuff.

The professor stopped at the doors. "I understand she's an artist. That's what your husband told me."

Her heart sank at the thought of Mark having tried, perhaps, to impress the professor, sensing what she had learned through her mother's many hospitalizations—that doctors, especially the senior ones, had a mysterious respect for artists and found them fascinating. She remembered the head of the orthopedic ward where her mother had spent a few days after breaking her hands, and the conversations Alona had had with him when he heard she was an editor. He'd told her which books he liked, and confessed that once, among his other transgressions—that's how he had phrased it—he too had taken pen to paper. And now this professor, too, was acting differently, more embarrassed and enchanted. He walked back and asked if Jane was a sculptor or a painter or what?

"Sculptor," she answered happily. "She's supposed to be taking part in a big show in New York next month."

"Really?"

"Yes, yes." She'd never thought of Jane as an important artist, but now she had become extremely significant. "It's a group show with a few well-known artists. I don't know exactly who, but I could find out if you're interested."

"That's too bad. I just got back from New York a week ago. My wife and I were there for two weeks for a conference."

"Well, you'll see her tomorrow, and you can ask her. I gather you have an interest in sculpture?"

"Absolutely." He told her it was his dream to study sculpture when he retired. At home he did a little work; he had a studio in his backyard. "Not exactly a studio, more of a hut, you know."

She nodded understandingly.

He made all sorts of statuettes; he had a few in his office. "If you want, you can come in to see me tomorrow and I'll show them to you. If you're interested, of course."

"Of course, of course I'm interested!"

"Good night, then." He walked back to the doors.

He seemed to grow smaller as she watched him leave, shrinking to the size of his statuettes, but next morning he would be giant-sized again. She wondered if he'd even remember having spoken to her tonight, if this talk about sculpture and retirement and the studio would envelop Roni like an angelic halo, see her through the reversal, redeem her from being merely one of four people lying in a room, naked, covered with yellow sheets, lights flashing on the instruments around them, ventilator monitors beeping like a canon, beat after beat, the second voice coming in on the first, then the third, and the fourth, a sort of "When the Saints Go Marching In" of monitors in an endless surrealistic loop.

She asked the nurse to call Mark. It was almost nine and time to go home. The kids would be exhausted and making her mother crazy. When he came out, his eyes looked red; he'd been crying again. She said, "Let's sit down for a few minutes and talk before I leave." He looked back at the doors, as if their being closed was a danger to Roni's life. "Okay," he said. She held his hand and they walked to the waiting room.

How long had it been since they had held hands like that? It seemed like years. In fact, she thought, they never had. Mainly because of her. Mark liked to hold hands, and in the first few weeks after they met, when they walked around together, his hand would automatically feel for hers, which squirmed uncomfortably, in a fist, like the hands of that professor. She wanted to tell Mark what he'd said about the glimmer of hope. But she wouldn't say *glimmer*—that might kill him now. She would say *chance*, a slightly fleshier word, an open word. After all, she was the one who'd complicated things with the word *glimmer*. Why couldn't she be like all the others who probably asked the same question without getting caught up in words? What do you think, Professor? she should have said. Will she live? Will she be a vegetable?

As if reading her thoughts, Mark stopped just before the waiting room, took off his mask, and said, "What's going to happen Alona? Will she get through this?" His voice cracked and his fingers grasped hers tightly, and before she could say anything he burst into tears. "Say she will, say she'll get through it. I can't take any other possibility."

She wrapped her arms around him, cradled his head in the crook of her neck, and whispered, "Yes, I think so. I think she'll come out of it." He cried louder, as if the word *yes* signified the opposite, the *no*, the lack of clarity: unclear whether your daughter will wake up tomorrow and, if so, whether she'll be able to breathe on her own, whether she'll open her eyes, whether she'll be the person she used to be, because we already miss her, we miss her so badly.

"I shouldn't have let her go to Tel Aviv," he said, pulling away from her embrace. "I knew she was lying, I knew she wasn't going to a demonstration. What was she doing there? Do you have any idea what she would be doing in south Tel Aviv? Where was she all night? Who is this Sivan woman? Have you ever heard of her? I have to talk to her. Does she even exist? Have you talked to Shiri? Does she know?"

"No, she doesn't know. Do you want me to call her?"

"Yes, don't forget. Maybe she knows something. I have to know what she was doing there. I need the truth."

She wanted to tell him that the truth wouldn't help now. The truth was a distraction. Roni could have been run over anywhere.

"Talk to Shiri, okay? At least she'll know. She's her best friend."

"Okay, I'll talk to her. I'll call her from the car." She wanted to say Shiri hadn't been Roni's best friend for ages, Roni didn't have any girl-friends, Roni was a lone wolf, and lately, in the last year, really—maybe because of her own impending fortieth birthday, which she now longed for so she could get it over with and move on—lately, every time she talked with Roni or looked at her, every time she saw her walking rest-lessly around the house, playing with the kids, or sulking in her room, she felt as if she were chasing her own long-gone shadow. There was an insult of sorts in that girl's presence, as if her every word and movement said: I am everyone you no longer are.

Mark's hand found hers again, and she held it and brought his fist up to her lips. She whispered, "It'll be okay. I talked with the professor and he said she has a chance."

Mark looked at her. "A chance? That's all he said? When did you even talk to him? I thought he went home."

She told him she'd managed to catch him a while ago, and he turned out to be an amateur sculptor and had invited her to see his statues.

Tears streamed from Mark's eyes. "Just a chance? That's all he gave her?"

"A chance is a lot. He doesn't lie, you know. He told Tzippi her son was in critical condition. He didn't tell us that."

"I'm exhausted," Mark said, and leaned back in his chair. "I'm just beat."

"I know. You had a crazy morning with the dogs, too. What a story, huh? Totally crazy. It's a good thing Ali took them, otherwise they'd be rotting in the yard right now."

"Yes," he said, and wearily asked her to go by his house on the way home and pick up Popeye. "You don't have a key, do you?"

"No."

He took a key off his chain and gave it to her, explaining that it sometimes got stuck in the lock and you had to jiggle it. "But gently, Alona," he said, predicting her impatience, "otherwise you'll break it."

She took the key with her free hand, refusing to disconnect her fingers from his.

He closed his eyes and yawned. "What time is it?"

"It's after nine. Nine-thirty."

"The kids have probably fallen asleep at your mother's." He sounded contemplative, his voice calm and routine, as if talking about the sleeping kids was a moment of reprieve in the storm. "You'll probably find her climbing the walls." He smiled.

She leaned her head on his shoulder. "Yeah."

"Call and make sure she hasn't killed herself yet."

She smiled.

"What did you tell them?"

She said her mother had let something slip, so she'd had to say they'd taken Roni to the doctor's together, in Tel Aviv.

"Oh, no. They must be really worried. Don't tell them about the dogs, okay?"

"No, of course not. What should we tell them? That they ran away?"

"Yes, something like that." She felt his chest trembling with a new sob about to erupt. "You know the way she's always protecting Popeye? So we won't put him to sleep? *He still experiences joy.* That's what she always says, doesn't she?"

"Yes," she whispered, almost to herself, and thought how funny it was that Popeye's old age had saved his life: had he been young, like the other two, he would have been as dead as they were now. The dogs' deaths, she realized, was the first thing that had been swallowed up in the storm. If not for what had happened to Roni, they'd probably be telling the kids now that Brutus and Olive had run away, and Roni would be alone in her room, grieving, maybe angry at her father, blaming him for their deaths. How badly she wanted to be there, in that domestic bubble of adolescent fury, instead of here in this twilight silence.

Mark said, "I have to get back. I don't want to leave her alone. Do you think she knows I'm there?" He kept his eyes closed, his head leaning back on the couch.

"Yes, she knows."

"It horrifies me to think that she's completely alone wherever she is right now."

"But she's here, Mark. She's just sedated." She suggested that he take a quick nap while she sat with Roni.

"No, I can't. I can't fall asleep until she wakes up." He nodded heavily and yawned.

Our children, she thought, are most ours when we can't see them. When we leave them at day care and send them out into a different existence. How many times had the teacher told her Maya was a perfectly behaved little girl? She was the teacher's right hand. "She's my assistant," she would say, "polite, generous, and so mature." How many times had she wondered if it was the same Maya, and who the real Maya was? And Ido? What about him? They never said anything about him, either positive or negative. And when they were with her, from 4 P.M. onward, she could never be completely theirs, present, absorbing—she could never be, just for four hours, the text itself, the strange, crazy text they were writing, and not the editor.

Like with the constant disorganization, the incessant movement of objects. She once told a single friend who was thinking about having a child that one of the things she liked most about being a mother was that nothing stayed static. She said that once, before she'd met Mark, she'd had a collection of toy lizards she used to buy at different shops. "Just one of those childish things, something the men I dated thought was cute, and I wanted it to be part of my image, you know? And now the lizards are in the bathtub, strewn around the living room, in the yard." It filled her with happiness to think that her previous life, the static one, was crumbling, and that objects that had been with her for so many years were being recycled, changing their purpose. And there was the little wooden box with the Buddha illustrations, which she didn't tell her friend about. That box had sat on the bureau in her Tel Aviv bedroom, and she'd kept condoms in it. Maya had eventually claimed it, and she used it to store barrettes and all sorts of nondescript little items, beads and threads and notes she collected, including the sticky notes she had removed every evening from Alona's computer screen during that strange, superfluous experiment. "Mom, can I? Do you need this?" she would ask when she padded into the study with her box. And she would leave armed with RELAX!, SURRENDER!, GIVE IN TO THE MOMENT!

Still, Alona found herself scolding the kids every afternoon because of the mess, demanding that they put their toys away, threatening, begging. And now, when she looked at Mark, who seemed to have fallen asleep after all, with his mouth slightly open and his fingers still clutching hers, she knew this was probably what tormented her so much: her children were her anchor, but also her storm.

She wanted to get up and call her mother, to apologize for being late and find out how things were going. She would say she was on her way, leaving right now, and she would tell her mother that if the kids were tired it was fine for them to fall asleep just as they were, in their clothes, on the couch. It was twenty to ten, and there was no chance she'd get there before eleven. But she stayed sitting, smelling Mark's sweat, looking at him. Underneath his corduroy jacket he was wearing the same gray sweatshirt he'd put on the night before, when they'd got out of bed and he'd walked her to the car. She remembered how he'd hugged her at the door, a strange, long hug that had concealed the big unasked question, which they probably would have discussed at length today over the phone, like two teenagers: What does it mean that we had sex? What's going to happen now?

It was strange how at night, before she fell asleep, when she reconstructed the evening with Mark—the cake, the conversation about Ido, the moment he took her hand and led her to the bedroom, and then the sex, which was quick but seemed long and complicated, divided up into chapters like a book—strange how that detailed reconstruction had omitted the embrace, which seemed to contain not only a separation but an opening, as if Mark were saying: let's go back to the beginning. Let's go back to that cold early spring morning in Ein Kerem, when you came out to the balcony and I was waiting for you like a prisoner anticipating a verdict, with a wonderful breakfast meant to disguise my fear. And you knew. You knew something had happened to you—something undefined, almost imperceptible, but huge, didn't you? And even though I knew you hadn't fallen in love with me the way I had with you, because you're not the falling-in-love type, and even though in every step you took from the bed to the balcony I heard a question mark, still I prayed you'd see what was waiting for you, trembling with hope.

That embrace, she thought now as she looked at Mark, the odor of his sweat spinning a familiar web around her, was not the question but the answer: let's go back to that morning in Ein Kerem, let's go back there with all our luggage, let's go back there with everything we didn't know then. Fall in love with me! it had said. It was no wonder she'd forgotten the main thing. Fall in love with me—it had demanded—because now you can.

He was asleep. She wondered if she would have been able to fall asleep like that in the waiting room if she were him, while her girl lay on the other side of the corridor. She admired his ability to cede control. She loved him for it. She got up to go and call her mother, but when she glanced at him again her heart shrank with compassion: he had allowed himself to fall asleep because he knew she was there. It was not loss of control but trust. She stopped at the desk where they kept the masks and robes, then pressed the intercom button to open the door.

Tzippi was sitting next to her son's bed reading a book. She looked up and nodded silently, as if there were different rules here at night, an almost routine tranquillity. She sat down by Roni's bed and touched her cheeks with her knuckles, as if checking for a fever. Although she knew the girl would not wake up, she resisted kissing her forehead, afraid to move a tube or disturb the instruments' operation. In her imagination she charged ahead to a week from today, two or three weeks, when they would tell Maya and Ido that Mommy and Daddy were moving in together again. She could hear their cries of joy, mainly Ido's, because obviously Maya's happiness would be diluted, as usual, with mistrust, with some miniature, unripe version of cynicism that still had years to mature. And Roni—what would she say about all this?

Knock yourselves out. That's what she'd say. Alona could almost hear her saying it, because she knew Roni would view their getting back together as a kind of failure, cowardly and lazy. Roni liked to proclaim her belief in totality. Total love, total life. Compromise is death, she said.

She looked at her, smiling in her heart at hearing these unspoken

words, the criticism not yet hurled, and the contempt. It occurred to her
that at some point, after they became completely sated, the word sponges
began to drip out everything they had soaked up over the years: compromise, love, death, totality. They lost their fluids and the words dried up
and maybe died a little. And there was something comforting in that.

Tomorrow she would meet Jane. For the first time in her life, she
would meet Mark's first wife face-to-face. She'd seen her only in photographs: a good-looking woman with a slightly unusual face, straight hair,
cat's eyes, a tangle of colorful beads around her neck like an Indian. It
would be strange to relay everything in English, to tell this woman what
had happened to her daughter and what the doctors were saying.

The nurse came up to her and said Mark was waiting outside, and
she got up and left. "I fell asleep," he said.

"That's good, you needed some sleep."

He said she had to leave now; they'd talk tomorrow, first thing; he'd
call her when she was on her way to the airport.

She said, "Yes," and thought about how the next time she saw him it
would be with Jane. She hugged him and said, "Good night, then." A
moment before he disappeared behind the doors, she called his name.
He turned around and she went over to him, looked into his eyes peering over the mask, and said, "Whatever happens, I'm with you. You
know that, right? I mean, this isn't the time to talk about it, but I want
you to know that. Last night did change something. Okay?" His eyes
said okay and welled up, and she wiped the tears off his cheek and said,
"You're getting the mask wet." He turned around and went in.

On the way home there was awful music on the radio. She flipped
through all the stations because she wanted to drive quickly, with music
on at full volume, like she had that afternoon with "Carry On," which
had been cut off right in the middle of her own reversal process: she
had crawled back in time, clearing cobwebs and junk from the road so
she could reach the place where she'd first heard the song.

She was fifteen, in the tenth grade, and had already started ditching
school and flunking every subject except writing. Some mornings she
went as far as Tel Aviv, where the only street she knew was Dizengoff.
She would walk up and down aimlessly, not really knowing what she
was looking for, running on the purest fuel she had ever known, the fuel
of restlessness, as yet nameless and shapeless. On one trip she met a girl

her age, Hadas, who came up to her while she was sitting on a bench in Dizengoff Square and asked if she had a cigarette. She smoked occasionally back then, secretly. She had one pack that she hid in her room, deep in the closet, but she didn't dare walk around with it in her bag. "I don't," she told the beautiful girl, who looked disappointed. "But we could buy some," she suggested, and Hadas happily agreed. They went to the kiosk and bought a pack of Time. Then they went back to the bench and sat smoking together. Hadas told her she'd skipped school, too. She went to a high school Alona had never heard of. "It's for gifted kids. Boring as hell." She told her she lived with her divorced mother, and her father lived overseas. They lived nearby, on Bialik Street. "Do you know it?" Alona said no, she wasn't from Tel Aviv, she lived on a moshav. Hadas found that funny: "A moshav? Like with cows and chickens?"

"No cows, but chickens, yes. Loads. The coops stink." She hated the countryside, hated, hated, hated it, and one day she was going to live in Tel Aviv. Hadas said she understood, and then she said her mother was a theater actress. She mentioned her name, but Alona hadn't heard of her. Hadas suggested they go to her place for some coffee. "We could have lunch, too. My mom's in rehearsals."

On the way, walking through unfamiliar streets, Hadas asked if Alona had a boyfriend, and what the boys on her moshav were like. Alona said not yet, and the boys were boring. "Yeah, ours too," Hadas said, as they climbed up the stairs to the second floor. She put the key in the lock of an old, tall, wooden door, and when they walked inside Alona gasped: the apartment was amazing. It had a sort of central atrium with an open kitchen, and mattresses on the floor with huge pillows made of shiny velvet and satin, and Bedouin-style embroidery, and rugs covering decorative floor tiles.

"This is the living room-kitchen," Hadas explained. "Here's where Mom and I spend most of our time, because it's the coolest room. And this is my room." She led her to another room with a high ceiling and huge window, a double bed with copper posts, an old bureau, a chest of drawers, and a table with a large copper tray. On the table were a cigarette roller and a pouch of tobacco.

"You smoke at home?" Alona asked.

"Sure. My mom does, too. Should I roll you one?"

She said, "Yes," and Hadas sat down cross-legged and expertly rolled two cigarettes. They sat on the rug and smoked, and Hadas went over to the record player and put an album on. She showed her the cover: "Crosby Stills. You know them?" Alona said, "No," and felt embarrassed. At parties on the moshav they listened to the Bee Gees and Rod Stewart. Hadas put the needle on and the room filled with that music: *Where are you going now, my love, where will you be tomorrow?*

Hadas said she'd had a boyfriend until recently, but she'd dumped him. She asked if Alona was hungry: "There's some good pasta sauce my mom made yesterday." Alona said okay, and then the door opened and a woman as beautiful as Hadas came in. "Oh, you're back?" Hadas asked, but didn't seem to mind. "This is my mom."

The woman said, "Hi, I'm Naomi. I'm starved—are you heating up that sauce?" She said someone in the production wasn't feeling well, so they'd cut the rehearsal short. She sat down at the large round table, on which Hadas set out plates and silverware. From a little tin box on the table, Naomi took out a small piece of something that looked like chocolate, crumbled a few bits off, went to Hadas's room and brought back the tobacco, mixed the crumbs with some, and, with quicker fingers than her daughter's, rolled herself a cigarette.

Hadas took the cigarette and took a deep drag, then passed it to Alona. She guessed it was hashish, even though she'd never seen it before, and so as not to misuse the great privilege that had fallen into her lap—the right to enter a new world that was harmonious, sophisticated, and mature, so mature—she took a small, hesitant drag and passed the cigarette back to Naomi. She felt as if all those months of aimless roaming around Dizengoff had been in preparation for this moment, at which the hands of her internal clock would move one hour forward and she would know that although nothing had really happened, her childhood was over.

She and Hadas had exchanged phone numbers and decided to be friends, but they never met again. On the way home, she sat on the bus feeling that someone had finally put some order in her longings, ranked them by urgency. When she walked into the house, her father was waiting for her with a meal, as usual. He asked how school was and she said it was fine, and wondered how he could not see the change in her—in general, but especially that morning. How could he not notice that the girl who'd left the house that morning was not the one who came home in the afternoon but a young woman who suddenly realized that her dad was getting in the way of her living?

She drove home from the hospital silently, completely focused on the attempt to reconstruct the unreconstructable, that moment when she felt she'd made the last great step from one world into another. Although she knew it was pointless, something inside her insisted on trying to get there, to the island growing ever more distant, peering out through the mist as an option that had already happened, windswept and flooded with salty water that had risen higher and higher over the intervening decades. She just wanted to be there, in the place where life was terrible only in theory, in the place where happiness was a massive thing that would one day happen to her, and not a microscopic thing she was afraid to lose.

The entrance to Eden was flooded, the main road blocked by a huge puddle. The same thing happened every winter, and the council kept promising to take care of it. She always managed to get through, but this time the puddle was deeper than she'd expected. The water reached halfway up the doors, and it was obvious she'd made a terrible mistake by driving in. There was no chance the wiring wouldn't get wet. As she kept pressing down on the accelerator, trying to feel the bottom of the car, the engine, every part, she waited for the moment when silence would flood the inside as the engine died. Then she felt a kick, as though invisible propellers had come to her aid and pushed the waters aside. She opened her window, watched the front left wheel turning into a sort of watermill, and whispered, "Just a bit more. Just a little farther, a little more." She felt the accelerator struggle, as if the gas were swirling and frothing in the tank, and suddenly the car came unstuck and lurched forward, and she kept going.

It was a miracle that the engine hadn't stalled. A miracle, she thought, as she drove past the grocery store. When she saw her mother's house down the street, the last remaining old house on the block, she thought: maybe not a miracle. Maybe she was just a good driver. Maybe she'd learned something from the one time she got stuck in that puddle. The driver who'd picked her up had said, "Slowly. You have to take it very slowly. You have to feel the car." She'd wanted to tell him, That's easy for you to say. You have an all-wheel-drive. But now, as she parked outside her mother's, she thought maybe she had internalized what he'd said about going slowly, about feeling the car, because it had seemed as if she'd actually known what she was doing back there. She turned off the engine, unbuckled her seat belt, and only then realized that her legs were shaking and her heart was pounding. She looked at the square of yellow light coming from her mother's kitchen. How could she have done that? How had she even dared to tell herself, as she'd sailed the car into that lake, that if she managed to cross it in one piece, everything would be okay tomorrow? As if the chance the professor had given her was not enough. As if risk was the true hope. And what would have happened if she hadn't done it? What if she'd sunk? If the engine had died?

She knocked on the door and heard her mother padding over in her slippers and the key turning twice in the old lock—how many times had she begged her to install a deadbolt? "They're asleep. How's Roni?" her mother said.

Alona whispered, "We don't know, Mom. We'll see tomorrow."

Her mother said the kids were asleep in her bedroom, because it was a little cold in the living room. When she saw Alona heading to the hallway, she said, "Wait, Alona, come here for a minute. I want to show you something. Ido wanted me to show you this. He wouldn't go to sleep until I promised to show you when you got here."

Alona followed her mother into the kitchen, where, on the table, was his little toolbox next to a dismantled camera. Her camera.

Her mother handed her the parts. "Wait, I'll get a bag." She dug through a cabinet, pulled out a supermarket plastic bag, shook it out, and told Alona about the evening's drama. "He felt so guilty. He thought they'd put him in prison." She took the camera pieces from Alona's hands and threw them in the bag. "It was weighing on him, but I promised him I'd tell you. I promised you wouldn't be angry. You're not angry, are you? I'm sure it can be fixed. There's a man in Petach Tikva who fixes cameras."

"No, I'm not angry. We're getting a new one anyway. Mark's buying one." Tears flooded her eyes, and she hurried to the bedroom and looked at Maya and Ido curled up under the big comforter. Maya was on her back, Ido on his stomach, his rear end up in the air, his pacifier next to him on a big pillow.

Her mother stood behind her and whispered, "Their things are by the door. Shoes, too. I can take the bags out to the car."

"Okay." She leaned over Maya, put her hands under her back and legs, and picked her up. Maya gave a dissatisfied mumble but did not wake up even when Alona carried her out and the cold air hit her face. She went back inside and sat on the edge of the bed next to Ido, gathered him to her, and stood up. The boy wrapped his arms around her neck and his legs around her hips. When she walked outside, her mother was standing by the open car doors like a guard who was sad that his shift was over, that these warm souls and chocolate stickiness and confessions and secrets were being taken away. When she put Ido in his seat, he opened his eyes and looked at her and asked sleepily, "Did you come to take us home?"

She kissed his forehead. "Yes, chickie, I came to take you home."

DAFNA

Around noon, after sitting in the café for over an hour, checking her cell phone twice to see if he'd left a message, ordering a salad after all since she'd left the house without breakfast that morning in her rush to get to the hospital for a blood test—she'd gone out of habit, to get it over with, to close a chapter or perhaps even end the whole story—and after finishing the salad and ordering coffee, she finally knew for certain what she'd guessed when she first got there: Adel wasn't coming.

Why would he? Had she really believed that an unemployed Palestinian floor tiler—he'd never said where he was from but had once mentioned the Nablus area—would be tempted to make the journey to Tel Aviv without an entry permit, just to get a Power Ranger? She couldn't phone him, because when she'd asked for his number he'd said it wasn't a good idea, and to Gabi's chagrin she hadn't insisted.

"What do you mean, not a good idea?" Gabi had grumbled, when she told him there was no way to get in touch with the man he'd been counting on as a media star. "What's he so afraid of? Does he think we're the police or something?"

Dafna had answered, "He knows what is and isn't a good idea."

Gabi scoffed. "Yeah, right, Dafna. Sure." Then he asked if there wasn't anyone else, some other Palestinian who'd called recently and might be more suitable for the job; someone they could put on standby. She said that there were hundreds of Israelis, if he wanted, but he said, "No. I need this guy."

After arranging the meeting, she'd gone to the toy store yesterday and bought a Power Ranger doll with her own money. They turned out to be difficult to find; they weren't very fashionable anymore, not in Israel. But she got one, and as she watched the checkout woman gift-wrap the box—"Exchange slip?" she asked, and Dafna said with a snort, "Yeah, I guess so"—she could feel the excitement of the little boy, the mythological Munir, as she thought of him, when his father gave him the box. She wished she spoke Arabic, so she could imagine the cries of joy, the father telling his son the wonderful story of the doll and what he'd done to get it. Maybe he'd have a kind word to say about CUSP or about her, the good Israeli fairy.

But Adel had bailed, and instead of imagining Munir's cries of joy she was now picturing the earful she would get from Gabi when she got back to the office. She knew he was waiting on pins and needles to hear if Adel had agreed to cooperate, because the minute he'd heard Adel was coming to get the doll, he'd quickly issued a press release about CUSP's humanitarian act, and they'd already found an Israeli campaign partner, a young man from Kiryat Malachi named Chaim who had recently lost his job as a carpenter.

Chaim and Adel, Gabi had named the campaign, after brainstorming with Dafna and the copywriter, even though she herself was too anxious to concentrate.

During the two weeks since the fertilization, she'd had no symptoms, nothing. But yesterday there was a moment, in the car on her way to Tel Aviv, when she thought her breasts felt swollen, like before she got her period. She knew the symptoms were similar but slightly different. She leaned her breasts against the wheel, trying to detect any sensitivity, and for a moment she thought there was some, but the next moment there wasn't. During the meeting with the copywriter she thought she felt a burning sensation in her nipples, a welcome, deceitful pain, and she raised her hand to scratch her ear so she could rub her arm against her chest, changing positions every so often. But no, she decided. There was nothing. And why should there be? When they'd implanted that one embryo, just six cells, she'd known it was a lost cause, and for the first

week of waiting, which was always easier than the second, she'd managed for the first time in her life to say the word *adoption* to herself
without the consonants tasting sour.

She planned to talk about it with Eli on Friday evening. She would
nonchalantly, heroically say, Okay, so what do you know about adoption agencies? Because she knew he'd already done the research, he
couldn't not have, and instead of getting angry and feeling betrayed,
she was almost grateful that he was going behind her back, doing something concrete with his despair. But Eli got the flu and spent the weekend in bed with a fever.

"So, what do you think?" Gabi looked at her expectantly, waiting
for confirmation.

"About what?"

"About *Adel: Chaim*. No *and*."

"Too refined."

"Okay. We'll go with *Chaim and Adel*." He pulled out a large computer printout with Chaim's picture. He was about twenty-five, good-
looking, black hair cropped short and glistening with gel, thick eyebrows
connecting over his brown eyes, his mouth slightly open, as if he were
modeling a bathing suit. "What do you say? Cute, huh? I just hope this
Adel guy is presentable." He pointed to the silhouette he'd marked next
to Chaim, the outline of another man, and Dafna pointed out that Adel
hadn't agreed to be in the campaign yet. "He will," Gabi said. "I guarantee it. You just have to know how to talk to him. You have to explain
that he's going to be a celebrity. No, don't say *celebrity*, say *national
hero*. People will come from overseas, foreign press; they'll do a Barbara Walters special on him. You'll see, he'll get international exposure.
And you know what comes with that kind of exposure? Immunity!
Protection. Can you imagine what this will mean for his family, for his
whole village? No soldier is going to touch them; no one will dare!"

Before she left for the café, Gabi said he wanted to be at the meeting
and personally give Adel the doll. As far as he's concerned, CUSP is me,
Dafna had explained, and Gabi eventually relented, agreeing that seeing a strange man might deter Adel. "You're right. Soften him up, and
I'll be there for the next meeting."

When she left the office and started walking in the rain to Sheinkin
Street, she almost hoped Adel wouldn't come. That he'd bail. That he'd

flee for his life from all her boss's good intentions. She knew Gabi's plans stemmed from childish hopefulness, but they'd become so cynical that yesterday, as she'd listened to the Ping-Pong of slogans flying over her head and watched Gabi and the agency copywriter passing the picture back and forth, turning it around, running their fingers over Chaim's body and Adel's silhouette—which looked like a police outline for a murder victim—she grew dizzy and had a strange taste in her mouth, something metallic and bitter. She got up to go to the bathroom, which unlike the one in their office was new and spacious. She washed her face and stood looking at herself in the giant mirror. She didn't want to go back to the agency office, with its big windows looking out onto the Ayalon Freeway.

She'd always hated skyscrapers and elevators. Whenever she visited Eli in his office she panicked. "How can you work in this place? What if there's an earthquake? Or a fire? How will you get out?" He would laugh and say he never thought about it. Lingering in the ad agency's bathroom, she thought about how in the last year or two she'd hardly visited Eli at work, simply because she had nothing to do there, and anyway their schedules never coincided. When she had a free hour, Eli was busy, and vice versa. The few times he called to ask if she was free and suggest she take a cab over—they could go to this new espresso bar he liked; they had a good lunch deal—he always caught her in the middle of something, or at least that's what she told him. He would say, "Okay, when you have a window let me know," and she couldn't tell if he was hurt or whether she even cared. She thought about the word *window*, and in her mind's eye she saw the windows in Eli's office, which couldn't be opened or looked in through, only out of. Just like the ones here, at the ad agency. As she tried to steady her dizziness, it occurred to her that maybe it was a question of men versus women, but she quickly reprimanded herself; it was sexist to think that way. Still, she was convinced that if anyone ever did a study, they'd find that men preferred skyscrapers with fast elevators and sealed windows, and women preferred to work close to the ground, with lots of escape exits.

She felt rude spending so long in the bathroom—the men would be wondering where she was. But she couldn't tear herself away from the sink and kept standing over it in case she needed to throw up. Then one of the secretaries she'd seen earlier at the reception desk came in. She was around twenty, wearing low-cut jeans and a short black sweater that exposed her navel. The young woman smiled at her and also stood facing the mirror. She smoothed over her eyebrows, then took out some lipstick from her jeans pocket. Since she couldn't keep standing there without doing anything, Dafna walked out into the hallway. She felt as if the carpet were sinking, the whole building shaking slightly.

She stopped a few feet from the office. Was she in the midst of her first-ever panic attack or was there some basis for her feelings? After all, there was a storm outside, and perhaps the building was swaying a little. She thought about how when she was overseas she never feared tall buildings and elevators. Once, shortly before she met Eli, she'd spent a few months in New York, living in a friend's apartment on the twenty-second floor. This new fear had something to do with Israel, otherwise how could you explain the selective geographical claustrophobia? But maybe it wasn't claustrophobia—she was covered with a thin layer of cold sweat, now, and took a deep breath before entering the room— maybe it was a crisis of faith, the idea that something here wasn't put together right. Because although she had no evidence, she was convinced that somewhere beneath her feet, no matter where she stepped, there was a seedling of negligence—an out-of-date phone number in case the elevator got stuck, an emergency exit that would turn out to be locked when disaster struck.

When she went into the room and sat down again, she smiled distractedly at the copywriter, who looked at her questioningly. Gabi turned to her. "Here's what we came up with. You know the Arik Einstein song, 'You and I will change the world'? So how about, 'You and I will *exchange* the world!' It's great, isn't it?" Without waiting for her response, he continued, "Make a note to find out about copyright and who wrote the song."

She nodded heavily and turned to look at the windows. The rain beating against them did not look dangerous but desperate, pleading, trying to tell them something, but what? She interrupted the men's conversation and asked was the building swaying or was it her. "It's you," Gabi said. She wanted to get up and flee again, but she knew she couldn't get in the elevator alone now, with the building trembling like this, with millions of moles gnawing at this very moment on the elevator cables, and the ground, the one the building sat on, the one beneath Ayalon

Freeway, and the roads, all the roads, and the earth on which their house stood, and Gabi's house and the copywriter's house and Chaim's house and Adel's house; the earth was full of holes and burrows and subterranean pits and everything built on it was pointless, ridiculous, and she wanted to get up and shake her boss's shoulders—how could she have believed him five years ago? It was one thing to believe that peace was relevant, that it could even be taken seriously, because even in the moments when it was obviously hopeless she had managed to convince herself that someone had to keep on believing in it, someone had to be naïve—and in recent months she'd seen herself as representing not peace but naïveté, because that seemed more important—but she knew that peace, if it ever came in any guise whatsoever, could not save us from ourselves.

Long hours seemed to go by before Gabi finally stood up, stretched, looked outside, and said, "Tomorrow, after the meeting with Adel, we'll be wiser. Right, Dafna?"

"Yes, if he shows."

"You're a pessimist, aren't you?" said the adman.

"That's why I like her," Gabi said.

They walked down the hall together on the soft, swampy carpet and stepped into the elevator. Even when the doors opened three floors belowground in the parking lot, she wasn't calm.

Now, at the café, she asked for the check. She'd waited for ninety minutes, and Adel obviously wasn't coming. Even though she was a little disappointed—after weeks of phone calls she was curious to see who he was, what he looked like, what he ordered, how he would look in this trendy café, how the two of them would look, perhaps like a couple on a blind date—she nonetheless relished Gabi's setback.

She put on her coat and took her umbrella from the plastic bucket in the entrance. She suddenly remembered a hotel she'd once stayed at in Amsterdam, a beautiful old building on a canal, with an umbrella stand in the lobby. She'd spent four rainy days there, and every morning before leaving the hotel, she would unfold the little umbrella she'd brought from Israel; it looked pathetic, not built for rain. Every morning she envied the other guests, who pulled out giant umbrellas from the stand and went off on their way with the nonchalance of people used to such weather. She'd walked the streets for three days, huddled under her little umbrella, which looked like a collapsed field tent, until on her last morning in the hotel she asked the front desk clerk where she could buy an umbrella like the ones in the foyer. He smiled and said, "They are for you."

"For me?" she asked, and he nodded and explained that they were hotel umbrellas for the guests' use. She smiled embarrassedly and thanked him, and when she went on her last outing, sheltered under a huge black umbrella, she felt a little foolish. Even her last day exploring the streets of Amsterdam, which by then seemed more familiar, even friendly despite the downpour, could not shake the discomfort she felt about being a tourist, an Israeli tourist: the other hotel guests were tourists too, but to them it was obvious who the umbrellas were for.

Her cell phone rang: Gabi couldn't resist after all. She picked up and answered with a defiance she could barely conceal. "He bailed. . . . Yes, I waited all this time. . . . No, I don't think he got confused. Yesterday he said ten. He said ten was good for him. But I'm willing to keep waiting. Do you want me to sit here for a while longer?"

She kept standing by the door, moving aside to let people in, and listened to Gabi whining. "I knew it! Fuck him. I knew it. No, don't wait anymore. I need you at the office. Fuck!" He'd already closed with *Ma'ariv* for an article in next weekend's supplement, and Chaim was coming to the photographer's studio that afternoon. "I thought you'd be able to convince this Adel to come. Shit!" He kept whining for a while, and then said maybe she *should* wait a bit longer, just fifteen minutes, because maybe there'd been a misunderstanding. "Does he even speak Hebrew? Did he understand what you told him?"

"He understood," she said, and reminded him that Adel didn't have an entry permit, and it was a little stupid of them to think he could even get in. She sat back down at her table, which the waitress had already cleared, and when she finished the phone call she ordered another latte. Then she remembered she'd already had two; if she were pregnant she should probably skip it. But she wasn't, she knew it, there was not a trace left of yesterday's nausea and dizziness. On the contrary, she felt great. Last night, when she and Eli had watched TV and he'd asked if she was nervous about the next morning, she'd told him about her panic attack earlier that day, at the ad agency, and Eli had looked at her and said, "I feel hot for you."

She asked if he was sure he felt well. He was still recovering from a bad flu, after all. He hadn't got out of bed all weekend, and on Sunday he'd skipped work. He said, "Great. I feel great. And you look great, and I love you, and I'm hot for you." He moved closer and asked what she thought, but he didn't do it like he had in recent years, submissively. He came closer and knelt down by her armchair and put his hands on her knees, moved them apart, then pulled down her sweatpants and underwear and threw them on the rug.

She kept sitting there, watching Eli watch her, on his knees, his hands on her lap, looking into her eyes, and she had the same thought she'd often had: his eyes were beautiful but sad. She was surprised to see so much sorrow in them, more sorrow than promise, as if he were apologizing while he spread her thighs and buried his head between them. How long had it been since he'd done that? Never mind, she thought, never mind, and whispered, "I'm sorry."

He looked up, his cheeks and chin covered with a thin shiny film. "What? Did you say something?"

She shook her head and told herself she couldn't, she shouldn't come, sex was forbidden until she found out if she was pregnant, and if she was, she should avoid it during the first trimester. But she wasn't pregnant. She knew it, and she might as well acknowledge it. Coming would be acknowledging it. She closed her eyes. Coming, she thought, would not only mean giving in to the pleasure she really, really deserved but letting herself have an intense orgasm now would be surrendering to Eli. Something had obviously happened to him, but what? Maybe the new-old fact that she didn't love him had percolated like a drop of rain into the soil, become absorbed in his skin and left a damp spot that now bothered him, gave him shivers.

Never mind, she told herself, never mind, because it wasn't Eli she was giving in to but some shared destiny, full of sorrow and who knew what else. The thought of leaving him appeared in her mind as a revelation. How strange that the idea had chosen this moment to introduce itself. It had always lurked there, hiding behind the day-to-day curtains, so why now? She knew it was there as a small consolation, a compensation for the static tedium forced upon her by the knowledge that she didn't love him, as if to say, *Here's something exciting to think about! Here's a possibility full of pizzazz and potential!* Because the fact that she didn't love him was a sort of closed case, gray and dead, whereas thinking about leaving him was full of life, almost like a pregnancy. She could grow it inside her, maybe feel it expanding and swelling, moving and kicking, and then she could think: there's the idea, growing a hand and a foot; there it goes, forming internal organs: heart, brain. There's a grain of sugar turning into something with hair and translucent eyelids and fingernails and a gaze.

She felt Eli's head between her thighs. The quick movements of his tongue always reminded her of a snake. When they were first together, she'd been disappointed to discover that when it came to oral sex Eli was a complete amateur: imprecise, hysterical. But then she got used to it, or didn't—now she knew she hadn't. Years ago, he asked her to teach him, to tell him what she liked, *what her style was.* She remembered the way he'd phrased it and it had turned her off, disgusted her in fact, like *Ginger* and *let me spoil you*, which sounded crass, unsophisticated. She thought about how innocent he was, and her boredom, which had been silenced by the immediate passion, now took on an added layer of compassion. "What's your style?" he'd asked earnestly, and she'd answered that she didn't have a style, she liked everything, and by doing this she'd actually told him to keep doing everything she didn't like. Or perhaps she'd just decided to learn to love the things he did, because she knew you couldn't teach a person how to fuck; it was a talent you were born with. And so she'd doomed that initial frustration to become the status quo.

She was close. She could feel her muscles, sentries standing on either side of a runway, making way for a wave of lazy pleasure that was just awaiting the signal. She thought about all the women who couldn't climax. She'd always felt sorry for them, but now she envied them a little, because their bodies spoke the truth while hers lied. She couldn't expect Eli to suspect that anything was wrong when she had such rocking orgasms, as he called them proudly. He enjoyed watching her come, shaking and squirming. "Yes!" he would encourage her. "Yes, my sweet!" When she thought about herself coming, she pictured the amputated tail of a lizard, and a moment before it was too late to change her mind, as she leaned back in the armchair feeling the currents gathering and linking inside her, she thought that if she wasn't so weak, if she had proper thigh muscles, she could have used them to clasp Eli's head like tongs and with one sharp movement break his collarbone. Because leaving him would be too complicated.

She heard him moan, knowing she was close, moaning his stupid encouragements into her, and it flooded her with sadness: all these years, all these fucks, he was in some togetherness he'd invented for himself, swept away by pleasure without asking himself any questions, like a child. And she would always watch him from above—climaxing, yes, but still cynical, and so lonely. She suddenly straightened up and slammed her knees shut, and Eli pulled back. "We can't," she said.

She looked in his face, searching for anger, disappointment, contempt, but his face was expressionless. He lay down on his back on the rug, and she could see his erection through the flimsy Bedouin *sharwal* pants he had recently started wearing around the house. Those pants, which usually made her laugh—why on earth would Eli wear *sharwals*?—suddenly saddened her: it was so *not* him that maybe it really *was*. She waited for him to say something cruel or accusatory, but he closed his eyes and said, "Let it go, Dafna. Just let it go."

She sat down next to him on the rug and said, "I can't." She put her hand on his stomach and slid it down over the surprisingly silky *sharwal* fabric. "But I can help you let go."

He held her hand. "No, Dafna, I don't feel like it. If you're not, then I'm not either. We'll just wait for tomorrow."

"Even though there's no point?"

He opened his eyes. "Even though there's no point." He closed his eyes again, and after a short pause he said he had to tell her something, something important that had been weighing on him for a long time. "But only if you promise not to make a big deal out of it."

"I promise," she said, but anxiety took hold of her. Why should she make that kind of promise?

Without opening his eyes, he asked if she remembered those prophetic moments he had sometimes, like on the day his father died.

"Yes, of course I remember."

He told her that six months ago, when they did the last IVF, he had one of those moments again. "And I didn't tell you because I didn't want to hurt you, because things between us were pretty lousy, remember?"

"Yes."

"And you wanted us to go to counseling, and I admit I didn't cooperate, and I don't know, it scares me, counseling, but if you want to, we
can think about it now."

She said it was okay, she understood, and the whole counseling
thing didn't seem that important to her anymore; it was just a temporary whim.

"I had that kind of moment then, that I didn't tell you about. I saw
us failing. And I saw our lives without children, Dafna. I saw us growing old together alone, just the two of us."

"Just the two of us?"

Eli seemed alarmed by his little confession. He held her body close
and stroked her hair. "Yes."

"So," she said, trying to sound matter-of-fact, "in this prophetic picture of yours, aren't there even any adopted kids? Or a child from a
donated egg?"

"Just us. Are you angry at me?"

"No, I'm not angry. Why would I be? You're entitled to have those
moments. And maybe it's true, who knows? But it's a good thing you
didn't tell me back then, I was pretty broken up. And it's good you told
me now. It's good that we're talking." But it wasn't good that they were
talking. Why talk? And about what?

He twirled a tuft of her hair around his finger and whispered, "Ginger. I haven't called you Ginger for ages."

"Which is fine with me."

He opened his eyes. "Really? You don't miss that?"

"No," she said, and thought, *Fuck those moments of his.*

"And you know what? You know why I'm telling you this now?"

"Because you feel guilty?"

"No, because I feel that maybe we can manage, just the two of us,
Dafna. Maybe just the two of us isn't such a tragedy, is it?"

She kept sitting next to him on the rug, looking at the *sharwals*, which
she suddenly found fascinating and which seemed to be the answer to a
question that she could not define but which was hovering low above
them, almost touching their heads.

She turned away and gazed at the living room set she found too bourgeois, and the coffee table she'd bought in the flea market back when

she'd lived in Kerem Hateimanim, and the cabinet that held the TV and
VCR and DVD, the ugly cabinet Eli had brought home one day from
IKEA, and then her eyes stopped at the long drapes that hung over the
French windows, sheer drapes with delicately embroidered butterflies
strewn with little beads. "What's that Indian thing doing in my house?"
Eli had asked when he first saw them, and now here he was wearing
sharwals. She wondered if in some way he was trying to get close to her,
and she knew it was not her he was trying to get close to but some new,
strange man inside him.

She practically ran back to the office through the rain, the big toy-store
bag slapping against her legs. When she walked into the old building
and up to the second-floor office, the secretary rushed up to her and
whispered, "He's got it in for you. Watch out."

She took her coat off and put the bag with the Power Ranger down
next to her desk and heard Gabi's footsteps coming down the hallway.
He came into her room wearing one of his expensive suits, but he looked
crushed. He sat down in the chair opposite her and said, "We have to
talk. And I mean really talk, Dafna." Then he said he was deeply disappointed in her. "Maybe it's slightly my fault, for putting such a sensitive
project in your hands. Maybe there was some negligence on my part.
But I think, Dafna, that you screwed up. I think that if you'd conducted
your interactions with this Adel a little differently, he would have shown
up. He would have been there with bells on."

"How should I have conducted it?" she asked, surprised by how
little she was interested in the answer.

"I'll tell you how." He started pacing back and forth across the room,
as he always did when he was about to give a speech. "Aggressively,
Dafna. Aggressively, forcefully. Not like you did, all lovey dovey. *Adel,
honey, please come, Mommy will get you a doll, okay?* I know Arabs,
Dafna. I know them, I worked with them, I saw them working in my
factories. I even had a few Arab shift managers. They're smooth, they're
manipulative, they stop at nothing!" He beat his fist on her desk. He
went over and stood by the window for a moment, then turned around.
"But I'm not letting this go. I'm going to call a friend of mine from the
police, someone who owes me a favor. He'll get me this Adel's phone

number. Did he call you here or on your cell?" Without waiting for an answer, he picked up her desk phone and dialed a number, looking at her or through her.

"Benny? It's Drixler. Listen, do you have the number of that guy Kedmi? I forget his first name. You know, the one from National HQ? . . . Yes, yes, that's the one. Will you get back to me? It's urgent. Thanks, buddy."

He put the phone down and stood up again. "You see? I can locate him in two shakes, and he'll be standing right here later today. Tomorrow morning, tops. Where's the doll?" He looked worried, and she indicated the bag with her chin. "Good. What were you saying, he doesn't have an entry permit? Then he'll get one. By tomorrow, he'll have one. You're going to see how things are done. Watch and learn, Dafna. Learn how to get things done in this country."

He leaned over again and picked up the phone. "Shit!" He put the receiver back down. "He's overseas. I know someone, this colonel who was on reserve duty with me. Total asshole, but I just met a mutual friend who told me they were going skiing with him. Fuck!"

As he talked, Dafna noticed that his lips were coated with a white layer, like foam frothing out of his mouth and drying in the air.

He shut his eyes for a moment and mumbled to himself. "Let's think. Let's think. Who else can I call?"

In her mind's eye she saw Eli getting up slowly off the rug and asking if she was coming to bed, and herself saying, *Soon.* He went into the bathroom and she kept sitting there, hugging her knees, resting her head on them. She heard the electric toothbrush, then a stream of urine, a massive yawn, and then, "When should I set the alarm for? Six?" The rustle of sheets, soft thud of the comforter, a fart, and then, "Dafna? Should I set the alarm for six?"

Yes, she said, knowing she hadn't spoken but whispered, and there was no chance he would hear her. A chill came in through the windows, even though they were closed, and gave her goose bumps. She could see her fair hairs bristling on her arm, and from the bedroom Eli's voice came again.

"I'm setting it for six, okay?" She said nothing, only wondered why he didn't come back to the living room and find her. Don't set the alarm for six, stop calling me and just come over, hear my answer in my silence, be frightened, come here in a panic to look for me. She knew he was already in bed, under the covers, turned over to his side; maybe he had already closed his eyes and gone to sleep.

She thought back to that day when she was five and had played hide-and-seek with her sister and a few neighborhood kids, just after they moved to Eden, a few weeks before her father died. She hid so well they couldn't find her. She crawled under the hedges between their house and Sonia Baruch's. It had never occurred to her that you could crawl under that mass of greenery, and when she found a hole, she lifted up the branches like a screen and covered herself with them, and her heart started to pound because she knew she would be the last one to be found.

She could hear the other children screeching when they were discovered, and then Irit said, "Now Dafna. Where's Dafna?" She heard them scurrying around the yard, slamming the toolshed door, running past her only inches from where she sat. Irit's voice grew impatient, then worried. There were huddled whispers, and then: "Mom! Dad!" She was surrounded by a halo of green light, and a late afternoon ray of sun warmed her forehead through the leaves. Although she couldn't see out, she knew her mother had come outside, and then her father, and she heard him shout hoarsely, "Dafna! Come on! Where are you? We give up!" She heard the rustle of his long cotton pants when he walked past the fence. "She's not here," he said.

"I bet she ran away," Irit said.

Her mother called her, angrily, and then she heard her father say, "Maybe she got too far away. Maybe she's lost." He sounded worried, as if he were about to cry, and she felt tears trickling down her cheeks. They tasted like leaves and dust, and she wanted to come out of the hiding place and stand facing everyone and declare, *Here I am!* But something told her she'd gone too far, she really was lost, and the only way she could come out was if someone found her.

It grew dark, and there was a great commotion in the yard. Neighbors gathered and consulted, Irit bawled, and the other kids whispered among themselves. "Maybe she's dead," one of them said. Her father handed flashlights out to the other men, and his voice no longer sounded like her father's voice. The world in general stopped sounding like the world she knew, and that was probably what eventually motivated her to emerge from the hedges into the dark yard, which was empty now, and to slowly, dreamily, walk to the house, climb up the five steps to the front porch, where a single bulb gave off a paltry glow, push in the screen door, and hear her mother asking in a tearful voice, "Daddy, is that you?" And that was what made her keep standing there silently, until her mother came out of the kitchen with a strange expression and wild eyes, and bow her head when her mother rushed over with both hands outstretched, and surrender to the hug she could feel coming as quickly as a draft, and look up at her mother for one moment, much less in fact, before the slap landed on her cheek.

And then the bath, and the hands tugging at her hair to wash it, tugging angrily, as if to undo the tangles. The bath was accompanied by her mother's hum, just like the one that only moments ago had surrounded her in the green world. Then the pajamas, stiff from sun-drying, and the bed, and the sight of her sister sleeping with her mouth agape, and then the shadow of her father standing in the doorway, blocking out the light.

Years later, when she was sixteen or seventeen and had a fight with her mother—they fought about everything and nothing in those days—she asked to spend the night next door, at Sonia Baruch's. "Anything but sleep in the same house with you," she told her mother. She lay on Sonia Baruch's scratchy couch in her living room and listened to her recount, for the umpteenth time, how they'd looked for her that day and hadn't found her. But that night Sonia added a confession. "It's funny, you know? If there was one moment in my life when I didn't regret not having children, it was then, Dafna, the night you got lost. I saw your mother and father die. They died for a few hours and then they came back to life. And I realized how lucky I was that I would never have to go through this thing that happened to your mother and father that night."

Gabi's cell phone ran and he answered quickly, repeating a number for Dafna to take down. "Awesome. Thanks a lot," he said, and grabbed the note. "Okay, we're making progress."

He looked at her with surprise when she opened her desk drawer, pulled out a large brown envelope, slid it over to his side of the table, and said, "Here." Then she opened her handbag and took out a receipt for two hundred and thirty shekels from the toy store. "These are my expenses. The envelope was on your desk, but I took it back because you didn't do anything with it. There's roughly eight hundred shekels here for parking and meetings in cafés, and this is the receipt for the Power Ranger. I want a reimbursement by tomorrow at the latest." Then she announced she was quitting. And before he could say anything, she said she had to make a personal call, and if he didn't mind, she would like to be alone.

"Sure, sure. But we'll talk later about this ridiculous resignation of yours, right?"

"No. And I'm not charging you for this morning's coffee because I forgot to get a receipt, so that one's on me, okay?"

Gabi murmured, "But I'll pay you back, just say how much. Of course I'll pay. I don't need the receipt." He got up, gave her a strange and slightly frightened look, left the room, and closed the door behind him.

She kept sitting at her desk, knowing she'd locked herself inside a bubble. No one would dare come close to her now. But instead of suffocation she felt the exact opposite: her breathing passages had been opened and her lungs were expanding, and with them her arteries and veins and all the little capillaries—everything was expanding in a huge yawn of indifference. Fuck them all.

She leaned back and put her feet up on the table and looked at her shoes, which she now saw were muddy and soaked. They were crushing the forms with the names and numbers and requests of the hundreds of Israelis who'd called in the last few months. On the top of one pile were the notes about a single mother from a suburb near Haifa who'd contacted them a few days ago with a particularly sad story. She pulled the form out from under her shoe and glanced at it, remembering her phone call with the woman. She'd said she had nothing to give her children. She had three kids and she had no food for them except bread and margarine, bread and jam. Then she said she hadn't sent the two older ones to school in September because she couldn't afford the books and supplies. When Dafna interrupted the woman's monologue and said, "Okay. What do you need most now? How can we help you?" the surprised woman had paused, breathed heavily, and finally said, "What do you mean?"

Dafna had patiently explained that CUSP was not a welfare office but a peace organization, dedicated to bringing Israelis and Palestinians closer. Their goal was to exchange items between the two populations. "For now, there hasn't been a great response from the Palestinian side, but we hope that down the line more people from the Territories will get in touch and we can get these exchanges going. Let's say, just as an example, that a Palestinian family gets a TV from an Israeli family, and an Israeli family, like yours, gets clothes or something from a Palestinian family."

At this point the woman broke in and said, "Never."

"Never what?"

"You want my kids to wear a terrorist's clothes?"

"But that's just it. Israelis and Palestinians in distress need to understand that they have a lot in common, that they're a force to be reckoned with."

"Have you people lost your mind? If I had a spare TV, or something I didn't need, why would I give it to some Arab who might flip out tomorrow and blow himself up at a bus station? Why? Tell me why?"

Dafna promised to see what they could do. She thought there was a family that wanted to give away old textbooks, which might be helpful. The woman was quiet, and Dafna could hear her disappointed breaths, until eventually she said, "You know what? Never mind. Thank you very much, and may God bless you, you shits." And she hung up.

When she went home that day there was an innocent moment, truly innocent, but too short, when she waited for Eli to come home so she could tell him about the woman. He would laugh and say, "Those people think they deserve everything. Now do you understand why the poor are poor?" But that innocent moment vanished long before he got home, and when he did arrive and asked what was new, she said, "Same as usual." And he said he was beat, and she said, "Me, too."

She put the form back on top of the stack and listened to the water clanging in the old gutter. She was glad she'd had something to eat at the café, because she felt suddenly weak. Not anything scary like yesterday's weakness, but something sweet and comforting, as if this weakness were a tender stamp sealing a very difficult decision. The relief of failure, of failing in such a comprehensive, decisive way—it was wonderful.

From now on she would turn the volume all the way down, she

thought, and live in a bubble of silence like the one that surrounded her now. And indeed, the normally noisy office had gone completely quiet, and were she someone else, were she the person she'd decided to be from now on, she could even fall asleep. She closed her eyes. On the screens of her eyelids she saw a group of men doing a sad tribal dance around a little fire: Eli and Adel and Gabi and Professor Ferber, and her father, too, his orange hair burning in a light that shone in—but from where? She realized the room was lit up and couldn't resist opening her eyes. The sky was still overcast, but a single ray of sun had broken through and flooded her office. She closed her eyes again and the light disappeared, and she wondered if the room was dark once more. But she reminded herself that she didn't care. No, she was trying to fall asleep, and now she could see nothing. The dancing men were gone, and she was alone again. The phone rang—or maybe it didn't; she didn't care. Two, three, four rings, and then silence. Then a knock on the door, and she opened her eyes quickly. "Why aren't you answering?" Dikla said. "Someone needs you urgently. A woman named Etti."

Dafna said, "Okay, put her through," even though she couldn't remember who Etti was. She picked up the phone and said, "Etti?" as if eons had gone by since seven-thirty that morning, when Etti had sat behind the nurses' counter and given her the regular fingers-crossed sign, and Dafna had smiled awkwardly, as if to say, What for? Save the finger-crossing for someone else.

Now she heard Etti's voice: "Just a minute." She said nothing. Then Etti's voice again: "Dafna? Hold on a minute, okay?" She heard her talking with one of the other nurses, explaining something, then laughing hoarsely. Then she whispered into the receiver, "Just a minute, Dafna, okay?" And that minute seemed to stretch into infinity, until she heard Etti's voice again.

"Dafna? Are you with me? Are you sitting down? Didn't I tell you? I told you it would work out in the end! Didn't I tell you? I told you, didn't I? Well, who told you it would work out in the end, hey? Who?"

PART FIVE

JANE

What would she have done without Barbara? The Middle Eastern glare abruptly replaced the dim Atlantic skies, and passengers around her began to wake, stretching, yawning, blinking, walking back and forth to the bathrooms, numbly anticipating breakfast. All this roused her too, although she hadn't slept a wink the whole flight, and only now was she able to make a mental list of all the things her good friend had done for her the day before.

George had picked up the phone, and his "Hi, Jane. What's up? What time is it, anyway?" was meant to inform her that, as usual, she had interrupted their morning fuck. "Ever since I hit fifty," he liked to tell her, "we've been doing it in the morning. First thing. You should try it, it's another world."

Barbara would elbow him, or giggle, and say, *Oh, really, shush*. Not because she was embarrassed by the way her sex life, at fifty, had suddenly become wild and daily, but because she hated to see her new partner throwing salt on her old friend's wound: other than a desperate episode with a widowed painter, a pathetic beatnik, as she now thought of him, Jane had not been with anyone for ten years. No one. And although she envied Barbara a little, because there was no doubt that she had blossomed, physically at least, since meeting George—"Who would have thought I'd fall in love with an office-supply-chain store owner? Me!"—Jane couldn't understand what she was doing with that stuffed turkey. The only art he appreciated, or even understood, was a fifteen-foot-tall office stapler that stood at the entrance to each of his stores.

Barbara was at her house within fifteen minutes. Jane was waiting for her by the kitchen window, leaning on the sink, trembling. Only when she saw the Honda coasting into the parking spot and her friend jumping out with her big colorful handbag did she grasp the actual emergency that had prompted her to call, and when she heard the front door open and the deep, throaty voice call out, "Jane?" she collapsed on the floor and started to sob.

There had been other emergencies, many in the last decade: crises with Roni, gallery rejections, grants not awarded, and that terrible year with the beatnik who was so depressed and self-involved that he hadn't allowed *her* to be depressed and self-involved, which was why she'd been attracted to him in the first place—Barbara was right—to distract herself from her own self. And there had been countless minor emergencies, always conducted in the same exact way: a phone call to Barbara, at any time of the day or night, Barbara's "Wait for me, I'll be right there," the sound of the car door slamming, and the hoarse voice asking—panting—"Jane?" And then the collapse.

In the morning—which was yesterday, now that she had crossed the international dateline—Barbara had lifted Jane from the hardwood kitchen floor and positioned her heavy, slow body, which always reminded Jane of a camel, next to her, encircling Jane in her arms. She whispered, "Tell me what happened, tell me everything," as her large rear end squeezed Jane's thigh against the kitchen cabinet on which she leaned, exhausted. She couldn't speak, only whimper, because she realized that this time it was a different kind of emergency and that, unlike all the other times she'd claimed her life was over, this time it was the truth.

But there were things that had to get done. She had to call the airline, she had to let the curator know she wouldn't make it to Manhattan next week to set up the exhibition and someone else must do it for her, and she had to hear Angelica's sweet voice wishing her the best, wishing her a miracle, and adding, "I'll think about you over there in Israel. Take care of yourself—it's dangerous there, isn't it?" while remaining formal and slightly miffed at the sudden change in plans.

She had to get hold of the contractor who was supposed to come tomorrow to fix the heat, and she had to stop sobbing, which she could not do until Barbara had stood her up and said, "Jane, I know what you're going through, but you simply have to pull yourself together."

And she had to bite her tongue and not say, No, you don't know what I'm going through. You don't have kids. It was not just because she loved her friend, and not just because she was grateful for Barbara being in her life at all that she'd never said that, but because she knew what Barbara would say, because she'd said it before in all sorts of contexts: "You're a shitty mother, Jane. A shitty mother." And she was right. Barbara didn't want children for precisely that reason: so she wouldn't find herself one day shaken out of a deep sleep or a session in bed with some geriatric turkey and hear someone on the other end of the line informing her that her child was lying unconscious in intensive care.

The flight attendants started coming down the aisle with breakfast, and Jane reached out automatically to unlock the tray on the seatback in front of her, even though she had no intention of eating. She reconstructed what she'd done after Barbara had told her there was a seat on a flight that left in two hours; the next one was tomorrow, so they had to rush to the airport. "Now, now!" Barbara had harried her. She'd proceeded to pack Jane's flight bag. She'd run back and forth between the bedroom and the kitchen to ask if she should pack this shirt, that pair of underwear, this towel, that sweater. "Is this your comfortable bra? What's the weather like in Israel, did you ask him?"

Jane had nodded like a doll, saying, "Pack whatever you think is best," and wondered why on earth she would have asked Mark about the weather. He called when she was still in bed and told her tearfully that Roni had been run over that morning, three hours ago, and was in intensive care, unconscious and sedated, and they'd drained a blood clot from her brain, or near her brain, she couldn't quite understand, and now they were waiting until tomorrow, and it wasn't clear what would happen. She could barely understand him because he was calling on his cell phone. "We don't know what's going to happen, Jane!" She wasn't sure if he was yelling because of the bad line or from panic. "When do you think you can get here, tomorrow?"

Why on earth would she have asked him about the weather when the only thing she could say was, "Oh, God! God, Mark!" and ask, "But how does she look? Tell me the truth!"

The line had suddenly cleared and she'd heard him sniffle, swallow, and say, "Okay. She looks okay." Then he told her matter-of-factly about an abdominal injury. The car had flung her "almost twenty *meters*." Jane was afraid to ask if twenty meters was a lot or a little, because she'd forgotten what a meter was. "But the stomach isn't the main thing. She has really serious head injuries, Jane. She has loads of tubes in her now, and she's on a ventilator. They'll stop tomorrow and do something called a reversal."

When Jane asked, What? and he repeated *reversal* and explained it, she said Oh but she was confused, and in her mind she saw her girl being run over in reverse, as if the car that had hit her had been driving backward, and then it drove forward and back again, trucks and buses and cars and motorbikes, all of them running over her daughter, crushing her body back and forth, the same body that five months ago she had seen submersed in a bubble bath right here in her bathroom.

She'd walked in by mistake, disoriented by a fight they'd had a few minutes earlier in the kitchen and thinking Roni was shut up in her bedroom, as usual. Roni's breasts were hovering above the water and a black patch peeked out between the white peaks of foam. She was holding the notebook she always carried around. She stared at Jane and said, "Could I have some privacy, please? Do you mind?" Jane had apologized, and the girl had yelled, "Get out!"

After Mark's call she had dragged herself out of bed with great difficulty, padded into the bathroom, collapsed on the toilet, and sat there for several minutes, while Mark's truncated voice played like a sound track in her mind: *Not clear what will happen . . . reversal . . . twenty meters*. It was lucky she was still holding the cordless phone, because even before getting up from the toilet she called Barbara. She considered just sitting there until Barbara arrived, but she managed to lug herself to the kitchen, glance at the clock, try and figure out what time it was in Israel, and realize, like the touch of a blade in the midst of all this misunderstanding, that when she had turned off the TV and gone to the medicine cabinet for a sleeping pill (she objected to medication on principle, but the upcoming show had been making her anxious), swallowed the little pink pill, looked at the clock—3:45—and noted the time so she would know how many hours she'd slept when she woke up the next morning shortly before noon, both refreshed and blurry, as she had the last time she took a pill, which was in fact the first time in her life, last summer, the night before Roni went back to Israel, after a particularly bitter argument, and she had barely managed to get up the next morning to take her to the airport, and when she'd got out of bed and found Roni in the kitchen with her suitcase next to her and the notebook open in front of her, Roni had said, without looking up, "So now you're taking sleeping pills, Mom? That's what you're into now?"

She had replied defensively, "Oh, come on. One! I took one! For the first time ever. And the last, I hope." Roni had scolded her, but she hadn't bothered retorting that she knew Roni smoked, so she could lay off the health sermons, and since it was late, and since—yes, now she understood this, it was terrible to understand it then, and even worse to remember it now—since she wanted the visit to be over and for Roni to go back to Israel and leave her in peace, she'd said, "Yes, this is the last time, okay?"

Roni had given her a sideways glance that looked mocking and full of scorn, although maybe she'd wanted to make peace, who knows? Who the hell could ever figure out what she wanted? And then she'd just said, "Okay." And now, four hours ago, at 3:45, when she took the second sleeping pill of her life, probably at the very moment she swallowed it, guilty and determined, her girl had crossed that street.

"You're taking a coat, right?" Barbara's voice hummed over her as she led her from the kitchen to the bedroom and sat her down on the bed. She picked out travel clothes and started to dress her. When she had trouble with the stockings, she said, "Come on, help me out, get up for a minute." Jane tried but couldn't, and she said, "Never mind, just get me a pair of pants." But Barbara insisted: "Just one more second, lift up your foot." Then she stuffed Jane's fossilized feet into a pair of long boots, which squeezed her calves and were a bad choice for traveling but she couldn't find the strength to say anything, and Barbara zipped up the boots and got up off the floor and said, "Okay. You're ready."

When she followed Barbara to the doorway, she thought about the sleeping pill, which might have been timely, even though she should have been more alert now, so that each and every sense could taste the sharpness of the disaster. That was why she had wanted to give birth to Roni naturally, at home. When she stood outside, leaning on the frozen Honda, waiting for Barbara to unlock the door, she remembered the argument she and Mark had conducted throughout the pregnancy. "Okay, natural birth, no medication, but why at home, Jane? It's dangerous," Mark had said. And she'd argued—how self-confident she'd been back then, how at peace with the gamble—that statistics showed that giving birth at home with a midwife was much safer than in a hospital. She said that in a hospital they would drug her with painkillers, and she wanted to feel the pain: feeling was being in control. Eventually Mark gave in, only because Hadassah Hospital was a stone's throw away, in case of emergency. And how could she have known then—when the heavy, sedating pregnancy had distracted her from her regret over having agreed to go to that terrible country in the first place—how could she have known what would happen, as she sat in that big room with the stone floor watching Mark build a cradle. It was so wonderful to sit there by the stove and think that two or three weeks from then, right there in the continuously improving house, this incredibly natural thing would happen, right in their bed, facing the window onto the wadi, which looked especially green and almost not-Israeli that winter. She even thought that perhaps this place would become her home after all; perhaps, as Mark said, it was a question of time, patience, and hope, and perhaps she had to give birth there to feel she belonged.

"Where are you going to stay?" Barbara asked. "Do you have to get a hotel or something?"

Jane shook her head. "I imagine I'll be at the hospital the whole time. I mean, you know, if—" She couldn't go on. That *if* could not be completed. "If I want to, I'm sure I can stay with Mark. Or with Alona."

"She's great, Alona, isn't she?" Barbara said, and Jane found herself nodding in agreement. "Have you ever met her?" Barbara asked.

"No, she's picking me up at the airport."

Fortunately there was no traffic, and when Barbara asked in a panic if she'd taken her passport, wallet, and credit cards, she nodded heavily, leaned her head on the frozen window, and looked out at the weekend snow. Most of it had melted, but there were still some giant piles left by the plows.

She remembered Roni's first snow. It was in February. She remembered because they had just celebrated Roni's second birthday, and when they got up in the morning and saw the white powder covering the yard, Mark was excited as only an Israeli can be upon seeing snow.

He bundled Roni up in layers and layers, and she toddled around the house and screeched, "No, no!" They thought she didn't want to go outside, but when they went out and she picked up a handful of snow and put it to her lips and said, "No, no!" with a huge grin, they realized she meant *snow*.

Barbara asked what she was thinking about—they had reached the airport entrance—and she said she was remembering Roni's first snow, in Jerusalem. Barbara smiled and asked if she remembered that crazy weekend in Vermont—how long ago was it, three years? Four?—when the three of them had gone skiing. "How old was Roni then, thirteen? Remember how she had a crush on that cute ski instructor?"

"Jamie," Jane said, suddenly remembering his name. "His name was Jamie."

Barbara laughed. "That's right! Remember how she spent the whole weekend sitting by the fire with her back turned to us, writing poems for him, or whatever they were? She was so cute. All secretive, remember?"

They said goodbye at the check-in. Barbara hugged her and made her promise to call as soon as she landed. "Or whenever you can, okay?" Jane walked away and thought about that cute blond Jamie, who had treated Roni so chivalrously, even though it was obvious that dozens of little girls fell in love with him every day. Jamie, the perfect gentleman, seemed to be walking beside Jane as she boarded the plane, standing next to the flight attendant who greeted her and directed her to her seat, smiling his pearly-teethed American smile but clucking as if to say, *How? How could you let that girl go?*

Because maybe if she'd refused, maybe if she'd said *Over my dead body* when Roni had asked to go back to her father at the age of twelve, explaining with heartbreakingly didactic maturity that it would be best for both of them, that it would save their relationship, enable them to be what they'd always wanted to be: mother and daughter, daughter and mother, not two women who fought all the time—that's what she'd said, two women who fought all the time—maybe if she'd said *Never!* instead of capitulating—although truthfully it was not a capitulation but a huge sigh of relief—she wouldn't now be finding herself boarding this plane on her way to the country she'd fled twelve years ago, to see her daughter.

The older woman sitting next to her asked the flight attendant how long before landing, and she said two hours. She collected the trays, including Jane's, which hadn't been touched. "Anything to drink?" she asked, and Jane asked for herbal tea. The woman next to her, who'd slept the whole way, asked in broken English if she lived in Israel or in the States. Jane said, In the States. She asked if she was visiting or taking a vacation, and Jane said, Visiting. She leaned her head on the window and closed her eyes, hoping the woman would leave her alone. The increasingly bright light penetrated her eyelids, becoming bothersome and demanding. It reminded her of Camus's *The Stranger*. She'd always hated that light, a murderous glare that had persecuted her for six years, flooding the floor of their house every morning as it perched on the edge of a terrace, its single balcony suspended in midair. You could never escape that light except on a few rare winter days, like that snowy day in February and the morning Roni was born, when the sun had seemed to hold back, waiting for the baby to come into the world.

She heard the flight attendant saying, "Excuse me. Your tea?" and she opened her eyes and saw the attendant and the woman next to her looking at her worriedly. She smiled and said thank you, took the plastic cup of hot water and the herbal tea bag, and straightened up in her seat. She stared at a pastry on a little dish in front of her, a tiny swirl of cinnamon and raisin. "I thought you might like something to eat," the flight attendant said apologetically. "I noticed you didn't touch your breakfast." Jane thanked her again but pushed the dish aside and closed her eyes. The captain's voice came over the speaker, wishing the passengers a good morning and reporting their estimated landing time: six-oh-five, ten minutes early. He said it was raining in Tel Aviv, with a temperature of twelve degrees Celsius. She couldn't remember if that was hot or cold. She'd left home wearing a long beige suede coat with cuffs and a lining made of curly, sheeplike artificial fur. It was rolled up in the overhead cabin, on top of her flight bag. She had no idea what was in the bag, but she trusted Barbara to have known what she needed.

When she opened her eyes and lifted the cup to her lips, aware of her neighbor's curious or perhaps worried look, her heart winced when she remembered how much Roni couldn't stand Barbara. On her last summer visit, the terrible visit when they hadn't stopped fighting—and that time, she thought, they really had fought like two women—Roni had concluded that her relationship with Barbara was pathological and dependent. What had surprised Jane, or rather infuriated her, was the sudden change in Roni's attitude toward Barbara, a woman who had been there all those years like a sort of spare mother.

"What's your story with Barbara? Anyone would think you were some kind of lesbian, Mom," she'd said. "Not that I have any problem with that, God forbid. If you're into that, go for it."

There was no point in explaining or defending herself, and certainly not in stepping on the land mine again by telling Roni she wasn't mature enough to understand how important it was to have another person, a close friend, someone to rely on. But she had inadvertently stepped on a more lethal mine when she said, "Let's find out, Roni, what bothers you so much about my relationship with Barbara. Could it be that you're a little jealous?"

Boom! Things went downhill after that, as they sat in a diner trying to have a relaxed Sunday brunch like two friends. Her daughter's stunned, mocking eyes opened wide and shot out two laser beams. "Me, jealous? What exactly would I have to be jealous of?" She laughed bitterly. "Of the fact that Barbara has become your mother? Tell me exactly what I might have to be jealous of, because I'm interested, really. I'm saying this without any cynicism, I swear. Maybe you think I'm jealous of Barbara because she has some fat idiot fucking her? Or maybe you're the one who's jealous?" She thrust her fork into her stack of pancakes, leaned back, crossed her arms over her chest, and waited. And Jane, instead of answering, instead of staying there and fighting, did what she always did when they fought: she got up, ran out to the parking lot, and shut herself in the car to cry.

She had tried on several occasions, in their rare moments of tranquillity, to share things with her daughter. She'd tried to treat her like a friend: not an innocent girl who needed protection but a young, intelligent woman who might be able to understand intuitively what could happen to herself one day. She'd tried to tell her that, yes, she was right, in some way she did envy Barbara. She'd tried to tell her—but how?— that she had felt like a stranger to her own body for ten years. That even though she knew time took its toll, skin naturally grew less taut and started to sag, and something happened to the tissue, as if it suddenly had more space to move in, something in her was still convinced that the real damage was not caused by time but because no one had touched her for ten years. No one.

But Roni didn't want to hear. She said it disgusted her to talk about that stuff. "I'm not your friend, Mom," she announced. Jane secretly seethed: Wasn't that why they had separated, so they could be friends? What now? What would happen now?

That Sunday morning, Roni had come out of the diner, walked up to the car, tapped on the window, and said in a measured, mature voice, "You forgot to pay, Mom." She'd quickly pulled out her wallet and Roni had taken it and said, "I'll be right back. Pull yourself together, okay? I don't feel like sitting in the car with you when you're crying. That's not what I came here for. I didn't want to come at all, you know, but Dad made me. He said it's the only thing you have in your life." She went back into the diner to pay the bill while Jane only cried louder. In her imagination she could already hear the phone conversation she would have later with Barbara: "What am I going to do with her? What am I going to do with all that hatred?"

Now on the airplane, she panicked when she realized she would have to go through passport control soon. She thought back to her first probing interrogation, when she landed in Israel with Mark, burned in her memory even though it had been twelve years ago. "Lerner? That's a Jewish name, isn't it? But your mother wasn't Jewish, so you aren't either." That was the first shock. "How do they know? Where is it written?" she asked Mark, who had optimistically told her when they married that she could convert if she wanted to. At the airport, he answered, "They know everything." It didn't do any good that they'd been married at the courthouse in Chicago. On the contrary: for some reason that just made the officials even angrier, and they held her for three hours in a little room where, she now remembered, there was also a Muslim family from the same flight. A man, a woman, and a baby, and for all she knew they might still be sitting there in that little room, the baby now a grown boy.

Eventually she was given a tourist visa and sent out to Mark, who was waiting outside. He hugged her and, attempting to put a pathetic Band-Aid on a knife wound, said, "You don't have to convert for me. But if you do, we'll have an easier life." In the taxi on the way to Jeru-

salem he prattled on about immigrant rights, financial benefits, mort-
gages. "And if we have kids, you know. . . . Just think about it." Neither
of them knew she was already pregnant.

When they bought the house in Ein Kerem and moved in, she was in
her eighth month, and she quickly made friends with a few immigrant
women who lived in the area, but she kept insisting that she would not
convert. Not because she had any principles about religion, and not
because she didn't want to accept the state's barbaric laws, as she called
them, but because since the age of seventeen, when her mother had
swallowed a whole bottle of sleeping pills in a Chicago hotel room and
within less than a month her father had moved in with his new girlfriend, who might in fact not have been very new—he had tried to
explain but she hadn't wanted to listen—and asked her to come and
live with him and that woman and her two kids, and she'd refused—
ever since then she'd decided to erase her previous life, her father, and
the questions left behind by her mother, and to start fresh: no parents,
no identity, no anger.

Since turning fifty last summer, she'd started to wonder if perhaps
that decision to never belong to any place or any person, or even to any
idea, had been childish. She was fifty years old, and other than Mark
she'd never had a meaningful relationship with a man. She'd only recently
settled down, having bought the farm in upstate New York for pennies,
both because it was a fifteen-minute drive from Barbara's house and
because she was tired of moving and the community college where Barbara taught history had offered her a job.

"I won't let anyone dictate an identity to me," she insisted, when her
American friends from Ein Kerem warned her that it would be difficult
for her child.

"That's how it works here, you can't change it," they said. "What's
the big deal? It's just a ceremony, what do you care?"

She broke down about a year after Roni was born and started studying for her conversion. At first she treated the whole thing with bemused
cynicism, but as the ceremony grew closer she became more anxious,
and eventually felt such a surge of resistance that she almost didn't
show up. If not for Mark, who took her to the exam, waited outside,
and said, "When you finish we'll go to a bar and get trashed"—if not
for Mark she would have fled back to the States, where she had nothing

except the promise that she could be anyone and no one. When her conversion papers arrived in the mail, she sank into a depression, the same kind she'd succumbed to when she'd walked into the airport two years earlier and felt not like someone getting a new identity but like someone whose lack of identity—that private, untamed thing—had been taken away from her forever.

She never forgave Mark for that, and she could never explain it to Roni. But that was what had led her, three years later—when Roni was a Jewish, bilingual, happy five-year-old—to announce to Mark, who already knew, that she couldn't take it anymore. The fact that she hadn't learned Hebrew was no accident, even though she could get by when necessary and engage in small talk with the kindergarten teachers, the doctors, and the neighbors. And it was not by chance that she had not done anything with her career. When they'd left Chicago she was at the beginning of her path, a recent graduate, and now what? Should she join the gang of American women, "the ceramicists," she called them, who had forged a mini-identity for themselves: women with artistic tendencies who taught kids how to work with clay and sold their wares in all sorts of charming little stores? Now what?

Mark couldn't say, and in fact he knew she didn't want an answer but a release. She hoped with all her heart that he'd say, "Over my dead body are you taking the girl!" But he didn't. He just explained patiently that he understood her need to leave, even though he didn't think she'd even tried to live in Israel and had arrived with preconceptions, but all right. He said he was done with the American chapter of his life. "But if you feel a bit stifled in Jerusalem," he added, "let's move to Tel Aviv. Maybe that will help. Or to the country; do you want to live in the countryside?" He knew that wasn't it, and that even if he agreed to go back to the States with her, he couldn't cure her *lone-wolf syndrome*, as he called it. He couldn't alleviate the claustrophobia that overcame her whenever she was with another person, anyone, even if that person was her child.

The soft chime sounded when the seat-belt sign came on. She straightened up in her seat and buckled up. "We're landing," her neighbor said cheerfully, and Jane said, "Yes, we're landing."

Everything went smoothly. No one questioned her when she handed her U.S. passport over—her Israeli one had expired eight years ago and she hadn't bothered to renew it—and the clerk nonchalantly stamped it and wished her a pleasant stay in Israel. Since she had no checked luggage, she skipped the wait at the carousel, walked quickly past the customs officials, and found herself in a big new hall that hadn't been there twelve years ago. Suddenly it struck her: How would she and Alona recognize each other? She scouted around for a woman who looked like the one in the pictures Roni sometimes brought of her little brother and sister. She saw no one who fit the description in the crowds, and the contemplative, groggy fatigue that had cradled her the whole way vanished at once and gave way to panic. No one was here to meet her, and she didn't even know what hospital her daughter was in.

She put her bag down, and the coat on top of it, and was about to look for a pay phone to call Mark, when a woman rushed in through the automatic doors and stood on her tiptoes to scan the arriving passengers. Jane recognized the woman from the photographs immediately.

"Jane!" the woman called out and hurried over, and for a moment it seemed as if they were about to hug, but Alona put her hand on Jane's shoulder, and she put her hand on Alona's arm, and they exchanged sad little smiles. Alona glanced at her flight bag and coat. "Is that it?" She said yes, and the question seemed not to have been about the bag and coat but about something more general: *Is that it?* As if she'd expected someone else, not this short woman with graying hair and a ridiculous sweater with deer skipping across it.

"I'm parked really close," Alona said, in excellent English with almost no accent. They walked out quickly, and Alona reached out as if to help with the bag or coat. She had no purse, and wore a short leather jacket and flared jeans, the kind Roni liked.

"On the plane they said it was raining here," Jane said hesitantly.

"We had a couple of really stormy days, but it stopped."

When they got into the car, Jane asked if the weather had had anything to do with the accident.

"No, I don't think so. The driver, that asshole, was going too fast. He was doing ninety, the police said." Jane asked what that was in miles, and Alona said, "I don't know, but a lot." She told her the night had been okay; she'd just talked to Mark. "There's no change, which is good, at least for now, because you know, even though she's sedated, there could be a deterioration. But that didn't happen, thank God. Around noon they're going to taper off the sedatives and see how she responds, you know—see if she wakes up. You'll get really scared when you see all the tubes, but she's all right. I mean, she's whole. She looks like the same Roni, but . . ."

She nodded, and wanted to say, *But I don't know.*

Alona, quite the chatterbox, said, "You really look alike, you know? Much more than in the pictures."

"You think? People say that about us, but I don't see it."

"People say it about me and Maya, too, and I don't really see it either. Ido looks like Mark, that's definitely true. He's a baby Mark."

They both smiled at the idea, as if the combination of words had provoked maternal feelings in them.

"At least he got about an hour's sleep. I was afraid he'd stay up all night. You know how crazy he gets when he doesn't sleep."

Jane nodded, even though she didn't know what Alona was talking about.

"You probably didn't sleep at all?" She looked at Jane.

"No, not a minute."

"Well, sure. I didn't either."

And then Jane understood Mark. She understood why he'd fallen in love with this woman. There was something alive and full of energy in her garrulousness, whereas with her, she knew, life had been too quiet, too goyish.

They crawled behind a long line of cars trying to get onto the main road. "There's not a minute without traffic jams in this country," Alona said. "But it must be worse in the States, isn't it?"

She shook her head. "Not really. Not where I live."

"Roni says it's lovely where you live. She says it's so beautiful it's like a garden of Eden."

Jane looked at her and her eyes filled with tears. "Really? Is that what she said?"

"Yes, she really loves that place. What's it called?"

"Woodstock."

"Of course, how could I forget? Woodstock! Wow!"

"Yes, I live nearby, in a small town."

"Roni says it's amazing there, real countryside, not like here."

She wiped her eyes and saw Alona stealing a look—how often had Roni told her she loathed the place where she lived?

"There's some toilet paper somewhere," Alona said, when she heard Jane sniveling. She reached out to open the glove compartment.

"I'm fine."

"It must be somewhere in the back."

Jane turned back and looked at the two car seats, which looked very old and soiled, and at the pile of stuff between them: books, stuffed animals, empty snack bags. She smiled. "How old are Maya and Ido?"

"Maya will be five soon, and Ido's three and a half."

"Right, right. I forgot their exact ages. I saw pictures of them over the summer. They look cute."

After a pause, Alona said, "We should be there in about ten minutes, I hope." She let out a huge sigh. "Can you believe it? I can't even grasp that it's happened. She's supposed to be visiting you in three weeks, right?"

Jane nodded.

"Well, you can stay with us—with me and the kids, I mean—for as long as you want. And with Mark, too, of course. With one of us. Or both, if you feel like it."

She nodded. "Thanks, we'll see." And the tears started welling up again.

"Just so you know, in terms of a place to stay, it's really no trouble. We both have big houses and we live within walking distance of each other." After a while she suddenly said, "Fuck! Sorry. I thought if I took this route I'd save us a few minutes, but look at this!"

She looked at the rows of cars on either side. "Is this a new road?"

"No, it's Geha Highway. You haven't been here for . . . how long, ten years?"

"Twelve."

"So you haven't been here since Roni came back, not even for a visit?"

She shook her head.

"It's totally changed, hasn't it?"

She looked around. "There are more cars."

"You can say that again. Too many." She sighed. "I'm dying for a cigarette. Do you mind if I smoke?"

Even though she hated cigarette smoke, Jane said, "No, go ahead, it's fine."

Alona took a cigarette out of her coat pocket and pushed in the lighter. She explained that she normally didn't smoke in the car because of the kids, but this morning she hadn't had a cigarette yet, and at the hospital you really couldn't, you had to go outside, which was a pain. "Are you sure you don't mind?"

"I'm sure." She watched Alona blow smoke out the open window. "Roni smokes too, doesn't she?"

"Yes, she does. Mark has a tough time with that. You probably do, too."

"Yes, but you know—what can I do?"

"Nothing. You can't do anything. I also started smoking when I was fourteen, and I hid it from my parents."

"Fourteen? Has Roni been smoking since she was fourteen?"

Alona sounded startled. "Not really. Just a little. Here and there."

"And now? Is she a heavy smoker?"

"What's heavy?" Alona put her cigarette out in the ashtray.

"I don't know . . . a pack a day?"

"Honestly, I don't know. Maybe a pack, maybe less."

Jane looked at this handsome woman, who was drumming her fingers on the wheel as if to spur on the cars in front of them. She wanted to say, *What difference does it make now?* But she didn't.

As if reading her thoughts, or perhaps sharing them, Alona smiled at her. "We'll work on it when she recovers, right? Mark and I will have an anti-smoking campaign. We'll all help her together."

As they drove past the guard and into the hospital parking lot, Alona said, "So you haven't seen Mark for twelve years either?"

Jane said she'd seen him when he used to come and visit Roni.

"Oh, right. I forgot. So it's only five years, really." Then she added quickly, "He hasn't changed. Physically, I mean. A little more gray hair, but he's still the same."

They got out of the car. Jane wasn't sure what to do with her flight bag and coat.

"Leave them in the car, they'll just get in your way," Alona said. "If you want something later I can get it for you."

With a strange sense of anxiety, she left her belongings in the car.

She detected no trace of winter in the air, and as she walked with Alona she felt as if she were leaving behind her helplessness, not her bag and coat. When they entered the hospital, she could feel her body anticipating the encounter with her daughter and her ex-husband. Her limbs tightened up, charged, but her brain was still lax and slightly muggy.

"That's right," Alona said, as they got into the crowded elevator. "When she came back to live with us, she came on her own. It was just before Maya was born, in September. That's right," she repeated, as if it were important. "She did come on her own." They walked down the corridor and Alona said, "You know what I just remembered?" Her chattering was obviously intended to numb, to pad the hallway that ended with a pair of automatic doors and a sign reading SURGICAL INTENSIVE CARE in English and Hebrew. "I remembered that when Mark came home with her from the airport I was in my sixth month with Maya, and I was pretty big. And the first thing Roni did when she came in was to come up to me and hug my belly. Funny, isn't it?"

They walked through the doors and Alona fell silent, as if it were obvious that there was no talking on this side of the door and no reminiscing. "You'll have to put on a robe and mask," she whispered, "and they don't let more than one person in at a time. It's annoying, but you can't do anything about it."

She said she'd ask the nurse to call Mark, but just then the nurse walked up to them and smiled. "Are you Roni's mother?" she asked in Hebrew. She immediately corrected herself and asked again in English, and Jane said it was okay, she understood a little Hebrew. The nurse said she'd call Mark and went into the room.

He appeared immediately, coming through the doors wearing a pale yellow paper gown, open in the back, and a mask on his face. He hurried over to them. Jane noticed his hair had indeed gone a little gray but was still more black than white. He suddenly stood still, then went over to the wall, hid his face in his hands, and started to sob. Alona was about to run to him, but Jane sensed her body suddenly brake, uncertain which of them was supposed to go to him. She looked at Alona the way you look at an old friend who can tell you what to do, and Alona motioned—*Go to him*—so Jane rushed over and wrapped her arms around Mark and held him to her body, feeling his tears dampening her sweater.

"Jane," Mark whispered into her neck, "Jane." He looked up at her, and she thought she saw the same look from twelve years ago, when he'd said goodbye to her and Roni at the airport, next to the escalator. The look of a child whose child is being taken away, she'd thought of it back then, as she'd watched him pick Roni up for one last hug, smile, and say, "So we'll see each other in two months, right? Daddy will come visit."

"How is she?" Jane asked, and he took the mask off and said there was no change. The night had passed quietly, and soon the department chair would come and they'd decide when to start the reversal. "Don't be alarmed by the tubes," he said, as he walked her to the gown and mask station. "You can barely see her." She said Alona had already warned her. Then she looked back at Alona, who stood a few steps away.

"I'll be in the waiting room. Are you coming?" Alona said.

Mark nodded.

Jane said, "Why don't you go downstairs and get a drink? Because I'll probably spend a long time with her."

Mark and Alona looked at each other, as if consulting, and Alona said, "Okay, we'll go down for half an hour or so."

When she walked through the doors she saw a woman of around her age sitting next to a young man's bed. The woman looked up and smiled, as if she knew who Jane was and had been expecting her, and her eyes directed Jane toward the adjacent bed. But she kept standing in the doorway, taking in the room, the windowless walls, and the back of another woman's head, covered with a scarf, who sat next to another bed. At the edge of the room was one more bed, with no one sitting by it. A cloud of white hair was crushed on the pillow, tubes covering the face. Then her eyes locked on the bed she had at first skipped over, the one the first woman had indicated.

Roni. But so tranquil that at first she thought it was someone else, some other mother's calm and happy child. When she got closer and looked at the instruments and tubes going into her mouth and nose and winding around her arms and stuck to her chest, she felt as if the opposite were happening: tube after tube was pulling matter from her child's body, the air was escaping, the blood emptying out. Jane sat on the edge of the upholstered chair, still slightly warm from Mark's body, then immediately stood up, smoothed her hand over the soft black hair—

how she hated that short-cropped hairstyle; she thought Roni had only done it to annoy her—and then leaned over her face, kissed her forehead, and then her eyes, as in a fairytale—but she wasn't the fairy—and then her cheeks and the tip of her nose—as she used to do when Roni was a baby—and if she could have, she would have kissed her mouth, which was blocked with large tubes, much too large for that little baby-fish mouth, which would never again produce a word that could hurt her, make her angry, or depress her. She swore.

"This is my son," the woman said, and pointed to the boy in the bed. "Soldier," she said in English. It was obvious she wanted to have a conversation. She wanted Jane to ask what had happened to the soldier and why he was there, but Jane just smiled awkwardly, with empathy but also caution: *Let me be alone with my girl.* The woman backed off. She stood by her son's head and kissed his forehead. But when Jane sat down again, the soldier's mother came over and said, "I'm Tzippi, nice to meet you."

Having no choice, she held out her hand. "Jane."

"You're Roni's mother. You look alike."

"Yes."

Encouraged by the exchange, Tzippi jutted her chin toward the bed where the woman with the head cover sat and whispered, "He was also hurt in an accident. He's an Arab. And that one"—she pointed to the edge of the room—"had a stroke. Poor man, ninety-two years old, and he has no one. His wife died a few years ago, his daughter died of cancer, and he has a Filipina but she went home for the night. She'll probably be back soon. Poor man. I lost my husband, too. I also have a daughter, bless her. She'll come soon, you'll see her. She's a good girl."

Jane felt as though she were in a joke: a soldier, an Arab, and an old man lie together in one room. And Roni? Who was Roni in this scene? She filled with anger; Roni shouldn't be in the story at all. She said to the woman, not believing her own words, but still saying them, that if she had no objection she wanted to spend a few moments alone with her daughter. The woman, hurt, said she was sorry and went back to her chair.

Then the doctors came in, two older men and two young residents. The oldest, a very tall, thin man, spoke. "Are you her mother?"

"Yes."

He shook her hand and introduced himself. He said he'd heard she was a sculptor.

Surprised, she said, "Yes."

"And I hear you have a show in New York next month."

She said, "Yes," even though it was obvious she wouldn't be there.

He told her he'd been talking to Alona yesterday. "Alona is her name, isn't it?"

Jane nodded.

"So I told her that I also do some sculpture. Nothing serious, but you know, for the soul."

She smiled.

"If you'd like, later, I have a few statuettes in my office."

"Oh, yes, of course."

Then the professor became very formal, put his hands in his coat pockets, and said, "Okay, so what are we doing with her today?"

It wasn't clear if the question was for her, for himself, or for the two residents, but they answered in unison: "Reversal."

"Correct." He glanced at his watch and said they'd wait another hour or two and then try to wake her.

Jane straightened up. "What do you mean? How will you try to wake her?" She pictured the four doctors shaking her daughter's shoulders and splashing water on her face.

Tzippi, who had recovered from her insult, laughed. "It's when they stop the infusion, isn't it, Professor?"

He smiled. "She knows. She's an expert." Then his face turned grave and he went over to Tzippi and put a hand on her shoulder. "Is it going to be okay? What do you say?"

Tzippi lowered her gaze. "God willing."

He shook Jane's hand again and said his deputy would be back at around noon, and they'd keep him updated on Roni's progress. "And hopefully this afternoon we'll be wiser." He reiterated his invitation to see his statuettes.

Tzippi said, "Wow, you're an artist, too, Professor? That's very impressive."

He smiled awkwardly. "An amateur artist."

Tzippi asked, "But when do you have time, Professor?"

He said he didn't, and he looked sad as he hurried to the Arab man's

bed, his deputy and the residents close behind. Jane and Tzippi listened
to the professor chatter in Arabic with the older woman, who kept nodding, and then he went over to the old man's bed with his gang, and
then they all left the room.

Tzippi sighed deeply and sat back down, and said that when her
daughter came she'd go and eat something. Even though she had no
appetite, she forced herself to eat, she said, "Because I have to. For him,
I have to." She held the soldier's hand and then started to sob. "I gave
birth to him in this hospital." She added in English, "I born him here."
And she kissed his fingers.

Tears streamed down Jane's own cheeks, and she went back to that
night when everything went wrong, the February night when Roni was
almost not born. She had replayed that night hundreds of times in her
mind, always as a sort of justification, like pleading before a judge: We
couldn't have known; we meant well!

The contractions had started the afternoon before. She had calmly
walked around the house, and late in the afternoon she and Mark had
gone for a walk in the wadi. "I'm fine," she reassured him. "I'm absolutely fine." She stopped every so often to lean on him and breathe deeply
like she'd learned from the midwife, Lisa, who had come to them during the last few weeks of the pregnancy from her home on a moshav
near Jerusalem.

Lisa was a macrobiotic, with five kids of her own, and all Jane's
American and British friends swore by her. "Only Lisa. There's no one
like Lisa." Mark couldn't stand her from the moment they met, because
she made him sit cross-legged on the floor and take deep breaths, too.

When they got back from the walk, Jane managed with great difficulty to climb up the stone steps to their house, and Mark sat her down
in the big armchair by the wood-burning stove and asked if she thought
they should phone Lisa. She said, "Not yet, in a while. The contractions
are bad, but they're ten minutes apart." He asked if she wanted to lie
down, and she said, "No, I want to get up!" When he pulled her up by the
arms, her water broke at once, leaving a huge puddle on the stone floor.

"Are you sure you don't want to go to the hospital?" Mark asked,
throwing some old towels on the floor and looking at her standing just
as he'd left her, trembling with cold and pain. She said, "I'm sure, but
call Lisa. We should call now." She asked him to bring her a large pillow,

so she could sit on the floor by the stove, which had suddenly become her compass and she was afraid to leave it.

When Mark came back and said Lisa was on her way, sitting on the floor became intolerable, and she asked to get up and walk around. He helped her up and walked her back and forth between the rooms, as if they were strolling around an exhibition of pain. Every few steps she had to stop and hold on to something—Mark, or a chair, or the railing on the baby-blue crib they'd put ready next to the bed, foolishly not believing in the evil eye.

The nurse came over and said Mark and Alona were waiting outside. She got up and followed her out to the hallway. When she saw them now—Mark without the gown and mask, gray-black stubble covering his cheeks and chin like moss, and Alona, looking without her jacket like a little girl in a gray Mickey Mouse sweatshirt—they could have been a high school couple who'd ditched school and accidentally found themselves in a hospital.

"You probably didn't eat or drink anything on the flight," Mark said. He knew her well.

She said she hadn't, but she wasn't hungry.

"Still," Alona said, "you should go downstairs. They have decent croissants. Because soon, when they start to wake her up, you won't want to leave."

"Okay," Jane said. "Are you going in, Mark?"

"Of course," Mark said.

Alona asked if Jane wanted company. There was nothing for her to do anyway. But she said she would manage.

Waiting for the elevator, she felt bathed in sweat. The hospital was overheated. Outside an imaginary winter and inside a sauna, she thought, summoning up her age-old resentment of this place. But the bitterness didn't come; instead, someone called her name. She turned and saw the professor. He asked if she was going downstairs and she said, "Yes, I thought I'd get something to drink."

"Yes, you should. After all, you've been sitting on a plane for several hours." He thrust his hands into his pockets and looked down at the linoleum floor. He said he was on his way to his office, which was very close, one floor below, and perhaps, if she wasn't in a hurry . . .

She smiled. Where could she be hurrying?

. . . she would like to have a peek at his statuettes?

"Yes, gladly. Of course."

When the elevator arrived, they squeezed in and went down one floor. They got out and walked to the end of the hallway, and the professor pulled a key out of his pocket and opened the door.

The office was relatively small and well-lit. Its windows faced the parking lot. The walls were lined with shelves containing a few books, interspersed with framed photographs of people scribbled with handwriting. She couldn't read the inscriptions, never having learned to read Hebrew, but she assumed they were words of gratitude from former patients, patients whose lives this man had saved. Even if he saved her daughter, it would never occur to her to immortalize that victory with lines of thanks handwritten over her face, because the photo would always be a reminder of what could have been, of the other possibility.

The professor saw her looking from one photo to the next and smiled shyly. "Would you like a glass of water?"

"No, no, that's okay. I'm fine." Then she noticed that in the spaces between the framed pictures were odd little structures made of wires. There was something that looked like a dog, and something else that looked like a turtle, and there was a tall one, made of copper strands, that looked like a female body, with screws embedded in the thicket of wires where the breasts were supposed to be, and hair made of a cluster of springs. She almost burst out laughing, but she walked over to the shelf with a serious expression and the professor stood next to her, wanting to explain, perhaps to protect his statuettes from her grave look. She picked one up. "Is this a dog?" she asked.

"No. Everyone thinks it's a dog, but it's supposed to be a bear."

She turned the little object over in her hands. "Yes, it does look a bit like a bear."

"But I messed up the ears."

"No, it's very impressive. And the fact that it's unclear whether it's a dog or a bear makes the statue fascinating."

"Really? I hadn't thought of it that way. Maybe I'm a little too self-critical."

"All good artists are."

The professor smiled proudly, and when he saw her staring at the female figure, he said that he kept the better works at home. "These are just, you know, beginner's stuff."

"Not at all," she said, and praised him for the idea of using screws. "There's something antisexual about these screws, yet at the same time very sexual. The word, you know, the word itself."

He raised his eyebrows, fascinated, and said, "I never thought about that. Interesting."

"Yes, it really is interesting, the choices we make, sometimes without even being aware."

He asked which media she worked in, and she said her statues were more installations, made of household materials: furniture, fabric, food packaging. At first she'd used stone, but now she found it restrictive, and lately she'd been trying to incorporate video clips in her work: personal relics, family films. In one of her projects, she started to say, she'd used a short film of Roni as a little girl. She smiled. There was Roni, back in the room. Roni, whose existence had been briefly forgotten thanks to art and lies.

The professor's beeper went off and he apologized and sat down at his desk with his back to the window. As he spoke on the phone, the sunlight illuminated his gray hair and he went back to being an important, lifesaving man.

"I'm sorry, I have to get back to the ward." She said she was glad to have seen his work, and he smiled awkwardly again and said it was a hobby for now, but in the future, when he retired, who knew.

"Yes, you must," she said.

He opened the door and waited for her to walk out, then locked it behind them and said goodbye at the elevator. "I'll see you later."

"Yes," Jane said.

She got out of the elevator on the ground floor and walked to the cafeteria, wondering how it was that she, who had always been a bad liar—"You have to learn how to lie," Barbara liked to tease her, "otherwise you'll never get anywhere"—had now, of all times, in this place, on this day, spewed out such wonderful lies, one after the other, like cherry pits. She got in line at the cafeteria—she wasn't sure if it was a line or a crowd; how she used to hate that—squeezed her way to the counter, and asked in Hebrew for orange juice and a croissant. She realized that just now, facing that talentless god, she had learned how to lie because she had to, because her lies might very well be the fuel that would drive the professor today. He would ride her compliments like a cavalier, loving himself in a way that would allow him to be particularly careful and precise. And in return for the gift he had received from her, he would give her back her child, who was now, after the intimate meeting in his room, slightly his child, too.

She took the juice and croissant and sat down on a bench near the guard, who ran a metal detector over visitors' bodies and dug through their bags. Perhaps she should phone Barbara, as she'd promised—although she hadn't really promised—she could go upstairs and use Mark's cell phone, but she remembered it was nighttime in New York, and she suddenly couldn't figure out if Roni had been run over yesterday at eleven, or the day before. Yesterday, she decided. They said she'd been sedated for twenty-four hours. She threw the greasy bag with the croissant, still almost whole, and the rest of the juice into the trash.

As she waited for the elevator again, she felt an urgent need to call Barbara, as though she could not begin the reversal without her. But even though she'd said to call any time and that had always been their understanding, there was no justification for waking her up. She knew she did not need a justification, but she realized that their regular emergency procedures had become complicated since George had entered their lives. Yes, *their* lives. George, whom she viewed with contempt not necessarily because he deserved it—although he did, undoubtedly: Barbara could have found someone you could talk to and not just ride like an aging cowgirl; Jane always laughed at her friend's fake-leather vests and her pointy-toed boots—rather, she scorned him because there was something so simple and gluttonous about this fat man, so logical, that at times he seemed to be infecting Barbara with his attitude. "Life is beautiful, Doll"—that's what he called her—"so let's just live it, okay? And smile a little. It won't kill you."

When she got back to the ward she ran into Alona, who was on her way downstairs to look for her. "The department head was just here; they've started tapering off the sedatives. Don't worry, nothing's supposed to happen yet. It'll take about an hour, and then they'll slow the ventilator. They won't stop it at once, of course. They'll see how she responds."

She wanted to tell Alona that she'd visited the professor's room and seen his ridiculous statuettes, but she said nothing, because there was a new tension in the air now, the tension of excitement. The vacuum of the past twenty-four hours started to fill with content, with schedules, with a certain order of events, like the moment the passengers are told to go to the boarding gate. There was something reassuring about it but also frightening: a journey that was beginning and could not be stopped, with no way to tell where it would go.

"He said he'd be back soon to see how she's doing," Alona said, "and then they'll do something, I didn't quite understand what; he talked with Mark. They'll slow down the ventilator, that's what I understood, and see if she can breathe on her own."

"And if she can't?"

Alona looked at her with surprise. "I don't know. We didn't ask."

Jane asked the nurse to call Mark, and while she waited she put on a gown and mask. Mark came out and looked at her as if he had only just understood that she was really here, and with bright eyes he told her everything she already knew. When he realized he was abandoning his post and might miss out on the moments of awakening, he made her swear she'd call him as soon as anything happened, even something small. "I can't believe they won't let us both sit next to her," he said angrily. "We should both be with her, shouldn't we?"

She went into the room and nodded at Tzippi, who looked at her excitedly and said, "This is it, they've started." She pointed at Roni. While Jane sat down next to her daughter and searched for the initial hidden signs of awakening, Tzippi came over and pushed a miniature book into her hands: "The Bible, it's good. You know *Tehilim*?"

Jane whispered, "No, thanks," and gave her back the little book of psalms. Tzippi went back to her seat and Jane suddenly thought she saw movement out of the corner of her eye. It seemed as if Roni's right fingers had fluttered on the mattress. But when she stared, the hand was still, and very white, and much smaller than she remembered. She thought about Roni's birth weight: she'd been big, perhaps too big, almost nine pounds. She leaned back and shut her eyes, knowing that if she stared at Roni she might fall into the trap of imaginary movements. She tried to probe her daughter's hands with her eyes closed: perhaps she could sense the movement instead of seeing it. How strange, she thought, that back then she could hardly get her out into the world, and now she could not contain her.

Barbara was right when she said a person should have two mothers: one for day-to-day, and the other a ministering angel, available whenever the first needed to rest or fall apart without dragging anyone else down with her.

She opened her eyes and stood up, leaned over Roni, and touched her eyelids with her fingertips. Perhaps her touch would be like the flutter of a butterfly wing that could hurry up the process. She wondered why no one was coming to check on her. She was supposed to start waking up. But she was afraid to go out and call a nurse, so she sat down again and leaned over with her arms on her knees.

Waiting for Lisa, addled by chills of pain, she had felt like someone was trying to cut her back in two with a knife. Mark sat on the rug, holding her freezing-cold hands and rubbing them, as if the cold were the problem. His touch bothered her. Instead of distracting her from the pain it added the pain of another person, who once again asked gently, afraid to anger her, if she was sure they shouldn't go to the hospital. She yelled, "No!" When he said okay and got up and started to massage her hunched back, as he had learned from Lisa, she elbowed him and asked him to leave her alone and not touch her: "Find yourself something to do until she gets here. You're getting in the way instead of helping." It was the contraction, not her, who yelled, "Get out of here!" And she tried to get up as if she could run away somewhere.

The contractions were coming every minute. From the corner of her eye she could see Mark standing by the window and timing them, his face lit by the big scented candles that stood in a row on the dining table. They had lighted them together, with great ceremony, when they'd come back from their walk and realized labor had begun. Now it seemed there was even less than a minute between each wave of contractions;

before one died down the next washed over her. Through gritted teeth she asked when Lisa had said she would be there, and he said, "An hour and a half ago. It's strange that she isn't here yet."

Since not everyone had cell phones back then—they didn't, and the hippie midwife certainly didn't—Mark called her house, and her husband said she'd left over an hour ago. "How long should it take to get to you? Twenty minutes, half an hour?" He said he really hoped her car hadn't got stuck; lately it was giving them trouble. He told Mark he himself had got stuck yesterday on the way home from Jerusalem, and was supposed to take the car to the shop today but hadn't had time. "Let's hope everything's okay," he said, trying to calm Mark, "maybe there's a traffic jam or something." But they both knew there could be no traffic jam on a winter night on a rickety road winding from the Jerusalem hills to Ein Kerem.

"She's not coming," Mark said, when he went back to the room and found Jane sitting on the edge of their bed, crushing a large couch pillow against her stomach. "I don't think she'll make it, Jane." Then he hissed, "It's so irresponsible. You'd think someone aspiring to be a midwife would make sure their car worked properly!" Jane let out a strange screech in a voice that wasn't hers at all, the screech of a frightened bird, and Mark rushed over and asked if she needed to start pushing. She shook her head wildly, as if trying to brush away flies, and said she didn't have the urge to push. She asked him to help her lie on her side, but when she lay on her side she felt unable to breathe, and Mark helped her up, but her legs gave way and she collapsed on the bed again.

He asked what to do, how to help her. "Maybe you should kneel on all fours. Lisa suggested it, remember?"

She said she wanted to stand up, and she leaned her body on his and he walked her around the room.

"Take it slowly," he said, his sweat dripping onto her arm. "Slowly, Jane," he said, when he felt as if her feet were trying to get away. She said she needed fresh air and asked to go out onto the balcony. She was hot and she couldn't breathe. When they managed, after what seemed like an eternity, to get onto the balcony, she leaned on the railing while Mark held her waist, and looked onto the silent black wadi and listened to the nocturnal rustles, trying to draw encouragement from the tranquil routine of nature. Then suddenly that screech ripped out of her again without any control. Mark, who was completely panicked by now, joked and said it was a good thing they didn't have any neighbors. She gritted her teeth and cried, and thought perhaps she had been screaming at the absent neighbors. Maybe this was not some wonderfully primal scream, one of those womanly things Lisa had told them about when she'd explained that Jane might emit all sorts of noises and she should do so without being embarrassed, because it helped. No, it wasn't that sort of scream but a call for help—a call for the neighbors they didn't have to come and save her.

When they went back inside, her body was shaking uncontrollably. She lay down on the bed and felt as if she might need to push, but she resisted: it was dangerous to push before she was fully dilated. Mark hurried to the kitchen and came back with a bowl of ice water and started wiping her face with a wet towel. A strange tune was coming out of her mouth, musical sighs that frightened him, and he asked why she was crying like that. "You sound like a funeral weeper," he said, trying to joke, "not a woman giving birth." But she could no longer hear him. She pushed away the bowl of water, which spilled on her bare thighs—she couldn't remember when she'd undressed or whether she'd been naked when she went out on the balcony.

Roni's eyelids seemed to be fluttering, as if a tiny lizard were darting back and forth behind them, looking for a way out. She stood up and leaned over Roni, holding her breath. Yes, there was definitely a tremor there, and it seemed like one eye was trying to open. Just then, knowing the precise timing of the procedure, the head nurse came in, looked at Roni, and said, "She's waking up," without any excitement in her voice, just stating a fact. She went over to the ventilator and hit a few buttons that gave confirmation beeps, and said, "Your husband wants to come in, so why don't you step out for a while?"

Jane said, "No, I'm not leaving. Tell him not yet." Then she added, in a quieter but more determined voice, "I can't. Okay?"

The nurse looked at her and said, "Okay, I'll tell him. The professor will be in soon."

Jane sat down again and focused on Roni's eyes, which kept moving under her eyelids. Now she thought she could see movement in her lips, too, which were hidden by the large plastic tube. It occurred to her that they would have to fight now, she and Mark, over who stayed here and who waited outside, and she knew she wouldn't give in, not this time. The professor came into the room and grinned at her. He was accompanied by the two residents, and there was Mark behind them. The professor came up to her and said, "Your husband begged us to let him be here with you both, so I agreed. But don't tell anyone." He winked at the residents, who smiled awkwardly, and then he asked her to move aside for a moment. She got up obediently and stood next to Mark, whose fingers intertwined with hers but quickly let go. The professor glanced at the ventilator and asked the nurse something they didn't understand. He nodded, satisfied with her response, and said, "So far it looks good. There are signs of awakening." He leaned over Roni, gave the skin above her collarbone a sharp, expert pinch, and turned to the residents. "See that? She's responding to pain."

"Where?" Mark said. "Where is she responding? I didn't see anything."

The professor patted his shoulder warmly. "You don't have to see it. She responded."

"Would you ever have believed that the most beautiful words you'd ever hear were that your daughter is responding to pain?" Mark whispered to Jane.

The professor said something else to the nurse, then turned to them. "Okay. In the past five minutes she does not seem to have suffered any respiratory distress. She has her own breathing reflex. We'll wait awhile longer and decrease the machine's activity by one more notch. The first signs are encouraging, and soon we'll know more."

When the entourage left, Mark dragged a chair over and put it on the other side of the bed. But rather than sitting down, he hovered around Roni and looked at her, hunting for more signs. Although he said nothing, Jane could hear all the promises he was making to himself, just as she was doing: *If she wakes up, then. . . . If she's okay, then. . . .* She knew the *then* was giant, aspiring to redefine their life: no more haggling over the little things, no more wars, and mainly, as she had promised herself hundreds of times over the last few hours, no more anger. Gratitude would henceforth be the guiding principle of parenthood, she decided. It was what would pave their way from now on.

And suddenly they both saw Roni's right hand lift up above the sheet and fall back, as if she were trying to say something, perhaps in response to their thoughts.

"Did you see?" Mark said, excited, and she nodded. Tears streamed down his cheeks, and he started to tell her about a dream he'd had last night, during a quick nap on the couch. It was a strange dream. He'd been driving in his car, and in front of him was another car, with a little boy jumping up and down on the driver's lap. "It seemed weird, because why would a little boy be on his father's lap while he drove? And on a scary, winding road like that. Since I didn't believe it could be true, I stepped on the gas and passed the car, and there really was a little boy there, around Ido's age." Then he said he'd been frightened and angered by the irresponsible, criminal driver and felt he had to stop him. "At some point, I can't remember exactly when, the car stopped and I went up to the driver's window furiously. He was about my age and he looked nice, not the asshole I was expecting. I asked him what the hell he was doing. How could he drive with a kid on his lap like that? What if there was an accident? The guy said in a friendly voice that the boy was his amulet. He kept him on his lap, close to his heart, close to the wheel, as a good-luck charm. Some people hang a prayer for safe travels from the dashboard, but he'd come up with something else, something ingenious: the boy. The driver hit the gas and zoomed away with the boy, and then I woke up."

"Weird dream. What do you think it means?"

"I have no idea, Jane. I have no idea, but it was really scary. I keep thinking about that boy, wondering what happened to him, if he's alive or dead." Tears ran down his face again, and he rubbed his eyes and then put one fist in his mouth and dug his teeth into it, trying to gnaw at the fear instead of letting it gnaw at him.

Her pain grew thicker and made each minute feel heavy and pregnant. Shortly after midnight, when it was obvious that Lisa wasn't coming— her husband had called to say she was stuck near Ramat Raziel; she'd walked a few miles to a moshav to use the phone and had promised that if she didn't find someone going to Jerusalem who could give her a ride she'd get a cab; he said she was hysterical, absolutely hysterical, and had promised to make it there somehow—but two hours had gone by since the phone call and anything could have happened to her. She obviously hadn't found a ride or even a taxi.

"Who cares what happened to her," Mark mumbled. "I hope she gets eaten by jackals." He paced the room, tossing more wood in the stove even though there was no need, just to see the wood crackling in the fire. A little after midnight Jane wanted to push, she could feel it clearly, and she said, "Mark, I need to push." He hurried over and asked, "So what do we do now?"

And then anxiety gave way to business, as if not only the birth had entered a new phase but time itself. Suddenly the minutes started flying by, and it was almost three by the time they realized nothing was happening. She was kneeling while Mark sat on the bed and supported her, his hands in her armpits, just like the irrelevant Lisa had taught them. Every so often she asked to lie down, but she couldn't do it, and then asked him to help her stand, and then knelt again, but nothing was happening. She wasn't crying or yelling anymore, just making that groan, until suddenly she passed out. When she came to, she found herself sitting on the edge of the armchair facing the crib, wearing the clothes she'd had on that morning. Mark was rushing around looking for the car keys. "Hospital!" he declared.

The head nurse came over and looked at Roni, and without saying a word she hit a few keys on the ventilator again. Instead of leaving, she stood next to them and they all waited a few more minutes, until the nurse smiled and said, "Look, she's trying to breathe on her own." She pointed at Roni's face but they couldn't see anything. "It's great, it's really good, she's strong," the nurse said. She wrote something down on the chart, then went to the other side of the room, where the Arab man lay. The woman sitting next to him was not the older woman from before but a younger woman, possibly his wife. Jane and Mark looked around, as if only just having noticed that there were other people in the room.

Now Roni's hands lifted together. Jane and Mark got up. The hands reached up to her throat and face, and her neck seemed to be arching back. Mark called the nurse, who glanced at Roni and said, "She's uncomfortable with the tubes."

"Then let's take them out," Mark said. The nurse smiled and kept looking at Roni, who had put her hands back down beside her body.

"No, not yet. I think we'll be able to disconnect her soon. She really is progressing very well."

"But she's uncomfortable!" Mark exclaimed. "Look at her turn her head from side to side." Roni's head was thrashing like a fish out of water.

"It's all right, she's groggy," the nurse said. "It's a normal part of waking up. Everyone tries to pull the tubes out. The ones who wake up."

When she left, promising to be back in a few minutes, they both looked at Tzippi, who peered back at them over her magazine. She was obviously monitoring every sign, like they were, experiencing with them what she had not experienced with her own son, refusing to be banished from a successful reversal, even if it wasn't hers. As if reading their thoughts, she said, "Now they'll have to make sure there's no brain damage. I understand that can take a few days."

Jane looked at Mark's face and could read his anger at this woman who had dared to tarnish his happiness and jolt him back to reality. "I'm gonna kill her," he whispered.

They both held Roni's hands, she the right and he the left, knowing that she needed accompaniment for the remainder of her journey back to them. It was as if they were walking her to kindergarten or swinging her up in the air like they used to do when they all walked together. "She's squeezing my hand," Mark said, and Jane nodded, "Mine too." She asked if he remembered the night Roni was born, and without looking at her, his eyes fixed on his daughter's face, he said, "Do I remember? It was the worst night of my life." Then he smiled and said, "No, actually *last* night was the worst night of my life."

"You saved us," Jane said.

"No, come on. Someone had to make the decision, and you were in no state to do so. You were a mess."

"No, Mark, I was stupid. I was irresponsible. I almost killed her."

He looked at her and said, "No, Jane, you tried. That's all." He giggled and asked if she remembered the drive to the hospital. "How fast was I going? A hundred and twenty, I think."

She said she couldn't remember anything about that drive. She remembered everything that happened before, at the house, and what happened afterward, at the hospital, but for some reason the drive was completely erased.

Mark smiled again. "I guess your unconscious wiped out that connection between almost-death and life." He shook his head and felt a chill, trying to banish the image. "It was such a crazy drive."

She smiled, a real smile, for the first time in twenty-four hours or maybe more, and asked if he remembered the nurse-midwife who'd admitted them.

"Of course. She was an old witch, but a good one. The first thing she did was yell at us. *You're mad! Who gives birth at home? What were you thinking?*"

The nurse had examined Jane, subduing her yells by saying, "Shhh . . . shhhh . . . enough already." She said she was used to couples who turned up at the hospital after a failed home birth and announced that Jane was fully dilated but the baby was stuck in the birth canal.

"And when you told her you'd been pushing for three hours, the old witch almost dropped dead, and she said, 'Lady, what were you trying to do, kill the baby? What happened to the midwife? Didn't you have a midwife?' And when I told her what happened she said, 'Oh, yes. Sometimes they don't make it.' "

Then she'd hooked Jane up to a monitor, and suddenly everything had changed: no more anger, no more reprimands and jabs but simple panic: the baby had no pulse. A doctor arrived immediately. Unlike the nurse-midwife, he was young, too young. When he examined Jane, the monitor suddenly jumped back to life. "There's a pulse, but it's very weak, up and down," the doctor said.

"The nurse-midwife stood there with her hands on her waist," Mark said, "clucking her tongue the whole time, remember?"

Jane smiled. "Yes."

Roni was stuck in limbo and it was too dangerous to attempt a C-section, so the doctor decided to use forceps.

"And then they made you leave the room, remember?" Jane said.

"Kicked me out of the room, that son of a bitch."

Roni started to move her legs, folding one knee in, raising it up and down, and then the other, as if her brain were going through roll call to see who was present. Then she lifted her head up and seemed to open her eyes for an instant, but her head fell back down and her hands climbed up to the tube in her mouth again, taking Jane's and Mark's hands with it.

They both whispered to her, he in Hebrew and she in English, almost inaudibly, "Yes, little girl, yes, baby," and "Good morning, good morning, my love." Their faces were streaming with tears, and they heard Tzippi sobbing behind them, sharing their joy, or perhaps feeling her own pain. They heard her briefly but then turned their attention back to Roni. This was their moment.

The professor came in, glanced at his watch, and said, "Okay." He motioned to the nurse, pressed some buttons on the machine, and the nurse stood at the foot of the bed and said loudly, "Roni? Can you hear us?"

Roni sighed.

"We're going to take the tube out of your mouth now, honey."

Roni sighed again, as if to confirm.

It occurred to Jane that she could have tried to talk to her for the past few hours. She could have asked questions and sought answers in Roni's movements. Why had she not thought of doing that? Instead of looking at her, sending silent messages and whispering, she could have simply tried to talk to her, as she had talked that day in the delivery room, when the pain and the exhaustion and the terror seemed to carry her on their wings to a different place, while the doctor pulled with the forceps and the metal burned her insides like a branding. The pain was the totality of all the pain she'd ever experienced: the little cuts and bruises when she was a girl, scraped knees, a sprained ankle, a broken arm, meningitis when she was ten, and then the great abandonment. And it was the prologue to all the pain she had yet to experience. The witch had stood at her side and said, "That's it, that's it. One more moment. Just a little longer. He's pulling her out now." She tried to steady Jane's wildly shaking knees. And then Jane had spoken to Roni with simple words, even before she'd come out of her body: "Come on, come on already, come out *now*!" she'd yelled.

The doctor had grasped the forceps like a wheel, quietly and precisely, making small tugs but working so hard that it seemed he might have been wrong and that even the forceps could not liberate this baby from her prison, and they would stay that way forever, the two of them, bodies locked together. The old nurse's voice whirled around her and she opened her eyes for a minute to see the doctor's gaze narrowing with a focus she'd never seen before, and the nurse had screamed, "She's coming out! Here she is! Everything's okay!" And then her own screech, as if coming back to her in an echo from the wadi below their house, and immediately after that the baby's cry. The old witch couldn't resist: she had run a warm, rough hand over Jane's forehead and said, "Everything's okay, see? Everything's okay."

They pulled out the tube and nothing happened for a moment. Suddenly Roni coughed and spluttered, her shoulders rocked, and her breath froze for a minute, as if she'd forgotten what to do. Then she sucked air into her lungs, as if she were drowning, and coughed again. Jane felt as though she were choking, too, as if her own lungs had forgotten what to do. She couldn't understand how the professor and nurse could stand there indifferently, waiting. "Good, Roni. Breathe, like that," the nurse said.

Roni coughed again, a damp, strange, angry cough, and whimpered, and tears started running quickly down her cheeks. "Is she crying?" Jane asked.

The nurse smiled. "Yes."

With her eyes still closed, blinded by the neon lights, Roni started to move her lips. She made another whimper, coughed, and then uttered a long, hoarse wail, insistent and wonderful: "Mommy."

ABOUT THE AUTHOR

YAEL HEDAYA is the head writer for *In Treatment*, the acclaimed Israeli TV series adapted for HBO. The author of *Housebroken* and *Accidents*, which was a finalist for the National Jewish Book Award in 2006, Hedaya teaches creative writing at the Hebrew University in Jerusalem.